THE
FIRST
SACRIFICE

THE
FIRST
SACRIFICE

THOMAS GIFFORD

BANTAM BOOKS
New York Toronto London Sydney Auckland

THE FIRST SACRIFICE
A Bantam Book / November 1994

All rights reserved.
Copyright © 1994 by Thomas Gifford.

Book design by Donna Sinisgalli

No part of this book may be reproduced or transmitted in any
form or by any means, electronic or mechanical, including
photocopying, recording, or by any information storage and
retrieval system, without permission in writing from the publisher.
For information address: Bantam Books.

Library of Congress Cataloging-in-Publication Data

Gifford, Thomas.
The first sacrifice / Thomas Gifford.
p.   cm.
Sequel to: The wind chill factor.
ISBN 0-553-09252-9
I. Title.
PS3557.I284F57   1994
813'.54—dc20   94-11548
CIP

Published simultaneously in the United States and Canada

Bantam Books are published by Bantam Books, a division of Bantam Doubleday Dell Publishing Group, Inc. Its trademark, consist-
ing of the words "Bantam Books" and the portrayal of a rooster, is
Registered in U.S. Patent and Trademark Office and in other countries. Marca Registrada. Bantam Books, 1540 Broadway, New York,
New York 10036.

PRINTED IN THE UNITED STATES OF AMERICA

BVG   0 9 8 7 6 5 4 3 2 1

FOR PATRICIA
AND FOR RACHEL AND TOM

AUTHOR'S NOTE

Not even the slower students among us could be conned into believing that a novel as complicated as this one—with a plot so convoluted and seen from so many points of view—could have been made to behave by one lone writer hoping for the best and clinging for dear life to his computer. While the mistakes and fumbles doubtless infesting the text are entirely mine, I must share whatever strikes you as worthwhile and lifelike and possibly even instructive with the following people, who take pains in my care and feeding and never, ever stick their fingers into the cage.

As always, my agents, Kathy Robbins and Elizabeth Mackey, encourage me and calm me down and lift me up when I am low; they have even been known to humor me and smile wanly when I am sure I am at my most amusing.

My editor, a worker of miracles, Beverly Lewis, has never worked more miracles than with this novel and I am deeply in her debt; I have not the slightest idea how she works her magic. But it's a damn good thing she does.

Without the exquisite Beate Wolff of Cologne, Germany, there would have been no book. She took me in hand and with grace and charm and wit and insight led me through what I came to see as perhaps the most civilized city I have ever visited: Berlin. She had a sure instinct for what I needed to see and know and when I waved the white flag of exhaustion she dragged me ever onward. Sometimes, when you need really special people, they appear. Thank God.

Not often, I suspect, is a writer tempted to create a sequel to a novel nearly twenty years old. However, events in the new, reunified Germany were sufficiently disturbing to warrant revisiting the characters of *The Wind Chill Factor*. And I quickly came to realize that I needed to conclude the saga of the Coopers of Cooper's Falls, Minnesota, by leading them deep within another heart of darkness, a sort of Black Forest of the mind and will. I think that perhaps now they can rest in peace. Still, you never know.

Thomas Gifford
New York City

Conscience is the first sacrifice on the road to survival.

—Emory Leighton Hunn, Spymaster

I am not I;

he is not he;

they are not they.

I

———

1

MISSING GIRL

She couldn't remember when she'd last slept.

Three weeks ago her father had taken her to see Dr. Gisevius and they had told her about her mother . . . and she'd stormed out, blind with rage, and cried her way through the night, driving aimlessly through the dark vastness of Berlin . . . driving until she was nearly asleep, almost wishing her depression and exhaustion would engulf her, deposit her in the crumpled, wrecked Porsche at the foot of a light stanchion with her worries and sorrow behind her.

Had she slept since then? She didn't feel as if she had. She might have slept but she knew she'd had no rest. And then . . . then . . . just two nights ago . . .

Two nights ago she'd been with Karl-Heinz at his hideaway in the warren of dreary, run-down, damp gray pre-Communist rat traps, structures that had managed to survive the Allied bombing of fifty years ago. That was in the East, of course, where he was still most comfortable. They'd spent the night preparing for the latest Stiffel rally against foreigners. Preparing to face the mob with their red and white and black armbands bearing the new version of the Nazi swastika, their brown shirts, their sweating faces in the bright glare of the television lights. Karl-Heinz would cover the event for his little newspaper, yes, but they were also there to protest. That was a given. She had stayed up all night helping him with the design and typesetting for the underground giveaway sheet outlining, in bold Gothic faces, the similarities between Stiffel's bully boys and those of Adolf Hitler just a moment ago in Germany's history. The job had taken all night and then she'd gone to work at the chic little gallery in Fasanenplatz, all day. Then the rally.

It had turned into a riot, a bad riot, her first.

She'd somehow gotten back to her apartment in a building only a couple of blocks off the Ku'damm at the edge of Savignyplatz and put ice on her bruised, battered face and had started pacing and reading the newspapers and listening to the old Rolling Stones records that belonged to her mother. The ice had numbed her face but everything else—her entire life, it seemed to her—was out of control. She knew there was nothing she could do about it, that she would never be free.

Everything Karl-Heinz had said would happen was there in the newspapers. He'd made her see the truth of everything and he'd made her see that there was no way out. History was a great machine, a grinding of gears, and once you were caught inside it, there was no getting out.

Karl-Heinz said he had seen the future. It was called SPARTAKUS. He'd told her about it as they'd worked through the night on the giveaway sheets. He hadn't finished the story when she had covered her ears, cried out to him to stop. It was cutting too close to the bone. Tears had streamed down her face and he'd grabbed her by the shoulders and shaken her until she stopped. *Don't be a coward, you of all people can't afford to be a coward in the face of this . . .* He said that telling her was a measure of his trust in her. But she mustn't say a word. "It's a disease, my darling. It's a plague. You could die from SPARTAKUS." He'd said it with a grim little smile. "Believe me, Erika, it will kill on contact." He had kissed her cheek; she'd felt the soft smile, the gentleness that lay behind the feverish eyes and drawn features of the true believer.

It had been raining when she got out of the riot's clutches, got back to the flat, the blood licked from her lips and a Hermès scarf held to a bleeding cut on her forehead. Karl-Heinz had laughed at what he called her "riot gear," a Jil Sander jacket and a silk scarf, jeans and ostrich-skin cowboy boots. She'd told him she couldn't help being what she was, that she was new to his world—and he'd hugged her and kissed her and told her to stick close to him. And now a gray, soggy dawn had come, a steady cold drizzle, the way Berlin always seemed to her. A reflection of her life.

The flat, newly carved out of an old building, one of the many her father owned, was cold and elegant. It had suffered bomb damage but that had been the war and no one spoke about the war anymore, not in her circle. They were tired of the war. It was ancient history. She'd been ashamed of how she thought about the war, with all her friends telling her it just didn't compute, not in this day and age. Ashamed of her sense of guilt—until Karl-Heinz had come along and she'd learned that her friends, and God only knew how much of the German *Volk,* were all lying to themselves, that she'd had it dead right from the beginning. Karl-Heinz saw Stiffel for what he was—a man with his finger on the pulse of the people. The man who understood where the great new Germany belonged. "A man like Stiffel . . . ," Karl-Heinz told her that last night. "He wants to rule Berlin first, then all Germany."

She'd last seen Karl-Heinz when he'd pushed her out of the way of the thugs with the clubs and the armbands. She'd already been bloodied and he'd thrust her away into the crowd watching from the comparative safety of the sidewalk. She'd huddled in a doorway and she'd felt them surge past her and he was gone, waving his broadsheets of indictments in their faces, and she was so afraid for him, but she couldn't get to him and her head was throbbing and eventually she'd wandered up a side street and begun to think she had to get home before she passed out. Was he all right? Had he reached safety?

Karl-Heinz saw history for what it was. The same things happening over and over again. Nothing more, nothing less. He'd told her a hundred times in the months since they'd met. "History is easy," he'd said. "Surviving history is hard." Surviving at all was hard . . .

Time passed and she didn't know it. She threw herself down on the bed, stared out the window, thinking about her mother, hearing Fritz Gisevius's voice, the voice she'd known all her life, calming her, prescribing medicines for her childhood ailments, always there to counsel the family, her father's best friend but she didn't hold that against him, hearing his voice three weeks ago as if he were in the room now, speaking to her. *You must prepare yourself, Erika, there's no running away from it, your mother is going to die . . .*

"I have never seen a case quite like it. Usually the mind steadily deteriorates but in comparatively small increments—this, it's progressing so quickly, so erratically." Dr. Friedrich Gisevius shrugged his massive, rounded shoulders, and the leather-upholstered swivel chair behind the desk groaned beneath his three hundred pounds. "I know this is not what you had hoped to hear, Erika, but it would be far worse not to prepare you. Do you understand that, my dear?"

She could smell his cologne, the same brand he'd always worn, even when he'd come to see her as a child when she had a sore throat or flu and he'd dispensed candies wrapped in bright, twisted papers. He always succeeded in making her feel better. And now he was watching her solemnly, eyes deep in their pouches, his fat-fingered hands clasped across his tightly buttoned vest.

She glanced at her father sitting next to her, at the noble profile. Wolf Koller turned, smiled slightly, nodding as if to confirm what the doctor was telling her, reached out to give her hand a squeeze and she pulled away. She wouldn't look back at him, fixed her eyes on the doctor. Her father watched her for an instant, the look of disappointment and humiliation flickering across his face, then ran his hands back through his hair, which was perfectly barbered once a week by a man named Anton who specialized in celebrities. "Fritz, are you sure? Can you provide us with no hope at all? This is Lise we're talking about. You've known her for more than twenty years . . . I don't want her discussed like a specimen in a laboratory. I don't want to hear how it's the first such case in medical history—" Wolf Koller suddenly banged his hand down on the arm of the overstuffed chair of cracked leather. Erika looked away, hating his theatrics. Gisevius blinked but otherwise took no notice of the violent gesture. The chair was very old, had been passed down from Gisevius's famous ancestor, the psychiatrist Walther Gisevius, contemporary of Freud. It was the color of dried blood. "Erika and I are watching Lise lose her mind. You don't see what it's doing to Erika but I do, it's tormenting her—"

She said something softly and Gisevius leaned forward, said: "What was that, dear?"

"He sees nothing," she said curtly. "He has no idea what I feel." She turned to her father. "I hate it when you try to make people think we're one big happy family—there's no point in trying to convince Dr. Gisevius. He knows the truth."

Wolf Koller sighed, let his chin rest on his chest, his long legs crossed before him. "Erika . . . can't you declare a cease-fire for the moment, when we discuss your mother's condition? After all, we both love her, we both care—"

"You *say* you love her," his daughter replied, "you always *say* the right things—but why can't you be honest with me, just this once?" She finally looked at him, as if she were pinning him beneath the microscope of her intensity. "You keep forgetting that I've seen the way you treat her, your coldness and impatience . . . Dr. Gisevius has seen it, too. So what's the point in the performance? Who are you trying to convince? Yourself?"

Wolf Koller said nothing for a moment, then: "Fritz, forgive us— we're both under a great deal of pressure. Erika's not herself—"

"What nonsense!" Erika interrupted sharply. But she let it drop.

Wolf Koller returned to his original train of thought. "Her mind, her personality," he said, speaking of Lise, "it breaks away in chunks, Fritz. Otherwise she's the same as ever. She's beautiful, she's healthy . . . but her mind is crumbling away."

He ran his hands once more through the mane of thick, silver-gray hair that swept back from his aristocratic forehead in long immaculately groomed waves. He looked as if he should have been the conductor of the Berlin Philharmonic. But he had a tin ear. He was a shaper of German society, of the German state. He was an industrialist and a financier, which covered in his case a multitude of diverse enterprises sharing a single quality—they made money. He had known Fritz Gisevius all his life. Their fathers—a doctor of such prominence that he treated the General Staff and Hitler's inner circle, and a judge who had been a leading academic as well as a pillar of the legal system during the thirties and forties—had been friends. The close relationship had been passed on to their sons. There were no secrets dividing them. Each was the other's most trusted friend and advisor. They were always partners, prompting Gisevius's former wife to remark during some long-ago unhappiness, "You'll march into hell together!" To which Gisevius had replied with equanimity, "Singing the old songs, too, I'll wager."

"Fritz," Koller continued, "I don't know if we as a family can stand it . . . I'll speak only for myself," glancing hesitantly at his daughter, "and I've never felt so lost, so helpless. One day she's her normal self, the next she's hardly there at all. The sadness is tearing me to shreds."

Relentless, Erika murmured: "Next will come tears . . ."

Gisevius frowned, looking from one to the other. "You must be strong. There's nothing else to do. Strong in the face of inevitable loss. Whatever happens, life must go on. Life must go on . . . and you will both be stronger if you can face the facts together . . . father and daughter. You're both suffering a great loss."

Gisevius clipped the end from an enormous cigar, moistened the leaf in his mouth, drew through it, and carefully applied a wooden match. On the dark paneled wall opposite his desk, surrounded by gleaming, carefully polished bookcases, hung the painting *Siegfried Waking.* Waking from his long sleep. Germany, the true Germany. It was a solemn sight, destiny playing itself out. A moment of hope. Which was what he'd always shared with Wolf Koller. And now their hopes were so close to realization. He expelled an enormous cloud of bluish smoke, watched it hang over his ornately carved and inlaid desk. He wished he knew just how to handle the daughter. Erika took a constant toll on Wolf's attention. Now, of all times, Gisevius hoped she wouldn't distract him from their great work.

"Listen to me, both of you. We're dealing with a chemical deterioration. To put it bluntly, garbage is clogging the spaces between the cells of Lise's brain. An autopsy will show exactly that."

Koller scowled, as if anger and frustration might keep him from breaking down. He looked like an actor who was deep into his role. His face was reddening.

"We're working on a new test with the Americans at the Salk Institute and the University of California. We know what it's going to show—but it's not operational yet. Six months, a year, two years—"

"You're telling me you could save her in six months or a year? For God's sake, Fritz—"

"No, that's not what I'm telling you. In six months or a year we will—maybe, just maybe—have the key to the disease, we will have the road map that may lead to a cure, or a way of blocking its development . . . no one knows how long that could take." He puffed again. The smoke filtered through the glow of the lamp on his desk. The room smelled of his cigars. "This new test will measure the presence of a substance called PN-2. PN-2 is normally cut and spliced by certain enzymes—and when the cutting and splicing is done properly the levels of PN-2 are high, as in you or me, for instance. Conversely, they will not be shown to be high in Lise, you see. *I'm telling you what the autopsy would confirm.* In an individual with Alzheimer's that peptide takes a different route, the wrong enzymes cut the string of the peptide in the wrong place . . . instead of getting the healthy PN-2, you find a different peptide, beta-amyloid . . . and that is the debris and garbage clogging the brain cells. Thus, Alzheimer's disease. You must both prepare yourselves —she will need to be institutionalized."

"Nonsense! I will see that she is cared for at home."

"It will be very unpleasant to watch. A woman you have loved will turn into an organism you will hardly recognize and may indeed come to despise—and she won't know either of you from Adam."

Wolf Koller waved his hand impatiently.

"You, Erika, must think ahead, you must find a way to cope with this—you've been very close to your mother, I know that—"

Wolf Koller drew back, his mouth tightened. "Like anyone else, Erika will simply have to deal with a family tragedy. She is a Koller."

Erika bit her lip, said nothing.

Gisevius said: "Will you tell Lise about her condition?"

"What's the point?" Koller laughed bitterly. "She'll just forget it. Isn't that the whole idea of Alzheimer's? Everything runs out through the cracks? What's the joke? The best thing about Alzheimer's is that you meet new people every day?" The faint laugh was hollow, empty.

Erika cried out, a wordless sound, leaped to her feet and strode angrily to a window. Her arms folded across her chest, she stared out at the huge concrete pots full of shrubs and trees lining the verandah of Gisevius's home.

"Yes, yes, but telling her now might be the kindest thing. There may be matters she wants to attend to. Wolf, my old friend—I understand, believe me. It's a sad time. There is no way around it."

In the silence that followed, Gisevius rolled the ash from the tip of his cigar and let it fall into the cut-glass ashtray. He rested the cigar in the groove and opened the middle drawer of his desk. He extended a finger and pushed the off button, felt the cassette click upward into his palm. He placed the cassette on the leather top of the desk. He put the cigar in the corner of his mouth and uncapped his fountain pen. He carefully printed the words *Wolf & Erika Koller. November. Regarding Lise Koller.* on a label, then affixed the label to the audiocassette. He looked up and caught Koller's eye. "Housekeeping," he said softly. "It saves constantly taking notes."

When it was time to leave Wolf Koller tried to engage his daughter in conversation. They were standing in the circular drive before the imposing house. "Erika, we must talk about this. I can't have you just leaving . . . I want to help you, do what I can to get us both through this—why won't you talk to me? Can't you at least put aside your anger for the time being? I might be able to help you . . ."

She stood with her legs apart, pulling on her gloves, her eyes steady behind the dark tinted lenses.

"Go to hell, Father. You're almost there as it is." Her boots clicked on the paving as she went to the little black Porsche.

Koller watched her drive away. Loving her, hating her . . . She saw it all in the rearview mirror as she swept around the driveway. Love and hate. And she knew she was becoming a problem, a real problem, to her father.

Now, three weeks later, forty-eight hours after the riot and Karl-Heinz's telling her about SPARTAKUS until she couldn't stand hearing any more, she stood at the window, felt the hot tears burning in the scrapes and lacerations on her cheekbones. She saw through the spitting mist the huge Mercedes-Benz symbol rotating ceaselessly in the gloom. The economic power of the new Germany rising from the barren bombed-out darkness of the past, built by men like her father who hadn't forgotten the old glories.

She leaned her face against the cold window, shivered. It wouldn't be much longer now.

She turned back to face her surroundings, all the nonsense of negative space she'd once, only a few months ago, thought was so bloody important. The furniture was low and sparse. There was a neon sculpture, alternating numbers in various colors, blinking, blinking, across one wall. And on the floor sat an installation by a promising young artist she'd delivered to the gallery, her first find. It was a pile of broken chunks of cement, pieces of the Wall, and if you looked at it in just the way the artist intended, in the perfect light, you might see the shadow of a howling wolf behind it, on the floor and across the wall. He was a very bright young man. He liked to shock people by wearing a yellow piece of cloth, the Star of David, on his shirt when he went among the lovers of art, the patrons of the gallery. Erika had, on one or two occasions, actually seen the howling wolf made by the pile of rubble. It wasn't easy. The artist said you had to *want* to see it. That was part of the art, surely she saw that.

At right angles to the howling wolf wall was a blown-up black and white photo of the Brandenburg Gate shot by her friend Beate. The details were blurred by sheets of rain. Against the gray sky the Goddess of Victory whipped her great gray horses onward, the old iron cross of Prussia back in place on her staff. After the war, when the Communists had repaired the statuary atop the Gate, they'd refused to put the symbol of Prussian militarism back in its place. But once the Wall had come down and the East Germans and the West Germans, the *new* Germans, had set about fixing things the way they were supposed to be, the iron cross had mysteriously reappeared. *Ya gotta love the Krauts, they never give up.* A young American student had told her that and they had laughed and had another beer. *No keeping you Krauts down. No wonder the rest of Europe is already scared shitless.*

When the Wall came down, when the Gate opened, when Checkpoint Charlie became a party, the space at the bottom of the Brandenburg Gate became a flea market where the former East Germans sold souvenirs, bits and pieces of their old military uniforms mostly. There wasn't much of anything else to call a souvenir. It hadn't been much of a country. What must it have taken to make a country of Germans unproductive?

The old Germany, the new Germany. In the end it was all the same. She could hear the jackboots marching, see the gray uniforms . . . *you wore blue, the Germans wore gray* . . . Bogart . . . She'd had to find it all out for herself and still she knew so little, but she knew enough . . . she'd seen the swastikas spray-painted on walls by the punks in leather and chains, posturing tough guys, bully boys . . . nothing had changed. And she was part of it, Erika Koller. She was part of the problem. Karl-Heinz had told her that the slogan made sense. *If you're not part of the solution, you're part of the problem.* It was true. He didn't understand what it was like to be Erika Koller. There was no way to make him see it. She was part of history in a way he wouldn't understand. She was part of the problem. In the end, he'd never have been able to forgive her . . .

No escape. No way to get out of it, nowhere to turn, no innocence to recapture, not for her.

She was at the heart of it.

Well . . . it was time.

She went to the kitchen. It gleamed, perfect, shiny and new. The Brauns, the Krups . . . the bright knives of Solingen steel.

Then she went into the bathroom. Preposterously bright and shining.

They had believed in blood rites. It was part of the Wagnerian, Teutonic soul. The Black Forest . . . Externstine . . . the Spear of Destiny. They loved all that. Destiny. Blood. Never enough blood.

She stared at her face in the mirror. She wasn't quite so pretty now that they'd finished with her in the street.

But it didn't matter anymore.

She felt the knife slip from her fingers, heard it clatter on the cold tile.

She could barely see her face through the blood sprayed across the mirror.

Burke Delaney hadn't wanted to leave the dogs to fend for themselves all day. That was in the first place. And he certainly hadn't wanted to drive that damn Range Rover—with a suspension that dated from T. E. Lawrence's day, he was certain—all the way to this dreary little oil slick of a village on the far side of Potsdam. That was in the second place. And the third thing was, experience had taught him not to deal with kids any more than he had to. Kids didn't know what they were doing, that was the problem, and some of them had the notion they were going to live forever, no matter what fool tricks they played. Well, they weren't going to live forever, and if this kid he was waiting for didn't turn up soon, he was going to find out how short life could be.

It was raining and it was cold and you could smell the mud and it reminded him of the Battle of the Bulge, which hadn't been any fun either. It smelled like snow. Darkness was coming earlier every day, that gray metallic darkness that leaked oil and sweat and sadness and the anger you always found in the East. Some folks were saying they were getting perkier over there nowadays but he hadn't seen it. And sure as hell not in this dump. It wasn't much different from Checkpoint Charlie in the old days, at its worst.

He had parked the Rover against a grimy shed that must have held something goddamn important when you considered the size of the dog rattling around inside. It sounded like he threw himself against the padlocked door every so often just for the sheer sport of it. The motorcycle garage and filling station were lit by three or four twenty-watt bulbs made in Ukraine. The village idiot was banging at an ancient Harley with a wrench built for lug nuts. Delaney wondered just how low he would sink doing things for his country. He had the feeling he was scraping bottom. Being home listening to Schuyler barking his head off and sporting a big red woodie—that was where he should have been, not in this outer edge of beyond.

He banged the bowl of his pipe on the heel of his Orvis boot and set to packing it full again from the oilskin pouch. It had been a three-pipe wait so far.

He heard the putt-putt-putt of the motorcycle first, then saw the figure of the man astride it, splashing through a pothole and skidding a bit coming out, then splashing through the oil and muck that served as a driveway. The kid swung the bike around and stopped it beside the Rover, dismounted, and swatted the kickstand down with his booted foot. The boots were the sort of thing that drove Delaney nuts. They had little leather wings with silver buckles up the side. Along with the scarred bubble helmet, they made the kid look like a panhandler from another planet. He tipped back the visor as he came up to Delaney, said something in German, but Delaney was staring at the face. It was swollen and bruised. The lower lip was split and the scab was pulling away. One eye wore a dark purple mouse and was puffed nearly shut.

Delaney laid a finger beside his nose, said: "Hit a van lately?"

"Very humorous. I nearly died. Stiffel's brownshirts." He sounded like a man trying to talk with a catcher's mitt in his mouth. "Street riot."

"You were obviously on the wrong side. English football fans versus the Ku'damm pansies?"

"You are not a serious man, Mr. Delaney. It worries me. Sometimes I think you do not take me with the proper gravity." He swallowed hard, tough with the catcher's mitt in his mouth.

"Sometimes you're right. You're an idealist, kid. In my line of work idealists are the ones always trying to get *me* killed for *their* beliefs." It was raining harder and the village idiot had stepped up his attack on the Harley. "Come on, you need some of my special coffee. You want Tylenol-3, the prescription stuff? Your face must hurt like hell, soldier."

They got into the Rover and Delaney switched it on, got the heater working. The young man pulled his helmet off, sliding it gingerly up over his ears, one of which was puffed to twice its normal size. He took the tablets Delaney shook from a bottle, sucked up enough steaming coffee to get them down.

"We ran into a mob of Stiffel's people. They were after some Turks . . . you can imagine the rest. These people are out of control. Very well organized, gaining support." He flinched when the hot coffee stung the raw crevice in his lower lip. "There's evidence of an alliance among the various neo-Nazi groups all over the country."

"So you say. There's some interest in your product in the home office. Understand?"

"It is logical. It is not logical to refuse to help us . . ." Behind the puffed flesh his eyes darted, surprised, panicky. "These people must be stopped."

"Relax. I need more time to sell them on the idea. You can't blame them, it's a little far-fetched."

"History is far-fetched," he snorted.

"It's just another bureaucracy, if that's any consolation. Drink your coffee."

"Americans never know what they want," he muttered, warming his hands on the plastic cup. "That's always been America's problem."

"Oh, is that right? We knew what we wanted in 1941 and '42 and '43 and '44 and '45—ask some of your old man's friends. We always knew what to do back in the old days—"

"The old days," the kid spit contemptuously.

"Back when there was right and wrong. But that's too sophisticated a concept for you, isn't it?" Delaney sighed. "My young friend, you told me it was important for me to meet you here in this pesthole today. I haven't heard anything important yet." He grinned, wolfishly, beneath his long soup-strainer mustache. Delaney always wore an old watch cap, which made his weatherbeaten, blunt-featured face look all the tougher. He always smelled slightly of dog.

The kid drew a buff envelope from inside his leather jacket. "For this, your friends should give us their support—for this alone." It was dark outside now. The dog was still throwing himself at the metal door of the shed. Faint rock music was emanating from the garage. "I must go. I cannot be late for the meeting."

"You're a busy boy. Meetings all day long. You going back to Berlin tonight?"

"Yes. I'm staying with my parents."

"No shit. If your father knew what you were up to—"

"Don't worry about my father."

"What's in the folder?"

"It's worth my life, I promise you that. It's self-explanatory. I can't wait to explain it. I must go." He had opened the door. "I'll be in touch."

"Oh, I'm sure of that, soldier."

Delaney watched him mount the bike, give it a kick, and settle back on the seat as it started to whine. *Bon voyage, my young friend.* He drove off through a series of puddles, sending up fans of muddy water.

Delaney fiddled around with his pipe again, scraped the inside of the bowl, and packed it with tobacco. He lit it and puffed reflectively, wondering just how long a kid like that would stay alive with guys like Joachim Stiffel running around with clubs and knives. They'd killed a Turk, some kid probably never hurt anybody in his life, and everybody knew who did it. Except the *Polizei*. He damn sure wouldn't be selling young Karl-Heinz Schmidt any life insurance.

Delaney didn't open the folder until he was well on the way home. He pulled off onto the side of the road and took out a flashlight, had a peek.

The kid had typed up a report. It was the second installment of SPARTAKUS—whatever the hell that was. He'd fax it from town the next morning, at the commercial copy and fax shop. To an accommodation number in Georgetown. Strangely enough, it was the most secure route.

Ned Cheddar could figure it out.

But it didn't take a genius to know that something was up.

Dreiser, the chauffeur, gave her a sidelong look of disapproval when she told him she wouldn't need him. Lise Koller swept on past him, keys to the Porsche Carrera—the twin of her daughter's—jangling in her hand. She'd had to give him a talking-to a couple of weeks before and then she'd laid down the law to Wolf. She might not be quite herself these days but they hadn't locked her up in a hospital yet and until they did she was going to drive her car. Wolf had backed off. She knew he had talked with Fritz Gisevius about her spells of memory loss, the days she spent in a haze of lethargy; she knew what Fritz must have told him, at least in outline, but not because the doctor had told her. She had instead gone to a doctor friend of Erika's and the young man had told her that, while he was not an expert, he could be quite sure she didn't have a brain tumor, which she had feared. He couldn't find anything; her symptoms fit with an onset of Alzheimer's—but, again, he'd assured her he wasn't an expert. There were other possibilities and he'd innocently suggested she consult the best man in Germany, in Europe, in fact. Fritz Gisevius, of course.

Fritz was the expert, she realized that, but he'd tiptoed around the diagnosis in her presence. And as far as Lise Koller was concerned, he was too much Wolf's creature to be entirely trustworthy. Wolf would control him—for whatever reasons he might have—just as he controlled everything else in his world. She was never sure what Wolf was after but their marriage was by now just a matter of appearances: nearly twenty years together had left her drained, unsure of what she believed but knowing she could never believe in Wolf. And Fritz was Wolf's man.

But the illness had taken a good deal of the fight out of her. Fritz was treating her with some kind of new injections that might reverse a protein deficiency which he said could in rare instances produce Alzheimer's-like symptoms. She was up against the wall: she had no choice but to try anything, and if it came from Fritz, so be it. Some days

—her good days—she was sure he was on to something. The bad days were a blur, blank spots. Terrifying. And it was Erika on whom she leaned for support, for hope, though she hadn't told her daughter yet how bad the news might be.

What was frightening her now was that she hadn't been able to get hold of Erika for several days. That was unusual. Yesterday she'd gone to the Café Einstein for their weekly meeting, a time to gossip, and Erika hadn't shown up. And there had been no answer at the flat. She had called the gallery and they didn't know where Erika was; she hadn't called in. Now Lise could wait no longer. Much as she hated to play the intruding mother, she was going to find Erika, one way or another.

She left the great house in Grunewald and felt the Carrera pulsing beneath her. The rain of the past several days had finally stopped, grudgingly, and the gray clouds still hung low over the trees of autumn, some dark-leaved and brooding, others skeletal. The road was slick with wet leaves. Her mind was racing. Was she losing her mind, was she going mad? Could it possibly be happening to her? She'd read up on the disease, going to libraries, privately learning the worst, but the good days made it all seem like a bad dream. Then she'd miss a day, two days, and it hadn't been a dream. She truly was losing her mind . . .

And now Erika—where was she? How could she just disappear? Karl-Heinz, the newish boyfriend, came to mind but she didn't have a theory as to how Karl-Heinz could make Erika disappear. She knew little about him: he seemed to be marginal in some way, not the sort of boy Erika chose to bring home with her. He was not the boy—she supposed she'd have to get used to thinking of him as a man—Lise would have chosen for Erika but, my God, she was just dating him. How much harm could there be in that? She told herself to lighten up. So, where was Erika? Why wouldn't she have called the gallery?

Even as Lise moved into her fifties she was a strikingly beautiful woman. Her pale brown hair, shot through with honey blond, was a work of art, casual, swinging when she walked, yet short enough to keep her from looking like a woman struggling to seem younger than she was. The result—with the attention paid to her face, the little nipping and tucking at discreet clinics in Switzerland, the smoothness of her skin, the perfect caps on her teeth, the figure that hadn't changed dimensions in twenty-five years—the result was that she looked to be in her late thirties. She wore clothing by Chanel and Balenciaga that she'd had for years, clothing that defined her image of herself. Today she wore a burnt-orange suit by Chanel with bone-colored shoes and earrings and bracelets. The skirt showed a lot of firm, shapely leg. The coat was by Joop, leather with lots of lashing at the edges, like something out of *Dances with Wolves*. Her sunglasses were by Claude Montana. At a distance, or in the flattering light of a party or a ball, she was rather more than a knockout still. But being a knockout was no defense against what was happening to her brain, and all the private crying wasn't doing her face any good.

When she inspected that face in the mirror the shock of reality hit her like a blow to the solar plexus. In the past few months, ever since she first began to feel things slipping out of control, she had seen a toll taken in her face. Her eyes were dulled. There was pain etched in the corners of her eyes and mouth, in the muscle flickering along her clenched jaw. Her mouth was held tight. Everything about her was tight and tense and tired, as if by constant vigilance she might stave off the inevitable.

She never knew what the next day would bring. She sometimes found herself living in memories that seemed to belong to someone else. She seemed to remember the bombing in London, the Blitz, hiding beneath a dining table while the Luftwaffe battered the city, seeing the ceiling crash down on her mother in an explosion of plaster dust and kindling . . . But she had never remembered her mother's death consciously. She had been too young. Now her mind wandered and sometimes Wolf would shake her and tell her she'd been screaming. Sometimes she thought she was in the cockpit of her father's Spitfire out over the English Channel, diving and twisting among the Messerschmitts, firing the heavy cannon in the nose of the plane, but none of that could be a memory. She'd never been inside a Spitfire. She only knew her father had died in the Battle of Britain, an American flying for the RAF, but why was it all raging through her mind now? What was the point? What was the source? It was all part of the mystery of what was happening inside her brain . . .

If only she could trust someone other than Erika. If only she could trust Wolf . . . But there was only Erika, no one else.

She left the Porsche among the wet leaves at the curb. The concierge's desk was unoccupied, as usual, and she went directly to the small, self-service elevator. It was an old building that had suffered during the war and been carefully restored. The quiet dry coolness, the permanent smell of plaster always made her think of Wolf: he owned the building and many others and years ago while he was restoring them she had helped with decorating schemes, had spent many hours among the plasterers and carpenters and electricians. Maybe, a long time ago, she'd felt differently about Wolf, back when she'd refused to admit the truth about herself, her own life, and his. But that was all over now. She knew she couldn't trust him now. Erika had made her see all that.

She had her own key to the flat, given on the condition that Wolf would never have it. Erika had been very clear about that. No key for her father. Erika's hatred ran deep, made all the worse because she'd worshiped him as a little girl. Erika was very like her mother. Within limits, they understood one another.

The spare, jagged edginess of the rooms bothered Lise, made her wonder what a psychiatrist would have said about them. Lise hated them. The flashing neon numbers, the pile of rubble with the light shining across it, the shadow on the wall. The splintered quality, the lack of depth, made her feel as if her own shattered mind were on view, mocked by the harsh environment. Yet she understood Erika, the girl's vulnerability and the conscience that Lise found so lacking in her own life, and she loved her as she'd never loved another soul. Now, taking in the room, she knew immediately that the place was empty.

Where could Erika be? Lise stood at the window, staring down into the street, already wintry and dun-colored, then let her eyes wander up to the huge photograph of the Quadriga on top of the Brandenburger Tor, to the great horses charging, thundering toward her beneath Victory's cries. Where might she have gone? For days? Without leaving word? She went to the slab of glass Erika used for a desk and shifted through papers and datebook. There was no explanation. Erika. Darling Erika. Where are you . . .

Without a plan, she meandered through the rooms, felt the coffeemaker; it was cold. The white walls were closing in on her. She went to the bedroom, where the bed was made but rumpled as if Erika had lain on it, covered with a blanket, and been unable to sleep. Unable to commit herself to sleep, perhaps. The mist streaked the windows.

The light was on in the bathroom.

She went to the doorway and reached in to turn it off.

There was blood everywhere. Sprayed on the mirror, streaking the porcelain sink. Puddled on the floor.

Lise felt her stomach turning, felt herself growing ice cold and dripping with sweat, felt her eyes losing focus, knew she was falling . . .

They were sitting where they'd been sitting three weeks before but now they were discussing Erika rather than having to deal with her in person.

They were three weeks closer to SPARTAKUS. Time was running short and Friedrich Gisevius was trying to calm himself: he was still worried about the relationship between Wolf Koller and his daughter, how it might be affected by the death of Lise Koller. All his life Gisevius had depended on Wolf Koller: on his strength of will, the power of his character and intelligence, and the immense influence commanded by all that money. SPARTAKUS was the culmination of all these elements and the doctor didn't want to run the risk of anything's bringing their plan to grief. There was no longer any reason to worry about Lise ruining everything with one of her irrational outbursts. But Erika was another matter.

"But is she stable enough?" The doctor had all but forgotten about his cigar, which smoldered, dying, in the chunk of cut glass. "These questions must be asked—I apologize for them. But can she handle both Lise and the effect of SPARTAKUS?" He spoke very softly. He knew who was the dominant figure in the room; there was nothing to be gained by tapping into the fury Wolf always contained within himself.

"I don't know . . . she hates me so much. I can't reach her, Fritz. You know the way she thinks—"

"Can you trust her?"

Koller stared at the Siegfried painting, eyes narrowing.

Can you trust her?

"No more than I can trust Lise. Who knows what either of them might say or do . . . Lise has poisoned her mind." Wolf Koller shrugged. "And that boyfriend, Karl-Heinz . . . he's the worst sort of influence on her. But I don't have a crystal ball, Fritz. When it comes to one's family, one can never be sure."

"There are risks . . . but you know that." Gisevius considered the storm gathering behind Wolf Koller's eyes and dropped the subject. "And there's the matter of telling Lise of her condition—"

"No. That's out of the question. Who knows how it might set her off?"

"Yes, yes . . . but she may wish to prepare. Wolf, my old friend —none of this is going to be easy."

"I know. I'm relying on you in this."

Gisevius nodded solemnly.

Wolf Koller stretched his long legs out before him. His chalk-striped suit from Huntsman in Savile Row, London, was rumpled, losing its shape. The problem presented by his wife was taking a toll on the best-dressed man in Berlin. He was in a very rare confessional mood. He was always the senior partner in his relationship with Fritz Gisevius: that had always been a given, something in the natures of the two men. But sometimes even Wolf Koller needed to confide in someone. Invariably it was Fritz Gisevius. "I don't know . . . she's not a happy woman. Death may be a release for her. She's never been happy. Our marriage has been a trial, you know that, almost from the beginning. She turned against me a long time ago. And I'm the one who rescued her from the mess she'd made of her life, I was there waiting for her when Gunter Brendel was killed twenty years ago, I'm the one who stepped forward to take her hand. But she's never been happy, never been willing to forgive me for rescuing her. Without me I think she'd have ended it all back then. Women—such *monsters!* I've only known one who wasn't, one woman who loved me . . . But that was a long time ago, wasn't it, Fritz?"

"Yes, a very long time ago, and she was damn near the end of you, let me remind you." Gisevius had rescued his cigar and now watched his old friend through the veil of smoke. "You haven't been all that lucky with women, Wolf. A sad fact."

"I think we're doing the right thing, the necessary thing." Wolf Koller heaved a frustrated sigh. "I can't trust Lise to behave anymore. God only knows what she might say about me . . . I don't know what poison Erika has been telling her, they've been cross-pollinating one another, infecting, then reinfecting . . ." He shook his head in contemplation of a peculiar phenomenon. "Women," he said again. *"Monsters."*

Gisevius waited, sensitive to Koller's moods, familiar with the mercurial temper. Then he said: "She still has some family in the United States." He didn't want to belabor the point but it had to be confronted.

"You mean that brother she hasn't seen in twenty years." He shrugged dismissively.

"The one who made all the trouble twenty years ago."

"When I rescued her from the mess he made—"

"She might want to see him again."

"She never speaks of him. Maybe her 'illness' has wiped out the memory—"

"Don't let her see him, Wolf. She might get it in her head to . . . well, it would just stir everything up again. That wouldn't do anyone any good. I advise against it most strongly. Her time is running out."

Koller nodded. "Yes, yes, I know she mustn't see him. That mess twenty years ago when Brendel was killed . . ." He was tired, his voice at half strength. "Her brother's part in it, yes, it might all come back to her . . . and God knows what she'd tell Erika about it . . ." He stood up, shot his cuffs. He was tall and slender, more relaxed now for having let Gisevius look within. "You've given me good advice, Fritz. I know I can trust you to do what is necessary for my wife. I thank you." He turned and walked across the room, past the globes and the books and the cabinets. He opened the heavy paneled door, then stopped, turning back to Gisevius, then was gone.

Later she was awake and remembered that she had revived and called Wolf at his office and they had switched her to his car telephone and then she had lost her bearings again and now she was hearing his voice in person. He was giving someone absolute hell, his voice steely quiet, but she wasn't quite sure why. She opened her eyes for a moment and saw the man with the gray brushcut hair taking the knife edge of abuse: she recognized him, Wolf's head of security, but she couldn't remember his name. He responded quietly and Wolf then put his hand on the man's shoulder in a comradely gesture. A moment's warmth in the glacier of fury.

Then she remembered the bathroom and the blood and fought off the surge of sickness in her stomach.

There had been no body, no lifeless Erika on the cold bloody tiles.

Lise fixed her mind on that. There was hope. Someone had found her, had helped her, had taken her somewhere . . . to hospital. Obviously. That's what Wolf was going on about now. The hospitals must be checked. Private doctors. Anywhere she might have been taken for treatment.

"What about the police?" That was the security man.

"Not a word of this must get out—this is my daughter. *Wolf Koller's daughter.*"

"With all due respect, Wolf, if you want to find your daughter you may have to deal with the police." The security man spoke with familiarity, calling Wolf by his given name. They'd known one another for a long time.

"Not until we must. You yourself found the knife under the bathroom cabinet. You've just proven to me that the only prints on the knife are hers . . . so it's not a murder case. We needn't call the police in yet."

"But we have such limited resources. I can have Sebastien turn his people loose on it but—well, hunting for lost girls is not their specialty."

"Tell him his life depends on finding her. He'll do as he's told. And if we have to deal with the police, you know who I want."

"Adler. Yes, I know."

"Well, don't just stand there. Find my daughter."

The voices floated around her as she lay still on the couch. Her head ached where she'd hit the floor. Wolf was kneeling beside her now.

"How are you feeling, my darling? Can you talk?"

"Of course. But there's nothing to say. She tried to kill herself."

"We don't know that. Don't be melodramatic now of all times. Try to keep yourself under control. It might have been an accident. We don't know."

"Don't be foolish. She wasn't peeling potatoes—"

"She wouldn't know how. I agree with you there."

"It doesn't matter."

"Lise—are you there? Do you recognize me?"

"Yes, Wolf," she said impatiently. "I recognize you. I'm all right. I want to go home. I can drive my car."

"I don't think that's wise, darling."

"You're a powerful man. Don't waste your power trying to frighten me. Just find my daughter. Don't worry about my going home."

She got up from the couch. Wolf tried to help and she pulled away. Two of his aides hovered in the background, one speaking in a determined whisper on the white telephone. Wolf paced, watched her, wondering if she'd suddenly come apart.

"It's raining hard out there." He watched her expectantly. "You're quite sure you'll be all right?"

She knew what he meant: it really had nothing to do with the rain. She turned and strode out of the flat, the leather coat swirling behind her.

If her daughter was dead, if she had somehow succeeded in killing herself, Lise would exact revenge on him. If Erika was dead, she would kill Wolf Koller.

For the moment, thankful that her mind was holding firm, she was thinking through a plan of action. Time was her enemy. She never knew when her mind would go. When she wouldn't know a goddamn thing, wouldn't remember what she'd done. She had to move fast.

There was someone she had to see.

And, miraculously, she had thought of someone else. Someone she could trust.

She hoped.

———————————

There was something a little funny about Clint Kilroy but not everyone picked up on it. You couldn't give it a name. He just sort of made you wonder. He was a nice enough fellow, no scandal had ever attached itself to him, nothing unsavory, but still, you always had the feeling there was a helluva lot you didn't know about him. Folks in Dallas weren't given to asking too many questions, not if you had Kilroy's kind of money, and his late wife had been as solid a customer as Neiman Marcus could have hoped for. You'd see them out at Turtle Creek and they were regulars in the skyboxes at the 'Boys games and Clint Kilroy was just one of a lot of people with pretty vague pasts who turned up in Texas one way or another.

And that was just the way Clint Kilroy liked it. He couldn't think of a time when you didn't want the other guy just a little off balance. Hell, it just stood to reason. The worst mistake in the world was to indulge in an excess of trust. It was the kind of mistake other people might make, but not Clint Kilroy.

He was seventy-three. Something like that, he was never quite sure. Thin and ropey, lots of sinew, dark leathery skin from years of being out in the sun in the oil fields or on building sites. Pale blue eyes, white hair cut short and brushed with a part on the left. He had developed a tendency to dress like a shitkicker with too much money, in Western business clothes, arrow-pockets and some leather trim and fancy-dyed boots some beaner in Waco made for him. The bullshit getup had helped get him into the part in the beginning and now it was second nature. His accent was indefinable—West Texas drawl but there was something else in there, too, and that was what fooled people. Nobody had ever guessed right yet and it was damn lucky for them they hadn't. He'd have had to go for his gun in that case. Kilroy himself attributed his accent to "varieties of hell-raising all over the world from oddball places like Bhutan and Belize City and an absolute shithole like Kaduna to some German hotspots during and after the big show over there," at which time he was, as he said, "a very tiny cog in a very big fuck-up called Military Intelligence, and if that ain't one of them oxymorons I'll eat my Stetson."

All in all, he'd had a full life and he often won people over by telling stories on himself. He was a millionaire so many times over he'd lost interest in counting it up. He'd shown up in Dallas one sunny day after the war was over, no family, no connections, plenty of nerve and lots of ready cash. He never let on where it came from but it was widely supposed that he'd come out of the war with a stash of dirty money— some folks said it was Hitler's money, some said it was blackmail because he sure as shootin' looked like he knew where somebody had buried the bodies. Others said maybe he just plain stole it. Clint just winked at them with his pale blue eyes and said he didn't think they really believed all that blood and thunder, did they?

When Ned Cheddar dragged him back into the deep shit for about the umpteenth time, Kilroy was lying in his pool, drinking vodka and tonic, pushing a yellow inflatable dinosaur at his granddaughter, who kept giggling and splashing him, chubby in her six-year-old's polka-dot bikini. It was unusually warm for late fall, one of the last good pool days. He had a snootful of Prozac and Wellbutrin, chased with a Valium and some Alka-Seltzer Sinus Medicine, so on the whole he had no complaints, other than a ticker that was paying the price for being seventy-three years old and having some pieces of a forty-five slug in it. No complaints until the telephone next to him on his pink plastic raft rang and he heard the familiar nasal voice and knew he had to switch the fucking scrambler on.

"Cheese," he said with a sigh of resignation. "So my sources told me the 'Boys would cover the six, so how could I know the 'Skins would get that Peruvian kicker outa detox? Is that my fault? Be honest for once, don't off the fuckin' messenger. Do we really need to scramble this shit?"

"Football has not prompted this call. Chitchat is not what I have in mind. What does the word 'SPARTAKUS' mean to you?"

Kilroy thought. It was a test, just like in the old days when he had to be up to the mark on all this shit because they were always springing little tests on him to see if he'd blow his cover. Was it a trick question? He swigged at the vodka and tonic. Little Jennifer came up underneath him and rammed his balls with the yellow dinosaur. Thirty seconds before, it had been such a nice day. "Kirk Douglas," he said at last. "Jean Simmons. Olivier plays the fruity Caesar or some damn thing. Howard Fast wrote the book. The downtrodden slaves revolt against their Roman masters. All the right-wingers said it was Commie propspeak. Fast was blacklisted—I defy you to flunk me on this one."

"That was *Spartacus* with a 'c' and you omitted the name of the director—"

"Kubrick."

"—and I'm saying 'SPARTAKUS' with a 'k.' "

"Well, how the hell was I supposed to know? You think I'm telegenic?"

"That's telepathic, Clint."

Kilroy sighed. "Lighten up, Cheese. It was a joke."

"So what does 'SPARTAKUS' with a 'k' mean to you?"

"I don't know. Nothing. So if that's all, I got me a dicey ticker here, a tender prostate that might mean any damn thing, and my granddaughter is trying to shove a pretty goodsized plastic dinosaur up my ass. So leave your humble servant be, okay."

"We've got a possible Code Red, Clint."

"Aw, shit! That kinda talk went out with 'the eagle has landed.' "

"Don't be that way. We can get you out of Dallas on American late this afternoon. Get you a nice dinner on board there, you'll be at Logan in time to get to the Harvard Club for a nightcap. Clint?"

"You're in *Boston*?"

"Good lord, no. I'm in Georgetown. *You're* going to Boston. There's a man I want you to check out." He began to lay out Kilroy's instructions and when he was done Clint Kilroy slammed down the phone and it slipped off into the water, bobbed away. "Aw, fucking crappola, crapper, crapperino!"

"Grandpa! You are being bad! Mom? *Mommy*—Grandpa is saying those bad things again!"

Kilroy was paddling his raft toward the edge of the pool. It was slow going. He'd spilled his drink. Cheese was after his skinny ass again. It was always something.

2

BERLIN WAS CALLING

They sat in the bright sunshine on the restaurant's deck overlooking the Boston Harbor marina. Faneuil Hall and the Quincy Market and Government Center and finally the brilliant gold dome atop the State House on Beacon Hill seemed foreshortened, as if they were all jumbled together. Wind caught in the sails of the boats bobbing in the choppy, glittering water, pennants whipping, canvas covers battened down at the end of the season. John Cooper took it all in absentmindedly, his attention on the rather peculiar gent across the table. Cooper was wearing chinos and a maroon boatneck sweater he'd bought in 1960 at Filene's Basement. The wind was cold enough to notice and he sat facing the sun, feeling it on his face. Gulls honked and dipped.

Clint Kilroy's thin mouth had formed what Cooper believed must pass for a smile out there on the trail. The man had a spare, wintry look. He was a mixture of good old boy and con man from the sound of the noises he was making. He wore a leather jacket with some fringe on it and whipcord pants and very subtle black cowboy boots with almost invisible black stitching. He was thin as a piece of jerky and looked twice as tough. Funny accent, not quite Texas but what else could you hear? Cooper wasn't sure.

"You came all the way to Boston to try to buy my theater and the bookstore? Long way to come on a smile and a hope and a shoeshine, Mr. Kilroy."

"Oh no, you misapprehend me, sir. I came here to buy the theater and the bookstore, not to try. 'Course, a fella doesn't always get his own way. But I figure you ought to think it over. I could make you a moderately rich man."

Cooper laughed softly. "I'm already a moderately rich man."

"Well, you never know, you might change your mind. What have we been eating here? Tasted almost like fish."

"Scrod. You might say the red stuff with the peppers and tomatoes in it makes the dish."

"Scrod. Well, I've eaten worse, I'll give you that. Lived on grub worms for a time in the jungle. Not half bad but I never figured out which half wasn't bad." He produced a weathered smile. " 'Course, I *know* you're moderately rich. I do my research. You've had an interesting life, Mr. Cooper."

"Have I, indeed?" Cooper sipped some steaming coffee. The guy was right. The scrod hadn't been up to snuff. "Am I so easy to find out about?" There was something going on in this chat that he didn't know about. Kilroy was so cool, so sure of himself.

"I didn't say it was easy. I'm just the kind of man who's got ways of finding out. You know that fellow who hired his own army to go after the MIAs, always running for President? I always call him Parrot. Drives him nuts. Well, he sold me some computers when he was working for Big Blue, found me some folks to run 'em. It's amazing the stuff I can find out. Your age, your birthplace, your daddy, your granddaddy. Now take you—you had an interesting adventure in Germany a while back. Twenty years ago."

What was going on here? "You have the advantage of me."

"Germany interests me. I was there during the war and for a time afterward. Munich, Frankfurt, Berlin. Spent some time in the East looking for folks. Very rewarding. Offering folks a better life."

"I'm having lunch with a saint."

"The East was *anus mundi* in those days, if you want the truth. It's still not much, from what I hear. Hangdog, you might say. Anyway, when Germany crops up, I notice."

"I must have missed Germany cropping up," Cooper said. He was on his guard now. *Germany.*

"Now I don't want to tread on anybody's toes here, but you're

Austin Cooper's grandson, am I right?" Clint Kilroy leaned back, blithely watching the diving gulls and the sun dancing on the water.

Cooper said: "What's this got to do with buying my corner of the world?"

"Hell, I don't know. I just collect knowledge. Always have. I like to know the man I'm dealing with. You never know when you might spark a friendship. Then you can make a deal. Mind if I smoke?" He took out a cheroot, cupped his hand around the lighter, and sent forth a plume of smoke. "Do you ever go back to Cooper's Falls?" He smiled. "What there was left of it when you and your pal Peterson got done with it. I've got some good friends out there. Lot of money in Minnesota. But you'd know all about that."

"No, I don't go back to Minnesota."

"Why's that? Too cold for you?"

"I just don't go back. That's my story and I'm sticking to it."

Kilroy laughed. "You haven't been back in twenty years? That's a will of iron. Made quite a story, 'the Siege of Cooper's Falls.' Emily, that's my head researcher, she got pretty wrapped up in all that when we were putting together a dossier on you. So you never went back."

Cooper nodded. "Look, I'm beginning to get a little pissed off here, so let's quit while we're ahead. You've proven your point, I suppose. You know about me and I don't know a damn thing about you. That's fine with me. But I'm not going to sell you my movie house or my bookstore. Let's just pretend none of this happened and we'll never see each other again. Sounds good to me, how about you?"

"Don't rile so easy, boy. You'll never make a poker player this way."

"That's okay with me too."

"Still have any old contacts left in Germany? Anybody from the old days?" He gave the funny little smile again. "Or did you kill everybody you knew?"

Cooper stood up. At six foot three, he loomed over the table. "You're out of time, pal. I've taken care of lunch so you can just saddle up and mosey on down the trail."

"You've still got a sister over there, right?"

Cooper was walking away. Kilroy caught up with him, still smiling. "You writing books these days? I got me a couple of the earlier ones, just couldn't get into 'em, somehow."

"A critic on top of everything else."

"I'm just saying, don't give up the day job." Kilroy followed him through the restaurant. The lunch crowd was thinning. "Did we get off on the wrong foot, son? Was it something I said?" Kilroy was enjoying himself.

"I'm not your son. You're wasting your time and mine. That's all, okay?"

"Don't be too sure. You gotta wait for the story to play itself out. Damnedest things been known to happen to folks. Right in the prime of life. Well, you take care now, hear? And if you change your mind you can leave a message for me at the Harvard Club."

"The Harvard Club?"

"Now, you see, I thought that'd get you. I've got friends." He shrugged. "Well," he said, laying a palm briefly on Cooper's back, "it's a long way to Abilene. Maybe we'll meet up again."

"Maybe not," Cooper said.

Kilroy was still smiling, not a care in the world, when Cooper climbed into his '78 Mark V. It looked like a brand-new car. The last view of him Cooper had, Kilroy seemed to be admiring himself in the mirror-like paintwork.

Before going to his office, which was upstairs, he ducked into the theater proper and took a seat. Kilroy had put him in a crummy mood and the movie might help get him out of it. He was running one of his quarterly "Ten Best Movies" festivals, which were intended to show the audience just how many wonderful movies there were and how one man's list was bound to be different than another's. Sergio Leone's *Once Upon a Time in the West* was playing and he sank into it, into the operatic power it had to move your emotions, to twist the knife of love in your heart. The story was nearing its end and was coming up on his favorite line in all of the movies of his life.

Jason Robards is talking to Claudia Cardinale. Her heart has been broken by love and he himself is gutshot and dying, though she doesn't know. He looks into her huge melting eyes—there were never more beautiful, engulfing eyes, a genetic equivalent of a time bomb going off in your emotional center—and considers her sadness, all the sadness that goes into a life that is after all too short and not so very important, and he says it.

"Make believe it doesn't matter . . ."

The point was, it really didn't matter, and that was as close to wisdom as he was going to come that day. Soon enough you were going to be gone, and what difference would any of it have made? You and all the people you loved and who loved you, you were all going to be gone and forgotten, and new people would be playing out all the same old plots. It didn't matter and nobody ever learned anything.

He'd been going to the movies all his life and those five words, remembered again and again, had made it possible for him to live his life, to hold it all together, after what happened twenty years ago. He had tried so hard to make believe it didn't matter. It had been a struggle.

Sure as hell this Kilroy character didn't matter. He'd just pushed the Fear buttons. But it didn't matter, that's what John Cooper was thinking as he left the comforting darkness. Maybe it was a lie but it could get you through the night, or the decade, or the rest of your life.

Sammy Desmond managed the bookstore for him. When it came to the bookstore Cooper was primarily a customer, constantly browsing, reading, and occasionally insisting that a particular book be stocked. Without Sammy the wheels would have quickly come off. Sammy was one of the perpetual graduate students who were everywhere in Boston and always had been. He looked underfed, undershaved, and overeducated, all of which were true. He habitually wore black pants and plaid shirts and was seldom seen anywhere but at his desk. He also often affected a green eyeshade and was wearing it when Cooper climbed the rickety stairs to the office and dropped onto the couch beneath the speakers. Today he recognized Roger Kellaway's recording *Come to the Meadow*, which meant Sammy was in a good mood.

Sammy looked up from a nostalgia radio cassette catalog and jammed his mended glasses back on his nose. He picked up a piece of notepaper. "You had a visitor, Boss. I would say at least an eight. So close to an eight it doesn't matter."

Mona Brooks sighed wearily from the other room, where she was pasting several thousand old movie reviews into scrapbooks, a job that did not in her mind jibe with the age of computers. She sighed loudly. "Jesus, what a sexist you are. Both of you! And you know it, too. Dinosaurs."

"Dinosaurs," Cooper agreed. "My lunch date was definitely not an eight," he said to Sammy. "What did I miss?"

"Great-looking girl, straight blond hair down to the line of her jaw, eyes as big as fists, sort of gray blue."

"Give me a looks-like."

"Right. Ummmm—okay, got it. Mai Zetterling in *Only Two Can Play.* My favorite romantic comedy. Definitely Mai Zetterling."

"Did you hear that, Mona?"

"Mai Zetterling. I suppose she's an eight, too."

"A nine. Maybe nine-five. All-time, all-star. Make a note, Mona. Put it on the next Ten Best list." Cooper turned back to Sammy. "So what did she want with me?"

"Sort of mysterious, Boss. Great accent."

"What kind of accent?"

"German. She had that low, throaty German voice."

"Listen to him," Mona said. "Hot for a Hun."

"She was wearing a black leather coat, creaked when she moved. Very sexy and sort of Gestapo-ominous. Love interest in a Helmut Dantine picture, maybe."

"What did she want, Sam?"

"Oh, want, yeah. To see you—said she couldn't leave a message with me. Too complicated. She'd just come in from Berlin yesterday. Funny thing, though. You never said you had a sister—"

Cooper felt the ground giving way beneath him. "What did you say?"

"She said she has a message from your sister. I didn't know you had a sister. What's the deal? She lives in Berlin?"

"I haven't seen her in twenty years. It's a funny family. That's all."

"Yeah, families are very funny creatures. Take mine . . . *please.* Heh, heh. Well, anyway, she said she'd get hold of you later. Since it was about your sister and all, I gave her your home number—that okay?"

"Sure, okay, it's all right." His mind was already elsewhere, spinning back through time. Kilroy had set him off on a track going backwards, hurtling into the black hole of time, and now this. And people said there was no such thing as coincidence.

"You okay, Boss?" It was Mona, standing in the doorway, holding a jar of paste. "You look like . . . like you've seen a ghost." She shrugged at her lack of originality.

Cooper came back to the present for an instant and smiled at her. "Sort of like *The Uninvited*?"

"Weeelllll, you're not exactly my idea of Ray Milland. Nothing personal, you understand." She went back to the other room and Sammy Desmond said: "So, what's up, Boss?"

But Cooper had gone on past him and into his own little office, seeing some shows that weren't listed, remembering how he'd found his sister, Lee, in the first place.

3

BEATE

He hadn't caught her name when she'd called back at the office. Her voice was indeed dark and throaty, as if she had a slight cold, but the name was unfamiliar.

"Bee-att-uh," she said. "Beate. Last name, Hubermann."

"Like Ingrid Bergman in *Notorious*," he murmured.

"Only she was Ilse. Aren't you clever!"

"It's my job."

"Being clever?"

"Knowing old movies."

"Well, can you tear yourself away from the old movies long enough to see me?" Her voice grew suddenly serious. "I have a message from your sister. It would be easier in person—"

"Yes, of course." Again he felt a chilly breeze of fear. Was it safe? Was she telling the truth or was there something else going on, something he couldn't see? He had the same feeling he'd had at lunch with Clint Kilroy—as if he were being left out of the joke. That was what Germany meant to him. That was the way it had been twenty years ago when so many people had died. Cooper had never quite known what was going on, and the fear and desperation had gotten worse and worse . . . Now, out of the past, a woman's voice, the German accent, and it was all coming back. "Do you know my sister well, Miss Hubermann?"

"Ah, what is it you say? *Not really?* I'll explain when I see you. But

I was coming to Boston and she chose to use me as a messenger, that's all.
I'm not quite in her social circle." She laughed.

"I wonder why she couldn't just write to me. Or call."

"I really have no idea. It's none of my business."

"Of course. What brings you to Boston?"

"I am a television reporter and producer," she said with a somewhat impatient sigh. "I'm here, Mr. Cooper, to cover a story. German
business investment in the Boston area. Not so very exciting."

"Well, how about seven thirty?"

"Excellent."

He gave her the Louisburg Square address. "Up on Beacon Hill.
Can you find it?"

"Oh, I wouldn't be surprised. I'm very resourceful, Mr. Cooper.
I'll tell the driver."

Cooper walked down Newbury and across on Arlington Street.
Workmen were raking leaves into piles near the Frog Pond. A jack-o'-
lantern left over from Halloween looked down from a window in one of
the condos overlooking the Public Garden and the Common. Darkness
was falling and the wind swirling up out of the Back Bay was cutting and
cold. When he'd climbed Beacon Hill the gaslights were flaring in Louisburg Square. His breath puffed out damply before him as he unlocked
the street door to the town house and let himself in.

The house was warm and comforting—shiny wood and the smell
of furniture polish and fresh flowers and the lingering aroma of his own
cigar and pipe smoke. Stan Getz's saxophone, the *Focus* album, could be
heard coming from recessed speakers. Cooper had bought the place
nearly twenty years ago, once he'd decided that somehow he was going to
recover from what had happened in Germany. He had coped with his
fate in this house, pulled himself back to earth, gathered the scattered
pieces of his psyche and stuck them back together. And he had gone on.
But not quite as before. No woman had ever spent the night. That was
part of the deal he'd made to keep himself sane. No woman had been
allowed so close. In twenty years he had had his relationships, but no one
had gotten close. That was the rule.

Not long after he'd acquired the house he had found Grahame,
who maintained both the house and its owner. As Grahame kept pointing
out, it was "a larf, mate, doing for you. Not much to it. Mainly just
'angin' about the 'ouse." Grahame was a wiry Englishman the size of a
steeplechase jockey who looked upon service as a way of life far preferable to actually working. "Chap never broke 'is arm polishing the silver"

was another one of his favorite observations. He came up from the kitchen while Cooper was lighting a cigar, sifting through the stack of mail on the hall table.

"Thick veal chop and salad strike you right?"

"I'm not sure. There may be two for dinner. Could you manage that?"

"Might I suggest you order in a lovely pizza?"

"Or you could push yourself and grill two veal chops."

"Leave to inform you, sir, I had the spare for lunch."

"Naturally. Well, let's just see how it goes."

"Good plan. Drinks, then?"

"Right. Set up the drinks table in the study. Light a fire. Load a bunch of Stan Getzes on the CD changer."

"Lower the lights? Turn down the bed?"

"Very funny. Take the night off. Hang out with the gang at Cheers, Sam and Woody and that mailman—"

"That's a television show, sir. You must learn to differentiate or we'll have to pack you away. I might go to the movies. *Mr. Blandings Builds His Dream House.*"

Cooper went upstairs and took a shower and watched Dan Rather's news. There was an investigation going on about human rights in Germany. A couple of Turks had been murdered in a street riot. Police had arrived too late to catch the neo-Nazis, skinheads, brownshirts, whatever they were calling themselves this time around. A pasty-faced man named Stiffel was their leader. Germany, Germany, some things never changed. The people interviewed seemed to be taking it seriously. Their memories were almost visible in their eyes.

He slipped into gray flannels and a double-breasted blazer and went back downstairs. Grahame was gone. An early Getz recording was playing now, from back in the forties when it was called "the Long Island Sound." He could lose himself in Stan Getz. He had closed both the theater and the bookstore to mark the day of Getz's death.

Somebody in a videotape on the *MacNeil/Lehrer Newshour,* a German official of some kind, had referred to "the Turkish problem," and a protester had yelled through a megaphone at him, "It's not a Turkish problem, it's a German problem!" Somebody was interviewing this fat-faced, purse-lipped, condescending bastard Stiffel, who said his followers had certainly never gotten the idea of killing Turks from him . . . but could you blame them, really? Killing Turks, unwanted foreigners, seemed to Herr Stiffel primarily a breach of taste. Cooper shook his head.

The drinks table was set out perfectly, including the ice bucket with the silver tongs, shining glasses, the best single-malts among the arrayed bottles. Grahame was never one to scrimp with Cooper's money. Cooper was still smoking the cigar and there was enough left to double off the Green Monster at Fenway. He was trying not to think about the dead Turks and the unexpected questions from Clint Kilroy and the call from Beate with a message from his sister, Lee. He wished he believed in coincidence.

On the mantelpiece and on a small library table that stood beneath one of the windows there was a jumble of framed photographs. Family photographs, the kind that dug at him and made him remember, but they were his family and he wouldn't hide them. A stranger might have looked at that room and concluded that John Cooper was a man in the fierce grip of the Shintoist tradition. The stranger would have struck the truth only a glancing blow. The fact was, John Cooper did not worship his ancestors; he was involved in a struggle to the death with them, a kind of terminal psychological confusion of love and hate.

The pictures of his mother and father: handsome and beautiful and young, up in Cooper's Falls and on the north shore of Lake Superior with whitecaps breaking on the rocky shore behind them. They wore sweaters and slacks and looked like those Ralph Lauren advertisements, both of them with long, streaky, dirty-blond hair, back in the mid-thirties. A perfect couple. Pictures of himself and his baby sister, Lee, and his brother, Cyril, silly pictures in bathing suits and snowsuits, at the beach and building snowmen in front of the great house in Cooper's Falls. All so unaware of what the future held for them. Death in the cockpit of a Spitfire over the English Channel, death in the bombs raining down on London during the Blitz, death for the little girl in the bombed-out rubble . . . death and then resurrection for the little girl who grew up to look exactly like her mother. It was the startling resemblance—that had been the key to it all: Cyril seeing a photograph in a newspaper in Scotland or someplace, Cyril being sure it was the little girl who had died so long ago, Cyril knowing that somehow it was little Lee all grown up . . . That was the thing that had set John Cooper's brother off down the dusty road to death.

There were a couple of pictures of his grandfather, who had known Lindbergh and Göring and Hitler, who had believed in his own misplaced ideals; photos of the guards patrolling outside the mansion in Cooper's Falls, there to protect the Cooper family from placard-waving anti-Nazi demonstrators. He thought of those nights, watching from his bedroom windows as they gathered, chanting about the Coopers, and a spring night came back to him, the smell of wet, cold earth as the snow-banks melted, the sound of the falls roaring like a mammoth beast on a quiet night, the mystery of the dark forested hillsides, the shadows of the guards moving soundlessly across the lawn looking for intruders . . . it was all there in the photos in their silver frames, like little time bombs just waiting, ticking, set to go off when he least expected it . . . But when would that be? Was it now, was Beate Hubermann coming to set them off?

Over the mantelpiece was the oil painting of his mother, so patrician and haughty and seductive, her gaze seemingly directed at something wonderful going on just past your shoulder. She was exquisite, quite beyond his powers of description. Her daughter, Lee, looked exactly like her. But Lee had had the privilege of living into middle age, something the Blitz had denied their mother. And she had sent someone, after twenty years, with a message for her brother . . .

The doorbell was ringing.

She came in with her cheeks pink from the cold, her hair blond and silky, eyes blue as a clear winter sky. She'd changed the black leather for a waist-length black and red buffalo-plaid jacket and black slacks tucked into the tops of cossack boots. She was about five-seven, smiling, saying something in her slightly accented German, her voice very deep like the voice of a certain kind of cabaret singer. When she turned her head to look at the mirror in the hallway, combing her hair with long slender fingers, he noticed that she had the prettiest ears he'd ever seen.

She nodded back at the doorway, said: "This is what I thought Boston would be like. Cobblestones, gaslights. What a wonderful place to live, Mr. Cooper! You must be very rich." She laughed openly, eyes flashing. He ushered her into the study and she gasped, put one hand to her mouth. "It's like a movie! How do you keep it so perfect?"

"I don't, I'm afraid. I make an incredible mess, wherever I go. I have a fellow called Grahame who keeps all this in order."

"You have a man! Like Jeeves! Wait—a, a, what is it? A gentleman's gentleman! So you must be Bertie Wooster in disguise—forgive me, I learned much of my English reading Wodehouse."

He nodded, took her coat, and laid it across the back of an oxblood-leather club chair. "I'm not much of a gentleman, I'm afraid, and I'm certainly not rich. The eighties made every thirty-year-old broker in town richer than I. I've owned this house for twenty years and my 'man' is a rather peculiar story, which I'll spare you. Would you like a drink?"

"Some mineral water would be fine."

He uncapped a bottle of San Pellegrino. "Ice?"

"One cube, please."

She had settled down on the leather couch facing the fireplace. She was smiling at the fire. "America," she sighed. " Money," she added, taking the glass, the lonely ice cube tinkling. "It's all so perfect. I'm sorry, I'm acting like an idiot. What is it you say? *Gushing!* But you must realize that I live up under a rooftop surrounded by dirty dishes and am grossly poor . . . underpaid, is what I mean. TV reporters don't make so much money in Germany." She made a face. "Shut up, Beate." He liked listening to her. She couldn't possibly be one of the dangerous ones. He was safe. A Hun had breached the defenses of his realm but he believed he was safe.

He poured himself an Edradour over ice and stood at the mantelpiece. Everything in his world was controlled, exactly the way he wanted it. His windowpane-check shirt, the blue wool tie with the foxes' heads. Everything in his world insulated him from the Huns, from the pain and the memories and the sense of loss that dwelt inside his head and heart.

"I don't want to seem abrupt, Miss Hubermann, and I do hope you'll join me for dinner in some terrible dive, but I must get to the necessities. Your request to see me was pretty provocative. You are bringing me a message from my sister—to say you're a surprise is a hell of an understatement. What's she up to?" The knot in his chest wouldn't let go. He was afraid of the message, afraid to bring Lee back to his life.

"She just showed up one evening, at my apartment—we'd met a couple of times when I was doing some pretty stupid stories about the social life of the rich and famous. Balls and charity affairs. She'd be there, among the sponsors. She is very rich, of course. Yet, here she was climbing my stairs. She'd called to talk to me about her daughter—I'll get to that in a minute—and I mentioned I was going to be traveling, that I was coming to Boston." She widened her eyes expressively. "You know who her husband is?"

Cooper shook his head. "I haven't heard a word in years."

"She is married to Wolf Koller. What can I say about him? One of the two or three richest men in Germany. The chairman of Koller Industries. He is prominent in everything. *Very* prominent in politics. Aggressively pro-American, a big supporter of NATO, pushed hard on rearming the German forces to achieve parity with other major powers. He *made* the present Chancellor, Heinrich Glock."

"How did he do a thing like that?"

"With money, endless reserves of money. And with speeches and backstage maneuvering. He threw the support of the Germany First group behind Glock. Nationalists. He's helped the Germany Firsters gain seats in Bonn—he's blended his support of American policy on Germany with his support of the rebirth of pride in Germany. He ran into a little bad publicity—I played a small part in the story—when it came out that one of his companies sold chemicals to Saddam Hussein for poison gas and for developing a big bomb. But that blew over because the Americans themselves had been the main suppliers of arms to Saddam and Koller's known to be close to the Americans. Some people say he's an American 'tool.' Which may be true." She paused for breath. "He is, what do you say—a man in a smoke-filled room? Is that right?"

"That means my sister's mixed up with another politician!" Cooper marveled, remembering how mad that would have seemed at one time. "How long have they been married?"

She shrugged. "Their daughter, Erika, is eighteen. So, that long. In fact, it is about Erika that she wanted me to speak to you."

"She has a daughter," he mused. "It's surprising, how much you miss in twenty years. Erika Koller. So what's the message?"

"Well, your sister came to me because she knows that I am a friend of Erika's. Erika is not the haughty rich. She is very real, very bright. She is too genuine for the art world—she works at a very trendy gallery—but she is young. I am ten years older. But we get along very well." She said: "May I smoke?"

"Of course." He struck a fireplace match and held it to her Lucky. She exhaled quickly. "Not good for you," he said.

"No! You're kidding me! I know, I know. I quit until yesterday, when I got to Boston." She sighed, leaned forward. "Erika has disappeared, you see, and Mrs. Koller is very worried. She asked me to tell you and—this is the hard part—she says . . . she wants you to come to Berlin. She told me that I must *make* you come—that I must convince you to come to her in Berlin. I told her there was only so much I could do." She swallowed and inhaled smoke quickly, nervously. "She told me you might not want to do it and that I was to tell you if you don't come now, then it could be too late."

Cooper sighed. "Her daughter's disappeared, and I must come before it's too late. In other words, it'll be my fault—*something* will be my fault. What is she talking about? Too late for what?" It was all coming back to him. The fear, the not knowing what was going on, not knowing if you could trust anyone . . . "How do you know Erika if she's only eighteen and you're twenty-eight?"

"I met Erika through this guy she's going out with. I'd run into him here and there—he's from the old East Berlin, a journalist on a little left-wing paper. Actually he's the one who uncovered the business of Wolf Koller being involved in the Saddam Hussein story . . . and Erika made him come to me with the story. Because she'd seen me on TV. They both came—"

"But she was ratting on her father," Cooper said.

"She thought it was important . . . she's very complicated, very German when it comes to her father. But that's none of my business. Your sister can tell you all the family stuff." She tapped the ash into a chunk of cut glass. She moved away from that subject, turned to his question. "Too late for Erika possibly. She thinks Erika may have been kidnapped. But there is something else . . . I don't know how much to say, it's none of my business—"

"Stop saying that. My sister, Lee, has made it your business. That's the way Lee is. Her problems have a way of becoming everybody's problems. So just spill it, tell me what matters—"

"All right. She's not well. Your sister, I mean. She didn't tell me that. It was Erika. Erika said there's something very wrong with her mother. Something serious. She doesn't know what it is but she—Erika—was very worried about it when I last saw her—"

"And then she disappeared. Is that the story?"

Beate Hubermann looked into the leaping tongues of flame, nodded. "That's the story." She sighed wearily. "Now I've done my duty. I hope you're not too upset."

"I don't know. It's like a message from another planet light-years away. Like one of those stars—we see the light in the darkness but the star died millions of years ago. I don't know. But you took it all seriously?"

"Yes, of course. But Germans always take everything seriously, don't they? Your sister was very serious, I assure you."

"But why didn't she just pick up a phone and call me—"

"I think she didn't want to hear you say no. She was afraid of that, I think. It's sad, really—she thought I might convince you when she couldn't. I know nothing about you and your sister, of course. Were you ever close? I know, it's not my place to ask. Shut up, Beate."

"Yes, we were close there for a while. I've only actually had contact with her for a week or so. As adults, I mean, and that was twenty years ago. We were separated by the war when we were children . . . it's a long story. And not a very happy one."

"She needs you, if that matters to you. I could see that. There's another reason why she needs you. She told me—she said, 'He's the only person left I can trust, now that Erika's gone.' "

"What about her husband?"

"Mr. Cooper, it was not my place to ask Lise Koller such a question. My job was to be gracious and comforting toward a very prominent woman—do you want to know how I felt? I felt honored that she came to me. And I can tell you this, Erika loves her mother more than anyone else on earth."

"All right, let's say the kidnap gag is just filler, let's say Erika's just taken a holiday. If that's the case, why would she leave her mother at a time like this, when she's sick? What's Erika's excuse?"

"She's very sensitive."

"As we Americans say, Gimme a break."

"Now just listen to me. She's easily depressed, she's had therapy . . . Being Wolf Koller's daughter is not easy for her . . . Look, I'm not her psychiatrist and I can't go into this any further. If you're interested, come to Germany—your sister can tell you all about her daughter. It's none of my business."

"Well, I'll think about it." She wasn't going to tell him any more. There was something nobody wanted to tell him. Not Kilroy, not Beate Hubermann. He should have known. It was Germany again. A country of the mind where they did things differently.

They went out to an Italian joint in the Back Bay, lots of tomatoes and garlic and paper tablecloths and cheap raw red wine in woven baskets and the Tears of Christ in green bottles shaped like fish. She smiled determinedly against the tension of their meeting, the emotional wallop of the message she'd carried across the Atlantic. The candle stuck in the bottle was dripping wax. "This is a 'joint'? It's like something from an old movie—do you feel like you live inside an old movie?"

"No, but I wish I did. That's why I brought you here—anybody who says things remind her of the movies is okay with me."

He made the conversation go easily. She hadn't known what she was getting into, all the layers of Cooper history, and now he was easing up. His mind was processing all she'd told him, twenty years of history laid out in a few minutes. What had happened to the girl? Was she in danger? Was Lee really sick? Why would Wolf Koller's daughter make trouble for him? And was this boyfriend involved in her disappearance?

And at bottom, more important than all the rest of it, what had happened to the poor lost woman Cooper had left in the big house in Munich twenty years ago? The woman who had chosen to stay there, more prisoner than anything else. Prisoner of her own fears and choices.

"Are you originally from Berlin?"

"No, I was born and grew up in a town called Bielefeld. You've never heard of it." She saw the look cross his face. "Don't tell me you know Bielefeld?" She was surprised. "You know Dr. Oetker's Puddings?"

"No. But I know Bielefeld."

"But why? Nothing important ever happened there."

"Oh, something very important happened there during the war."

"I don't think so."

"Nobody ever told you about the first thousand-bomber raid? Pretty historic."

"What are you talking about?" Her eyes were wide with curiosity. She sipped wine and mopped up sauce with bread, her eyes on his face. "Tell me. Don't tease me."

"The first thousand-bomber raid the Allies made during the war was on Bielefeld. The city was reduced to rubble and dust. Didn't you ever notice that there weren't any old buildings in Bielefeld?"

"I just thought it was prosperous, up-to-date. You're telling me the city was destroyed? I can't believe that. My father was a soldier . . . surely he'd have told me. Or in school . . ." She paused, smiled sheepishly. "Listen to me—what do I think I'm talking about? German kids don't learn much about the war. We learn that Hitler came to power after an unjust peace that threw us into depression, that he was a nationalistic leader who did some good things for Germany but was a very bad man in the end, that he lost the war though the German army fought hard, that he murdered the Jews in camps, that he killed himself rather than face the consequences of the evil he did . . . and the Americans helped rebuild our country and so on. Not much in the way of details, I'm afraid. It's everybody's least favorite subject, particularly if they're old enough to remember it. Except for those who still feel guilty—they call it racial guilt. So, Bielefeld really was bombed?"

"Really. Well, it was a long time ago. And I guess the Germans probably don't want to think about it too much. My father was an American who joined the RAF and fought the Luftwaffe in what we call the Battle of Britain. He never came back. My mother was in London and she was killed in the Blitz. Up until twenty years ago I believed that Lee, my sister, was killed with her. And then my brother found her by accident . . . and I found her with his help."

"Is he here in Boston, too?"

"No, he's been dead for twenty years."

"Quite a lot happened twenty years ago."

Later he asked her what exactly she was doing in Boston. What was this business story she was covering?

"Well, maybe it will be on your television here tonight. Is there someplace where we could watch the late news?"

"Follow me," Cooper said.

It had gotten seriously cold outside. She said she thought it would be good to walk and burn off some of the pasta with puttanesca sauce they'd eaten. She was out of breath from the climb up Beacon Hill and stood beneath a gaslight, her breath in clouds before her. She took his arm. "I *like* Boston!"

His mind was still on Lee and Erika and Germany. At least most of his mind. She looked at him quizzically.

"I like it, too. The home of the Bean and the Cod."

"What does that mean?"

"It means we should go in and have a coffee and watch the late news."

Her perfect ears were pink with cold.

He left her in the study and went to the kitchen on the bottom floor. Grahame had left the Starbucks coffee beans out, Sumatra decaf, and the green Krups grinder and the Bodum infusion coffeemaker. Grahame liked things just so, which made life that much easier for Cooper. He boiled the water, ground the beans, poured the water into the glass cylinder, stirred in the coffee, put it on a bamboo tray with cups, sugar, milk, and sweetener, and carried it all back upstairs.

She was holding a silver-framed photograph in her hand, staring into it as if it were a page she could read if she looked hard enough.

"The checkered family history," he said, putting the tray down between the fireplace and the couch. He poked the dying embers and placed a couple of Grahame's specially dried-out birch logs in a sort of teepee position so they'd draw quickly. He pulled a big shiny black television set out from its place against the wall and clicked it on. She was still looking at the photograph, then held it up so he could see.

"I don't mean to be too inquisitive but I am a reporter. And I don't mean to bring up anything uncomfortable—so tell me if I'm off base. Okay? What does off base mean? No, wait, it's not important—so, look, is this the famous Austin Cooper? The American Nazi?" She shook her head. "I'm hopeless, you don't have to tell me . . ." She was blushing. "Shut up, Beate."

"How come you don't know about what happened to Bielefeld but you're an expert on American Nazis?" His internal sensors were quivering. Did she have some agenda after all?

"I don't know, it just popped into my head. I'm sorry—"

"No, I'm serious. Tell me. How did you know about Austin Cooper? Did my sister tell you about the family's history? You couldn't just *know* it—"

"Look, I apologize. It all happened so long ago, I didn't think it was *verboten,* you know?"

"Look yourself," he said. "Do you want this incredible coffee which will not under any circumstances keep you awake? Well, you won't get any of it until you tell me how you came to know about my grandfather. And I'm not angry. Just curious. It's not the sort of thing people know anymore."

"It was Erika. She mentioned it once. She said her father told her all about this Austin Cooper—"

"Her *father?* Not Lee? That's sort of weird, don't you think? What's Austin Cooper to Wolf Koller?" He frowned and depressed the plunger in the coffeemaker, feeling the solid resistance. The coffee was ready. "I don't get it. What did Erika say? What brought it up? I didn't realize you were such close friends—I mean, you don't seem terribly worried about her—"

"I'm not her mother. In my view, it's not unreasonable for a girl like Erika to want to be alone, to just take some time off. She's only been gone a few days. But Lise is her mother, and mothers are mothers. So, you're very smart to see that I'm not terribly worried."

"Right enough," Cooper said. He clipped the end from an enormous Casa Blanca cigar and lit it.

"So you and Erika are actually close friends. She confided in you about her family's past—"

"Where are you getting that? I didn't say that." Her eyes, so bright, were boring into him. "Are you a detective or something? I know her, that's all. We were having coffee one day and we got to talking about our parents. I told her how mine fought in what you Americans called the Battle of the Bulge."

"You see, you do know about the war."

"My father fought in that battle. That's why I know. He fought under a man called Sepp Dietrich. He worshiped Sepp Dietrich. That's practically the only name I ever hear him mention from the war. And then Erika told me about her great-grandfather—she said he was a Nazi, a famous one in America. She didn't know any real details—"

"Wouldn't she have told you if she were planning to disappear for a few days? I don't care what you say, it sounds to me as if you're good friends."

"She wouldn't necessarily tell me. We weren't on a talking-every-day schedule—I don't care what *you* say."

"Well, here's your coffee then, as promised." He poured the cup and handed it to her. She took a sip.

"You're right, this is excellent."

"It's time for the news. You still want to watch?"

"If you don't mind?"

"Not at all."

"I love television. Over here, I mean. Not in Germany. There's nothing to watch at home . . . except my favorite old show. *The Rockford Files*. James Garner. I love him."

The news was blurting away on the tube when one of the talking heads said: "And now for a story about yet another step in the direction of international economic interdependency." The other talking head said: "Or the buying of America. This time it's the Germans. Our Haley Seabrook was at the groundbreaking ceremony today. Haley, have the Germans landed?"

It seemed that the Germans had indeed landed. They were building a huge data storage facility off Route 128. It would serve customers in the Americas, North and South, but the data would cover the world. Nobody was being too specific about what kind of data. That was the kind of detail that scared hell out of everyone. Cooper didn't even really know what a data storage bank was. Or why the Germans needed to have one here.

"What is this outfit?" he asked.

"Wolf Koller's conglomerate. A holding company. It's all about money," she said. "It sounds like it's about computers but it's not really. Computers today, chemicals tomorrow, high-tech machinery. It's all about money." She sipped her coffee. "I don't suppose you have an Oreo cookie, do you? They help me not smoke." He shook his head. "No, I understand. I must be strong."

"The triumph of the will," he said. "Everybody seems to think that nations are dead as dinosaurs. The great conglomerates will replace them. Maybe they're right. And my sister's husband has one of them. Why should I be surprised? Lee could always pick 'em."

"But one thing I can tell you about this deal today you might find interesting. Wolf Koller is the chairman of the conglomerate, yes, but you have to realize that it's everywhere. South America, the Middle East . . . and he has really moved into Russia in a big way. Everybody talks about going in there, beginning new industries, making a statement—but Koller, so far, is the main player. It's money, it's transportation, it's electronics for new kinds of communications. He's betting on the future of Russia. Wolf Koller is known as the Berlin Connection and that's why I'm here—the Berlin connection."

"Is he here? Personally?"

"He sends his emissaries. He hardly ever leaves the country—you don't have to go anywhere now, of course. The communications links are so sophisticated. The only place he's been going to lately, it's no secret, is Moscow to cement these new enterprises. Otherwise it would take World War Three to get him out of Berlin." She saw the shadow pass his face. "That's just a, a figure of speech, World War Three, okay? Wow, you really do have a thing about Germans. The war was a long time ago—"

"You're right. I'm all wet when it comes to the new Germans. I apologize. It's not your fault you're a German."

She burst into laughter. "Well, thank God for that!"

"Ah, that rare thing. A German with a sense of humor!"

"Even Germans know that joke. What is the world's thinnest book? *The Anthology of German Humor.*"

Suddenly Cooper's attention was nailed to the screen. There was some German corporate official speaking to the interviewer, but over his shoulder, still in focus, a thin-faced man with leathery skin, eyes with a thousand-mile squint in the autumn sunshine. He was watching the man speaking; then, as if he noticed he was in camera range, he suddenly moved away. "Did you see that guy? The one in the background?"

"I don't know. I guess not. I was thinking of another joke—"

"I know that guy. I'm sure I know him. Damn, he was there and then he was gone. I had lunch with him today—"

"Who is he?"

"Well, he's a guy called Clint Kilroy. Texan. He wanted to buy some property I own here."

"And?" She urged him onward with her hands.

"And I said no, not for sale." He finished his coffee and set the cup down. He puffed the cigar, watching the clouds of smoke draw toward the fireplace. "Never heard of this guy and now he turns up twice in one day. He didn't say anything about doing business with the Germans. But he was the first person today who knew all about Austin Cooper and the Nazis. Nobody mentions Austin Cooper and the Nazis to me in twenty years, now two in one day."

"Maybe it wasn't the same guy."

"Sure as hell looked like him. And why would he be a part of the German invasion of Boston today?"

She shook her head, stood up. "Well, you've had a lot of Germany for one day. I've got to do some work here at WGBH in the morning and then I'm going down to New York for a UN story and back to Berlin. I'd really better head back to the hotel. Copley Square."

"I'll call a car for you."

"You don't have to do that—"

"No trouble. I've got this service."

He watched her get into the short red and black jacket again while he telephoned. She had a vaguely klutzy manner, a kind of self-consciousness that was endearing. But somehow she looked graceful. Maybe it was because she was pretty. Maybe it was the ears.

"It'll be five minutes," he said.

"So, are you coming to Berlin to see your sister?"

"I don't know. As you say, maybe she's just worried over nothing. Panicky." He knew that wasn't the case. He was trying to sound normal.

"What should I tell her when I get back?"

"Tell her I'll be in touch. Maybe I'll talk to her tomorrow. Before you get back. I'm just not sure."

"All right." She shrugged. "Whatever you say."

When the car pulled up outside he followed her into the cold. He opened the car door.

"We Germans do have a sense of humor, you know. I have one. I know a joke. Why did the CIA have Einstein killed?"

"I don't know."

She looked up from the backseat as he closed the door. *"Because he knew too much . . ."*

She was laughing when the door clunked shut.

4

SPOOKS

When Beate Hubermann got back to the Copley Plaza she was still wide awake and wound tight from the intense activity of the day, particularly the evening spent with John Cooper. Her initial response was curiosity: what had made him so closed off and enigmatic? And where did his distrust and possibly even fear of Germans come from? What had gone wrong in his life? And what did Germany have to do with it?

He was full of psychological tics: his awareness of his family sat at the center of his psyche, from his sensitivity to discussions of them to the table full of photographs and the imposing portrait over the fireplace, which she at first had thought was his sister. It had turned out to be his mother but that made no difference: in fact it underlined the validity of her analysis. The portrait dominated the room the way the family seemed to dominate his life.

She didn't doubt for a moment that he'd come to Germany. This was *family* and he wasn't going to turn the family down. So, yes, he was probably going to turn up in Berlin, which meant she would have to deal with him.

She bought a newspaper and found the hotel coffee shop where she could get a cup of decaf and unwind. She sat down, and was immediately drawn to the front-page piece on the crisis in Moscow. Yeltsin was threatening to force a vote of confidence in the legislature, or maybe even a vote of the electorate, and the opposition was rattling its sabers in a muted way. The implication was there and it wasn't all that subtle. The old Soviets weren't done yet. And their philosophical descendants, now in their thirties and forties, might not hesitate to try another coup. Beate had spent some time in Moscow: if they tried another coup, it might be a close thing. She knew there were old names and faces behind the scenes, men from the second rank in the old regime who might grab for power, might force themselves into the front rank once they gauged the severity of Yeltsin's weakness. Chancellor Glock in Bonn wasn't saying much but there were all sorts of implications for Germany . . . a huge armed and angry Russia to the north and east was something that could shake all the presumptions about the new Europe and the new Germany to their foundations. And what would the Americans do if Yeltsin went down? It was all too involved for late-night thinking.

She found the story about the Germans coming to Boston on the business page. What was the man Cooper knew, Kilroy, doing in the pictures on television? Who was Kilroy? How was he involved with Wolf Koller's interests in Boston? But, wait a minute, she was getting ahead of herself . . . maybe Kilroy was involved in the Boston end of the deal. That must be it. He'd wanted to buy real estate from Cooper and there had been a lot of real estate involved in the deal with the Germans. She was trying to follow that train of thought but the type blurred together and she found herself staring into space.

There was no getting away from her thoughts of this man Cooper. What had the Germans done to him twenty years ago? Something, a mystery. Her reporter's curiosity was joining her personal interest in the man. What had happened? He'd seen his sister in Germany twenty years ago, then nothing . . . A brother and sister, no contact for twenty years —that in itself struck her as slightly crazy. Yet, when the sister is really worried, really desperate, who does she turn to? Her rich and powerful husband? No. Instead she sends this odd, urgent plea to her brother. And what does the brother do? *He says he'll think about it!*

It was beyond her. Time to go to bed.

She finished her coffee and took the elevator to the sixth floor. In her room she tossed her jacket onto the bed and headed for the bathroom. And stopped.

The light in the bathroom was on, just as she'd left it. But something was different in the darkened bedroom.

It was a smell. Smoke. She spun around, wondering where the light switch was. A cigar . . .

"Who's there?" She tried not to sound frightened but her voice cracked. "Is someone there?"

Her heartbeat was suddenly rocking her. Everyone's worst fear about America . . . a murderer . . . a rapist . . .

The lights popped on.

A man was sitting in the armchair by the window.

"Who the hell are you?" she demanded angrily. She was backing away, putting distance between them.

He stood up; she thought she recognized him.

"My name is Kilroy," he said. He was smiling like a crocodile.

From the windows of his kitchen Burke Delaney commanded a long, unobstructed view of the meadow rolling down to the country road that connected him to the rest of the world. Or at least to the humbler precincts of the rest of the world. The path up to his old stone house was a dark, smudged trail of mud. Black evergreens lined the roadside and the rest of the view provided him with a wide field of fire should anyone come visiting without an invitation.

The morning was gray and drizzling and he was soothed by the endless yapping of the dogs out in the barn. He raised rottweilers and bull terriers, which he'd intended as a cash crop. He'd train them to rip and tear and kill the bad guys for whoever felt threatened by bad guys. That had been the idea. But the problem was he didn't much care for the training. It involved being more or less unpleasant to the dogs all the time and that rubbed him the wrong way.

In Burke Delaney's view dogs were much nicer than the bipeds they were supposed to rip to shreds, or to serve, for that matter. So the business never amounted to much and he gave dogs to his old friends and kept a lot of them around just to talk to. The bull terriers were the funniest dogs on earth and Burke Delaney often found himself in need of a good chuckle or two.

As he sat at the kitchen table drinking his steaming morning coffee he was watching his personal house dog, a bull terrier called Schuyler, named after an old boss of his back in OSS days. Schuyler had no idea of his own strength. One of his amusements was to scrunch down and slide under the rungs of the heavy, carved chairs at the kitchen table. Once firmly under a chair, Schuyler would glance around to see if he had an audience, and then, reassured that Delaney was paying attention, he would stand up, lifting the huge chair on his back. Then with a devil-may-care grin he would stroll around the kitchen with the chair, showing off. Delaney had once decided to give Schuyler a test. When he watched the dog calmly clench his jaws down on the fat end of a pool cue and just snap the damn thing in two, he called an end to the testing. Fuckin' dog was plenty strong to bite off any bad bastard's leg, which was the point of the test.

His German wife, Anna, had enjoyed the dogs, too, but then she had died, which took the fun out of everything for quite a while. And most of the fun had never really come back. He'd met Anna back in OSS days during the war. She'd been one of his agents inside Germany, bravest goddamn woman he'd ever known. Bravest goddamn person he'd ever known. And when the war ended he stayed on, took up residence in Germany, did his part to bring in the Gehlen network with all their information about the Communists, did his part to recruit lots of the old Nazis to work for the Army of Occupation. You had to be fast on your feet and willing to turn a blind eye on some fairly nasty shit in those days, but there was "the greater good" to think of, and it covered one helluva lot of sins.

Anyway, it was the dogs who had kept him sane when Anna went down with the cancer and had kept him sane while she got through the business of dying. Now they were his family.

It was time to stop horsing around with Schuyler and get to work. He opened the envelope the German kid had given him. Karl-Heinz. He put on his Ben Franklin glasses, leaned his head back, and licked his thumb to get a purchase on the first sheet.

SPARTAKUS

He went through it slowly, stopping to fill his coffee cup again, stopping to stare out the window into the blowing rain, thinking, then going back to the report. The kid knew something, whether he could prove it or not. There were more installments to come and the evidence of their validity would build. But validity had to be assumed. In Burke Delaney's world proof wasn't always required. There wasn't time. He sighed. No wonder the kid was nervous.

Finally, he pushed the papers back into the envelope and went to the fireplace, blackened from years of use. He knelt on slightly arthritic knees, which made him wince, and snaked his arm as far as it would go up into the chimney. Soot dribbled down. He loosened the brick in the inner chimney and pulled it out. He folded the envelope and reached up into the darkness again, shoving it into the hiding place. Sneezing in the dust and soot, he replaced the brick. He went to the sink and washed his hands. Schuyler was out from under the chair and looking up at him expectantly. "Come on, Sky, let's go walk the perimeter."

He wore a green Barbour waxed jacket and wellies, threw a chewed-up rubber pork chop to give Sky a sense of purpose. They walked down the long slope of thick, wet grass to the fence where he knelt again, cursing, and fumbled around in the long grass at the base of a post. He armed the sensor there and twice more along the fence. He was thinking about Karl-Heinz and the bruises on his face.

And now he knew that Erika Koller had disappeared and her father had his ass in an uproar and Max Adler was in a tizzy about finding her and trying not to let anybody know she was missing. Stiffel was on the march. Jesus H. Christ. You just get the Cold War over and sure as hell nobody could leave well enough alone. There was a lot of pressure building, like a boil saving up pus. Sooner or later there was going to be a mess.

Cheddar himself was sitting up and taking notice. Coded messages. Delaney had driven to town to fax the pages to Georgetown and parked his car near the drugstore and when he came back damned if there wasn't an envelope on the floor by the gas pedal. Games again . . . Well, it was something to do. He'd dreamed during the dark and quiet and rainy night of an army of spooks moving along the tree line. Marching in the mist. It was like the old days.

He checked the tripwires. He checked the halogen lights that were set to flood the surrounding landscape with a very disconcerting glare. He checked the speakers in the shrubbery and the tape deck hidden by a pile of firewood that never seemed to dry out.

By the time they got back to the house Schuyler had somehow managed to lose the stupid rubber pork chop. He'd have to remember to get him another one. Rubber pork chops seemed to be the only thing Schuyler didn't actually eat until it was gone. He lost them instead.

In the kitchen he opened the boot chest, lifted out the jumble of boots and junk, and took out the six Uzis. He checked the action, made sure they were loaded, checked the extra ammo. He thought of the boot chest as the armory.

Then, whistling "Danny Boy," he went out to the barn to chat up the doggies. He wondered what SPARTAKUS actually meant. There was more to come, and in due time there was always the possibility that it would make sense.

He wondered if the kid would stay alive that long.

———————

She'd put on pearl-gray woolen slacks, pleated, with an orange silk blouse and gold necklace and bracelets. She remembered doing that. That much was perfectly clear. But somewhere in the hallway she'd somehow gotten turned around and for a moment she wasn't quite sure where she was. There was a bed in the room and she sat down. She knew it was happening again and there wasn't anything she could do about it. She tried to fight it but it came in waves. In one wave she asked herself why she'd come to Erika's old bedroom. In the next she was shaking her head, wondering who Erika was, struggling to identify Erika . . . Goddamn it! There were tears streaking her face, it was all so bloody frustrating! *What's my name? Jesus . . . what* is *my name?* This was impossible. She closed her eyes, waited. No, it wasn't going to right itself . . .

She heard someone downstairs, a door closing, something falling on the floor, then nothing. That was Hilda. The housekeeper. Yes, Hilda downstairs . . . A door closed again. Was it Erika? No, something had happened to Erika . . . What was it? What had happened to her? A door closed. Was Erika home? No, try to remember that. No. But who the hell was Erika! A door closed. Oh, it was John! Of course, it was John, John had come to save her again . . . John, John, he'd saved her before. John who? Why couldn't she remember?

She took a deep breath and wiped her eyes and got up from the bed. A door closed. She went out into the hallway, walked carefully to the top of the stairs . . .

She smelled the rain blowing in from outdoors.

There was a man down below in the foyer, standing on the parquet, a very handsome man looking up at her. His hair was a beautiful gray and waved back from his temples; he was saying something to her but she couldn't quite make it out. Who was he, what was he saying, why was he in her house?

She took a step toward him. She'd better go down and see what he was up to, and she took another step, seemed to step off into space and for a moment she was sure she was flying, flying, the way she'd flown as a child . . .

Kilroy was slouched in Ned Cheddar's Eames chair, his cowboy boots stretched way out in front of him.

"Well, Cheese, you fat fuck," he said genially, "now's the time you better tell me what's going on. 'Cause I'm too old to go in blind. And, as you know, I don't give a shit who I kill. I might even get a round or two into that big gut of yours. We all clear on that, Fatty?"

"You are such a child," Cheddar said. He was full of tolerance. "Fatty, indeed. At your advanced age you must calm yourself. No one wants your sunset years to be more restful and enjoyable than Ned Cheddar does. Trust me."

Kilroy laughed at the suggestion. "I am going home unless you tell me what all this Boston nonsense was. I felt like an idiot. Sneaking around the Copley Plaza, waiting in her room . . . and that lunch with Cooper! What a load that was. I'm done playing the fool for you, Cheese." Having spoken his piece, Kilroy seemed to curl his personality around himself and withdraw. His reptile brain had taken over.

Ned Cheddar had overcome a lot of die-hard criticisms of his weight during the years he'd served his country in a variety of what were sometimes called "black" or "wet" jobs. The objection was that he was too damn recognizable and memorable because, in the words of one since-disgraced DDI (Deputy Director, Intelligence), "Ned's just too fucking fat!" Cheddar defended himself by observing that if the gun, the knife, the plastique, or whatever agent of destruction was called for somehow failed he might still succeed by the simple expedient of sitting on someone. In the event, his weight had never proved to be a problem, beyond the extra expense required in buying him first-class airplane seating. He'd never had to kill anyone by sitting on him, though he had used his vast bulk to push a few people around. He'd been gutshot once and hadn't noticed it for nearly twenty-four hours. The bullet had just given up the struggle to get at a vital organ. Chalk one up for blubber.

He was very smart and very devious and eventually he got to the top of Covert Ops, a makeshift position that didn't exist in any budget and that put him beyond the control of just about anybody you could think of. The President needed deniability so you couldn't tell him a damned thing; and within the intelligence community no one wanted to go up against Ned Cheddar because Ned could go all violent on you, or so the stories went, and, as Harvey Kerper said from behind the bandages in his secret room at Bethesda about six years ago last Christmas, getting Ned's dander up could be "pretty counterproductive." At least that was what it sounded like he said. He couldn't move his head, lips, jaw, or upper torso, a condition which had resulted from a prolonged discussion with Ned over irregularities in his expense account while on a mission that found him in both Beirut and the Indian Ocean. All in all, it took Harvey about six months before he could be understood, and by then it was said that his star was no longer on the rise in the world of intelligence gathering.

At six-two, 388 pounds, Ned Cheddar was still a growing boy at the age of sixty-one. Golf was his game but when he wasn't chasing whitey around the links he didn't like to move much. So, when the two Marine assassins who served as his security guards at the unassuming house in Georgetown reported over the closed-circuit TV—which Cheddar believed provided the most tedious cable show in town—that Clint Kilroy had arrived, he just bellowed a welcome down the hall from his office in the back of the house. He liked having it in back because, frankly, that way it was near the kitchen. Sometimes a man wanted a ham and cheese sandwich, some potato salad, a couple of Asahi beers, and a nice big chunk of pecan pie to tide him over until dinner, and sometimes it was easier to rustle it up for himself than to set the involved food chain rumbling into motion. A man could lose his appetite if he had to wait too long.

When Kilroy had ambled in Ned Cheddar had said: "Now be sure to speak up. You always drawl like a spastic cowpoke who's afraid of waking the baby. Drives the sound engineers crazy. So make an effort. I think the taping system dates from just before Ike's day. How are you? Not still smoking, for heaven's sake?"

"It'll be the death of me, Cheese."

"Look, you really must speak up. And try to enunciate more clearly. What good's a bugging system if you can't understand what everybody's saying?"

"As you wish," Kilroy said loudly, clearly.

Cheddar nodded. "That's more like it."

"You didn't drag me in here to talk about the More or Less Pretty Nearly Evil or At Least Distasteful Empire, did you? Yeltsin's tit's in a wringer—how's that for mastering idiom? It's his own fault. And ours, I guess. You haven't been listening to that fat asshole Rush Limbaugh, have you? You should never listen to that guy. He's just trying to be funny—"

"No, that's not the problem." Cheddar was shaking slightly with mirth. It was not unlike watching Mount St. Helens hiccup. "But we do have a little blip on the screen." The chair groaned as he swiveled behind his desk. He picked up a pad and stared at it. As far as Kilroy could see there was only one very short word written on it but it was a little too dim in the room for him to make it out. "Something's going on over there and it's a little ripe around the edges. I don't like it."

"Where?"

"Germany, of course. Where the devil do you think? Nobody gives a clipped groat about the Serbians, Clint. It's the same old story. The Germans and the Japs. You watch, before you know it, the Japs are going to declare they can send troops abroad again after all these years. How do you think that will set with some of their neighbors? So be glad we're dealing with the Germans. At least we're on the same page, give or take." He pulled on his immense lower lip. "Well, at least it's the same book, anyway."

"So what about the Germans?" Which was the point at which Kilroy had prefaced his demands with the Well-Cheese-you-fat-fuck opening move.

"Ah, well, it is somewhat complicated. Let's see . . . there are three issues. There's the SPARTAKUS-with-a-'k' thing I mentioned. And when I start hearing code names my dick gets hard, if you'll pardon my French. There is the issue of John Cooper. And there is the Hubermann woman. Let me explain. SPARTAKUS. I'm getting product from a source in Berlin. Via Burke Delaney." Kilroy nodded approvingly. "Source is new but looks good. We've just scratched the surface of the product but there's more to come. I'm of two minds. I can't go into the content with you, Clint. It's strictly need-to-know."

"Big deal. Go on. SPARTAKUS. Revolt of the slaves. So it's something to do with a revolution. I'm not exactly a genius but even I can figure—"

"Just so. I neither confirm nor deny—"

"It's a revolution, right?"

"Mmmm . . . well, maybe. Depends on your point of view, I suppose."

"How about *our* point of view, just for the sake of argument?"

"You want a beer? A chicken leg? Something? I worry about you. You're getting awfully skinny in your old age."

"Just keep talking."

"When two things happen together and I hear about them from different sources—I always get a little shiver, can't help it. I learned a long time ago that there are no coincidences in this line of endeavor."

"Two?"

"We've got a missing person, too, you see. There's a kind of a fit here, and I start seeing things. It's like hearing the house creak in the night, footsteps on the gravel . . . just before you get your brains blown out your ass—"

"Who's missing?"

"Wolf Koller can't seem to find his daughter."

Kilroy's face brightened. "Ahhh. Well, I see your point, Cheese. But what kind of a fit could it be?"

Cheddar smiled and shrugged his shoulders. "Our source for SPARTAKUS is young Erika Koller's boyfriend . . . How does it fit? We're going to find out, you and I. It's going to be just like the old days."

Kilroy stood up and went to look out the bulletproof glass window into the garden, which was lit by floodlights. He knew the entire garden and lawn beyond were a maze of electrified fences and laser sensors calculating changes in sound, movement, pressure, and who the hell knew what else. More than one bunnyrabbit had regretted wandering into Ned Cheddar's garden.

"Now," he said, "tell me about what the hell I was doing in Boston. Cooper and the Hubermann woman."

"Yes, well, the Hubermann girl is a bit easier. She told you the truth at the hotel—and why shouldn't she? Cooper's sister asked her to bring him a message. She wants him to come see her in Berlin. But she refused to tell you any more. Well, she was within her rights and I hadn't given you enough information. Miss Hubermann was strictly a courier, so far as we know. Lise Koller wants John Cooper to come to Berlin, no doubt because of the disappearance of her daughter, Erika."

Kilroy sighed. "Bingo."

"Precisely. Bingo. Wolf Koller, Lise Koller, Erika Koller, and John Cooper. One big happy family."

"The sister turns to the brother, not to her husband. I hate dysfunctional families."

"Well, you've put your finger on something there, Clint. The Coopers are dysfunctional in a rather large way. The grandfather, Austin Cooper, was something rather special. I told you he was a Nazi . . . I was understating things a bit, Clint. He was part of the Nazis' plan for world domination, for governing from within. We think, and have thought for many years, that he was the man chosen to govern America when the Nazis won the war. The American Quisling, so to speak. And that was just the beginning . . . Are you sure you wouldn't like a pizza or something? Some roast chicken?"

"Is it a long story?"

Ned Cheddar shrugged. "Long enough to eat a pizza."

"All right. Where the hell does this John Cooper come into the story?"

Cheddar smiled and called one of his guards. He told him to order a pizza and for God's sake not to shoot the delivery man.

"So, Clint, we begin the story of John Cooper and the Coopers of Cooper's Falls. You'll appreciate it."

Ned Cheddar began by pointing out the obvious: that none of the subsequent Coopers knew about the depth of Austin's involvement with the Nazis. Well, except for Austin's son, Edward Cooper—that was John's and Cyril's and little Lee's father. In the end, he'd turned out to be a Nazi, too, though the official story was that he'd gone to England and joined the RAF and been killed in the Battle of Britain—that was all true but for the last part. He'd flown to Germany or some damned thing and his ultimate fate was uncertain. Ned Cheddar acknowledged that the final facts of the Cooper story might never be known, at least not to him. "Time passes, as you well know, my friend," Cheddar said, "and it's probably all for the best. A great deal is forgotten or lost in the files and there you are, eternal mysteries."

So, the war was over for a long time, it was the seventies, John Cooper was divorced and a recovering alcoholic—a term that brought a fed-up look to Clint Kilroy's face—and living in Boston, writing potboilers. Little Lee had been killed in the London Blitz along with her mother, an heiress of almost legendary beauty. And brother Cyril was a sort of shadowy figure, moving about the world in one business after another—moving money, shipping goods from one spot to another, something of a soldier of fortune. He would turn up here and there, send John a Christmas card or a wire. "The simple fact is," Cheddar noted, "they hadn't seen each other in years. Their lives had taken very different paths. But they were still brothers, still Coopers, and when Cyril summoned him, John was quick to move."

"Someone's always summoning John Cooper," Kilroy said.

"Oh, twice in twenty years doesn't seem so outrageous to me," Cheddar demurred.

Anyway, the telegram originated in some offbeat spot, Cheddar thought Buenos Aires or Cairo but he couldn't be sure after all this time. Kilroy smiled to himself. What a bullshit artist! The Cheese had boned up on this particular file over the past day or two, or Kilroy didn't know his man. So, the telegram came to John in Boston, said Cyril was coming home to Cooper's Falls after all these years and he damn well wanted John to meet him there at the old family home where they'd grown up with Austin Cooper the head of the house.

So John Cooper hauled ass out there, arrived in the middle of a hell of a snowstorm, went to the big house and what did he find? Brother Cyril. Dead as a doornail. Murder.

Now, Cheddar was at pains to explain, it got very complicated very quickly and he wanted Kilroy to grasp the main points and not concern himself overmuch with details. Before Cooper could turn around the guys who had killed Cyril began some sort of siege of Cooper's Falls. It was quite a story. A bunch of people got killed. There was a big damn fire, the whole town almost went up. What was the point? Well, the killers apparently wanted some evidence that was squirreled away in Cooper's Falls about a plan the Nazis had that involved Austin Cooper and maybe his son, Edward, a plan that might have disclosed that the Nazis were still alive and well in the seventies . . .

Cheddar spoke slowly, between bites of pizza. "I was just on the edge of the case when it finally broke in Washington. I kept hearing all these wildass stories about what was going on in this little town out in the middle of nowhere, this little town that was snowbound, completely cut off. Incredible stuff. And then, before you knew it, it was over . . ."

The dead were buried. Cooper and his newfound ally, the local chief of police, a guy by the name of Olaf Peterson, still had no idea what the devil had happened . . . but they had a clue. Now this was the best Cheddar could recall but he was sure he had the essence of the thing, even if some of the details were a little hazy. Which meant to Kilroy that the Cheese might be giving him a slightly doctored version. Or not. But, anyway, they had this newspaper picture of a woman, a beautiful woman, that Cyril had found somewhere and John came up with . . . and it looked exactly like their mother! But the time was all wrong, she'd been dead for thirty years, and John Cooper had a brainstorm. It had to be their little sister, the one who died in the Blitz—but now she's alive and all grown up and according to the picture she's a woman called Lise Brendel, married to a German businessman, tycoon maybe, called Gunter Brendel . . .

"Now I may have some of this wrong, Clint, but what I'm telling you is basically the true story. Like I said, I wasn't really part of it. But it became a bit of a legend among the few people who did know anything about it. Now John Cooper took a fatal step. He decided he'd backtrack and find out what his dead brother, Cyril, had been doing. Somebody should probably have stopped him but maybe nobody knew what he was up to until it was too far along—I don't know—and this Peterson character got involved and they proceeded to raise absolute unholy hell all the way from South America to Germany . . . and what they found was, well, you can just imagine . . ."

What they found was little sister Lee, now Lise Brendel, alive and well and married to this German and she was right in the heart of the Fourth Reich. The Nazis were alive and well, too, they had a bigtime HQ centered around Brendel and some of his pals in Munich and it was a worldwide conspiracy, however nutty that might sound today. "It sure as hell wasn't nutty back then. And it led all the way back to Cooper's Falls . . . *again.*" Cheddar smiled at Kilroy, who was paying pretty close attention. Cheddar licked hot pizza sauce from his fingers and finished another beer. He liked holding a smartass like Kilroy more or less spellbound with a story. It was hard to do: Kilroy had seen damned near everything.

"Well," Cheddar said with a happy sigh, "Peterson and Cooper went bananas over there in Germany. They took the whole Nazi thing apart, piece by piece, killing people and stacking up the stiffs like firewood, rescuing sister Lee from the big bad Nazis . . . only to find that Lee liked it there! She'd been raised among these people, she'd married one of them, she was Queen of the fucking Darkness as far as they were concerned—we never figured that she knew politics from third base, she was just a creature of circumstances. My guess is that she wasn't exactly aware of what was going on around her." He shrugged. "As fate would have it, among those killed by Peterson and Cooper was her husband, Brendel. Or at least he was killed as a result of what they did to the Nazi movement. The point is, when our John tried to get Lee to come home with him and make a new life . . . she wouldn't do it." He wiped his chin, balled up the paper napkin, and took another piece of pizza, drooping from the overload of sausage and pepperoni and onions and green pepper. "That's all you need to know, my friend, about the past of John and all the Coopers. Everybody involved then is dead now, except for John Cooper and Olaf Peterson and Lee, who is now Lise Koller.

"John just about flipped out when he came home. We debriefed Olaf Peterson in Washington—that's where I came into it personally. I was just observing, not asking any questions—I was *analyzing.* I was just another suit as far as Peterson was concerned. John became kind of a hermit in Boston, wrote some mystery novels, bought the bookstore and the movie theater, and finally we forgot about him. Peterson is back in Cooper's Falls, I guess, enjoying a richly deserved anonymity, in my view. I don't like to admit it, but that guy is very, very hard. He's as hard as you are, Clint." Cheddar skipped on past that, said: "I didn't think I'd ever hear about any of these people again . . .

"And now John Cooper's niece, his sister, Lee's, daughter, goes missing, and Lee is married to another bigtime German with an iron in every imaginable fire—seeing the pattern here, Clint?—and the niece's boyfriend is providing us with this SPARTAKUS thing . . . and John Cooper is back from twenty years' vacation, like Rip Van Winkle, and his sister, whom he hasn't seen since he killed all those people for her twenty years ago, she's calling to him for help . . .

"And, let me be frank with you, Clint. John Cooper scares the shit out of me. He is the definition of the wild card, you understand? I don't want him anywhere near Germany. Things are very tense in Germany these days, okay? You know that. It's the sort of situation that a man with Cooper's record could turn into a dog's breakfast in about thirty seconds. I know it, I feel it. Does this Hubermann girl think he's going back?"

"She said she doesn't know—"

"Damn! That means he's going back. That sister of his has got him in some kind of spell . . . How can a man be so dumb?"

Kilroy said: "You want me to make sure he doesn't go?"

Cheddar slowly shook his head, his big lower lip pushed out. "I've got some people who'll make our case to him. You just stay here, you can move into the back bedroom." He cleared his throat and sucked at a tooth. "You know Wolf Koller from your days in Germany." He was thinking aloud. "I'm going to need you for some rather delicate work. Watchmaking, we used to call it. I need to think it over. In the meantime," he said with a sunny, sudden smile, "we can talk about old times."

"All right, Cheese. I'll wait it out with you."

He listened carefully while Cheddar outlined a plan of action but Clint Kilroy had a two-track mind. He was making some plans of his own. On occasion his own private agenda was not entirely congruent with the Cheese's, and he was enough of an outlaw to have earned the nickname Jesse James back in Munich years ago. He sneaked a look at the pad on Cheddar's desk.

WOLF. That was the only word.

5

COOPER'S FALLS

John Cooper had never seriously doubted that he'd go to Germany in answer to his sister's cry for help. But he didn't trust Germans and Beate Hubermann was a German and there was no reason to tell her his plans. He wished Lee had left the reporter out of it but then Lee wasn't the steadiest person he'd ever known. She'd been fragile twenty years ago. Afraid. A moral coward. There was no point in pretending anything else. But, of course, he'd go to her. She had turned out to be the one enduring point on the compass of his life. Lee.

He settled back, listening to the Northwest Air jets whining as the late-afternoon flight headed west out of Logan. He had straightened everything out with Grahame and left a message on Sammy Desmond's phone at the office. He had attended to some errands, all the while reviewing the meetings with Kilroy and Beate.

Kilroy.

Cooper hated the German connection. Without it, Kilroy was just an eccentric old fart who was too big for his britches. With the German connection, God only knew what he was up to. *Kilroy was here.* The World War II slogan. Why did he have to be named Kilroy?

Cooper shifted restlessly in his aisle seat. His biggest job at the moment was to keep fear at bay. Fear and Germany, they were synonymous for John Cooper, and he knew that everyone was going to be afraid of Germany before it was over. The Russians were collapsing in on themselves, threatening a return to the old ways, poised on the edge of a black hole of revolution and violence. Eastern Europe was in a million pieces, and a new generation of Nazi thugs was roaming the streets of Germany, breeding chaos and fear. The million pieces were beginning, already, to coalesce, drawn like iron filings to the magnet at the center of Europe, the power source, Germany. Whole peoples were crying out for order and certainty. It was a goddamn powder keg . . .

He woke up when dinner was being served and the guy across the aisle was grumbling. "What is this crap? You're telling me this came off a chicken once upon a time? Good gravy, they think we'll eat anything." He was struggling with the hermetically sealed bubble of plastic utensils. He looked over at Cooper just as Cooper bit through the corner of the plastic wrap.

"Good idea," the guy said. He was roly-poly and fifty or so, black hair combed across his dome from a low part. His fingers were fat and stubby and there was a lot of black hair on the backs of his hands. Quite a crop bulging from his ears and nostrils, too. "Thanks for the tip, pal," he said. "You fly a lot, do you?"

Cooper shook his head. "Hardly ever anymore. I hate it. I always wind up someplace I wish I weren't."

The guy chuckled. "Ain't it the way, though?" His wife leaned across her husband's thick chest and shook her fork at Cooper.

"Now what's worse than two men getting together, talking about how they'd rather be home watching the Vikings or somebody! I just love to travel."

"You're a travel agent, naturally you're in favor of travel." Her husband grunted. "And it's the Twins, bunny, the Twinkies."

Cooper said: "You're from Minnesota, I take it."

"Oh, sure, North Oaks. Real nice community. Gotta gate, yet. The wife, Audrey, she's in travel, I'm in electronics. Bob Denlinger. Got me a store out at Rosedale. Big shopping center." He stuck his hand halfway across the aisle and Cooper shook it. It was nice to remember that there were just folks out there, not a damn thing to do with Germany.

"Bob, now you let the man enjoy his dinner," the wife said. Bob and Audrey Denlinger. North Oaks. North of St. Paul. Minnesota.

"Enjoy? This stuff?"

They chatted amiably back and forth. It was a relief to talk about the Twins and the Braves and their classic World Series. Later the subject matter switched to Herschel Walker and why the Vikings had never made the slightest attempt to use him as an offensive weapon. "Pissing contest," Bob Denlinger said. "Mike Lynn makes the deal for Walker, gives away the fuckin' store, and then Burnsie gets his back up and won't use the guy! And who gets the shaft? All of us Viking fans, the season ticket holders—poor dumb slobs like me."

Cooper went back to sleep.

The jet hit some turbulence as they drew nearer to the airport serving Minneapolis-St. Paul. Things were shaking around and it was dark outside and finally the captain came on the intercom and said they were getting a little snow out there, several inches building up. "Little early for a big snow," the captain observed. "But the kids will enjoy it, I guess. We should be on the ground in about twenty minutes. Nothing to worry about. We're on time."

Snow.

Twenty years ago, coming back from Boston because his brother, Cyril, had popped up after years and summoned him home, there had been snow, more snow than he'd ever seen. He'd driven his mighty, majestic '66 Lincoln across the country and when he'd been attacked by men who didn't want him to get back home for the meeting, the huge Lincoln had saved his life, had sheltered him with its warmth as he lay bleeding and beaten by the side of the snowblown road.

Snow. They'd followed him all the way home, they hadn't given up, and finally the gaunt man had come out of the night on the ghostly snowmobile and the time had come to kill or be killed in the frozen blowing night . . .

The lights of the city were smeared behind the snow blowing past the window as they banked and began the descent toward the strips of glowing dots lining the runway. A sudden downdraft shook the plane and then, softly, it settled down and landed, skidded with a squeal, straightened out and braked with the jet backthrust until they were rolling slowly. Snowplows were out in force, heaping giant mounds of what looked like white boulders on the spaces to the sides of the tarmac.

The wind was blowing hard, whipping the tops off the mountains of snow. Maintenance crews leaned into the gale, moved about with flares and flashlights, motioned and yelled soundlessly to one another. The main terminal appeared and then was gone behind the rolling curtains of snow.

Bob Denlinger grinned at Cooper. "Now this looks like a real snowstorm. Can't wait to get my snowblower fired up. Snowmobile, too. If the damn environmentalists ain't outlawed 'em yet."

Audrey chimed in: "He's just like a little boy with that thing. Me, I hate the noise, I'm not a winter person, when you come right down to it."

But Cooper wasn't paying any attention. He was back in the storm twenty years ago, watching the gaunt man on the snowmobile running him down, sending out the great plumes of snow as Cooper waited with the shotgun . . . then pulled the trigger . . . He shook his head, not wanting to remember what it had done to the gaunt man . . . the body hurtling through the windscreen, pieces of the man flying away in the night, the blast of the shotgun in the stillness.

He was clammy with cold sweat and felt vaguely faint by the time they'd disembarked and were trudging down the endless corridors. It wasn't exactly an anxiety attack: it was more like the icy grip of paranoia. The fear that somehow it might all be happening again . . .

He was picking up the rental car when he saw the Denlingers walk past, heads down into the wind. Bob waved and called out something but it was lost in the whining wind. Cooper found the car and threw his bag into the backseat and closed the door, breathing hard, sweating. Calm down, for God's sake. But he was having a hard time. He turned on the radio once he had pulled out of the parking lot. He found WCCO. He knew they'd be talking about the storm.

A foot had fallen already and there was no end in sight. The temperature was hovering in the high twenties but the wind chill factor was below zero. Travel advisories were out for the whole area and you were nuts if you were thinking about taking your car out. As he headed the car toward the city he felt the ruts grab the wheels and jam him into the tracks worn in the snow. The highway was freezing over and a mixture of sleet and snow was turning the windshield into a smeared, nearly impenetrable, constantly shifting sheet of wetness.

As he fought to keep the car on the mostly deserted road his mind began running down the corridors of the past again. They'd been following him twenty years ago, and he felt the paranoia twisting and turning in his brain. Was he being followed again? Was there something going on he didn't understand? He'd been innocent then but he didn't have that excuse now. Twenty years of nothing, no hints of the past, and now, suddenly, here he was again, the snow all around, the cold and the wind and he was alone again . . .

He maneuvered the long sweeping turn onto the highway leading toward St. Paul, then angled off to the left, the two cities almost mirages in the night. But who could possibly be following him? Who would care all these years later? Who might be afraid of him now? It was ridiculous.

No one knew he was coming. He'd told no one but Grahame and the people at the office. Beate Hubermann didn't know and neither did Kilroy. No one else knew he was back. Just Bob and Audrey Denlinger. He smiled at the thought, then felt the smile fading. Who the hell were they really? He knew what they'd said. But the men who'd followed him home twenty years ago hadn't told him the truth either. He wiped his face, straining to see through the mess on the glass before him. He saw two cars up ahead in ditches, their taillights glowing red. The highway ahead was empty. The light stanchions lining the road shook in the wind, shadows shifting across the snow. There were three or four cars spread out behind him, burrowing along through the night. He wondered if Bob and Audrey were back there, worrying about getting home to White Bear Lake.

What about Bob and Audrey?

Something was wrong—but what was it? Cooper was sure it wasn't just paranoia, not just the old fear. They'd been friendly, they'd seemed harmless, they'd bickered and teased like a long-married couple, they'd paid a helluva lot of attention to him. Were they too good to be true? They'd said something. Or done something. Something all wrong . . . but what was it?

He was yanked back to the present as the car shuddered and jumped the ruts, slid wildly sideways across the road. He spun the wheel, felt it fishtailing in the snow and ice, then fought it back into the ruts and slowed down to a crawl. He'd heard himself shouting as he'd struggled to control the car. Christ. He hated this, all of it. Then he swallowed hard, biting back the sour bile, turned the radio up, concentrated on keeping the car in the tracks.

He saw the empty blackness of the countryside up ahead; then he was in it, the lights of the highway fading behind him as he swept down the ramp and onto the two-lane road. He felt as if an envelope were being sealed around him. No lights, no stars, just the swirling snow in his headlights and the throbbing of the battling wheels. The snow whipped across the road, fetched up against anything in its way, and the wind hammered the side panels. The sides of the road were filled with snow; up ahead a truck had skidded into the void, sat nose down and deserted, disappearing beneath the snow.

They were driving a rented car . . .

He was watching headlights barely visible behind him, watching the lights bounce and swerve in the snow, trying to remember everything about Bob and Audrey Denlinger, remembering Bob's jaunty wave as he

called something, trying to get the door of the car open . . . and it was
in the rental lot where Cooper had picked up his own car. Bob and
Audrey of North Oaks were driving home in a rental car and it just didn't
ring true. You don't rent a car to get home from the airport in your
hometown . . .

The car behind him now was drawing closer, still sliding in the
ruts, steadily closing on him. The driver had the brights on and they
reflected blindingly in the rearview mirror. Cooper adjusted the mirror
slightly to get the glare out of his eyes. He slowed down, waiting for the
other car to overtake him. Were they following him, or did they want to
waylay him? Or was his imagination out of control? He couldn't let it go.
He had to find out. Maybe it was nothing. But in his guts he knew, he
was sure . . .

*They weren't Bob and Audrey Denlinger . . . They'd lied to
him . . .*

He was moving into an attack state. Olaf Peterson had taught him
how to do it and his instincts were taking over. It wasn't remembering,
not consciously. It wasn't a choice. It was just happening. It was a little
like losing your mind, losing the ability to differentiate between the past
and the present. A part of him he'd thought was dead was coming back
to life.

The other car was drawing closer. He squinted into the mirror,
trying to make out how many people were in the car behind him. The
blowing snow and the glaring brights made it impossible. The car itself
was just a black shape bearing down on him. Cooper slowed again. He
wanted to force them to make their move. Maybe they were just trying to
get home. Maybe they'd go around him and drive off into the night. But
he knew they wouldn't. It didn't matter why, didn't matter what he
represented to them. They were watching him. They wouldn't go away.
They stuck to his tail.

Suddenly he hit bare ice, felt the car starting a skid, felt it begin
spinning, then felt the solid blow as the car behind him smashed into his
bumper, jolted him forward into a wilderness of blowing snow. He desperately tried to correct the direction again, slid off the shoulder and
pulled it back onto the level, he had no idea how, and then the car was
coming at him, slowly, sideways, its headlights wandering away into the
emptiness. The cars were like two elephants trying to tango, back and
forth, slamming into one another and then floating away, it seemed to go
on forever, a *pas de deux* in pachyderm time. He tried to get in behind
the other car, to force the followers into the lead, he was braking, they

were drawing even now, but the road was turning sharply, nothing but blackness lay ahead, the four headlights sweeping across a stand of wind-blown fir trees. He pushed hard on the brakes, his legs cramping, hoping the wheels would find some purchase, some traction, they were both braking, trying to stay on the road, sweat dripping down his forehead and stinging his eyes, and he ground to a halt almost without realizing what was happening, but the other car hadn't found the traction, Cooper saw it spinning on through a rickety guardrail, saw the wood splintering, saw the car moving away like an astronaut with his line cut floating away in space, saw the car pitching forward into the darkness and then disappearing in a halo of light that swung this way and that as the lights reflected on the falling snow . . .

He climbed out of the car, leaning with all his weight on the door, pushing against the wind to get it open, feeling the brutal wind and the icy snow on his face, and realized he was at the edge of the drop-off, almost propped against the wooden fence himself. He staggered, slipped to his knees in the snow, then slid clumsily down the rock-strewn ravine into the infinity of snow, a terrible roaring in his ears, drowning out even the sound of his own panting, realizing it must be the deafening sound of the falls, he was nearing Cooper's Falls much before he'd expected to. His own headlamp beams pierced the darkness overhead, but the ravine was in shadow. It made no difference, he knew it by heart now, he'd hiked in the steep, slanting ravine as a boy, he knew that hard left turn in the road, it was all coming back to him, he knew exactly where he was. The snow was blowing in his face, he felt as if he were being sliced to shreds as he clambered down the steep rocky face of the cliffside, the car had to be at the bottom, he kept on going, he had to know . . .

It was like a dream, a nightmare of cold and pain, as if he were floating in slow motion, as if the pain were drifting away, he kept crashing and falling through the snow, through the crusty drifts up against the boulders and trees and piles of broken branches that gave way like trap-doors when he leaned on them. The earth was shaking from the roar and power of the falls, thousands of tons of water spilling into the river only a hundred yards away, so loud he could barely think . . .

He fell the last ten feet, banged up against the car which looked like another drift, already building a coating of snow, flipped on its back, like a cockroach on its shell. One body had gone through the windshield, the face when he found it a pulp of glass-sheared blood and bone . . . He reached for the body, felt the mink coat. Christ, it was the woman from the plane, it had to be, it was . . . His heart stopped and he knelt in the snow, gasping, feeling faint . . . it was happening all over again, they were coming after him . . . He got up, steadied himself on a wheel stuck tight on a twisted axle, then leaned down and yanked at the front door, yanked until it screeched open and the overhead light came on, and there he was, thrown sideways on the floor with his feet tucked upright under the glove compartment, his head turned to the roof. Cooper had to be sure. He crawled into the upended car, moving along the roof of the passenger compartment which had become the floor. He had to be sure . . . He maneuvered past the steering wheel which hung like a broken limb, snapped in two . . . he reached down, tugging at the man's leather trenchcoat, yes, it was the right coat. The man's head flopped into view, blood coming from the mouth and nose and cuts across the broad forehead and bald scalp . . . suddenly the closed eyelids popped open, like a doll's, and Cooper lurched backward, screaming, banging his head against the foot pedals . . . the eyes were staring at him, poor dead Denlinger, whatever his real name was . . . he made a long sighing sound, lips fluttering, then nothing . . . if he wasn't dead he was so close it made no difference . . . Cooper was shaking hard, uncontrollably, and had a hellish time getting out of the car, scuttling along in the snow once he was free of the beast, then he turned and was scrambling back up the steep incline, a wild half-hysterical climb back up the slippery, icy wall, falling, propelled forward by a blind fear of the two corpses . . . the fear of all the corpses, the new ones and the ghosts of twenty years ago . . .

They'd been after him. He repeated that to himself again and again. They were after him . . . It couldn't have been some crazy coincidence, thinking about coincidences was how you got killed . . . it was Part the Second of a story begun years before, not just twenty years ago, but in his grandfather's day . . . they'd come after him and they'd failed again . . .

He reached the top of the ravine and stood outlined in the headlights, deafened by the roar of Cooper's Falls, horribly afraid, barely feeling the clenched fury of the night, remembering why he was here and letting himself give in to it for the first time, giving up all the coolness and distance he'd cultivated while structuring a new life for himself, feeling the tears streaming from his eyes, freezing on his face, and he cried into the wind, as if he could make her hear him even now, in Germany, in Berlin where she'd stayed on when the first stage of their war had ended —he faced the explanation . . .

I love her . . .

I love her . . .

6

A MAN WITH
A BROKEN LEG

He woke up in an overheated motel room that smelled of cedar chips and mothballs and ancient cigarettes. An old colored newspaper photograph of Cooper's Falls, in a thick wooden frame, hung on the wall across from where he lay trying to swallow in the oppressive heat and dryness. A radiator was hissing.

I love her . . .

His cry was still bouncing off the bulkheads of his brain. He still saw the night's dead, the fingers of light from the cars probing the snowy blackness, still heard the deafening crash of the falls.

He struggled out of the tangle of blankets and realized he had a headache. He dug around in his bag for Advil and took four and padded across the turquoise shag carpeting to stand at the window. It was early morning; the darkness was slowly fading beyond the frosty glass. The snow was still falling. He cranked open the window and breathed in the damp, cold air. The desk man from the motel office was huffing and stomping around in the parking lot, brushing snow off the cars with a broom. He was wearing a red and black mackinaw jacket, which reminded Cooper of Beate Hubermann's more stylish version, and a hunting cap with the earflaps pulled down. His big mustache was white with snow. He could have been a Norman Rockwell *Saturday Evening Post* cover from 1943, a description which could with equal accuracy be applied to just about all of Cooper's Falls. The image was timeless but it struck him as an illusion. What had happened in the snow twenty years ago was no *Saturday Evening Post* cover. Norman Rockwell wouldn't have thought much of what happened last night either. It was the wrong kind of Americana.

In the shower he wondered when somebody would find the car and the bodies. Once the wreckage was found, they'd sooner or later start looking for the car that matched the paint scrapings from the scrap in the ravine. Sooner or later there'd be hell to pay. But for the moment, he was okay. And, if luck was with him, he'd be gone before anything bad could happen. He was already thinking in the old ways, thinking about surviving, thinking about how frail your lifeline could be. He was already making a plan all about staying alive.

Whoever they were, they didn't know yet what had happened last night. They weren't going to like it.

The municipal snowplows had been fighting a delaying action through the night. A few cars moved slowly through the falling snow, appearing at corners like apparitions from behind piles of hardened snow ten feet high. Cooper eased his car out of the parking space and into the street, then drove out the old familiar road until he reached the limit of what the plows had cleared. Then he slipped on the black buckle galoshes the desk clerk had found for him in the broom closet, and set off the last two hundred yards on foot.

He was sweat-soaked and gasping for breath by the time he reached the two stone buildings flanking the entrance gate. Beyond the open gate the driveway stretched away toward the great mansion where he'd grown up, where Austin Cooper had been held under a kind of house arrest during the war, where he—John Cooper—had come twenty years ago at his brother Cyril's urgent request, where he'd found Cyril dead . . .

Poplars still lined the road, stark black against the shifting whiteness. To the right of the gate was one of the two stone buildings. It had a heavy oak door. The soldiers guarding the house had once used it as their command post. Austin Cooper had sent out containers of soup and sandwiches every day. Snow was now drifted eye-high against the door.

There were elms and oaks and groves of firs scattered across the lawn as it dipped and swooped in a perfect white expanse toward the six squared white columns ranged across the front of the house, rising all three stories to the roof with its cupolas and brick chimneys. Home.

There was no other name for it but that. It was home, would always be home.

But as he slowly toiled up the driveway, sinking into the fresh snow, leaving prints like potholes, he knew that the home he'd known was yet another illusion, something that was no more and had, when you faced the bitter truth, never actually been at all. When all the illusions had ended twenty years ago, he'd given the house to the town to replace the little gingerbread library, which had been destroyed during the Siege of Cooper's Falls. Now it was both the library and the home of the Historical Society of Cooper's Falls, which had come to serve much of the state for the preservation of documents. Standing on the porch, he felt like a stranger for a moment, almost overwhelmed by the dignity of the place. He looked at his watch. No, it didn't matter. He'd come a long way. He had to see it again.

The windows glowed a refined yellow through the falling snow and the front door was unlocked. He smelled coffee and heard women talking, heard faintly a radio tuned to WCCO in Minneapolis. There was a long list of school closings. The airport was socked in. It was all so familiar.

There was the parquet floor, the long, gently curving stairway with the rail where he and Cyril had done their boyhood sliding and Grandfather Austin had caught them, scooping them out of the air before they landed on their rear ends. On either side of the entry hall, sliding doors led to large parlors . . .

The women were still chatting away. The staff had been snowed in, he gathered, had simply stayed the night. He passed on through one of the parlors, which had been fitted out now as a reception area, with a new computer and some very old card-file cabinets. The same carpet he remembered, somehow the same smells. Across the room the doorway stood open; he swallowed hard. The library.

The huge leather chairs were still there in their same places. He remembered the windows shattering, gunfire from outside in the snow and darkness, glass sprayed across the carpet . . . Over there were his grandfather's standing globes, the maps on the wall—but his pins marking the progress of the war had been removed. He could still catch the aroma of the old man's cigars, trapped forever in the fabric of the drapes and in the spines of the volumes filling the shelves. The brass student lamps were still there, the leather-topped desk, the andirons and the logs laid in the grate waiting for one of the old man's long wooden matches. And, out of some respect for celebrity perhaps, the framed photographs of Austin Cooper with some of his friends still sat on the tables, signatures preserved under glass.

Puffing a cigar with Winston Churchill back in the thirties, when the future Prime Minister was lost in the wilderness, put out to pasture and not yet summoned back to his rendezvous with destiny . . .

Sitting in a slatted lawn chair in the late-afternoon sunlight, talking with Hitler in some flower garden . . .

Chatting with Hitler and Eva Braun at a luncheon table with heavy carving and massive woodwork, on the walls tapestries, a couple of German shepherds dozing at their feet, Hitler's white hand hanging at the side of the chair, his fingers scratching behind a dog's ear . . .

Inspecting a bottle of wine with the onetime wine merchant von Ribbentrop . . .

Standing by an immense open Mercedes-Benz, smiling almost shyly while Göring shook with laughter, leather-gloved fist resting on the elaborately jeweled handle of a hunting knife in a scabbard affixed to his belt . . .

Pictures of Cooper's father and mother with him and Cyril, their beautiful mother holding their infant sister, Lee . . .

The engines of memory were roaring in his mind—

"May I help you?"

A stylish gray-haired woman had come in behind him, was peering curiously at him as he turned, her half-glasses perched on the tip of her nose.

"I'm sorry for just barging in," he said. "I used to live in this house. I wanted to . . . I don't know, I guess I just wanted to have a look around—"

"John Cooper! Of all people—I'm Helen Roark, John, we were classmates in high school. Remember? Miss Downer? We were in the same homeroom."

"Of course. Helen. Of course, you took me by surprise, that's all."

She was smiling at him. "John, it's so good to see you again. We didn't think you'd ever come back . . . You'll be wanting to see some of our model reconstructions, won't you? I'll bet you've heard about them —we had a designer from the Guthrie do them for us . . ."

He heard her voice going on and on.

We won't have many visitors today, maybe no one, with this weather . . . I can't believe you came out in all this snow . . . Are you back for long? . . . Have you seen any of your old friends? . . . Dr.

Bradlee passed on almost ten years ago, you know, and so many oth-
ers . . . of course, the Siege itself took some lives, but you know all about
that . . . but Olaf Peterson's still the law and order in town . . .

But he wasn't listening.

He was staring at the glass-encased display on a library table, the carefully detailed model of the major events that came to be known as the Siege of Cooper's Falls.

In the tiny fields and streets of white snow it all came back to life. The little library was in ruins, flames leaping into the air. Another building was burning. Olaf Peterson, mustache prominent, stood in the street before the old hotel, looking at the burning library. Was Olaf the sheriff or the chief of police? Damned if he could remember. There was a model of the Cooper house, a little figure standing deep in the snow with a shotgun at his shoulder, its muzzle belching flame; he recognized himself, and he saw the snowmobile smashed to pieces in the snow and the body of the gaunt man flying through the air, atop an elongated toothpick, the figure covered with blood . . . It was all there, reduced to a museum display, a part of the history of the town . . .

A large board on an easel bore the title "The Siege: An Enduring Mystery." Carefully laid out below the headlines, the story began.

> If anyone understands the full meaning of what happened
> in Cooper's Falls over a few days in the winter of 1972, he
> has never come forward. But we can at least make some of
> the facts clear for researchers of the future. . . .

The upper floors of the vast house were closed to the public but Helen Roark thought John Cooper was entitled to a trip down memory lane if anyone was. He climbed the long staircase by himself. Snow rattled against the windows. Wind shrieked far away in the eaves among the lead drainpipes. Ahead of him he saw the room in which he'd been born with Dr. Bradlee doing the honors. The long hallway was nearly as dark as it had been that other night, twenty years ago, when he'd made the long journey with Paula Smithies, the librarian, beside him. Up here the house hadn't changed at all. Twenty years ago seemed like yesterday . . .

Paula had said, "John, there's a light down there . . ."

He'd turned and seen the glow, a strip of light stretching dimly across the floor and up the wall opposite. Something was banging against the back of the house. He'd felt for the light switch but it hadn't worked.

The light was coming from what had once been his grandfather's bedroom. He'd laughed nervously. "This is ridiculous," he'd said. "Why are we tiptoeing around?" Paula had taken his hand, squeezed it. They went into the room together.

The man was sitting in a wingback chair by the window. His eyes were closed. He was tilted to one side, his head turned away, lolling down on his shoulder. His left arm extended stiffly over the arm of the chair.

"Cyril!" His cry had echoed in the silence.

His brother, Cyril, was dead . . .

Now he stood in the doorway looking at the same chair in the same dim room but Cyril was long gone. Slowly he moved past the huge four-poster on its platform, stood at the window looking out into the storm. Below he saw the snowbound lawn where the gaunt man had tried to run him down on the snarling snowmobile, where he'd pulled up the shotgun and blown his nightmare to shreds, bloody shreds . . .

That had been the beginning, not the end, of the nightmare, and it had lasted a long time and now it was beginning again and none of the story was told on the display board downstairs. No one knew the whole story but John Cooper and one other man. They knew everything about the Fourth Reich twenty years ago.

John Cooper and Olaf Peterson.

A snowplow had just finished clearing the narrow country road that led along the top of the bluffs above the river with the falls thundering off behind a heavy stand of firs. Cooper waited for the plow to turn back onto the paved road and then swung into the newly cut path. The snow was still falling and WCCO was reporting that it had a chance to become the biggest twenty-four-hour snowfall in Minnesota's history and that was saying something.

The house came into view slowly, emerging like a ship in the fog. It was a big place, stone and wood and brick and mammoth logs, a big glassed-in sun porch angling off at one end. The plantings were majestic and enormous with the topping of snow. He parked the car with its nose just short of a snowbank. Smoke drifted up from a couple of chimneys, the wind whipping it away, losing it in the blowing snow. It was noon and the storm was thick enough to make you drive with the lights on.

He followed the shoveled walk up to the door, rang the bell, waited. Nobody came to greet him. He rang again, then pushed the door open.

A voice he recognized from across the years was yelling from somewhere inside.

"Yeah, yeah, come on in for Christ's sake, I'm just a poor son of a bitch, helpless cripple, you might as well come on in and just rob me blind and then cut my throat . . ."

Cooper went inside. He smelled the same cigar smoke. The voice from twenty years ago . . .

They'd come back from Germany and were standing in front of the Ritz in Boston and he'd looked at his watch and shrugged and caught Cooper's eye. "Well, it's time for me to go," he'd said. They had seen it through and finally it was over.

"Me, too," Cooper said.

"Well, then," Peterson said. The wind was tugging at his very expensive hairpiece. He smoothed it down. "Always think the damn thing's going to blow away." He laughed. "You were the first person who ever spotted it, you bastard." He grabbed Cooper's arm. "Look, this is getting silly. Stay well, John. And try to forget it." He was shaking Cooper's hand, squinting in the bright sunshine, backing away.

Make believe it doesn't matter.

"Everybody dies," Cooper had said but the wind blew the words away.

"I'll be in touch, Johnnie." He waved one last time and they both turned around and went their own ways.

But they hadn't stayed in touch. It just hadn't worked out that way. Cooper had needed to forget. And now Cooper was following the voice, through a huge room with island-sized hooked rugs and a glass wall looking out across the river to Wisconsin beyond, a vista of blowing snow with shapes of color here and there, the river, the bridge, the steeple of a church on Main Street rising darkly through the snow.

Olaf Peterson was sitting in an immense plaid armchair. One of his legs was in a cast stretched out on a hassock that matched the chair. A fire burned brightly in an oversized stone fireplace. There were gun racks with a variety of weapons on the wood-paneled wall. Crutches leaned against an end table within easy reach. Peterson looked up impatiently from the television screen.

"Well, Cooper, long time no see. Take a load off." He waved at a chair that matched his own. He was watching *The Third Man*. The cat sniffed at Harry Lime's shoes; then the light fell on his fleshy, boyish face as he hid in the doorway. Orson Welles.

"Long time no see? After twenty years, that's it? Long time no see?"

"Shut up and sit down."

"I'm touched."

"Cooper, try not to be a sap. Try hard." Peterson's eyes never left the screen. "Another hour won't matter. Just be quiet—there's a pot of coffee and some Danish on the coffee table. Eat, drink. Watch the movie. I never get tired of this movie. Best I ever saw."

So they watched. The ride on Vienna's mighty Ferris wheel. The cuckoo speech. The hunt through the sewers . . . Harry Lime trying to escape, the shot from above the ground with Lime's fingers snaking up through the grating, struggling to get away, knowing he must die . . . the scene after the funeral, Joseph Cotten standing at the roadside smoking a cigarette, waiting for Alida Valli, and the long shot of her walking down the narrow road . . . and walking right on past him.

Make believe it doesn't matter.

Peterson was in his early sixties now and looked hard and fit as ever, once you got beyond the leg. He was wearing a Minnesota Vikings sweatshirt and sweatpants, purple and gold and white, one leg cut away to make way for the thick plaster. His bandit's mustache was flecked with gray and the hairpiece had undergone a similar costly transformation. He was still dark, Levantine in appearance, the backs of his hands covered with dark, wiry hair. If ever a man didn't look like an Olaf Peterson it was Olaf Peterson. While watching the movie he occasionally held heavy handweights out before him, raising and lowering them without seeming to notice what he was doing. When the last frames of the movie flickered past, he clicked the VCR remote and stared at the screen for a moment, transfixed.

"Man, that stuff in the sewers . . ." Then he snapped out of it. "So, Cooper, where ya been? Seems like years and years—"

"It has been."

"—and like only yesterday." He shifted his leg and grinned wolfishly beneath the thick mustache. "All those guys trying to kill us. That was fun! Yeah, those were the days." He scowled. "So what brings you back? Feeling homesick? That's kinda strange after all this time."

"I'm never homesick," Cooper said. "I carry this place around with me, it's always there. No, I came back to talk to you."

"You don't say."

"To ask you a favor."

"After twenty years you want a favor."

"Well, from the look of you, I'm not so sure."

"You could have saved yourself a trip then. You could have called."

"No, I had to see you." He nodded at the cast. "What happened to you?"

"Broke my fucking leg playing racquetball with that big bastard Wisneski, you remember him?"

"Used to have lunch with him at Nye's Polonaise."

"That's the guy. Used to be a newspaperman in the Cities. Real smart."

"Funny fella."

"Yeah, he's funny, all right. Tells a helluva story and a few of them are about me. Now he's got a new one. We were playing a month ago, he was beating hell outa me, I went for some shithead killer shot, tripped over my own racquet, fell down, snap, broke my leg, old Ken's laughing his ass off, I thought he'd have a coronary. I don't know, I'll be up and around in a few weeks. And then I'm going after that bastard—he'll get me out on that boat of his and try to catch a fuckin' fish and then it'll be my turn. You know what he catches? Dickfish. They're all about the size of his dick . . . Well, you sure got Cooper weather. I haven't seen this much snow since the Siege." He shook his head. "So what's the favor you came all this way to ask?"

"Well, lean back, let me tell you the story . . ."

Cooper told him what had happened in the last few days. Kilroy from out of nowhere dragging up the Nazi part of the family, the German TV reporter showing up unexpectedly with the message from his sister, Lee, and the disappearance of her daughter, Erika, then Kilroy turning up in the TV coverage of the German investment in Boston. "So, Lee wants me to come to Germany."

"Lee." Peterson repeated the name with an expression on his face that was hard to interpret. "She's a head case, you know that. No, don't say a word. I know about these things and you know damn well I'm right. Head case. Always was, always will be. She didn't have to stay in Munich when we'd finished with those crazy Nazi bastards. She could have come home, she could have come with you—"

"It was complicated."

"Bullshit. She decided to stay. Mama Nazi—"

"That's unfair and you know it."

"Okay, okay, but she always pissed me off." He sighed and lit another cigar only slightly larger than a ballbat. "Look, remember what Dr. Roeschler said about her, that night in Munich? I can hear him now —he said she'd never be sure who she is . . . She's nuts, schizoid, he said. I told you then, and I tell you now, she is all trouble. And all this German stuff—I don't like it much. Hell, all you gotta do is read the papers. I mean, it's not exactly subtle. There's a precedent, right?" He waited in the quiet, then said: "So, are you going back to the Fatherland?"

"I wanted you to go with me. That's the favor."

"Old times' sake?"

"No. I'm afraid to go alone."

Peterson laughed abruptly. "But you're going, no matter what?"

"I've got to. You know that. It's Lee."

"You've never gotten over all that Lee business, then. I've always hoped it would wear out over time."

"Look, I'm going back. I wanted you to come with me. I didn't know about your leg."

"Yeah . . . well, it's a different Germany you're going back to—"

"Get serious," Cooper said. "Germany doesn't change. It just gets bigger. Bigger means scarier."

"You're thinking about the old Nazis? Hell, Cooper, those guys are all dead now." He laughed huskily at a memory. "You and I killed most of 'em." Milo Keepnews, had he been a Nazi? Cooper couldn't remember but he remembered Olaf Peterson killing him in a dirty, scum-caked toilet . . . When it was over Peterson had appraised himself in a long, thin splinter of mirror. He touched his hairpiece, adjusting a lock or two at the front, and stood back to look down at the body. One of Milo's sleeves had slipped off the rim of the toilet bowl and his hand floated, an amorphous blob, in the filthy water. His eyes were open. He stared unblinking at the floor, saliva dripping from his mouth. "Goodbye, Milo," Peterson had said matter-of-factly as he pulled the string on the one dim light bulb. A long time ago . . .

Peterson stood up with some difficulty and balanced on one foot, grabbed his crutches, and hobbled over to the expanse of glass. " 'Course, from what I read and see on the TV, there's a whole new crop of them."

Cooper turned abruptly. "Of what?"

"Come on, Cooper, pay attention, willya? We're talking about the bad guys here."

"I was just thinking about poor Milo Keepnews—"

"Whoever the hell he is! Let's think about Germany. Think about what you're getting into—okay?"

"Peterson," Cooper said patiently. "Always a smartass."

Peterson ignored the comment. "I pay attention to Germany these days. I read whatever I can get hold of—Germany's not exactly a secret. It's just that America's got this crazy obsession with Japan . . . I never gave a damn about Germany until you dragged me into it, you and your weird fucked-up family, twenty years ago. Didja ever think, John boy, that you're the only one of the bunch who's not a living, breathing lie? You should be proud of that. Even your hero father didn't die over the Channel after all . . . even he was a Nazi—"

"Drop it," Cooper said quietly. "Let's talk about Germany."

"Well, like I said, I get a big kick out of all these folks scared shitless about the Yellow Peril, the Fuck-Babe-Ruth Japanese . . . *Banzai,* right? It makes you wonder, am I the only one left with the vision thing? People ought to be thinking about Germany. About *Europe.* Japan's going to have its hands full in ten, fifteen, twenty years—with Korea, with China moving into a capitalist economy and undercutting them on prices. Think about China versus Japan on a level playing field. Hell, we could live to see that, pal, and I'll tell you one thing, we're gonna use China to pay back the Japs . . . but the big point is simple, we're a European country. It's history, it runs so deep. Our future lies with Europe . . . We're going to have to develop a partnership with Russia, Ukraine, all the Ivans. Oil alone indicates that. They're sitting on the world's biggest supply—did you know that? More oil under the old Soviet Union than anywhere else in the world. We're the ones who can help 'em get it out of the ground and refined. We gotta be the firstest with the mostest. And ask the sociologists who've been studying national character the past fifty years . . . You know who the Russians are most like? The Americans. Natural allies, John boy . . . but there's one big worry. Know what it is?"

"Go on, your erudition makes me weak."

"The worry is Germany. We can't let the Germans, the dear old Huns, beat us to Russia. Think—we've got through this whole damn Cold War, we rebuilt Europe after the war and more than anybody else we rebuilt the Huns, we waited forty-five years thinking the Russians were going to nuke us and all the time the meter was running on them—

they self-destructed. And now the marbles are all over the place, just waiting to be picked up . . .

"And it beats hell out of me why! Anybody who thought seriously about the Cold War must have realized that there had to be two parts to it. First you wanted to win, sure, but there was the inevitable second part —you wanted to turn Russia into your new best friend—sure as hell you didn't want to make them somebody *else's* new best friend!"

Peterson had climbed onto a stool at the bar, sat dangling his cast, staring at Cooper, waiting.

"Well, that's just fine, but isn't it a little macro? What I've got to do is more micro—I've got to go see my sister. The future of Europe doesn't matter much to me. Lee is what matters to me."

"So what the hell are you worrying about going to Germany for? Her daughter will probably be back safe and sound by the time you get there. Lee, she'll be all calmed down—you'll be back in a couple of days, you won't know why you were so worried."

"But what about Kilroy? Beate Hubermann?"

Peterson shrugged. "Just people."

Cooper sighed. His stomach was knotted tight. "There's one other thing."

"Just like the old days." Peterson smiled behind the drooping mustache. "There was always one more thing. Okay. What is it?"

"They tried to kill me last night."

"Aw, come on, Cooper, please, spare me some fantasy—"

"Now it's your turn to shut up and listen. This is Cooper talking."

"Okay. You're right. Tell me."

When he was done, Peterson frowned and blew smoke at him. "The Denlingers! Jeez. Just a couple of poor unlucky bystanders."

"They were following me. They were lying. They didn't take a turn-off to that fancy suburb, North Oaks . . . in the end they were trying to knock me off the road—"

Peterson held up his hand. "Okay, okay." He picked up a cordless phone from the bar and called the police station. "Mike? This is Peterson. No, *Chief* Peterson. Mike, I know you're new but you gotta get with the program. Look, there was a car, took a header off that tricky turn just before you get to the falls . . . Last night, no, coming in toward town, right during the worst of the storm . . . Yeah, Mike, I know the roads are bad . . . Well, try it, or wait until Orville gets back in . . . Sure, okay, Mike, yeah, I understand. Can you get LaVonne to patch me through to Highway Patrol? . . . Thatta boy, Mike . . ." He winked at

Cooper. "He's just a kid. We're not exactly used to crime waves out there." He waited for the call to go through. "Lester," he said, "you boys probably just sittin' around the checkerboard today, right?" and he laughed, then ran over the story of last night's car wreck with more urgency than he had with Mike. He listened for a few minutes, then said: "Well, look, call me back as soon as you get anything, okay, Lester? I'll be waitin' by the phone on this one."

While they waited Peterson filled in some blanks for Cooper. "Yeah, the wife is already out in Scottsdale getting the house opened up. We got a helluva place out there. Best thing I ever did was marry a beautiful heiress. But I'm still chief in this little burg. I just take off every winter. Leave Orville Forrester in charge, he's a good man. I'm getting pretty near ready to pack it in, tell you the truth. I'm thinkin' about opening up a little joint, hire a good cook, live the quiet life down in the Keys somewhere or maybe out in Sausalito. Mind you, I'm still a hardass, but I was a helluva lot younger when you and I were runnin' around terrorizing Nazi wannabes . . . but what a time that was!" Peterson stared accusingly at the leg and the cast. "Remember that creep Lee was married to in those days. What was his name?"

"Brendel. She was Lise Brendel back then."

"Lise. I forgot that was her German name. Always think of her as Lee. Well, what a bunch they were. Man, that sister of yours could really pick 'em." He looked at Cooper, then out the window. "You know what I mean. She was a looker, though. Jesus."

Silence had settled over them and Cooper put some pizza from a couple of nights ago into the oven, following Peterson's instructions. Dribble a little olive oil on it, scatter some red pepper flakes, put it on the pizza pan with all the little holes. Set the oven at 450. Give it eight, nine minutes . . . The telephone rang.

Cooper couldn't stand hearing a one-sided conversation so he went back to the kitchen and waited for the pizza. When it was ready, he brought it in on a couple of plates, with a pair of beers. Peterson was watching the afternoon darken.

Cooper said: "So?"

"No ID of any kind. Not a piece of paper. Except two plane tickets in the name of Denlinger. No car rental agreement. It wasn't a rental car. Had a phony Minnesota plate. The car—they call 'em 'blanks.' I've heard about 'em, never actually seen one before. The government uses 'em, they call it 'drawing a blank.' They use 'em for surveillance and God only knows what else. Can't trace 'em, no way to identify 'em. The car has been lobotomized. It has no memory, no history. Same with the guns."

"Guns?"

"Two nine-millimeter Berettas. No serial numbers, no nothing."

"But they were on the plane. They had to go through security points—"

"Cooper. The guns would be in the car. Waiting for them."

"Of course. I'm not too quick . . . Do you have any suggestions about a course of action for me?"

"Be incredibly careful, that would be my first. Or just get back to Boston, act innocent, stay there. They'd leave you alone."

"I can't do that. It's—"

"Lee. Don't say it. I know. Well, I hope to God she's worth it. I really do. Look, why don't you stay the night?"

"No, I think I'd better keep moving. They probably don't know where I am now."

"Hell, they don't even know their people are dead."

"One question. Who are they?"

"Cooper, I'm just a small-town cop. But I don't think they're Germans, okay? Smells like Feds to me."

"I've got to get to Lee," Cooper said.

Peterson sighed, scratched at his cast as if he could feel it. "It's another fine mess, pal . . ." When Cooper was leaving, Peterson grabbed his arm and squeezed. "I wish I were going with you, pal."

Peterson stood in the doorway watching until the car was almost out of sight, its headlamps only a faint glow against the snow. "On his own," he said regretfully. "And on the run. God be wi' ye, John Cooper." The last was just a whisper and, in any case, there was no one to hear him.

7

NIGHTWORK

The chair groaned and squealed beneath Ned Cheddar's immense girth. He was staring balefully at Kilroy, whistling an old college song he re-membered from somewhere, "Buckle Down, Winsocki." It wasn't from a college Cheddar had attended, so far as he could recall, but he liked the song. You couldn't have proven any of this by Kilroy, whose taste in music presently ran to Kinky Friedman and the Texas Jewboys.

Kilroy's Stetson rested on his knee and he was smoking one of the long cheroots. The Georgetown house seemed to hum and almost quiver with the variety of security and technological systems implanted within the walls and under the floors and crisscrossing the outer shell. Kilroy wasn't sure if the house made him feel secure or very vulnerable. He wasn't sure it mattered, what he felt.

"Sad news, I'm afraid." Cheddar had held off making a sound for some time, trying to build a little suspense. When he spoke it was with a sigh or a wheeze, Kilroy wasn't absolutely sure about that either.

"You don't say." He placed his crossed boots on the corner of the Cheese's desk. Cheese frowned at them.

"Our friends the Denlingers have gone to their reward."

"As in dead? Well, frankly, Cheese, I don't give a damn. I've never heard of them." Kilroy blew smoke at Cheddar and provided a leathery smile.

"They had an unfortunate automobile accident in Minnesota. Drove off a cliff, apparently. Killed outright."

"Minnesota, you say."

"I do. They were observing our Mr. Cooper, who made that trip back home. An incredible snowstorm. A kind of constant in his trips back home, if you remember his history."

Kilroy nodded. "Seems like folks who get hitched up with this character have a way of getting killed."

"An understatement. Though we have no direct evidence that he was involved in this incident. I leave it to the Minnesota authorities to figure out the details . . . and to ascertain who the victims were." He very nearly smiled. "They're going to have quite a problem with that, I'm afraid."

Kilroy nodded again, waiting, smoke drifting up from his nostrils.

"We're not exactly sure where Mr. Cooper has gotten to . . ."

Kilroy began to chuckle and the chuckle turned to a harsh cough. Cheddar watched impassively. Kilroy wiped his mouth with his bandanna and peered at the spittle. "God, Cheese, I love it when you get caught with your great big trousers down!"

"I'm always pleased to be the cause of merriment in others. But you'd be well advised to consider our relationship and keep a civil tongue in your head. Cooper is off the screen at the moment. We'll find him in due time, of course. Certainly if he leaves the country. I really don't see him trading in phony passports."

"What difference does it make? He's going to head for that sister of his. Berlin."

"Indeed. I'm rather tempted to let him go. Can he serve our purposes?"

"Don't look at me. How the dickens would I know what your purposes are?"

"If only I could truly believe that. Still, you have a point. We know he'll go straight to his sister. I really need to have a word with Delaney and . . . and the Professor. You know, Clint, the Professor is bound to understand Cooper better than any of us . . . yes, I should have a word with the Professor. Must be very careful, the man's a graveyard full of secrets . . ." Cheddar was speaking softly now. The past had him in its grip: Ned Cheddar knew too much about the Professor and John Cooper and so many others, the quick and the dead. Once in a great while it was hard to keep it all to himself: once in a while he'd have liked to tell some of the truth, unburden himself, but he couldn't and that was the price he paid for knowing all those secrets—he had no choice but to keep them, each in its own little compartment, and God have mercy on his soul and his ass if he ever mixed up the compartments.

His tiny, glittering eyes, sunk so deeply beneath his brow, discovered Kilroy again. "And having spent a great deal of time studying the lengthy dossier on Mr. Cooper, I must say he just might find the daughter, Erika . . . he's a determined man. Or he was twenty years ago."

"He had Olaf Peterson with him then."

"I realize that. And I've looked into Peterson's current status—he has a broken leg. We can count him out—which is a bloody good thing. The man's a maniac. In a way it's a shame he won't be over there. He'd find the girl and doubtless kill a bunch of our friends in the process—"

"Is that what you want, Cheese? To kill some of your superfluous friends?"

"I wouldn't comment on that, of course. But *if* I were to comment, I might say that it wouldn't break my heart. It depends."

"Always does, doesn't it?"

"So, I say, let him go to Berlin."

Kilroy shrugged.

"You'll have to go over as well, of course," Cheddar said.

"Crap. Crapperino. Crapperoo."

"I'd have thought you'd be pleased. Old times in Berlin, memories flooding back, beer and fräuleins in the old rathskeller, the occasional jackboot echoing on the cobblestones—"

"Oh, shut up, Cheese."

"You can pay your respects to Herr Koller."

Kilroy made a sour face. "I don't want to get back into this. I'm old. Haven't I served my time?"

"Not you, my friend. Not you, not ever. You are serving consecutive life sentences. You belong to me." He truly smiled at last. "You, truth to tell, will never be rid of me."

"There's always one way, Cheese. You know that I might avail myself of that one way."

"Oh, for the love of mike. I'll pretend I didn't hear that. False bravado. Deep down I'm going to believe that you love and respect Ned Cheddar. You're one of my boys."

"Nearing the end of the trail. Keep that in mind. So, when do I leave?"

The three men sheltered from the cold rain, their backs to a wet brick wall. They were standing on the roof of a four-story building in a block made of small businesses topped by two or three floors of flats. The brick wall was part of a low shed containing a water tank, workmen's tools, odds and ends. Chimneys poked up here and there. The rain was slanting into their faces.

Across the street was a long low building, three stories, once a school, later a barracks, later still a hospital for recovering mental patients after the war. Now it served as living quarters for refugees, mostly Turks, Armenians, Bosnians. They were held there in a kind of political limbo: they existed, but only barely. The case of each and every individual had to be evaluated by the authorities: were they real refugees from oppression, or did they merely want to better themselves economically in the new Germany? If they were found to be fleeing from political enemies, Germany would accept them, though of course they couldn't become citizens. There was, however, no limit on their numbers. The policy had stood since the end of World War II, when Germany, as a kind of atonement for Nazi crimes, opened its doors to anyone suffering under a cruel government. For a long time it hadn't been a problem. But now times had changed. Now it was a problem.

The economy of the new Germany was in an enormous recession, a recession that was sapping the will to greatness, sapping the will of Chancellor Glock and those around him—this was quite clear to the men on the rooftop. The unification of East and West had proven more difficult than expected. Jobs were scarce. Money was tight. The foreigners kept coming. They were given money and free housing while they lived in the refugee centers; these hostels had become the flashpoints of the firestorms of hatred. The Germans who were having trouble themselves now felt betrayed. The Germans from the East, who had always been provided with work by the Communist government, missed being employed, resented being "sacrificed" to unification. Resented these newcomers' being subsidized by the government.

Out of the mixture of economic and ethnic confusion and discontent and bitterness had come the neo-Nazis. Thugs, skinheads, hoodlums, anyone with a grudge and the intellectual capacity to make a Molotov cocktail. Taking out after foreigners, after refugees. It was something to do if you were young and stupid and didn't have a job or didn't want one. It had begun in the East and in the boondocks and it had been ugly. There were rumors now that it was going to get a lot uglier and it was going to hit center stage. Not off somewhere, places like Rostock, not out in the provinces. Not a little skirmish, like the Potsdam incident. Major violence. And it was going to hit Berlin itself.

And when the neo-Nazis were coupled in the headlines with *Berlin* there was going to be a shock wave that would scare not only nervous European neighbors but the rest of the world as well. The neo-Nazi groups would inevitably begin to coalesce around one or two leaders, would inevitably form an openly acknowledged political party and choose candidates . . . It would be the same old story. And then, within Germany, you'd have to choose sides, you'd have to demonstrate and sign up, and soon the pikes would be flashing, there would be blood in the gutters . . .

There would be chaos.

There would have to be a crackdown. The government would have to show itself as made of steel, after all.

The men on the rooftop waiting in the dark and the rain knew all that. They were the kind of men who made sure they knew everything. They knew that in every crisis there was opportunity. It was their business to see things that way. But now they were just getting wet and cold. They were impatiently stamping their feet to keep the blood circulating, blowing on their fingers, tightening their mufflers.

Wolf Koller, his hat pulled low on his forehead, moved out of the shadow of the wall, stood near the roof's edge, and stared down the length of the rain-washed street. Dr. Fritz Gisevius came forward and joined him. He was sucking a lemon cough drop. They could all smell it. Behind them in the shadows stood Max Adler, chief of detectives of the Central Police. Wolf Koller's cop. He was smoking his ever-present pipe. He looked briefly at his watch. Across the horizon the lights of what had once been West Berlin lit up the stormy sky with a blurred pink radiance. The sky over what had been East Berlin was dark as always, almost as if there were no city there at all. Adler sighed, sucking at the pipe. Lights, no lights. That told the whole story. Adler was accustomed to taking the long view, accustomed to weighing his options and toting up where his loyalties might, in various situations, lie. He'd been taught by a master. Werner Paulus hadn't taught the great truths to many of those who worked under him, but he'd taken a shine to Max Adler when Adler was new in Homicide Central. He'd thought Adler might have some promise, might be worth teaching. So, Adler smoked his pipe and watched his two companions.

Wolf Koller was lost in thought, remembering a conversation he'd had in the Daimler with Fritz Gisevius an hour before, as they headed through the stormy night toward the rooftop. Gisevius, in a reflective mood, had asked him what, in the end, Koller wanted for himself, what did Wolf Koller truly see as his role in the future of Germany and the world. It wasn't the sort of question they often faced up to, but the darkness of the back of the limousine, the sound of the rain outside and the flicking of the windshield wipers in front, the sense of solitude—all of those elements made the question somehow quite reasonable. Perhaps it would make its way into the book Gisevius would someday write about Wolf Koller poised at the edge of his greatest achievement.

"Richelieu," Koller said after a long moment's contemplation. "Cardinal Richelieu. That's how I see myself. What do you make of that, Fritz?"

"I would say that . . . it fits. Oh, you don't fit the vulgar, popular myth of Richelieu . . . the sinister, remote figure at the center of his web of deceit and lies and intrigues, the man consumed by ruthless vindictiveness, the ultimate spymaster surrounded by his fourteen cats . . . the man universally feared in France . . . in Europe. That's not you at all. But then, it wasn't Richelieu, either. You do seem cut from the cloth of the real man, the real Richelieu." He paused, waiting for his old friend to elaborate.

Finally Wolf Koller had spoken.

"Richelieu saw the chaos of seventeenth-century Europe. He brought his intelligence, his will, his ability to convince—he brought the weight of his station and his personality and his vision to bear on the chaos all around him. He saw that disorder was the enemy of greatness. He saw that man alone possessed reason and therefore reason must always be brought to bear on the evils of society—reason was the ultimate weapon." He smiled in the darkness. "I would not say this to anyone but you, but I understand what the times require and I understand how to accomplish it. Therefore, like Richelieu, I must work diligently my miracles to perform. I am not a politician. But I have power, I have leverage, and I am right. Therefore, I must make the politicians do the right thing. That is what I am about, Fritz. The future can still belong to us, old friend. We can steal it back from those who would throw Germany's greatness away . . ."

Koller turned back to the present, wondering if he'd been foolish to speak so candidly. But that was nonsense. Gisevius was a man of comparable seriousness. Gisevius had the courage to do what had to be done. Someday, Wolf Koller knew, Dr. Fritz Gisevius wanted to be Foreign Minister. He had undertaken diplomatic missions of some delicacy during the last twenty years. A man of science as well as a man of letters, Fritz Gisevius went down very well in the international community. He had played a key role in the Wall's coming down and he had spent the spring and summer of 1989 in Moscow as an advisor to various diplomats on when and how the Monolith might best come undone. Gisevius had gone on record in academic and foreign affairs journals early on, saying that the Soviets were done. He knew that the United States had simply spent the Reds into the graveyard. When the Red money was gone, the West would have won. He had said as much in '86, when he had gone to Harvard and shared a podium with Henry Kissinger, discussing before an august crowd just what the future held for what was and would still be for a short time the Soviet Union. It was widely believed that Fritz Gisevius knew more about the reality of the Soviet Union and the Russia that was to be than almost anyone. No, he'd been quite within bounds to confess his vision of himself to Fritz. Fritz was the sort of man who had the capacity to understand.

Wolf Koller was not quite so sure about Chancellor Glock. Of late, and in private, the Chancellor had shown signs of chafing under Koller's yoke. Glock was—Koller had been informed by men who'd overheard him—increasingly jealous of the power Koller wielded over him and over Germany, as well. And bothered by the fact that more and more the people looked toward Wolf Koller at a time of crisis than toward their Chancellor. When Germany moved to help the Russians get through the winter, it was Wolf Koller's plan: Wolf Koller's planes transported the food, Wolf Koller *was* Germany at that moment. When an earthquake demolished a region of Yugoslavia, already raped and pillaged by the civil war, it was Wolf Koller who came forward with a European Relief Plan. Wolf Koller, not Chancellor Glock. When the time was at hand for huge investment in Eastern Europe, it was Wolf Koller who stepped in, built a factory here, a sawmill there, revitalized a harbor somewhere else. Wolf Koller was *becoming* Germany in the eyes of much of Europe . . . not Chancellor Glock.

What Glock might do to reassert himself was a mystery—almost unimaginable—to Koller. But the bottom line seemed to be that Chancellor Glock wouldn't have the guts to move against Wolf Koller . . . wouldn't know where or how to strike a crippling blow . . . Chancellor Glock owed his own prominence—however it might have been diminished by Koller—to the political and financial support of Wolf Koller. All the power in the relationship lay with Wolf Koller. As usual. It was always the same with Wolf Koller.

Koller, having made peace with his doubts, turned and took a few steps toward Adler.

"They're coming. Get over here. You don't want to miss this." Max Adler did as he was told, wedging between Gisevius and Koller. He could already see the headlines in the morning papers.

BERLIN IN FLAMES.
THE NAZIS ARE HERE.

At the end of the street, below them in the rain, just turning the corner and coming toward them, was a band of perhaps a hundred young men. Punks, hellraisers, delinquents, all around jack-offs of one kind and another. Brown shirts tucked into black trousers, the red and black and white armbands so reminiscent of the past, the dark past. Hoods, bully boys, car thieves, you name it. They were illuminated by very bright, hand-held floodlights, which would help the TV people when they arrived. They came marching down the street, boots thumping, voices raised in an angry, meaningless chant. Snatches of old songs you hadn't heard sung in a long time. Adler knew the TV people would arrive at any moment. They would have been tipped off by the thugs, no doubt of that. TV was really the point of the whole exercise: they were selling their views and activities to the nation. They were followed on the sidewalks by less heroic supporters, just plain onlookers. The protesters would arrive as soon as they got word of the evening's entertainment. A lot of people were going to make a night of it. Max Adler thought the whole thing was insane.

By the time the marchers reached a point beneath the three unseen onlookers, squarely opposite the refugee hostel, the chanting had turned into general yelling and screaming, obscenities and racial insults and political slogans hurled across the fencing separating them from their target. People were appearing in lighted windows; other lights were going out, as if darkness might hide the watchers from their tormentors. There was no security force guarding the hostel, just the fence. The windows were no more than fifty feet from the gang gathering on the sidewalk and in the street.

The floodlights picked out the familiar, stout figure of Joachim Stiffel, stuffed into black leather, his round spectacles catching the glare and reflecting it. He looked as if he were wearing goggles. He was addressing his troops, urging them not to resort to violence but nevertheless screaming that the foreigners, these lesser creatures, these non-Germans must have no doubts as to the message being sent.

"They are not welcome here!" Stiffel screamed into an electric bullhorn. His face was wet with rain and sweat. "This is not *their* Fatherland—it is *our* Fatherland and they don't belong here! They take our jobs, they are living off our tax money! They must go! We must help send them on their way! Germany is for Germans!"

The crowd began to pick up the chant. Stiffel turned toward the building and began addressing the refugees. Some were leaning out of the windows, hurling epithets of their own at the mob. Several young men, Turks, had come out of the building and were facing Stiffel. They shouted back at him.

"This is our nation," Stiffel bellowed at them with the bullhorn. "Our Fatherland, the Fatherland we Germans have fought and died for. It is not your land, you have done nothing for Germany. We will not cede this country to you, no matter how many of you come, no matter if you are a tidal wave . . ." His voice had reached a shrill scream, the words blurring together, like a rock singer yelling lyrics no one could possibly understand—yet somehow the meaning was clear. "We will fight to the death to keep Germany pure . . . Germany is for Germans! Germany belongs to us! We will fight with our German blood, we will spill our blood for our Germany! We will fight with God's help to save our Fatherland from you, the scum of the earth, the mongrels who seek to feed off the country that is ours, the filth who would steal it from us!"

It began with a stone, a breaking of glass, another stone, cheers, howls, blood on a white shirt, then a stone thrown back at the mob, another bouncing off one of the floodlights . . .

At the other end of the street a television van was screeching around the corner, skidding to a halt. Out came the videocams, the reporters, more lights; Stiffel was turning toward the cameras, his face pale and glistening with the rain, his eyes blinking in the glare behind the thick lenses speckled with rain . . .

"You see," he pleaded into the advancing cameras, "what we are up against? They throw rocks at us, they come to our Germany and this is what they do . . ."

His voice was lost in the shouts of the crowd as the first Molotov cocktail waggled through the air, trailing its burning tail like a wounded pheasant. It landed on the bricks among the refugees who had ventured out to exchange comments with Stiffel's people. The gasoline sprayed up in flaming jets and one of the dark-faced men stared in amazement as his pants ignited.

In quick succession three more firebombs were thrown, each wobbling almost comically, tail aflame, then the crack of the glass shattering and the spreading swirl of flame. The man who had caught fire flailed away, trapped in a layer of barbed wire between the building and the fence. The mob saw him, sensed his hopelessness, and pushed. The fence went slowly but steadily and they were pouring over, surrounding the fallen man, exaggeratedly acting as if they were helping him put out the flames. In fact they were kicking him to death, didn't stop until he lay still, smoldering.

One of the bombs had broken a window. Smoke was funneling out the window. People inside were screaming and women were coming out the main doorway holding tight to their children's hands. The little kids hid behind their mothers or stared, wide-eyed, at the fiery craziness all around them.

The mob was moving toward the people cowering by the doorway, trapped between the spreading flames and the advancing, threatening killers. Their arms were raised in something very like the Hitler salute. The leaders flaunted the brown shirts and armbands with the insignia so like the outlawed swastika that it made no difference.

The building was burning. Several firebombs had broken windows, and flames leaped out of the windows into the rain. The upraised arms, the salutes, were silhouetted against the red and orange of the fire.

Suddenly a man burst out the main door. He was holding a baby in his arms. His back and shoulders were on fire. The mob, laughing and pointing at the sorry bastard, parted, let him run through their ranks until he was in the street. He was burning more brightly by then, yet he made no sound. Holding the baby, he ran down the rainy, shining street, caught in the eyes of the videocams, the cameramen running beside him, until he was alone in the dark street, a human torch; then he was sinking to his knees, the fire eating him, the baby falling and bouncing away and coming to rest, its blanket burning, the thin wail of the infant in the sudden silence as everyone watched, stock-still.

When the refugees began swarming at the club-wielding mob, when the battle was truly joined, the sirens sounded a warning—first the police, then, a few seconds later, the fire trucks. The cops in riot gear advanced with batons and shields on both groups.

The metallic crack of a gunshot was heard from somewhere and one of the cops fell, clutching his leg, his shield falling at his side. The police drew weapons and in a quick burst of fire two refugees and one of the brownshirts were blown away. Another cop went down hard.

The automatic-weapon fire broke the back of the show. Stiffel had not been seen for some time and now his followers were drifting away in the street, insolently daring the police to follow them.

"I count five, maybe six dead." Koller turned to the other three. The rain was blowing across the rooftop. "Something must be done!" he said. "And where were the protesters? Have they lost interest? Germany cannot lose interest in this outrage!"

No one answered. Adler was already heading toward the stairway, which would take them to the waiting Mercedes a street away. Koller followed with Gisevius, driving home his points . . . already preparing a speech.

Burke Delaney, short and stocky, built for power and endurance, stood in a doorway down the block from the burning immigrant hostel. The ancient navy watch cap was pulled down on his forehead. He stood deep in shadow.

The gangling German boy, Karl-Heinz Schmidt, stood beside him. He was cold and wet and nervous. He couldn't keep from worrying about Erika. Where was she? Was she all right? Why hadn't she contacted him? He wondered if she'd been found by her father's people, wondered if she was dead by now . . . He was sure Wolf Koller wouldn't hesitate to have her killed—if he discovered how much she knew . . . Erika could do him too much harm. Koller was afraid of his daughter, just as he was afraid of his wife. Karl-Heinz fought the fear he felt for Erika: fear and loss were inevitable in fighting a man like Wolf Koller. You had to be a zealot, willing to die for what you believed. But had Erika been willing to die? Maybe she hadn't run away at all: maybe her father's men had seen her at the rally and finished her off in her own apartment . . . Karl-Heinz knew it was all his own fault. He knew he played on her class guilt but it was so natural, she wore it on her sleeve. He clenched his fists in his pockets, he was so damn cold. He used her, yes, but she wanted to be used: it was good, it was healthy, and it was historically necessary. The flames were jabbing through the windows, poking at the night sky, into the rain.

The man with the baby lay in the street about twenty yards away. Karl-Heinz's natural inclination was to dash out, smother the flames, try to save lives. But Delaney's grip was fastened on his arm like a steel clamp. Not a word needed to be said.

When the worst of it was over, when the Stiffelites, as some were calling them, had traipsed off into the rain with their clubs dangling and their own wounded screaming their final insults and moaning in pain, the street slowly began filling with local residents. Some seemed to approve of what they had seen—after all, the foreigners were taking their jobs, or so they reasoned, and they wanted the immigration policy changed. This was a step in the right direction. You had to hand it to Stiffel . . . Others were staring in horror at the aftermath of the violence, crossing the street to comfort some of the dazed victims, women with children, terror-stricken. Some of the local householders shook their heads and wiped their eyes, while ten feet away others were strutting, making the weird little salute and shouting insults and feeling pretty good about themselves.

Delaney put a heavy hand on the young man's shoulder. The attack had come right on the schedule Karl-Heinz had given him. "Kid, I'm impressed. You've made a believer out of me." He blew his nose on a crumpled white handkerchief. The rain was playing hell with his arthritic joints. "I want more product, though."

"Of course you want more product. What I need to know is what you're doing with it." Karl-Heinz's lips were still scabbed and split, the bruise around his eye fading. "And you have to tell me if you know where Erika is . . . I want to know if you are the guys who kidnapped her."

"What would we want with her? Don't be silly. And you know what I'm doing with the product. I'm passing it on. It has to be evaluated. We've got to validate it—make sure you know what you're talking about. This thing tonight is a pretty good confirmation. Beyond that, what can I tell you?"

"You don't understand—the girl I love has disappeared!" His whispers were growing in vehemence and Delaney put his finger to his lips. "She's *his* daughter—do you people have anything mounted against him? Would you kidnap his daughter? I'm not accusing you of it, I'm asking you . . . and if the answer is yes, that's *good* news, because I don't think you'd harm her. Would you? Damn it, I might as well be talking to myself . . . Are your people going to act on SPARTAKUS? What are they going to do? Can't you apply pressure, get the government to do more than issue nice, responsible statements, and do fuck-all?"

"Son, you've got to be kidding. How am I going to pressure the government of the United States? And besides, we don't need to pressure the government, just one fat bastard in—"

"Something has to be done before it's too late."

"But that's what we don't know," Delaney said, trying to be patient. "We don't know what's going to happen if we don't act . . . This product you're giving us would carry a lot more punch if we had the intended results. All we've really got now is some speculation on—"

"I know what you've got. I'm giving it to you."

"We can't do a damn thing until you give us more. That's what I need to have, *more*—and I need it soon. Do you understand? My masters don't go off half-cocked, they want to know what the hell they're getting into. So it's up to you, son."

"Look, it's obvious it's leading up to something. I got you this, I'm obviously going to be able to get you more . . . There's something going on, more than just this window-dressing . . . SPARTAKUS is more than Stiffel, I'm convinced of that."

Delaney squeezed his fingers inside his gloves, trying to keep blood circulating. "Look, I don't shape policy. I provide raw data. Policy is a swamp, pal, you get sucked into that dung pit and you can disappear without a trace. You just get me the rest of the product . . . that's all that guys like us can do . . ."

"Same old bullshit, then." Karl-Heinz swore under his breath. "Chain of command while people are getting killed and the Nazis are adding supporters every day—"

"Nothing you can do about that, son."

It was raining harder, rattling on the street.

"Tell me where you get it," Delaney said softly. "Then we could lend a hand, help you out—"

"Do you think I'm some fool from the East, just fell off a turnip truck? You'd kill me. You wouldn't need me and you'd kill me. I know how you guys work. My father told me all about it." The bitterness was palpable.

"Your dad was an old STASI hand. I knew him." The East German Secret Police. He'd produced Karl-Heinz. Somehow.

"He always told me that when the pros get into it people start getting killed."

"I've said the same thing about amateurs. Your father was a pro. What's he up to now? Retired?"

"Sure, retired. And you're right, he was a pro and that's why he knows what he's talking about."

Delaney shook his head. "The pros or the amateurs, either way. People always start getting killed. The stakes are high enough, shit happens."

"His point exactly."

"Look, kid, I'm a pro. And you got me into it."

"That's what worries me."

"Your father and I knew each other in the old days. We'll both tell you the same stories. You gotta trust me, son. Give me that product, keep giving it to me, and something will happen—maybe good, maybe bad. Maybe your girlfriend gets out alive. Maybe she doesn't. You're in it now, see. It's like dog shit on the sidewalk. You step in it, it sticks to you. Once you're in it, you're in it."

"Yes. And you'd sell me out just for practice if you didn't need me."

Delaney watched the tall, loose-jointed kid set off down the street. Black leather jacket, black jeans, black high-topped shoes. No motorcycle tonight. Where the hell was he tapping into SPARTAKUS?

Delaney didn't envy the young man his youth, his moral commitment, or his fear. The kid was an innocent and in Delaney's experience the innocents were always the first to die.

An hour and a half later Burke Delaney was picking his way through a rubble-strewn open field in what had been East Berlin. It was spitting sleet now. When he'd driven over from the site of the fire there hadn't been another car moving on the Unter den Linden and only a few buses to pick up isolated groups of huddled travelers. Now he stumbled over some broken packing cases, slipped in the mud, and swore at the inconvenience of it all. Ice was forming. The mud was stiffening underfoot.

He heard the sucking sounds his boots made in the muck. The rain was blowing in his face. He hated this shit. He was too old.

The building looked like a dark, deserted ruin, a single low-wattage bulb burning over a boarded-up back door. He kept on through the tin cans and dog shit and garbage until he reached the door, which he pushed open. Inside there was a blue glow and a stairway leading down to the basement. The stairs felt as if they might give way at any moment. Wallpaper was peeling and drooping. At the foot of the stairs he pushed open another door and stepped into another world.

It was called Rio.

Bossa nova gently filled the smoky room, scenes of life on the beach: brown breasts bouncing, hips squirming to escape thongs; dark luminescent eyes swallowed you from huge video screens. The room was full, dark but for the light of the video screens and work lights behind the bar. The crowd was hip, trendy, mostly from the West. It reminded him of Paris after the war in the fifties, all the black turtlenecks, guys trying to look like Belmondo and girls trying to look like either Juliette Greco or Bardot. The girls were all young, the men of every age. It was not Burke Delaney's kind of place. But he'd been there several times in the last six months. Business.

Only one drink was served, a "Rio." It was too sweet but it was supposed to be good for you. Laced with vitamins and God knew what else. No alcohol. What was the world coming to? Times had changed.

On the nights he came to Rio there was always a small corner table waiting for him. He pushed his way through the crowd. The girls were very pretty but not really as pretty as his dogs. Still, fräuleins were his favorite brand of girl. He loved listening to the whispered gutturals of the language. He spoke it well but not like a German. He sat at the table and the waiter, dressed in a tuxedo with a wing collar, deposited a tall Rio before him. He took a sip, leaned back, surveyed the scene. Languid dancing, cool, calm, lots of haughty looks from enormous uncaring eyes. It was a game, a performance. Gray-haired men in Armani suits and 1940s ties; young men, beefy, shaved heads, leather vests, white skin with tattoos. A girl with a teardrop tattooed on one exposed breast, right by her nipple. Delaney didn't feel self-conscious because it was dark enough to hide him. It was like being a voyeur.

Then he felt the presence of someone standing over him. He looked up, nodded, and the man sat down. "Quite a show you boys put on," Burke Delaney said.

Joachim Stiffel smiled. "It had its moments, I agree. So, how are you, Mr. Delaney?"

Delaney considered the question and the range of possible answers. "Watching my back," he said at last.

Lee Koller was having one of her better days. She sat in the wheelchair, which she didn't really need. The nurse, Gretel, had brought it up to the bedroom and Lee hadn't wanted to appear unappreciative. It was rolled near the window and Lee sat looking out most of the day at the Hasensprung. The exquisite path was shrouded with trees, hung like a rope bridge over the stream that ran behind the house and grounds. The

Hasensprung, or Rabbit Run, had been her favorite spot for taking Erika on her first outings as an infant. She remembered the lovely wicker carriage, Erika bundled in layers of blankets, peering out from beneath her bonnet, her little hands flexing into fists in the air or waving at the breeze, or grasping a golden leaf as it drifted before her . . .

As the walkway bridged the stream, they would stop, and Lee would hold her up to see the collecting pool that surged away into the stillness of the little lake. Leaves floated on the surface like tiny rafts. And on either side of the walk was a stone rabbit, a pair that Erika had named Hans and Franz when she was four, Hans and Franz, the two guardians of their home . . . mighty, magical rabbits who came to life in the darkness when ogres walked the night . . .

With the leaves now covering the walk she could see the bridge railings and the magic rabbits through the naked tree limbs. She spent much of the afternoon crying, tears coursing down her cheeks. Crying for the past, crying for her daughter . . . where had Hans and Franz been when Erika had needed their magical powers? Where in the name of God was Erika now?

In her fall down the steps to the foyer, she had badly wrenched an ankle. She remembered nothing of it, had only Wolf's word to go on. She had fainted, perhaps, been momentarily knocked out when she hit her head, had awakened in Wolf's arms . . . When her memory took over she was in the doctor's office at a private hospital run by a Dr. Lipp. She'd been on a table and her leg and arm throbbed. And she had a nasty headache. Then her ankle was being wrapped and she was being wheeled home by the nurse Wolf engaged on the spot. Fritz Gisevius had been there somewhere, she couldn't quite recall . . . They'd given her a sedative and it was already taking effect before she left the hospital.

It was raining now and darkness had wiped the Rabbit Run away and she and Gretel were watching television as the evening wore on. She couldn't concentrate on anything but she watched anyway, glad for Gretel's company. She couldn't stop thinking about Erika, still hoping for a call, hoping that her own mind wouldn't let her down, at least not until Erika was safe . . . She'd cried out to Fritz Gisevius, begged him to tell her what was wrong, but it was always a matter of a shrug, more tests, it was nothing they could pin down. She knew it was bad, it had to be bad . . . a brain tumor they couldn't locate, or maybe they weren't telling her the truth . . . Or epilepsy. She had read that it often struck in middle age . . .

The next thing she knew Gretel was pulling the sleeve of her robe, pointing at the television screen. Lee had nodded off and needed to refocus. When she did she wished she hadn't. There was a live report from the scene of another attack on an immigrant hostel . . . this time in Potsdam, on the edge of Berlin. The reporter stood in the rain with the fire burning behind her; the camera panned quickly away down the street to the bodies, both burned, of a man and a baby . . . "Call them neo-Nazis, skinheads, or just the predatory animals they are, they struck again tonight here at the very edge of Berlin itself . . ."

Lee covered her mouth with one hand. The horror of it!

Gretel looked at her, pursed her narrow mouth, and drew herself up primly. "Oh yes, it's a shame, but you can't tell me the foreigners didn't bring it on themselves. If they'd stayed in their own countries where they belonged we wouldn't be having all these problems. We can't go on letting just anyone in—"

Lee waved her into silence. The camera had come back for the reporter to sign off.

It was Beate Hubermann.

II

8

BERLINER LUFT

When Cooper left the TWA 757 at Tegel Airport and cleared passport control without their giving so much as a glance at him or his passport, the first things he noticed were the headlines in the newspapers. While his German was far from conversational, he could study it out in written form if he took the time, thanks to Miss Berger in high school. The headlines and the photographs on the front page were enough to make him sick. He paused to scan the story.

Eight people were dead, six refugees from the hostel in the Berlin suburb of Potsdam, one of the skinheads, one policeman. Half the hostel had been consumed by fire. The Mayor of Berlin was mortified, Chancellor Glock was viewing events with white-faced alarm. His top aide had been dispatched to Berlin and was in meetings with Berlin's city fathers— of whom the only one named was Wolf Koller. So, Cooper thought, he really is one of the heavyweights, the kind of man the politicians like Chancellor Glock turn to in a crisis. Politicians of both right and left were outraged and calling for a crackdown on the violence and disorder —the former suggesting the foreigners be deported and the immigration laws rescinded, the latter calling for simultaneous investigation of the police leadership, the suspiciously slow responses to all these outbreaks of nationalistic hatred, and the political establishment generally. One city official asked, as best Cooper could translate it, "What did all of Hitler's victims die for? *This?* If so, then they died absolutely in vain. When will the *Volk,* the people of Germany, wake up to the fact that the Nazis are back and on the march?" But other opinions were voiced as well: "Now is the time for Germany to turn itself around and fill the vacuum at the center of Europe. Rearm, let rearmament fuel the economy, and make Europe stable again with a great fortress of iron at its center, make a German proud to be a German again . . ."

The whole thing made John Cooper shudder. Twenty years ago everything had been going on behind the scenes, it had been the last gasp of the old Hitler Nazis and their direct descendants. Now a new genera-tion was taking enthusiastically to the old ways, and somehow it was worse. They weren't afraid to bring it out into the open.

Leaving the terminal lobby, he was struck full in the face by some-thing like the blush of spring, almost—but not quite—enough to blow away the sinister clouds of fear and hatred he'd seen in the newspapers. Natives called it the Berliner Luft, the perfect sunny, breezy weather the city was known for. Bracing, invigorating. The smell was fresh, the after-math of rain. He grabbed one of the endless line of Mercedes cabs. He gave the driver the address in the Kreuzberg section and sagged back, turning again to the newspapers. A sidebar dealt with the phenomenon of missiles, tanks, guns of all kinds being sold throughout Russia and Ukraine to organized crime and middlemen who were selling out of the old Soviet Union, a kind of deadly bazaar where the things the Soviet Union had left behind when it died were going to the highest bidders.

He was so tired. Worried about what in the world Lee was up to, wondering just why her daughter had disappeared, what it might have to do with her father, the estimable, quotable Berlin leader, Wolf Koller.

Most of all—and he felt it in his stomach—he was nervous about seeing Lee again after all these years. What did she remember of the days they'd spent together? Did she remember that he'd told her he loved her and didn't give a damn if she was his sister or not? The knot in his gut felt like lead. He could think about Wolf Koller and Erika and neo-Nazis all he wanted, but nothing made the knot go away. Lee was at the bottom of everything. She always would be . . .

He could use a second wind right about now. He had driven cross-country from Cooper's Falls to Washington, assuming that if it was someone in Washington who had set the deadly tail on him, then that would be the last place they'd expect him to turn up. From Washington he'd taken a bus to Philadelphia, having left the rental car on a crowded twenty-four-hour ramp, and in Philadelphia he'd switched to a train for the last leg to New York. He'd picked up as much money as he could during the first two days at cash machines, hoping that the storm in Minnesota would slow down the news about the two bodies in the car. Peterson would impede the process as much as possible. He had to get to Germany before they found him and stopped him and Lee had to go it alone . . .

When he got to New York he called Beate Hubermann in Berlin. He tried to explain why he was coming and what had happened, but it was nearly impossible to make any of it sound sensible. So he mainly told her he was on his way. She gave him the address of her flat, told him to come there, they'd work out something. She lived in Kreuzberg, the Greenwich Village of Berlin. She laughed when she said it.

He wasn't kidding himself. He knew that his flight from Minnesota, from Cooper's Falls, would mean nothing if they really wanted to find him. If they were people from the inside, from the government. The cash machines would tip them off, the car on the ramp would be found, they would be watching all foreign flights, particularly any to Germany. They'd been watching him from Boston onward.

Maybe Kilroy was one of them. How did he know Beate Hubermann wasn't one of them? He didn't. But sooner or later you had to take the leap of faith. Otherwise, you'd go home and hide. Which was what he'd been doing for twenty years.

The apartment building was a block long, or seemed to be: it might have been several buildings, dating from before the Great War by the look of them, all the detailing intact. Diagonally across the street was a pretty green park with benches, some children's swings, naked trees guarding wet mounds of yellow leaves. An ornate cast-iron pissoir stood in elderly dignity near the corner. All around were buildings similar to his destination.

He was ringing the street-level bell, about to give up, when he heard the approaching roar of a Harley. He turned and there she was, straddling the broad saddle in boots, black slacks, the red plaid jacket, her short blond hair whipped by the wind. She killed the engine, slid her Rommel-type goggles up onto her forehead.

"The Desert Fox," he said.

"Mr. Cooper! I'm so glad I got here in time. Oh, it's good to see you—did you just get here? I hope so . . . Something terrible happened and I've been working on the story nonstop. Come on, you must be very tired." She was unlocking the high double doors that opened onto the street. Inside there was a huge echoing hallway with stairs going up one side. "Help me with this mother of all hogs," and they wheeled the

Harley inside. It came to rest alongside several bicycles. The smell of cold oil was everywhere. She took the helmet she hadn't been wearing, along with a backpack that had been tied on behind the seat, and set off up the stairway. "Take a deep breath, it's five flights. And how was your trip? Whoever was chasing you," she said, referring to their garbled telephone conversation, "must not have caught you—"

"Climb now," he said, "talk later."

At her door she turned, swiped the yellow hair back from her face. "Still with me?"

"I'm in my elevator years."

"Don't be silly. We Germans would say you are in your prime. Come on in and try not to say anything about the mess."

He could see two rooms, part of a third, part of a kitchen with dishes stacked in the sink. Everywhere there were stacks of newspapers, magazines, videocassettes, books. An open stairway along one wall went to a second floor. She threw her coat onto a couch. "Just drop your bag where you stand. Go on upstairs. I'll make some coffee. Instant. Okay?"

"Fine with me." He climbed the staircase and arrived in a room with slanted ceilings and skylights cut into them. Huge exposed beams looked like twelve-by-twelves, big enough to prop up a castle on the Rhine. He sat down on one of a pair of low couches, looked around at black and white photographs she had taken at events she'd presumably covered, including the coming down of the Wall; a stereo, a television set, bookcases, some plants that looked a little stringy . . .

"Wake up," she was saying softly, "coffee's ready. Earth to John Cooper."

He shook his head to bring himself back to the surface. He must have drifted off. The coffee was scalding. He was suddenly wide awake.

Beate opened the skylights. He felt the fresh air, saw the view of the blue sky.

She sat on crossed legs on a floor pillow, facing him, warming her hands on the coffee mug. Her blue eyes were bright and clear but red-rimmed. Her face looked gaunt, her cheeks slightly hollowed. She saw him examining her. "The real me," she said. "Awful, isn't it . . . well, I've been up for a long time, I'm very tired and very upset and very angry . . . welcome to Berlin! It's my usual state, I'm afraid."

"Are you talking about the thing in the papers this morning—the riot?"

"It wasn't a riot, it was a well-planned attack. It was premeditated murder and nobody did a damn thing about it . . . and the idiots who run my life at TV Center jumped all over me about editorializing! Was I supposed to deliver the report from the scene with a happy weatherman's brainless grin?" She bit off the sentence and sipped some coffee. "But we can talk about all that later. Listening to me complain about things isn't the way to begin . . . I want to know what's going on with you. After that phone call—well, it wasn't very clear." She waited, anticipating.

He began with the trip back to Minnesota once she had left Boston, the man and the woman on the plane, the car hurtling off the cliff, the guns and the lack of identification cards. Then he backtracked, telling her how the storm had transported him back two decades to another storm that had culminated in another trip to Germany.

"You mean that your *whole* family was involved with the Nazis? I thought it was just your grandfather—I don't know what to say. Are you serious?"

"Oh, yes. Very serious."

"And your brother was murdered and you found your sister here in Germany? Married to one of them?" She bounced up from the pillow, began pacing, ducking under one of the huge beams again and again as she went back and forth, listening intently. Then: "And you and this Peterson guy wrecked the whole Nazi setup?"

"I don't know. When it was over and Peterson and I went back home, well, to us it was just over. Until you and Kilroy showed up. Then, whammo, the whole nightmare began again, and here I am."

"I'd say I'm sorry to have dragged you into it, but Lise Koller would have gotten hold of you one way or another. But I am sorry that it's all beginning again—or is it? You can't be sure—"

He smiled. "The point is, Beate, I'm the one who should be apologizing to you. Listen to me—my being here could put you in danger. If they come after me here, they're not going to care who gets hurt—"

"But why? Why would anyone be after you now? And who are they?"

"I just don't know. CIA maybe. That couple—it has all the earmarks of something coming out of Langley. But they were definitely watching me. They knew I was going to Cooper's Falls. I ask myself, how could they know? And I have no idea. The only thing I can think of is this—they're afraid of me, maybe they're afraid of the past I represent, or afraid of something I know . . . Maybe I'm like Einstein, I know too much. But what is it I know? How can I hurt anyone? What are they afraid I'll do?"

"But what if it's not your government, your CIA? Could it be the

Nazis? Or the neo-Nazis? But there's no connection between them, John. The neo-Nazis are just thugs, they're not smart enough to have a great plan—"

"I sure as hell hope so." He was twisting around to watch her. "Why don't you settle in one place?"

"I'm hungry. I'll make something to eat. Can you put up with Italian?"

"Are you kidding?" He followed her downstairs and watched her clear a space in the kitchen. She put a pot of water on to boil. She began chopping tomatoes. Then onions. She looked up at him: "Anchovies okay?" He nodded. Black olives. In the end it turned into a puttanesca sauce. He opened a bottle of Orvieto. She grinned at him: "As you can see, I enjoyed our dinner in Boston! You don't mind it's the same?"

"I think you're something of a wonder," he said. "That's what I think."

They carried dinner upstairs and she put several Chet Baker CDs on the changer. He hadn't heard Baker sing in ages, and while they ate he was struck by how much he liked what he was hearing. All the great old songs. "Dancing on the Ceiling." " 'Tis Autumn." "You'd Be So Nice to Come Home To." "There Will Never Be Another You." It seemed as if Chet Baker had been dead a long time. The brain dive in Amsterdam, someplace like that. But here he was. In Berlin. Singing again.

She told him about the massacre at the hostel, how Stiffel's gang had done their usual job. What made it somewhat unusual was that one of their own had been killed—that was a first. Then, typically, they had melted away into the night. The police had let them go. "It's getting crazy," she said. "Honestly, no one ever believed it would reach Berlin. Way off in Rostock, that's one thing, but this . . . Something's going to happen soon—"

"Like what?" He was soaking up excess sauce with crusty bread.

"The demonstrations are going to get bigger. On both sides. Against the foreigners and the immigration policy. Against the Stiffel gang. The government's coming under more pressures every day." She shrugged. "Gutless wonders. But they'll have to do something."

The day was gone. The Berliner Luft had turned cold. She went to the skylight windows and pulled them shut. The city was aglow over the rooftops toward the west. The night sky over the east was much darker.

She'd had a fairly rotten day. Sometimes working for the state-run TV seemed like a nasty and irritating waste of her life. But not always, not enough, because she stuck with it. Early on she'd been determined to make them take notice of her—that rarity, a *female* reporter, the very last thing her bosses ever wanted to deal with. It wasn't like American TV, where most of the reporters seemed to be women. And then, when they did notice her, they enjoyed making it tough on her, but she was damned if she'd crack. At least not when they were watching. And slowly she was convincing at least one or two of the men on the slippery pole above her that she could do more than fashion and art shows and whatever fell into the wastebasket called "women's news."

There was something about John Cooper that made her want to talk—maybe it was that his situation made hers seem like nothing more than killing time. For all they knew there might be somebody who wanted to kill Cooper. From the way he talked about it, it seemed like a pretty good chance. And yet he was calm—outwardly, anyway—and single-minded and just getting on with it, qualities she much admired and fancied she possessed herself. She liked listening to him talk. She liked the sound of his voice and she liked the sadness that lurked deep inside the story he told. There was something for her to learn hidden within John Cooper. And he treated her as if she amounted to something. It made for a powerful combination.

She set about making coffee and while it dripped through into the glass pot she curled up on the couch under the slanted roof and told him about the riot at the hostel. She'd worked all day in the editing rooms, fighting for the time on the machines, putting together a piece for the weekend omnibus show. Part of it was on the tape she'd dubbed and brought home. Not the riot at the hostel, but an earlier skinhead outing. She wanted to watch it calmly with a cup of coffee and a plateful of Oreo cookies. She had quit smoking again and had brought the Oreos back from Boston.

She brought the cookies and coffee to the couch where Cooper was sitting, staring up at the gallery of photos on the walls. "Quite a show," he said. "I'm impressed."

"Would you like the tour?"

"Of the pictures? Sure. Start with the Wall."

There were shots of the Wall coming down, all in black and white, printed with a fairly high degree of contrast to give them the stark look she wanted. Thousands of people milling happily, nervously at the foot of the Wall, singing, staring in wonder, drinking beer, carrying hammers to chip off souvenirs. One of her colleagues had taken a shot of her atop the Wall. Among the revelers hers was the one serious face, her compact Leica held in one hand, raised to her eyes, focusing on the crowd below . . . she was wearing a leather jacket and her hair was spiky and almost white, her stare intense, caught up in observing the events rather than taking part in them. A boyfriend of the moment was crouched behind her, holding a bag of film and another camera loaded with color film . . . She liked the intensity in her face. She liked the shot because it was the way she saw herself. There were shots of the Brandenburg Gate through a gray mist of winter, the Gate open, people passing through unafraid . . . Shots of the Tiergarten, the flea market, then a panoramic, wide-angle shot in color of the vast crowds surging toward the Wall on that extraordinary night . . . then a change of pace, a head shot of three men at a political gathering, some kind of banners arrayed behind them, not identifiable, their faces immaculately detailed, Wolf Koller and Dr. Fritz Gisevius and a very old man with wisps of white hair, a cherubic face with lifeless eyes, a man whose past was part of history, of a world long gone . . . the old man, dead now, was Wolf Koller's father, Erhard Koller . . . and next to them a shot of a tattooed skinhead rushing toward her camera, eyes like bulging prosthetics, fist drawn back, mouth twisted with rage, and she'd just kept shooting.

"More cookies," she announced and bounced up out of the deep cushions of the couch and went downstairs, loaded up the plate and refilled their coffee cups and went back.

"Let me show you a tape," she said. "It's part of a piece I'm doing about the skinheads and brownshirts and their leader, Herr Stiffel. Would you like to see it?" He nodded. "Yes, I'm sure you should see it," she said.

She rummaged through an oversized leather shoulder bag, came out with an unmarked videocassette. She slid it into the VCR and turned on the television with a remote control. Then she fast-forwarded through images of herself, an elephant, and a zookeeper who bore an unfortunate resemblance to the late Herr Himmler. Then static, then her face filled the screen. Her blue eyes were huge and clear. She decided the lipstick was a mistake. Uve Ganz, her boss, was going to tell her the blouse was all wrong, made her look like a tart rather than a TV reporter, a journalist the viewer could trust, and what the hell was she doing wearing only one earring and not only that, it looked too much like a Star of David and people didn't like that sort of thing, didn't like to be reminded of all that.

And he didn't like any of his reporters making fashion statements, political statements, or any other goddamn kind of statements, and why was it always the females who were doing the dumb things that made his ulcers act up?

"Here we are," she said.

The screen was now filled with another face that was becoming as well known as Chancellor Glock's. This man was younger, his face fleshy from the jawline so that it seemed to bulge slightly, like an overfilled bag of sand. His lips were full and he habitually pursed them between words as he spoke. His eyes were narrow and close-set behind circular wire-rimmed glasses. His forehead bulged above the eyebrows, then sloped upward to a sharply delineated widow's peak of dark, shiny hair. His voice was nasal, the words clipped and precise. His thoughts were carefully organized, professorial, his tone calm and reassuring.

"I am indeed sorry that there was violence," he said slowly, calmly, precisely. "I abhor violence in any form. But we must ask ourselves, who was first sinned against? Is it not the first cause that must be understood? Is it not only human to react when one is provoked? Treated unfairly? How many times must one turn the other cheek?"

She heard her own voice, trying hard to keep any kind of judgment out of her tone. "But we need to make this clear, Herr Stiffel. Your supporters murdered two young Turkish workers in the street—are you saying that this is unfortunate but how can the murderers be blamed? That it was the fault of the Turks themselves that they were murdered?"

"Come, come, Fräulein Hubermann. First, you say these men were my supporters—am I then responsible for the personal actions of anyone who happens to agree with me on certain principles? That is preposterous on the face of it. How am I responsible? Do you posit cause and effect? I have not suggested that anyone kill anyone else—I abhor anything that smacks of violence. I am on the record, again and again. I merely observe that there is something deeper here than what appears on the surface. Second, is it wrong to say that this is a nation of Germans? Is that somehow immoral? Is it immoral and subversive to suggest that our loyalties must first be to the welfare of ourselves—of us Germans? If these are examples of incorrect beliefs—then are we living in a world where minds must be controlled, where we cannot express freely our thoughts about our homeland? I cannot accept that. I must express the truth as I see it. It is our Fatherland . . . *your* Fatherland. Are we to be outcasts in our own homeland? I cannot accept that. Thus, while I never condone violence, I can understand it . . . I merely say that Germans have the right to defend themselves and their country from the takeover by outsiders. Is that unreasonable? I hardly think so. And, thirdly, I can only say that if those Turks had not come to Germany, taken the jobs of Germans, had instead remained in *their* homeland—then, then they would still be alive." He shrugged ever so slightly, as if it were absurd to subscribe to any view but his own.

"Then you refuse to accept any responsibility for what happened three nights ago?"

"Obviously. All I'm saying is that Germany, the new Germany, must first look to its own children. Germany for Germans. If there is blame in that . . . then, Fräulein Hubermann, I am guilty." He smiled, the thick pursed lips loving, almost kissing the moment. "I am ready to accept the judgment of my fellow Germans. I could not ask for a fairer jury."

The total effect, at least in the eyes of much of the German public, was to reveal Joachim Stiffel as a perfectly pleasant fellow, a patriot, perhaps a bit to the right, but wasn't that maybe just what the country needed today? A touch of pride. A bit of the old spirit. And they would also see Beate Hubermann as a snot-nosed, sharp-tongued bitch who clearly had it in for anybody who wasn't a Turk-loving liberal, and wasn't it the liberals, the ever-apologizing liberals, who'd gotten us into this mess to begin with?

The second half of the piece would deal with the nightmare of fire and murder at the hostel, the burning man and his baby, the brownshirts, the cool premeditation of it all. And then the German audience could judge the man Stiffel, who abhorred all kinds of violence. At least Ganz had okayed the piece to run on the Sunday show. Probably because he felt Stiffel had made a fool of her and he could use it to send her back to covering the annual dumpling and strudel festival in the Harz Mountains . . .

Well, so be it. The piece was on. There were bound to be some viewers out there who shared her view of Joachim Stiffel. That he was the most dangerous man in Germany.

The piece of tape that followed was something very different. It looked like a *cinéma vérité* exercise from a talented film school graduate. Jagged, blurred images, clubs swinging, faces white and snarling, others grim-lipped, efficient, clubs smashing, flailing, two men at the center, blows snapping down, you had to flinch when you saw them cleave the air, smash into bone and flesh, the camera jerking and images cascading, swirling, faces, hands, backs and sleeves and people falling, crawling on hands and knees, more faces, more blows raining down, boots slamming into bodies, a hand suddenly in front of the camera, Beate yanking the camera away, turning, a face she knew, a beautiful girl with black hair and straight eyebrows and a slightly tilted nose, a wide straight mouth, blood trickling from her nostrils, a vicious scrape on her cheek, blood on her forehead, the look of shock and curiosity, a club flashing in from outside the frame and striking her across the front of her coat, she's falling back and is grabbed by a pair of hands trying to keep her from falling among the stamping boots, a man's face, another face she, Beate, knows, one eye puffed shut, blood running out of his mouth, teeth smeared with blood . . . trying to hold the beautiful raven-haired girl so she won't fall . . . and then the camera was smashed from her grasp and the screen went black.

She told Cooper what had happened when her boss had seen this particular piece of tape.

"God in heaven!" Uve Ganz had turned pink, staring first at her with his mouth gaping, then staring at the faces on the screen, then at someone standing in the background while the blows were falling. "You don't think we're going to show this film on television! You must think I'm crazy! Do you know who these people are? That girl? What am I saying? Of course you know who they are! That's why you're doing this to me!"

The faces on the screen: the raven-haired girl was Erika Koller, the daughter of the enormously important Wolf Koller. Ganz sputtered. "And he will personally see to it that we're fired, both of us, blacklisted, never allowed to work in our chosen field again . . . the idea, Erika Koller getting beaten up right in everybody's very own living room! Offend Wolf Koller—is that what you want to do, slap him in the face in public? You must be mad!"

Cooper listened to the story, said: "So that was Erika . . . Could you run that back and freeze a frame so I can get a good look at her? What the hell was going on, anyway? Where was that taken?"

"A small brownshirt rally, over in the East. East Berlin, I mean. Nothing like this riot at the hostel you read about in the papers today. Very small."

"But when you see it shot that way it looks like the end of the world. Was Erika hurt badly?"

Beate stopped the frame with a close-up of Erika's face, blood streaking across one cheek, her eyes wide with surprise or fear or pain.

"I don't know. I lost her in the crowd, she was just swept away. But I wasn't worried then—"

"Why not?"

She used the handset and moved the tape, stopped it again on the man who was trying to protect Erika from the mob swirling about her.

"Because that is her boyfriend, Karl-Heinz Schmidt. He brought her to the rally that turned into the mess you saw—he was protesting, of course, and she got caught up in his idealism. So to speak."

"But you've seen her since?"

"No. That was the last night anybody saw her. Anybody that we know, anyway. She's been missing ever since." She clicked off the VCR. "And you're here to find her for your sister. I wish you luck."

He was tired and she knew she had to let him sleep. But she wanted him to go back over his story; she wanted to know more about Kilroy and why the CIA would be involved, or if not them, someone else, like the Nazis . . . The whole story was so melodramatic—or would have been if there were no brownshirts rioting in Berlin.

As if he were reading her mind, he broke the silence. "There's one other possibility, of course. It could be a rogue operation. Rogue CIA, or some other crazy secret outfit. Our government seems to abound with them—they crawl out of every nook and cranny." He paused. "That damn Kilroy, he bothers me . . ."

"And I showed up at the same time," she said. She was curled up at one end of the couch, sipping the last of her wine. "Maybe you've chosen to trust the wrong person." She watched his sad eyes, watched the lines at the corners crinkle when he grinned.

"Maybe. I won't know until you betray me. And if you do it well enough, or kill me, I may never know. Well, it's too late, it seems. You look trustworthy. I have this tendency to trust pretty women."

"Such a sexist!"

"Only human."

"Fatal flaw."

"Not yet. Look, I have to trust somebody. I need a guide. I'm lost here. You can help me. If you're willing. I need to know how best to get hold of Lee, I need to know everything I can find out about Erika. Where she lives, what kind of person she is, who's investigating her disappearance, who are her friends, what's the story on this boyfriend . . . What's this thing with her father? What's the problem?"

She sighed and ticked points off on her fingers. "Erika is still missing, no leads I've heard of. The story hasn't gone public yet—Wolf

Koller has kept the lid on. You can't blame him, really. If word got out every creep in town would be trying to get some ransom money . . . he's probably got his own security people looking for her—"

"And the boyfriend?"

"I really don't know. Karl-Heinz Schmidt. He's pretty self-absorbed. Takes himself very seriously. That's all I know."

"You said you worked with him—"

"Only on that one story, the Saddam Hussein thing when Koller Chemical supplied stuff for gas. He came to me because he knew his paper was too small to handle it."

"The police must know something—"

"Two things. They're not going to welcome an American amateur poking around in their business. And men like Wolf Koller live by their own rules. He undoubtedly has friends so high up in the Berlin police, he'd treat the police like part of his own security force. I have to tell you, John, you just can't go poking around over here. Before you know what you're getting into, they'll be stretching you out on the rack down at headquarters. Take my word for it."

He was almost out on his feet when she showed him to a small second bedroom.

She said: "Tomorrow morning I'll help you get started."

"How?"

"I think we should start with your sister, don't you?"

9

MR. PAULUS HAS
A BIRTHDAY

Werner Paulus was seventy years old, that fine autumn day being his birthday. He didn't remember it was his birthday until he had massaged the liniment into his aching shoulders and knees, ground the morning's coffee beans, and started the brewing process. Then he saw the date printed out on the little television set he kept on the chopping-block counter. He picked up the newspaper to double-check.

Good lord, it was true! Seventy years!

It sounded like a hell of a long time, true, and he'd seen far more of life and the world than most men, but it had gone by quick as a train out of Zoo Station, bound for God knows where. Rattle, bang, stop, start, all out, end of the road. It's over. How could so much raw material have been packed into just a few moments, a grinding of gears, the squeal of brakes? Quick as a wink, the Americans said. They had it right.

It didn't seem altogether fair, a lifetime in a wink. Still, you could waste a lot of time trying to think of something that was fair. Just one fair thing . . . Well, he for one couldn't think of such a thing and he supposed everybody at seventy felt pretty much the same way, a bit cheated out of time. Too fast. Life went too fast.

He'd outlived so many of his colleagues, comrades in arms, pals. He'd dreamed of Karl Bach during the night. He couldn't imagine why.

Karl Bach had been piloting the Messerschmitt 109 off his left wing when the Spitfires had engaged them fifty years ago in the glaring, molten sunshine over the desert, a ribbon of blue water way off at the edge of the world, and the lead Spitfire's cannon blast had chewed through Karl's fuel line and on through the cockpit, and black smoke had billowed up like octopus ink and the last he'd seen of Karl, he was slumped over dead and the ME 109 was falling away toward the cement-hard flats and dunes of North Africa and Airman Paulus had to attend to getting out of the mess alive.

Fifty years ago. Half a century. His father hadn't even *lived* fifty years, to say nothing of seventy. It wasn't fair. None of it was fair. Count your blessings, Werner Paulus, drink your coffee and read your paper and watch your television. Karl Bach. What would he think of television were he to parachute in from Valhalla this morning? What would he think of how the war had turned out, how Germany had recovered since the war . . . what would he think of this morning's news?

Werner Paulus watched the television for a bit, video footage of people running, children sobbing, flames darting through windows, the terror and anger in the dazed faces of the dispossessed.

He turned to the newspapers, stared at the front page. There was no escaping it.

The hell that had thus far been kept at a distance, in Rostock and along the Dutch border and elsewhere out in the sticks, had reached Berlin. The Nazis were back, the country was overrun with foreigners, the left was turning violent as well.

The headlines screamed at him.

TIME FOR A FIRM HAND!

Which could mean damned near anything you wanted it to mean.

Paulus had a habit of being able to sweep his mind clean, as if it were the kitchen countertop or his desk at Berlin Central when he'd run the Detective Bureau. He was famous for his ability to scrape away the details and obfuscations of the most heinous, unsettling crimes and go out to a cheerful dinner or the opera or a bit of cabaret. He saw nothing surprising in it. What he couldn't understand was colleagues who took their work home with them, who couldn't get free of it. How did they keep from going mad? Maybe they didn't. He'd known enough of them who'd killed themselves or become, after a certain time on the job, rather peculiar.

On the morning of his seventieth birthday, after the daily dose of terrible news on the television and in the newspapers, he cleaned up the kitchen as well as his mind, and went out into the Berliner Luft whistling an old favorite. "Don't Fence Me In." Mr. Bing Crosby from the old days. It was funny how they'd nicknamed him in German.

Der Bingle.

He drove his three-year-old Mercedes sedan, solid and predictable in middle-class dark blue, to the cemetery to visit his wife. She had died in Berlin during the bombing in '44 while he'd been picking oranges and living in an American POW camp in Southern California. A town called Stockton. Helga. Bless her. Dead forty-eight years. He remembered her imperfectly but with great, undying affection: a sturdy blond girl from a village in the Harz Mountains, pretty, with her hair done up like a movie star's. Most of the snapshots had been destroyed in the bombing and he regretted that, but war was war, nobody to blame but Herr Hitler, and that sorry son of a bitch had been burnt to cinders a long time ago.

Not far from Helga's grave was that of Willi, his son, dead fifteen years, an overwrought artistic type, too sensitive to live with the accumulated past for which he thought the least he could do was bear symbolic responsibility. A Christ complex, some shrink had said. A suicide. A ritual suicide. It didn't matter anymore. Germans of Werner Paulus's generation weren't terribly impressed by or frightened of death and didn't dwell on the phenomenon of brutality through which they had lived. It was the generations that came after the Nazis—or at least some members of those generations—who were so frustrated, guilty, depressed, and ultimately despairing—that was the true Nazi legacy.

After paying his respects to Helga he knelt at his son's grave. Paulus didn't pretend to understand the phenomenon that had produced his son's suicide, but understanding wasn't required. Since the 1960s there had been a constant rate of suicides among the nation's youngsters —say those from fifteen to twenty-five—related to their sense of guilt over Germany's role in the Second World War. The genocide carried out against the Jewish population was, of course, the primary cause of the guilt, which seemed not to stem from the suicide's actual connection to the Holocaust. Apparently, there was no need for a father or an uncle or a grandfather to have been directly involved with the Nazis or the slaughter of innocents—though having a few Nazis in your family tree might increase the individual feelings of guilt. That's why parents so often felt such helpless confusion: the family might have been spotless, might have given its own members to anti-Nazi groups who were rooted out and killed by Hitler's thugs—it made no difference. Psychologists suggested that what was happening was the birth of a racial, or national, memory. Henceforth, they speculated, there would be a certain percentage of young, impressionable Germans who would be drawn to suicide because of their obsession with the enormities committed by the Nazis. In other words, German mothers and fathers, get used to it. The only remedy would be to rewrite history and when historical guilt lay so heavily on a people it might take a couple of hundred years of good works to cleanse the national conscience completely. So, Willi Paulus had been chalked up to the suicide phenomenon. Another victim of the Nazis.

He reflected on the call he'd received from his old protégé in the department, Max Adler, a week or so ago. Erika Koller was missing . . .

Would you have understood this girl, Willi, this Erika Koller? If I had understood you better, would I be able to find her? Might you still be alive? Is she alive, Willi? If she succeeded in killing herself, who took the body away? Or did someone snatch her back from the precipice? Was she like you, my son? Could she not live with the past? Or am I on the wrong track? God in heaven, how I miss you, Willi my son! How I miss the wisdom you'd have grown into by now . . .

He left the cemetery and drove to his late-morning coffee date, parked the car a few blocks from his destination, an old habit. He walked the rest of the way. He was a tall man who carried himself with military erectness. He wore a long blue raincoat and a long Invertere muffler from Sabo & Sabo on the Ku'damm. It was too warm for the muffler but it was new and he couldn't wait another day. Anyway, he thought he'd caught a whiff of snow in the morning's breeze. His long forehead sloped back to straight combed hair the color of a cold, silvery winter sky. If you looked closely enough, you might catch a hint of a limp, a souvenir of North Africa.

He turned at the corner and headed for Checkpoint Charlie. There were always tourists coming in and out of the rather remarkable museum, snapping pictures of the guard tower, walking back and forth where the Wall had stood. He glanced at his watch. He walked down the street to the memorials and the fresh flowers commemorating some of the would-be escapees who hadn't quite made it over, or through, the damn Wall in those terrible years. Terrible, yes, though they'd been good years for one of the two businesses he'd been in. Being a cop was his daytime job, so to speak. He had also been a "mole" for an American spymaster, the fat man, Ned Cheddar. An entirely benevolent mole: Ned Cheddar, these past twenty years, had just liked having a friend in Berlin who could keep him up to date, keep him in the big picture. He hadn't had much contact with Ned Cheddar since his own retirement from Berlin Central. A couple of Christmas cards from the fat man, that was about it. Very thoughtful, though, those cards, and the European money orders folded inside the cards among the snowmen and reindeer and the jolly St. Nicks.

Now he stopped at one of the markers. One of the remembered dead, marked by a bunch of Holland tulips, had died a scant two months before the Wall had come down. Shot by a border guard. Just two months. Some kid. He remembered his own youthful impatience. It was tough being a kid if you were dumb or unlucky, or both.

He turned away from the markers, pushed through the crowd of visitors. He walked back to the corner and went into the Café Adler. It was a place where you could be invisible. Tourists tended to stop in for coffee and cake. The café sat kitty-corner from the guard tower. It was a natural stop. The Wall had stood only a few feet from the café windows.

He slid into a seat in the second room with a view of the front entrance and ordered some coffee with milk and a chocolate pastry. What the hell, it was his birthday. He unfolded a newspaper left on the seat next to him and took a look at the photograph of the attack on the hostel. His reading glasses perched at the tip of his long Roman nose. He waited. It looked as if the convulsions in Moscow were far from over. The anti-Yeltsin forces, which he translated as meaning the anti-American forces still wandering around the corridors of power in Moscow and Kiev, seemed to be gathering steam. Where did they think they'd be without the United States as big brother? Who did they think they could join up with to face the future? They were running an arms bazaar over there, they didn't know if they could survive the winter without mass famine, they had to know that Communism was a dead issue . . . what could they be thinking of, trying to mount a return to a hard line? Did they have a plan? Had they any idea what the hell they were doing?

It wasn't long before Max Adler appeared. He was a short, swarthy man with thick black hair that had in recent years begun to show some gray. He wore a leather trenchcoat and a soft felt fedora. He bounced on the balls of his feet when he walked like a fighter stalking an opponent. He had been a cop all of his adult life and on Paulus's retirement had been named to replace him as chief of detectives, Berlin Central. He was a very busy man so Paulus had suggested they always meet at the Café Adler so Max wouldn't forget the name of the place. Café Adler. The Eagle.

Adler dropped his hat on the corner of the table, shucked his coat off and draped it over the back of his chair, and sat down. He fumbled a packet of cigarettes from his suitcoat pocket and lit one with a Zippo. "My wife won't let me smoke at home anymore. I lead a dog's life, Chief." He always thought of Paulus as the Chief and always would. "What's on your mind?"

"Have a cake. Have some coffee."

"I will, I will. By the way, take a look at this." He dug a flat silver-wrapped and beribboned package from his trenchcoat pocket.

"What's this, Max?"

"It's your birthday, Chief."

"You didn't need to—"

"Just open it."

Carefully Paulus unwrapped and refolded the paper. He opened the box. It was a soft leather wallet. Expensive. Ku'damm all the way. He smiled at Adler. "You are very, very kind, Maximilian. Much too generous."

"I know. I'm all heart. Just remember and give me something nice on my seventieth birthday."

"Hmmm. I'll be ninety. I might forget."

"I'll be there to remind you, Chief. And you'll have had plenty of time to think of something very nice." Coffee and cake arrived. Adler sipped the coffee black. "My wife thinks I should drink it black. What a foul taste." He poured cream and added sugar. "Now what's up?"

"Have you seen much of Wolf Koller lately?"

Max Adler made a scowling face. "More than I'd like, I promise you. How did you know?"

"You know."

"You mean I'm Koller's tame cop."

"You know what people say. In my day they said I was Henry Popper's man. Krupp's man. There's always somebody to spread a rumor."

"Were they right?"

Paulus shrugged his wide shoulders. "Sure. When it was convenient. It pays to have friends in power. People always forget that the street runs both ways. I used them at least as much as they used me."

"Things never change. I've seen him a couple of times. He had me out in the rain watching that mess at the hostel. Somehow he'd got wind it was going down. With that security force of his I guess he hears lots of things. He wanted me there to watch. He's bothered by the police response time. He wants a bigtime crackdown . . . I told him there's a

fine line. We're on the slow side now, admittedly, but we don't want to
start machine-gunning crowds either. We're trying to find the right balance." Adler sighed, looking across the room at the crowds milling beyond the windows. "Granted, we *are* pretty damn slow. I'm not sure
why."

"You said you'd seen him a couple of times."

"I was summoned to the house."

"Grunewald or Wannsee?"

"Grunewald. He wanted me to assign half of Berlin Central to
look for his daughter. Erika. You know about this Erika thing? Of course
you do, what am I saying? You know what I had for dinner last night.
Anyway, he knew I couldn't devote that kind of effort to it—he was just
giving his tongue a workout. I told him I'd do what I could. What am I
supposed to say? And all this without publicity of any kind. He thinks
he's a dictator."

"Seems to be working. Not a word in the press." Paulus nibbled
at the last of his cake. "She could be dead, you know."

"Possible."

"Or kidnapped."

"More likely. But there's been no contact made. You wonder
about all that blood."

"She might have tried to kill herself."

"Most likely. But then, where is she? She tried to kill herself,
screwed it up, then decided to take a vacation?" Adler sighed. "So I've
got a couple of guys looking around. It's an impossible job if she has
people helping her and wants to stay hidden and we can't use the media
to help find her."

"Did you tell him that?"

"More or less."

"And how did he react?"

"Usual thing. He'll end my career if I don't find her, he'll have me
put in the deepest dungeon in the darkest prison, then the death of a
thousand cuts." Adler chuckled. "What could he say? He had one of his
flunkies hanging about. He couldn't lose face. Why are you so interested?"

"I wouldn't mind finding her myself."

"What the hell for?"

Paulus smiled. "I'm an old man with nothing much to do."

"Oh, that slipped my mind, Chief," Adler observed with heavy
irony. "Who are you working for?"

"You have a suspicious mind, Max."

"You taught me to be suspicious of everyone, Chief."

"Did I?"

"You did."

"Well, I'm sure I didn't mean me."

They sat smiling together.

Paulus left the Café Adler several minutes after Max Adler departed. He strolled apparently aimlessly, and ten minutes later he stood before a grassy expanse. A sign had been erected, black letters on white.

Topographie des Terror

It was the former site of the Prinz Albrecht Hotel, headquarters of the SS, for many years the most feared address in Europe. If you were taken to Prinz-Albrecht-Strasse, you were finished. Now, across the green carpet of well-tended grass, there was a small, low, flat-roofed building. He had visited it several times, the museum relating the history of the SS. At the end of the grass, walking along the sidewalk on Prinz-Albrecht-Strasse, was a portion of the Wall left standing. It wasn't very thick. Shrubbery and weeds grew up all around it. It had been spray-painted in a variety of colors. He wondered why it had been left standing. Tourists never came there.

He walked back across the damp grass, feeling the sunlight growing hazy and the breeze on his face. At the little museum he stopped for a moment, watching a group of thirty or so German schoolkids lined up, following their teacher inside. Behind them another group, a bit smaller, waited. He heard them speaking with English accents. He'd seen such groups before, coming from all across Europe. Dutch, Italians, French, Spanish, Scandinavians, Scots, they came from everywhere, class trips to Germany, seeing everything, having a good time, but stopping here to learn something from their grandfathers' days. It was a good thing.

He walked back to his car and drove into the heart of what had been West Berlin. Past the magnificent ruin of the bombed-out Kaiser Wilhelm Church, which was the official symbol of the city, past the nearby Europa Center with the huge Mercedes insignia endlessly turning on the roof, the unofficial symbol of Berlin. Past the zoo with the great Oriental gates, up Kantstrasse, with the S-Bahn trains streaming by along the overpasses on his left. He hung a sharp right and parked on a cobbled street near a park with a statue of somebody who must once have been important. He didn't think it was Kant.

The bar was thick with smoke and overheated. Through the resulting fug he saw Burke Delaney waving at him. He and the Professor were deep in a corner. Delaney was eating a dish of the day's curry. His pipe sat in an ashtray, smoke curling from the bowl. The Professor was drinking beer. Paulus made it three, old warriors full of memories. Delaney was a few years younger than Paulus and the Professor was not yet sixty although, as with everything about the Professor, you were never quite sure.

"You're running a little late, Werner." Delaney mopped his mouth with a napkin. "Busy morning?"

"Just the usual. Madonna called to wish me a happy birthday. The Chancellor. President Clinton. The usual."

"Your birthday?" The Professor blinked at him. He had only one good eye but Paulus could never remember which was which. And he was wearing dark glasses anyway. "No one told me."

"This is a terrible place," Paulus said, looking around. "It's hard to breathe. I liked the other place . . . What was it? Diener something, wasn't it?"

The Professor said: "Diener Tattersall? It's quite near."

"Full of actors," Delaney said, as if that settled the matter.

"So?" The Professor raised an eyebrow. "I have spent some time over the years in amateur theatricals. I'm quite a master of disguise, if I say so myself."

"I don't know, something about actors—they're so actorish—"

"Well, I don't think it's open for lunch," the Professor said.

"We're here, so that's that," Delaney said, shoveling in some more curry. "Let's talk SPARTAKUS." He dropped his voice to a low grumble.

"Good," Paulus said softly.

"My masters are obsessed with it," Delaney began. "I've never seen them so hot for anything. I'm damned if I know why. We don't know where it's leading . . . if it's leading anywhere. And they're acting like it's the Manhattan Project. Only one thing solid so far—SPARTAKUS is somehow linked to the Stiffel bullshit, that little crowd-pleaser he pulled at the immigrant hostel. The SPARTAKUS product told us about the hostel attack before it happened." He grinned suddenly. "It's driving the Cheese nuts back in Georgetown. He rolls over, he sits up, he begs, soon he'll be fetching."

"There ought to be some money in it for you then," the Professor murmured. "A bonus. He's such a tight bastard—always has been." Delaney wondered just how much the Professor knew about Ned Cheddar. Every so often he'd say something that made you wonder just who he was exactly.

"And what," Paulus said, "about the young man, Karl-Heinz?"

"He's good and scared. He's worried about the girlfriend—the Koller girl."

"Does he know where she is?" the Professor asked. Paulus smiled: not more than a handful of people even knew the girl was missing.

"Hell no," Delaney said. "He thinks the bad guys have got her but he doesn't know which bad guys. In his mind, we're all bad guys. Us, Stiffel, Wolf Koller's palace guard, the Nazis. He thinks maybe we've got her. He also thinks we'll kill *him* if he tells us where he gets SPARTAKUS. I can't"—he chuckled—"promise him we won't."

The Professor said: "The young man finds himself in a legitimately frightening world. Would you think I'm crazy if I tell you I envy him? Sometimes I miss those days."

"You can have 'em," Delaney said darkly. "I'm not out of 'em yet and they're for the birds."

"You don't mean that," the Professor said, peeling the coaster from the bottom of his beer stein.

Burke Delaney rolled his eyes. "Karl-Heinz was right on the money about the attack on the hostel, though. He took me to it. So, he's plugged in. But he won't tell me how . . . I sometimes wonder about that STASI colonel father of his, is he involved in this somehow?"

Paulus ignored this last flight of fancy. "I wonder where the girl-friend fits in."

The Professor said at last, impatiently: "I think she's a red herring. I think she's just a kid who's run off somewhere. It's a waste of time trying to tie her into all this. She's probably sick and tired of the whole thing, her lefty boyfriend and her tycoon father with their demands—"

"You *know* her," Paulus said. "She used to hang around you in that café in the East, the one where you held court. She was one of your protégées—" The Professor taught at the Institute for the Study of European Politics, Literature, and History. It was a creation of the immediate post–Cold War period. Even Paulus couldn't say it all in one breath, in German. It was a *very* serious place.

"Nonsense. I knew her, yes. Hardly a protégée."

"Karl-Heinz met her there, right? Isn't that what you said? Did you introduce them?" Paulus smiled genially. "If you did, then I'm sure Wolf Koller would say you have much to answer for."

"I certainly didn't introduce them. You can be very wicked, my friend." The Professor was watching him from behind the dark lenses.

Delaney said: "It's his Berlin sense of humor. The one Berliners never let you forget about."

The Professor continued with his thoughts about the girl. "I don't know if they actually met there. But I saw them talking a few times. I'm convinced she's just an airhead girl, spoiled, rich, pampered. We're all making too much out of it."

"Aren't you forgetting all that blood?" Paulus asked.

The Professor shrugged. He had a short beard with a lot of gray in it, an old blue beret, wore the dark glasses and an oiled Scandinavian turtleneck. A duffel coat of green loden wool was folded in an empty chair. He looked like a beatnik in Greenwich Village, circa 1954.

He had an interesting history, what Paulus had been able to find out about it. He was an American, had appeared behind the Iron Curtain in the early seventies. He had arrived more dead than alive: at least that was the story. You never knew what to believe. He might have walked in off the street whistling "Blue Skies," for that matter. Nor was it clear where he'd come from. In the following years, he'd been in and out of East Germany, Poland, Hungary, and some people swore he'd been a regular analyst at Moscow Center for a time, though proof was in short supply. There was a minority opinion that he'd been an American mole but that was thought to be a touch of melodrama. More likely he'd actually defected for a time. Or he'd been CIA and snatched by the KGB to keep in reserve as a trading chip. Whatever, it was all behind him now. Paulus, of course, had ways of finding things out, and he'd found out that the Professor's name was either Adam Eager, which was what his passport said, or Kiril something or other, which had been his name in Moscow. When he came out of the East at the time the Wall was about to come down, it was courtesy of Ned Cheddar. Cheddar and Burke Delaney went back forever, but Paulus and Cheddar went back nearly thirty years themselves. It wasn't quite clear how far back Cheddar and the Professor went. But Paulus's professional opinion was that the Professor had been an American agent inside the KGB. In any case, he was truly retired now, so far as Paulus could discern. Which meant that he was either still working for Cheddar or was a bit of a freelance or, yes, was retired. He'd heard somewhere that the Professor had been through something so bad that Cheddar had actually let him quit. If that was a true story, it must have been something very bad indeed.

Paulus was unsure of the Professor's role in the present proceedings, but then, the Professor was probably curious about what Paulus was up to. It was a world where questions were sometimes most unwelcome. Better to find out on your own. They had known each other for a few years, in the brave new Germany. There was something in their relationship that reminded Paulus of stories he'd heard about spooks, terrorists, and arms suppliers all thrown together by the coincidence of sharing a safe house on the same night. Delaney told the story of how he'd played cards all night with the man who was Carlos the Jackal, as if they had checked their real identities at the door. Carlos had been the most hunted man in the world at the time, yet they'd played cards and talked about their parents and what it had been like growing up. When he looked at Delaney and the Professor, Paulus remembered the story.

Delaney finished his curry, wiped his mouth again, and sucked on the pipe, which had finally gone cold. He applied a match and puffed out an enormous cloud of smoke. "Well, the girl's uncle has arrived from the States on a white charger. Bent on finding the girl."

The Professor looked up, a flicker of alarm crossing his face. "What are you saying? I have a pathological hatred of wild cards . . . particularly when they're played by amateurs."

"Her uncle, John Cooper . . . Lise Koller's brother. Just got here this morning."

"How would you know such a thing?" The Professor was rotating his mug of beer on the wet spot on the table.

"The Cheese told me he was on his way. Well, he's here."

"But why? Who's responsible for his coming?"

"Apparently his sister got a message to him through a friend."

"His sister? Good lord. What friend?"

"Beate Hubermann. Ring a bell?"

Paulus said: "TV. She's sexy, sort of Scandinavian-looking. Not bad if you like them perfect."

"Where is he staying, Burke?" The Professor was showing more interest than Paulus thought logical. He couldn't help making such observations. A lifetime's training.

"With Hubermann."

The Professor frowned. "I hope he stays the hell out of the way. Cooper! We've got to keep an eye on him, see what he gets up to. I trust none of us needs to be reminded of what happened the last time he stuck his nose into Germany's business?"

Paulus wondered how the Professor knew about all that: where had he been twenty years ago? Moscow? Working for Cheddar? Had he somehow been involved in that old mess?

Delaney puffed. He didn't seem to think the question strange. "None of us needs to be reminded. It's the stuff of legend now. Thank God Cooper's a lot older, without that crazy pal of his—what was his name?"

"Olaf Peterson," the Professor said.

Paulus smiled sadly. "Look at us. *We're* a lot older, too, and where's it gotten us? Still caught up in this nonsense."

"Gotta fill the time," Delaney muttered.

They laughed rather ruefully but the Professor didn't think it was all that funny. "We need to keep after SPARTAKUS. We can't let Cooper screw it up. We have to learn where it's leading—what is the point of SPARTAKUS? Why is it called SPARTAKUS? It can't just be Stiffel and his crowd raising hell . . . these things always make sense if you dig deep enough."

Paulus nodded. "To someone." He wondered who was employing the Professor. Cheddar, still? Hmmm. What if the Professor belonged to Wolf Koller? Stranger things had happened. He'd never seen the Professor quite so interested in anything before, almost agitated. Usually his interest was academic, how to solve a problem. He had once confided to Delaney and Paulus that he was writing a book. Usually that amounted to a death sentence for an old spook, if the word got out. Paulus didn't know whether or not to believe him. Maybe it was just a feint. Or a joke.

Delaney said: "I don't like relying on Karl-Heinz. He's gonna get his ass shot off and I don't want to be the poor bastard standing next to him. So, where is he getting the product? He comes, he goes, he's never in the same place, never home, doesn't *have* a fucking home so far as I know. That paper he writes for, they never know where he is. I'm saying he's just a kid for chrissakes and we're depending on him to provide product Cheese is dying for! It's Mickey Mouse, is what it is. You get that, Werner?"

"Yes. I'm familiar with the term Mickey Mouse."

"Well, I don't like it."

The Professor was the first to go. "And I don't like this Cooper thing. Steer clear of him. But somebody's got to keep track of him."

"How about you?" Delaney said.

"Not a chance."

They had known each other long enough: they could communicate in a language of their own. They were, in effect, all vouched for by Ned Cheddar, that disembodied voice in Georgetown. In a way, thought Paulus, they were three sides of the same object, each with a slightly different agenda, each with his own private relationship with the Cheese. But they knew their business. And they trusted one another. If not all the way, then most of the way. If one of them someday turned on the other two, well, he supposed it would serve them right.

10

LEE

Beate looked freshly scrubbed, blue eyes shining, tiredness gone, when Cooper greeted her the next morning. The sun was shining and the kitchen had benefited from a scrubbing. For the moment he'd forgotten about the corpses in the snow, the nervousness about meeting Lee again that had wakened him several times during the night. The coffee was fresh, there were three different kinds of bread on the pine table, a boiled egg in its little cup, and two pots of jam. Beate laid aside the morning paper and grinned at him while he went to work on the egg's shell.

"I've been thinking," she said. "It'll be better if I call Lise. Lee. Your appearing suddenly might not be such a great idea if she's as delicate as Erika told me. I'll tell her you're here and we'll set up a meeting for the two of you."

He nodded. "I hope she's up to it. You don't know how sick she really is?"

"We're going to find out. But first I want to take you out for a drive. It's too early to call her now. And you should see what you're getting into. We want to give Wolf Koller plenty of time to get to his meeting with the Chancellor."

"Glock?"

"Mmm. That's the only Chancellor we have."

She drove a Volkswagen her brother had left her when he went off to study medicine at UCLA. She seemed to be under the impression that it was a Ferrari, a style of driving that made conversation imprudent at best. The ride went on forever. Cooper spent most of the time watching his life pass before his eyes. The sun had gone, the sky was gray. Eventually they were out of the traffic, woods all around, and she was slowing down. She eased off onto the shoulder and stopped. The earth was damp and soft, matted with golden leaves.

She pointed at a path leading away at right angles from the road. "The Hasensprung. That means 'Rabbit Run.' Come on. I'll show you." She put her arm through his and pulled him with her.

The wide brick path was strewn with golden leaves. Most of the trees, thousands of them, were nearly bare. The path slid downward; the shrubbery was deep on either side, and he heard the running of a stream. It was like something from Disneyland. Goofy was bound to jump out from behind a bush at any moment, making dumb noises.

"During the day this is where the nannies and the au pair girls, sometimes even the mothers, take their babies out in carriages. No vehicles, just people walking with babies. Perfect symbol of a privileged existence. Some people think it's the most beautiful spot in Berlin. I might be one of them. If I married a rich guy and we lived out here this is where I'd take my baby . . . but, of course, I'm too wrapped up in my career—" She laughed. "Oh, shut up, Beate. Just look around, John . . . look at those."

They'd reached the bottom of the slope, the bridge crossing the stream that fed into the pool on his right. It made a perfect, idyllic, almost musical sound as it bubbled over the stones. The pool was smooth as an old worn coin.

On the railings on either side of the bridge sat, larger than life, stone carved rabbits, smoothed and caressed by the hands of thousands of children through the years. Beate was running her hand across the nose of one of the huge rabbits. "Bugs," she said. When he looked at her quizzically, she added: "Bunny. Bugs Bunny."

"My favorite actor." He was watching her long slender fingers. When she turned to smile up at him, she might have been in just that instant a photo in *Vogue*.

"So, what are we doing here?" he said.

"Look up through the trees. We'll just keep walking. See . . . Those are private homes."

"They look like hotels."

Looming ahead on the right side of the Hasensprung was a massive building of gray stone, four stories high with a slate roof, balconies,

black ironwork grilles on the windows, beautiful hothouse flowers—
somehow, in November—dripping from baskets. Something about it—
the weight, the scale—reminded him of his grandfather's house in
Cooper's Falls. There were cars and vans, six in all, parked on a blacktop
surface. He realized he was looking at the back of the house.

On the left side of the path an even larger house seemed to cas-
cade down the slope in the direction of the gurgling stream. Next to it
were a greenhouse and a summerhouse, a miniature in the style of the
huge main house, which was made of white stucco or plaster with a red
tile roof, its peaks and gables set out in a symmetrical scheme. The bottom floor seemed to be two stories high; above it a white balcony ran the
width of the house with countless rooms, French doors opening out to
the fresh air. Above the long balcony were two more floors, windows
recessed beneath the overhang of the roof. There were willow trees still
laden with leaves and drooping heavily. Two uniformed servants carried
things in and out of the back doors and the garage.

"All of the houses out here are built on something like the same
scale but some are just more equal than others. Like this one."

"Who lives in them?"

"Business tycoons, doctors, lawyers, bankers, financiers. The rich,
the powerful. It's always the same people who live in such places."

He pointed at the vast white house. A gardener was moving behind the glass of the greenhouse. "This place . . . Who would live in a
place like that . . . it's a kind of palace—"

She was smiling when she said: "That's Wolf Koller's house."

Cooper strode down Fasanenstrasse—Pheasant Street—from the
Ku'damm with a faint mist in his face and his heart pounding. He hadn't
seen her in twenty years, hadn't seen a picture of her, and he found that
now he couldn't catch his breath. Up ahead was Fasanenplatz, splendidly
autumnal, golden leaves and green grass and the smell of damp earth. It
smelled like the graveyard he remembered from his grandfather's funeral.
Fasanenplatz, that was where she'd told Beate she'd meet her brother,
John.

He saw her from a block away. There was no mistaking the angle
of her shoulders, the way she held herself, even leaning on a cane. She
might have been their mother, the resemblance was so strong. It was that
resemblance that had made the whole thing come together twenty years

ago. Cyril Cooper and the photograph of her in a newspaper. It had stopped him in his tracks: it had seemed to be a picture of their mother . . . and he had had to know who this woman was. It had been Lee and it had cost him his life.

And here she was again, the reincarnation of their mother, the fine features, the level eyebrows, the remote gaze, all the habitual movements carried forward by the genetic miracle. She had turned and was watching him approach, seeming calm and cool, honey-streaked hair gently waved to her collar like a movie star's, timelessly beautiful. She was wearing slacks the color of café au lait, an olive-green blazer fitted to the shape of her body, tailored to within an inch of its life. A scarf was puckishly pimiento silk.

Her mouth was straight, like her eyebrows, and she kept her eyes on him as he drew close. He felt his heart struggling to escape from his chest. It had been twenty years since he'd felt anything like it and he was afraid, afraid of the power she had over him, afraid that at the moment of seeing her he would lose her yet again.

They had made love once, more accurately he had made love and she had withdrawn to her cell of alone-ness, back in the days when he had tried to convince himself that she was not his sister, that she couldn't be his sister, that God couldn't make such a joke of his life.

Now . . . she was so beautiful he couldn't speak. The past—the brief time they'd shared, the hatred and passion and fear—lay between them like a minefield littered with the corpses of past battles, old losses.

She was older but it didn't register, didn't lessen her, somehow added to her appeal in subtle, indefinable ways. There were lines at the corners of her mouth, not those of laughter but possibly of pain or confusion. There was sorrow in her eyes: or was it that he didn't want her to have been happy without him? She had lived all but a few days of her life without him, had married twice, had a child, reached middle age, and now . . . what?

She was strung so tight he feared she might snap when a sudden hint of a smile traced the corners of her mouth.

"My God, John, you're so big—I'd forgotten . . ." She came forward, leaning on the cane, her hand clamped around the carved bulldog's head. "Can't you say something, John?"

He put his arms around her and felt her leaning against him, like a fragile bird flying to the protection of a huge, sheltering tree. Holding her, trying to think, seeing the beautiful architecture of the low blocks of apartment buildings lining the small square, the red and yellow leaves thick on the ground, the grass damp and green, he tried to slow the procession of images through his mind. He was imprinting the moment on his brain. Lee again . . . Twenty years and here she was again, the only woman he had ever truly, deeply, unforgettably, hopelessly, inescapably loved.

His little sister, Lee.

She had once told him he had demolished her life, told him he was something evil that had come to destroy her life and leave it barren, told him she didn't hate him but simply wanted to forget about him. She'd said she was a German and was strong and he meant nothing to her . . . He had gone away then, leaving her with a good old man called Dr. Roeschler, had told him to take care of her . . .

He remembered the last time he'd seen her.

He and Olaf Peterson had gotten into a Mercedes on a dark, rainy morning. Dr. Roeschler had been standing on the step, watching the Mercedes pull slowly away. At the last moment Cooper had looked back at the house. On the third floor of the narrow, spindly building a light clicked on in a window, the white curtains parted, and then the car had turned the corner and that was the last of Lee. The parted curtains, a vague shape.

"It's good to see you, Lee." At the most crucial moments of a lifetime, the most ordinary utterances. He wished that eloquence were not beyond him.

"Thank you for coming, John. I didn't know if you would. You'd have had every right not to. I wouldn't have blamed you . . ." He could hear the German in her voice. He was still holding her, she was whispering in his ear. "I remember the last night, the last time we spoke." He almost couldn't hear her. "It might have been yesterday . . . I've never forgotten—"

"Well, I came back. Maybe I never was very bright, maybe I don't know when I'm licked. Maybe I'm just a sucker for a pretty girl. Anyway, I'm too old to change now."

He released her; she held on to his arm with her free hand. She looked up at him, for once searching his eyes with her own. "I should have asked you sooner. In better times." She spoke with a dying fall.

"You should have come with me twenty years ago."

"Ah, that. You do get right to it, don't you, John?" Holding on to his arm, she turned, using the cane, and they began to walk slowly along the leaf-carpeted sidewalk. "I couldn't."

"You could have, Lee. But that's all too long ago to argue about now."

"We're old now," she said. "Life changes. Everything changes. Everything you thought you knew, it all turns out to be wrong. Not what you thought at all."

"You're not old. You'll never be old. You are as beautiful now as you were then."

"Oh, cling to your illusions." She smiled faintly, the cane tapping. "If you only knew."

"We're not old. But life went on without us."

"No, John, that's maudlin. We went on, too. Without each other, that's all. It had to be that way." She reached up, stroked her hand along the side of his face. He smelled the richness of the glove leather. "I've thought about what I'd say to you if you came. I knew you didn't understand why I stayed behind in Munich. I gave you a lot of reasons . . . I said terrible things to you but I was hurt and lost and I was afraid to let my guard down, my emotions were killing me, I was bleeding . . ."

"I wasn't feeling so hot myself."

She went on, thinking about herself, as if he hadn't spoken. She'd thought it out. She needed to say it. "You and Olaf Peterson had arrived out of nowhere. As a result my husband was dead, my lover was dead . . . I was afraid of what might happen to me, I'd lost my grip—"

"I understood," Cooper said. He tightened his arm on hers, felt her return the pressure. "You belonged to them. To the Nazis. Just like our father, like our grandfather—" He wanted her to have an excuse. He wanted her to share the feelings of family guilt he'd never been able to shake.

"No, John, that wasn't it, it had nothing to do with that."

"What do you mean, Lee? Think of it. You needed them . . . They took care of you. They owned you and you owed them everything— the life you were used to, the money, the luxury all around you." He tried to remove some of the sting. "It's over, I don't blame you anymore. It wasn't that you sympathized, or even understood, their political ideas— I'd never accuse you of that. Anyway, it was a long time ago and I don't blame you."

"But you blamed me then and I couldn't tell you everything in my mind—"

"I was an inconvenience, Lee. Peterson and I made a mess of your life. I know that."

"You loved me, John. You went all over the world looking for me. You fell in love with me when I was a ghost you couldn't quite see, then you found me and fell in love with me again when you saw me as a person . . . you killed the dragons but the maiden in the tower was afraid to come down and leave with you . . . You weren't supposed to fall in love with me, not with *me,* John . . ."

"The inconvenient Mr. Cooper," he said, his voice tight.

The sky was darkening now for rain. Lights shone in the windows, lives were being lived, in Potsdam the smoldering hostel grew damp and smudged the sky. Life had gone on without them and Cooper felt half mad with the waste. All that mattered in his life was what had happened in those few days twenty years ago.

"But you don't understand." She took a deep breath. Now she wouldn't look at him. "Maybe I didn't know it then but I knew it soon enough . . . I loved you, too, John." She sighed, out of breath. "I was in love with my brother. My brother . . . the man who had just destroyed my life. I couldn't face the fact that I had the feelings for you that I did— it was all so wrong, don't you see? There's no way to prepare yourself for that, is there?"

"I couldn't prepare myself either," he said.

"Maybe you're stronger than I am—"

"Hardly. More likely I was weaker, I gave in to it. But no, I can't buy it, Lee, I can't buy it when you tell me you loved me. I saw your face. You weren't loving me."

"I denied it. To myself and to you . . . but when you were gone and I was left with the emptiness of my life, I knew why it was empty— you were gone. It took me a long time to get used to the idea of loving you. To this day I don't know why I did . . . except that it had some-thing to do with what you'd gone through to get to me. And I'm not very sophisticated, John. Even after I faced how I felt about you I couldn't imagine what else I could have done. Think, John—what would have happened to us if I'd gone back with you to America? Oh, we could have told people anything we wanted, we could have gone to Boston and I'd have been a widow you met in Germany, Lise Brendel, nobody would have known . . . I knew that much, I thought that much of it through . . . but, John, for God's sake, *we* would have known, and it would have been there every day. Brother and sister. What would we have let ourselves in for, over the years? Whenever we fought our minds would have flown to the truth about us. Where would rancor and anger have led us?" She made a soft sound, deep in her throat, despair or relief or hope, it was impossible to say. "Forgive me for the long speech, John. I've waited twenty years to say it . . . I was sure I'd never have the chance . . . and I've thought about it every day for twenty years."

Cooper shook his head. Was it the one thing he'd waited all this time to hear? She'd loved him.

Or was it in some awful way the worst thing he could ever know? That she'd loved him and done nothing?

Did it make a tragedy of his life? A waste?

"And now I'm sick," she said, "and Erika's gone and there was no one else to turn to."

"But why not? Why not your husband? She isn't just your daughter, she's his daughter, too."

"Erika hates him. She's always hated him. No, that's not true. She worshiped him when she was small, even in her adolescence . . . but then it began to change and it was an implacable hatred. Like one animal instinctively hating another . . . They're at cross purposes. It can't be changed."

"But why? What is it all about?"

She impatiently rapped the tip of her cane on the sidewalk. "It doesn't matter anymore. It's too late to change any of it. And I don't have the energy left to cope with them."

"Does he know you've asked me to come?"

"He wouldn't have understood. It would have made an impossible situation in our lives. You must try to understand—Wolf hates me, I wasn't what he thought he was getting. He married me for sexual access to me, that's what drove him. And he came to realize I was someone else than he'd been told. He looks upon me now as a weak link, a liability, I might bring shame to him . . . He sees Erika and me as the Furies in his life—two women out to destroy him. Because we know him . . . Erika knows *something* that terrifies him, that's what I think." She took a deep breath, looked up at Cooper almost as if she were pleading with him to believe her. "And he thinks I might do almost anything and he can't stand that. He's afraid I might do or say something that will expose him —only I have no idea what he means, expose *what*? . . . And then I became ill . . . That's why I think he hopes I'll die and he'll be free of worrying about me. Now that Erika is gone, I wonder if he even wants her to come back. She can be wild and unpredictable, she has her own mind . . . I don't know if he wants her found. And you were the person I could turn to . . . ." She shrugged away the inquisitive expression on his face. "The only one."

They were having lunch at a restaurant called The Fasanerie, set in a courtyard well off the street. The glass roof came to a point overhead, like a tent. There was a rumble of thunder and rain began spattering the glass. The lunch crowd was beginning to thin out. Very dressy in a casual way. Mostly women, a fortune in clothing, but Lee was different, she caused heads to turn. They knew who she was. He heard a woman whisper the words *Lise Koller, Wolf Koller's wife,* as they passed by on their way to their table by the glass wall.

They ordered omelettes and Rhine wine and stared into each other's eyes. But they weren't high school kids. Being lovesick now was for the birds, surely. But what to say now? Desultory conversation until the food arrived and the tables near them had emptied.

"What do you mean you're sick? Is it something to do with the leg?"

"No, no, I just had a fall. I'll tell you about the rest of it later. I'll either get better or I won't—but I've lived my life, Johnnie, most of it, at least. Dr. Gisevius doesn't know what's wrong with me anyway."

"Are you sure he's good?"

"It doesn't matter. Yes, yes, he's an old friend of Wolf's, I've known him forever—John, it's Erika we should be talking about—"

"All right. I understand that she's disappeared, gone off somewhere. What would she do that for? She must know how you'd worry—"

"She didn't set out to run away, John." She was trying hard not to be impatient. "She set out to kill herself. Her prints on the butcher knife, no one else's. That's a fact. Her blood was all over the bathroom. I don't know what could have happened, but in my heart . . . I know she's alive."

"Could it have been a murder attempt gone wrong?"

She winced when he said it.

"No, no, the fingerprints . . . only Erika's." She put down her fork, left the omelette half eaten. "That leaves the real question, why would she try to kill herself?" She finished her tea, set the cup down, rattling, in the saucer. "When you're ready, I'll take you to her flat. If you're going to help find her for me, that's where you should start."

She was trying so hard to hold on. He said: "Are you all right? Do you need anything?"

"All I want is my daughter back. After that . . . well, I can handle whatever comes." She stood up, holding on to the table's edge, clutching her cane. "Come on."

The building was in Bleibtreustrasse, an elegant street of boutiques and restaurants just off the other side of the Ku'damm, near Mommsen-strasse. A faded pinkish-lavender structure, lots of windows, balconies, turrets, cupolas, tiled roof, five stories, expensive clothing shops on the ground floor. The concierge's desk was unattended. A small wire cage of an elevator carried them to the top floor. Lee said: "The concierge had a toothache the day it happened. He was at the dentist for hours. No one else was on duty. Nobody saw anything. He went home and took pain-killers, didn't come in until the next day. Maybe he's had a relapse." The elevator jiggled to a stop and he opened the door, followed her to the end of the hall.

The apartment was spare and oppressively minimal, if Cooper un-derstood the word correctly. White walls, a bunch of neon numbers blinking against the emptiness. The few paintings were so self-referential that they meant nothing to him. There was a pile of junk, doubtless masquerading as art, laid out on the floor. It was all so icy, so remote, that it chilled him to the marrow. He turned to Lee. "I know why she ran away."

"What are you saying?"

"It was either run away or kill her decorator."

"She's young. She lives in the art world. You can't hold it against her."

She took him from point to point, showing him where the blood had sprayed on the mirror and the sink and the bathroom floor.

"These are the knives." She took him from the kitchen back into the main room.

"Poor little rich girl," he said.

Lee's temper flashed at him. "Don't be condescending. You don't know her. She's not shallow or stupid or spoiled. She's alone and afraid and something made her want to kill herself."

"Were you really close to her, Lee? Tell me the truth."

"We wanted to be close. Most of the time we were. But she couldn't be sure of me, she was always afraid I might betray what she told me to her father, and I couldn't convince her that there was almost nothing left between Wolf and me. She and I had coffee every week at the Café Einstein. We talked about her job, we talked about art, we talked about all the things mothers and daughters talk about. Until a few months ago. Then *she* began to tell *me* things about Wolf . . . But I was beginning to suffer these spells of mine and . . ." She stood looking out the window. Across the street, between two buildings, Cooper could see the huge Mercedes-Benz star slowly revolving on top of the Europa Center.

"What did she tell you about Wolf?"

She shook her head. "I don't remember—"

"Think, Lee. This could be the key—you must see that—"

"What I'm saying is . . . that I can't remember. She told me things that meant a great deal to her but I had begun to have these blank spots. I remember listening, I remember looking into her face while she spoke—but what she said is all blank, it's just gone—"

"Maybe you don't want to remember. Maybe you're repressing what she said—"

"Please don't try to psychoanalyze me, John. I don't remember. *Believe me.*"

"I do believe you. That's not what I'm saying, that I don't believe you." He didn't want to argue. He changed the subject. "How well does she know Beate Hubermann?"

"Beate? I don't know. Beate has a view of things we don't often see—because of her job, I suppose. She's unimpressed by our money . . . it means nothing to her."

"Don't kid yourself," Cooper said. "She's impressed."

"Maybe in the sense that she's aware of the money and how Wolf's influence stems from it. But I don't believe it affects the way she treats Erika or me. I found her very refreshing. She's the kind of new German woman who infuriates Wolf. She doesn't know her place . . . She's not overcome by respect for men like Wolf. Or anyone else for that matter. Beate figures that people have to earn her respect." As her voice died away she passed her hand in front of her eyes, touched her temples.

"Are you okay?"

"Just a headache. Erika admired Beate, her career in television. Erika thought her own life was parasitic, she was convinced she got her gallery job because of who she is. And Beate was a person who did something that mattered, something important. Erika saw no relevance in her own life—"

"Is there any?"

"Look, John, she's not Mother Teresa, and she's not Petra Kelly, either, thank God. She's not devoting her life to the Greens or good works but she thinks she should. She's an idealist who doesn't believe she's living up to her ideals. I think the death of Petra Kelly, the peculiar circumstances, bothered her . . . sad things, tragic things colored her moods. And all this neo-Nazi stuff, we talked about that the last time we were together, she said that Karl-Heinz, her boyfriend, told her about something, some plan, some code word . . . I do remember that bit of the conversation—it was SPARTAKUS . . . she said he'd discovered some master plan and it had something to do with the neo-Nazis, the demonstrations—it sounded so far-fetched." She turned away from the window. Her face was pale. "I didn't want her seeing this boy, he was always out waving a placard or passing out leaflets, I didn't want her to lead that kind of life, riots and demonstrations, it never leads any-where—"

"That's not always true," he said. "It got the United States out of Vietnam. And made a President of ours call it quits—it played a big part in the downfall of Communism. And it made Hitler the man who ruled Germany."

". . . and she hates Wolf, as I said, and it's gotten worse during the last few months." She wet her dry lips with her tongue. "Would you bring me a glass of water?"

He went to the kitchen and filled a glass from the tap.

When he got back she sipped, then popped a pill and swallowed. "I know she's out there somewhere, not knowing what to do, knowing she tried to kill herself . . . what if she tries again, John?"

He was standing at the window, looking across the street, the rain coming down harder, slashing in the wind. It was growing dark. Between the two buildings, in a slice of open space, he saw the revolving Mercedes symbol. Behind him he heard a sigh.

He reached her just as the glass of water slipped from her fingers and hit the floor, shattered. He caught her as she fell, lowered her onto a white couch.

"Oh, God," she murmured. Her eyelashes fluttered, her fingers dug into his arm. "I hoped this wouldn't happen . . . I'll be all right, John, just wait a minute." He watched her struggling to force herself out of it. "Sometimes . . . I can't remember where I am . . . or who I am . . . please forgive me, John, I'll be all right. Just hold me for a moment. Oh, Johnnie, I'm such a fool, such a mess." She clung to him as he sat down beside her, pulled her head to his chest.

"No hurry," he said. "Just relax, we can sit here forever. I've waited a long time to hold you, Lee."

She began to breathe deeply again. "It's terrifying. I black out, I have memory lapses, some days I can't remember at all, the day I fell—that's how I hurt my leg—Wolf said I had no idea who he was . . ." She huddled tighter against him. "Wolf says he cares about me, he says he wants me to get better, but I know he thinks I'm losing my mind. I can see it in his face, he thinks I'm going mad and he hates me for it. Wolf Koller's wife, better off dead than stuck away in one of our Grunewald hospitals with the other rich, crazy people. The embarrassments to their families." She sighed. "I'm tired, John. I've lived too long, I'm just running down. Wearing out. Time to die."

"You can't die. I've only just found you."

"Oh, John, you haven't learned a thing in twenty years."

"Tell me what your doctors say."

"I told you. They don't know. Lots of tests. Maybe some kind of epilepsy. Dr. Gisevius won't tell me if he really does know something. They give me antidepressants, shoot me up with some other stuff—"

"What does Erika think about your condition?"

"I haven't told her much. I don't want her to worry. She's confused enough." The pulse in her throat flickered. Her eyes searched his face. Her eyes were huge, bottomless. It was dark but for a single lamp lit on Erika's desk.

He kissed her. Her mouth was soft and dry, her lips trembling. She began to move her head away but he whispered no against her mouth and she slowly began to kiss him in return. He ran his tongue along her dry lips and then their tongues were touching and she opened her mouth just enough to allow him inside. They kissed like that for a long time, hours, years, the rest of their lives, and finally he let her face slide back to his chest and the only sound was their breathing.

"John," she whispered, "the time can never be right for us."

"The love that dares not speak its name?" What the hell did he know? Maybe she was right. Maybe it was nuts to think they could be together.

She shook her head, ignoring the joke. "You've seen too many movies. You're different than you were before. But you can't joke the truth away. You mustn't want me." She wiped her eyes. "Aside from everything else, the next time I see you I might not know you, you might be a stranger—"

"Don't worry. I'll remind you."

He felt her shaking against him, sobbing. He kissed her tears. She held tight to his jacket. If she'd done the same thing twenty years ago, their lives would have been entirely different. It might have been a mess but it would have been their mess. It would have been their own personal mess. They'd have been together, he'd have been with Lee. It was all he'd ever wanted. To be with Lee.

While she rested he prowled the apartment, trying to plumb the barren artiness, looking for the essence of his niece. The very absence of warmth, Erika's elaborate distancing of herself from emotion, produced what he supposed she'd refer to as "negative space" where there should have been the evidence of a human being.

In the kitchen he stood before a sleek chrome-framed bulletin board: the only indication of the girl's life in the process of living. Snapshots of friends in summer weather, at a café sitting outdoors, laughing at the camera. He unpinned one of the snapshots, noticed something written on the back of it, put it in his pocket. Someone had scribbled an address and telephone number and circled them twice.

Lee was up and staring out of the window at the real world beyond her daughter's artificial contrivances.

"What do you know about Karl-Heinz, the boyfriend?"

She shook her head. "She hides him. I don't know anything. Beyond his leftist political leanings. East Berliner. Counterculture journalist. He's always investigating something . . . like this SPARTAKUS thing he told Erika about. She resents any questions about him. I gather he's not of our class, as my husband would say. Well, she's young, she's going to do what she wants . . . I tell Wolf to relax and he accuses me of encouraging her in a relationship with what he calls a bum. The truth is, I'm afraid to push it, I don't want to lose her. We talk, but never about boyfriends."

"Not about boyfriends, not about sex, not your illness, not any problems she might have?"

"We seldom talk about dangerous things."

"So you don't talk to anyone about dangerous things . . . or do you?"

"Just you, John, lucky you. Lucky John."

11

RAINMAKER

Cooper was back in Fasanenstrasse, on the far side of the little square where he had met Lee, standing before a plate-glass window trying to see past his reflection. The art gallery was called UDO.

Lee had given him the name and called the owner to let him know that Cooper was on his way. She'd summoned her driver to pick her up at the Bleibtreustrasse address. She was shaky and Cooper hadn't liked leaving her but there was no choice. She had to get home, get off her ankle. Now he was peering past his own reflection into the stark white room. A girl with an equally white face and a severe black haircut that looked like polished ebony was staring back at him. Slowly she raised her white hand, crooked a finger, and beckoned him inside.

When he went in she was gone. He was alone among the glaring white walls, the polished blond wood floor, the white pedestals with Plexiglas cubes on top, a few installations arranged on the floor, one a jumble of industrial fittings, another of naked dolls that had apparently been smashed to bits with a sledgehammer since the hammer was there, too. An occasional eyeball peered up at him. Some huge paintings hung defiantly on the white walls, primary colors in raw wood frames. A diptych was unavoidable: a red wolf falling backwards out of a green building in one frame and in the other the red wolf falling through a black starlit night with blood pouring from his mouth. The blood was an almost luminous cobalt.

The white-skinned, black-haired girl materialized at his side. "Herr Cooper?" He nodded. "Udo," she said, pulling him gently by the arm. *"Bitte . . ."* She tugged him toward a narrow white hallway that was all but invisible until you were in it and left him at a white door in a white wall. Before she left him she pushed the door open, smiled, and began to dematerialize.

Udo would have been scary if he hadn't been so short. He was clad in black leather and buckles, earrings, storm-trooper boots, wire-rimmed glasses with triangular lines in the round frames, hair in rainbow stripes and tied in a ponytail: all in a five-foot package. He spoke in a soft, rather gravelly voice, excellent English, very precise. He looked Cooper up and down, clicked his heels. "You are very large." He paused. "I am less so."

"Good things come in small packages, or so I've heard."

"I disagree. I believe in the Napoleon complex. Short people are always trying to prove how big they are. I'm a perfect example." It was delivered deadpan.

"This getup you're wearing. The only thing missing is a coal-shovel helmet and some barbed wire from Auschwitz for a belt."

"Not very imaginative," Udo sniffed. "But then, neither is this outfit."

"It appeals to the art crowd?"

"Not exactly the cutting edge crowd. My outfit appeals to the moneyed bourgeoisie. They find it a little daring . . . that's all it's for, setting oneself apart in their eyes. A boy needs to be noticed." He thought for a moment, then sat down in a large black leather chair that seemed to swallow him. "I hope to reinvent myself soon—but for now I'm in no danger of being mistaken for one of the solemn gallery types, or for any of my clientele. I have a profitable business. I deal with very conventional people."

"And they like you the way you are," Cooper said.

Udo smiled slowly. "These people expect something wicked. A whiff of sulfur. I give them that. A hint and they let their tiny imaginations do the rest. It's all very innocent really. The self-deception that believes the lie, so to speak. Now, what can I do for you?" He pursed his thick lips and waited.

"Erika Koller."

"Ah, yes, yes. You have but to ask."

"I'm her uncle."

"Yes. Well, good for you. John Cooper."

"Her mother is terribly concerned, as you can imagine."

"As am I." He looked as if he could bear it, though. "I'm not at all sure that this cloak of secrecy about her disappearance is for the best. But it's none of my business, of course. I comply with the Kollers' wishes."

"I'd like you to tell me what you know about her. For instance, how did she come to work here?"

"She simply applied for a job. She is very beautiful. My first requirement. Also a bit warmer and more approachable than the other zombies I've hired. She was a student of art—she's only eighteen, nineteen, isn't she? How much could she know? The answer is, she knew *enough*. And the fact is that somebody around here should know *something* about art—"

"Where did you learn your English?"

"Good, isn't it? New York. Columbia University. Back in the heyday of Area. Limelight. Many low dives. I am not HIV-positive. Why am I telling you this shit? It just doesn't signify."

"Erika. Somebody should know something about art . . . what's that supposed to mean?"

"Erika was good to have here since I obviously know nothing about it and really can't be bothered to learn. It's all bullshit. It doesn't signify. Art galleries have to do with a lot of things, but nothing whatever to do with art. Sex, power, society, media . . . *money*. That is the art world of the late twentieth century, pure corruption and big money— that's why I love it. I love to listen to the tearing of flesh, smell the blood and the jazz, suck up to the money. It's bullshit. A perfect metaphor for today, don't you agree? And I dress up like part Nazi and part queer and the patrons beat a path to my door."

"And Erika felt at home here?"

"Ah, Erika. She's not like any of what I just described. She knows some art and that's nice. She realizes what goes on here is pure theater. But . . . *but* . . . she's *Wolf Koller's daughter!* Her most important qualification, I assure you. She has the connections that are necessary . . . high society, political figures, her father's fellow tycoons, everybody with huge amounts of money and clout. She brings them in. Lawyers in New York have a name for it. Rainmaker. Erika's a beautiful rainmaker. She makes it rain money. She understands that, of course."

"And it's all working out? She's happy here?"

"Yes and no." The leather creaked while he shifted his odd little body. "It certainly worked out for me. People came. They bought. The openings here are social events. So, yes. But Erika wasn't happy with it."

"Not happy?"

"Look, Mr. Cooper, Erika Koller has a brain so how could she be 'happy' in such an environment? And I wouldn't say this to Lise Koller, but Erika is a bit of a flake. Moody, very quiet, you never know what she's thinking. You always have the feeling she's a step and a half from bringing the bloody temple down around your ears . . . she has *values,* you understand? She should never have come to work here. She would have left soon, I'm sure. And who could blame her?"

"What sorts of things did she have on her mind?"

"I was educated in a Jesuit school in France and I can tell you this, she'd make a good Jesuit. Always mortifying herself over everything—the plight of the poor, the starving children God knows where, the injustice of just about everything. She went through a period of visiting the concentration camps and she was depressed for days. Most of us have heard enough about the war, it's ancient history. Yes, *those* Germans were awful, we agree, but it was over a long time ago. Okay?"

"Whatever you say."

"But not Erika. The war was yesterday for Erika. She can hear the doors on the cattle cars heading east, she can still hear those doors clanging shut, the cries of the little children on their way to the ovens. She hadn't been born yet, her *mother* had just been born in *Minnesota!* But Erika can hear them!" He yanked on the ponytail so hard his head jerked sideways. "She worries about the poor East Germans having to deal with a new world in which they're free but pretty low on the ladder. She worries about the immigrants and the hostels and all this hatred, these thugs, the poor Bosnians and the Turks and the Gypsies. She is a victim of an overdeveloped conscience in my view. Conscience is a luxury I definitely cannot afford. I mean, did you see the crap I sell out there? And the prices? Ridiculous! It's all I can do to keep a straight face. Beyond that I don't know much about Erika. She withholds herself. A kind of Vestal Virgin. You know the kind of woman. Girl. Whatever you want to call her."

"The boyfriend. I understand she has a boyfriend. What's his story?"

"To begin with, Erika isn't the sort of girl who has lots of boyfriends. I wouldn't be surprised if I was told authoritatively that she's the only virgin her age in Germany. This boyfriend . . . I met him a couple of times here at the gallery. Another breast-beater, morally pure. Every-thing was politics. Life is the class struggle—nothing else. Always pro-testing one thing or another." He glanced at his watch. "And now I have a client coming in. I must go sell some of this junk."

"Did Wolf Koller and his wife come to some of these opening parties you held here?"

"Absolutely. That was the point, wasn't it? Lise even convinced him to buy a couple of pieces. Dr. Gisevius . . . some of Wolf Koller's new-rich tycoon friends."

"When you say new-rich you mean . . . ?"

"Well, new meaning post-1935 to them, I suppose. Old money goes back much further than that. But a great many people came into money once the Nazis came to power. And Wolf Koller multiplied the family fortune in the years since the war. The German Economic Miracle —he was one of the big beneficiaries. I guess you would call Wolf Koller's money both new and new-new. You see what I mean. Now, please, I must kick you out of here. I'm striving for new-new-rich status myself, you see." He was grinning like a conspirator when Cooper left.

12

KINGMAKER

Cooper took a cab back to the Kreuzberg apartment building and let himself in with keys Beate had given him in the morning. The place was empty. He found a beer in the refrigerator and took it and a couple of Oreo cookies and sat down on one of the low couches on the lower floor. There were more blown-up photographs on the walls. As far as he could judge, she was a very good photographer. He figured she had a lot of nerve. And her own agenda. What was her role in this whole complicated business? She was too smart not to have an angle.

For one thing, there was the picture he'd taken from the bulletin board in Erika's apartment. Beate sitting beside Erika, one blond and spiky, the other dark-haired with enormous doe eyes, and on the other side of Erika a solemn-looking young man with a scruffy, thin beard and pointed features. The girls were laughing, it was a sunlit scene outdoors, and in the background the bombed-out ruin of the great Kaiser Wilhelm Church loomed darkly. At the foot of the Ku'damm. *Friends.* Beate, Erika, and Karl-Heinz. Beate's arm draped around Erika's shoulder. He looked up at the photos on the walls, back at the snapshot. Politically, the three of them had a lot in common.

When Beate came banging up the stairs and into the room she called his name, her face flushed with cold, the motorcycle helmet wet with rain. Her eyes were bright. "I'm so glad you're here! I've had a horrible day, everyone's been mean to me, and I've been wondering what's been happening with you—how's Lise? Is there any news of Erika?" She had thrown her backpack down, shucked off her jacket, and was in the kitchen getting the cork out of a bottle of white wine. She came back, took his arm, and led him upstairs to the sitting room with the slanted ceilings. "The Chancellor is coming to Berlin, probably to-morrow, to consult with city officials and the, the, what do you call them? The top people—"

"Power brokers, heavy hitters—"

"No, it's big-something—"

"Bigwigs?"

"That's it. He'll talk to the bigwigs! And the biggest of all, Wolf Koller . . . about the Nazi violence. It's out of control . . . the politi-cians in Bonn went crazy today, yelling and shouting—it was supposed to be a debate. There's talk about a huge anti-Nazi demonstration . . . but a new report on the economy was issued today, it's even worse than was expected." She sighed deeply and stuck out one leg at him. "Boot," she said. "Give it a pull." While he tugged first at one boot, then the other, she looked at her watch. "Now tell me everything."

He told her the externals of the story, leaving out what had passed between him and Lee that was personal. He mentioned the word "SPARTAKUS," told her of Wolf's fear of Erika, his fear of Lee's some-how saying something to embarrass him publicly. He'd begun to get a picture of Erika and her life. Karl-Heinz interested him. He was next on the list. But he wasn't going to be easy to find, from what little Cooper had gathered.

"Your turn," he said. "Who was mean to you?"

"Oh, don't get me started. Those TV bastards can't stand having a woman around who cares about her job. It pisses them off because I'm not a cynical hack or a corporate snake like they are . . . but enough of that. Today—yes. There was a luncheon and a conference at the Kempin-ski—you're a rich American, I'm surprised that you didn't book a room there. Scotch and water, fifteen dollars in the lobby bar."

"You haven't told me what kind of rate I'm getting here, have you?"

"The conference was set up by the bigwigs, announcing a commit-tee to take a serious look at the Nazi arrival in Berlin. Hurray! A serious look! They announced the visit of the Chancellor, they're setting up a fund for the help of the families of the dead Turks and Gypsies and the dead cop, as well."

"Who are these bigwigs?"

"I'll get to that. I dubbed a cassette of my report and brought it home. It's edited by someone else and I want to see how badly it's butchered." She shoved the cassette into the VCR. "It's in German but it's what I've just told you. Your job is to look at the pictures. I'll translate when there's something worth it." She punched the play button.

It was a conference room immediately after an establishing shot of the main entrance of the Hotel Bristol Kempinski. Several men in dark suits were arriving. Then Beate's voice cut in while the men sat around the conference table, camera panning their faces.

"Right there! That's him." She backed the tape up, then let it shuttle forward, then froze the frame. "Nothing ever happens here unless he's involved . . . and now he's behind this committee. He's giving the government absolute hell, warning that the Chancellor had better get involved because this was a German problem, not just Berlin's . . . blaming the police for not reacting more quickly, calling for a new get-tough policy, calling for right-thinking Germans to take a stand and demand some order—" She jabbed a long finger at the screen. "Wolf Koller. A kingmaker. Or in this case, a king-unmaker. It's going to be an interesting show when the Chancellor shows up. Wolf's going to try to remake Chancellor Glock in his own image. If Glock doesn't mind becoming a puppet, then Wolf will turn him into something . . . *someone*. He could keep Glock in office forever, one way or another."

"But if Wolf's one of the anti-Nazis, one of the good guys, then why does Erika hate him so? Whose side is Erika on?"

"Karl-Heinz's. Now, first, I didn't say he was a good guy. And daughters can hate fathers for rather less public reasons, don't you think? Little girls start out worshiping their fathers and then when they're discovered to be mortals with feet of rocks, no, whatever the saying is—"

"Clay."

"Maybe Erika hates the idea of power and influence, maybe she hates the idea of insiders . . . well, her father is the ultimate insider, all power and influence. He's the man the politicians always consulted."

"If we can find out why she hates him maybe we'll get a lead on where she might have gone—don't ask me to explain my reasoning. I'm an amateur at this—"

"I'd say you're taking your detective work pretty seriously." She was teasing him.

"Look, somebody tried to kill me back home. Erika tried to kill herself and has disappeared—all that concentrates the mind most wonderfully."

"It would have just scared me off. So why didn't you just say no, leave me out of it?"

"My sister. That's all. Just my sister."

"It's funny—I nearly told you not to come. When you called me from New York, I thought, no, he should stay there, or if you came you'd better not include me. Really. I'm not kidding you."

"But why?"

"Remember the evening we spent in Boston?"

"Of course."

"And I left your place, went back to my hotel in Copley Square. There was someone waiting for me when I got to my room . . . it was terrifying, John . . . a man, just sitting there, waiting for me—"

"What the hell did he want? Did you know him?"

"All he wanted was to ask me some questions. He wanted to know about you—were you going to Germany, why were you going, what did you tell me of your plans, why had I come to see you—"

"And?"

"I told him the truth. I didn't know what I'd gotten into and—"

"Who was he?"

"Well . . . it was the man who came to Boston to see you, he wanted to buy your—"

"Kilroy! Clint Kilroy." Cooper paused, about to finish the last Oreo. Finally he put it back on the plate. He watched her take it in her long slim fingers. She pulled the two halves apart with a screwing motion, lifted the half with the white filling attached. Slowly she licked the white filling from the brown disk, her eyes on him.

"Look," he said at last, "I don't know where Kilroy fits into this. But I'm wasting time thinking about him until I know more. Seeing him on TV in Boston linked him to Koller or Koller Industries somehow, but how? Is Wolf Koller interested in me? Does he know Lee was trying to get word to me? We just don't know. Tell me more about Wolf Koller. Where does Koller's money come from?"

"Well, it's not just the chemical industry, or the transportation business, or all the investments abroad—probably the biggest single part of it is real estate. He's one of the biggest landowners in Berlin. Maybe the biggest. He's one of the major forces behind the development of the Potsdamer Platz. It's a huge area just beyond the Brandenburg Gate in the East, just to the right when you go through the Gate. It will be the biggest real estate development in Europe. People used to say the Potsdamer Platz was the center of Europe . . . Koller and others say it will be again. Now it's just a big, muddy, empty field. It was the heart of the Nazi empire. The Reichschancellery was there, the Führerbunker. Hitler died there when the Red Army had reached the tunnels leading in toward the bunker. It was the center of the Nazi world. Well, it's going to rise again, the commercial heart of Europe. Skyscrapers, luxury housing, concert halls, the works. All within a five-minute walk of the Reichstag that Hitler didn't quite burn down, the Reichstag where the central government of Germany is supposed to be returning by the year 2000." She took a deep breath. "More than anyone else, Wolf Koller is the future of Germany."

"But what about his past?" Cooper said. "What's his history? I need to get my bearings."

"I don't know all the details. His father was a judge or a professor . . . But we can find out."

"Let's do that."

She was throwing her jacket back on, her face lit from within again, the bad mood fallen away. He put his hand on her arm, held her in place.

"And one other thing, Beate." His nerves were doing the rhumba: seeing Lee had turned him inside out and he'd fought it all day, tried to ignore it while he interviewed Udo at the gallery, tried to keep it under control while carrying on a civilized conversation with this woman. He was trying to present the calm exterior, the mask he'd been wearing for twenty years. And the mask was slipping. "We don't know each other very well, do we? You may think I'm a nice, easygoing guy, kind of a sweetheart, pretty confused and saddled with a fairly weird past—"

"I don't think you're a sweetheart. Not yet. But you have possibilities." She grinned slowly. "For an older man."

"Well, the truth is a little different. You've been seeing only one side of me, I'm afraid. Because at heart I can be a very nasty man. I learned how from an expert. Fellow called Olaf Peterson. He's the kind of man who does what's required. I can be that kind of man when I need to be. It's all coming back to me. How to save myself, how to trust nobody . . . Now, I want you to cut the bullshit and tell me what you know about this Karl-Heinz character. Everything."

"I told you, I don't know much." She was staring at him as if she were confronting a dog that just might turn on her. He'd surprised her.

He kept his voice low and calm. "Don't fuck with me, okay?" Her face registered something he couldn't quite identify: it wasn't good. He hadn't seen it on her face before. "I can very easily go back to blaming you for just being another Hun. Take a look at this very chummy picture of you and Erika and Karl-Heinz." He waved the snapshot in front of her face. "Direct from Erika's bulletin board. You don't know these people slightly, as you suggested. You know them well. Erika's a close, very close pal of yours, isn't she? And since she never talked to her mother about personal things, who would she talk to? Maybe you . . . maybe her pal Beate? I think so. So don't hold out on me. God help you if you know where she is—"

"Maybe you are the ugly American," she said softly.

"It's an outdated concept. Everybody is now ugly *to* Americans. It's the world's favorite social game. Well, frankly, my dear, I don't give a damn. I truly don't. I just want you to level with me." He stood up, adrenaline pumping. "What's the big mystery about Karl-Heinz? I've got an address and a telephone number. Do you have anything to tell me? Is he dangerous? Is he crazy? Will he know where Erika is? Is he a lovesick nitwit who hacked her up and stuffed her in the trunk of his VW? Could she be hiding out with him? Should I just call him? Show up at his place? Are you listening? I got to Berlin alive—I can't just sit around and turn into a target—somebody wants to kill me!"

"You have his address?"

"Erika wrote it on the back of the snapshot I found on her bulletin board."

"Look, I'm not trying to give you a hard time, okay? Try to keep your nasty streak under control. You've only been here thirty-six hours."

"You've been warned," he said.

"All right. Do you feel better?" Her blue-gray eyes were colder now, but she'd taken his hand. "Now let's go find out about Wolf Koller. I've got someone you should meet."

13

ARCHIVIST

They went down green corridors, then entered the gray zone accompanied by a hum, a sense of electronic life pulsing quietly, sucking everything that mattered out of the ether and ultimately doling it out to the waiting public ear. All the news that was fit to be seen and heard, well edited, given some pizzazz, topped off with a weatherman wearing a dumb tie. TV was TV, universal, all one world. The lights made his eyes burn.

Two women were taking a coffee break, giggling about something sexual—it was in their eyes. They waved to Beate, who pressed on, then ushered him into a smallish office with a couple of computers, a blue face and a green face, giving off too much heat. Maybe it was the printers giving off heat. There were metal shelves loaded down with videocassette boxes, stacks of unboxed tapes, and computer printouts dripping like hanging gardens. A woman sat drinking coffee, smoking a cigarette, staring at the green screen, scrolling through endless listings. She was pale and dumpling-shaped with a broad, innocently curious face. Mousy brown hair a couple of decades out of date, drab cardigan, because she obviously didn't care. It was possible she hadn't been out of this room in a couple of decades. Cooper felt sweat blooming on his forehead.

"Bruni is the Keeper at the Gate of the Past."

"How mythological," Cooper murmured. "She doesn't sweat, either."

"Bruni, this is my American friend, John Cooper. We need to access your memory."

The woman finally looked up from the screen as if she hated to ditch a pal. She shook hands with Cooper, all business. "Beate," she said. "Nice work on the hostel story." She spoke in German but he was pretty sure that was what she'd said. Cooper looked at Beate.

"I'll translate but only the parts that matter." A moment later she said: "She says she can't remember what she had for breakfast but she can find out by looking in the garbage can. She has no memory, she only accesses The Memory. She says she picks through the garbage can until she finds the right rubbish."

"A philosopher and a poet. Tell her we're looking for the works on Wolf Koller."

Beate spoke, then listened, then turned back to Cooper. "Any names we can connect to his?"

"How about his father, Erhard Koller. And Lise, too."

"Ah. The judge." Bruni nodded and began punching the keyboard and the blue screen began jumping and stretching and bopping. She kept chatting with Beate, smoking her cigarette, knitting her brow and squinting at the screen. Then she began to speak in perfect English. Beate did a double take and raised her eyebrows. Bruni tapped the ash into a coffee cup and said: "Beate has a habit of thinking she's the only one with any brains, Mr. Cooper. She's frequently wrong." She laughed and Beate made a face at her. Bruni continued.

"The father, Erhard Koller, will be difficult. There wasn't TV back then, of course. Lots of newsreel footage but it was on film that's degraded now. Besides, most of it was lost during the war and the Occupation. A lot was destroyed 'accidentally on purpose,' as you say—too many people were running around trying to edit history into the story they wanted told. Much of the film was incriminating, guilt by association, you know . . . The Allies, the Russians particularly, the Nazi-hunters, the war crimes commissions, they were all looking for evidence in those days —they wanted to know who knew Hitler, the courtiers, the henchmen, the flunkies. If the wrong man was in the picture, important people would make sure the film got lost . . . It must have driven the hunters crazy not to be able to put people into pictures where they wanted them —you saw the movie *Zelig* by Woody Allen? Just think if they could have created historical film the way he did in that picture." She lit another cigarette, staring at the screen.

"Nowadays, of course, we keep everything. Germany's a nation of record-keepers—somebody must have said that at some point." Beate was standing with her arms crossed, watching the screen, watching the printer purging itself of all the stored-up trivia. Bruni was going on. "You want to find out about Erhard Koller, you should go to the museum at Wannsee, the Wansee Conference House where Heydrich and Eichmann and the others decided to go ahead with killing all the Jews. I'm a Jew, by the way—I know a lot about the Nazis. My family's history. And I'm learning more all the time. Wannsee is a monument to record-keeping. They have lists kept by the people running the camps, meticulous records of Jews' belongings, a twisted spectacle frame, a blue fountain pen, a worn leather wallet with a tear at the corner, so on and so forth, all the details noted as if they were ever going to get any of the stuff back . . . Okay, we can print this stuff. Now we'll go find the cassettes. Everything's on new cassettes now."

When Bruni came back she racked one cassette after another into the VCR and they saw snippets of film and tape, a mosaic of Wolf Koller's public life, even his marriage to Lise Brendel. Wolf Koller with a variety of politicians, Wolf Koller playing tennis, Wolf Koller at a big tennis match talking to Jimmy Connors and Steffi Graf, Wolf Koller the civic leader somewhere with Gorbachev, then with Ronald Reagan at the Bitburg ceremony during the blowup about the American President visiting an SS cemetery, Wolf Koller dedicating an imposing building, Wolf Koller the businessman greeting a variety of junkets led by Mexicans, Japanese, Chinese, Arabs . . . And most recently Wolf shaking hands with a smiling Boris Yeltsin, celebrating some investment venture or other, a meeting of Wolf and a couple of generals who were helping with the distribution of foodstuffs using army trucks, a smiling Wolf shaking hands with a stern-looking man in a wheelchair: "That's Egon Rossovich," Bruni said, and Beate added: "He used to be head of the KGB. Some sort of accident crippled him. He's been lying low for a while. Here he is, congratulating our boy on some big deal . . . Wolf knows everybody."

Bruni looked up hopefully when she'd ejected the last cassette.

Cooper shook his head.

Beate said: "Go back a little further."

Bruni began on the keyboard again. Cooper and Beate went into a nearby office and poured coffee for the three of them. She sniffed and made a face. "Burned. It's probably been sitting there for hours. I'm still mad at you, you know. That wasn't a nice speech you made at my place. You don't know who your friends are."

"I told you. It was a warning, not a speech."

She took two of the cups and carried them back to Bruni's lair.

Bruni showed them what she had. Nothing. Then she said: "Let's try friends, business associates, anyone Koller worked with. Sometimes you find things in the damnedest places."

"I don't know who his friends and associates—hey, wait a minute." He was staring at the screen. "Jesus Christ, the mother lode! Look, that's Gunter Brendel!"

Beate followed his pointing finger. "Brendel?"

"My sister's first husband! He died twenty years ago, not long before she married Koller—"

"You're sure it's Brendel?" Beate's fingernail was tapping the screen.

"Right there, looking just like he did when I knew him!" Bruni had frozen the picture. She backed it up and ran several seconds of tape.

"But this is a Wolf Koller tape," Beate said. "Where is *he*?"

Cooper couldn't understand the German being spoken on the tape but it was obviously coverage of something being celebrated. Brendel was being congratulated by other business executives while the voice-over droned on.

Beate let out a little cry of excitement, grabbing his arm, poking at the screen.

"There he is. There's Wolf Koller!" She put her fingertip on a man in the background, as if it were a replay of the moment they had found Kilroy in the Boston clip. "John"—she was clutching his arm again—"they knew each other . . . they were partners in business—"

"And they each married my sister. In sequence. It's a small world."

Beate regarded the picture, once more frozen on the screen. "Body language. Looks like Brendel was the senior partner. You're a genius, John. Well, someone's a genius . . . Bruni is!" Her face fell slightly. "But what does it mean?"

"I'll tell you later."

They went through a half hour's worth of paper files, Koller biographical material that indicated in clippings from newspapers and magazines the extent of his real estate empire, his chemical and steel holdings, the banks he controlled, the transportation companies.

Finally Beate thanked Bruni and led Cooper back to her own office, a large cubicle. She sat behind the desk and looked past the video playback equipment and computer terminal. "So, what does the late Gunter Brendel have to do with anything happening now?"

Cooper propped his feet up on a box of videotapes. "It's all part of what happened the first time I came to Germany, when I wound up in a hive of Nazis. Gunter Brendel was one of them. He was deeply involved in the Fourth Reich. Now I'm back, and I discover that Wolf Koller was Gunter Brendel's partner . . . and two things occur to me. Two bad things.

"Like, one, I was up to my neck in the murder of Gunter Brendel. I didn't do it but it wouldn't have happened if I hadn't been around. So, I figure Wolf Koller must know about me and my part in the screwing up of the Nazi plan back then. Koller was close to Brendel—he just about had to know. He was probably at the party outside Munich that night, the night Brendel got killed and Olaf Peterson and I took Lee away from them—"

"You *kidnapped* her?"

"Well, you know . . . we *rescued* her, like Cary Grant carrying Ingrid Bergman down the staircase and out of Claude Rains's house in *Notorious*. You know—"

"I know. Shit happens. I read the T-shirt."

"It's a long story. She went back to them in the end. The point is, Koller is going to be on the alert when he finds out I'm back in Germany. And I'm hanging about his wife . . . He's not going to like it. Maybe he holds a grudge." He smiled thinly.

She laughed. "I wouldn't be surprised. You said two things occurred to you—"

"One of them's personal."

"Oh. None of my business. Well, you're saying that Koller was a Nazi then and therefore he's still a Nazi?"

"I don't have any idea, not really. But there's a nasty little Nazi movement going on, who's to say there aren't some nasty big Nazis involved. I know, don't say it, he's Mr. Berlin, Mr. Concerned Citizen, Mr. Potsdamer Platz—" Cooper turned and pointed a finger at her: "That's it! He's Mr. Berlin . . . so here's a question about old Wolf that hasn't crossed my mind until just this minute—Does he want to be Chancellor someday? Is that shot on the table? Is he going to shove Glock out of the way and grab the top job for himself?"

Beate was shaking her head. "Never in a million years. For Koller to become Chancellor would be a *demotion*—he *owns* the Chancellor.

Koller wants to own things, run things, he wants to write the script and then direct the production . . . and he would never, ever leave himself open to the vote of the rabble. Do you see? Koller can't be voted out of office—"

"Yes, but he seems to be so much in the spotlight. No different than a politician. You'd think people would know if he had dirty little secrets—"

"No, they wouldn't. No one in the press covers Wolf Koller the way they cover a politician like Glock. For one thing, they're afraid of him. And they're certainly not afraid of this Chancellor or any other Chancellor. But if you know what's good for you, you write about Wolf Koller very carefully. Besides, he's a kind of hero to much of the public. That's just the way it is.

"Look," Beate said suddenly. It was almost eleven and she was hungry. "You like Luciano Pavarotti?"

"What a question. Of course I like Pavarotti."

"Good. We'll go to his favorite restaurant in Berlin. Maybe we can think better on a full stomach."

"And maybe you can level with me about your pal, Karl-Heinz." And Erika, too, he thought to himself.

Or maybe she already had.

14

MANTOVANI

The restaurant was called Mantovani, which to an American recalled an extremely romantic orchestra conductor of the fifties and sixties but in Berlin seemed to have a lot to do with operatic tenors. The photographs of Pavarotti and Domingo and others were everywhere, blown up, their smiles engulfing the diners, and the sound of opera in the background never stopped.

Beate ordered dinner for both of them, and they were too tired to talk until they'd started to eat. Then she looked up at him as if she expected the worst. Her clear blue eyes had a weary patina of gray, and she was smiling by effort of will.

"Look," he said, worn out himself, the jet lag creeping up on him, "I need you to be honest with me. My sister is half mad with worry about Erika . . . Is this kid alive? Is she just a body in a ditch somewhere? I don't know Erika, but I see what this is doing to Lee. And the snapshot tells me you could give me more information than you have. I don't care why—you've got to cut it out." He rubbed his eyes and was surprised when they didn't plop out into the linguini and white clam sauce.

She was chewing on fettuccine with thirty or forty kinds of cheese. She kept chewing, making little waiting motions with her hands. "Stuck my tongue to my teeth. Very cheesy. *Quel fromage!*" She sipped some wine. Pavarotti hit a high note. "Okay. Yes, I know them both better than I've implied. But I don't know you. Or I didn't. Now I do and I think you're okay. I can trust you. We're dealing with Wolf Koller here . . . and the fact is you're a member of the family. You probably haven't thought of it that way, have you? But to this particular German, *the first thing you are is Wolf Koller's brother-in-law.* I have to go very carefully before I take the wrong step with Wolf Koller's brother-in-law—"

"This is crazy. I'm not a member of the—"

"But you are! You could have been on Koller's side in some plot of his . . . but that was just me being wary of the unknown. Now I think Erika would have liked you. She would have trusted you." She half-blinded him with the smile, the teeth. She was overcoming her weariness.

"You can trust me, all right."

"I'll tell you what I know, but it's not a lot. You know that Karl-Heinz calls himself a journalist and I guess he is. Left-winger, East Berlin underground. He's a creature of the night. Do you understand?"

"Sure. Film noir. Lives his whole life at night. Dark, rainy. *Out of the Past.* That might be the best one."

"Everything is a movie for you."

"No. Everything is a movie. Period. If it's not in the movies, people have never done it. I promise you."

She fought it out with her dinner. "It's just too much cheese." She kept swallowing until the mouthful was gone. "He's an idealist. Communism was all he had to believe in and now it's in the wastebasket. His father was in the police. STASI, I think. Karl-Heinz's whole life was spent learning how monstrous the West is. Did you know that? Growing up over there, the kids were indoctrinated with the idea that *West* Germany was the Nazis, the *bad* Germans, and after that, that they were the puppets of the United States, which was even worse. Corrupt, immoral, believing in nothing at all but the power of money. That's Karl-Heinz.

"Erika. Okay. Erika had a secret life. She could *afford* to have a secret life. She could *afford* Karl-Heinz. She could *afford* anything. She could afford the luxury of a very political life—there were no little realities of everyday life to stop her. That's why I worry about her. She's a perfect candidate to become, well, a terrorist. Very privileged background, lots of resentment toward her father, more than her share of German guilt—it's practically the profile of a terrorist."

"So you're going to tell me somebody kidnapped her and is brainwashing her into becoming a terrorist—like maybe old Karl-Heinz? Is he a terrorist? Is that why he's so hard to find all the time?"

"No, no, not Karl-Heinz. I'm talking about Erika. I'm just saying she's a typical Patty Hearst kind of kid. She's hyper about the Nazis, hyper about the neo-Nazis, she's over the edge. Before Erika met Karl-Heinz, she had no idea what to do with all her anger. She had no idea how to become a political activist—it would have been a joke. People would have thought she was trying out the new fashion, the latest trend, no one would have taken her seriously . . . Karl-Heinz was the answer to her prayers. He enabled her to become political . . . *Plus*, he knew a lot about *her family*. That was the key. Erika said Karl-Heinz told her about her grandfather, Erhard Koller . . . no, she didn't tell me *what* he told her. I learned that tonight from Bruni. He also told Erika things about her father but she wouldn't tell me any of it. And that's the truth."

"What about his father in the East Berlin police? Could he have dug up the Brendel-Koller connection?"

"I don't think so," she said. "How would a cop in the East have known about the most secret Nazi plan of all? No, he wouldn't. Whatever Karl-Heinz told Erika about her father it wasn't ancient history."

"What I want to know is what triggered her attempt to kill herself. Did she take drugs? Was she depressed enough to kill herself? And where is she if she's alive? Where would she go?"

"She wasn't into drugs at all. The thought would have horrified her. Depressed? She was always sort of depressed. She'd go to these demonstrations with Karl-Heinz, I told her it was dangerous, then she got beaten up at that last one—"

"Are you sure you didn't see her that night? Maybe you covered that demonstration—"

"I did. You know that. You saw the tape."

"—and then you went to see her the next day, after she'd been to work and gone home feeling crummy, maybe you were with her, trying to help her out, and she tried to kill herself in the bathroom while you were having a cup of coffee and . . . I don't know . . . And you helped her disappear . . . I was just wondering." He shrugged. "That's all."

"You're such an insulting bastard! You need me, may I remind you of that?" She was brushing the pale blond hair out of her eyes, which were flashing danger signals. "You still think I'm lying to you?"

"You might think you're helping her by hiding her. But my sister is in bad shape . . . I'm not going to hold it against you. Trust me."

"You've got to make up your mind whose side you're on, Yank. I'm not the enemy."

"I'm just trying to find Erika. Doing the best I can. When did you last talk to her?"

"Well . . . you're right, she did call me that night. I was asleep—

my days and nights get all confused, with my schedule. She called me when she got home from the riot, I don't know where she was, I don't know if Karl-Heinz was with her, she was pretty upset, she said she'd gotten hit in the head and she thought he was hurt much worse—"

"And you haven't seen her or talked to her since."

"That's right. I should have made certain I did, I ought to have seen her right then. I didn't."

"And you haven't seen him since?"

"No, I wouldn't have seen him. Except through her."

"Didn't you pick up on her state of mind?"

"She was upset. Did I think she might try to kill herself? Of course not." She motioned to the waiter for their checks.

As they were leaving the restaurant, he said, "Look, I haven't got a hotel room yet."

She gave him a pitying look. "Oh, Cooper, Cooper," she sighed. "It's okay. My place is headquarters. I can stand it. I've gotten used to the idea that you're a hard man to get rid of. But don't push the cross-examining. Who knows what I might do to you once you fall asleep?"

"I'll sleep with my eyes open. I saw a guy in a movie do it. *Designing Woman* with Gregory Peck and Bacall—the sleeper was a punchy fighter with a smashed nose. Lauren Bacall looks at him and says migod, he doesn't have a nose. And Peck says sure he does, it's on the inside."

That made her laugh and, looking at her, just for the moment he forgot his sister. Just for the moment.

Werner Paulus was sound asleep when the call came through from Max Adler. It took a few moments for him to get the message straight. Adler's voice was shaking; there was a great deal of noise in the background, voices and sirens and God only knew what else.

"Chief, you've got to get over here, Zoo Station, there's a helluva mess. Two bombs took out a bunch of cops. Remote control . . . it's a nightmare, Chief. And you won't believe who did it . . . they left their calling card." The Chief of Detectives' voice was being drowned out by the sound of ambulances and fire trucks and police vans.

Paulus couldn't say he'd been expecting this particular kind of violence but, on the other hand, he realized he wasn't surprised. But Adler hadn't told him who was responsible. When he got to the scene—

well, he could have guessed the identity of the bombers for a thousand years and he still wouldn't have had it right.

From where he stood now in the bright floodlights that had been erected in the aftermath, he saw the general areas where the two bombs had exploded. Walls and floors had shattered, masonry and twisted metal lay helter-skelter across the broad area, one stairway was blocked with rubble. All train service had been stopped and transportation in Berlin was going to be screwed up for days. Track had been blown up, broken glass and railings and . . . it was hard for him to realize that somehow, magically, the station's main building hadn't simply collapsed. Proof of both God and Satan in the same event.

What had happened? It was a matter of putting together various bits and pieces of information. There had been a call to the police, word of a bomb that was set to go off at the Zoo Station at midnight, which gave them nearly an hour to find it and defuse it. Bomb experts and a couple of vans full of cops arrived, worried, on top alert because of all the other violence that had been hanging about like clouds of poisonous gas the past week or so. While they'd cleared the area and pissed off the late-night travelers and set up emergency medical systems in case they needed it, the dogs and the bomb squad had found the suspicious package . . . and as they bent to their work it had been detonated. Two dogs and four men had been killed more or less instantly. It was a fragmentation device and the lethal contents had sliced their way through the entire length and width of the area, taking down nine more cops and several civilians who'd been making nuisances of themselves hanging about for a view of what was going on. Once the tremendous cracking blast had just begun to fade there had been a second in a stairwell that had taken out the side of the building, the stairway itself, and a large chunk of the tracks it was leading to. Four people outside Zoo Station were seriously injured by the rain of debris.

It had been a massacre.

The bodies of the dead and wounded had been taken away and the streets outside were clogged with television news vans and reporters and all the newspaper people and the photographers and soon Max Adler was going to have to make a statement as to casualties and what kind of explosive device had been used. And why? Who might have done it? What was Berlin coming to? How was order going to be restored? How could Berliners go about their lives with some degree of safety? Did the authorities have a plan? Was it an IRA bombing? Could it have had anything to do with Queen Elizabeth's impending visit to Germany?

The questions would go on and on and Werner Paulus was devoutly thankful that he wouldn't have to answer them.

Even in all the rubble, he could see ugly smears of blood, bits of clothing, a forlorn shoe; a forgotten finger lay among cinders where he'd seen a technician carrying away an arm clad in a police uniform. The techies and the lab people and the scene-of-crime teams were all hard at work, trying to erase the horror of the event from their minds by means of plain, hard work. The smell was overpowering. It reminded Werner Paulus of the war.

It was terrorism but not entirely: the targets had been the police. They were proving how easily they could kill, how helpless the police and everyone else really were. Someone in the Zoo Station, watching the police preparing to defuse the bomb, had pushed the button. One of those hangers-on, someone in the crowd, faceless and deadly. The stakes had been raised, a line had been crossed. These victims weren't immigrants. These victims were representatives of authority, of the people themselves. The police represented Order. Order had been made a joke.

It was chaos, from the mouth of hell, intended only to destabilize society.

That was all bad enough, but there was more. This act of terror had come swirling out of the shadows of the past like a river of blood. The act had been signed, with a handful of red roses thrown across the rubble by the stairway, the signature of one of the groups that had spread murder and terror years ago, the signature of the Dorfmann gang.

It took Paulus back to his own days as chief.

Max Adler had come over and stood beside him, hands in his pockets. Staring at the mess. "They've gone too bloody far, that's what they've done." He blew his nose, which had been irritated by the fumes and the gritty dust. "But the red roses. I don't understand that, Chief. The trademark."

"Dorfmann . . . Rafaela Dorfmann."

"Yes, of course. I understand that much. But it doesn't compute. I mean, they're all dead . . . they've been dead for years and years."

"Makes you wonder, doesn't it, Max?"

15

FÜHRERBUNKER

The next morning Cooper woke to the sounds of Chet Baker singing "You'd Be So Nice to Come Home To." Beate was messing around in the kitchen. He smelled the coffee. By the time he tottered to the pine table she was reading the morning papers, eating sausage on black bread, scribbling notes. The coffeepot stood by his plate and cup.

Without looking up she said: "Busy day. The Mayor, the Chancellor, hearings on the skinheads. Queen Elizabeth is on her way and there will be the inevitable protests. Elvis was seen last night at Zoo Station."

"Elvis. No kidding." He poured himself a cup of coffee and took up a knife to slice some sausage. "I need you to do me a favor before you go. I'm going to try to get hold of Karl-Heinz. The number on the back of the snapshot. If he's there—which I don't expect—I may need you as an interpreter. If he's not there, I'm going to go looking for him over there, starting at the office of the paper he writes for. Assuming they have an office." He piled slices of sausage on the bread and added some strawberry preserves. "Okay?"

"He speaks English."

"East Germans, too? I thought it was probably a sin over there."

"In Karl-Heinz's case, the better to know the enemy. The Western Devil. But I'll hang around while you call." She reached across the table and poured him the last of the coffee, then got up and started rinsing dishes. With her back turned, clattering dishes, she said: "What are you looking at?"

"Your behind. And very nice it is, too."

"Hmmmph. I knew it." She turned around. She wasn't smiling but the blue eyes were. "Make the call, Cooper."

"What call was that?" What was he doing? Did he think he was funny? He was old enough to be her father. "I can't remember anything. I was looking at your behind and what can I say, my mind went blank." He wondered if he was laying an egg. Yes, probably. "Look, I'm trying to show you my playful, winsome side. Nothing about the Fatherland."

"I wondered what it was. Winsome. That's a new word for me."

"It means cute."

"Like my behind."

"That's it exactly. A very winsome behind."

"Are you going to make your call?"

"Yes, ma'am. Right away. Coming up."

A man answered the telephone.

"I don't speak German. But I'm trying to find Karl-Heinz. Is he there?"

"I don't know any Karl-Heinz."

"Wait, don't hang up." He caught her eye. Beate was listening on some funny little European thing, an earpiece attached to the phone with its own cord. She was nodding: *It's him.* "Look, if you see Karl-Heinz, tell him it's about Erika. Tell him I have information about Erika. I need to talk to him. He'll want to talk to me. You got that? Erika." There was a long pause. "You still there, pal?"

"Who are you?"

"He doesn't know me. I've come all the way from Boston. I'm Erika's uncle. Look . . . where does he hang out? Any place I might run into him? Believe me, it's important."

"He might be willing to meet you out of doors. Maybe."

"Okay. Name a place. Anywhere at all, I'll be there."

"An open space. Do you understand?"

"Sure, sure, but where?"

"Do you know Potsdamer Platz?"

"I'll find it."

"It's big. Come through the Brandenburger Tor. To the right. It's a big empty field. There's a circus at the far end. Walk to the field. Behind an apartment block. Coffeehouse and restaurant on ground level.

Muddy field. There is a mound at the circus end of the field. You under-stand?"

"Yes."

"If he wants to see you, he'll be there. You wait. Karl-Heinz will be watching."

"Okay."

"Come alone. He's very nervous. Understand?"

"Right. Wait, hold on—what time?"

"Five o'clock."

That was it. Click.

Beate said: "That was Karl-Heinz himself. He can't resist the magic word. Erika."

The phone rang a few minutes later. She answered it and her face fell immediately. She covered the mouthpiece, said: "My boss . . ." She listened, the expression on her face changing dramatically, then spoke quickly in German and hung up, already moving toward her coat, which hung on the back of a chair. "Something terrible has happened—a mas-sacre at Zoo Station. It'd be like a bomb at your Grand Central Station. Last night, about midnight. They thought they had enough people to cover it but with all the other stuff happening today they're down to the bare bones. So I'm heading for Zoo Station—"

"Who massacred whom?"

"It's crazy but it sounds like the Red Underground Army and the police massacred each other. But that was all so long ago. It's a mess. And it just gets added to the Stiffel stuff—and it's going to produce some right-wing repression from the government. The public will demand it. The Germany Firsters are going to love it." She kissed him goodbye, impulsively, stood smiling at him, eyes twinkling. "Take care, Coop. Don't take any stupid chances. See you later."

The taxi swung past the massive statue of the Soviet soldier memorial-izing the Red Army's arrival in Berlin in June of 1945. Sharing the space was a tank said to be the first of the liberating army's to fight its way into the city. The marble slab was supposed to have been taken from Hitler's office in the Reichschancellery. They were driving down the broad ave-nue leading directly through the Brandenburg Gate, which stood up ahead in the gloom and fog. It was as much a symbol of Berlin as the

Eiffel Tower was of Paris. Massive, solid. The Quadriga—Victory and her rampaging steeds—faced into East Berlin, toward the Museum Island and the other awesome architecture that had been cordoned off behind the Wall for so long. The Unter den Linden, Under the Linden Trees, once the greatest, widest, most fashionable thoroughfare of Central Europe, stretched away into the East as the taxi passed under the mighty center arch of the Gate.

He paid off the driver and stepped out into the cold and damp, the wind whipping through the bustle of the flea market that had sprung up as soon as the Wall had come down. Red Army watches and insignias and patches and badges, Peruvian necklaces and jewelry, knockoffs of Rolexes and Breitlings, carved chess pieces and inlaid boards from Pakistan, bits of cement hastily rainbow spray-painted and guaranteed to be pieces of the Wall, drawers of jewelry hung by straps looped around necks and shoulders of Afghanis, East German army uniforms, caps, boots, knives, compasses, camouflage jackets, bits of Persian carpet, wind-up cars modeled on vehicles never seen in the West, all sold by Arabs and Hamitic-faced men with dark, dramatically hollow-cheeked faces, deepset eyes burning like coals, men who looked as if they'd been left for dead in Kabul or had somehow attached themselves to the evacuating Soviet divisions as they bailed out of Afghanistan. It was a Third World bazaar selling wares to impoverished tourists from across Europe, Americans who moved among the hundreds of dealers as if checking out a peculiar zoo, and West Germans slumming, looking for a bargain. The heavy lifting and carrying seemed to be done by dark-faced women, fleshier than their men but with glazed, distant eyes, the eyes of people almost devoid of hope managing to carry on out of habit and sheer stubbornness. Rain blew like Agent Orange across the blighted landscape. It was that time of day, dying time.

Cooper pushed his way through the crowds, came to a brightly lit, utterly deserted carnival of six or seven rides. Something called the Spider spun to the canned music, the bucket seats empty, no one at the controls, and behind it other rides lifted and turned and lowered without any apparent human component. The rain drifted across the scene. It looked as if a small, distant, bedraggled planet at the far end of the galaxy had thrown a party and the word hadn't gotten around. Cooper stood still, watching, momentarily transfixed. He felt like a man trapped within one of Graham Greene's more ominous entertainments, like a man marked for a sorry fate, a man watched, set up, doomed.

He came to a corner and turned right. There was almost no traffic.
The sidewalk was muddy and deserted. Up ahead he saw what might be
the apartment block Karl-Heinz had mentioned. He headed for it. The
lights of the street-level restaurant and coffeehouse swam into view.
Ground fog hugged the weeds and shrubs. He turned right again, saw a
few people behind glass reading newspapers, guarding their cups of coffee. A small church seemed deserted. The bare trees had a bombed-out
look and there were large black birds arranged here and there on the
black branches. A couple of motorcycles sat in the rain, tires and flaps
muddy.

Dead ahead, across a makeshift mud and cindered path, lay a vast
field. Was this Potsdamer Platz? The future center of the new Europe?
Wolf Koller's playground? It needed work.

It was dark now. The cold rain was seeping down inside his scarf.
He pushed his gloved hands deep into the pockets of his old bush coat.
Way down to his left, several hundred yards away, he saw the cluster of
bright lights and heard the faint, tinny music of a calliope. The circus . . .

He set off down the muddy path. The field was full of trash, odd
lumps of this and that. Broken boards, bits of torn fabric blowing like
flags of surrender but the battle was long since over here, had moved on,
raged in some other place. He was suddenly beset by a depression that
seemed to attack like the cold and damp, getting under his skin and into
his nervous system, destroying his spirit as it went. Was he on a fool's
errand, not just to this godforsaken spot, but to Germany? Had he been
suckered into someone else's nightmare, this time alone, without Olaf
Peterson to save him? What the hell was he doing? What did any of it
matter . . . why not just go home?

Lee. Erika. Beate. Wolf Koller. Kilroy. Karl-Heinz. Each life, each
strand, twining and intertwining, and then there was a web and he was
caught before he knew it. He felt as if he were in someone's crosshairs,
wondering if he'd even hear the shot.

He was trying not to think of Lee. He had fought off any thoughts
of her since he'd seen Brendel and Koller on the tape last night. Married
first to Brendel, then to Koller . . . He should have known. People
didn't change. You were what you were. He had held her in his arms only
yesterday and kissed her and longed for her and when he wasn't looking,
the steamroller had been creeping up behind him. People didn't change.
He hadn't changed, he hadn't learned. Longing, yearning, loving had

blinded him in an instant, in the explosion of seeing her, smelling her, touching her, tasting her. It took about a second and a half to fuck up your whole life . . . to blow what you'd struggled so hard to learn into ashes and dust.

And all he'd learned was that you never learn. Maybe that was all you could ever hope to learn. That you just never learned.

The mound rose and he picked his way through the rubble toward it. There were smashed slabs of waste concrete, large pieces of stained plasterboard, craters in the earth where barbed wire, scrap lumber, lengths of discarded sewer pipe, all seemed to be struggling to crawl out. Forty yards beyond the mound the circus glowed merrily.

The American Circus.

The rain was blowing in his face. The idea of a Graham Greene novel had been replaced by the sights and sounds of a Fellini picture. It was perfectly surreal. He blinked against the rain.

The happy shouts and laughter of children floated across the desolate expanse of muddy rubbish. There was clown music. A man in a white suit with gold epaulets and huge boots was busily lining up several ponies wearing handsome and jaunty cocked hats, pushing them into line for their big entrance.

At the side of the entrance to the tent there were three large, heavily barred cages, red and gold with large gold-spoked wheels. From behind the bars a couple of lions stared impassively into the rainy night, their breath hanging like clouds, their eyes somewhere else, dreaming of some high plains in Kenya, someplace, the past. Two tigers next door prowled restlessly, occasionally letting out a perfunctory, cavernous growl. The kids in the tent were screaming with delight. A couple of men in black jeans and leather jackets watched the lions, smoked cigarettes, waited for something.

Cooper turned back to the mound of earth and rubble.

Two men stood at its summit. There was a bench beside them, a thick attaché case on the bench. They were staring off toward the West, toward the lights of Berlin twinkling in the rain, as if hoping to catch the first glimpse of the column coming to relieve them.

Cooper climbed the mound. One of the men turned around. He wore round dark glasses. He was looking past Cooper. He said something in German. He put out his hand, tentatively feeling for something in midair.

"I don't speak German."

The other man turned. He wore a black leather cap and a black raincoat. He spoke in German to the blind man, then to Cooper: "Can I assist you?"

"I'm meeting someone here. Are you Karl-Heinz?" He couldn't see the face that well in the darkness.

"No. Are you interested in this place? Someone sent you here?"

"I'm meeting someone. Potsdamer Platz?"

"All this." He waved an arm. "The Reichschancellery stood here once. Are you interested in history?"

"The Reichschancellery. Of course." It looked like the end of the world.

"*Ja*, here. Over there the Führerbunker itself. Underground, of course. He died over there . . . and there his body was burned . . . the Red Army—"

"Who died?"

The man stared at him. He was middle-aged but white hair curled from beneath the cap. "Adolf Hitler."

"Oh, I see—of course." How stupid could you be?

"The Red Army had reached the entrances to the tunnels . . . Are you interested in history? We have a monograph you might find worthwhile." He turned to the bench, opened his umbrella, and popped the clasps on the attaché case. "It is a history of the Führerbunker itself as well as of the Reichschancellery. People forget our German history." He held out a stapled sheaf of papers. He flipped through them. "Architectural drawings, you see, reproductions of photographs of an archival nature . . . in English, though not perfect English, I'm afraid. I do the best I can. Here"—he tapped a hand-drawn map—"we're standing here. Over there is where the Russians tell us Martin Bormann died . . . some of us question that."

Rain blew across the mound, spotting the papers.

The horses were prancing into the tent, the whip cracked, the band struck up their signature tune.

A sudden gust of wind snapped at the umbrella, blew it inside out. It twisted in his hand like a huge, maddened bat. He fought with it for a moment. Cooper pushed the attaché case shut to keep it dry.

"*Danke.* Would you perhaps like to take this monograph with you, sir?" He put the ruined umbrella down on the bench.

"Sure. How much?"

"Ten deutschmarks, sir. Please."

Cooper handed him the money and folded the papers, stuffed them into his pocket.

He saw no one else in the vicinity.

"Danke, danke, danke . . ."

The man was bowing slightly, his voice fading as Cooper left the mound. Here, it was here that the Third Reich had all finally come crashing down.

Götterdämmerung. Had Bormann really died? Or had he escaped, had Skorzeny and the Condor Legion seen him out through Madrid and on to South America? It was raining more insistently and the wind swirled on the vast open field. Far away the Brandenburg Gate was a blur in the lights.

Where the hell was Karl-Heinz? What was the point in standing him up? Maybe it hadn't been Karl-Heinz at all . . . Maybe Beate had been mistaken. Maybe she and Karl-Heinz had wanted him out of the way . . . He was always at home with paranoia when he crossed the border into Germany.

Cooper cast one long last look into the darkness, toward the apartment block, toward the Brandenburg Gate, past the two men on the mound, all the way back to the circus.

A figure slowly detached itself from the shadows at the back of the tiger cage. He watched Cooper for a long minute, then waved briefly with his right hand. With his left he cradled a motorcycle helmet against his leg.

Cooper plodded across the scrubby, patchy weedbed, avoided a few gaping holes, climbed across some shattered concrete and an expanse of gravel to reach the street. The music was playing loudly in the tent, acrobat music, man on the high wire music, accompanied by the shrieks of the kids. Cooper imagined trapeze artists reaching for the one instant when their hands might come together. He crossed the street to the waiting man.

"Karl-Heinz?"

A lion said something, a sound rolling deep within, like volcanic rumbling at the movies.

The man stepped out of the shadows again and Cooper saw his face, the straggly beard. He was a boy, a kid. There was a scabbed abrasion on one side of his face and a black eye was getting some age on it. There was a deep scabbed wedge cut out of his lower lip.

"I'm Karl-Heinz. Maybe. Or he sent me."

"You're Karl-Heinz. I've seen your picture. Erika had it on the bulletin board in her kitchen. You, Erika, and Beate."

He nodded. "So, who are you?"

"Erika's my niece."

"She never said anything—"

"I'm Lise Koller's brother. I came from Boston to help find Erika."

"So what do you have to tell me about Erika? What can you do to find her?" Suddenly his eyes were pleading. "Have you found her? Is she all right?"

"I don't know. I wanted to meet you. I had to get you to meet me. You're said to be a hard man to find."

"That's right. I am. I have enemies, Mr.—what?"

"Cooper. John Cooper."

"I have enemies, Mr. Cooper. And you've lured me out into the open. With nothing to tell me. So now I am leaving—"

Cooper reached out, laid one huge hand on the slight young man's shoulder. "No, you're not leaving. Not until I have time to ask you a few questions." He closed his hand on the shoulder. "Let's not have trouble, son. I need your help. You want Erika found, don't you?"

"Take your hand off me if you want it back."

Cooper smiled. "Will you give me a few minutes? We really are on the same side." He took his hand away. "You were the closest person to her. She loves you. You had tremendous influence over her . . . she was an unformed young girl when she met you and you became her mentor. Don't be modest—isn't that about right?"

"I suppose it is." There was a note of pride in his voice.

"So you're the fella I have to see. Your face—did you fall off your motorcycle? It was nasty, by the look of it."

"I'm very good on my motorcycle, Mr. Cooper. I don't fall off. My face is the result of that bastard Stiffel and his bunch—you've been here long enough to know about Stiffel?"

"Oh, yes. Was this the same demonstration where Erika got knocked around?"

Karl-Heinz moved back into the shadows, underneath an awning. The rain plopped on the canvas overhead. It seemed to be making the tigers nervous.

"Yes. The last time I saw her."

"You took her home that night?"

"No. I tried to get her out of the way—the crowd was crazy, clubs and pipes swinging, I was swept away and I couldn't get back to her. I got hurt pretty bad, you can see, and I passed out. When I came to I was on the way to the hospital, they patched me up, I was pretty groggy. When I got home I felt half dead, I slept for quite a while, when I woke up I called her but there was no answer. Next thing I knew, she was gone."

"How did you find out she was gone?"

"Beate told me when I called her—she said she'd gone to the building but nobody had answered, then she told me about what Lise Koller had told her . . . about the knife and the blood."

"What do you think happened?"

"I don't know. I can't believe she wouldn't have let me know if she'd just taken off—"

"But she didn't just take off, did she? She slashed her wrists instead."

"I don't know what happened." There was a catch in his voice. He was near tears. "She may have been weary of me, fed up with my investigations, my marches, my demonstrations . . . I think I may have gone too far."

"Weary of you? Come on, son, I doubt that. What I've heard, your word was gospel with her—"

"But she was afraid. She was afraid of what I'd shown her, she was afraid of the violence, she took things very hard . . . that last demonstration, Stiffel's people singled us out, gave it to us good. They came after us in the crowd . . . after me, really. They're small stuff, Stiffel's thugs, but they're just the tip of the iceberg."

"What's the rest? What can't we see?"

"It's bad enough that the polls show a quarter of the public agrees with the Stiffel bunch . . . but what's worse is that the real Nazis—oh, yes, the real Nazis, nothing neo about them—they're the ones running the show. It was too much for Erika."

"You're not trying to tell me—"

"I mean what I say! The spiritual descendants of the old Nazis are using these thugs and creeps to raise hell and get people ready for a return to a strong, nationalistic, right-wing Germany-for-the-Germans kind of government. And that Reich will be run by these people behind the scenes . . . they're the ones we need to be scared of."

"It's a little imaginative, isn't it? Just a little overheated?"

"You don't understand Germany or Germans."

"Well, you've got me there."

"Nobody's motives are ever clear, Mr. Cooper. But one thing you can be sure of. No matter what is happening, the Nazis are always involved. It's not a movie, it's not a cheap thriller—it's historical reality. And the worse it gets, the more likely you are to find the Americans dipping into the blood for their own ends. Remember the Baader-Meinhof gang—"

"Easy, boy, easy."

"Listen. I'm pointing out that since Hitler and the rise of Nazism, there is no getting away from them. They're in everything." He turned to stare at one of the huge cats, which was staring back at him. "The Nazis are like the lions and tigers. Always hungry. Always watching. And Erika . . . I confided in her, all of my fears . . . she was too frightened."

"And depressed? Enough to try to kill herself?"

He shrugged. The strain of Erika's disappearance was showing on him. He was thin and worn as a rock star. Pipestem legs in tight black jeans.

"But she wouldn't"—Cooper pressed him—"try to kill herself over *politics* . . . it has to be a lot more personal than politics—"

Karl-Heinz laughed, then winced when his lip pulled painfully at the deep scab. "Americans!" Cooper heard the lifetime of indoctrination, the built-up hatred and contempt. "Out of the question, dying for politics! Who cares about politics. Americans will accept any system as long as their money is safe—"

"Listen to me, kid." Cooper felt himself trembling out of all proportion to the insult. Who gave a damn what the kid said? But he felt himself boiling over. "Americans don't care . . . right. All those Germans, East and West—wasn't it wonderful the way you Germans rose up and threw Hitler out . . . what a bunch of heroes! Well, bullshit! We're the ones, the Americans and the Brits, we buckled on the old six-guns and came over to this rotting, putrefying mess and cleaned up Dodge. And we're the ones who coughed up the dough to rebuild the shithole that Hitler left behind. We paid for your economic miracle and opened our doors to your cars and cameras and goddamn coffeemakers—and we did it all just so you can stand here, some fucking little punk, and tell us what assholes we are." Cooper narrowed his eyes and wondered if he'd caught the right mixture of John Wayne and Jimmy Stewart. He wasn't sure how it would play in Berlin but he had to get some kind of an angle on this kid. A very large man leaning over you and screaming in your face often helped reveal character.

Karl-Heinz was staring at the ground. Cooper could almost see the wheels going around in his head: should I argue about how the fucking Americans used us as the biggest CIA station of all, about how well they've done financially out of rebuilding us . . . Finally he looked up. "Erika was afraid of everything. Afraid of Stiffel, afraid of the real Nazis, afraid of Germany's 'demon within,' that's what she called it . . . she was afraid of what it means to be a German. She was afraid it was all happening again . . . and there was her father."

"What about her father?"

"She was afraid that her father believes in all of it, all the political stuff from the past—"

"She believes her father is a Nazi?"

"More or less. Yes."

"What gave her that idea?"

"I did."

"Were you trying to impress her? Or did you know something?" He waited a moment. "What's SPARTAKUS?"

Karl-Heinz's body stiffened; then he kicked a stone. He was trying to get his equilibrium back. Cooper saw the change SPARTAKUS had wrought. The music from the tent was louder, reaching the final grand march of the participants. All that was left was the lions and tigers, the climax. Men had come and were pulling the huge cages toward the tent. A paw flashed like a catcher's mitt at the bars.

"I don't know what you're talking about."

"Ah. Well, Lise Koller—that's my sister—told me Erika had mentioned something to her about SPARTAKUS, some code name . . . she thought it had probably come from you."

"I can't talk about it anymore. I was a fool to see you . . . you tricked me, Mr. Cooper. You've added nothing. You don't know where she is. And I've taken a very great risk talking to you. I have enemies—"

"Something to do with SPARTAKUS?"

"I have enemies—you don't understand any of this—"

"So you told Erika about SPARTAKUS. Why not tell me? Maybe that will tell me where she is."

Karl-Heinz was shaking his head, backing away.

Cooper pressed on. "Sure, sure, we've all got enemies. I understand—what I could tell you about enemies, believe me. I once had to kill a man with a shotgun, both barrels. I know about enemies. So where do you think she is? Did she leave on her own after somebody rescued her? Or was she taken, kidnapped? Or—"

"I think . . ." He swallowed hard. "I think she's dead. I think somebody murdered her. Not a suicide . . . why does everybody think it was a suicide attempt?"

"Hers were the only fingerprints on the knife."

"So what?"

"Why murder her?"

"Because she knew things . . . they were afraid she might tell what she knows . . . she might become an embarrassment—"

"But what the hell does she know?"

"What I told her. Now—that's it. I'm not going to say any more. I don't even know who you are, maybe you're CIA, how should I know—"

"CIA?" He thought: the snow, the couple in the car, the guns, no ID . . . "What are you talking about? What do you know about the CIA?"

"Do you work with Delaney? Go ask Delaney . . . get your answers from him. Maybe you're the reason he's got all those tripwires and dogs and—how do I know who you are? I've talked enough. You can tell me . . . if you're CIA, what do you want? You want the SPARTAKUS man, don't you? You want to cut Delaney out of it . . . Shit, maybe Delaney knows too much now, maybe you were sent over to . . . God, you all make me sick." His teeth were chattering uncontrollably; the buckles on his jacket were clicking against the helmet.

"Wait. Hold on—what's the CIA got to do with it?" He looked down on the kid. "Maybe I'm CIA, maybe I'm somebody else. Somebody a lot worse. Think about it. Maybe I'm looking for Delaney . . . Maybe I'm not, maybe I'm just here to kill people. But so far you're alive, so you must be doing something right." He slapped the boy on the shoulder. "Just humor me, son. And nobody gets hurt." The dialogue came easily. He'd heard it all before in a thousand darkened theaters. "You tell me why you think the Company is after you."

"There must be a leak somewhere. They know my source . . . so who needs me? They're watching me. When they're sure they don't need me anymore, they'll kill me. It's cleaner that way. They're always watching—"

"Whoa, babe. Slow down, son, you're scaring me—now let me get this straight. Is that why they want to kill Erika? Because you told her all about SPARTAKUS? And they know she knows . . . is that it? But why would the CIA want to kill her? What's it got to do with them?"

"Everything, you idiot! It has everything to do with them! Don't patronize me—they know everything, they're everywhere."

"The CIA? You've got to be kidding. Haven't you heard about the quality of our intelligence? You'd be better off reading *The Washington Post*—"

"I am not a fool," he snarled. "You play the joker, it's nothing to me. They want to kill me now. They're all part of it, they're in it together, the CIA and Stiffel and . . . I know them. I can recognize them." He stopped. His voice dropped to a whisper. The children were shrieking at the arrival of the lions and tigers. The ground underfoot trembled slightly. The U-Bahn. There was a station nearby. "There." He came close to Cooper's ear. "That man."

Cooper turned his head.

"That man, the tall man with the limp."

Cooper saw the man, ramrod straight, elderly, out for a stroll in the rain. He probably lived in the apartment block. He stood momentarily in the penumbra of a streetlamp, the rain caught in individual droplets in the light.

"I've seen him before." Karl-Heinz was trying to compose himself. "I can spot a tail. My father taught me how. This old man has been following me. I don't know who he's working for . . . but he's one of them."

"One of whom?"

"My enemies. You don't listen to me. I have *enemies*. They *know* . . ."

The lions were growling, like the crack at the end of the world, the sound that comes from the bottomless pit, and the kids were screaming with delight and fear.

Karl-Heinz clutched at Cooper's arm. "I'm telling you, Mr. Cooper, whoever you are, get out . . . just get out of Germany while you can . . . don't kill me, don't kill anyone . . . Erika's dead, I'm telling you that, believe me . . . they don't care who they kill."

Karl-Heinz suddenly bolted around the corner, running hard past a deluxe mobile home where some circus people, in costume, were standing in the kitchen, laughing at some story a blond woman was relating.

Cooper went after him, stopped abruptly, winded. He had no chance of catching the kid. The darkness had swallowed him and then he heard the nasty roar of a motorcycle kicked into life.

Cooper turned back. At the circus tent's entrance the children were pouring out, coats half buttoned, mufflers trailing underfoot, traipsing heavily in the puddles, mothers in raincoats with scarves over their heads, kids yelling, reliving the excitement of the show. A little girl put her hands up and growled like a lion at an unimpressed little boy.

Under the light of the far street corner, over the sea of bobbing children, he saw the tall elderly man push his hands down into the pockets of his raincoat, and slowly, deliberately walk away.

Once he was through the swarm of children, Cooper set off following him. He wasn't sure why. The kid was paranoid. It was an old guy out for an evening constitutional.

He followed him the length of the apartment block, then toward the East Berlin landmark TV tower with the observation deck near the top, faint lights giving it the look of a flying saucer hovering overhead. Then past an ancient church in splendid isolation, rain dripping, buses going slowly past, wipers flicking. The old man gave no indication that he knew he was being followed but his pace quickened.

He headed into a small flea market lit by some naked bulbs that popped and hissed in the rain. A crowd milled about, women with string bags and pinched faces and worn coats, men looking at sweatshirts hung with clothespins beneath makeshift canvas awnings. A small man smoked a cigarette, stood behind a table with six hopelessly small, wrinkled potatoes for sale. A woman haggled over the price of a Fred Flintstone T-shirt. The next booth offered a dozen Hawaiian sport shirts made of a synthetic material that shone like plastic in the light.

When Cooper looked up the tall man was gone.

"Listen to what I'm saying, Cheese. Just give me a chance to get two words in edgewise—it's not my fault and you know damn well it's not—"

"Where are you, may I ask? A speedway?"

"I'm at a call box. There's traffic. And a goddamn train going by . . . what'd you say? I'm having a helluva time hearing—"

"I said, 'For God's sake.'"

"Sure, sure. Now listen to me—I'm telling you, I can't find him. What part of that don't you understand? I. Cannot. Find. Him. He's just disappeared."

"Gone to ground. He's afraid. What's he afraid of, deep down?"

"Us! I'd say that's obvious—"

"I'm not happy about this, Burke. I want the rest of SPARTAKUS. Or should I say the *last* of it? What part of that don't *you* understand?"

Horns were honking, gears grinding. Ned Cheddar was in a bad mood. "We've got to find out what it's all leading up to. How much money is involved? What is Koller buying? Or selling? Why do I smell a Russian? Look at all the time he's spent over there. We know Koller played a part in arming Saddam . . . is he arming some other son of a bitch? And now you lose the kid!"

"I wasn't tailing the kid, Cheese. Now don't give me this shit. And you don't have to tell me it's important—I'm only an old field man but I know that much. The kid has gotten lost on purpose—he's scared shitless. He thinks we're going to kill him as soon as he gives us the rest—"

Ned Cheddar sighed. "Jesus wept."

"Well, you can't blame him. It's a legitimate fear."

"Nonsense!" Cheddar exploded and then pulled himself back together. "Moving on for a moment. John Cooper?"

"Well, he's in place. With the TV reporter, Beate Hubermann."

"Isn't he just a trifle overage for her?"

Delaney ignored him. "He went to see his sister."

"And?" Cheddar rasped impatiently.

"They had lunch. Went to the daughter's apartment. I can't read the man's mind, Cheese. We don't have bugs in all these places."

"We don't have bugs in *any* of these places. We didn't know we were about to have a *situation,* did we? Tell me, the Professor—what does he have to say about Brother Cooper?"

"He thinks Cooper's a wild card. To be avoided at all costs. He hates wild cards."

"Good. I must be thankful for small blessings. You know, I can't believe you lost Karl-Heinz—"

"I didn't *lose* him for chrissakes. He just isn't there anymore. You ought to know that sometimes these things just bloody well happen!"

"Well, I'm putting in another party. I've got to find out what SPARTAKUS is really all about. I've been in the dark too long on this—"

"Come on, we're talking about a few days here!"

"At the risk of sounding melodramatic, hours could matter when something like this is beginning. Whatever it is, when it goes, it will go fast. And I don't want my drawers around my ankles. I'm putting in another man. I need people on the ground, taking the pulse, feeling the tremors."

"I don't like the sound of this—"

"I'm putting an assassin in play—"

"Oh shit. Who's he gonna kill?"

"We'll just wait and see, won't we? Maybe he won't have to kill anybody."

"Oh, that's good, that's rich! When was the last time you put an assassin in and nobody got killed?"

"There's always a first time. And in any case I put a fellow into Africa once—he was going to kill Idi Amin and in the end he didn't."

"I never heard about that."

"With good reason. I think Amin may have eaten him and mailed us back the bones. Something like that. It made a bit of a stink when the box of bones and his ring and watch showed up one day at Langley. Amin let us know in back channels that it was his idea of a joke—but they were undoubtedly the fellow's own bones. Ah, well . . . I'm putting the assassin in. One must keep one's options open."

III

16

RAFAELA

Werner Paulus drove through the afternoon traffic, just another not-quite-new blue Mercedes sedan, as close to invisible as he could be. Up ahead, usually just within his view, was the rakish, elegant old Mercedes convertible—bulky and squared off and imposing, the padded fabric top like a beacon in the clot of cars. It was nearly thirty years old, a slap in the face to what was up-to-date. Paulus was not a student of automobile history but he knew something special when he saw it. He didn't really know the year it was made but he remembered when they were new. This one had a forest-green body, polished to a diamond shine. It was rain-spotted at the moment. Most of the time he kept the Mercedes convertible in sight. It didn't matter. He knew where it was going.

He was beginning to get a picture of the larger situation as it took shape behind the fog. He was beginning to grasp the elements in play and there were plenty of them. He'd finally gotten a line on Karl-Heinz and it had paid off. He'd had a look at the American, John Cooper—who so bothered the Professor—meeting Karl-Heinz at the American Circus. Cooper wasn't getting anywhere yet with the hunt for Erika Koller but he was quick off the mark for a man in a foreign country.

He occasionally regretted he couldn't call for help on a tailing job. That was nearly the only advantage he'd had as King of Berlin Central. Now he was on his own, old Werner. Well, old Werner knew what the hell he was doing, which put him a leg up on the competition. That was

what he had in common with Burke Delaney and the Professor, that was
the bond between them. They never just flopped around like something
about to die. They knew what the hell they were doing. So, the miles sped
by, while he listened to his tape of the great Erika Pluhar singing some
sad songs about loneliness. His favorite was the one about the Loneliness
Hotel.

Paulus knew what he was doing. And he—alone among them all—
knew what had really happened last night at the Zoo Station. He understood the truth behind the horror and the red flowers scattered across the
scene. The truth about the Dorfmann gang reaching out from the past,
striking again. Nobody else knew. Just Paulus. So, he was on the road,
heading into the Harz Mountains, a seeker after deeper and still deeper
truths.

As they began the climb in the darkness of the night the headlights
picked out the damp, melting patches in the road, then the mounds of
snow at the shoulders, then patches of icy snow and the road's narrowing,
the pine boughs heavy with wet snow brushing at the side panels like the
outstretched hands of beggars or ghosts.

The road was winding, clinging to the side of the slopes, and
several times the single set of lights up ahead came into view as the road
curled back. It wasn't much of a challenge in terms of tailing.

The lights of a village glowed around the bend, a dim light indeed,
since it was a very small village and it was very late. The blue haze of
television screens shone through some of the windows. There was a light
on in the bakery. The service station was the busiest place in town. Two
men in coveralls were closing down, shutting off the lights.

Several kilometers past the village the big convertible turned into a
narrow road and Paulus pulled off onto a skinny shoulder. He waited ten
minutes, then pulled back onto the same road, felt the tires slide into the
frozen ruts, and proceeded upward. A kilometer on he saw the chalet, an
A-frame of considerable dimensions, facing out across the valley. The
convertible was parked in the lot by the doorway, where a single decora-
tively shielded light burned a hole in the surrounding darkness.

Paulus had been making this trip for six months, once a month.
He knew a good place to park up above with a fine view of the chalet. He
was a very calm man who planned ahead, avoided surprises. He settled
back in the seat with a battery-driven reading light and began rereading
Hans Hellmut Kirst's classic novel *The Revolt of Gunner Asch*. He adjusted his muffler, lost himself in the story, without missing a sound or
movement in the night. It had been a good deal more comfortable during

the summer nights. Now winter had come to the mountains and he had to turn on the little auxiliary heater from time to time. He was always prepared.

Dawn came early and Paulus was awake drinking coffee from his thermos. He stretched his legs outside and had a pee, watched Wolf Koller come back out of the chalet to his wonderful convertible. He wore a green loden greatcoat and dark glasses and driving gloves. He slid in behind the wheel. Paulus heard the heavy clunk of the closing door, heard the crunch of the tires on the gravel forecourt below. Slowly the car drew away. Wolf Koller was going home. Not to his house just up the road from the clinic, but back to Berlin.

A few minutes later Paulus had parked in the forecourt and was rapping gently on the door. When it opened he was confronted with the sad face of Dr. Christian Milch, who looked up into the icy blue eyes and smiled slightly beneath the unnaturally black mustache. The grin only made him look sadder. He stood aside. "Come in, Chief Paulus. Your coffee is freshly brewed and I have some sweet cakes. Did you have a good trip?"

Paulus handed him the empty thermos and followed him across the polished hardwood of the foyer outfitted with potted palms and cheery wall hangings. Sunlight streamed through a skylight. Milch led the way into the administrator's office. There was a VCR in a corner; in the Krups, coffee dripped its last. Milch turned expectantly to Paulus. "You had quite a lot of excitement in Berlin, eh? The Zoo Station of all places —who would do such a thing? It's out of control, Chief, it's all out of control—they miss you at a time like this."

"Was our guest his usual self this morning?"

"Much the same, Chief."

"And how is your patient, Milch?"

Milch's black eyebrows rose in a gesture of realistic acceptance. The eyebrows, the mustache, the hair were all coal-black. His skin was unusually pale. Paulus knew Milch to be sixty. He supposed Milch thought all the dye made him look younger. Instead he made you think of a superannuated Bela Lugosi.

"The same as ever, Chief Paulus. No change. There will only be one change for our Lady of the Shadows, you know that." Milch couldn't bring himself to speak her name. It was worth his life to keep the secret.

"Well, let's go see her."

Christian Milch had run the private sanitarium for thirteen years now. And for all those years and several more there had been only one constant patient. The facility's cost per patient was surely the highest in the world now that Hess was dead and Spandau Prison was no longer in the running. But for Wolf Koller money was never an issue. Wolf Koller may have thought he owned Christian Milch but that was an illusion. Milch was the personal property of Werner Paulus.

Paulus had nailed him for providing the drugs, impure as it turned out, that killed several wealthy wastrels in Berlin in the mid-seventies. Paulus had offered him a deal: his freedom, relatively speaking, and in return, Milch had become an informant serving a life sentence. Milch felt it was all slightly Faustian, but then, Chief Paulus could have dropped him down a hole and forgotten about him. Paulus made a benevolent Satan if you had to make that kind of deal. Milch had proved invaluable during the Cold War when there was always somebody or other, East or West, it didn't matter, who needed to be shot full of drugs and kept under wraps for a few days or weeks or years. Some had not survived. There was a small cemetery of unmarked graves on the slope below the A-frame. Life was cheap in those days. One deal at the Glienicke Bridge in Potsdam had gone wrong and a Russian colonel, a double agent, slept forever under the gaze of Dr. Milch.

And once upon a time a man had needed a place to store Rafaela Dorfmann, a place where she would receive perpetual care, and, unseen and unnoticed, Werner Paulus had made sure she wound up in Dr. Milch's care. Paulus looked upon her as an investment that was bound to pay off sooner or later. After all, he was investing, so to speak, with Wolf Koller's money, and Koller could spare it. There was no downside. It was, in the term mathematicians liked so much, a fairly elegant solution for everyone, though Wolf Koller would have been shocked to learn Paulus had a hand in any of it.

They walked down a tiled hallway into a bright, airy room with an astonishing, sunny view across the snow-patched mountainsides. Paulus was always surprised by the extreme beauty of the view.

The only sound in the room came from some sort of machine that assisted the patient in breathing. Or maybe it monitored the breathing. It meant nothing to Paulus one way or the other. It made a faint wheezing and clicking sound.

He turned from the view and went to the bed.

Part of Rafaela Dorfmann lay beneath a single sheet. There was really only half of her, the right side. She had only half a head and only one side of a body. The rest, or where the rest had been, was swathed in bandages and dressings.

Milch gazed down at her. "Twenty years and still she will not die. God is punishing her."

"Maybe she knows what He has waiting in store for her on the other side. It's nice to know that He occasionally pays attention to this small planet and gets it right. It doesn't happen often. You know, Milch, I love it when God unexpectedly takes the moral view."

"Just often enough to keep us hoping He exists."

"Why, Christian, you're a philospher."

"I have so much time to think here, Chief Paulus."

"Not complaining, are you, Christian?"

"Certainly not, Chief Paulus."

Paulus sat down on the wooden chair beside the bed. The figure on the bed had a mouth into which a tube disappeared like a worm down a hole. She had a nose with only one distended nostril and only the cheek on the right side. She had an eye and it was closed, though the lid had a tendency to flutter sometimes as if it were being tickled. She hadn't spoken since the bomb went off eighteen years ago but she might not have been able to speak even if she'd regained consciousness. Brain damage, throat damage, chest cavity blown open, left with half a lung. What remained of her hair was visible from beneath the bandages. It had once been black as Milch's but had looked a good deal better on her. Now it was a wispy iron-gray. He spoke her name softly, as a formality, out of respect, in case she could hear.

He picked up her limp claw-like hand, all tendon and bone and long nails, which Milch kept manicured, probably to pass the empty hours. He kept up a flow of words, as if he were comforting a child, just chatting really, but he was thinking about what she had been a long time ago . . .

She was once a girl who got her picture in the papers and the glossy magazines. When she had been Erika Koller's age she was one of the most famous fashion models in Germany. All the girls in those days tried to look like the wondrous Rafaela. She'd only had the one name then: Rafaela. Straight raven hair to her shoulders, hip-huggers low on her long-legged narrow body. She had led two lives, though, which was too bad. When Wolf Koller met her she'd only been leading one: he was a rich man about Berlin, in his thirties, an expert on the beautiful women of the day. And there was none more beautiful than Rafaela. He'd annexed her as Hitler had annexed Austria.

Back in those days Wolf Koller had been tied up with a cell of Nazis who fancied themselves the Fourth Reich. One of them had been his friend Gunter Brendel, who had the beautiful wife, Lise. Paulus hadn't been involved with all that since it had been centered in the Munich area. But in the aftermath he had picked up gossip about what Brendel had been up to: and he'd learned far more once he'd tapped into the knowledge of his secondary employer, Ned Cheddar.

When Cooper and Olaf Peterson had demolished the Nazi conspiracy, Wolf Koller had escaped unscathed. Even then he'd stayed well behind the scenes, out of the line of fire. By then he was deeply involved with Rafaela Dorfmann—and she had gone from being one of the world's top models to being one of the world's most wanted terrorists, with the red rose signature. Paulus had often theorized about what had brought about the change in her. He had never fully satisfied himself. Psychologists had had a field day psychoanalyzing her in absentia; the general conclusion was that she was acting out of self-hatred, another example of German guilt dating back to the war. Well, they were the experts, but Paulus had his doubts. His own son's suicide was the more understandable act for a guilt-ridden German youth: Rafaela had seemed to snap, she had become worse than the worst of the Nazis, acting without a political agenda, embracing terrorism for its own sake. She was a terrorist for hire . . . by anyone, left or right, anywhere on the spectrum. As far as Paulus could figure it out, simple was better. He decided that Rafaela Dorfmann was nuts, and why she went nuts was an addendum he'd given up trying to understand.

Wolf Koller had been drawn to her in the first place by her beauty; had he been further seduced by her will to commit mayhem? Had he envied her ability to act, to strike out and kill and maim without fear of the consequences for herself or anyone else? Wolf Koller was a high-pressure operator but exercised a great deal of control over himself: did he admire her ability to let go of sanity, to go over the edge?

Paulus had often wondered if the Fourth Reich had planned to use her as an enforcement arm of its organization. Possibly. It was all conjecture now. Eventually she had exploded into madness, and then she'd literally exploded, in that bomb factory in Munich.

Now Rafaela was in her early forties. Had she lived a normal life her modeling days would have been long gone by now, she might be on the far side of a career in films, married to a rich man, maybe a man like Wolf Koller.

Maybe Wolf Koller himself.

When Werner Paulus finally stood up beside her bed, Dr. Milch had gone. Paulus found him in the office filling the thermos for him. Milch wasn't a bad chap, really.

Paulus said: "I'd better have the tape."

Milch handed over an audiotape he'd extracted from a recorder attached to the underside of the hospital bed.

Paulus nodded toward the VCR. "And . . ."

Milch went over to the machine, pressed the eject button, and handed Paulus the videotape. Paulus looked at it and handed it back. "Let's see a test."

Milch pushed the cassette into the slot, depressed the play button, and on the screen a surveillance tape appeared, black and white, not the best lighting, shot from the camera concealed in the ceiling above Rafaela Dorfmann's bed. Wolf Koller was sitting beside the bed, speaking softly, unintelligibly. The sound on the audiotape would be much better. Paulus watched for a few minutes. The tape was marked across the top with the date and the time, the numbers constantly jittering along.

"He always talks to her about Lake Constance," Milch said. "Why not? Happy memories, I suppose."

Paulus nodded. "In his heart he believes she can hear him."

However inexplicable some of their story was, Paulus accepted the one great immutable truth about it. Wolf Koller had never stopped loving Rafaela. The heart has its reasons.

17

OUT OF THE PAST

So, the Cheese smelled a Russian in the woodpile . . . Russia behind the facade of SPARTAKUS . . . But what the hell did the neo-Nazis of SPARTAKUS have to do with the newly impoverished, chaotic Russia?

Burke Delaney was sitting in bed with three pillows behind him, his Ben Franklin glasses perched on the end of his nose, reading a book that weighed damn near as much as Schuyler, the bull terrier beside him on the blanket. It was titled *Smoke and Mirrors* and it was a thousand-page biography of Emory Leighton Hunn, the great spymaster who had recruited Delaney himself. Delaney was smoking his pipe and remembering the great man. Cheddar himself revered Hunn more than anyone else; the Cheese said Hunn had shown him the pure joy and satisfaction of intelligence work, of recognizing the truth behind the lies of others, and of making everybody else accept as truth what you knew to be false. He wondered what Hunn would have made of SPARTAKUS—was it true or false, information or disinformation . . . but if it was disinformation, then what was it calculated to make the Cheese think and do? That was the hard part. Nobody seemed able to figure out where disinformation might lead, so the stuff was probably genuine. Either that, or they were up against someone too bloody smart for them. Now there was an idea to sleep on.

Still, Delaney kept trying to develop theories. Never his strong point. Strictly a field man; his was not to reason why, his was but to get out there and kick some serious ass. He liked to simplify and then break arms and legs. But still he wondered, what was going on in the Cheese's mind? Russians. Putting in an assassin. He couldn't see where Cheese was heading and that always made an old spy, an old spook, question himself, wonder if maybe he was past it. Had someone decided the time had come to bundle him up, trot him out onto the ice floe, and let him drift away into the cold? No coming in from that cold. Not ever.

If it was Koller and the Russians it had to be some big money thing. Wolf buying nukes and brokering them to some hairy-assed little shithead who wanted to rule the world from his own pile of sand. That had to be it. Some huge billion-dollar kind of deal, an alliance of money, maybe a line of franchises, Nukes-R-Us . . .

He had been sleeping for a while, he didn't know how long. The heavy book had slid off his chest; he'd turned out the light. The wind was harsh. During the afternoon it had blown a large tree limb down and some of the wires arming his security system had gone with it. It had been snowing lightly at the time and when he went to bed there had been nearly two inches on the ground. The frozen mud and the browned-out winter grass had been frosted white. He'd gone out and fucked around with the wires. The falling limb had set one of the tape recorders playing and he'd disconnected it. Sinatra's recording of "On the Road to Mandalay" had played loudly for several minutes and he'd loved it. Would have scared the living shit out of any hotshot would-be killer sneaking up on him during the night. You had to have a little fun, you had to be creative. But it was too damn cold to fart around out there in the wind restringing the wires in the trees and hooking everything back up. Tomorrow. He'd do it tomorrow.

Now, as he slowly came awake, wind blowing like a mad bastard at the windows and a couple of the dogs bitching out in the barns, he wondered what had jogged him from sleep.

Then he heard the noise . . . the sound of Schuyler's toenails snicking on the bare polished wood of the hallway. The bull terrier's place on the bed beside him was still warm. Snick, snick, snick . . . In the winter it was most unlike Schuyler to rouse himself and forsake the warmth of the bed to go prowling around in the cold house. Bull terriers had the strength of ten but Schuyler wasn't exactly a kid anymore, more like middle-aged, and he enjoyed sack time.

Snick, snick, snick.

What the hell was he doing out there?

Then the snicking stopped for a moment, then began again.

Goddamn it! Delaney seemed to remember he'd been having a good dream, whatever the hell it had been about—

He got up, grabbed the Army-issue Colt forty-five from under his pillow, and went to the door of the bedroom, took a look down the hall.

Schuyler stood in the faint moonlit patch at the end of the hall. Staring.

Delaney padded down the hall barefoot. Still in the dark, unable to see into the large main room with the fireplace and the couches and the eight-foot-high bookcases, Delaney knelt and hoped the intruder didn't hear the fucking racket his knees made going down.

Schuyler was still staring at something Delaney couldn't see. Delaney whispered into the dog's ear.

"Eat 'em up, kid."

Schuyler departed like a sixty-pound mortar shell. There was a hellish noise when he knocked over a chair, then a louder noise, like somebody chopping wood and practicing cannibalism at the same time. A scream Delaney wasn't ever going to forget. A gunshot that banged off one of the heavy cast-iron skillets hanging from the huge cast-iron hooks at the far end of the kitchen. Deep growling in the throat of a very playful bull terrier that had somehow been transformed into the hound from hell.

Delaney stood up and snapped on the lights.

A man wearing a ski mask and half a sheepskin coat lay on his back beside a broken chair. The other half of his coat was bloody and torn and was hanging from one of Schuyler's incisors. The dog was shaking his head, trying to get the coat off his tooth. He looked at Delaney as if to apologize for turning a scene of high tension into a comedy.

The man's left arm lay beside him, inert, apparently connected by a thread. Blood was welling up beneath him, and the coat, in Delaney's estimation, was just plain beyond repair.

The man rolled away with a gurgling groan. His left arm didn't move, just lay there. "Jesus Christ," Delaney murmured, looking over at the dog. "Schuyler! Bad dog!" Schuyler looked back at him indignantly. Delaney got a kick out of Schuyler. A real sport.

The man couldn't speak. His mouth was moving behind the ski mask but he was no longer able even to scream. Shock, Delaney thought. Loss of blood.

Delaney advanced, holding the gun on the reclining figure.

Delaney said: "Dog doesn't know his own strength. He gets all enthused and . . . well, you see what can happen." Delaney shook his head, chuckling, as if Schuyler were an unruly child.

Schuyler was growling again, this time at the half of the sheepskin coat that he couldn't seem to disentangle from his teeth.

Delaney said: "So, who the hell are you, soldier?"

He began to lean down to pull the ski mask away, sensed a movement in the man's right hand, leaned out of the way as the slug took out part of his pajama top and laid a hot poker about a hundredth of an inch deep just below his armpit.

Delaney made a sour face and pulled the trigger on the forty-five.

The bullet blew the man's chest out between his shoulder blades and that was that.

"D'ja see that, Sky? That's what you can do when you got fingers and an opposable thumb. Which is why I'm the master and you're the pet. It's all in the thumb."

He knelt down beside the remains and worked the ski mask up off the stiff's face. He took a long look. He was just beginning to get the full whiff of death's stench. He sat down in an armchair by the fireplace, staring at the man's face.

"Well, for chrissakes," he said softly.

He knew the dead man by the scar that angled down across his forehead and across his cheek, souvenir of some forgotten dustup. He hadn't seen Kuno Meinhold since when, back in '70 maybe? Hell of a long time.

Gray hair and not much of it. Kuno had been a kid, twenty or so, back then. Now he was a gray-haired corpse. Jesus, he'd aged quickly, but that was all over. You couldn't get any older than he was now.

Schuyler finally rid himself of the damned coat and came to stand beside Delaney, looking up with what passed for an eager grin.

Delaney stroked the back of the bull terrier's head. "Kuno," he said softly, still staring at the face, "where the hell have you been? And what in God's name brings you back?"

18

CHARLOTTENBURG

Cooper wasn't quite prepared for the size of the Charlottenburg Palace. On a foggy morning it seemed like a somewhat smaller version of Versailles, the two long wings extending on either side of the yellow, white-columned center section as far as he could see, and there were bare-limbed trees between the palace and the traffic in the street. Frederick I had built it, the center building, at the end of the seventeenth century for his wife, Sophie Charlotte. Then she died and wasn't that always the way? During the Second World War it had been badly bombed but now it was restored, as if it were new. The golden figure of Fortuna on the dome was smudged by fog. He stood on the lumpy cobblestones in the courtyard, at the foot of the famous equestrian statue of the Great Elector, that first Frederick.

He was early. Beate had arranged the appointment with Lee and he'd taken a cab to the palace. She'd said to go inside and take up a stand at the main-floor picture gallery, which featured the paintings of the nineteenth-century Romantic Caspar David Friedrich. In his present frame of mind that was all he needed—lovelorn, depressed, windblown Caspar David Friedrich.

He hadn't been able to sleep, had been up pacing Beate's apartment, going outside in the cold predawn hours and walking for an hour in the quiet streets of Kreuzberg. He was sinking into the complexity of the situation as if it were quicksand. Koller and his connections to the

Nazi Brendel and thereby to Cooper's personal past, Stiffel's people on their murderous rampages, the horror of the bomb attack at Zoo Station, which had kept Beate on the run since the word came in . . . Cooper was beginning to feel the fear that was consuming Karl-Heinz. He had dreamt of the man Karl-Heinz had pointed out, the man he'd followed and lost near the sad little flea market . . . Erika had been part of the dream. First she'd been walking with the man Cooper had chased into the flea market, then he'd seen her with her father, screaming at him with tears running down her cheeks while he sat stone-faced behind a desk until she was finally quiet and Wolf Koller took out a huge Luger, swollen all out of proportion, from the desk drawer and fired it at his daughter . . . water squirted out and the BANG! flag fell from the barrel, a joke, but Erika had nevertheless fallen dead . . . only she had turned into her mother, it was Lee by the time her body hit the floor . . . He sighed, remembering the dream, comparing it to the Dali dream sequences in the old Hitchcock picture *Spellbound* . . . On the whole, his dream had nothing to be ashamed of. Dreams were bullshit, he lied to himself, hoping.

He found the Friedrichs without difficulty. They immediately began reaching out, pulling him into their throbbing center. Ultra-Romantic, haunted, half doomed, half hopeful. Lonely figures on promontories with their backs to you, looking out into the haze; a sense of loss, a turn into despair; the longing for what had been and might never come again, what was lost, lost, lost. He thought of Lee, suggesting this place. *Give me a break, sister.* This was worse than his dream, for God's sake.

"I love his paintings. They usually match my mood." She was standing at his side, her voice hushed as if she were trying not to break the mood of the paintings. He smelled her perfume.

"Not exactly cheery."

"Neither am I. Of course, I'm not an American. Americans are the cheery ones who can fix anything, no matter how badly it's gone wrong. How are you, John?"

"Frustrated. Getting nowhere."

"Miss Hubermann said you were making some progress."

"I don't think I'm any closer to Erika than I was when I got here. I'm sorry, Lee."

"It's unfair to expect you to find her. I know that. I don't believe that was ever my real motive. I wanted you to come so I'd have someone to depend on . . . I wanted to see you before I died, that is, if I'm really so sick . . . How could I have thought you'd come to Berlin and turn up a needle in a haystack? But . . . tell me what you've been up to. And, John, every day they don't find her body is a good day for me—"

"They. Who is they? Really?"

"Wolf's succeeded in having Max Adler—the police chief—assign several policemen to the search. And Wolf has his own security people. He depends on them, swears by them. No one has turned up anything."

"Are you sure Wolf wants her found?"

"What are you saying?"

"Maybe your husband is the one who took her away."

"Are you serious? But why, why would he do such a thing?"

"I don't know. Get her out of the way . . . get her away from her boyfriend. I've met this kid—he's a piece of work, Lee. He's not exactly what Wolf would have had in mind."

"Nor I. I told you that. How did you find him?"

"Called him on the phone. Nothing to it."

He told her about the meeting in the rubble of the Potsdamer Platz, the mound over the Führerbunker, Karl-Heinz's fear of being watched by his enemies, by the CIA, by the bogeymen . . . the fear of real Nazis behind the neo-Nazis.

"He's a fanatic, one of the Easterners," she said. "I've known some fanatics, Wolf used to know some, a long time ago, people who would do anything to achieve their aims, which were usually crazy and pointless. They were terrorists like the Baader-Meinhof gang. The Dorf-mann gang . . . not really political, politics wasn't the point. Wolf took the bull by the horns, or so he told me. He didn't want to be murdered or snatched off the street and have his companies stuck for some incredible ransom. Do you know what he did? He got the word out to them that he wanted to meet with them . . . and he did. He talked to them, let them air their views, he negotiated with them and treated them as if they were important which, God knows, they were . . . and his approach worked. They left him alone—"

"Out of the goodness of their hearts? That's pretty hard to swallow. What did he have to give them?"

"I don't know. I've thought about it . . . He might have convinced them that he was more ruthless than they were. It's possible. He'd research them, he'd find their weak points, the pressure points, and then he'd talk to them, tell them what he was going to do if they came after him or his business or his family. But I don't actually know."

"Maybe he just hired them, have you thought of that?"

"No, I never have."

"People like these gangs, the Baader-Meinhofs and the Dorfmanns, they don't really have pressure points—not if they're true nihilists—"

"Well, it's just a story he told me, John. I don't know anything about it or about nihilism or any other -ism. I'm telling you how Wolf does things. And no, I don't think he kidnapped Erika—"

"Maybe not. But say he truly loves her . . . say he kidnapped her *to keep her safe*. Maybe he figured Karl-Heinz is heading for a nasty accident and he didn't want his daughter to be anywhere near him when it happened. Look what happened that last night they were together. She could have been killed. Maybe it was the only way her father could control her and make sure she was safe. And keep her away from all the information Karl-Heinz might be sharing with her. She sure as hell wouldn't have paid any attention if Wolf had told her to stay out of it."

Slowly she turned away from the gloom of Friedrich's painting. "Do you seriously believe that's possible?" She wore a thoughtful expression, as if she might have just glimpsed a corner of reality. "Could he have done that . . . and not told me? In his way he does love her— immensely. She doesn't see it, of course, hasn't seen it since she was small, I think. You're a man—might he love his daughter still, even knowing she hates him?"

"How should I know? I've never even met the guy. Is it possible? Probable? You tell me. But I'll tell you one thing . . . I've been doing some research on your husband. And you know what, Lee? Wolf Koller is capable of just about anything."

She moved away to another picture. He followed her.

"Are you trying to scare me, John?"

"I don't know. Am I?"

"Well, you needn't bother. I'm already scared of Wolf. I'm as scared of Wolf as he is of me . . . It bothers me, you know, the way I feel myself claimed by these paintings. It's like seeing a painting of my psyche. I have a feeling that Friedrich's appeal is mainly to adolescents. Do you like them, John? You're a gloomy romantic."

"Right now they're giving me the creeps."

"Because you see yourself in them."

"Did Erika get you to look at them?"

She looked up almost dreamily. "You're so smart! She brought me here . . . how did you know that?"

"Kryptonite. It's this eerie gift I have. I like the paintings, too, the same way a person likes biting down on an abscessed tooth."

She moved away again, to the next picture. Cooper went to a window in the corridor connecting the rooms in all their gilt-encrusted, ornate splendor. Scaffolding had been erected in one of the long rooms; men were fussing with the ceiling, up among the chandeliers. Wisps of fog were blowing away and the watery sunlight filtered past the Grosse Kurfürst. The Great Elector. He turned and went to the opposite window, looking out the back into the vast, geometrically laid out formal gardens.

Anything was better than looking at Lee.

He was keeping his emotions in check, balancing them, loving her and despising her, wanting to hold her again, wanting her to be well and strong, wanting to find her daughter for her, wanting to make her happy and take her away with him . . .

And hating her for being so weak, so cowardly, so self-indulgent, such a willing victim.

She walked past him, saying nothing, and he followed her, watching her move. She wore a heather-hued English tweed suit with a fitted jacket, the skirt snug across her full hips, boots that reminded him of English coaching inns in old prints he'd found in Cecil Court, dark purple leather gloves, the cane.

Her limp was nearly gone. Her hair was sleek as polished, satiny wood. The way she moved, all confidence and swagger today—what was she thinking? He wondered if she actually loved him, if she'd loved him twenty years ago. He wished he could believe her. But he couldn't. She'd been telling him what he wanted to hear, perhaps out of pity, perhaps because she wanted him to help.

He wanted her, in his heart, in his guts, in every way a man can want a woman. He didn't want to hear any more sister shit. He'd known her for a handful of days out of his life. So, she was his sister. Big deal. But so what? Being his sister was nothing. An accident. Being his sister wasn't the worst problem with Lee Koller.

"Tell me, how did you come to marry Wolf? What sort of a man was he then? Has he changed? How well did you know him when Gunter Brendel was still alive?" He kept his voice steady but couldn't look at her. He felt the weight of the gray sky bearing down on him. The sun was fighting a losing battle; their shadows were disappearing. They were alone in the gardens. He saw in his mind a moment from *Last Year at Marienbad.*

"Forgive me, John, but what has this to do with finding Erika? I know what I need to know about my husband, and what has any of it to do with you? It's Erika who's tearing me apart."

"My God, Lee, she says she hates him. It's the main passion of her life . . . and you want to know why I need to learn about him? He, Erika, you—your *family*—are at the center of her disappearance. Your *family* made her want to kill herself—"

"How can you be so sure? You don't know!"

"You and Wolf, you're her family. She didn't do what she did to get away from you, Lee. So, it was her father."

"You're telling me that she hates him *so much* that death was better than being his daughter . . . How can that be?"

"In your heart you're still an American—and it's been pointed out to me lately that Americans cannot conceive of dying for an abstraction . . . for politics. You don't share her feelings because *she* is German. She has a conscience, Lee, something you can't imagine. You're a survivor, whatever the cost, but she's not. She's a German, she thinks more than we do, she accepts her dark side just the way we deny ours . . . she knows how one dies for an abstraction when we'd just shrug and say stop being such a drag, get a life! Can you understand? Conscience, in your life it's the first sacrifice on the road to survival—in hers, it's the last."

She wouldn't answer. The cane scraped among the crushed stones of the path. He was beginning to crack her and he hated himself for doing it. But he hated her more for making it inevitable.

"Tell me about marrying him. Why was it all so fast? Your husband was just dead—so what was the hurry?"

She lashed out at him, almost physically, fighting for her life. "You had left me!"

"That's revisionist history, Lee. You ordered me away. Told me I had destroyed your life."

"I was alone, helpless—"

"You're always helpless. And you're never alone. That's the point, *they* were there."

"—and I was afraid. I had nowhere to turn and Wolf was there."

"Peterson used to say you were nuts, 'crazypants' he called you. He's not a romantic, Lee. He knows bullshit when he steps in it. What you're trying to palm off on me is self-indulgent bullshit. We've been through all this. I didn't leave you . . . get that straight, okay? You chose to stay. A grown woman, perfectly capable of knowing right from wrong. That's right, isn't it?"

The tight set of her mouth was crumbling, the fine pointed features, the perfect clarity of her face. "You tell me about conscience . . . I'm telling you about fear! You know nothing of fear. I was afraid, you and Peterson had wrecked it all—why is this so hard for you to understand? Wolf stepped in and cared for me, I let him comfort me, he took care of everything. Erika didn't exist . . . how could I know what lay ahead?"

"Right. You were afraid . . . let's cut a little closer to the bone, shall we? How close was Wolf to your first husband?"

"They were in business together."

"Did they think alike, Wolf and Gunter? Did they share a set of political beliefs?"

"What are you going on about? Just say it! Why are you attacking me? You say you love me, but you try to wound me—why? I didn't make Erika run away, why punish me this way? What is it you want me to say?"

"Just admit the truth, goddamn it! Wolf Koller is a Nazi, just like Gunter Brendel! Wasn't he in it with Brendel and all the rest of them twenty years ago? Isn't he in it now? Isn't that what drove Erika to take that knife and start in on herself? The fact that her father is some kind of latter-day Nazi?"

She steadied herself against a bench; she was fighting back the tears. She didn't want to give in.

"For God's sake, stop it, stop, stop, stop! Don't do this to me! Don't talk to me about Nazis! I'm not a Nazi, John, I'm your little sister, Lee . . . oh please, please, John—"

"I want to find your daughter. You and Wolf have made her part of the shrieking madness of your lives, of all the Nazis stood for . . . I have to understand what she's running away from, or if she's dead—"

She began to sob, sank onto the bench, shoulders quaking, the purple glove at her mouth.

"If she's dead, I have to understand why . . . if she's dead, Lee, then this is the last act of what began twenty years ago. Look, I'm sick in love with you, I can't look at you and not feel my legs go weak, and I couldn't possibly care less that—by some accident which has had no bearing on our actual lives—you're my sister. That's absolutely immaterial to our lives, it means nothing, we're just two people . . . I've known you for ten days of my life, your being my sister is a supreme irrelevancy . . . *but you've let yourself be passed from one Nazi to another,* *you're their goddamn property, their queen! You don't have the strength or* *the desire to get away from them, not in twenty years!"*

"My God, how I hate you!" she cried out, her voice breaking.

"You called for help and I came."

"Then go home, just go home! You make me hate you, you never stop judging me, and I'm never good enough for you . . . I never measure up. My God, I'm the one who's sick and I can't stand fighting with you . . . I'm sick and I don't have the strength anymore."

Tears were running down her face. He watched her let it happen, make no attempt to stop them and pull her face back together. There was nothing left to accuse her of: he'd unloaded all of it. One Nazi to another, handled by them, passed on . . .

"I'm not going home. I'm going to do what I can because your daughter has the courage to fight it, fight for herself . . . she deserves to be saved and helped and given a reason to go on . . . but you've got to help me—"

"I can't help you, John. I don't know how—"

"You won't, you won't pull yourself together and fight the fight with me! If you don't have a conscience, where's your courage? The worst of the Coopers at least had courage!"

She got up from the bench, pulled away from him, stumbled as she tried to run away. He watched her go. She reached the door of the palace, disappeared within.

He was out of breath, emotionally spent.

It was the hardest thing he'd ever done. He'd found her after all these years, and now he'd driven a stake through her breast.

He'd had to do it but he couldn't have done it more destructively. He knew that. He didn't know how to handle her and she didn't understand what lay at the core of his life.

She didn't get it.

He had to be the one in the family who did something worthwhile.

He'd spent twenty years living down the family. He was the last one, the only one who could be an honorable Cooper. His brother, Cyril, was dead these twenty years and Lee might as well have been dead. She didn't understand what it meant to look back at a family of traitors and know you were the last one with a chance to save the family from ignominy . . . They might as well have come from different galaxies. The Nazi past, the central evil of the century, meant nothing to her, he'd never heard her mention it, it wasn't her guilt . . . which was why John Cooper had more in common with Erika than Lee did.

It was John Cooper and Erika Koller who shared the guilt.

19

WOLF

Cooper emerged from the palace, back onto the cobblestones, cursing his own foolishness, his lack of feeling. Why had he treated her so brutally? What was the point of raking over the errors of the past . . . what the hell business of his was what she had done twenty years ago? It was a world ago. He'd been talking about two different people at different times in their lives. It was now that should have mattered. It was now that she had turned to him, reaching out across the chasm of years. And he'd responded by throwing a fit like a jealous, angry schoolboy. She was what she was, did what she'd had to do, and she'd never claimed to be strong or perfect. And now, had he driven her away for good? How could he make it up to her, how could he even get in touch with her again?

He was out in the middle of the cobblestones, passing the statue of the Great Elector, when he heard someone calling his name. "Mr. Cooper, over here . . ."

He turned and saw an immense old Mercedes convertible, dark green, reflecting the Charlottenburg Palace and the Great Elector like a mirror. The passenger door had been swung open and a man in a slouch hat and a gray herringbone jacket and black turtleneck was leaning across the leather seat toward him, waving.

"It is Mr. Cooper, John Cooper of Boston?" He was smiling. He wore driving gloves. Cooper had never seen a more beautiful car. The creamy fabric top looked fat and perfect. "Let me give you a lift. And introduce myself . . . I'm your brother-in-law. Wolf Koller. Come on, climb aboard." He had a slight English accent. Cooper remembered seeing somewhere in Bruni's archives that he'd been educated at Cambridge in the late fifties. "Let me give you a lift, old chap."

Cooper slid into the seat, which approximated a large leather club chair. The car looked as if it had just rolled off the assembly line. They shook hands. Cooper said: "This is unexpected."

"Yes, I suppose it is. The palace is quite a sight, isn't it? Did Lise show you the Friedrichs? They're her favorites, my daughter's, too, for that matter. Was Lise all right? I saw her leave just now looking a bit fragile—she'd have killed me if I'd stopped her. She drove herself today and that scares me but there's just no stopping her. She didn't have one of her spells, I hope?"

"No, she was fine. She's under a lot of stress, as you know."

"She and Erika have a lot in common. Very serious people. I've always found that a leaven of humor makes life a good deal more endurable. Do you have the time for a get-acquainted chat? I think I'd better fill you in on what's going on—you may just possibly be getting a garbled version. Can you spare me the time?"

He was incredibly handsome in a way that other men didn't resent. His face was rugged as well as chiseled. The eyebrows were thickets and the silvery gray hair swept back over his ears was thick and didn't look as if he spent a lot of time worrying about it. His clothes reflected his Cambridge years. Pearl-gray slacks, dark brown suede boots working the gas and clutch and brakes.

"Sure. I don't have a very tight schedule."

"Good. I know a horrible little corner bar not too far from here." He pointed out another museum as they entered a broad avenue with a grass strip down the middle, said: "Have you seen Nefertiti? She's in there. Worth the trip out here. Well, I'm glad Lise didn't have one of her faints or anything. She's very brave, won't accept that she's ill, but not always wise. So, what do you think of your sister after all these years?"

"It hadn't occurred to me that she would be so beautiful still."

"Even now she makes my heart stand still," Koller said. "It's all in the genes according to my medical friends." He sighed, his eyelids drooping sadly in a bed of fine wrinkles. "Her beauty makes her condition all the more heartbreaking. Medically, she's a bit of a mystery thus far. I've got a good man but he's being very cagey, doesn't want to commit himself. Fritz Gisevius. He'd be glad to talk with you while you're here, I'm sure. I've known him forever. His father and mine go way back." He pulled the car over against the curb and parked. "Follow me and I'll put you in the picture."

It was a simple bar, windows on the street, nothing dark or atmospheric about it. Koller was known. The woman tending bar flashed him a subservient smile. He nodded. "Mr. Cooper, will you try one of my specials?"

"Why not?"

He held up two fingers in a V-for-victory gesture. "Watch." The woman expertly made two perfect martinis and then, as if by magic, she waved a beautiful bottle of blue Bols curaçao over the glasses, and the martinis turned an ethereal cobalt. "Blue martinis. Fellow I knew in Saudi years ago introduced me to them. They taste all right. It's the color that won me over. Come on, let's sit down over in the corner."

Wolf Koller made himself comfortable, put his hat on the empty chair, crossed his legs, slouched in the chair with his back to the window. He looked far more like an artist than a business tycoon. He was probably fifty-five and looked it but there was an immense casual dash about him. Cooper knew what it was. He'd been watching it all his life at the movies. Star quality.

"In the first place, let me apologize for not welcoming you to Berlin sooner. Obviously, you should be staying at the house with us—my wife's brother, after all. But things are a bit unsettled here these days, as you know if you've been reading the newspapers. I get dragged into these things in one way and another—probably because I'm willing to express myself with relative candor. Then there's Lise—would you rather I called her Lee?"

"I know who you mean either way."

"I think of her as Lise, then. She has such a lot of identities and nationalities. Born American, her childhood in London, then here in Germany. Confusing. Well, I'll call her Lise. The difficulty, as you may have guessed, is that she is full of secrets these days—it may well be part of her illness, we can't be absolutely sure. But she has chosen to keep your presence in Berlin secret from me—thus my very poor hospitality."

"But you knew to follow her?"

"Yes, one develops these little stratagems to discover what she's up to. It's a long story, Mr. Cooper, and a sad one at that. She's been in failing health for several months, actually, closer to a year, I suppose—mental health, let me assure you. Physically she's still strong—another aspect which makes it so terribly poignant. But her physical health could go, too, you see—we just don't know what to expect. Her illness—it started with her forgetting things, occasionally saying inappropriate things, having fainting spells and not remembering where she was. One of the first instances of it occurred at KaDeWe, our great department store. You must make a visit there while in Berlin, by the way. The top floor is devoted entirely to foodstuffs—think of Harrods food halls only much, much larger. She was shopping there one day and suddenly was making a disturbance, had no idea where she was, or who she was, and then fainted. They got hold of me at my office . . . it was a bit of a mess. We had to keep it out of the newspapers for her sake—we labor under the curse of being a moderately well-known family and the vultures are always hovering around looking for scandal. As in the case of Erika, which we'll come to in a moment. Fritz Gisevius, the doctor friend I mentioned, offered to have a go at diagnosing her illness. It's been most confusing—he's the best and he doesn't know if it's some kind of brain fever, a tumor too small to be detected, a very early onset of Alzheimer's disease. The point is, she seems to be getting progressively worse and he thinks that she may need hospitalization soon. She had a terrible fall not long ago, might have broken her neck, landed at my feet in the foyer of our home, looked up at me and had no idea who I was . . . Of course, I hold out hope that they'll discover it's something simple, a dietary thing, some minor body chemistry that cornflakes in large quantities will cure." He smiled the sad smile again. "Hope sustains one, you see. I look at her, I cannot believe she's beyond repair—she's like a thoroughbred automobile, she should be fixable, but unlike a car, she has a soul . . . and I believe that her illness stems somehow from the soul. Her soul is infected and we cannot understand how to cure it." He stopped himself and took a sip of the blue martini. So did Cooper: miraculously it wasn't bad.

"This business with our daughter isn't doing her any good, either. Erika can be, like all children, I suppose, exceedingly self-absorbed. I'm afraid I'm rather put out with Erika these days."

"That's why I'm here. That's what Lee contacted me about."

"I gathered as much once I learned you were here—which happened only a few hours ago. Tell me, how did she contact you? A letter? No, there was hardly time for that—"

"Someone she knew was coming to the States. She had her deliver a message."

"Ah, I see. Well, it's none of my business and in case she's sworn you to secrecy, I won't ask any more questions. I congratulate you on being a very devoted brother. I've always wondered why she didn't make more of her relationship with you. I mean, you're her only relative and she won't contact you—struck me as odd but she made it clear to me that my opinion was not required."

"Well, it cut both ways. I didn't contact her. I didn't know she'd remarried until all this present stuff—"

"And it's been twenty years!" He shook his head, ran his fingers back through his hair. "Where does life go, eh? We're at that stage, all of us. I find myself taking note of the obituaries, checking the ages . . . it's a universal experience, I'm told."

"So why were you following her today?"

"Well, it worries me when she insists on going out alone, particularly when she refuses to have our chauffeur drive her. And so, if I'm aware of it and at home, I occasionally follow her."

"It was a coincidence then, that she was meeting me?"

"No, no, I was hoping we'd meet somehow. Or I'd at least get a look at you. You see, she's well aware of her infirmities now. The blackouts, loss of memory, spasms of fear and emptiness in her mind. So she writes herself notes, insurance against forgetting . . . So, I found a note she'd written to herself about meeting you. *John at the C'burg,* and it clicked in my mind. We don't know any John and I thought of brother John Cooper . . . it might just fit in, so I thought, with the Erika problem and her health worries—wouldn't it be logical to want to get in touch with her brother? And here I am. I am so glad, John, that it was you."

"I am, too, of course."

"I thought it was important that we meet and talk. About her medical condition more than anything else. I'm still hopeful she'll come round and be all right. But for now Gisevius tells me that she mustn't be excited, or upset, or subjected to any more stress than is necessary. She's like an unstable element, an explosive. He says she might blow herself to smithereens at any moment. It could short-circuit, you understand? It's all electricity in the brain, he says, chemical reactions. And I know you'd want what's best for her. You wouldn't want her to do herself any harm."

"Is she suicidal?"

"Who knows about such things?" He shrugged. "One hopes to God she isn't, but one doesn't actually know. Her mind seems to be a loose cannon—"

"I understand Erika tried to kill herself."

"Oh, good lord, Erika—she has a flair for the dramatic."

"You don't take it seriously? I understand there was blood everywhere—"

"Yes, yes, but no Erika. Suicides don't cut their wrists, die, and then walk away."

"You don't think it was Erika's blood?"

"Oh, no, it was Erika's blood. Or blood type, anyway. I'm willing to believe she cut herself. But Dr. Gisevius tells me that suicides often do themselves a superficial injury and then wait for friends to come rescue them. I'm sure that's what happened. Erika had the added pleasure of knowing that it would drive me absolutely crazy—which it did, of course. But I'm angry not about what it did to me—Erika has been fighting me, and alternately worshiping me, since she came out of her mother's womb, it seems. She has a will of iron—which she tells me she got from me. Well, perhaps she did." His face softened at the thought of his daughter, wayward, but his daughter nonetheless. He shook his head, full of a father's confusion. "No, I'm angry that she could cause her mother so much pain so heartlessly—and now she's off on the Costa Brava, Ibiza, God knows where, having a fine time, paying us back for all the horrible things we've done to her . . . While enjoying the life we've been able to provide for her, she can never forgive me for being who I am. Are you a father, Mr. Cooper?"

"No, I'm not."

"Well, it's not an unmixed blessing."

"You take a pretty dim view of your daughter."

"I love my daughter. That's immutable. But my daughter and her friends are part of what's wrong with Germany these days. Rich, arrogant, self-indulgent, able to afford philosophies and attitudes which make men like me the villains . . . it's not exactly a new story, is it? We will tame them sooner or later, of course. Life will tame them."

"The daughter you describe is not the one I've heard about from others I've spoken with. Who is the real Erika? Theirs or yours? What is it about your daughter?"

"Americans have a unique way of looking at things."

"So people keep telling me. But it's never the prelude to a compliment. Are you about to join the multitude?" Cooper kept sucking at the blue martini, which gave the whole scene a certain appropriate air of unreality.

"I dislike being as predictable as all that but perhaps I am. It seems to me that you Americans don't really have a gift for the study of history—maybe because you have less of it. Look at us—Europeans have not only the history of their own little countries to digest, but all the other little countries, some of which they may have been part of at one time or another . . . you see? It's a full-time job being a European and grasping the essence. One does what one can. It is terra incognita to Americans, in my experience, or to Australians, for example. So, not understanding Europe's hopelessly complex history, you glance over at us from time to time and see Napoleon and Disraeli and Queen Victoria and Freud and Hitler and the concentration camps and the Wall and German reunification and the EEC and a Pope or two and Charles and Diana . . . just isolated events, never the seamless continuum of history—"

"Does your daughter figure in this somewhere, or is this the standard gratuitous lecture on what hopeless stupid shits we Americans are?"

"Bear with me. Lenin comes, Stalin—the greatest butcher of the century—comes, then Khrushchev bangs his shoe on the table at the UN, the Bay of Pigs, Kennedy dead, the Wall goes up, the Wall comes down, Communism staggers off into the darkness from whence it came . . . all isolated moments, headlines in the papers, nothing more to the Americans. Well, Mr. Cooper, you Americans—as the expression goes—just don't get it! Another blue martini?"

He lifted his empty glass and the woman at the bar nodded.

"Don't get what?" Cooper asked. It was growing darker outside.

"Nothing ever ends. Try to remember that when you're dealing with Europe. *Nothing ever ends.*"

"Your daughter? You mean she's a Nazi or something—nothing ever ends?"

"Erika? A Nazi? Good God, no! She's a Communist, I should think. Though I doubt that she's ever had a coherent political thought. It's easier just to hate, isn't it? Start with your plutocrat father, hate him very thoroughly. Then get cracking with the class struggle. Such things do still exist—"

"Plutocrats?"

"Communists. Leftists. We're due for another wave of anarchist, leftist terrorism. Terrorism for its own sake. Things like this nightmare at Zoo Station the other night. It's all a cycle, nothing ever ends—remember? We're due—not for the Nazis. What you think of as Nazis, they're always with us, here, America, everywhere. Nazism is now a state of mind that has nothing to do with the excesses of Hitler—these neo-Nazis like shocking people, invoking Hitler's name, but they're thugs, creating civil unrest—they should be stamped out. But I'm afraid of the Red Brigades, whatever they'll call themselves this next time . . . I'm afraid of your CIA, for that matter . . . I'm afraid of a great many things, as any thinking man must be, but I am most afraid that my daughter will align herself with the wave of leftist terrorism, anarchist terrorism, Arab-Islamic fundamentalist terrorism, whatever it turns out to be—*because she resents her father.* She resents the fact that people listen to me, that I have some small political influence. Can you imagine what a trophy Erika Koller would make for these bloodthirsty imbeciles? Patty Hearst and the Symbionese Liberation Army magnified a thousand times because Germany is a smaller place, the world watches Germany so closely . . . Rich, beautiful, 'bent' as the English would say . . . that's what I fear most, and I cannot share this fear with Lise because of the condition she's in."

The two new blue martinis arrived and Koller stared into his for a few moments. The bar was filling up.

"Are you quite serious? Or is this somehow for my benefit?"

"Quite serious, I assure you. I have my own people combing the logical spots looking for her but you can see how difficult it is. I don't know where she might go—or with whom. Everything is so volatile, isn't it? What about Russia, for example?

"Now the Russian Bear is loose again, cut down in size, but nothing ever ends . . . he has his destiny. We all have our destinies, Mr. Cooper, nations and individuals, and I very much suspect that we keep playing them out over and over again. Sometimes I feel we are all very old souls, Mr. Cooper, living our lives again and again, never really learning anything but struggling to achieve our destinies. The Russians feel Europe is still theirs, a continent of weak, self-absorbed sybarites, easy pickings for the Bear, but the Bear can never get it quite right. He worships the Europeans, their wit and sophistication, and he despises them for their decadence—the Bear is a little short on brains, I'm afraid, but very determined. He knows things never end. The Bear is a fierce defender, an uneasy winner—look at General Kutuzov swallowing Napoleon, look at Hitler's armies disappearing in the frozen wastes, German soldiers in summer uniforms staying alive by eating their fallen, frozen comrades— the Russians need someone to tell them what to do. Then they'll be all right."

"And what about the Germans?" Cooper asked.

"Ah, the Huns. The Teutons. The Germans. We are the great intellectuals, the intellectual fools of Europe. Without us there is no real depth to European culture, we produce the greatest music, the deepest thinkers, the great philosophies, the really massive depressions, the great political leaders with the vision to unite Europe in one Reich . . . and we blunder out into the world thinking how everybody is bound to agree with us because we are so obviously the brightest of the lot . . . and we are inevitably hurt and surprised when everyone hates us with a bloody passion!"

"It's probably because you start by killing them," Cooper observed.

"No, you've got it exactly backwards, Mr. Cooper. That's not what we do. We *end* by killing them! And they remember! They always hate us from the last time. Whenever it was. It's the German tragedy!"

"But it's their tragedy, isn't it?"

"Their tragedy comes midway through the opera. The last act is our tragedy. That's when *they* kill *us*. We can't seem to grasp the obvious. Am I more than routinely boring today, Mr. Cooper? I'm trying to make up for having treated you so badly since you've been here—"

"Look . . . are you a Nazi? In any sense of that word?"

Wolf Koller broke into loud laughter. No one paid any attention. Maybe he was a regular, maybe he laughed a lot. "You do sound like my daughter! Me? A Nazi? Good God, what an imagination!"

"I take that as a firm no, then."

"Firm. Although a real Nazi might not just blurt out the truth in a neighborhood bar. It would depend on the neighborhood, I suppose."

"But Gunter Brendel was. You were his partner."

"Brendel? Dead for twenty years! Yes, I suppose he was. Murky chap, Gunter. I've heard he was a Nazi. Then he was murdered . . . Baffling. Lucky for Lise that I came along. God, I was in love with her before I ever had the nerve to touch her. Women have such power! Gunter was a weak man, a fool, but I am neither. A Nazi! No, Mr. Cooper, I am not a Nazi. A believer in Germany, the Fatherland. But that's hardly a crime."

"But your daughter thinks you are a Nazi."

"Well, she likes to accuse me, in any case. She's a kid, maybe it's just that I like the Beatles or something. She's got friends who think anyone with money is an SS man in disguise. Her boyfriend is from the East. He pours the nonsense into her ear and it comes out her mouth— not a damn thing I can do about it. She'll turn up. Lise is the one I'm worried about—"

"If you're not a Nazi—"

"All right, Mr. Cooper, you've had your little joke."

"—then what are you?"

"I'm a German nationalist, that's all."

"What's Joachim Stiffel?"

"An idiot. A violent idiot."

"Do you know him?"

"I know almost everyone. Yes. He came to us once, to some men I know, wanted us to back him financially, said he wanted Germany for the Germans, said he was just a nationalist and all the rest was bad PR! Cheeky little bastard!"

"And what happened?"

"He was crazy. Not the sort of investment I would want to make. Or be associated with. My God, he's vermin."

"Frankly, I don't know who or what to believe about anything. And that includes you, Herr Koller."

"I fully understand how strange all this must seem to you. I sympathize. And I even have a suggestion, if you won't think me inhospitable. May I?"

"Fire away."

"You have come, through no fault of your own, at the worst possible time. Erika making a fool of herself. Lise in a bad way. I'm involved in some fairly explosive negotiations myself, with our social unrest as it is . . . have you thought about going home and waiting for things to calm down? We're going to find Erika. I'm sure we'll get Lise properly diagnosed and set her on the road to recovery. We'll take care of the Stiffel problem and the immigrant problem . . . I'll be delighted to stay in touch with you, by telephone or fax or letter, any way you choose, keep you informed . . . and come spring, why don't you plan to return to Berlin? The whole world is going to look different by the spring. I'll take you out on my boat in Lake Wannsee, Erika will be there, Lise will be there, the sun will be shining, we'll have a family reunion. We'll be laughing about what we all went through during the winter—and we'll wonder what the hell we were all so upset about. We'll go on a Rhine cruise, we'll take my big boat! What do you say?"

"But what about German destiny?"

"Well"—he laughed—"I think we've pretty well proven that war doesn't work! We'll just have to realize our destiny some other way. Deep down, you know, we're just Americans without a continent to call our own."

Koller was still smiling with good humor when they got back to the car. "Where can I drop you? Where are you staying?"

"I'd just as soon go for a bit of a stroll," Cooper said.

"Absolutely. I know just how you feel. I'm very glad we could meet. I only wish it were under more normal circumstances. But next time, come spring, we'll do it right. As for now, why not just go home? Here's my card—you can always get me at my office. We'll stay in touch." He reached out and they shook hands. "John Cooper, let the Germans try to make sense of Germany. If we can't do it, no one can."

Cooper watched the exquisite car slowly pull away, watched it until it was gone.

20

ORLOVSKI

When he saw the man standing next to the enormous gray mouse, the Professor did a double take that snapped his neck violently enough that he heard vertebrae cracking. Then he very nearly called out to him. It was like running into an old pal at Macy's during the Christmas rush, someone you hadn't seen in a long time, someone from another lifetime. He almost called out, he almost . . . Then all his training took over and he clamped his mouth shut and became invisible, became just another guy in the crowd. Salt-and-pepper beard, beret, shearling jacket, only one eye that focused if you were really paying attention. The beard covered scars put there by a onetime SS interrogator he had run into in Buenos Aires twenty years before. Hugo Waxman. One of those who slipped through the nets after the war: everybody said Hugo was long dead but the Professor had found him down Argentine way in that other lifetime, even before the lifetime that had included Orlovski, who was still standing next to the big fucking mouse, and the Professor had made a mistake and had wound up with the late Hugo Waxman pushing knitting needles through one side of his face and out the other. It had been a disgusting few hours and then, what with one thing and another, by dint of superior intelligence and stark terror, the Professor had turned the tables and pushed the needles through Waxman's throat and then all of Waxman's friends had decided to pursue the man who was now the Professor to the ends of the earth . . . and so he had become the Professor, and never gone back to America, and had wound up in an office with Konstantin Orlovski . . . alive.

And now here he was, good old Konnie, and if they'd been in other lines of work they might have gone for drinks and told each other old war stories, new lies. But the surprise of seeing him in Berlin, at the KaDeWe, talking to a seven-foot-tall mouse, was just enough to give the Professor pause. He shrank back into the crowd of parents with their small children staring round-eyed at the dream world before them.

He had been to the food floor on top of the KaDeWe, picking up a few pounds of his favorite Sumatra coffee beans, and he'd come back down with his parcel on the escalator. On the way out on the ground floor he had stopped to watch the finishing touches being put on the Christmas fantasy display in the high rotunda. Kris Kringle's wintry castle, frosted with dripping snow like wax on a candle; all manner of trolls and elves and very large mice and bunnies and squirrels: and there he was wearing a fur coat, from the look of it sable, bald head with a ruff of gray hair from the ears around the base of his bony skull, dark aviator glasses squatting astride his broad, brutally Slavic nose. The mouse was miming the eating of a massive wedge of Swiss cheese and the man was chatting him up, grinning broadly, to the delight of the kids gathered around them. One small boy tentatively put out a foot, lowered it on the mouse's long tail just to see if he noticed. He didn't.

Several other animals wandered among the crowd, handing out bits of candy in bright wrappers while Christmas music played. The scene reminded the Professor of the small town where he grew up—a white Christmas was just about guaranteed there. It had all been a long time ago and in another country.

Watching the man in the sable coat, he thought that the Christmases spent in Russia and the East didn't make the final cut for the holiday hit parade. He was thinking about a bleak Christmas day spent in the sweaty, carbolic-soap smell of Moscow Center, the gray and grimy walls in the overheated corridors that wound around like a tub of guts, waiting to learn the fate of a man who had no more chance than Frosty the Snowman on that last hot summer day, and when he looked back at the consumer fantasy before him he couldn't quite believe his eyes . . .

He was watching Major Konstantin Orlovski, KGB, who'd spent

that day with him, playing cards, exchanging the latest gallows humor, smoking the terrible cigarettes, waiting for news of the man out there in the gap, was it to be life or death?

About ten o'clock Christmas night word had come through from Deputy Director Egon Rossovich himself on the scene in Prague. The word wasn't so good. Their man had turned up with his throat cut, hidden beneath a snowbank. So much for our man in Prague. Orlovski and the Professor had given each other weary, forlorn, resigned looks and stubbed out their smokes, entered the time in the log, bundled up in their greatcoats and fur hats.

"Happy Christmas, Comrade," Orlovski said softly, as if Rossovich or one of the other bigwigs might overhear and raise an official eyebrow.

"The same to you, my friend," the Professor said. Orlovski was a kind man. He wasn't overly bright and the KGB liked that in a man. Loyal, hardworking, and no genius. He had hitched his star to Rossovich, who was rising fast, and as time went on he became as indispensable to Rossovich as Rossovich was to him. They made a good team, like Sancho and Don Quixote, Orlovski the pawn paving the way for Rossovich, his knight.

Now Orlovski stood before the Professor, surrounded by laughing children, in his sable coat, carrying a shopping bag in one hand and a suitcase he'd obviously just purchased in the other—the luggage department was only a few feet away. It was an emerald green plastic or Lucite or fiberglass suitcase the Professor had admired while strolling on the ground floor an hour before. It was the most beautiful and the most expensive suitcase he'd ever seen. He'd wondered just who would ever buy such a thing. A suitcase that looked like something Burton would have put on Taylor's finger. Well, now he knew. An ex-KGB major, high in the party apparat as well, who was supposedly retired to a Black Sea dacha. Orlovski was in his mid-fifties. They had been born within a few days of each other, thousands and thousands of miles apart. Orlovski had sent him a birthday cake when the Professor was new in Moscow, showing his goodwill. *Happy Birthday, Kiril, and Welcome!* had been written across the cake in bright red script. He'd had the cake made in the shape of a hammer and sickle in a fancy government kitchen by the boys and girls who catered official dinners. It was the sort of trick a KGB major could get away with without arousing any comment.

So, what the hell was Konnie Orlovski doing in Berlin looking like

Sol Hurok introducing the Red Army Chorus to the cultural establishment of the West? Buying a three-thousand-deutschmark suitcase? It had to mean something.

Orlovski had been the primary KGB operational liaison with the terrorist groups popping up all over the West back in the old days. Baader-Meinhof, the Red Brigades, the Dorfmann bunch, Carlos the Jackal . . . dozens more, big and small, both "Red" and "Black" as they were called. Now he was too busy talking with a bearded Christmas troll of some sort and keeping the kids laughing to have noticed the Professor, or Kiril as he'd have called him. The Professor faded back deeper into the safety of the crowd and decided he'd keep an eye on Orlovski. Just for the hell of it.

When Orlovski left KaDeWe he set out on foot, the dry snowflakes speckling his exquisite fur coat. He carried the green suitcase and the shopping bag and he was hard to miss. He was a man without a care in the world. He walked all the way up Tauentzienstrasse past the immense interlocked tubular *Berlin* sculpture, which the natives called *Entwined Entrails*. Berlin's residents could never quite take anything pompous too seriously. It was what set them apart from other Germans. The Berlin attitude.

At the Europa Center Orlovski went inside, strolling through the constant bustle, consumers wandering from shop to shop, teenagers lounging, smoking. He stood transfixed for several minutes watching the glass-enclosed Water Clock, forty-three feet high with all its workings visible. There was always a crowd at the Water Clock. Orlovski stared at it like a child fascinated by a new toy.

The Professor was yawning. Come on, Konnie, what's the big deal? Finally the Russian checked his wristwatch. From where the Professor stood it looked like a gold Rolex. A knockoff maybe, but probably not. The suitcase and the coat, they were the real thing.

When he left the Europa Center he continued on past the Kaiser Wilhelm Memorial Church, a bombed-out shell from the war. A tragic monument. But the locals couldn't resist calling it *the hollow tooth*. The snow was blowing around in busy little swirls. The sky was slate-gray and going darker.

He crossed the street at the bright Ku'damm corner where the famous restaurant Café Kranzler glowed behind its red and white striped exterior. It seemed supernaturally bright and cheery and welcoming against the dour afternoon. It was said that more tourists dined at Kranzler's than any other restaurant in Germany. It glowed like a great ocean liner seriously off course but docking on the Ku'damm, making the best of it. And, God knew, Orlovski was far from home.

Orlovski went inside and climbed the stairs to the second floor with the grand unobstructed view of the endless activity on the street below. The Professor waited, then followed him up the stairs. He had checked the suitcase and the shopping bag. He was sitting by himself at a window table. The hostess took the Professor well across the room, far enough away for safety but with a clear view. It was nearly two o'clock. The Professor ordered a large beer and a plate of lasagna. Orlovski was drinking a beer and staring out the window.

The Professor unfolded his newspaper and began to read. The Zoo Station massacre was still dominating the news but there wasn't much progress to report. The red flowers signifying the old dead Dorfmann gang were obviously a kind of joke but beyond that nobody seemed to know much. The stories concentrated on the outrage that was sweeping across the city and the nation. If you weren't calling for an end to the mindless violence, for a return to a law and order program while there was still time, then you just weren't a public figure.

The next time the Professor looked, Orlovski was shaking hands with a new arrival. He was tall, wore a brown suit, had fuzzy remnants of red hair that were going white at his ears. But there had once been a lot of wiry red hair and the Professor recognized him. He'd been known as Sebastien the Red some twenty years ago. The Red was for his hair in those days, not for his politics. History had passed him by. Most people believed he was dead and the rest had forgotten about him, which was just the way Sebastien had wanted it.

The Professor wasn't sure what Sebastien was doing now. The last he'd heard Sebastien had gone into something comparatively respectable in light of his previous enthusiasms. With a new name, a new identity, and official membership in the upper middle class. A hell of a far cry from the old days when he'd been a gunman in one of the Black terrorist gangs in West Germany and, hell, all over Europe.

The Professor thumbed through the index file in his mind. It had been Rafaela Dorfmann's bunch, and when Rafaela had been killed in the explosion in their bomb factory the word had gotten out that Sebastien had perished with her. There had been four or five bodies reduced to bits of this and that in the rubble. Identification had been on the sketchy side. But the bright boys back at Moscow Center had known Sebastien was in The Hague the day the bombs blew up in Munich. He'd been kidnapping a business executive and had botched it. He'd had to kill the guy, his wife, and a teenage daughter, had been lucky to get out of Holland with his poor scared ass intact. Orlovski and Egon Rossovich had engineered the snatch and would have killed Sebastien with their bare hands if they could have gotten hold of him.

But times change. You cool down. Now they were having lunch, laughing about old times. Terrorist and spymaster having moved on, living new lives.

What the hell were they up to?

21

STORKRAFT

"He's a liar! Smoothest goddamn snow job I've ever heard. Mr. Reasonable! Whatta guy! And it was just all bullshit, every fucking word of it!"

When Cooper got back to the flat in Kreuzberg, Beate had just finished washing her hair. She did things like that when she could find the time. Her life was made of squeezing things into her schedule, coping with the full-time anxiety of her job. The Zoo Station massacre had increased the anxiety. Now she was sitting at the kitchen table in a white terrycloth robe with her hair wrapped in a towel. She was watching and listening to Cooper blow his top on the subject of Wolf Koller. "That very polished Cambridge accent . . . He was more like an upper-class Englishman than a German—maybe he thought I'd fall for that quicker. Wants me to go home and come back next spring and we'll all go out on his boat, his little boat or his big boat on the Rhine—Jesus! Erika will be back and Lee will feel fine and we'll have a fucking picnic or something . . . Nazi? Me, a Nazi? What a joke, I'm only a German nationalist and that dirty little Stiffel person, just scum . . . And he thought I was sitting there lapping it up like a grateful hick from the turnip farm!"

She watched him with a smile slowly spreading across her face. "But could he be telling the truth about Lee?"

"Not a chance. It was all calculated, with just enough truth in it to make him think I'd fall for all of it—there's something so weird going on with this Erika thing . . . but Wolf just takes it as the self-indulgent act of a snotty rich kid who wants to bug her parents—the girl tried to kill herself! And he says she's just being a bitch, trying to bug him!"

Cooper was blowing himself out, beginning to feel the adrenaline rush fading. He poured himself a cup of coffee and sat down. He told her about the meetings with Lee and Wolf without quite so much editorializing.

She grimaced at what he'd done to Lee. "You were a little too hard on her, if you don't mind my saying so. She's a victim in this mess. Isn't she?"

"I don't know. She's always a victim and it pisses me off. She could have just kissed those jerks goodbye twenty years ago—I'd have helped her through anything—"

"You have very strong feelings for a sister."

"Yes, I do." He didn't want to try to explain it to her. It was too long a story and the fact that he found Beate so attractive didn't make it easier.

"Blue martinis," she said. "Erika's told me about his blue martinis. His trademark. The magic is lost on me. I've never tasted a martini of any color—"

"You're the same way, you don't seem as worried about Erika as you should be—"

She shook her forefinger at him. "Drop it, John. I'm not going to run around beating my head on the wall—I can't *do* anything. We'll wait and see. And don't make me mad—I can't afford the time and energy." Her eyes were flashing at him. He nodded, and she went on. "You should know that this lovely English-accented fellow you met today is very busy. The hot rumor is that because of the Zoo Station massacre Wolf Koller has decided to push everything into high gear. Change has got to come quickly and it has to come all across the board, from the Chancellor on down . . . They say that Koller wants a crackdown on the violence, maybe martial law, he says the Germans must once again take their destiny into their own hands, nationally and internationally—"

"What does he want the Chancellor to do? Can he just get what he wants?"

"Well, the Chancellor isn't known for standing up to Wolf Koller —but what's it going to be? That's the big question. If things don't go Koller's way, he might do anything—back a popular movement, back his own man, call on the people to choose a new leader, he could undermine the Chancellor's power . . . Koller wants in Bonn a man who'll do what he's told. Better yet, a man who'll do it enthusiastically . . . Maybe the

Chancellor is that man. If not . . ." She shrugged. "The point is, something is going to happen soon. You can feel it—everywhere I go on a
story it's all anyone is talking about. Everybody is talking about the
breaking point—"

"But I don't care about your politics," Cooper said. "I'm only
interested in helping Lee."

"Maybe not, but it doesn't matter anymore. You're inside the perimeter of Wolf Koller's world now, he's taken notice of you—I'm not so
sure you can just walk away."

"I'm not walking away, not until we find Erika. In fact"—he
winked at her—"I have a plan. But explain it to me—what started these
political rumors? I mean, does Wolf Koller call a press conference, like
Ross Perot?"

She was unwrapping the towel from her head, running her hands
through the thick blond hair. "No, no, it's not like that. The Chancellor's
been seen going out to Koller's place at Lake Wannsee. It's totally sepa-
rate from their public meetings. Totally secret. They even use a double, or
the Chancellor's car goes off in the wrong direction . . . anything to
throw us off. And Koller has his security people at his houses to keep
anyone from getting too close. But it's reliable, the Chancellor was seen at
Koller's place on the lake. Glock is due back in Bonn for some hearings
tomorrow—people are watching to see how he behaves once he's back at
the office. Will he start making changes and pronouncements? Will it
look like somebody's finally in charge? Koller's way, though, is to work
on things from offstage. He can be irresistible. You saw that—he breaks
off a session with the Chancellor to follow Lee and then spends another
hour winning you over. Such a sweethead—"

"Heart. Sweet*heart*."

"Okay, okay," she said impatiently. She stood up and looked
down at him. "So, what's this big plan of yours?"

Cooper was saved from having to reply by the telephone's ringing.
She picked it up. The first thing he heard her saying was: "Yes, he's
sitting right here." Then: "No, he's all right. He just had a meeting with
Wolf Koller. He's tired of being lied to." Then she lapsed into German
and he couldn't make any sense of it. She listened, staring at him, then
spoke again. Then to Cooper: "Are you free tonight?"

"No, I'm going to the nearest disco."

She said into the mouthpiece, "Yes, he's free," then went back to
German.

When she hung up the phone she turned to him with a quizzical expression.

"The Chancellor calling with a scoop?"

"Karl-Heinz."

"About me?"

"He called to tell me about his meeting with you. I think he was planning to warn me. He wanted to know if you'd approached me—"

"I didn't mention you to him. I didn't want to drag you into it."

"Well, he's on his way. He has a plan for tonight."

"News about Erika?"

"That's part of it. He says there's something important he has to tell you about her—he didn't say what."

"And what else?"

"He wants us to go to a rock concert."

"I was a bad host when we first met. I thought I should try to make it up to you." Karl-Heinz was leaning against the kitchen counter by the sink, rolling an icy bottle of beer back and forth across his split lip. "You must see some Nazi rock while you're here. You must try to understand what we're up against. It would be unforgivable if I allowed you to miss it." He forced a little laugh.

"Tell him what he's getting into," Beate said. She seemed comfortable having him there, Cooper noticed. "John should be warned."

"Nazi rock, it's our new art form. It's big over in the East. In Hungary it's much more vile than it is here, but ours is bad enough. The concert tonight is back in my part of town." He named some venue that meant nothing to Cooper. "The name of the group is Storkraft. They're a Düsseldorf skinhead outfit. The name means 'destructive force.' Their biggest hit was two years ago, 'Kraft für Deutschland.'"

"'Strength for Germany,'" Beate translated. "The lead singer, he's a guy called—what's his name, Karl?"

"Jurg Petrisch."

"I did a piece on Nazi rock for the BBC about six months ago. I remember the lyrics to the song . . . something about fists 'hard as steel' and making Germany 'clean.'"

"But the music," Karl-Heinz said, "sounds like somebody cutting up a football team with a chainsaw."

Beate said: "And it ends with the words 'Germany Awake!' That's a Nazi slogan from the thirties. And no, I didn't just happen to know that. I found out when I did the story. Of course the powers I work for wouldn't touch it—it was as if admitting it existed might encourage it."

"Who likes this crap?" Cooper asked.

Karl-Heinz pushed off from the counter, his black leather jacket creaking. He wore a black T-shirt and black jeans. "People who think civilization has been going downhill ever since the Third Reich went down. It's selling everywhere—Europe, England, South America. Look, it's time to go."

On the stairway Cooper grabbed Karl-Heinz's arm. "What's the news about Erika? What's going on?"

"Later. After the concert. There's much to tell you that you don't know. And you won't believe it unless I can explain it all to you—but she's not the person you think she is. Do you understand? She's not what you think."

"What do you mean?"

"Later. Just listen to the words. She's not what you think she is."

"Then what is she?" He looked back at Beate. She was locking the door and coming down the stairs behind them.

"Something else." Then Karl-Heinz was heading down the stairs and that was all. It was enough to set Cooper's mind spinning once again.

The crowd was on its feet in the large dark hall. It looked and smelled like an auto warehouse, the smell of very old oil and grime, the bare steel rafters almost lost in the shadows overhead. Cooper felt claustrophobic, too many smells, too many blank stares, all too close together. Sweat, perfume, smoke. There was no way to judge the size of the crowd. A thousand? Two thousand? Canned music blared out of big speakers on the blacked-out naked stage. Not much light, a couple of spotlights, playing across the crowd, seething, swaying, stomping their feet, yelling.

"I hate this," he said.

Beate was holding his hand because she didn't want to lose him in the surging crowd. "Really?" she shouted in his ear. "There's no place I'd rather be." She squeezed his hand. Karl-Heinz was scanning the faces in the crowd. Cooper saw mouths moving but understood nothing. Then the dim light was going black. The crowd was quieting, holding its breath. Pitch blackness. Bodies pushing against him.

Suddenly torches exploded into flame on the stage. Long poles wrapped with rags at the end and soaked with something you could smell, kerosene or gasoline, like the villagers marching through town, pissed off, in an old James Whale movie. Looking for the monster. Flames licked at the inky darkness, shadows flickering across the crowd. A couple of red spots came on and machines began blowing thick billowing clouds of dry ice fog past the torches and out into the crowd. Occasionally someone screamed.

A sudden deafening screech from an electric guitar sliced through the crowd like a guillotine whistling down the track, and four bodies seemed to plummet from the rafters down onto the stage. The noise seemed to be out of control inside Cooper's head. His eyeballs begged for mercy. The crowd was going crazy, jumping, shouting, arms thrown up in the Hitler salute. And the singer began howling, his mouth distended, touching the mike, nothing identifiable as a human sound. His face seemed a misshapen mask, lit from below like Rondo Hatton as the Creeper in the old horror movies. The smell of the torches settled like a cloud of insecticide, filtering through the waves of fog, the amplified, distorted squeal of the guitar, the pounding, throbbing drum line, the guy screaming on the stage, veins bulging on his pale skull, in his throat . . .

Cooper shouted something of a critical nature into Beate's ear but she was taking pictures of the crowd, the nightmare onstage, and she didn't hear a word he said. He felt as if his brain had liquefied and was running out of his eyeballs.

And it wouldn't stop. It was like the mother of all dental appointments, no Novocain, a drill that made a lot of noise, Laurence Olivier leaning over you, seen through a blood-red haze of pain, asking, Is it safe? Is it safe? Is it safe? No, Cooper thought, it isn't safe, none of it's safe.

And then the building cacophony hit a throbbing peak and the spotlights were spinning wildly through the darkness. Two guys jumped out of the crowd and onto the stage and they were unfurling a red, white, and black battle flag from the Hitler days, the sight of the swastika hurling everyone into the past . . . or was it the future?

"Sieg Heil! Sieg Heil! Sieg Heil! Sieg Heil!"

The crowd was chanting, stamping, arms outstretched in the stiff-armed salute. The walls were shaking, the floor vibrating, Karl-Heinz was pulling them backwards through the crowd. He kept looking over his shoulder. Something had changed. He'd seen something, someone; he was afraid. He was pulling hard on Beate and she was yanking on

Cooper's hand. Karl-Heinz was out of breath, panting, as they neared the doorway to the outside world. He grabbed Cooper's shoulder, put his mouth close to Cooper's ear. "If we get separated . . . remember this . . . Bayreuth . . . you understand, the town Bayreuth . . . Warmolts, the man is Warmolts—" And then he was jerked away.

The concert was over but the crowd was still roaring as they got outside. The street was dark and narrow and the anti-Nazi protesters were waiting with placards and banners and some bats, marching around, working themselves up to a fit of righteousness. When the concert crowd blew out, carrying the three of them on the crest, the protesters waded in swinging bats, and suddenly there were TV lights and production trucks and people with videocams and the hopped-up thugs from the concert were swinging heavy-gauge chains and some knives were coming out.

Cooper never saw the iron pipe that glanced off somebody else's head and slammed into the side of his neck, sent him spinning, vision going black. He couldn't breathe, fell sideways, couldn't see Karl-Heinz or Beate, caught himself on the side of a car, grabbing at the door handle, but he couldn't keep from falling. People were yelling and swearing and grunting, all in German, and he felt blood on his face like a sprinkle of rain from above, and he was trying to stand up. He felt his way around the side of the car and saw Beate crouched in a doorway snapping pictures. She stood up, began moving out from the doorway, and a man with blood running down his forehead came out of the darkness with a chain, swinging it around his head, going for her.

Cooper lunged at him, saw him turning at the last moment, sensed the chain altering its course and coming at him, ducked his head at the last moment, too late, felt the chain whipping into his cheek, felt his own flesh splitting like a melon, felt the impact of his shoulders hitting the guy just below the sternum and driving him back into a brick wall. The guy hit the wall like a sack of cement, cried out when the breath exploded from his lungs, and Cooper took his head and slammed him by the ears against the rough brick wall four or five times. There was blood oozing out of the guy's ears and his eyes were glazed over. Cooper let him fall like a dead man. He saw Beate on the sidewalk, trying to protect herself from a skinhead with a hobnailed boot drawn back to kick her abdomen. Cooper swung the chain he'd liberated as hard as he could. It smashed the skinhead's kneecap like a light bulb and he went down screaming, his face a ghastly white. Cooper stood over him and took out some of his frustrations. By the time the guy had pink foam bubbling out of his mouth Cooper threw the chain into the crowd and Beate was up and tugging him toward an open alleyway, toward a pile of crates and trash-cans.

"Your face," she gasped. "Are you all right? You're all bloody—"

The riot was surging away, bottles crashing, sirens wailing, music blaring, accompaniment for imbeciles, *Sieg Heil!* It was farce, it was tragedy.

"I feel amazingly fit," he said. She was trembling and he put his arm around her, felt her quaking against him. He realized he, too, was shaking. He couldn't quite grasp what he'd just done but he knew he'd done it, all right.

"You wouldn't stop hitting that man—"

"Olaf Peterson would have been proud of me." He was winded, sucking air. "I think I may have killed the first one. And the second one." He felt an irresistible smile crossing his face, felt the pain of the chain tracks across his cheek and it felt strangely good. "He may get better . . . but he'll never get well."

"You went crazy."

"No. Just working out some frustrations." He held her for a moment, almost one of those private moments, but he was too conscious of its being like a movie, and he let her go. He wasn't John Garfield, she wasn't Jennifer Jones. She'd never heard of either of them. "Where's Karl-Heinz?" He was standing in the entrance to the alley. Half a dozen of the wounded lay in the street. A medic from an ambulance was bending over a girl who was lying on her back, vomiting into her own throat. The medic was trying to keep her from choking to death.

The first man Cooper had dealt with didn't look so good. His eyes were stuck open and they weren't seeing much. The second man, the skinhead, lay on his side clutching his leg. He was vomiting, too, from the shock of the pain. He held his hand out to Cooper, wanting help. Cooper stared at him until the hand fell hopelessly onto the pavement. Cooper thought about it for a moment, then stepped heavily on the hand. The son of a bitch sobbed. Cooper looked down and said: "You should see the other guy," but he didn't hear.

Karl-Heinz was nowhere in sight. The street was emptying. The riot was wearing out somewhere else.

She sighed. "That was too close. You went crazy, Cooper."

"Did you get some good pictures?"

"Maybe." She was still shaking.

"None of me killing anybody, I hope."

She gave him a sidelong glance, shook her head.

A second ambulance had pulled up, another police car, and more medics were moving about the battlefield. Car windows had been shattered and the street was full of glass. One of the medics spoke to Beate. When he went away she turned to Cooper. "He wanted to know if we needed help."

They were back in her brother's car—the brother at med school at UCLA who'd left his car in her keeping, the brother who could have stitched up his face. No sign of Karl-Heinz.

"This is his turf," she said hopefully. "When we got separated he may have headed for home."

Cooper nodded. "Do you want to hear my plan?"

"We've got to get your face cleaned up. Are you all right?"

He looked at his watch. "Let's get it done right away, then."

"We'll go to my place. Fifteen minutes. I'll wash it up and put a bandage aid on it—"

"Band-Aid. Not bandage aid."

"Does it matter, John?"

"No, I guess it doesn't." His face and neck were throbbing and more than ever he wanted to smash things. It had helped to let go on the thug who was going to kill Beate, who was going to kill her when she was unprotected and helpless, shooting pictures. But it wasn't enough. It hadn't gotten him any closer to Erika Koller.

22

SNIPER

Ned Cheddar was sitting at his desk in Georgetown eating his fourth chicken leg and thinking about some grilled catfish with red pepper relish on a pillow of polenta. He was thinking about how that was just about what the doctor ordered when the green telephone rang. He felt in his cardigan pocket for the packet of antacid tablets.

It was Burke Delaney at the other end.

Cheddar listened for several minutes. "Wait a minute, for the sake of Beelzebub!"

The line broke up for a moment. Delaney said: "What? Who was that?"

"No one, forget it. Now I want to know who the hell this Schuyler is—and what do you mean exactly, he tore the assassin's arm off?"

"He bit it off, Cheese. I said 'bit.' "

"What in the world are you talking about?"

"Jesus, Cheese, you remember Schuyler. I told you all about him. He's my bull terrier."

"Like the Booth cartoons?"

"What? Whose cartoons?"

"Booth, *Booth! The New Yorker.* You're saying Schuyler is a *dog?* Do I have that right?"

"Yes, yes, he's a dog. I don't know many men who could bite off a whole fucking arm."

"All right, all right. Go on."

"Well, it just bothers me."

"And well it should. Somebody tried to kill you."

"Not just somebody. I used to know this guy."

"To know you is to want to kill you."

"That's rich, Cheese. But it wasn't too damn funny when he pulled the fucking gun—"

"And what did you do?"

"Before or after I shit my pants? What do you think I did? I killed the sumbitch. I'm still trying to clean his lungs off my floor."

"You knew him? Who was he?"

"Brace yourself. Kuno Meinhold."

"Kuno Meinhold? Hard to believe."

"You remember him?"

"The Dorfmann bunch. Not much since then."

"Good for you. Where were you twenty-five years ago, Cheese?"

"Rome. Cairo. An unfortunate few weeks in Belize City and a ghastly trip into the wilds of Paraguay looking for Martin Bormann—"

"Jeez, I'm sorry I missed that. I spent an evening taking shots at Kuno Meinhold, and six months later I was buying him a beer in the Oslo airport, trying to hire him and the Dorfmann bunch to take out a former friend of ours. Now he comes out of the fucking night and tries to kill me. Who wants an old fart like me dead? What am I doing that could call up an old gunsel like Kuno? Don't bother to answer, Cheese. The answer is—can only be—this fucking SPARTAKUS product . . . and I still don't know what the hell it's all about—"

"Think. If it is SPARTAKUS, and Kuno wasn't just paying you back for sleeping with some long-forgotten girlfriend of his, then somebody knows how you're getting SPARTAKUS . . . they know about you and Karl-Heinz . . . and it's worth killing you for." Ned Cheddar sighed and stared at the last bedraggled chicken leg. He was losing his appetite. "Now there is a downside to all of this."

"What can be worse than having Kuno Meinhold show up in my house in the middle of the night with a Luger and a ski mask?"

"Listen carefully. Having Kuno Meinhold or someone like him showing up in *my* house in the middle of the night with a Luger and a ski mask." He paused. "Really? A Luger? He didn't keep up with the times, did he?"

"It'll kill you just as dead." Delaney was laughing into his hand.

"We've got to track back on Kuno. Start over there. I'll dig a bit from here. It's got to be somewhere in one of my computer programs. I don't like this, Burke."

"He doesn't like it," Delaney said mockingly. "Walk a mile in my moccasins and see how much you don't like it then."

"Nonsense. You love it. Makes you feel young again. Excuse my indelicacy, but what did you do with the stiff?"

"Dropped it down that old well. The lid fits pretty tight. I'll worry about it in the spring."

"Down a well. The arm, too?"

"No, I hung the arm over the fireplace for the holidays. Jesus, yes, of course the arm, too. I would have buried the whole mess but it was too much work, and Schuyler would just have dug it up and dragged it back to the house to play with."

"You lead a peculiar life, Burke."

"You should talk."

"Keep me in the picture, Burke."

"Yeah, yeah."

"Remember that I am your paymaster. You make a good living and you're, in your own words, an old fart."

"A ruthless old fart, Cheese."

"Precisely why you still have a job. Goodbye, Burke."

Sitting alone in the darkened office in Georgetown, Ned Cheddar flipped through the files in his mind. Kuno Meinhold. The Dorfmann gang. Rafaela Dorfmann. He could see her in his mind. Tall and dark with long legs, staring out at him from the pages of the fashion magazines. She'd been on every cover. And then she'd gone bad, she'd turned against the world that had produced her. Kidnapping, extortion, murder . . . living underground, striking without warning, conscienceless. It was a kind of terrorism you didn't see much anymore, an outgrowth of the sixties. Not political at its heart. Just the spirit of evil set free. Rafaela Dorfmann.

At the height of her fame as a model she'd been seen always on the arm of a rich German industrialist and financier. Not a movie star, not a rock singer. People said she was smart, she knew what she wanted. And she'd found him . . . Ned Cheddar saw the picture file in his mind. The beautiful model and the tall, tanned tycoon . . .

Wolf Koller.

And then she'd gone crazy and started killing people and blowing up jewelry stores and kidnapping people who seemed an awful lot like Wolf Koller. But not Wolf Koller. And in the end she'd blown herself all the way to hell. Served her right.

But why did Kuno Meinhold, one of the Dorfmann leftovers who hadn't been heard from in years, want to kill Burke Delaney? It had to be SPARTAKUS.

And that was Wolf Koller.

Wolf Koller had gone to Lise's bedroom and was trying to be patient. It wasn't easy.

"You followed me?"

"I've explained all this. I'm worried about you."

"You're afraid of me. Of what I might say. You're afraid of John. You know what he did last time he was here . . . You don't want me to tell what I know—"

"What are you talking about? Who would believe you?"

"You're afraid."

"I'm worried. I can't let you run around and forget who you are and what you're doing . . . I explained things to your brother. He'd just had a full dose of your behavior. He'll be going home now. I told him we'd get your health taken care of and he should come back, join us at Wannsee this summer. You must stay calm, darling."

She drank some of the tea he'd brought her. He was right about one thing, at least. She had to stay calm. But it was so hard, the meeting with John had gone so badly. What he said about her, it had all been true. Would he really leave her behind in Germany, just wash his hands of her? She started to cry again and Wolf stared down at her, his face set in a mask of disgust.

"You should never have brought him here," he said. "He doesn't know what is at stake here. All he can think of is the past . . . Brendel, the old Nazis, he doesn't understand how times change—"

"Nothing changes!"

"Now you sound like Erika! Don't just repeat everything she tells you. That ridiculous boyfriend of hers—I spend my whole life trying to make something for the future, and this tattered Communist slinks up and drains the brains from my daughter—" He turned away from his wife, stood by the window staring at his reflection.

"You don't care what happens to her! You're not trying to find

her . . . Maybe you kidnapped her—maybe you had your security people kill her!" She was raving, saliva bubbling at the corners of her mouth.
"You killed our daughter! I know you did . . . you're sick, you're full of
sickness and hate and you're afraid of what she might say . . . and now
you're going to kill me, too! Admit it, just admit it!" She was raving at
him and couldn't help it. She didn't know if she believed any of it. The
ranting had a life of its own. She turned away, sobbing, remembering in a
shattered split second the worst thing, the time they never spoke of, the
time they'd taken her away and tied her down on the table and put the
pad in her mouth so she wouldn't bite her tongue off. She'd been sobbing then and she'd thrown a glass bowl and it had shattered like her
poor brain and she'd walked through the glass leaving bloody footprints
all through the house and he'd come home and found her dancing in the
blood and they'd taken her away, strapped her down and put her in the
place where they did the terrible, horrible things to her, she could hear
the hum of the machine and feel the lightning going into her body until
she knew she was breaking . . . It all came back to her as her body
arched with the crying out, with the sense that there was nothing she
could do to stop John Cooper from leaving and nothing she could do to
stop Wolf from . . . from . . .

Suddenly she heard glass breaking.

Wolf staggered back against the handcarved chest of drawers with
the inlaid pearl design, his arm sweeping the framed photographs of the
family off onto the floor. He was grabbing for anything to hold on to,
pushed the small reading lamp off onto the floor. There was blood all
over the wall behind him, and it didn't seem real to her, it was like a
scene from a movie, it was unreal and she felt something pulling apart
inside of her, as if time were coming apart, she felt herself escaping, saw
him sliding down the front of the bureau and the blood smeared on the
pearl, but it didn't matter, she wondered where her mother was, she was
coming to pick her up and take her to Hyde Park, the Serpentine, she
was late but Lee knew she would come, and she heard someone screaming and someone had been fingerpainting on the wall and the maid would
have to clean it up . . .

When he turned tail and ran away from the fighting, away from Cooper
and Beate, Karl-Heinz knew he was done. He'd been broken. They had
won. His anger and frustration and outrage had been overtaken and

sucked dry by fear. They dealt in fear, they had perfected fear and all its many uses, and now they had broken him with it. When he saw the chains and the pipes and the knives come out, it didn't really make any difference in whose hands they were—he felt the strength drain out of him, he could barely breathe, he had to run . . . he could think only of running, escaping . . . he didn't want to be hurt again . . . It was that simple and he didn't know if he could live with that.

He remembered the night with Erika, the beating they'd given him, the pipe slashing at his face, the blood in his mouth, the pain jolting him, then snaking through his nervous system . . . Watching them set out after Erika . . . It was the second time he'd been beaten. They knew who he was, he was a target. If he kept on writing about them in the poor rag nobody ever read, if he kept on showing up at the confrontations, they'd keep beating him and eventually they'd kill him and no one would be punished, no one would care, and they would have gotten away with it again . . . He was drawn to the violence, everything he knew about them drew him to the riots, the demonstrations, everything he believed about the evil, the wickedness of what they were doing, had pulled him onward until, like a blind pig, he eventually found the truffle . . . SPARTAKUS. And if—when—Wolf Koller found out where the leak was . . . well, that would be the end. Maybe he already knew.

He could still hear the sounds of the riot and the police car sirens and the ambulances winding through the dark streets toward the violence. He was trying not to run now. If they saw him running, they might pick him up . . . He was dripping with sweat and his breath was struggling in his chest. He wondered if Cooper and Beate were all right—or if they'd fallen victims . . . the way Erika had that night.

He could still see the blood on Erika's face where they'd hit her. He couldn't get it out of his mind. Her beautiful face, the kind of girl he'd never dreamed would be in love with him . . .

And now he was letting them down, running out on Cooper and Beate, running out on himself . . . Would they follow up on Bayreuth and Warmolts? He should have given Cooper more, maybe he'd call him again but there was no reason to think Cooper would believe the truth about Wolf Koller and Lee and Erika . . . He was counting on Beate to see it through, he knew how determined she could be on the trail of a story.

He found a tavern on a dim street. Snow was beginning to fall. He went inside, into the beer-smelling darkness, and found a table in a corner. He sat down, feeling as if he were in a trance, unable to focus his eyes. He ordered a beer and tried to hear the riot but he was too far away. What he could hear was in his mind. In his mind the riots never stopped, not anymore.

He was sure Erika was dead. They'd killed her and before she died they'd have made her tell what she knew and how she'd found out . . . She'd have contacted him otherwise. She loved him. They'd come and taken her away and they'd killed her and no one would ever find her body . . . he knew where they disposed of bodies, one of the big dumps, they'd run the bodies through the grinders used for the mountains of trash, they could get in at night, there was a deal made, maybe if you dug deep enough you'd find that *he* owned the haulage companies . . . He owned everything else . . . There was no way to escape him, his people were always watching, eventually they found out everything, they were bound to . . . there were so many of them.

But still he could hurt them—he had SPARTAKUS.

When he first began to uncover it, it was all an accident. He'd been wanting to find out more about the man . . . Karl-Heinz had known Wolf Koller was behind something, his kind were always tinkering with something, carrying out their pacts with the devil . . . and he'd stumbled into the gold mine, SPARTAKUS . . . He hadn't quite known what to do with it. It was too big for his little newspaper, it was too big for any newspaper. And then he'd remembered his father's talking about the OSS man he'd worked with during the war. Delaney. Burke Delaney. Who had married a German girl, had stayed in Germany and was still in Germany . . . And Bernd Schmidt knew where Delaney lived, was sure he was still a field agent, maybe semiretired but that would mean nothing to a man like Delaney, still bound to be a Company man. So, Karl-Heinz had gone to Delaney with SPARTAKUS.

But now he was afraid of Delaney. As he'd told John Cooper in a roundabout way, he was afraid Burke Delaney would be ordered to kill him once he had the last of the SPARTAKUS product. He knew how the Americans worked. Life meant nothing to them. Yet the Americans were the only people he could take SPARTAKUS to, they were the only ones who might be able to stop it from happening . . .

But then, fearing for his life, he hadn't been able to give it to Delaney after all. He'd had to think of another plan. Some other destination for the last of SPARTAKUS . . .

He drank another beer, trying to work up his courage to go back outside. He'd seen them at the concert, the same faces, the ones who were after him, and they'd seen him, too, their eyes had met. He hadn't acted entirely selfishly, either. He couldn't drag Beate and the American into it. They'd die, too, these people wouldn't think twice about it. And they had to survive, because he'd made them part of his plan, part of his legacy . . . But where to go now? Where could he go that they wouldn't find him?

The men drinking in the bar were what East Germany had come to. For the first time in their lives they were out of work. Always full employment under the Communists, now they'd lost their jobs, they were losing hope on a larger scale than they had under the Communists. Now it was more than grumbling and bitching, now it was serious, and when you saw them drinking beer and staring morosely into space or talking hatefully of the foreigners you could understand where their confusion and unhappiness and hatred came from . . . Their lives had been taken away from them. The West was extracting its final pound of flesh, leaving them with nothing.

No, that was no way to think! But the problem was, Karl-Heinz didn't know how to think anymore . . . he was tired of trying to force it all to make sense. Anyway, it was out of his hands now. He'd spent his courage and ingenuity on getting to SPARTAKUS and now he was through.

They would never guess what provisions he'd made for the last of it.

Still, would it be in time? Had he made the proper judgment?

Finally he left the bar, back into the cold and snowy night. Early snow this year but it wouldn't last, it would be gone by morning. The night was quiet, no sirens, no sounds of rioting, no bright lights, no traffic. Three men were standing at the corner, smoking cigarettes and looking cold beneath the only streetlight on the block that worked.

Karl-Heinz walked directly toward them.

There was no point in running away.

23

MAN WITH A PLAN

They sat in the car, watching the large snowflakes drift down through the light of the streetlamps. Most of them melted on contact with the ground, but just enough accumulated to give the street and sidewalks a slippery, gleaming look. Cooper's face ached dully, a result of the riot after the concert. But his adrenaline was under control. They'd gone to Beate's apartment, where she'd patched him up and he'd convinced her to set out for Grunewald. What the hell, the night was young and they were both still alive. He didn't want to think about the riot.

Cooper was watching Dr. Fritz Gisevius's large, square gray stone house and office, which sat next door to his private convalescent hospital. It was one of the Grunewald retreats for the very rich who were deemed "not well," which could mean almost anything. Gisevius's compound was situated about a twenty-minute walk from the great house of Wolf Koller, and the mood was much the same though the homes of Gisevius and his neighbors were somewhat smaller. All the lights were out in the house. Cooper was trying to get up enough nerve to follow through on his plan.

Beate Hubermann was smoking a cigarette, wondering if she could confine herself to just the one. Or two. She was also biting her lip, intent on trying to make a connection between the words Karl-Heinz had left with Cooper: Bayreuth and Warmolts.

"I've been to Bayreuth, of course. The Wagner festival, the operas and concerts. It's in Southern Bavaria. I have no idea what it has to do with Erika . . . or why she is not what she seems to be. Or whatever he said. And Warmolts means nothing to me—but I can find out." She exhaled smoke nervously. "Maybe we can just find Karl-Heinz and ask him. If he doesn't do one of his disappearances."

Cooper didn't respond. He rolled the window down, as if that would answer his questions about the dark house. "I wonder if there's anyone home."

"How's your face?"

"The least of my worries."

"I'm not overwhelmed by your plan, you know that."

"I'm not overwhelmed by it either. But I've got to force the issue. I say Wolf Koller is lying about Lise's health, I just don't buy this mystery disease nonsense—like the 'brain cloud' in *Joe and the Volcano*. Or was it *Joe Versus the Volcano*?"

"It's not important, Cooper."

"Right. It's not. So, if anyone knows what the hell's the matter with her, it ought to be Gisevius."

"Yes, but why not call him up and ask him? Why break into his office?"

"Because I can't think of a single reason why he'd tell me the truth if his pal Wolf Koller won't. Come on, it's just like a movie—where do you think the movies got the ideas?"

She gave up, shaking her head.

"I'll surprise him if he's at home or I'll look around, see what he's got in the way of files—"

"And what if you set off an alarm system?"

"Look, I didn't say it was a perfect plan, did I?" He went back to the process of working up the adrenaline to set out for the unknown.

Suddenly, from behind them, an old Mercedes gullwing coupe came swerving out of the darkness, looped around them, and with a squeal of tires and brakes hurtled into Gisevius's driveway, the head-lamps playing across the face of the house. Two young men clambered out of the car, one skulling himself on the upswept door and finding his own clumsiness hilarious. They were wearing evening clothes, the white shirts and wing collars flickering in the darkness, and they were some-what drunk. Smoking cigars. Going up the few steps to the terrace that ran alongside the house, perpendicular to the front, they burst into song for a moment, then loudly shushed one another, giggling. A long white scarf fluttered to the terrace stones. One tottered over to a large concrete planter and threw up while the other hurried him on, talking loudly.

Beate translated. "He said their master will be home soon and they must prepare themselves for him."

"What are they? Staff?"

"Boyfriends of the good doctor, I should think."

"Ahhh."

Arm in arm, like a pair of figures from another era, they skipped along the terrace, trying the handles on French doors until a set opened and they battered their way in past heavy curtains, which blew out into the night, caught for an instant in the wind. The doors banged to and fro. Moments later lights appeared in what must have been the foyer, then on the second floor. The light in the foyer went out and there was only the dim yellow glow above.

Cooper took a deep breath. "Now or never," he said, "and honk if he gets home." Then he was out of the car, feeling like a man jumping out of an airplane.

Two minutes later he stood on the terrace, feeling naked and obvious in the slanting light from the street. The curtains billowed out through the open doors. He looked up into the drifting snowflakes. "Thank you, God," he whispered, and stepped through the doorway.

A small table lamp had been left burning in the front hallway; he glimpsed it through heavy open doors. He would have to have more light. He found a table lamp, turned it on, and realized that luck had put him in what appeared to be the doctor's study or office. In addition to some very large, very Teutonic paintings and massive carved furniture, there were a fax machine and a copier and a series of old-fashioned wooden filing cabinets stretching along one wall, fat volumes of medical references in glass-fronted bookcases. Every time the draperies flopped against the French doors he nervously snapped his head around to face God only knew what. He could hear the occasional peal of laughter from the lads upstairs, the dropping of what sounded like a bottle, the slamming of doors, the pounding of bare feet on the floors. It sounded like a slumber party at a girls' boarding school.

He wondered what Olaf Peterson would have thought of him just then.

He was flipping through the filing cabinets when he saw it, *Lise Koller,* and heard it, the honking of a horn, followed by the sound of a car pulling up in the forecourt.

Peterson was laughing, a hollow sound from somewhere in deep space.

Jesus, there was no hope of copying it, he'd have to steal it . . .

and when Gisevius next went to look for it, it would be gone . . . but there was no choice . . . With the file folder in hand he turned, saw a pile of tapes on the desk, took one step toward them, and then the front door opened into the hallway. A heavy footstep, a snap of a light switch, a much brighter light falling across the parquet floor and reaching toward him. He couldn't move. The light was in his eyes.

A squat, fat man stood in the hallway, tired, slipping out of his overcoat, throwing it across a side chair, placing a homburg on top of it, peering for a moment into a gilt mirror above a bowl of flowers. He was wearing a blue pinstriped suit. Behind Cooper the goddamn draperies swooped in and smote the French doors, a cold draft swirled through the room. Slowly Gisevius turned toward the sound, took a step toward his office as Cooper darted into the shadows, back toward the draperies and the doors. "Kurt?" Gisevius asked, moving slowly, unsure of what he'd heard. "Kurt?" He took another step toward the office, where the light was on for no good reason he could think of.

Cooper stepped through the draperies and doors as quietly as he could, slipped on a stretch of snow, fell to one knee, and gave up any pretense of sneaking away unseen. He bolted along the terrace, heard Gisevius entangling himself in the leaden draperies and coming out onto the terrace, shouting something in German. Yet he was fat and tired and he wasn't going to win a footrace and the lithe young men were upstairs and there was nothing he could do about that . . . Gisevius shouted something into the night as the figure slipped around the corner. Then he turned, waddled slowly back to the office.

Clutching the file folder, Cooper got into the car and was relieved to note that he didn't seem to be having a heart attack as she pulled away from the curb, moved calmly out into the dark street.

He told her what had happened, what he'd stolen. "You're going to have to translate but we've got to see what's in here." He was out of breath from the sprint. "I could use a drink. Let's go somewhere—"

"I got a page on the beeper while you were out committing burglary—I have to call."

She found a call box near a drugstore and he waited in the car while she phoned Television Center. He flipped through the pages, hardly legible in the dim light, realized he understood nothing. He hated the anticlimax. And he wanted the answers about Lee right now. But when Beate came back she was running.

"It's going to have to wait."

"Are you kidding? I just pulled the heist of the century and you're telling me—"

"There's been a shooting at Wolf Koller's house—"

He felt his breath come to a stop: "He killed her!"

"They don't know who was shot. They want me over there to find out."

She accelerated, and he was slammed back into the seat, clutching his folder, wondering which news was going to be worse.

24

BREAKING EGGS

Grunewald was not the sort of neighborhood where you would ever expect to see an indecorous police presence. But that night all the rules went out the window. People were peering out of windows and standing on the sidewalks straining to get a view—the curious rich. What they saw: the curving narrow street, the imposing homes, the piles of raked leaves at the curb being frosted with snow, the crowd of police cars overflowing the driveway into the street, bright lights on tall collapsible standards throwing both the front and back of the house into antiseptic, unreal relief, the silent snow drifting through the penumbra of the light, the coppers moving around looking for signs of any damn thing, two television vans with their attendant crews and a third, CNN's, looking for a place to park.

Beate pushed her way to her familiar van, spoke with the crew, and crowded up to the gate in the long black iron fence. She was in her element, eager, determined. A guy with a minicam on his shoulder went with her. Cooper stood beside the sound man, who didn't speak much English but smiled a lot and accepted Cooper's presence as a given. An Associated Press guy was asking questions of a man in a tweed overcoat who was standing beside a uniformed police officer. The man in tweed identified himself as Erich Haas, public relations officer for Wolf Koller's conglomerate. Haas was waiting for the six or seven newspeople to shut up. The AP man was an American, and the resulting conversation was conducted in a mixture of German and English so Cooper was able to keep up.

"Mr. Wolf Koller was shot about two hours ago. The assailant was not in the house. *Not in the house.* That's correct. He was the only victim. No other member of the household was shot or harmed in any way. The single bullet was fired through a window at the rear of the house. Mr. Koller has been taken to the hospital." The name of the hospital was a jumble of German that Cooper couldn't understand.

"What's his condition, Erich?" It was the AP guy. "Is he dead?"

"No. He was seriously wounded."

"Unconscious? Could he speak?"

"He was conscious. Very conscious, let me say. You people know Wolf . . ." There was an appreciative laugh from the newspeople. "Let's just say he was not happy with what had happened. As always his concern was for others—was anyone else hurt? . . . He was very much alive."

"What did he say?"

"That is not for the tender ears of your audience, Mr. Miller." More good-natured chuckles. "As you all know, he is a fighter."

"Did he walk out of the house?"

"No, he was on a stretcher. No, actually on one of those rolling things. A gurney?"

"What shape was he in? Shock? Loss of blood?"

"I promise you that *I* was in shock," Haas said. He was very good, very easy with the press. "I'm not a doctor, I can't say what his specific condition was. He had lost a fair amount of blood."

"Let's be candid, Erich—is he going to make it?"

"I'm not his doctor. I'm not *a* doctor. My guess is that he will recover. I'm confident he will."

"Where was he hit?"

"You mean where on his body? It seemed to me that he was struck in the shoulder, collarbone area maybe, upper body. I can't be more specific. When I got here he was on the gurney thing and they were taking him out to the ambulance."

"Did you speak to him?"

"More accurately, he spoke to me."

"And?"

"He was angry. He told me not to worry. He was concerned about his wife. She was in the room with him when it happened."

"Did you see her?"

"Yes. Not to speak with."

"How was she taking it?"

"Ah, Karl, how do you imagine? She was having a conversation with her husband in the privacy of their home and suddenly he is shot by a sniper—how would your wife react?"

"My wife? She'd pop a bottle of champagne and invite the neighbors," the reporter observed thoughtfully, waiting for the laugh.

Erich Haas waited, too. "Yes, but she would have had good reason, Karl. Frau Koller was naturally upset. Now, that's about all I have to say. I'll be speaking with you again tomorrow at the hospital. Koller Industries may even feed you. Lay it on for noon." He started to pull away.

"Where is she?"

"Really, I have nothing more to say about Frau Koller. Herr Koller wants her privacy respected. I must ask you to do as he suggests. Now, I'm through here, Chief Max Adler has made himself available for your questions . . . Chief?"

Chief Max Adler wasn't about to offer much in the way of elaboration. He answered half a dozen questions, covering exactly the same ground that Erich Haas had, then asked if they would all excuse him, he really had some work he should be doing—

"What about Erika Koller? Was she at home when her father was shot?" That was Beate, always thinking.

"I have nothing to say about anyone but the victim himself. Herr Koller's family is off limits as far as I am concerned."

"Why the special treatment?"

"Nothing special about it. You know that, Fräulein Hubermann. The families in this sort of investigation—"

"What sort of investigation *is* this, Chief?" she asked.

"—have the right to their privacy." He grinned at her. "The hounds of the press must be kept at bay."

"Is that original with you, Chief Adler?"

"No, Fräulein Hubermann. That was original with Chief Paulus as you damn well know."

"Is it true that Chief Paulus taught you everything you know?"

"A vicious rumor. No doubt begun by you or someone very like you." Everybody was smiling and having a good time by now. Cooper was almost giddy with relief that Lee was safe. "Now, listen, you're all going to have to go howl at the moon. I've got work to do. See you tomorrow. Unless I can think of a way to avoid it." He gave a little wave and he and the PR man set off toward the immense, baronial house. The TV lights flicked off.

Beate came up beside Cooper. Her eyes were sparkling. She was caught up in the work. "Wolf's a lucky man," she said, pulling him away from the knot of reporters. "I know one of the cops. He said it was a high-powered rifle. Blew a hole in Koller and knocked down half the wall behind him. He said if it had been a head shot they'd be looking for his brains in Potsdam. He has a way with a phrase."

Cooper said: "I'm wondering—how much does Erika hate her father? Could she have disappeared with some real terrorists? Could she have something to do with this?"

Beate shook her head, snow melting in her hair as it swung around her face. "No, it's impossible. She's not violent . . . she hates violence."

"What did your cop friend say about Lee?"

"She was hysterical. He was in the room when they sedated her. They shot her up with something that knocked her out. She's still in the house."

"Out cold."

"Out cold?" She looked puzzled.

"It means she's asleep."

"Out like a . . . ah, light?"

He couldn't resist her. He hugged her and kissed her forehead, feeling cold snow on his lips. "Exactly," he said. "Can we go now? I need to see what's in this folder I stole."

She didn't want to leave right away. "Always wait around for the scraps. You never know what you might find." She talked briefly with her crew and came back. "I'm going to drop you off at my place—yes, we'll look at the folder, I want to know, too, you know. But I'll have to go back to the studio and work on this tape and write a piece for the morning news people." She looked at her watch. "It's nearly two o'clock now. We'll go in a minute." She ran after her people, who were loading equipment back into the Mercedes van. She had more instructions.

Cooper walked back to the fence. Though the television lights were gone, the police lights were still turning the dead of night into daylight. Cops were combing the driveway, the front lawn, looking for anything that might help. They knew it was unlikely but they were being very thorough anyway. Cooper could imagine how hard they were looking in back. They had blocked off the beautiful path, too, the Hasensprung where Beate had taken him on their first outing. The sniper must have fired from the Hasensprung or the hillside across the stream. The guy had to be a hell of a shot.

He was watching the cops when he noticed a man in a dark suit coming out of the front door. He stood in the bright light watching the same cops. After a few minutes he turned and went back into the house.

The sight of him had stopped Cooper's heart for a brief, eye-popping moment.

Clint Kilroy.

Beate dropped Cooper off at her apartment with another quick apology. She had to get to Television Center, but they'd go through the stolen files in the morning. She smiled sheepishly. "Okay?"

"Okay," he said. "I'm beat, anyway." He stifled a yawn. "It'll keep." At half past three, in the dark and the snow, the great heist didn't seem so important. It would be important again in the morning.

He slept as if he'd been drugged. It had been an incredibly long day, the meetings with Lee and then Wolf Koller, Karl-Heinz and the concert, the riot and the sound of the man's head smashing and crumbling, the burglary at Gisevius's and the shooting of Wolf Koller . . . every day was long but this was the longest. He'd put Chet Baker on the stereo and let the sound drift across him as he allowed his nerves to collapse. He wasn't thinking of the man at the riot, the man he might have killed, he was thinking only marginally about Wolf Koller and who might have shot him, he wasn't thinking of Karl-Heinz's cryptic message about Bayreuth and Warmolts . . . What thoughts remained in his consciousness as he felt himself going, going, were of Lee and Erika.

He woke out of a dream that had been making him sweat. Anxiety. There was a girl in it, he couldn't remember her face but he'd been trying to impress her with some sort of show he put on . . . He used a couple of big rag dummies in the show and he'd carelessly left them behind somewhere and he had to go back to get them but when he got there he fumbled around and couldn't find them and the girl was growing impatient with him, she wanted the show to go on, and he couldn't find his goddamn dummies and he kept making excuses and finally she just grabbed the arm of some guy and turned to Cooper and said something he didn't like and then, in the illogical continuity of dreams, he heard her talking on a telephone in another room, just out of sight, and she was talking about another man, maybe the guy she'd gone away with a few seconds earlier, and she was telling someone *I don't know what came over me, it never happened to me before, but he just turned me into a nymphomaniac, I was so hot, I would do anything for him, I was doing things I didn't even know you could do* (laughter, shy and almost shocked), *and I didn't want to stop* and as he heard her speaking he knew they were the things in the world he least wanted to hear, to know were true, that she hadn't been that way with him but had found it irresistible with someone else and it was not a really great dream and he woke knowing it had to be all about his own insecurities and fears and God only knew what else but the thing was, what had awakened him was a mystery but what he was hearing, now that the dream was over, was a woman talking on the telephone.

Beate was home from the studio. It was past six o'clock and he had been sleeping with every muscle clenched and he felt as if he'd break if he stretched. He heard her voice and he yawned . . . he had to get some more sleep.

". . . No, I don't think he's going to die . . . No, I understand that, but after all he is—I think she's about ready to crack, she saw her brother today and I guess that could have gone better . . . No, he was pretty bothered by it, I guess . . . If they know who shot him, they're not telling . . . I'll call you when I can . . . Are you all right up there? Plenty to eat? . . . Yes, it's snowing here, not enough to last . . . Don't worry . . . He's all right, at least he was tonight . . . I think he's afraid . . . Of course, who could blame him? . . . All right, go back to sleep."

She hung up and he heard her humming to herself, yawning, and crawling into bed and he tried to make sense of the conversation, the end of it he'd heard, but it wouldn't quite fit. *After all he is . . . what? . . . a pretty tough guy? After all he is . . . your boss? After all he is . . . your lover? After all he is . . .*

He told himself he had to remember that last one in the morning.

25

GRUNEWALD NOON

It was late morning with a gray light filtering in through the skylight when they settled down with strong coffee and the file. Melting snow was dripping from the eaves and a breeze freshened at the window. Cooper's cut face itched, which he took for a good sign, and Beate's eyes were bloodshot with rings of tiredness beneath them. But she was ready to go, primed. He sat watching her reading. At one point she nodded and looked up. "Here's Bayreuth. Let me just go on and finish."

When she finally looked up her lips were pursed and she was thinking aloud. "I've got two days off coming. I'd better take them. I'm going to have to go to Bayreuth."

"For God's sake, explain."

"Well, in the first place, the file contains a brief medical history. Wolf Koller contends that Lee is given to occasional outbursts of temper and irrationality, both in public and in private, which are extremely embarrassing to him. She attacks him verbally, accusing him of all sorts of things—including being a Nazi. There are some examples of Lee's behavior at parties and balls, making scenes about Koller . . . it isn't always Nazi-oriented. She claims he's in love with another woman, there are references to an alleged affair he had with the model Rafaela Dorfmann before she became a terrorist—"

"A *what?*"

"I was a kid but I can remember that story, the tycoon and the model, they were an item, a grand romance. It would have been back when Lee was married to Gunter Brendel—it wasn't a scandal or anything, just a very visible love affair. Then she gave it all up, including her relationship with Wolf Koller, and the next time she surfaced was in the role of terrorist—a very, very bloody one. I can remember how worried my mother was when I would go on school field trips in a bus, because Rafaela had blown up a school bus and killed a lot of children—"

"And she was Wolf Koller's girlfriend?" Cooper said. "Unbelievable."

"But she wasn't a terrorist then, so far as anyone knows. Don't get obsessed with this—honestly, it hasn't even occurred to me before this moment. The point is, Lee—according to this file—kept accusing him of having affairs, bribing politicians, on and on. Koller thinks she's crazy . . . and/or sick." She consulted the file again. "Lee's been blacking out, she claims not to remember certain events, she's even accused Koller of trying to poison her. So Koller finally seeks the help of Friedrich Gisevius."

Beate peered through her glasses at the report for a moment, then slipped them off. "It appears your sister has a history of mental problems. You were here with your friend Peterson in the winter of 1972, is that right?"

Cooper nodded. "She's no crazier than I am, damn it."

"According to this she married Wolf Koller within six months of your leaving. May 1973. Erika was born in April of 1974." She put her glasses back on, checked back with the file. She bit her upper lip slowly, a picture of concentration.

"All right. What difference do the dates make?"

"Well, that's what bothers me . . . In late October of 1973 she suffered a severe nervous breakdown, that's a quote, collapsed in a public rest room after trying to kill herself with a butcher knife apparently taken from her home. She went to work on her wrists." She paused to watch Cooper's face. "Like mother, like daughter."

"I wonder if Erika knew that?" Cooper mused.

"So, Lee is pregnant, in fact she may just have found out that she's pregnant, maybe that's why she tries to kill herself . . . whatever the reason, she tries to kill herself and would have succeeded except that the rest room she used was at KaDeWe and somebody found her. The police were called and it got into the papers . . . after all, she was Wolf Koller's wife. Gisevius notes here that this was the culmination—after her outbursts at parties and so forth—of the public humiliations for Herr

Koller and, indeed, for Herr Koller's family, meaning his parents, who were still alive and extremely imposing people. The result of this rather public failed suicide attempt was that Frau Koller was put in a 'clinic' for an extended period of recovery and rest. You're a very bright student—where was that clinic?"

"Bayreuth," Cooper said.

"You may go to the head of the class. And who was the doctor who owned the clinic and cared for Frau Koller?"

"Dear lovable old Dr. Warmolts!"

"Exactly! You are such a bright boy, John Cooper!" She was grinning widely at him, leaned across the coffee table and gave him a kiss. He licked a crumb of bread and butter from the corner of her mouth, listened to the sound of her laughter as she leaned back.

"So, what's the big deal that Karl-Heinz has to make such a production of telling me?"

"I am not absolutely sure but it may have something to do with the fact that Lee did not leave the clinic until April of 1974—"

"When Erika was born. So Erika was born in the clinic while her mom was in treatment . . ."

Beate nodded. "And Karl-Heinz told you Erika's not the person you think she is. It has to do with Bayreuth and Warmolts. Does that mean she's somehow different because of the circumstances of her birth?"

"He could mean that Erika is the daughter of a crazy person and it's hereditary. And I suppose that's possible—I'm not exactly an expert on mental illness. Or it could mean that he thinks Erika has been affected by some kind of medication Lee took while she was pregnant. That's all the rage these days—anything an expectant mother ingests is scrutinized very carefully, at least in the States."

"It's the same here. And when he said she's not the person you think she is, he meant you don't know she's got something wrong with her . . . Well, we're going to have to talk to him again and get some straight answers. Maybe she knows, maybe Karl-Heinz found out somehow and told her and that's why she tried to kill herself. It all hangs together, John." She put her hand on his arm. "I know it's sad—"

"It's too mysterious to be sad yet. What else does he say about Lee's condition now?"

"Much the same as Wolf Koller told you—various scans, doesn't have a brain tumor, doesn't have epilepsy, shows signs of Alzheimer's disease. Gisevius is of the opinion that it's progressing very rapidly. Less than a week ago he made a note to the effect that he felt she would need to be institutionalized very soon and he gave this opinion to Koller. He thinks, oh John, I don't want to tell you this—"

"You'd better."

"He thinks she could be gone in a few weeks."

Cooper shook his head. "It's so hard to believe. She seems quite normal considering everything . . ." His voice trailed off. "Think of the stress she's been under—maybe the son of a bitch really is trying to kill her. That might make you a little stressed out, right? And she's been worried about Erika and Karl-Heinz since before Erika tried to kill herself and then disappeared . . ."

"So," Beate said decisively, "I'm going to Bayreuth just as soon as I get an okay from my boss. There must be somebody down there who can remember, somebody who'll talk to me."

"I'll go with you. But right now I'm going out to Wolf's house. I want to see my sister—even Wolf ought to understand that."

"I'm going to catch that press briefing at the hospital, see how our boy is doing today." She took his hand in hers and looked worried. "Do you know how to be careful?"

"Look, I'm just going out there to check on Lee."

"I couldn't sleep when I got home last night. I lay there—"

"That's what I wanted to ask you—who were you talking to last night? On the phone."

She looked at him curiously. "What are you talking about? I was practically unconscious by the time I got home last night. I didn't talk to anybody. I had the radio on for a few minutes. Then I went to bed."

"I must have been dreaming, then. I thought I heard you—"

"I couldn't go to sleep last night, I kept thinking about the man you were hitting after the concert—I tried to find out if he died but I couldn't tell from what they were reporting when I was at work—"

"You've got to forget it. He was going to kill you or somebody else and if he died, he died. It was a riot. I was defending you and me and everybody else—"

"I didn't question why you did it. I'm just afraid that you might try it with somebody who has a gun. You've got to keep your temper—"

"If I'd kept my temper last night there'd be some other dead people today. I'm not sorry. I'm glad he's dead, he wasn't even human—"

"I just want you to be careful—"

"I will. But I've got to make some headway."

"You're not exactly the person I thought you were." It was almost what Karl-Heinz had said about Erika.

"I warned you."

"Maybe it runs in the family."

The streets in Grunewald were narrow and winding and tree-lined and he made a few false starts until he recognized a landmark, a tall gray house with blue trim and a blue roof on a corner. He'd noticed the large plaque on the side of the house before and when he asked her what it meant, Beate said: "They're on several houses out here. It marks a house that the Nazis confiscated from a Jewish owner—it's another way of making sure people don't forget." It was always a surprise, when he discovered some overt memory-evoking effort: he'd come to Germany thinking they didn't want to be reminded of their hideous past. But it wasn't true. The reminders were everywhere.

From the house bearing the plaque he knew how to reach Koller's house. It brooded beneath a dark gray noontime sky, heavy clouds so close you could almost touch them. There were police guards on duty at the black iron gate and a police car pulled up onto the sidewalk. The Hasensprung was still roped off and a police van was parked behind the rope. Cops were visible down at the low point where it bridged the stream between the two stone rabbits.

Beate had told him that the cops in Berlin were so afraid of seeming uncaring or brutal, so obsessed by the need to disappoint anyone who brought that preconception to Germany, that if they were on duty at Koller's he might be able to bully his way right past them. As it was, they stopped him at the gate and apologized for the inconvenience but told him the house was off limits.

Cooper looked perplexed. "Look here, you guys, I'm a member of the family. Lise Koller, Wolf Koller's wife, is my sister. I've come all the way from Boston, Massachusetts, USA, to see her and I'm damn well going to see her. Some cop told me last night that since I was family there was no problem. I took him at his word."

"Excuse me, sir, do you happen to recall his name?" The young man spoke nearly perfect English.

"Max Adler. He told me to use his name. Chief Adler. I was speaking to him last night, right on this spot, when I came to see my sister, right after my brother-in-law was shot. Please, check with him—"

"That won't be necessary, sir. He's at the hospital attending a press briefing on Herr Koller's status today." He motioned to his colleague and spoke a few words in German and the gate was walked open by the second cop. The first cop cleared his throat and almost blushed when he said: "I will have to check you for . . . ah, weapons, sir."

"Fine, fine. I don't want any nuts with guns getting in there to do any harm to my sister." He lifted his arms while the cop patted him down. "Here, have a look at this, too." He showed his passport. "I'd suggest that you check the identity cards of anyone you let in here. My sister is very important to me."

"Yes, sir. You're absolutely right."

"You're doing a fine job," Cooper said as he walked through the gate. In Boston somebody would have broken his nose by now and had him cuffed.

The front door was answered by a man in a black alpaca jacket like the majordomo would have worn at Edward Arnold's estate in a thirties movie. Cooper had forgotten that there were still people who had staffs like in the old movies. The man's English was rudimentary. Cooper was trying to get his point across and wasn't sure he was succeeding. The man's face gave nothing away but he remained firmly planted in the path toward the great staircase leading up from the foyer. Finally, Cooper caught his eye and began to advance, pushing him backwards, gesturing out toward the cops and saying that Frau Koller was his sister. The majordomo gauged Cooper's size and apparent determination and gave ground. Finally he nodded and said he would go get the doctor—Cooper was pretty sure that was what he'd said. Cooper smiled, nodded, said *Herr Doktor,* as if it were the best idea in the world. He watched the man back away, then turn and disappear down a hallway. Weird, it was all so weird.

As soon as the majordomo was out of sight Cooper was across the foyer and climbing the stairs. The house was quiet. Eerie. The stairway creaked for an instant and it sounded like a cry for help. The chandelier glittered like a bagful of diamonds. There was a statue of some mythological figure in the stairwell and a fountain coming out of the wall. Trickling very quietly. At the top of the stairs he waited, hoping for a sound to guide him. Nothing but the moaning of a water pipe somewhere, a cough in the heating system. Then, distantly, someone running a vacuum cleaner. To either side stretched the carpeted hallway, vases of flowers, mirrors, framed drawings and paintings, everything perfectly maintained. Some of the doors were open. He saw out the back, across to the oppo-

site side of the stream, where two policemen were crouched, looking at
the ground, which was damp with snow and matted leaves. He tried a
closed door and entered what he assumed was Wolf Koller's bedroom:
dark, heavy furniture, silver-backed hairbrushes and silver-appointed cologne bottles on the rugged chest of drawers, a dark manly hunting print
on the couch under the windows. It looked like a Ralph Lauren advertise-
ment. A piece of plywood had been placed over the broken window and
there were bloodstains all over the wall opposite the window. It looked as
if somebody had thrown some clots against the creamy paint and some
had stuck, some had run down in watery streaks. The carpet around
where Koller had fallen was marked off with tape. There was no one in
the room.

He went through the connecting door to the room on the other
side and saw Lee.

The draperies were drawn, creating an unnatural darkness, and he
smelled her perfume in the air, hanging gently, seductively all around
him.

A small lamp far from the bed glowed yellow.

She lay under a heavy comforter drawn up to her chin, in the
middle of a large four-poster bed. The colors of the room, the comforter,
the sheets and pillows, were pale strawberry and cream. Her head rested
on a big overstuffed pillow. The pillowcase was exquisitely detailed with
lace. Her breathing was a shallow rasp, her eyelids fluttered quietly. Her
lips were slightly parted. She looked almost dead.

Her skin was parchment white, looked dry and brittle. So pale.
Veins showed blue beneath the skin. Her hands on top of the comforter
were gray white and looked too much like claws. He gasped as he drew
near.

She looked old.

Like an old woman.

For an instant he didn't believe it could be Lee, but it was. She
might have been dead but for the faint whistling of her breathing.

He knelt beside the bed and spoke her name. Then spoke again,
more insistently, touched her shoulder. Slowly her eyes opened, she
blinked. There was something wrong with her eyes. She was doped up
and she was having trouble fighting her way back to the surface. He took
the cold, pale hand.

"Lee . . . it's me. I'm going to take care of you. I'm so damned
sorry for the way I acted at Charlottenburg. You've got to believe me, I
was just blowing off steam, acting like a jerk. Try to forget what I said,

just try to forgive me . . . everything's going to be all right . . . I'm going to stay, I'm going to help you get Erika back, I'm not going to leave you again, I'll never leave you again." She was breaking his heart, so helpless, so fragile. What in the name of God was the matter with her? Why did she look so old, so weak? "Lee, can you hear me? Are you there?"

She was staring at him but he couldn't tell if she was seeing him. She seemed to be looking through him. Or not really looking at all. She might have been blind. Her eyes couldn't seem to focus. He might have been dealing with an aged mother, someone who had once looked like Lee. She swallowed slowly, with great difficulty, as if she were dried out, dried up. He squeezed her hand and there was no answering pressure. Her hand felt cold and papery. Yet the day before she had walked through the palace at Charlottenburg with him, had fought with him, had been so alive, so angry. He'd have given anything to hear her anger again. Yesterday she had been desirable, he'd felt all the physical urges. He'd wanted her. He always wanted her. It was part of what she was. And now . . . this . . . She seemed to teeter on the edge of the grave.

Her lips moved and he felt a slight pressure on his hand. He couldn't hear her but she was saying something. He put his head down beside hers, stroked her hair. "What is it, Lee?"

She whispered into his ear.

"Who are you?"

He was still sitting beside her, holding her hand, watching her sleep, when he heard a sound behind him and the door from the hallway opened.

"Leave us the hell alone." He was ready to sob or shriek with rage, he didn't know which. What had they done to his sister?

"Mr. Cooper."

Cooper turned to see the majordomo lurking behind a squat fat man in a pinstriped suit, starched white shirt, and tie. Long hair, wavy, streaked with gray, heavy jowls, thick lips, a broad short nose with heavy hornrims squatting across it. "I am Frau Koller's physician. Friedrich Gisevius. I must ask you to leave at once or I'll be forced to summon the policemen from outside. You give me no choice." His fat hands were clasped in front of his vest.

Cooper stood up, walked over to him, and placed his flat hand on the doctor's vest and pushed hard. Why couldn't Gisevius have just been civil? What was the point? Gisevius went against the wall, double chins quivering, obscuring his collar and the knot in his tie. Cooper stared into the small dark eyes hiding in the pockets of flesh.

"What . . . have . . . you . . . done . . . to . . . my . . . sister? She looks half dead. Yesterday she was full of life. Raising holy hell with me. She looked so beautiful I . . . I—just look at her now, you bastard—what have you done to her?" He spat the words into the doctor's face, but quietly, not wanting to wake her.

Gisevius replied calmly: "It's a fiendish little trick we Germans have, Mr. Cooper. It's called sedation. Maybe it's unheard of across the sea. It calms people when they are hysterical. Now back away from me. Don't make matters worse for yourself and your sister. You are intruding here."

Cooper stared into the small, glittering eyes and didn't move. "This is my sister, you silly shit. The only person I'm likely to make matters worse for right away is you—so help me, don't fuck with me. What have you done to her? This isn't a couple of Tylenol and some Sominex—she's out on another planet somewhere. She doesn't know who the hell I am! Now talk to me!" He was holding the lapels of the doctor's coat, shoving him against the wall. Trying hard not to reach overload. His rage reminded him too much of what had happened after the concert—had it been only last night?

"Forgive me, Mr. Cooper, I am not answerable to you and your absurd threats. Take your hands off of me at once."

"You started with the threats, my friend." Cooper wanted to hurt him. Gisevius was going to pay for what was happening to Lee.

The majordomo in the alpaca jacket, with his balding bullet head and tiny ears so flat to his skull, had produced a gun, a pistol of some kind, and Cooper turned like something normally found behind bars in a zoo and smashed the man's arm, wrist, and hand against the frame of the door with his forearm. There was a gurgling cry of surprise and pain and the gun dropped loudly to the floor. Cooper and the alpaca jacket looked at it. "Try to pick it up," Cooper said softly. The man's hand hung limply from his wrist and he was fighting back tears of pain. "Please. Try to pick it up."

The man staggered back two steps, leaning against the wall in the hallway. He looked gray.

Gisevius turned to Cooper. "You fool!"

"I don't know my own strength. And I specifically said not to fuck with me. What he did—pointing a gun—that counted as fucking with me." Cooper shook his head, leaned down, and scooped up the gun. It was very heavy.

"Who's here?" It was Lee, moaning, speaking in English, maybe because that was what she was hearing. "Who are you people? What's happening . . ." She lapsed back into silence, her head turned away; she was asleep.

"Come, Mr. Cooper," Gisevius said. He was whispering placatingly. "We got off on the wrong foot—let's start again. I apologize for any misunderstanding on my part."

"Now that's more like it, Doctor. And diplomatically put. Though a little late for your friend." They could hear the man in the alpaca coat vomiting in a nearby bathroom.

"Shock. I'll attend to him in a moment."

Gisevius was leading the way toward the long stairway. "I was under the impression that Wolf had explained his wife's condition to you. Come, we need a bit of refreshment. And a moment to calm down—I feel as if I could use a sedative myself." He smiled. Apparently he hadn't connected Cooper with the break-in at his home. "We're all very tense today, I'm afraid." Cooper followed him down the stairway. The house had gone back to its quiet, insulated normality.

Gisevius led the way into a handsome study with a fire in the grate, the fireplace made of beautifully matched tiles depicting some kind of knighthood flowering in a mysterious black forest. A couple of immense, wonderfully intelligent-seeming giant schnauzers, like mutant Scotties, pitch black, looked on with great dignity and calm as Gisevius poured scotch and water for both of them.

Once they were sitting in two leather chairs by the fire he went through the entire routine, telling Cooper more or less what Wolf Koller had told him the day before and what Beate had read in his file. The tests, the lack of certainty about a diagnosis, though it looked more and more like Alzheimer's. "But we mustn't give up. She might respond to a treatment of drugs. Look what has happened to manic depression, schizophrenia, all kinds of once incurable mental illnesses. Great strides are being made—"

"She looks a hell of a lot like Ingrid Bergman in *Notorious*."

"I don't quite understand—"

"The Hitchcock movie. You must have seen it."

"I'm afraid not."

"My God, Doc, this is Germany, not the moon. Ingrid Bergman

looked the way she did because Claude Rains and his wicked mother were poisoning her. South America after the war, a band of Nazi leftovers . . . Cary Grant saved her."

"I assure you, this is no movie. And nobody's being poisoned. This is a very real condition and it's very serious. We are doing everything we can—"

"I'll bet you're not big on second opinions."

"—but strain seems to intensify the condition. To that extent it is psychosomatic—are you familiar with ulcerative colitis, for example? Stress triggers attacks. That's what we seem to have here. The disappearance of her daughter, your arrival, the attempt to kill Wolf last night— these are things she simply can't handle. She went completely to pieces."

"Has it ever crossed your mind that maybe she's just nuts? The well-known American expert on mental illness, Olaf Peterson—you must have read some of his work—once told me that he thought she was just plain nuts."

"Ah. I'm not familiar with . . ." Gisevius let the sentence trail off. " 'Nuts' is not a very accurate term, clinically speaking, but in its colloquial sense I've sometimes thought that she might suffer from some kind of schizophrenia. But I doubt it. Nothing delusionary. No particular paranoia . . . just this personality displacement, in the sense that she loses her personality, her identity, just misplaces it for a time, then she finds it again . . . Our fear is that one day she will misplace it and not be able to find it again." Gisevius looked up and then stood. "Ah, come in, Mr. Kilroy. Have you met Mr. Cooper? Dear Lise's brother?"

"Hell, Fritz, John Cooper and I go way back. How are you, Cooper?" Kilroy came into the room like a knife, thin and sharp, wearing a dark suit and vest and black cowboy boots. "You're a long way from Boston, boy."

"And you're a long way from Texas, Clint." Cooper was remembering: the way he popped up out of nowhere wanting to buy Cooper's building in Boston, the way he showed up on TV in Boston in the German investment story, how he was waiting in Beate's hotel room in Copley Square, how he was captured in the bright light of last night as Wolf Koller lay wounded in the hospital.

"Tell me about it. And I hate every damned minute and mile of it. Still, I'm a citizen of the world, John. I've got business everywhere. You're here visiting your sister, is it?"

"Didn't Wolf tell you?"

"Wolf didn't tell me diddly. I came along last night about five minutes after some sidewinder put a bullet in him. Jesus, talk about good ol' Texas boys with gun racks in their pickups—how about Berlin, eh? Snipers!"

"What brings you to Berlin?"

"Bidness, just bidness, as we say down my way. I saw the old family retainer puking his guts out a coupla minutes ago, I think he's got a broken wing. He says there was some trouble upstairs—is that right?"

Gisevius said: "Mr. Cooper was concerned about his sister and there was a misunderstanding. An accident."

"Ahh . . ." Kilroy smiled at Cooper. "I'll bet folks are just always havin' accidents around ol' Coop."

"What's the word on Wolf Koller this morning?"

"Well, Coop, he was up kickin' ass at the hospital. He's gonna be all right. But I tell you, he'll never throw that Nolan Ryan fastball again. But what the hell, right?" Kilroy sneezed and blew his nose on an immaculate white handkerchief. "I'm not kiddin' you, I'm too damn old for all this flyin' around, jet lag, changes in the weather, my resistance gets low, I get a fuckin' cold. Doc, you got anything to clean up my miseries?"

"Of course. It won't do much for the cold but it will mask the symptoms."

"Jesus, that's what doctors always say. What is it?"

"Don't worry. The Chancellor has the same cold and I gave him the same thing yesterday. It will dry up your nose."

"Shit. Contac. I can get that at home."

"But you are here, Mr. Kilroy. Just take what I give you."

Cooper interrupted: "What are you going to do with Lee?"

Gisevius said: "Watch and wait. She is not an easy person to deal with. Very headstrong. When she's herself, that is."

Kilroy said: "I understand there are days when she doesn't know herself from Katarina Witt. That about right?"

"It's a complicated condition. You might try prayer, Mr. Cooper. But I must insist that you leave treatment to me. And frankly, your presence is very upsetting to her. Feel free to call me at any time but allow me to tell you when you might see her."

"I'll be in touch, then," Cooper said.

"Then, if you'll excuse me, I should have a look at Bruno's wrist."

"Arm, I'd say," Kilroy said. He walked outside with Cooper, took a deep breath of cold air. He looked out across the forecourt at the cars. A Daimler-Benz, two Mercedeses, a BMW, a Jaguar convertible. "Hell of a lot of money on wheels right here." He was noting a fact, not passing judgment. "Back in Texas I got me a Bentley Turbo or two, cost more'n all these heaps. Ah, I'm about Krauted out, y'know? These Krauts give me a pain in the hindquarters. But bidness is bidness, as LBJ used to say. It's a small world, you get in bed with the guy you need. No matter who the hell he is. Small world. In fact, the world is a handkerchief, as an old friend of mine used to say. It covers us all." He gave a wintry laugh.

Cooper said: "I love it when you get all folksy. But one question—who shot Wolf Koller last night?"

"Well, you got me there, son. I don't know but I'm afraid great men always have enemies."

"Ain't it the truth?" Cooper said.

"Well, I've got work to do, Coop. I expect I'll be seeing you somewhere on down the trail."

"Hiyo, Silver," Cooper said.

26

ANOTHER ARABESQUE

Bernd Schmidt was worried about his son.

Karl-Heinz had been missing for two days and Bernd knew it was no fluke, not just a case of his kid's failing to report in. Their relationship was such that there were no flukes. It was too serious. They both knew that things could happen. Each had to be sure of the other. They were in this thing together. And he hadn't heard from Karl-Heinz for two days.

Both of their lives were in play. Father and son. German history reflected in yet another family: there were such families all over Germany, in the East and West. They shared the same framework, though their personal nightmares might be very different from one another. Germany the perpetrator, Germany the visionary, Germany the destroyer of nations, Germany the slayer of generations. Every German had his own private Germany. Bernd Schmidt's Germany was a chessboard and at last, after fifty years, he saw checkmate within his reach. He had been patient, more patient than he'd believed possible, and now he was almost there. There had been sacrifices along the way, opportunities he'd been unable to take . . . but now, now was the time.

But Karl-Heinz had gone missing.

Bernd had to be more careful than ever. But he couldn't lose the opportunity. He was past seventy. Logic told him he was looking at his last chance. The complexity of it all was, he supposed, taxing his brain's power. If he thought of his brain as a computer he might admit that there were faster models out there, capable of more calculations per second; but the value of a computer lay in the quality of the program, the software. The elegance and simplicity of his program was, he believed, in a class entirely of its own. Uncluttered. Simple goals. Yet immensely flexible, able to cope with half a century's worth of surprises and keep functioning. He had to keep the simplicity of it all in mind. He couldn't be diverted by the loss of a pawn here, a rook there, a bishop somewhere else. It was a question of knight moves, the piece with all the trickery and indirection in its very nature. Had Karl-Heinz been swept from the board? Could he adhere to the original program if Karl-Heinz had been lost?

Once Bernd Schmidt realized that he was, within the broad definition, a monomaniac he set out to discover if he was a psychopath. He turned, masking his intentions, to his wife, who was a professional psychologist. She discussed the issue with him, gave him some books with chapters marked to his attention. In the end Bernd decided he fit the description of a child-murderer his wife had dealt with for the police in a small town near the Polish border: "icily psychopathic," she'd called him. He rather liked the sound of that. He wasn't a raving maniac but he was very sure of what he wanted to accomplish. Bernd thought he was a good deal healthier than the farmer who dismembered living children because he knew it was his duty; but he shared with the farmer a calm determination to achieve his goals.

Bernd Schmidt's life had taken a turn at the age of twenty, in the year 1942. It had taken another blow during November of 1944. Henceforth, he'd known what he was meant to do during his time on this earth.

He hated Nazis.

Specifically he hated the Family Koller, which at present amounted to Wolf Koller, son of Erhard Koller.

Bernd had the best reasons in the world for being an icy psychopath.

Bernd was born in Berlin in 1922. He was a young soldier during World War II, serving on the Eastern Front with great distinction, and managed to survive the endless retreat. He came home laden with battlefield decorations. He was chosen during the autumn of 1944 to serve under the extraordinary six-foot-seven adventurer Otto Skorzeny in one of Hitler's wildest schemes, Operation Greif. Skorzeny was to train a group of English-speaking German soldiers, who would put on American uniforms and infiltrate American lines in the Ardennes, spreading confusion and havoc wherever possible. It was all part of the breakout, later referred to by the winners as the Battle of the Bulge, which was to shock and demoralize and ultimately defeat the advancing Allied forces, who thought they were primarily sweeping up the last pieces of the Third Reich army on their way to Berlin.

Bernd Schmidt looked upon his involvement in such an important offensive as a high honor. Until he learned that Skorzeny himself was not accompanying his men in Operation Greif. It was deemed too dangerous to risk such an important man. Then Bernd Schmidt realized that if he was captured wearing an American uniform he would certainly be stood up against a wall somewhere and shot. This issue was raised with Hitler, who scoffed at it. "Once the shooting starts, the battle begins—then strip off the American uniform. The Geneva laws will save you." Bernd and many of his fellow impostors found this altogether too whimsical. Still, there was no getting out of it. And by some incompetence on the Allies' part he survived the action near Saint-Vith and got home once again. Home to fight the oncoming tide rolling toward Berlin. Home to survive. It seemed that that was what he was, in addition to being a hero: he was a survivor. As a legendary hero after the war, he became part of the Berlin (Russian Sector) police, working with the Russians; he survived that test and rose through the East Berlin bureaucracy, moved on into the STASI, the secret police. It had been a remarkably good career. And when the Wall came down he'd moved into what people called the private sector, where he had prospered, even though he was getting on in years. Everybody said he seemed younger than he was.

Maybe his hatred kept him young.

His father, Alois Schmidt, had never joined the Party but had nevertheless been a respected officer, had sworn the personal allegiance to Hitler required of all. The old Prussians had had a fit about that. It was reprehensible to give your oath of loyalty to a man, an individual, rather than the state. On the surface they'd gone along with it, had given the oath, but it was only lip service. In private they spoke against it. Alois had gone along with the others, all the time finding Hitler and his followers loathsome, unprofessional, immoral, corrupt. Wasting so much time on the Jews was insane: a wise man would have co-opted them, turned them into a great resource of the state. But Hitler had decided not merely to humiliate them and put them in camps: Alois had good information that they were being murdered in huge numbers. Alois Schmidt had never paid much attention to Jews one way or the other but Hitler's policy was both stupid and inhuman. No rationale for it made sense to him.

When the opportunity arose in early 1942 to join a plot to overthrow the Führer, Alois agreed to play a small role. He was, in effect, a messenger moving among the main plotters, men of standing and family and power in the military. Bernd was never even quite sure if his father had known it was a murder plot. It was quite possible that he thought it was a plot to overthrow Hitler, hold him under house arrest, and offer peace negotiations to the Allies. What was known through interviews Bernd had conducted with men who'd known his father during those years was that Alois was among the middle rank of officers who opposed the war on the grounds not only that it was wrong but that it was absolutely unwinnable from the moment America got in. Their view was the sooner you sued for peace the better it was going to be for the greater German *Volk*.

When the plot was uncovered, as many such plots were, Alois Schmidt was swept into the same sack as the major players. He was tortured into confessing along with the others and then he was tried by a military and civilian tribunal in one of Hitler's courts. *In camera*. It was a touchy issue, how public such proceedings should be. The Führer certainly didn't want the people to get wind of the fact that his officers were always trying to kill him—the people might begin to wonder why. But it was important that word get around the officer class. Betray Hitler and you were a dead man.

Alois Schmidt was found guilty and sentenced to die by the presiding magistrate, one of the flowers of Hitler's judicial system, one of Hitler's personally picked judges . . . Erhard Koller, former professor of law, author of law texts, who had been to America to meet and study with no less a man than Oliver Wendell Holmes. Erhard Koller, Wolf's father. Erhard Koller, who had been one of the representatives of the Third Reich's judiciary at the Wannsee Conference.

Alois Schmidt had disappeared after the trial. His son, fighting the war and becoming a hero, was never notified of his father's fate. Neither was Alois's wife, Bernd's mother. That good woman, who always smelled of *Hasenpfeffer* and cookies and baking bread during Bernd's childhood, was hounded as the traitor's wife among the other military wives, and finally went to the kitchen, where she was most at home, and took her own life with a carving knife of Solingen steel.

Then, in October of 1944, just before he was to begin training for Operation Greif under Skorzeny, a mysterious package arrived for Bernd Schmidt. Mysterious in the sense that it had originated at the Secret State Police Office, Prinz-Albrecht-Strasse 8, Berlin.

There was no letter, nothing. Just a set of carefully enlarged photographs, meticulously printed. The photographs showed several members of the plot against Hitler, Alois Schmidt among them.

They had been stripped naked. Their faces and bodies were covered with marks of torture: burns, cuts, bruises. One of his father's ribs had been broken and was protruding several inches through the flesh of his chest.

They were hanging from meathooks in a packing house. Blood ran down their bodies, formed pools on the floor. Some were upside down with the hooks driven through their rectums and back out just above their genitals. Their legs hung every which way. The others were right side up, the hooks driven through their spines and back out at the bases of their skulls. As the years passed Bernd could no longer actually remember which way it had been for his father. He had forced it, the picture, out of his memory. And he supposed it hardly made a difference.

He supposed also that he was lucky not to have been shot himself for being Alois's son. Then he thought that maybe the Operation Greif thing was enough like a suicide mission to qualify as an execution.

Which was why he had let his hatred for the Nazis and the Family Koller dominate the rest of his life. He was not made particularly unhappy by his obsession. In fact he was known to his coworkers as a relatively sunny fellow. His wife having died, he married a second time, the pretty psychologist from Potsdam. Their life together had been a happy one, all things considered. Life in East Berlin under the Communists had been hard but he had adapted, endured, and succeeded. He liked to think that having a deep sense of purpose was what kept him in a relatively good mood and free of illness during his advancing years. Bernd Schmidt was as committed to exacting his revenge on the Nazis and the Kollers as another man might be to discovering the cure for cancer.

Sitting in his office at the printing company, staring out into the gray day at the fleet of trucks, the men unloading supplies, the massive rolls of paper, the warehouses that stretched away, a world of warehouses, he wondered if Burke Delaney had figured out that he, Bernd Schmidt, was the hand behind the SPARTAKUS product. Was Burke still quick enough? Would he see it for what it was? Or would he believe that Karl-Heinz had dug it up himself?

When Bernd learned that Karl-Heinz had met Erika Koller and begun seeing her, he saw his opportunity. Fate had played into his hands.

First the Wall had come down and Germany had been united; now, miraculously, access to the world of Wolf Koller. He could now lay a tiger-trap for Wolf Koller, using Erika Koller and his own son, the grandson of Alois Schmidt. He provided Karl-Heinz with background on the Koller family, the extent of Wolf's holdings, the Nazi connections of Erhard Koller, Erika's grandfather. He knew that Karl-Heinz was telling Erika, filling her in on the family's Nazi past. She already hated her father for his arrogance, for the way he treated her mother. Now Bernd was completing the job of ripping her away from him.

Finally he revealed to Karl-Heinz that he was not simply the manager of a large printing company, that instead the printing company was part of Wolf Koller's holdings and that he, Bernd, was not the manager . . . that the job of managing director was a cover for what he really did.

Bernd Schmidt's success in the STASI had led to a job as director of security services for the Koller Group, reporting directly to Wolf Koller.

It was time to confide completely in Karl-Heinz. The time had come to strike at Koller, whatever the cost. Bernd had worked it out carefully, combining what he knew of Koller's political operations with what he surmised and was damn well in a position to find out.

The key to it all was that flat in Knesebeckstrasse. It had turned up in the Security pay sheets without an explanation. If it was Security, then Bernd Schmidt should have known about it. But he didn't. And neither did anyone in Accounting. Real Estate said it didn't show on their computer printouts. But there it was on his budget. It didn't exist; but there it was.

Somebody had to pay for it. So it came out of Security. And Security—Bernd Schmidt—had never heard of it. It was the sort of thing that anyone involved in intelligence work would pick up on; but most heads of intelligence services were not the ones who sifted through their budgets. They had people who took care of accounts. Unfortunately for Wolf Koller, Bernd Schmidt was from the old school, a perfectionist.

So, when he first spotted the Knesebeckstrasse flat and didn't get the answers he needed, Bernd stopped asking questions, began looking around. He spent the better part of two weeks watching the building. He had a couple of his oldest Security field men videotape it. And then he got a surprise. The primary visitor to the Knesebeckstrasse flat was Wolf Koller himself.

Bernd's first assumption was that it was a love nest. But it wasn't. Koller met only with men. Maybe he was a pansy, then, meeting his boyfriends. Like Gisevius. And Gisevius was among the visitors to the flat. But the pattern of visitors, and Koller's nature, made that possibility absurd.

So Bernd Schmidt turned his son loose on the flat with a few special instructions and an electronic toy or two. Karl-Heinz was an eager student. He was satisfying his own morality. And he was being a good son.

And Karl-Heinz discovered SPARTAKUS.

Father and son now had the key to the rest of Wolf Koller's life. What to do with it?

The first thing was to have Karl-Heinz get hold of an old warhorse by the name of Burke Delaney. Which he had done and the SPARTAKUS product had begun to flow.

But now Karl-Heinz had vanished . . .

Bernd Schmidt knew he now had to meet with Delaney.

Bernd had known Delaney since the CIA had tried to build that crazy goddamn tunnel in the fifties. They'd both been up to their asses in that one, though at opposite ends of the tunnel. Bernd had always called Delaney "Digger" after that. The Yanks had dug the tunnel all the way from the American Zone to its terminus directly beneath Soviet Military HQ in the Russian Zone. They had listened to what was going on overhead with the most sophisticated eavesdropping equipment possible. The product was then sent back to Berlin and Washington for analysis. It was a huge, time-consuming job but it was an intelligence coup of almost unbelievable proportions.

Or would have been if the Soviets hadn't known about the tunnel almost from the beginning. Once the CIA found out they were compromised, countless millions of dollars had been spent deciphering worse than useless product—sheer disinformation. It was the nightmare of a lifetime for a spy and it took the Agency years to recover, both from internal bloodletting and the loss of respect in the outside world. Many believed that it had driven the legendary genius of the CIA, James Jesus Angleton, most of the way to madness.

Delaney still liked to think of it as a triumph of a sort—a triumph of tunnel-digging, if nothing else—and fuck the betrayal. The suits always betrayed the poor bastards with the guns and the cyanide pills, anyway.

Bernd would point out to him that you had to keep your sense of humor in this business. Bernd had been helping the Soviets think up plausible disinformation. It had been fun, insofar as anything you did with those morons was fun.

But now nothing was fun.

He couldn't find Karl-Heinz.

27

OLD FRIENDS SHALL MEET ONCE MORE

Bernd Schmidt did, however, have plenty on his mind other than the disappearance of his son.

He was in charge of Wolf Koller's search for *his* missing daughter and it was hopeless. No one had seen the girl since she'd been roughed up by Stiffel's young braves at the riot. Koller knew she had been there with Karl-Heinz but he didn't seem to hold it against Bernd. Koller had said over a cup of coffee in his office, the morning after Lise had gone to Erika's flat and found the blood and the knife: "Bernd, I won't hold your son against you if you don't hold my daughter against me. You probably don't like having Karl-Heinz and Erika together any more than I do. But we're both smart enough to know we can't get our kids to do a damn thing we want them to—we'd only make it worse, isn't that right, Bernd?"

"Yes, Wolf, I think you're right. Kids will be kids these days."

"Kids have always insisted on being kids. Now they just don't hide their rebellion. They parade it, just to spite their parents. It's the direction life has taken. So, we'll forget they're *our* kids. And you'll just try to find my daughter. If she doesn't want to be found, you probably won't find her. She's smart. But you'll try, won't you?"

"I'll get on it immediately."

"You might as well start with Karl-Heinz."

"Just what I was thinking, sir. But first I'd better have a look at her flat."

"Good. I'll make sure Adler's men give you access. Get on it, Bernd. And good hunting. I want her found before she really goes off the deep end."

They'd never spoken again about the relationship between their children. Bernd wondered if Koller really wanted his daughter found: Did Koller know his daughter could destroy him and everything he'd worked for? All because Karl-Heinz was Bernd Schmidt's son.

And then somebody shot Wolf Koller.

Koller wanted to know who shot him. You couldn't blame him for that. But Max Adler was the man for that job. Bernd's security force protected corporate premises, checked out employees' backgrounds, made sure the computers were secure, swept for bugs on a regular schedule, dug around when there were incidents of white-collar crime. And then there were the strongarms whom Koller called the "facilitators." *Bernd,* he would say, *get the facilitators on this, right now!* They were the muscle and their intimidating presence was usually enough during labor disputes, for example. In a conglomerate as large as the Koller Group there was always something for the facilitators to do. They were the old hands, characters from the murky past. Useful. But none of them knew how to conduct a police investigation, which was what was needed to find out who might have shot Koller. And of course they couldn't find Erika either.

Once again Bernd found himself trying to get inside Koller's mind. He thought Koller probably had a pretty good idea who took the shot at him. When Koller knew he had an enemy he could be a very bad man. And now Koller wanted him front and center in his hospital room.

Before he left his office, though, Bernd Schmidt put in a call to Burke Delaney, who'd come to Berlin and left a message for him. It had to be about Karl-Heinz. Had something gone wrong? He didn't want to think about all the possibilities . . . It was such a dangerous game. The stakes were so high.

The Professor didn't like to call his behavior obsessive but his curiosity was certainly piqued by the sighting of first his old pal from Moscow

Center, Konstantin Orlovski, and then Sebastien the Red. It kept him from worrying so much about John Cooper descending upon them, screwing about in other people's business. But Cooper's presence was still eating at the back of his mind as he sat in his VW watching Orlovski pacing back and forth in front of the Berlin Zoo's famous Elephant Gate. Orlovski was waiting at the Elephant Gate for the third consecutive day. A short way up the street the police had still barricaded some of the entrances to Zoo Station itself in the wake of the bombing but that didn't bother the Professor. He had decided the Russian was waiting for somebody to pick him up in a car. And the Professor didn't want to get left behind when it happened. So, on this third day, he'd brought his own car.

It was late afternoon, turning into darkness. Crowds streamed to and from the enormous, sprawling, wounded Zoo Station with the gigantic bubble of glass looming up behind the tracks, the zoo's aviary. One of the biggest in the world. Most of the zoo's animals had been killed in one godawful bombing raid back in what, '43? Horrible mess. Orlovski was still passing back and forth like a sentry, peering down the street into traffic, holding his umbrella too tightly. His arm was going to tighten up. Why was he so tense?

It was odd when you thought about it, which was all the Professor was thinking about lately: Erika Koller disappears, then John Cooper shows up. Stiffel and Company bring their murderous bullshit all the way to Berlin. Delaney gets mixed up in some craziness with Karl-Heinz Schmidt, and pretty soon a broken-down terrorist, for reasons unknown, decides to make a run at Delaney and winds up dumped down a well . . . and the CIA or one of their equivalents might or might not be involved . . . then Orlovski shows up with a gold Rolex and a hotsy-totsy suitcase . . . and has lunch with another old terrorist, for chrissakes, also from the Dorfmann gang . . . and then somebody actually tries to assassinate Wolf Koller and damn near succeeds . . . and John Cooper is always there, mooching about the edges. Poor bastard. He had no idea, not a clue, of what the hell he'd gotten into . . . That was the one thing in the whole business that the Professor had hoped would not happen. The slaughter of the innocent. Because if there was one innocent in the mix it was John Cooper, late of Cooper's Falls, Minnesota . . .

The car finally came. He could almost hear Orlovski's sigh of relief from across the street. Gray Mercedes. Now there was a surprise. Sebastien at the wheel. What did it mean? Sebastien and Orlovski. And Orlovski was Rossovich's handmaiden once he took over in Moscow, his errand boy, his advance man . . .

They were in no hurry so it was an easy tail. Which was a very good thing. The Professor was out of his element.

Traffic was murderous. It was that time of day. It was dark, the rain slashing across the headlights, the highway hissing as if the tires were snakes. The rain was turning to sleet. The road was increasingly slippery and eventually he could smell the Grunewald forest all around and it was getting colder. The VW heater was not state-of-the-art. He hoped it was not going to be an all-night drive. Sooner or later he was going to have to take a piss. He was going to get hungry. He was already colder than the Chancellor's heart.

How did guys who tailed people for a living handle it? Lots of problems of a practical nature.

James Bond never seemed to take a leak.

The next thing he knew he felt a sharp wind flailing at the car. The wind was blowing hard off Lake Wannsee. Hmmm. Now this was interesting . . .

Wolf Koller was sitting in a chair by the window, his profile caught and held by the gray, cold winter light. His arm was in a sling. A Beethoven quartet was coming from speakers nestled among vases of flowers. Bernd Schmidt stood in the doorway of the hospital suite, watching the great man, his employer, his mortal enemy, the man he was betraying. Then he knocked softly and Koller turned and with a heavy sigh spoke his name.

"Bernd. Come in. Sit down."

It seemed to Schmidt that a good deal of the fire and snap had been removed along with the bullet. Koller's eyes had lost their shine. His face was drawn, eye sockets hollowed. "How are you feeling?"

Wolf Koller shrugged, winced. "I am inconvenienced. Otherwise . . . the wound is the least of my concerns. I'll be fine."

"You were a very lucky man." Schmidt sat down in an armchair, sneezed at the scent of all the flowers. He was allergic. "Have Adler and his people come up with anything?"

"No. Someone fired a high-powered rifle from the bank on the other side of the stream. They think they have some footprints in the leaves and mud but . . . it won't be of any help. They found a shell casing. In other words, nothing that matters a damn."

Schmidt shook his head, commiserating. "What can I do?"

"That's why I wanted to see you. I believe I know who was responsible. There's a plot against me."

"There is? You're serious?"

"Someone inside the government. Close to Glock . . ."

Schmidt tried to hide his astonishment. "I don't follow you. I mean to say, you and Glock . . ." He crossed his fingers to show how close they had always been, since Koller had picked Glock from the ranks of the politicians and pushed him forward. Schmidt wondered what the devil Koller was up to now with such a strange theory. "How could someone close to Glock . . ." He shrugged.

"It could *be* Glock."

"Chief, with all due respect, I find that hard to believe."

"Fortunately, then, I am not concerned with what you do or do not believe. Glock has shown signs of . . . jealousy. He resents me, my power, my control over him. I want bugs in his home and office."

"That's a federal crime," Schmidt said softly. "Treason. In addition to being very hard to do. The office, particularly."

"Occasionally you are required to accomplish difficult tasks. Just do it, Bernd."

Schmidt stood up, stood staring out the window across the green lawn going brown with the cold weather. Men were raking leaves beneath the bare trees. Did Koller know what he was saying? Could a wound such as his produce delusions?

"All right," he said. "I'll do what I can."

"You're very good with bugs, aren't you? Wasn't that the STASI specialty?"

"We relied more on informers."

"Ah."

"Well, I'd better get on this right away. I'll go to Bonn myself—"

"No, no, I want you close by. Send someone you trust, one of your experts. I need you here. There's Erika . . . Have you come up with any leads at all?"

"We're getting nowhere." Schmidt's mouth was dry, and there was a faint buzz of warning in the back of his mind. Something was wrong here. "But we knew the odds were heavily against us. I'm convinced she'll just turn up—"

"What does Karl-Heinz say?"

"He's very worried, of course. But I don't see much of him."

"I thought you were in close contact with him."

"No, not at all. He's 'outgrown' his parents. It's a stage. It's probably what Erika's going through, as well. Finding herself, as they say."

"Well, I hope it's working," Wolf Koller said bleakly. "Nobody else seems able to find her. But you're sure Karl-Heinz doesn't know where she is? You're sure this isn't some kind of game they've come up with?"

"Absolutely sure. I know the boy."

"Bernd . . . I believe we have a mole, a spy, somewhere inside our operation."

"Fill me in." Was it more paranoia? Or did he know about the SPARTAKUS leak? "Where? How do you know?"

"Secret material has fallen into the wrong hands." Koller turned to face his visitor. "There's no other explanation."

"Explanation for what?"

"I've been warned. Leave it at that."

"We can vet the main office, of course." Schmidt kept his voice steady but he felt the sweat breaking out. Koller had never mentioned anything relating to the SPARTAKUS penetration before, for the simple reason that Schmidt had not been told of its existence. Schmidt believed the leak had not been discovered. And now—was Koller talking about SPARTAKUS? "You'll have to give me something more to go on if you want me to take action. This is industrial espionage, I assume. Fill me in and we can handle it." He hoped he sounded confident.

"Yes, of course. We'll discuss this when I'm back in the office, when we've got this Erika thing cleared up. And when my wife is on her feet again." He stood up, pain etched in his face. "I have enemies, Bernd, enemies who will do anything to tear down what I am building." Koller patted Schmidt on the back, and as Schmidt reached the door Koller had an afterthought. "About Karl-Heinz . . . I'd like to speak with him. Yes, I know what he's written about me—I don't hold it against him, Bernd. He's young, he's trying to adjust to a new world. But I'd like to speak to him about Erika. Let me know how I might do that, my friend. When you see him, tell me. And I'll await your report on the Glock situation."

Once Bernd Schmidt was gone, Wolf Koller returned to the chair where he'd been sitting, sat down, and took something from the pocket of his woolen robe. As if it were an unpleasant task, he finally looked away from the window and looked at the object he held in his hand.

It was a postcard.

It was the proof that SPARTAKUS had been leaked.

Burke Delaney drove up the hill and into the vast parking lot. It was raining. Puddles stood in a random pattern, dimpling with the falling rain. The weather wasn't stopping an instructor who was putting a motorcycle rider through a series of maneuvers on a course laid out in the middle of the parking lot. The only other car in the lot was parked way up to the right, as close as you could get to the Olympic Stadium Hitler built for the 1936 games. At this moment it had to be the most deserted spot in Greater Berlin. He drove across the lot and pulled in beside the other car. He got out, walked across to the dimly lit ticket booth. A man peered out from inside.

"How much?"

"One deutschmark."

Delaney paid him and walked on in. You had to have a ticket to take a look at an empty stadium. Germans. He walked on into the stadium portal in front of him and in a moment he saw the green field stretching away below him. Most of the stadium seemed to have been hewn out of the earth below ground level. Maybe it was an illusion. Delaney had never been there before. Eighty thousand empty seats looked like a million. Far around on the right side he saw a man sitting under an umbrella, watching him. He waved and the man waved back. He hadn't seen Bernd Schmidt half a dozen times since the end of the war. About once a decade. Delaney walked beneath the overhang, smoking his pipe upside down, trailing smoke. He was smoking his favorite mixture, the one that stood the test of time. Barking Dog. It was a bitch, he had to have people smuggle it in from the States for him. For a while, he had Cheese sending it over in a diplomatic pouch he picked up every few months in Brussels. The rain was slanting across the field. The lights in the runway were very dim. Great place for a murder. He pulled his cap tighter, pushed the scarf under the Barbour coat closer to his throat, and stepped out into the rain, made his way down to where Bernd Schmidt was sitting. He wiped water off the seat with his gloved hand and sat down.

"This boy of yours," Delaney said.

"Karl-Heinz," Bernd Schmidt said.

"You know what he's been doing lately?"

"More or less."

"You told him to come to me."

"More or less."

"And you put him onto this product. SPARTAKUS."

Schmidt shrugged, smiled wistfully from under the umbrella. "And now I can't seem to find him."

"He hasn't contacted me either. We had a meeting set up. He likes to move around. Learned that from his father, I daresay. This was out at Tegel. I waited at TWA and he never showed up. I figured you might know . . ."

"Who's your master on this one, Burke? Bob Schlatter?"

"Schlatter! Jesus, Bernd, his liver got him two years ago. You're out of date, my friend. Schlatter, he'd been out to pasture for seven years."

"I'm in a different line of work these days."

"I know, I know. I never could figure out why you went to work for Koller. You had such a hard-on about the old judge. Then I thought about it and I had to laugh. You're a good hater, Bernd. I wouldn't be surprised if you've got his weenie in the wringer this time."

"I should probably have killed you years ago."

"Nah. Why? What the hell. It's all just a game anymore, two guys get up in years like us. No point in killing your old friends." He sucked the pipe. "You know, you sit here in this deserted place, more than half a century later, and it's like you can still hear the roar of the crowd, real faint, the place is full of ghosts . . . look down there, it's Jesse Owens . . . look over there, it's the Führer himself, havin' a fit . . . I believe in ghosts, don't you, Bernd?"

"You haven't said who your master is on this one."

"Jeez, I'd feel like a traitor if I told you that."

"It's Cheddar, isn't it?"

"I can't talk about that."

"But it is, isn't it?"

"Well, who else would it be? Now don't keep bugging me about it. You figured it out. I didn't tell you and I don't intend to go on talking about it. Now what do you think about ghosts?"

"Sometimes I feel like one."

"Well, you're not gonna believe this, but I ran into one a few days ago."

"Did he have a name?"

"Damn right. The thing is, he was a ghost all right but I had to kill him just the same."

"Who was it, Burke? Get to it—I've had a long and unpleasant day."

"Kuno Meinhold."

Slowly Bernd Schmidt's gaze moved from the rainswept field until it locked on Delaney's face. "Kuno Meinhold with the scar?"

"How many Kuno Meinholds do you meet in a lifetime? Jeez, of course Kuno Meinhold with the scar. Late of the Rafaela Dorfmann coven."

"Tell me the story, Burke. I'm sure there is a story. You didn't kill him just for practice . . ."

Burke Delaney sat in the rain and told him the story of the assassin in the night. He gave most of the credit to Schuyler, as was only fitting, and said he really regretted having to kill Meinhold. But he'd been left no choice. "Funny thing was, I just assumed he was dead. I'd have bet the farm that he died when Rafaela's bomb factory blew up. Had to be twenty years ago."

"Are you telling me this because you know something else?"

"I'm telling you because we all go back a long way and I thought you might find it interesting."

"Well, I do find it interesting, more interesting than you can imagine." He sighed the sort of sigh that came at the end of a rotten day. "You just said it's all a game, that we're getting on in years, that we're all going to be dead soon enough anyway . . ."

"That's what I said."

"Well, Kuno Meinhold did get blown up with Rafaela. But . . . not really. He had a helluva headache for a while, then we got him in the East, patched him up, put him to work doing jobs for us. One of our destabilizers—"

"Scaring the shit outa people in airports, right? Leaving the occasional old Citroën packed with dynamite and a timer on a street near an embassy . . ."

"Department of Fun and Games we called it."

"So how the hell did he wind up in my kitchen?"

"That's the part that bothers me. Nobody told me about it."

"Bernd, why the hell would anybody tell *you* what an old bastard like Kuno Meinhold was doing?"

"Because I pay his fucking salary, is that a good enough reason for you?"

After a long pause during which Delaney fruitlessly tried to decipher this cryptic piece of information, he stood up. "The shit's getting a little deep for me and I'm wet as old Kuno's remains in my well. Now let's get outa the fuckin' rain, Bernd. Whatever this is, it ain't worth getting terminal pneumonia over." He got up and climbed the cement stairs to the safety of the stadium roof. He shook out his cap, knocked the dottle out of the pipe, repacked it with Barking Dog, and lit it while Schmidt was climbing the stairs behind him and then wrestling his umbrella to a draw. Delaney got the pipe going and leaned against a pillar, watching the struggle with the umbrella. For just a moment there Bernd Schmidt looked like an old man. "So, what's the story? What the hell did the late Kuno Meinhold do for you?"

"He was part of Wolf Koller's private SS, so to speak. The facilitators. And as you know that makes me his boss. It's all under Security."

"So . . ." Puff, puff. "Why did you send him to kill me?"

"Burke, I'd feel a damn sight better if I *had* sent him to kill you. But I didn't. And he had no personal reason to kill you, did he?"

"A long time ago there was a girl—"

"Well, after the bomb went off, one of the things Kuno didn't have to think about much anymore was women. No, I don't think he'd carry a grudge twenty-five years—"

"Bernd, come on."

"Well, you know what's funny? Somebody else was giving Kuno orders. He didn't have enough brain power on his best day to think of something to do on his own. So if he works for me and somebody else is giving him orders—it's a very big worry for me. It means somebody's got access to Koller's SS . . . it would be like having control of a bunch of guided missiles . . . Remember those Japs, the kamikaze pilots? Well, that's what Koller's facilitators are like. They owe everything to this guy. Their very existence. Everything. Personal allegiance."

"Like the old Hitler days."

"Exactly. The possibilities are endless—what if somebody is able to turn them against Koller? Maybe one of his own boys shot him . . ."

"Maybe Koller has taken control into his own hands. Maybe he's going around you."

"But why the hell would Koller want to kill *you*? He has no reason even to know you exist."

"Guy like Koller knows a lot. Maybe he knows about the SPARTAKUS pipeline . . . Maybe he knows I'm the bagman."

"You don't think . . . no, that's impossible. Let's get out of here. It's getting dark and I'm scared of the dark." They walked back around to the portal where Delaney had entered. Their footsteps echoed on the wet concrete.

They went out through the portal and began walking toward their cars. Delaney said: "What don't I think? What's impossible?"

"Just a crazy thought . . . what if *your* people got access to Koller's SS?"

"Listen, the last thing they'd do is send Kuno to kill me. I'm the source of SPARTAKUS."

"No, Karl-Heinz is the source of SPARTAKUS. And he's among the missing. I don't like to make you worry, Burke, but what if your Mr. Cheddar already has all he needs of SPARTAKUS? Then he wouldn't need any of you, would he?"

"No, he wouldn't. But how would he get control of Koller's SS? I don't think so, Bernd. I told him about the attack and I've never heard him so quiet and confused. He's not that good an actor. I've known him too long."

"That may be the problem, Burke. You may have known him too long."

The rain was rattling in the trees and on the piles of leaves along the street and behind the gates of the Wannsee Conference House where Eichmann and Heydrich and Erhard Koller and the rest of them had reached the final solution to the Jewish problem. The gatehouse was dark but the long driveway was dimly lit by the lamps on the front of the building. It was a handsome old place, never intended for the spot in history it occupied. The Professor watched it as he slowly drove past and kept to the right where the road angled toward the lake. Up ahead the gray Mercedes was moving slowly on the wet road, which was doubly slick with leaf cover.

As he drew closer the Professor switched the lights off and barely crawled through the darkness. They were close by the lake now and he knew it in his mind's eye, the way it would be punctuated with countless white sails in the summer and people out on the pretty little island with its magic castle and children laughing. He'd never been here in winter before. He remembered that there was a good-sized hospital nearby, across from the Wannsee Conference House. The homes were all substantial, imposing. Some of them were summer places, down by the water, others were year-round places. The Mercedes up ahead was turning slowly into a driveway that nosed farther down toward the water, heading for a huge, low white house that had Frank Lloyd Wright lines and probably dated from the twenties. The Professor didn't know much about architecture. It looked like Wright. Maybe it was some German. Bauhaus or some damn thing, it wasn't his field. Anyway, it was a fancy house, an idiot could tell that. It belonged to Wolf Koller.

He rolled the VW to a stop in the shadows of a tall wall of shrubbery. He could see, down to his right, the Mercedes's lights going off, Orlovski and Sebastien getting out. A light went on over a side doorway behind a bank of evergreens, and he saw them for a moment. The door swung open and they went inside.

There was something parked in the shadows with the Mercedes, a panel truck maybe. A funny shape. An old-fashioned kind of shape, like a station wagon. What the hell was it? He got out of the VW and went swiftly across the road and crouched alongside a tree line. It was dark, nobody was going to see him and he wanted to know what the hell that shape was. He drew even with it, about thirty feet away, and shook his head. Of course, it was an ambulance. From a private firm. Echardt's Ambulance.

So, Wolf Koller was out of the hospital already and had gone to Wannsee rather than the Grunewald house. Why?

And Konstantin Orlovski was visiting him and had brought along Sebastien the Red.

Rain was running down inside his collar and he was cold and had to piss. He went deeper into the shadows and relieved himself on the side of Wolf Koller's four-car garage. It didn't set off any alarms. Then he went back to his car, got in, and tried not to think about the cold. In a little while somebody came out, two guys in white uniforms, and got into the ambulance. They backed around and came up out of the driveway head first. When they turned onto the road the headlights blinded the Professor momentarily and then they pulled past him and were gone, taillights flickering among the trees and then darkness. He was going to wait awhile and see what happened. The rain was drumming on the metal roof and the sound was rather comforting.

Werner Paulus was playing chess with himself in the parlor of his apartment, which had become his study, gradually and over a period of years. A Berlin Philharmonic performance was on the television, Solti was conducting. It had been taped a year or two before but it was good and who cared how old the tape was? He had been replaying a couple of Bobby Fischer's games from years before, trying to get inside his head and failing. Fischer seemed to operate in another zone altogether. It was a little like listening to Glenn Gould play Bach. You couldn't quite figure out what was in his mind but it didn't matter in the end. It was all being done on an entirely different level. It made him think of Stan Kenton, the American bandleader from California.

He knew a great deal about Stan Kenton. When he first heard him he knew he'd never heard anything like it before because there had never been anything quite like Stan Kenton before. Now he was thinking about Stan Kenton. He got up and turned the television off. He left the computerized chess set on because he was coming back. But first he had to find his Stan Kenton collection. They'd reissued a lot of the stuff on CDs now and he believed in keeping up with technology. He found a Capitol CD, *Kenton in Hi-Fi,* which had about twice as much music on it as his old LP with the same name. He inserted it in the CD player and stood at the window looking down into the street. The rain reflected in the pools of light. The rain had washed away all the snow but as the music started, it wasn't winter anymore, it was hot and there was an oscillating fan in the corner of his mind and he was back in California. Stockton, California.

He'd been shipped all the way from North Africa to Virginia to St. Louis to Stockton, California, where he'd come to rest. The luckiest German of the war in his own mind. He didn't know about what was going on in Germany, what was happening to his wife, but then a POW had to be glad to be alive. And in California. In the sunshine and working out in the fields picking fruit and living in the barracks and knowing that the war was over and the Americans were a decent bunch. They treated you like a man. They didn't seem to hate you for being a German, for having fought against their sons and brothers and fathers. They were, somehow, a forgiving people. And their kindness to him during his years as a prisoner was as important as any other experience of his life. At night in the barracks, after dinner, he would listen to the radio and work on his English and one of his favorite shows was Bob Hope. Something about the way he talked . . . And he saw pictures of him, that wonderful nose, and Bing Crosby the singer, of course. A man named Skinnay Ennis had been Bob Hope's radio bandleader but then he'd left and this man Stan Kenton had replaced him and then somebody, one of the young officers at the camp, had brought in a Capitol recording, a big 78, and played it on a portable, leatherette-covered Victrola, it was 1944, and the recording was from another world, *Artistry in Rhythm,* and nothing meant California more clearly to Werner Paulus that cold and rainy night in November of 1992 than Stan Kenton, dead now, born in 1911, but young then, in the first burnished glow of his greatness, broadcasting from the Rendezvous in Balboa, California . . . What he'd give to have it all back again, to be young and full of hope even after the war. He knew now what he'd have done, he'd have gone back to America and made his life there in California, he'd have met another woman on some beach and he'd have lived in California, happily ever after in the sunshine.

He was listening to the CD, which had been recorded in the fifties in hi-fi, new recordings of the old masterpieces from the Balboa days and beyond in the forties, with Maynard Ferguson and Pete Candoli and Mel Lewis and Laurindo Almeida and Bud Shank and always Kenton on the piano, he was back in Stockton, California, when the telephone rang and someone told him that if he wanted to see Karl-Heinz Schmidt he'd find him at the Loretta beer garden in Lietzenburgerstrasse.

The voice jolted him back to the present but the music was still going on. "Peanut Vendor." "Eager Beaver." "Minor Riff." He knew every note and here was this voice dragging him back to Berlin, and he didn't want to come.

"In the rain?" he asked.

"He'll wait for you."

The line went dead. He listened all the way through the seven minutes and one second of "The Concerto to End All Concertos" and switched off the chess computer and stopped the music.

The endgame was coming up. He wished he knew what game they were playing, though. But John Cooper was at the center of it because he wasn't going to give up and go home; he was going to blunder around and upset applecarts and scare people into doing stupid things. He was going to poke around until he found things out and he was going to confront people and it was going to get way out of hand and now it was much worse because Kilroy was in town. *Kilroy was here.*

It was time to give Cooper a scare.

Werner Paulus was all the way back from Sunny Cal, as they used to say.

Wolf Koller sat staring out at the blackness of Lake Wannsee, listening to the soft hum of conversation in the room behind him. He'd bullied his doctors into letting him go home. He was in a good deal of pain but they'd given him medication to take whenever he felt like it and a nurse was perpetually on call. He didn't give a damn about the pain. You get shot, you expect it to hurt. Now he sat by the wall of glass, staring into the night.

Several of his associates were gathered in the large room. Orlovski had come all the way from Moscow as a representative of the Russian end of the deal. Gisevius, who had whispered to him that there had been a break-in at his home the night he got back from Moscow. Sebastien.

The men gathered in the other room were expecting him to go over the timetable with them and there he sat, staring into space, seeing through the lies and the plots against him, then switching his attention to the postcard in his hand, half blinded with rage and fear . . . How could it all have come to this? His arm was on fire. His daughter was missing. His wife was going to die soon. A sniper had just tried to kill him. The word on SPARTAKUS had leaked . . .

The postcard in his hand was a photograph from a movie, the kind of thing you could pick up anywhere. It showed Kirk Douglas in a kind of loincloth with a net and a trident, standing his ground in the Roman sunshine, ready to do battle to the death. The film was *Spartacus*. In German there was a "k" rather than a "c." The picture alone had made his blood run cold.

The message was printed anonymously on the back of the card.

I KNOW WHAT YOU ARE DOING. AND I WILL STOP YOU.

BELIEVE ME.

It had been postmarked in Bayreuth.

Slowly he pushed it into the pocket of his robe and crossed the room to face his fellow plotters. He smiled. Someone was fucking with Wolf Koller and like all the others before them, they would live just long enough to regret it with all their hearts.

28

REALITY CHECK

Cooper lay awake in the predawn hours, unable to get the sight of Lee on the bed out of his head, looking so old and so sick, so helpless. The woman on the bed bore so little resemblance to the woman he'd seen twice before in Berlin that he wondered, how could it be? The woman on the bed had no future. She seemed to be near death, papery and dry and brittle with labored breathing, as if she were in a coma. What could he do? Did help lie in Bayreuth? Was there a magical secret there?

But that was just the start of it. He kept hearing the tag end of the phone call Beate had made while he was asleep, the call she said had never occurred. But he'd heard it. She was lying to him . . .

. . . *No, I don't think he's going to die . . . No, I understand that, but after all he is— . . . I'll call you when I can . . . Are you all right up there? Plenty to eat? . . .*

And Kilroy was here. Clint Kilroy had become a part of Cooper's life, had simply inserted himself. What was he up to? What did he do for Wolf Koller? Why had he shown up the night Koller got shot?

What about Karl-Heinz, who had talked to Erika about something called SPARTAKUS . . . He'd told Cooper the CIA wanted "the SPARTAKUS man" and the SPARTAKUS man was Karl-Heinz . . . *But what was SPARTAKUS?* Karl-Heinz seemed to think that maybe Cooper was sent to kill this Delaney . . . but who was Delaney? And why would the CIA want to kill Karl-Heinz? *There must be a leak somewhere. They know my source . . . so who needs me?* Cooper was shuffling through these concerns, trying to fit them together into some sort of identifiable pattern, but it was slow going.

And then the phone began ringing, the insistent little European sound like a gnat in your ear, and he heard Beate fumbling around, sleepily answering it, listening while the caller spoke; then she muttered something else and he felt her hand on his shoulder. She was yawning. "It's for you," she said.

"Who would be calling me? I don't know anybody—"

"Well, it's for you. A German."

"You listen on the earpiece."

She picked up the attachment and he sat down by the window, felt the damp breeze. "Yes, this is John Cooper."

"I apologize for the hour, Mr. Cooper, but this won't wait, I'm afraid. You don't know me but I know you by reputation. My name is Werner Paulus. Please believe me when I say you have nothing to fear from me." He paused and Cooper looked at Beate.

"Go ahead," she whispered. "It's all right."

"What's your business with me, Mr. Paulus?" The streetlamps were on outside. The windows were nearly all darkened in the building across the street. It was four o'clock in the morning.

"Your friend Miss Hubermann will know my name. I'm sure she will give me a good reference." Cooper glanced at Beate and she nodded, made a thumbs-up gesture. "I need to see you. There's something I have to show you . . . I would prefer that you come alone. I'm aware of the hour but this won't keep, I'm afraid. Will you indulge me?"

"All right, if it's so important."

"Good. Come to the Loretta beer garden in Lietzenburgerstrasse. Miss Hubermann will direct you. It is not difficult to find. And, Mr. Cooper, one word . . . be very careful. Do you understand? You are in a great deal of danger . . . I'll be waiting for you."

When Cooper hung up the phone he looked at Beate, who was running her long fingers through her hair, sweeping it away from her face. She looked very pale in the middle of the night. She stood up. She was wearing a long T-shirt with the head of a wolf staring out from her chest. It was from some environmental group. She shivered with cold, went away, and came back with a blue terrycloth robe. "Coffee," she announced and poured beans and ran the grinder, fiddled with the filter and the water. When she'd pushed the button she came back, yawning, said: "I'll never get back to sleep."

"So give me this guy's references," Cooper said.

"Well, they're pretty good. He's the great legendary 'Chief' of Berlin Central detectives. Retired a few years ago but he was the man, no doubt of that. He always tried to stay out of the news but sometimes it just wasn't possible. People were always trying to get him to leave the police and run for public office—for mayor, for Parliament, there were even people who would have been happy to see him become Chancellor. But he was too smart, he knew that once he went for the bait he'd lose the thing he valued most, his integrity. As chief he had to be politically aware, but he was more his own man. So he never fell for the flattery."

"So how does such a man know I exist? And then he tells me I'm in great danger—frankly, if he's so important, that scares hell out of me—"

"Maybe he just wanted to get your attention. We can hope so." She was taking coffee cups down from the cupboard, spoons, sugar, milk. "As for how he knows about you, well, he knows all sorts of things. He is said to have the most enormous network of informers . . . he has the knack of making people like him, making them want to help him. I interviewed him a few times. He told me the secret of being a great detective. He said the best way to close cases was just to have people call you on the phone or meet you for coffee somewhere and tell you who did it! He said there's almost always somebody who'll just tell you what you need to know, if you just find them and ask them. He said that was the secret. So he made sure he knew so many people that some of them were always going to be telling him the answers to the big questions." She was pouring the first of the hot coffee. The aroma filled the kitchen. "I liked him. And people used to say he was never wrong."

"Great," Cooper said, scalding his mouth. "That means I really am in great danger."

She was headed for the shower when he closed the door behind him.

He stood on the wet sidewalk, looking up at the swinging chairs at the top of the Ferris wheel. It was a dark gray, watery morning with the rain slowly turning into a spitting mist. The wind scurried in the street and shoved the Ferris wheel's cars, just enough to make them squeak on their axles. The sign stuck in the middle of the wheel said *Loretta,* painted in dark blue, flanked on either side by a gold star and on the left by a cartoon of a green parrot with an orange bill. He seemed to be smiling. The entire structure was outlined with light bulbs but they weren't lit. The place looked closed and deserted if not quite derelict. A few cars, headlights glowing, swished by on Lietzenburgerstrasse, the early shift coming on or the late shift calling it a night.

There was no one waiting for him. The box office was closed. It was a warm-weather place. He could imagine what it must be like on a hot summer night. A madhouse.

He walked around the Ferris wheel, which was up against the sidewalk, outside the main area of the beer garden, and found a wooden gate. He pushed it and it swung open. If you'd left such a site open through the night in Boston it would have been an empty lot by morning. He took a last look at the headlights going by, reflecting in the wet street, and went inside. The cold seemed to increase once the gate swung shut behind him.

There were trees everywhere, naked and wet now, but in the summer they'd have provided a natural canopy. Huge piles of wet leaves and still more to rake, a carpet of wet leaves in auburn and red and gold. It was a huge space, on two or three levels, seating at white tables for a hell of a lot of people. He saw several counters for buying beer; the taps were in place behind the counters. The tables stretched off into the dark mist at the far end of the space, a couple of hundred yards away—a sea of tables and an ocean of molded white plastic chairs, as if the crowd had just pushed them back five minutes ago and gone home. The big beer steins on the tables increased the feeling of a recent mass departure. But the steins were full of rainwater, and leaves floated with the cigarette butts.

The tall white statues placed randomly among the tables gave a peculiarly eerie feel to the deserted space. They were very kitsch, very erotic in a simpleminded nudge-and-wink manner. The god Pan with his head thrown back played on his pipe. A huge erection curved up across his belly. Naked odalisques posed, more painted images of the laughing parrot dotted the landscape. It was a childish, obvious idea of suggestive naughtiness but when the band was playing in the summer and the beer was going down and the nights were hot the images might have had a powerful effect. Now they just looked cold.

In the center of the garden was a large, round, covered food and drink center, more empty steins, hanging plants, ferns, dead or dying. It was utterly silent but for the wind moving the hanging plants and the distant creak of the Ferris wheel chairs tilting back and forth. Cooper felt as he had used to feel in the Harvard Yard, as if some magical force kept the sound and cacophony of the outside world from penetrating the cloister. Rain dripped from the roof over the center concession stand. Pan twisted and played his pipe, the naked women offered themselves with outthrust breasts and buttocks . . .

What the hell was he doing here?

He scanned the empty tables as if parting curtains of mist. The gray light of dawn was having a tough time getting into the Loretta beer garden. Shadows swallowed its edges. The buildings surrounding the garden seemed to be rumors of another world beyond the fences.

Cooper couldn't quite bring himself to call out in the eerie silence.

He walked deeper into the grip of the place, peering from table to table, searching for Paulus in the sea of chairs.

Finally he saw a man sitting at the far end, a shape in a dark blue raincoat, calmly waiting, wearing a dark gray fedora. Cooper stood watching him.

He felt at that instant like a man in a Hitchcock picture, facing the job of walking across the tableau of tables, an unknown landscape full of fear, a maze of white chairs and tables, the reverse of the black umbrellas giving cover to a murderer in *Foreign Correspondent,* a danger zone between him and the man in the raincoat who sat so stolidly, in such quiet . . .

The walk took forever but in the end the man slowly stood up. No shots rang out. Cooper was still alive. It wasn't a movie.

"Mr. Cooper, I'm Werner Paulus." He looked out from behind steel-rimmed glasses. He tipped his hat, old-fashioned, courtly. Cooper saw silver hair, a long nose, a long sloping forehead. He stood ramrod straight.

"Well, the man who disappeared," Cooper said. Potsdamer Platz, the meeting with Karl-Heinz Schmidt.

"Quite right. You followed me past the old church, the Marienkirche, St. Mary's. Have you read about that church? Mentioned in documents as far back as 1290 . . . the second oldest church in Berlin . . . well, I mustn't bore you with pedantry—in any case, you followed me . . ." He smiled in a kindly way, like the doctor Cooper and his brother, Cyril, had had when they were children, back in Cooper's Falls.

"You were following Karl-Heinz—"

"No, actually, I wasn't. I was following you."

"Me? Why follow me?"

"Because some of us are very interested in you, Mr. Cooper. In my kind of work I could hardly fail to learn about what you and Mr. Olaf Peterson did to the Nazi movement centered in Munich some years ago. Now you are back, your sister is married to Wolf Koller—and Wolf Koller, shall we say, *interests* us—their daughter has disappeared, you are the guest of Miss Hubermann, who is a friend of the missing Erika Koller as well as the daughter's boyfriend, our young friend Karl-Heinz Schmidt . . . and the boyfriend is moving stolen information about Wolf Koller to agents of a foreign power, namely the United States of America . . . and Karl-Heinz's father is head of security for Wolf Koller's various companies—you see, it's rather a tangled web, is it not? We would be remiss if we were not more than a little concerned with your arrival on German soil, wouldn't we?"

Cooper stared at him. "Wait. I don't know what you're talking about. I mean, I do to some extent, but I came here simply to help my sister find her daughter—"

"But you're not making much headway, are you? I wonder, how did you think you might help?" He spoke softly, without an edge. Soothing.

"I didn't think that far ahead. I came because my sister asked me to."

"And who can blame you, coming to your sister's aid? Naturally you came. After all, twenty years is twenty years. Except maybe in Germany, eh? Yesterday is very near, always, maybe Siegfried will wake from his slumbers today and a new world will dawn." He sighed at the mysticism of his countrymen. "But your sister has led you into the heart of darkness once again. It seems to be her nature, her destiny—"

"Well, I want to lead her out of it. That's why I came."

"I wish you success but I doubt if you have any idea just how dark it is. Come. Let me show you something . . ."

The body lay behind and partially covered by a pile of rain-soaked leaves at the farthest, murkiest corner of the beer garden. Paulus pointed with the ferrule of his neatly rolled umbrella. "You see, there is very real danger here, Mr. Cooper."

Karl-Heinz was lying on his back. His head had been nearly severed, a deep ragged cut across his throat as if it had been chewed rather than sliced. The cut went all the way through to the spinal column. His head lolled backward. He seemed to have two mouths. One huge and raw and gaping.

Cooper couldn't look away.

Paulus said: "I received an anonymous call not long after midnight. The man told me to come here if I wanted to see Karl-Heinz Schmidt. I was concerned about the young man. I got here not long after one o'clock. I found him as you see him. Then I walked up Uhlandstrasse over to the Ku'damm to the Hotel Kempinski, where I happen to have a few friends. I went to the kitchen. I drank some coffee and had some dark bread and jam and sausage and I wondered what to do . . . and I thought it was about time to have a chat with you. It was time you found out just what you'd put your foot into, particularly in light of your own history in Germany. What do you Americans call it? The perfect expression . . . ah, I remember. I thought it was time you underwent a reality check, Mr. Cooper."

29

EMPIRE

John Cooper hadn't seen anything like the body of Karl-Heinz since he'd last been in Germany. Time hadn't made such a sight any easier to take. His legs were a little rubbery and there was none of the adrenaline rush he'd felt during the fight after the Nazi concert. This was altogether pathetic, tragic even: Karl-Heinz had been both brave and afraid and Cooper had rather taken a liking to him. He had been doing what he thought was right and now somebody had very nearly cut his head off and dumped his body like a sack of trash. He was just a bag of bones with blood running out.

Maybe Cooper was in shock. Maybe he was just sad. But whatever it was it began to fade as he and Werner Paulus left the Loretta and walked toward the Ku'damm only a few minutes away. He felt the fire in his belly again, the sense of outrage that such deadly arrogance existed . . . He felt as if he were coming fully alive once more.

They walked over to the Hotel Bristol Kempinski, which should have been one of the glories of Berlin, old and full of history, but wasn't. It wore a somewhat nondescript, altogether modern, vaguely slapdash expression that didn't seem to merit the catastrophic prices. The name was there but that was all. Otherwise, a very fancy Marriott.

The restaurant was deserted but ready for the first customers of the day, those with insomnia or early planes to catch. They were shown to a perfect table up against the glass, looking out at the Ku'damm. A pot of coffee was forthcoming and before Cooper could start with the questions Paulus suggested he call Beate. "She's going to be very interested in all this, Mr. Cooper," he said quietly. "It might be simpler to invite her to join us. I wanted to speak to you privately and I wanted to spare her the first sight of her young friend's body. But she is in danger, just as you are. She needs to be warned. Go, call her from the lobby." His eyes were so calm, so intelligent: he was the perfect internist. His perfectly starched white shirt, the carefully correct blue silk tie, the gray suit and vest with a blue and red plaid so subtle it might as well have been in somebody else's suit. He wore a silver wedding band. It was embedded in the flesh. It had been there a long time.

Cooper made the call and Beate was breathless. "I've been waiting! So what's happening? What did he want? Where are you? Tell, tell, tell!"

"Look, I've got some bad news. Karl-Heinz is dead. He showed me the body."

"Damn! I knew it! I knew they'd get him sooner or later—he was such a fool! Wolf Koller found him and wanted to know where Erika is . . . no, I'm not going to cry, I'm not the type. But what did Loretta have to do with it?"

"Somebody called your friend Paulus and told him Karl-Heinz would be waiting for him at Loretta and he had to come right away. He was dumped on a pile of leaves with his throat cut. It wasn't pretty."

"I think they took him during that mess after the concert. They tortured him, Cooper. I'm sure they did. He knew something or they thought he did . . . Bastards!"

"Paulus and I are having coffee at the Kempinski. He wants you to get over here. He says we're both in danger. He says we were the last ones with Karl-Heinz and they're going to wonder if he told us everything he'd collected on Wolf Koller . . . or where Erika is. Paulus says they're not going to want to run the risk that he told us anything damaging about Koller. So, he wants you here."

"I'm on my way. I'll take the car."

By the time she arrived they were on their second pot of coffee and some bread and croissants were on the table. Several of the tables had filled. She slipped out of her red plaid jacket and dropped it over the back of the chair. Paulus stood to welcome her. "I'm so sorry we meet again under such unhappy circumstances, Miss Hubermann."

"I'm glad you remember me, Chief Paulus, under any circumstances at all." She brushed the straight blond hair back from her face, tucked it behind an ear. "This is terrible about Karl-Heinz. Did you know him?"

"Let's say I knew of him. I'd heard a great deal about him from a dear old friend of mine. A man named Burke Delaney. Did he ever mention Delaney to you?"

"No"—she looked at Cooper—"but he mentioned him to you, didn't he? He thought you were working with Delaney, or against him or . . . something."

Cooper said he'd told Paulus about that, added: "What I want to know is what the hell Karl-Heinz had found out and was giving to this Delaney . . . and why it got him killed. If that was the reason for killing him."

Paulus ordered tea for Beate and leaned back in his chair, legs crossed, calm and reassuring, as if the X-rays had come back and maybe there was some hope after all.

"All right," he said, "let us begin. Young Karl-Heinz discovered a great many things in his investigation of Wolf Koller. It wasn't just an attempt to impress Erika Koller, either. It had begun before he ever met Erika. And I doubt very much that Koller would have gone to the extreme of killing Karl-Heinz if Erika's whereabouts were the only issue. It was Karl-Heinz's investigation into his activities—it just took him a while to find the boy."

"Tell me, Chief," Beate said, "how do you know all this?"

Paulus smiled in a kindly way. "I have so many friends who tell me things. This came from a very good friend. Karl-Heinz and Erika were brought together by the fact that they were both students in a class given by a friend of mine, a new university program in the East, politics and history and whatnot. Extraordinarily bright man. They met at one of his classes, then they met again at one of the coffeehouses. After that they saw each other regularly at the lectures and the coffeehouse, which was near the basement where he put together that newspaper of his. And so" —he spread his hands, looking at Cooper—"it began. And now, you find yourself involved with all sorts of peculiar people—from the lovely Miss Hubermann, who obviously isn't peculiar at all, to the very strange Mr. Kilroy . . ."

"So you also know Kilroy," Cooper said.

"Oh, I've known Mr. Kilroy for a long, long time. How did you come across him, if I may ask?"

"Before Beate and I met in Boston, this Kilroy appeared out of the blue, a Texas millionaire who wanted to buy my property in Boston—a theater and a bookstore. He said he'd done some research on me, he knew my whole life story. It was irritating—"

"And then," Beate said, "we saw him on television—I had come to Boston to cover a development in Boston being financed by German interests, mainly by Wolf Koller, and we saw the local piece on the news that night. And there in the background was Clint Kilroy! It didn't take a doctorate in intrigue to make some connections—Kilroy comes to see John, I come to see John about his sister, who is married to Wolf Koller, and Kilroy is at the press conference about Koller's investment in Boston—"

"But that's not the end of Kilroy," Cooper said. "I went out to Koller's house in Grunewald that night after he was shot . . . and I spotted Kilroy there, looking right at home. He was there again the next day. He acted as if we were great chums and he seemed to know Dr. Gisevius pretty well." Cooper finished his coffee and poured more from a recently delivered pot. "So," he said into the silence, "what does it all mean?"

"It means that Kilroy is a very dangerous man," Paulus said. "But then I already knew that."

"I don't understand." Cooper was watching Paulus's face, trying to divine if he was the real thing, or only another actor in this saga of duplicity.

"Clint Kilroy," Paulus said, choosing his words carefully, "is a professional killer. An assassin. He works for the Americans, probably because they've got something on him. He has to work for them."

"When you say the Americans," Beate asked, "what do you really mean?"

"The CIA and any of their other covert operations run out of God knows where. Occasionally, I've heard, he carries out a private contract. But the government is his main employer." Paulus leaned forward, his sharply tailored elbows on the tabletop. "Now we must factor him into the present equation."

Cooper said: "If he works for the Americans, what was he doing at Koller's house? I mean, he acted like he owned the place."

Paulus smiled, as if congratulating a good student. "Either he is working for the Americans and betraying Koller . . . or the Americans are working with Koller. We will need to learn the truth about this, you see. If the Americans are working with Koller, then what part do they play in this plan Koller has . . . this SPARTAKUS that keeps cropping up? We have much to discover, that's what we know for sure."

Cooper was suddenly desperately hungry. He ordered eggs and sausage. It was fully light outside and traffic was heating up and the restaurant was just about full. Berlin had come to life. Cooper wondered when someone would find the corpse in the Loretta beer garden. Had the boy been tortured? He couldn't think about it.

While they ate Werner Paulus returned to the subject of Karl-Heinz's investigations into the career of Wolf Koller, the making of an empire.

"It all began with the great jurist Erhard Koller, perhaps the pre-eminent judge in the nation. He became a Nazi in the mid-thirties for the same reason that lots of people became Nazis then. To gain an advantage, to have his books published more profitably, to get the most prestigious lectureships, to make money from inside information, to make money from his own judicial rulings that various Jewish property was to be confiscated—all the things that were part of Hitler's coming to power. A man could be a cultivated art lover, a patron of the opera and the symphony and the art museums and the theater, he could be internationally regarded as a leader in Germany's justice system, he could lecture at Harvard and Oxford—and he could be a Nazi. To be important, to be rich, and to be treated with the ultimate respect, it was best that you were a Nazi. In other words, it was a matter of simple greed and the requirements of ego.

"Within a few years Hitler began rewarding Dr. Erhard Koller with what such pirates can only call 'booty.' Plunder. Treasure. He rewarded him with parcels of land and real estate taken from Jewish owners —including even real estate that Koller himself had ruled on. There was a warehouse here, an office block there, a hotel somewhere else, a block of apartments, individual homes in places like Grunewald. And so Erhard Koller became one of Berlin's biggest landowners . . . but was he a war criminal? Certainly he was part of the Wannsee Conference . . . he cooperated.

"Well, he survived the war. Did the Allies try him and hang him? No. Instead he was made the most prominent German member of a committee charged with rebuilding the German legal system. He wasn't hanged. He was honored by the victors. Because the Allies needed him. He was one of those Nazis whose crimes were conveniently forgotten, intentionally overlooked . . . In fact, they went out of their way to *honor him.*" The more forceful his point, the quieter his voice became, as he tapped a forefinger on the tablecloth. "No one moved against his vast holdings. I don't know if the Americans ever realized just how enormous they were, during his lifetime. That was all left up to the Germans. And he was one of the men deciding what was to be done. Say half the buildings in Berlin were destroyed or damaged in the bombing and the fighting—then half of them were not. He surely held both kinds of buildings, agreed? Of course. He set up a variety of corporations which owned the real estate, the office buildings, the warehouses and the apartment blocks—it was the basis of what we now know as Koller Industries International. When he died it was all left to his only son, Wolf . . . and it became Wolf Koller's empire. Based on the stolen properties of Jews his father helped to send to their deaths in the camps and the ovens." He smiled bleakly at the irony of it. "We must give Wolf Koller credit. He has made the most of his opportunities. He has expanded into a variety of other areas, into steel and electronics and chemicals and paper products and leasing warehouses and a vast transportation network. But he still owns fifty-nine residential buildings in what was West Berlin alone. Where do you think Erika Kohler lives?"

"Oh, no." Beate shuddered.

"In one of those buildings stolen from the Jews who were murdered. I suspect Karl-Heinz told her all about that . . . I can only guess what that did to her."

They finished up breakfast. It was nine o'clock by the time they left the hotel. On the sidewalk outside Paulus said: "Come, I want to show you something. There's a woman we might run into . . . Do you have time, Miss Hubermann? You'll find it quite interesting."

"Yes, of course. Let's go." Beate was looking at her watch. She glanced at Cooper. Bayreuth awaited, but they couldn't resist the spell Werner Paulus had cast.

30

THE HOUSE ON BLEIBTREUSTRASSE

The house on Bleibtreustrasse was in a state of immaculate restoration. The high carved wooden door with the heavy iron knocker, the new white plasterwork outside, the smell of varnish and fresh paint. There were no windows on the front, giving it the air of a church or a library. Large potted firs flanked the wide double door.

Paulus surveyed it. "Impressive, isn't it? It's being restored for the first time since the bombing of forty-four. It only suffered a little damage so they left it. The restoration, the woodcarving particularly, has taken two years so far and they're not done yet." He took off his hat as a woman's voice answered the call box and then buzzed them in. Inside, the open foyer was two stories high, dark above them with more carving on the wooden panels leading up the walls beside the staircase and on the facing of the balcony railing. There was a small, cage-type elevator tucked away under the stairs.

They climbed the stairs so Paulus could show them the quality of the fresh carving. "Not many craftsmen left who can do this sort of thing," he remarked. "Progress. Ha."

When they reached the balcony a door swung open and a woman in her mid-thirties came out to meet them. She wore a print housedress and her hair was tied back with a ribbon made of the same material. Behind her a small boy wearing jeans with turned-up plaid cuffs sat on the floor maneuvering a plastic airplane. She wore slippers with rabbit faces on them. Her son wore what appeared to be pint-sized Reeboks. "Oh, Chief Paulus," she exclaimed, "is there anything I can do for you today? It's so good to see you. Is everything—you know, upstairs"—she gestured with her shoulders—"all right?"

"Yes, yes, I'm sure it is. Helga, these are my friends, Beate Hubermann and Mr. John Cooper from Boston."

The woman nodded to Beate. "I see you on TV." She shook hands forthrightly with Cooper. "Welcome to Berlin, Mr. Cooper." She turned back to Paulus. "Are you going up there?" She gestured again with her shoulders, a kind of stage gesture, as if it were a secret. She had the broad quality of someone onstage. Every word, every gesture was larger than life.

"Yes. My friends are interested in your landlord, Helga. So . . . not a word to anyone."

"Silent as the grave, Chief. So, you're interested in Wolf Koller . . ." She cast a quick glance over her shoulder to make sure her son hadn't divebombed some native villagers. She had been speaking in a mixture of English and German with Cooper fitting it all together as best he could. Now she was working up a head of steam and switching all the way into English for Cooper's benefit. "Wolf Koller," she repeated the name, like an incantation. "Well, I know a thing or two about Wolf Koller, I've made it my business to know—let me tell you a thing or two about Wolf Koller. This building is in his wife's name, but it's all the same, no difference at all. No matter which one of them owns it, this building is soaked in blood. Jewish blood and, frankly, I'm not a Jew, I've only met one Jew in my life that I know of—I mean, Germans my age don't know many Jews, you understand what I mean? But I know what we did to Jews in this country, what everyone did or went along with, don't you believe they didn't know about the pogroms—who cares if they knew about the death camps? The rest of it was bad enough! What kind of people were these, who stood by and let the persecutions take place? Was it only the death camps that were bad? And everything else was okay? Such hypocrisy! Marching them around and taking their property away and chasing them through the streets, *that* was okay, it was only bad when Hitler started pushing them into ovens? German logic baffles me, Mr. Cooper. But I know what went on in this country . . . and I ask you now, how can anyone, anyone at all, live on the money they make from property stolen from Jews who were murdered by the state? What kind of people do such a thing? I have a friend, she lives in a building owned by a woman of fifty or so who owns thirty-seven buildings she got exactly the same way Wolf Koller got this building—from a Nazi family who left them to her . . . It sickens me, it disgusts me, it disgusts any decent German, it disgusts Fräulein Hubermann here, you can see it in her face . . . And you Americans are as much to blame as we Germans, your hands are just as bloody. Who won the war? Who let the Nazis go free and who paid them to set up the new state? And who made money from rebuilding Germany? Who got rich? Americans, that's who got rich! And after you got rich, then we got rich, too . . . but who among us got the richest? The old Nazis!"

She stopped talking abruptly and blushed bright red. "He does this to me, gets me started," nodding toward Paulus. "Can't keep my big mouth shut." Her son was yelling about something in the background. "I'm too opinionated—my mother says it's my father's fault. He is an American, he was serving here during the Occupation and they fell in love and they stayed here. In Germany, I mean. She says I take after him. Maybe I do. Don't hold it against me, please. Could you join me for coffee or—"

"Now, Helga," Paulus said, "you have a full day ahead of you. We're just going to take a look around upstairs." He put his forefinger to his lips and she nodded, made the gesture back at him.

She went back inside and they got into the elevator cage. While they were slowly ratcheting upward Paulus said: "I've known Helga since she was a child and I had just become chief. She's a wonderful girl. She looks upon me as a kind of great-uncle. I know a lot of people in this city. I have spent a lifetime taking an interest in them. You'd be surprised how many times this habit has helped in my police work. It's my belief that people want to be good, they want to help, they are essentially decent if we tempt them to be good rather than tempt them to be bad. It goes back to the fairy stories—somebody, a witch or a troll, is always tempting a child to be bad, and the child is always then subjected to something very unpleasant. We must be tempted by the good, we must allow ourselves to be good. It's simple. Isn't that so, Miss Hubermann?"

At the apartment door Paulus produced a key, opened the door, and led them inside.

The aroma of new plaster hadn't quite faded from the room. It was bare—no carpet, no furniture, a couple of boxes left by workmen, some nails and caulking guns on the floor. Paint smell. Stuffy with the windows closed. It was the top floor of a five-story building and the windows gave onto a courtyard with some wrought-iron furniture far below.

Paulus let them have a look, get a first impression, and then directed their attention to various points on each wall of the two-room apartment.

Cooper stared. He could see nothing where Paulus had pointed. "So?"

Paulus smiled. "Microphones. The newest, the best, the smallest. Implanted in the walls. This is the source room for SPARTAKUS. This is where all the trouble really started—"

"What is it, this room?" Beate was tapping the wall to no avail.

"This is the room where Wolf Koller conducts his most secret meetings. His inner sanctum. His security people have given it their most thorough attention. Wolf Koller and his friends are safe here. . . friends like Dr. Fritz Gisevius, several politicians he owns, a man who may be the closest advisor to the Chancellor, some important newspaper owners and industrialists . . . yes, some lawyers and professors as well . . . Wolf Koller's *Kabinet,* you might say. Why, Joachim Stiffel has even come to this room to visit with Koller . . . all because"—tapping the walls himself—"Koller knows he is safe here." He swept his hands wide, taking in the entire flat. "No nooks, no crannies, no hiding places for bugs and cameras, a couple of simple bare rooms—"

"Look," Cooper said, "if there are mikes in those walls any really good security people would find them in a flash—"

"Absolutely," Paulus agreed, "though soon there will be a window of time when there will be mikes that are undetectable. Then the window will close with new sweepers being invented. However, you are quite right."

"I don't get it."

"Koller has it swept for intrusions, swept personally by the head of his security forces, a man named Bernd Schmidt . . . who just happens to be Karl-Heinz's father."

"You mean they're both—"

"It is here that Karl-Heinz installed the bugs that recorded SPARTAKUS for him to deliver to the Americans. We know all this, we know how Bernd Schmidt worked with his son to destroy Wolf Koller, we know that Karl-Heinz turned to Bernd's old opposite number in the

CIA, Burke Delaney . . . we know all this, but we know only the little things, we have an accumulation of interesting detail—"

"It sounds like you've got a helluva lot," Cooper said.

"Forgive me, you're an amateur, Mr. Cooper. You've got nothing until you get the whole picture. It's like a puzzle, a picture puzzle. We have the frame, we have filled in some of the picture, but at the center? Nothing. Let me explain. We know that Wolf Koller has been using Joachim Stiffel and his neo-Nazis to stir up trouble—Koller funds them, he has virtually created them, do you see? They're nothing. They're a diversion. They make trouble, they throw some firebombs, they murder a few refugees, they create an atmosphere which makes people cry out for order. It isn't so much that Germans *hate* things—it's that they *love* order, an established framework. They need the playpen like the baby needs it, to reduce the number of options for behavior, then they're happy. So Stiffel runs around banging on the playpen, he breaks it open, it's a mess and people want it fixed, they want their orderly world back. This Stiffel stuff is noisy, they arrange to blow up the Zoo Station—of course it's a Wolf Koller operation, designed to drive people into a frenzy, making the mob cry out for order . . . it gets a lot of coverage in the press around the world, CNN throws it—plop—into your living room, pictures of broken bodies and bloody walls and terrified citizens, all onto your breakfast table. With CNN I guarantee there would never have been a Hitler. People would have sat at home watching and they would have gone crazy. Anyway, people get all worried about Germany— are we on the verge of another xenophobic madness over here?—but it's all sleight of hand, it's there to distract us. Wolf Koller can snuff out the neo-Nazis before breakfast any day he wishes, but what is he *really* up to?" Paulus was staring out the window into the courtyard, the withered vines, the dead flowers, the gray of another day.

Cooper and Beate waited, unsure of what to say. It was as if, for a moment, Paulus were alone with his thoughts. He was a man who had spent his life working out puzzles. He was at home in the maze.

"I don't know," he said, turning to face them with a faint smile on his long, solemn face. "We have the shell of SPARTAKUS. But what's inside? That's what we have to find out. That's why Karl-Heinz is dead . . . Wolf Koller knows there is a problem. He knows that this room where he thought he was safe is where he was in fact betrayed. Will he believe he has found the only leak? Or will he believe there are others? How can he be sure? Will he blame Bernd Schmidt? Will he believe that his daughter learned the truth from Karl-Heinz and now threatens to destroy him? He must move quickly, don't you see? To achieve SPARTAKUS, to complete it before he is stopped . . . whatever *it* is . . ."

Paulus was pacing the room, thinking aloud.

"He knows Karl-Heinz knew what SPARTAKUS is but he doesn't know if he told anyone. *I* know he didn't tell Burke Delaney. That is what Delaney says and I choose to believe him. He never got it. And now somebody just tried to kill Delaney. They thought he'd gotten the last of it, so he had to die. A slight miscalculation—the other man died. But Koller doesn't know who knows . . . you see? Try to get inside his mind, try to imagine the terror and fear and anger and frustration and outrage, and he's a man used to commanding everything. He must have order, order above all. He has a plan for everything, SPARTAKUS is his plan, maybe his master plan, his life is wrapped up in it. And now maybe it's all coming apart and people are getting killed and maybe he's going to be one of them. Do you grasp all this, you two? Koller is watching his life come apart and he'll do anything to keep that from happening . . .

"And that's why you—and you, Miss Hubermann—are in very real danger. You were with Karl-Heinz twice, Mr. Cooper, and you were Karl-Heinz's friend and you are Mr. Cooper's friend, Miss Hubermann. I'm rather afraid that the bad guys are going to think that Karl-Heinz may have passed it on to you . . ."

"Now that I am scared absolutely shitless," Cooper said, "I have one more question. Who tried to kill him?"

"I don't know. But it's nice to know that he's in danger, too, isn't it?"

"Is he afraid of Erika, too?" Beate asked.

"Afraid? Of course. Who knows what Karl-Heinz might have told her? And when she finds out Karl-Heinz is dead she's going to be sure her father is responsible . . . Yes, he's afraid of her. How afraid? Enough to do her harm? I don't know . . . But there are killers on the loose out there and I would advise you both to be very careful. Do you understand what I am saying?"

31

BAYREUTH

Cooper chartered a small plane, which was one of the advantages of having unlimited credit cards. Beate corrected him. It was one of the advantages of being rich. He didn't argue. He wanted to find out what she'd learned about Warmolts and his clinic.

Beate had made three telephone calls before they left for the airport. Dr. Warmolts had died in the late seventies. His clinic had ceased to exist—that is, it was taken over by another group of doctors and turned into a psychiatric center. The clinic under Warmolts had handled a variety of psychological illnesses, had provided apartments for long-term guests such as Lise Koller, had contained examining rooms, an operating theater, treatment rooms, and a padded cell or two. Now it consisted of offices for psychiatrists, therapists, marriage counselors, and hypnotists for smokers and fat people. The doctors who had worked with Warmolts had retired, scattered, or died.

"But," Beate said, eyes bright, blond hair swinging, "Warmolts's head nurse is alive and well, waiting for us. She'll talk, John, I heard it in her voice. She sounded almost eager."

It was dark and a chilly rain was blowing when they got to Bayreuth and then to the large gray stone house at the end of a long narrow drive bordered by heavy, glistening wrought iron. The trees were neatly trimmed and the lawn was immaculate, the flower beds geometrically shaped, but now the flowers were gone and clumps of this and that had been carefully wrapped like children prepared for the Bavarian winter. The light under the stone portico glowed welcomingly and Joan Freundlich, who looked to be in her mid-fifties, was equally warm in her greeting.

"Tea," she said with a vestigial English accent, "or something stronger perhaps? Come, come, there's a fire in the study. What a night for travelers! Miss Hubermann, Mr. Cooper, you've come at a perfect time. Rolf is out and Helene . . ." She nodded toward the heavy, carved stairway. "Our daughter Helene is deep in her studies. Do sit down. Hannah will bring us some tea and there's the drinks cabinet, Mr. Cooper."

While they waited for Hannah, who arrived with a silver tea tray and curtsied before departing, Joan Freundlich showed a masterful hand at small talk. "I'm English, you see, married to a German businessman, but he came along after I left Dr. Warmolts and the clinic. Rolf is out somewhere tonight treating his top salesmen to a lavish German dinner, the *old* cuisine I call it, dumplings and sauerbraten and blood sausage—they should post a medical unit in each restaurant, shouldn't they? . . . Ah, Hannah, here's something to warm our insides."

Once the tea ceremony was well underway, she continued: "I'm a great one for bringing people together—an English trait of mine. I devote most of my time to creating a greater understanding between the English and the Germans. I know, my husband tells me it's a quixotic task, he says the English and the Germans know each other better than any other people in Europe, they've shared a royal house of England, they've fought two wars . . . I suppose he's right"—she smiled a trifle wistfully—"but I do enjoy setting up tours back and forth, housing people with families much like their own . . . I'm an idealist, aren't I? Well, I make no apologies for that." She had a long English face, a comfortable, toothy smile with long teeth, a large English bosom on a tall, spare frame. "Now, you have questions about the clinic and Dr. Warmolts?"

"As I mentioned, I'm with National TV working out of Berlin—"

The woman nodded, pursed her lips as if about to speak, but waited.

"And we're inquiring about Wolf Koller. We're doing a major documentary on his rise to political influence . . . and his wife's current physician, Dr. Gisevius, has told us that she spent a period of time here at the Warmolts clinic roughly twenty years ago. We're just following up on that."

"And I'm Lise Koller's brother, from America. Lise isn't too well now and I didn't want to bother her with questions—but I am concerned about what happened so long ago."

"My, my, this is all so very strange. I don't quite understand—"

Cooper said: "What's the problem?"

"Well, just a few days ago I spoke to your colleague, Marlene Schleuter, didn't I?" She looked inquiringly at Beate. "Yes, that was her name, she said she was your producer—and she asked me the same question. What did I know about Lise Koller's stay at the clinic. And I told her what I knew—surely she must have told you?"

Beate smiled. "Marlene, of course. Well, this is a case of the right hand not knowing what the left hand is doing. We're both on the road so much. A story of this magnitude requires quite a lot of research. I do some, Marlene does some—and she must have gotten confused. You're sure it was Marlene?"

"Yes, she said Marlene Schleuter."

"Short, rather pear-shaped, about forty—"

"Oh no, nothing like that. She was so young, I was amazed that she could be a producer. She rather reminded me of you but she couldn't have been more than twenty—of course, everyone dresses like teenagers nowadays. She was rather *punky,* is that the word? Spiky hair, very blond. Black jeans, black turtleneck. And quite probing with her questions—not the woman you described at all—"

"Ah, no, what was I thinking of? I was describing someone else entirely." She glanced quickly at Cooper. "Well, I haven't spoken with Marlene. Would you mind terribly going over the material again?"

Cooper finished his cup of tea. What the hell were they talking about? Marlene was a new one on him. And there was no major documentary about Wolf Koller. So, who else was doing research?

"Yes, of course," Joan Freundlich said, refilling the teacups. "I can quite understand how wires can get crossed in a complex undertaking. I don't mind at all." The fire crackled and spit out an ember, which lay glowing on the tiles. She got up and poked the fire, pushing the ember back onto the grate. "But I would like to make clear to you the reasons why I am willing to speak about such matters. In the normal course of events, one would be rather reticent to discuss private medical affairs, wouldn't one? But this is different." She took a deep breath and squared her gaunt shoulders. She wore a gray wool dress with a chain at the waist, some understated, very good jewelry. "I came to disapprove of how Dr. Warmolts conducted his practice. And I think people have a right to know some of his, and other doctors', primitive methods. Which are still being practiced in some places. And I particularly didn't like what was done to Lise Koller. It was not only unnecessary, it was wrong . . . it was evil. Oh yes, doctors are quite capable of evil, and often they don't even recognize it for what it is. And, finally, Wolf Koller, the man he is today, offends me and should offend every thinking German. I feel no need to keep the silence of the confessional where he is concerned." She sat back down, crossed her long legs, and refueled with hot tea.

"What did Warmolts do to my sister?"

"And why should every thinking German object to Koller?" Beate added.

"Excuse me for a moment, Mr. Cooper, but let me just say this about Wolf Koller. He is a powermonger, he is without principle. He tries to influence events, he parades about with the Chancellor, he wants us to believe that Germany belongs to him . . . and he risks nothing. The people never vote on the Wolf Kollers of the world, so you can't get rid of them. And I object to that. So—I will keep no secrets for Wolf Koller." She sighed. "Though I hardly think I can affect him one way or the other . . ."

"What did Warmolts do to my sister?"

"Oh, I'm sorry—yes, it was terrible. I was her special nurse, I liked her, I was with her for hours every day, and I couldn't make them stop. Today, I'm a different woman—I'd have raised the dead now, but then I wasn't, oh, as fully evolved." A small secret smile played across the wide mouth. "They treated her mainly with electroshock. I attended. It was like something out of a concentration camp. But I couldn't say that to a man like Warmolts. The poor little thing, she lived in fear from day to day that they'd come for her again, strap her down, and . . . you know, give her the shocks. Twice they broke one of her ribs."

Cooper clenched his teeth, kept calm. "But why? What was the point?"

"Oh, they said one thing and another, they had their excuses, but I'll tell you what it was—the idea was to break her spirit, crush the life and the fight out of her. Wolf Koller complained to Dr. Warmolts that she was irrational, that she'd been under great strain, that her first husband had died violently not long before, that she was living under some delusion that her husband and some lover she had were Nazis, that there was some terrible Nazi conspiracy and that he, Wolf Koller, was also a part of it—Koller wanted her 'cured' of this madness. He said she was paranoid, schizophrenic, and vengeful—he was convinced that electroshock was the only way to rid her of this delusion . . . which was why he brought her to Warmolts in the first place. Warmolts was known to be the virtuoso of the electrodes. So, they did it to her again and again and again . . . she was nearly catatonic for months, whether with fear or from the shocks to her system I don't know . . . And now I see pictures of her in the press and I think of that poor little thing, huddled in her bed, sobbing, afraid that they were coming for her. Now she's very grand, of course, but I've often wondered what lasting marks the treatments left on her. You don't just forget such things."

In the quiet that followed, rain hissed in the chimney and rock music could be heard from upstairs somewhere.

Finally Cooper said: "That must have been very hard on the baby."

Joan Freundlich looked up at him quickly, her blue eyes suddenly curious, piercing. "I don't understand it—that's precisely what Marlene Schleuter said. 'It must have been hard on the baby.' I tried to explain to her . . . there was no baby. Lise Koller wasn't pregnant, nothing of the kind . . . I think even Dr. Warmolts would have refused to use electroshock therapy on a pregnant woman."

Beate said: "But she did come home with a baby. That's a matter of record."

"Miss Hubermann, look at me—would I spend months and months with a young woman, day in and day out, and not know if she were having a baby? I know nothing of what the record may show, but Lise Koller had no baby at the Warmolts Clinic. And that is exactly what I told your young colleague. Really, I can't imagine where you got this idea."

"All right, who the hell is Marlene Schleuter?"

"There is no Marlene Schleuter. There is no documentary on Wolf Koller. Someone is impersonating a TV producer, which is one of the strangest—"

Cooper held the cold beer to his forehead. It was hot in the hotel bar where they'd stopped because he damn well needed a drink and they had an hour before they were cleared to fly back to Berlin. "It's Erika," he said.

"Erika?" Beate scowled into a glass of white wine, then at him. "I thought it was somehow one of Wolf's people . . . but, no, you're right. Of course it is—it's Erika."

"Karl-Heinz must have told her about Warmolts and the clinic. Can you imagine, if he told her the same thing he told me—she's not who she thinks she is? What must that have done to her? First she tried to kill herself, then she must have set out to find out who the hell she really is." He shook his head. "She's either right on the edge of a nervous break-down or she's made of flame-tempered steel . . ."

Beate was thinking, staring at her reflection in the mirror behind the bar. She came back to the surface. "She's strong. Sometimes I think she's too strong. She's been battling her past, her family's past, her father —for so long. All her life, really."

"So, who is she?"

"Erika? Well, she must be adopted."

"No, Wolf Koller would never adopt a child. Believe me, I'm a man, I know what kind of man he is. Fruit of his loins and so on. I'll put money on Koller being the father. It's just that Lise isn't the mother."

"You're calling her Lise, not Lee."

"I guess I'm thinking of her as Lise. Someone foreign. My God, I hate the son of a bitch for putting her through all that horror in the clinic. I'm beginning to think I'd like to kill him."

"Please don't talk like that."

"Let's just hope I don't get the chance."

"So now they all know," she said. "Wolf, Lise, and Erika all know that . . . Lise isn't Erika's mother."

"You know, it seemed so . . . so simple when I started out to come over here and help Lise get her daughter back. Scary, yes, because it meant coming back to Germany . . . but it got so complicated so fast." He looked over at her, saw she was smiling at him the way women sometimes do, as if they're indulging a little boy. "You don't seem all that relieved to hear that Erika is alive—granting that you think it's Erika."

"Somehow I'm more worried than ever. If she's alive and investi-gating along the path Karl-Heinz set for her, I'm afraid Wolf will find out. And he'll go looking for her. Especially if he knows she's been here, to the clinic . . . well, I don't like to think about what he'll do."

Cooper finished his beer and set it down on the bar. It was time to go. "There's another thing. What about Erika? What will she do when she finds out that Karl-Heinz has been murdered? She's going to have to know it was her father . . ."

32

FINGERSPITZENGEFÜHL

In the bleary-eyed morning Beate had to leave to get to work and Cooper remained with his coffee and toast for a few minutes in the empty room. It was so hard to keep track of it all: it was like coming in late on a play that began twenty years ago. There was so much to catch up with . . . It hadn't been any of his business, either, not until Lee called out to him. And now, in light of what they'd learned in Bayreuth, Lee was more at risk than ever. What Wolf Koller feared from her now was what he'd feared when he'd sent her to Warmolts's clinic: He feared all that she knew, all that she'd been through, he feared the eruption of her soul. And now, more than twenty years later, Cooper knew he had to pry her loose from this nightmare. He didn't quite know how it could be managed but the idea had begun to consume him. It had begun with the sight of her on the bed looking so old and frail and helpless, like the victim of a vampire. Or, some might say, the vampire herself, starving . . . And last night, listening to the woman who'd nursed her through the tortures, he knew he no longer had a choice.

All these years, all his life, it had all added up to this. His job was to save his little sister, Lee, or die trying. It might not be much of a monument to the life he'd lived, but it was all that made sense anymore. She couldn't make it without him. There was no family of his own, no lasting accomplishment, a few mystery novels, a movie theater, a book-

store, not much, his life hadn't amounted to much. But if he could save
Lee, then living would have meant something. Something.

He felt in that moment like a figure in a myth. He felt like the man
who was threatened by the trolls living beneath the bridge and up in the
tree, waiting to prey on him before he could rescue the poor, helpless
princess in the tower. It didn't matter if the princess was worth saving, it
was only the quest that mattered . . . He was the quest, he would pass
through the tests and furies and fire to get to the maiden and save her and
bring her home and if it all went the way it was supposed to, he, and
maybe she, would be transformed into something worthwhile, maybe
even glorious in a way . . .

It was early but considering how early Paulus had called him the day
before, he didn't hesitate to pick up the phone and call the "Chief." The
phone was answered on the second ring. He could hear the sound of a
television or radio in the background.

"It's me. Cooper. I need to talk to you."

"All right, Mr. Cooper. I am at your service."

"Tell me where to meet you."

Paulus suggested Kranzler's on the Ku'damm. "It's a landmark.
You really should see it."

"Okay. In an hour. Chief Paulus?"

"Yes?"

"Erika Koller is alive."

"Yes, of course she is, Mr. Cooper. In an hour, then."

Paulus was waiting for him, looking freshly barbered, smelling of a
quiet, elegant cologne, lighting a Dunhill cigarette, letting the smoke drift
lazily away. The table was on the second floor, looking out over the busy
street and the shops across the way, the news kiosks, the crowds. Umbrellas bobbed against the slashing fits and starts of rain. As Cooper got
seated, Paulus said: "I was just sitting here thinking of the sentimentality
of the German people. Bleibtreustrasse, where we were yesterday. Do
you know what the word means?"

"No. Not a clue."

"Well, let's see . . . true love, or fidelity, faithfulness . . . Fidelity Street. Something like that. It's a pretty street. Like a movie set.
Sentimental. We are a sentimental people. Part of the contradictions,
don't you see? Capable of the most horrifying enormities . . . yet crying

over the beauty of a flower, a snatch of remembered song." He sighed. "Perhaps I am feeling poetic in my old age. You know, I only smoke two cigarettes a day. This is very early for my first." He took a deep breath.

"Look," Cooper said, "there's something I think I should tell you but I don't know—well, hell, if I can't trust you, who can I trust? Right?"

"I suppose that's possible." He smiled like the old family doctor. "You must decide for yourself. But I'm a good bet." He smiled again over the rim of the coffee cup.

"I told you that Erika Koller is alive."

"Yes."

"A few days ago she was in Bayreuth. She was checking out something Karl-Heinz told her—something he told me, as well. Lise Koller spent some time in a clinic in Bayreuth shortly after she married Wolf Koller. She was subjected to inhuman electroshock treatments. In effect, she was tortured. To let her see what could happen if she ever spilled the beans on the nest of Nazis I fell into twenty years ago, if she ever denounced Wolf Koller as one of them. So far . . . so far it has worked but she's near the edge again, he's scared all right . . . that's why he's going to kill her. Make no mistake, that's what he's moving toward. In Bayreuth, Erika Koller found out the truth about what happened to Lise in that clinic twenty years ago. And when Lise Koller left the clinic she also brought home her baby . . . little Erika . . . that's been the story. But Lise Koller was not pregnant. Lise Koller had no baby. The nurse who was with her every day in Bayreuth swears that there was no baby . . . Yet there was Erika when she went home with Wolf. A baby, yes. But not Lise Koller's baby. And a few days ago Erika Koller learned that fact, too." Cooper leaned back from the table, watching Paulus's impassive visage. "Karl-Heinz told me that Erika Koller was not who I thought she was. Now I know what he meant. Can you imagine what she must have felt when he told her that? And when she found out the truth? Can you imagine what that must have done to her?"

Paulus asked him to run through the whole story and he did, while Paulus seemed to be taking involved mental notes. He interrupted only a couple of times for more explanation, otherwise listening raptly until the story was finished.

After a lengthy pause Paulus said: "You and Miss Hubermann amaze me, Mr. Cooper. You have uncovered something I didn't know. I congratulate you. Frankly, it's a very nice touch, this Warmolts Clinic and the electroshock treatment and the central question, Who is Erika Koller?"

"I've thought about this next item on my agenda," Cooper said, "and I've wondered what I should do—well, I'm going to get it off my chest. I'm trusting you, for better or worse. It's Beate Hubermann. I keep thinking there's something wrong—I've had this feeling about her from the very beginning . . . that she's never quite taken me into her confidence. I felt it even in Boston when she brought me the message from my sister, Lee. She was holding something back . . . and when I got to Germany I learned that she was a much better friend of Erika Koller's than she admitted. She knew *both* Erika and Karl-Heinz, and she knew them well . . . now why would she lie to me? I couldn't figure that out. And I still feel that way about her. She knows something, I just feel it."

Paulus was smiling at him, looking down the long nose, eyes a piercing gray.

"Fingerspitzengefühl."

"What the hell is that? Lunch?"

"Fingerspitzengefühl. It's an attribute people have always said I have in more than my share. And it's true, I think. It's a sense, you can feel something *in your fingertips.* It's a tingle, it's heat, you know you're on to something but you can't quite prove it. That's what you're feeling about Miss Hubermann."

"Yes. But then I came up with some more evidence that she's got her own agenda." He told Paulus about the early-morning phone call he had overheard. "I haven't been able to forget what she said. I think she was talking to Erika Koller. I think she knows where she is." As soon as he'd said it he felt relieved. "And then, last night, she didn't seem particularly interested in the discovery that Erika's alive—but only worried that Wolf Koller might find out what she's up to."

Paulus snuffed his cigarette in the ashtray and finished his coffee and the sweet roll. "My experience is, always trust your *Fingerspitzengefühl.* Come, I'll call a friend of mine at telephone headquarters. He will do the old Chief a favor. I will ask him to check calls going out from Miss Hubermann's telephone on that morning. He'll tell me who or where she called. Of course, the call might have come in—but probably not. You would have heard it. We shall see, Mr. Cooper, we shall see."

Cooper waited while Paulus made the call from a phone box on the corner. He came back from the booth and said his friend would try. "I'll call him back in a little while."

They went to a brasserie in the passageway leading out of Savignyplatz, underneath the elevated S-Bahn, and bought coffee.

Cooper stood in the open doorway, watching the rain and sipping the steaming coffee, while Paulus phoned his friend.

"Miss Hubermann placed the call," he said when he returned. "She called a number in a little town in Bavaria. Mountain village. Quite near Berchtesgaden. Shades of the Führer, eh? The number is listed in the name of some other Hubermann. A relative, I suppose. Father, grandfather. A summer home, a vacation home, in any case. Very probably deserted this time of year. Unless one is harboring an unexpected guest who's trying not to be found." He smiled at Cooper. "What do you think, Mr. Cooper?"

"I think just what you think, Chief."

"You should probably have a talk with Miss Hubermann."

"What are you going to do now?"

"Try to decipher the code of what's going on here. Talk to my friends. I think we're running out of time, Mr. Cooper." He spoke calmly. "Whatever you do, be more careful than you have ever been in your life. I want you to survive this."

"What are the chances? No—don't answer that. I'll be in touch, Chief Paulus." Cooper liked calling him Chief. It made a lot of sense just then.

Cooper rented a car, yet another Mercedes, and worked his way through a street map of Berlin with the aid of the rental agent. If he drove straight out the Ku'damm for a while—following a bus was one suggestion—and turned off to the right he'd find himself in Grunewald. Then he would just have to curl around the winding street and . . . right, he got the point, he could handle it. In the end, it was less trouble than he'd expected and the manners of Berlin drivers were absolutely civilized. An hour after parting from Paulus he was staring through the fence at the Koller mansion.

The gates were swung open and there was only a single uniformed guard having a smoke up by the front door. Cooper drove up the driveway and stopped near him. The man watched him through the cigarette smoke, squinting. He was solid and middle-aged. *"Ja?"* he said with a wary look.

"Frau Koller," Cooper said by way of an opening conversational gambit. "Herr Kilroy, the American. Or Doktor Gisevius?" So much for the language of his hosts. He wished he knew it. There was something so perfectly right about German compound nouns. *Fingerspitzengefühl.*

The guard left the cigarette in his mouth but lightened a bit at the sound of Gisevius's name. He nodded at the door and made a sound indicating that Cooper could have a go, he was on his own.

Cooper buzzed the door and when no one answered he tried it, found it unlocked, and went in.

There was something different about the house. He knew it the instant he was inside. It was devoid of life. Empty or emptying. "Hello," he called. "Dr. Gisevius?" No answer. He poked his head down a hall, into the room where he had had the conversation with Gisevius and Kilroy. The hearth was cold. He was looking out the window onto the back driveway, where two servants were loading things into the back of a long Daimler, when he heard a sound behind him. It was Gisevius.

"Mr. Cooper. An unexpected visit. May I be of any help?"

For a moment all Cooper could think of was Gisevius, plotting with Koller in the room at the top of the house on Bleibtreustrasse. "I was hoping I might see my sister again. She seemed to be in such bad shape the other day . . ." Had it been just yesterday? He was losing track of time. "How is she?"

"I'm very sorry to say that Mrs. Koller is not at all well. She's taken a bit of a turn." He put his thick, meaty hands out, palms up. "Of course, we knew it might happen this way . . . her case has been so unpredictable."

"How bad a turn?" His throat was suddenly dry and his chest ached. He didn't want to hear this.

"I can't say. She could rally. She could stabilize. She could sink. We're exploring terra incognita here, Mr. Cooper. I can only do so much."

"She's my sister—"

"I'm aware of that."

"Where is she? Can I see her?"

"She's not here, Mr. Cooper. She has been removed to a private hospital where they can give her more comprehensive care. She's receiving the best care imaginable, as you might assume. Mr. Koller would stand for nothing less, obviously. Now, I must—"

"Where is this hospital? I need to see her for myself . . . I need to talk to them—"

"Mr. Cooper, please, you must understand that after your display here at the house and all that Mr. Koller has gone through I cannot divulge that information. I want to spare these two people all the excitement and confusion I possibly can. Frankly, I don't want you charging like a wild animal into the hospital, demanding to see your sister—that's not the way we do things here, whatever you may be used to in your country. Her treatment is the best possible. Let that satisfy you. Beyond that, you must apply not to me but to Mr. Koller for information regarding his wife. Now I must be leaving. Please." He indicated the door.

"You know, I could develop a real dislike for you, Doctor."

"I'm sure that is possible. I'll have to live with that, Mr. Cooper. Now . . . please . . ."

"I'm an irrational and frequently violent man, Dr. Gisevius. And, to make matters worse, just look at me. Big, too."

"Attacking me would be a mistake, Mr. Cooper. I still wouldn't tell you Lise's whereabouts and you might be gravely injured."

"By you?"

"No. By this gentleman." He said something in German and another man appeared in the doorway. He was tall and lean with once-reddish hair going gray and white. His face bore no expression at all. It was as if he were empty but for the program that made him function. Gisevius spoke to him in German, then said: "I'm not dependent on a mere butler this time . . . Would you see Mr. Cooper out, please, Sebastien?"

The man took a step into the room and made that same gesture toward the door. *"Bitte,"* he said. *Please.*

Cooper was very sure there was no bullying Sebastien.

Cooper waited in the rented car just at the edge of the curve leading down to the Koller house, slouched down behind the wheel. The afternoon was darkening and the windshield was covered with dirty water. Nannies were walking their little charges up and down the Hasensprung. He could hear the trilling laughter of children. Eventually a large black Daimler slid quietly out of the Koller gates and down the street. Leaving his headlamps off for the moment, Cooper followed the Daimler. Gisevius was in the passenger seat in front and the man called Sebastien was behind the wheel. Cooper hoped very hard that he would never run into Sebastien in a dark and lonely place.

Cooper had no idea where they were going but there was plenty of traffic and no danger of being seen by Gisevius and Sebastien. Half an hour later he saw the sign that said they were at Lake Wannsee, and there was a big parking lot and some ferries lit up and looking rather forlorn, ignored. They took a turn off to the right and it was too dark to notice much in the way of surroundings as they passed beneath tall trees, a hospital with a lighted parking lot on the left, down a road that rustled and squished with the leaves and the puddles. He dropped back again, not wanting to be more obvious than necessary. The Daimler was moving slowly, the turn indicator flickering, and then it pulled off to the right toward the water and a big low house, very modern, hard to make out in detail. It looked like a large ship drawing in to the shore.

It had to be Koller's lake house. Cooper figured Koller was in residence. With Gisevius. Who else? He was surrounded by bodyguards, presumably, after the attack on his life. If everything Paulus said was true, then Koller believed he had his back to the wall.

As Cooper drove slowly past the house he registered a VW pulled over at the side of the road. The streetlights were far enough away so that their glow didn't penetrate the darkness. But he thought he saw the figure of a man beside the car in a certain stance.

He'd have sworn the guy was having a piss.

Ah, hell. He didn't know where Lee was. He was pretty sure he knew where Erika was. Paulus said the little town was near Hitler's Eagle's Nest. But he couldn't get to Erika until Beate laid the truth before him.

He was going to have to face her.

33

BLOOD SPORT

"Why didn't you tell me you know where Erika is? That you're keeping her in your house in the mountains?"

She was throwing down her backpack and helmet and had her back to him. He watched the hesitation, the slight stiffening of her back, and then she let the stuff fall onto the couch. She took an Oreo from the plate on the coffee table. It was the last one, had been there for a couple of days, and he heard it snap as she bit into it.

"Turn around, damn it, I'm talking to you. What was the point? Knowing I was trying to find her, knowing how worried my sister is— what was the point in keeping your little secret?"

"How long have you known?" She was sinking into the couch, looking at him defiantly, daring him to be angry.

"Since this afternoon. It was Erika you were talking to the other night on the telephone when you thought I was asleep. You told me it was my imagination. But the more I thought about it, the more I knew I'd heard you . . . I told Paulus today and it took him all of fifteen minutes to nail it down."

She laughed quietly. "What did I tell you about Paulus? He knows everybody in Berlin and they're all working for him."

"You owe me an answer. You're the one who got me to Berlin, all the way from Boston. You knew the truth even then . . . Two people were going to kill me in Minnesota and now people have started dying over here, just like last time. You got me into this—and you knew it was all a fool's errand. You knew Erika was all right and you've let me risk my neck and you've refused to stop my sister's pain. What the hell is going on with you, Beate?" He realized he was shaking and his hands were clenched into fists. She was looking up at him as if she might be wondering just how to make her escape if things got out of hand. She was right, he wanted to start breaking things. "You'd better say something," he said.

"My only loyalty in this situation," she said, her voice unexpectedly brittle, near cracking, "is to Erika. She's my friend. I didn't know you existed. And her mother is an erratic, emotionally unstable woman—that's what Erika says, regardless of how much she loves Lise. You were an unknown quantity, and Lise . . . if I told her about Erika she might start raving and blurt out what she knew. And that would completely defeat the point of everything . . . Erika is trying to get away from her father, from everything Karl-Heinz has told her about Wolf Koller, all the Nazi business. She carries Nazi guilt at the center of her soul—there's no point in arguing about whether she should or shouldn't, that's beside the point. I'm not a shrink. But it's there. I don't know if she can ever get rid of it. I couldn't run the risk of letting her fall back into Koller's hands when she's this vulnerable . . . she has to come to grips with it—"

"Fine, fine, but what's that got to do with me? Why couldn't you tell me? Why did I have to play the fool, running around thinking I was looking for leads to find Erika—"

"Because you'd have told your sister! But you were also tracking down Koller's story . . . and you weren't a fool."

"I could have handled Lee, I could have been better with her, I could have—"

"Look, I know all about you and your sister! Don't tell me you could have been near her and seen her so upset and not told her—I don't believe it!" She thrust herself out of the grip of the couch and stormed past him and into the kitchen.

"What do you think you know about me and my sister? What's that crack supposed to mean?"

"I know. I *know*. Erika told me, and she found out from Lise, Lee, whatever the bloody name is! I've known from the time I went to Boston to deliver the message, I've known from that night with Erika . . . the night she almost killed herself. She told me why she believes her mother acts so crazy sometimes, why she's always been so kind of knotted up and had these depressions all her life, all of Erika's life, anyway . . . Erika told me how you tracked all across the world until you found her, how you just had a random newspaper photograph to go by, and you found her and . . . and wrecked her whole life." Beate was out of breath, standing by the kitchen sink, trembling, as if she had no idea why she was there or what she was intending to do. She bit her lip. She was crying. "She told me that you and her mother, your sister, had had a love affair . . . she didn't know if you'd actually realized then that you were brother and sister, but eventually you did know, and her mother has been trying to live with the idea and figure out what to do about it ever since. Erika told me all about it, how you were so madly in love with Lee that you nearly got killed and then Lee wouldn't come with you . . ."

Cooper's stomach had disappeared in the general direction of China. He felt as if he'd been hit in the belly and couldn't get his breath or swallow ever again. He felt completely disoriented, as if everybody had removed their masks and they were all strangers. "I don't understand—how could she know all this?"

"But it's true, isn't it?"

"Some of it's true, yes. But how did Erika—"

"That proves my point—you love Lee now, too, don't you? And you'd have told her, you wouldn't have been able to let her suffer—I don't want to get into the middle of the problems you and your sister are trying to work out . . . I didn't really believe her when she told me, but now that I've seen you after you've been with Lee, I've seen what it does to you—you do love her and it's none of my business but—"

"Wait a goddamn minute! How did Erika know all this? Are you saying Lee actually told her?" He was trying to get his equilibrium back and he wished the tears would stop running down her pale cheeks. Why was she crying?

"Of course Lee told her. She rambles, she takes her medicine, she talks on and on, has no memory of it. Erika told me it's as if Lise is in a dream sometimes, and you're there, and your brother, Cyril, and your parents, past and present all mixed together . . . Yes, of course, she told her . . . all about what had happened twenty years ago. And she's been on the edge ever since. Twenty years, Cooper, and every bloody bit of it is your fault . . ." She grabbed a towel from the countertop and wiped her eyes. "So . . . You'd have told Lee all about where Erika was—I knew it, and I couldn't tell you." She rubbed her nose. "How angry are you?"

"What kind of a question is that?"

"I saw what you did to that man when you were angry—I don't want you to do that to me . . ." She looked out from behind the towel.

"Stop crying. I'm begging you, stop crying."

"You're not going to hit me?"

"I don't think so. I'm unpredictable."

"Do you understand why I didn't tell you?"

"I accept your reasons, I guess. But look—tell me about Erika. Does she know about Karl-Heinz's murder?"

"Yes. I told her before we went to Bayreuth. There's an answering machine . . . where she is. She had to know. They might come for her—"

"Near Berchtesgaden?"

"Paulus told you, of course."

"But you didn't know she'd been to Bayreuth?"

"I had no idea. But if they find out Karl-Heinz told her so much—"

"You really do think Wolf Koller would do something to his own daughter?"

"She might be somebody else's daughter."

"She's Wolf's daughter," Cooper insisted.

"I'm not so sure. But, yes, I think Wolf might kill Erika if she's a threat to him and his grand design. I'd say he's capable of anything."

"I want you to call Erika now. I want to know that she's all right."

"You're in charge now?"

"I'm always in charge. It's just that sometimes nobody knows it. So call her. Right now."

The telephone rang and rang at the other end but there was no answer.

"She's probably out for a walk. Or taking a nap. We'll call later. She'll be back."

"Oh, really? She's been to Bayreuth. Now she knows her father probably had her boyfriend killed. She's got reasons to be damn near anywhere so long as it's on the warpath. Tell me—what happened that night? The night she tried to kill herself."

"I called her, just to talk, and nobody answered. She'd left a message on my machine at work, she'd said she would be home . . . she sounded like a zombie. She said she'd been banged up at the rally, the riot—"

"And you went over to see her and found her all cut up—"

Beate looked at the big black watch on her slender wrist. "Time to go. We'll talk later."

"Where are you going?"

"The mother of all rallies."

"This thing at the Brandenburg Gate? The *good* Germans?"

"That's the only rally I know about. Three hundred thousand people who are supposed to be protesting the Nazis and the violence. In reality, it's just going to be a lot of people—every possible point of view will be out in force, I promise you. The Chancellor's back in town, a handful of ministers, the Mayor, the Angel Gabriel—"

"I'm coming."

"Promise not to get angry and kill people?"

"No."

Ned Cheddar was finishing a cheeseburger and a double helping of cole slaw when he got a call from Burke Delaney. He wiped ketchup from his chin, noticed that some had dripped onto the papers on his desk, and listened to what Delaney said. He felt as if he were sliding away into quicksand.

"We got a dog's breakfast over here, Cheese, and we're getting close to some damn thing, but I guaran-damn-ty you I don't know what it is. Clues, Cheese, we got clues."

"Fine, Burke, fine." He was trying very hard to control himself. He poured ten Rolaids in different pastel colors on to the desktop and began chewing them up. "Let's get to them." He was busy trying to get absolutely clear in his mind what Delaney knew and what he didn't know. He was jotting down a note, making sure he didn't misspeak himself to his faithful old Delaney, when he jerked to a stop as if the brisket and banana cream pie were about to make a repeat performance. "Say again, please, Burke."

"I said that the Professor has seen Sebastien the Red and Konstantin Orlovski in Berlin. Orlovski's the advance man for that cocksucker Rossovich, the great white hope of the Russian right wing." He paused a moment, hearing the silence. "Aha, I thought that might just grab your attention—first Kuno Meinhold, now Sebastien . . . and then Orlovski comes sneaking into the mix. Can Rossovich be far behind? Though the Professor says Konnie wasn't sneaking at all, he was feeding his face at Kranzler's. Talking to Sebastien."

"Hmmm. Rossovich wants to run a new government if they can just give Yeltsin the push. Have you heard the latest? In a speech yesterday in St. Petersburg, Rossovich made it pretty clear that . . . *he wants*

Alaska back! You want to work on that one, Burke? So—is the Professor sure it was Sebastien? He's dead, you know."

"Well, he's sure as hell handling the bad news real well." Delaney was enjoying himself. Cheddar could positively hear the big smile.

"You're still in Berlin?"

"No, Miami Beach for the winter. Jeez. Yes, of course I'm in Berlin."

"Give me your analysis."

"I don't have one. But I've got a lot more news—like how I can't find the Professor anymore. He's gone, disappeared."

"Damn it! Is he off being Nancy Drew? I hate that. He's not at all comfortable with the wet work. He's essentially something other than a field man."

"I don't know. But there's more. Brace yourself."

"Oh, please."

"The cops found Karl-Heinz in a beer garden with his throat cut . . ."

Silence.

"Did you hear me, Cheese? The kid, my *source,* is dead."

Silence.

"Cheese?"

"Yes, I happen to know that, old man. But thanks all the same."

"How the hell?"

"The Cheese has his ways. Try to keep that in mind." He smiled to himself. "And I don't suppose he'd delivered the rest of SPARTAKUS before his untimely demise?" It was like a disease: the worse the situation got the more he wanted something to eat. A pizza. Pepperoni, meatball, some anchovies . . .

"If he had, *I* might've killed him. No, just kidding, Cheese. Ah, no, he didn't deliver any more of SPARTAKUS."

"So we don't know where it's going. Is that what you're telling me? *We just don't know?*"

"Now, Cheese, don't get your shorts all bunched up. I don't know. But I wonder sometimes, what do *you* know? Maybe you know and just aren't telling me. All I can say is, *I* don't know where SPARTAKUS is going. It has to be Wolf's lads who did the dirty."

"That's neither here nor there. I'm missing the last of SPARTAKUS."

"So, Wolf Koller—he must've found out about the SPARTAKUS leak. He must've found out it was the kid. And had him killed."

"Do you think Wolf knows the boy's father's role?"

"Don't ask me. I just work here."

"I'm beginning to think you're past it, Burke."

"Pardon me, but bullshit, old chap."

"And insubordinate, as well."

"So, call a cop."

Cheddar chuckled.

"And now I gotta go to this fucking rally, a bunch of Krauts all worked up about politics and persecution, my idea of a helluva good time. Wish you were here."

"Are you keeping an eye on the young Master?"

"Yeah. Little shit. I wish I didn't have to deal with him—it's like touching something wet and—"

"It sounds like you're in the middle of a Chinese fire drill. Try to safeguard our friend. We may still have uses for him."

"He's a guy I'd really like to kill. Those glasses, that fat face—"

"Well, don't. Not yet. And stop calling me and whining about your problems."

Cheddar felt the reverberations as the phone slammed down in his ear. He looked at his watch. He was expecting another call in fifteen minutes. Not really enough time to ease the pizza deprivation.

Sometimes Cheddar grew perplexed by his own motivations. He was supposed to be the spider at the center of his web, weaving the masterpiece, the one man who knew all the parts of the pattern. He wasn't always sure that he did. For instance, things had gotten so confused and fucked up with Wolf Koller and the Old Firm's policy toward Germany that Cheddar sometimes wondered if just possibly he wasn't outsmarting himself. Now that would be a hell of a thing . . . He wished U.S. policy toward Germany and the old balance of power could be a shade more overt. But then they wouldn't need Ned Cheddar.

What frustrated him was that he had created so much of SPARTAKUS himself.

I mean, it was my idea, damn it! If you come right down to it, I fucking created Wolf Koller! And now I'm in the dark . . . the son of a bitch has used my SPARTAKUS as a jumping-off place . . . My SPARTAKUS has turned into something else . . . His SPARTAKUS! Where is he jumping? Is there any water in the pool? Do I want water in the pool? Or do I want Wolf to do a brain-dive into a cement hole . . .

Alone with his own thoughts, Ned Cheddar wondered if Clint

Kilroy's shot had gone accidentally astray so that Wolf Koller was only wounded. Or had the wily old bastard done it on purpose? He had the feeling he'd never get a straight answer out of Kilroy.

Maybe it was for the best, having Wolf Koller alive. Or maybe for some inexplicable reason God—through his cherub Kilroy—had chosen to spare him . . .

The call from Clint Kilroy came through on schedule, fifteen minutes later. Cheddar ran through what Kilroy was supposed to know and what he couldn't be told. He had to jot down another list.

Clint Kilroy said: "Koller's still alive. He's going to be all right."

"But you did make an attempt to kill him?"

"I followed your orders."

"Did you shoot to wound or kill?"

"It was a terrible, wet, cold night. I sneezed."

"All right, all right," Cheddar said. He was impatient but he was trying hard not to let it bubble over. You had to be careful with artistic types. "What's he up to now?"

"Out at Wannsee with a houseful of guests, including some fucking Russian."

"That would be Konstantin Orlovski. Have you seen Sebastien the Red?"

"Seen him? We're living in and out of each other's pockets. He's part of Koller's Praetorian Guard . . . those who'll die for their leader."

"Men with nine lives, I'm beginning to think. Any more word on the last stages of SPARTAKUS?"

"Koller isn't telling me shit."

"He hasn't forgotten who you *are,* has he?"

"I don't reckon so, you fat—"

"Don't let him forget that you're a hero of his. And, Clint—"

"Yes? What? *What?*"

"Calm yourself."

"You're not over here in the middle of all this crap. Here I am, putting a slug in Koller, then turning up five minutes later acting like his faithful PR man in America. This operation is just about out of control, Fat Man . . . And what about Orlovski? He's got to be the messenger boy for somebody."

"I wouldn't be entirely surprised."

"The shit is gonna hit the fan for sure tonight. This rally's gonna be a ballbuster."

"Yes," Cheddar said softly. "What else?"

"Well, there's this goddamn Cooper all over the place. We never should've let him leave the States. You know, I've been wondering, Cheese—is he working for you, by any chance? Something you're not telling me?"

"Perish the thought. I'm the one who sent the unhappy couple to dissuade him from making the trip—remember?"

"You want him out of the way, then? I can do that. He's gonna gum up the works, I'm telling you."

"You're not suggesting that he be terminated, surely? Oh, Clint Kilroy, what are you saying?"

Cheddar began to chuckle. What tangled webs we weave, when first we practice to deceive . . .

The Professor had a cramp in his leg. The VW was not meant for long-term surveillance. It was the second night he'd waited outside the low-slung modern house at the edge of the lake. He wasn't at all sure why he was doing it: it was such a hit-and-miss proposition. He was quite sure that Orlovski and Sebastien were in residence; Orlovski had never left. Sebastien came and went but had been at home for some time. He'd seen Wolf Koller come out to greet the Chancellor. Fritz Gisevius had arrived with Sebastien. Clint Kilroy, whom he knew on sight, was also on hand. Lots of booze going in and empties coming out. Catering services. It was like a very fancy frat house party. Heading into the second night.

When darkness approached the house would light up, shadows would drift past windows, men would shimmer across the lawn and disappear in the shadows. Now the rain was beating down on the VW's roof and he felt very sleepy. A pair of limos had driven away, doubtless headed for the big rally at the Brandenburg Gate, which was probably just kicking off. He yawned. Sitting, waiting for them to come back, trying to get a feel for what Orlovski was doing in their company. He was surprised they hadn't spotted him. But the security seemed lax, as if it hadn't crossed their minds that they might need it now, in this place, at this time.

As was so often the case in this particular line of work, the moment he began thinking there was something wrong with the security, he heard the steps beside the VW and there was a pistol barrel tapping on the window. A flashlight was being shone in his face, obliterating the man behind it. He was yelling at him in German to get out, get out. He seemed not to be kidding. The pistol slammed into the window again and a crack traced its way across the surface.

The Professor opened the door slowly. "No need to be so rough." He planted one foot to lever himself out of the car.

"Out, please. What are you doing here?"

"I was pulled over intending to empty my bladder."

"Papers, please."

"You sound like an old movie, you should hear yourself. Papers? What papers? My driver's license? My passport? Who the hell do you think you are? I'm not going to show you a damn thing."

The muzzle of the gun swung low, pointing into his face. "Papers."

"Oh, for God's sake!" The Professor reached into the copious folds of his ancient Burberry. "I can't find my papers . . ." He was muttering and the guard leaned close, trying to hear more clearly.

"Hurry up!"

"Yeah, yeah, I'm hurrying . . ."

In the dark, with the flashlight pointed at the hand fumbling in the pocket, the guard didn't see what the other hand was doing. He might have looked over at just the last moment. But it was unlikely that he ever saw the gun with the long snout of silencer. The Professor shot him directly in the middle of his milky face. The man fell as if he'd been dropped in a lump from the sky. He slid in the wet, icy leaves like a bag of garbage and went about halfway under the car. He was dead before he hit the ground.

The Professor got back into the car and drove over the body, feeling the wheels slip in the leaves and bump across the dead guard, then rolled on down the street past the house. He left the lights off until he was well past. Then he started up the engine, flicked on the lights, curled around a few blocks, and pulled off into the hospital parking lot. Time to collect his thoughts.

Koller's people were going to find the body sooner rather than later. Somebody was bound to miss the guy. He wouldn't show up at check-in time and they'd go outside and look up and down the street and somebody would see him. He wondered if the flashlight was still turned on. Damn it! Why didn't he think of that? Maybe the guy was lying on it. Maybe he'd driven over it and crushed it. And maybe it was shining like a lighthouse welcoming the intrepid home from the sea.

They were going to find the guard and then there was going to be hell to pay. The whole Wolf Koller thing was like a poisonous cyst, working its way to the surface, the pressure building, the infection spreading through the body. He dropped the metaphor.

Well, he had something to do before it was too late. He checked his watch. Long drive coming up, and he didn't want to make it in the VW. He would have to take a pass on Orlovski.

Time to get a move on.

It was too bad about the guard.

Desperate men were capable of desperate measures. That was what his grandfather used to tell him, and he'd known for a long time just how true it was.

The cold mist blew in shimmering, shining sheets across the crowd of three hundred thousand gathered at the Brandenburg Gate. The spotlights caught the raindrops and reflected a million times from each one. It looked as if a giant, fragile, gossamer chandelier was swaying over the heads of the crowd. The lights poked and snooped at the crowd like the suggestion of a cattle prod, and when the light moved and tracked away across the mass of bodies, the bodies seemed to jump as if shocked. It reminded Cooper of a crowd he'd once been a part of at a Janis Joplin concert. They were there but they weren't altogether there: they were off in a solar system of their own where they thought they could be one with Janis, one with the emotions of the event. It was frightening.

Voices lumbered out of huge loudspeakers mounted on the backs of flatbed trucks, and way off to the left, down across the wasteland that was the Potsdamer Platz and barely in view, were the lights of the circus where he'd met Karl-Heinz. In the darkness between he couldn't make out the rise in the ground where the two men had served their time as sentinels. The German sounds coming from the loudspeakers—there was also a pair up on the stage that had been erected for the occasion below the massive sculpture of chariot and horses and the great goddess atop the Gate—assaulted his ears, the way the unintelligible sounds came at you from the hidden speakers in the New York subway. And the crowd was chanting, stomping their feet, waving their fists in the air, stretching away toward Unter den Linden and Alexanderplatz and the grayness that was old East Berlin.

The Mayor of Berlin was on the stage staring out through the rain and amid a bustle of bodyguards and aides the burly, dour Chancellor appeared from nowhere, suddenly there, his face a solemn, lined mask, heavy as a slab of beef. He was roughly the size of a telephone booth. At the moment he was shrouded in a black raincoat, standing bareheaded in the mist. He and the Mayor made eye contact, something passed between them, and then the Chancellor stepped to the back of the stage and reached down to help someone up the steps and onto the stage.

The man wore a camel-hair coat draped over his shoulders like an Italian movie star, or a gigolo for that matter, and one arm was in a sling. It was Wolf Koller, with Chancellor Glock grimacing in the rain as he helped Koller toward the center of the stage. It didn't seem to make much difference to the crowd that he was there but Beate caught Cooper's eye. "He's here for a purpose. He's being identified with the Chancellor and the Mayor. Whatever Wolf is up to, he needs the Chancellor—*that's* a change—" She was shouting over the crowd and her voice cracked. She was in constant danger of losing her camera crew in the throbbing mass of people.

Someone bumped into Cooper, knocking him sideways, and pushed on past. All Cooper saw of him was a dark green Barbour jacket and a tweed hat smashed down on his big square head. When he looked back he saw Beate's blond hair bobbing in the crowd, the bulk of a camera on one of the crew's shoulder, and then she was gone. He moved off in the direction he thought she'd gone, and for just an instant he was staring into a familiar face.

Joachim Stiffel. He had a pasty, pudgy face with puffy bags under his eyes, wire-rimmed glasses, and he wore one of the armbands with the insignia that looked like a swastika but wasn't, and several of his followers were milling around him. He was shouting at someone, turning, twisting, looking for someone with a tinge of panic in his voice.

This was supposed to be a crowd protesting against Stiffel and the violence, but in the end it was just another gigantic mob. He had created the mob to a large degree, but now that he was among them, he didn't look overly enthusiastic about it. The noise was deafening, there was some kind of martial music blaring from the huge speakers, and Cooper was being swept away, past Stiffel in his black leather jacket with his armband, past his own private guard of toughs, past everything that was gathering like a storm threatening to break over Berlin . . .

Burke Delaney, having damn near knocked over some joker who looked like a lost soul, couldn't hear himself think, for chrissakes, what with the music—whose idea was that? fucking Goebbels?—and the drunken teenagers and the druggies and the pushers and the soldiers and the cops and the displaced flea marketers who wondered what the hell was going on that was so important that the flea market had to close down. Cheese ought to see what he was up against in a zoo like this. That'd serve the fat bastard right . . . There were a few hundred supporters all around Stiffel but he, Burke Delaney, was the minder insofar as the Cheese was concerned, Stiffel was Burke Delaney's responsibility although only he and Stiffel knew it, and the Cheese ought to get his butt over here in this crowd and try to fucking protect somebody! Jesus! He saw Stiffel up ahead but Delaney was being swept away by an undercurrent running through the crowd, like one of those undertows he used to find off the coast near Malibu, and he set off, struggling against the crowd, trying to get close enough to keep an eye on his miserable Kraut asshole . . . He looked up at the stage, which seemed to be about three blocks away . . . was that Wolf Koller up there? What was he doing with the Chancellor? Aw, why did he even give a shit? . . . Burke Delaney was a foot soldier, he left the strategy to the desk jockeys . . . but where the hell was Stiffel? Ah, there he was . . . somebody was bellowing through the loudspeakers and he couldn't make out a fucking word and from the looks of what was going on around him neither could anybody else . . .

He was looking up at the stage again, trying to figure out what was going on, why people were cheering and shouting and clapping now, why the Chancellor was waving at the sea of people, and when Burke Delaney looked back for Stiffel it was too late . . . the attack had come from behind, now they were all being pushed toward the stage and it wasn't three blocks after all, it was close as hell, a man who had seemed totally out of place in the crowd, a man almost his own age, stepping forward out of the crowd and moving close to Stiffel, and a riot was breaking out and people were charging the stage and the beast, the crowd, was screaming, and a huge speaker toppled off the stage into the crowd and helmeted riot police were suddenly forming a human wall, shields up, between the people and the Chancellor, people were swinging clubs all of a sudden and Delaney felt blood spraying across his face and yes, he was

2

too old for this crap, but it was fun in its own silly way, and he saw some cops knocked down meaning there'd be hell to pay and sirens were going off and the huge spotlights were pouring down like boiling oil on the center of the fighting, turning everybody ghostly white, and people were holding flickering candles, there were always stupid shits with candles in the crowd as if they were about to join a holy procession, these people were dropping the candles and burning themselves and others and you could smell the candle smoke and then there was the inevitable woman with her hair on fire because she had so much hairspray on and she was going up like a rocket, you could always count on the woman with the burning hair, maybe she went from riot to riot all over the world, and people were trying to throw coats over her head and God it was a mess and people were crying, nightmares came to life so quick you couldn't quite hold them down, they just happened and then everybody was covered with shit before you knew it, and Delaney was struggling to keep his feet, you didn't want to leave your feet in a crowd of this magnitude, that was a no-no, but he was feeling his age which was about 112 and then he was going down and he grabbed some big guy but got pushed away and suddenly he was down and ready to be trampled to death, figuring that there were worse ways to die, a helluva lot worse, and he tried to crawl across another body on the ground and holy shit, it was Stiffel, oh crap, Stiffel, and he wasn't moving and the crowd was sort of making a space around them, the Berliners were so goddamn civilized sometimes, the real Berliners, and he turned Stiffel over on his back and his eyes were open and they had that look, they were seeing some shows that weren't listed, and Delaney bent down close and was whispering in his ear when he noticed the bullet hole right below his ear, a small hole, very professional, an execution in a crowd, harder to do than you might expect, it was murders in crowds that were comparatively easy, not this neat kind of an execution, and the lights were playing across him and he was kneeling beside the corpse saying you little Nazi fuck, you little Nazi bastard queer, you weren't supposed to die, asshole, you stupid little Nazi piss-pot, the Cheese is gonna blame this all on me . . . He looked up and there was a man watching him, looking down at him, and it was the man who hadn't belonged in the picture a few moments before, the guy with the Tyrolean hat with the feather in the band who looked like he should have been attending the monthly meeting of his Oompah Band, it was Gunter Kohlberg, big old turdface Gunter Kohlberg, but Gunter had been killed in that messy business in the U-Bahn when he was shepherd-ing the cipher clerk who decided life in the West was the answer to the biggest puzzle of all, but here he was, Gunter, another of the army of the dead, Meinhold and Sebastien and now Gunter whose idea of a big joke was to light his farts with a match, Gunter was looking down at him and the bullet hole beneath Stiffel's ear was Gunter's doing, he was fucking winking at Delaney!, he was mouthing something, saying something and winking, and then moving away in the crowd and Delaney was trying to struggle to his feet but he couldn't, he was fucking glad not to have been trampled to death, and the crowd took him with them, the crowd was surging over Stiffel's body, and at the end Joachim Stiffel was a man consumed by the same monster he'd created which was one of those poetic moments you'd miss if you weren't paying attention . . .

The man and the woman wore rough woven bags over their heads, tied tightly at the throat with ropes. Their hands were tied behind their backs. They stumbled as they were pushed across the cinder driveway and parking lot toward a long gray warehouse. There was a constant low rumble of sound, a moaning of some kind of machinery, coming from behind the concrete walls of the warehouse. Three men were pushing and pulling at the two wearing the bags. The captives said nothing and the others spoke in whispers and seldom. They left the ten-year-old Cadillac Sedan de Ville parked in the shadows of a long shed. There were only two lights on poles casting shadows across the cinders and the lights of Berlin seemed far away, tinting the black sky at the horizon. The small door, almost unnoticed in comparison to the great sliding doors where the trucks went in and out, swung open and the woman tripped over the sill, fell to her knees with a grunt. Then she began to sob, whatever words she was speaking muffled by the gags beneath the hoods. The hooded man turned helplessly, trying to find her, and he was yanked back, pushed ahead. The woman was helped to her feet, shoved forward.

The noise inside the warehouse was loud and insistent, like the growling of a giant. The woman turned again, fell to her knees. One of the men swore and looked at the apparent leader. The leader inclined his head, nodded. The room was empty of people. Trucks lined up in rows, dwarfed by the surprising height of the building, its vast width and length. It was a waste-disposal plant, immense compacting machines making the low rumble as they turned tons of rubbish into small packets. The trucks brought the trash in, the compactors mashed it into cubes, other trucks took it away.

The woman was on her knees, shaking with her crying. Once the leader nodded, the man standing over her took a pistol from his pocket, held it to the back of her head, and fired. She flopped forward, the sound of the shot lost in the cascading rumble. Her body jerked and flopped around for a few seconds. Then she lay still. He lifted the body onto a rolling cart.

The hooded man turned, struggling to ask a question but unable to speak. He was whirling like a madman, the frustration of his situation causing his brain to slip its moorings—knowing his life was over, knowing his wife was also bound to die but not knowing, perhaps, that she was already dead. With his hands tied and unable to see, he quickly lost his balance and fell heavily to the oil-stained cement floor. The smell of oil, of the trash, of the hydraulic machines was faintly nauseating.

The man lay on the ground, his body convulsing, quite possibly choking on his tongue.

The leader made a sour face and took his own gun from the pocket of his trenchcoat and put a single bullet into the back of the man's head.

He gestured to the third man to hoist the body up onto the same cart.

With both bodies flung across the cart they moved to one of the huge compactors and succeeded in feeding them into the massive jaws. The jaws closed. The three men glanced around to make sure they'd left nothing behind. Then they went back outside into the cold rain. They climbed into the Cadillac and drove off down the empty street.

34

ERIKA

Once she returned from Bayreuth—dazed, in a kind of shock, but driven by anger and hatred and frustration, unaware of her own identity—Erika Koller got the message on the machine from Beate. Karl-Heinz murdered, dumped in a beer garden with his throat cut. For a period of several hours she walked among the trees, staring out across the mountain valley, seeing nothing, and boiled over with tears and rage and regret and sorrow until she was finally exhausted. Then she went inside, dragged herself to a couch in the main room before the fire, and sank into oblivion.

And in oblivion she found salvation.

When she awoke, the fire had long since died and lay coldly before her like the ashes of her own previous life. She was beginning anew. She had slept sixteen hours. And now she was ready to go to war. Her father ought to be proud of her. A Teuton, a Hun, at last . . .

After Beate's friend, the medical student, had stitched her wrists, Beate had taken her to the two-story apartment in Kreuzberg and put her to bed. When she awoke, they went to work changing her appearance. Conspiring like a couple of children. Erika was dark, her eyes smoldered, though in her relative innocence she didn't really know it: she was tall and slim and people often took her for a professional model or possibly an actress. Everything had to change.

"You're not just another girl walking down the street now," Beate had said, taking charge. "You're Erika Koller and your father is going to have half of Germany looking for you. You must disappear. We start this way . . ."

Within a few hours she was a blond with punky hair. Different eyeshadow, different eyelashes, thick applications of eyeliner, different lip color and a slightly altered shape to her mouth. Different clothes: leather pants, a turtleneck, a motorcycle jacket. It wasn't just a case of changing the look: they changed the kind of person she was. Given the chance, her own mother and father might not have recognized her.

The medical student had stopped by, checked on the bandages and wounds, complimented Erika on the cleanness of the cuts. When he left he gave her pills for sleeping, pills for staying awake, pills for pain. Then Beate packed a bag and gave her some money, and they drove into the countryside, where Beate stopped. Beate told her her destination, gave her the keys to a car she'd find there, made sure she understood the directions, took her to a train station for the rest of the journey, and kissed her goodbye.

The Hubermann family had a cottage in the Bavarian Alps, in the shadow of the snowcapped Watzmann near Austria. The closest town of any size was Berchtesgaden with its steeples and turrets and mountain ways and its memories of Hitler and his country home.

That first morning, she got out of bed to a vista of sun gleaming on the virginal mountaintop, which shone like crystal. From the porch overlooking the valley, she could scan the east face of the Watzmann, all the way down into the perfect lake, reflecting the mountain and the drifting clouds. Edging Lake Königssee was the village of St. Bartholomä. She could see the odd rooftop through the heavily forested mountainside stretching down below the schloss. She felt as if none of it was quite real, as if she were still safe within some sort of dream. Maybe this was the afterlife, cool and clear and very beautiful . . . But no, she knew she was alive, knew it was real, when she looked into the mirror at her new self. They'd never let her into heaven looking like this . . .

She refused to think about why she had tried to kill herself. She couldn't give in to it again. She couldn't let it matter so much. She would do the best she could. But she kept thinking of her mother; she hated not telling her where she was, that she was all right, but she had to have time, she had to pull herself together and think it through . . . God, what a mess! And what must Karl-Heinz be thinking? But if Beate told him her whereabouts he'd come after her, which was precisely what she didn't want, so he'd just have to stew a bit . . .

And she had to face all the things Karl-Heinz had told her. About her father. About this thing called SPARTAKUS. Could it really be happening? Or was it some crazy dream Karl-Heinz had had? Could he have understood it all properly? And what had he meant when he told her he had something else to tell her, something about the Warmolts Clinic in Bayreuth and her mother's nervous breakdown . . .

The cottage was really rather elaborate with its carvings and finishing touches and comforts. It had once belonged to Beate's great-grandparents. Her great-grandfather had been a military advisor to Kaiser Wilhelm in the Great War, now called World War I. The cottage still seemed suffused with his personality. A portrait of him hung in the long hallway, which served as a balcony above the main room. He was wearing his spiked helmet and many decorations, and with his piercing blue eyes and stiff gray mustache he looked like a god of war. At least that was Erika's view. She had no grasp of that kind of militarism, the impulse or need or obsession with destruction that was the history of the tribes of Europe, her own tribe foremost.

In a cabinet in one of the bedrooms behind glass doors was the very same spiked helmet, as well as a variety of mementos related to the old man. There was also a photograph of Beate's grandfather as a young soldier in the First War and of her father as a boy, regarding his father and grandfather with considerable awe and pride. Father and son were holding up the banner of some forgotten regiment.

She drove into town and picked up provisions, coffee and bread and sausage and meat and spaghetti and tomatoes, whatever she could think of, whatever made her hungry. She prepared a simple dinner and lit a fire and kept the door at the front of the house open to help air it out. There was a powerful scent of clean evergreens and the smell of water rising up from the Königsee. She ate and read a newspaper she got at a stand in the town. As yet, there was nothing about her disappearance, and she could imagine her father working on it privately, wanting to keep everything out of the press.

Later in the evening, with darkness complete and only the night sounds of the forest to keep her company, she decided it was time to write some reflections on her suicide attempt. In her heart writing was what she wanted to do as a career, though she'd never really admitted it to anyone. Now, if she didn't have something to say to herself about the act of self-murder and her rescue—well, then she wasn't much of a writer.

She went to the large, very old rolltop desk and opened it, looking for pen and paper. There was a notebook in view but no pen and ink. She pulled the drawers open and found a fountain pen. Ink, ink . . . She was making her way through all the collected junk, pencils and clips and rubber bands and scraps of this and that, when she found a Luger pistol and a box of shells, untouched for years. She shivered uncontrollably, dropped the pistol on the desktop as if it were a huge insect, as if it could hurt her.

Beneath it in the drawer was a framed photograph of three men, faded, put away long ago and forgotten. Two young men and a young priest wearing his collar. They stood with their arms flung over each other's shoulders, grinning like kids in party dress. The men on either side of the priest wore the dress uniform of the SS.

She slammed the drawer shut, went out onto the porch, stood staring at the night, at the mountain.

This was Hitler country. Every German knew that. The Eagle's Nest. Berchtesgaden. Obersalzberg. The Berghof Hitler had acquired after reaching power in 1934. He'd put Martin Bormann in charge of its growth, watching it attain ever larger proportions. Hitler. The Lonely Man of Berchtesgaden.

She hugged herself against the cold night. She felt a faint mist on her face.

She felt dead at the center.

Now she looked back on her first day on the mountain as a time of unspoiled innocence, however upsetting it had been then. Now she knew so much more, had thought so much more, had truly hardened her heart . . .

She had purchased a video camera in Bayreuth. She had thought long and hard about how she would use it. She had found out from Beate how things stood in Berlin. She had heard about what an unusual man her uncle John Cooper was . . . He sounded like a bit of a maniac but she knew her mother's life had been turned inside out by him, that the power of his emotions had changed her forever. Erika knew that her mother had never quite gotten over, or gotten past, her one meeting with her brother, John Cooper. And now, Erika wondered, what was Cooper's reappearance going to do to her, sick and fragile as she was? Lise was her mother, would always be her mother, though Erika now knew that another woman had given birth to her . . .

It was all Wolf. All Wolf's responsibility, all of it.

And now she was going to make him pay up, pay for this, pay for his whole life. In the end somebody always presented the bill. In Wolf Koller's case it was going to be his daughter.

She looked into the camera on its tripod. She flicked the timer switch.

And she began to talk.

IV

35

THE LONGEST NIGHT

They took turns behind the wheel every hour or so, leaving Berlin behind and heading out through what had been East Germany and into the old West Germany, all shrouded in the thick darkness of midnight. Beate knew the best route. She'd driven it many times before, heading for the seclusion of the mountain lodge that had been in the family for so many years. Being a more practical creature than Erika, she wasn't bothered by the Nazi past of her family—and therefore of the lodge itself. A house didn't soak up the failings of its owners. Which was what she had told Cooper when he asked her about the place. A house was just a house, and this one had a beautiful view across the mountain valley to the snowy Watzmann near the Austrian border. And it didn't make her think of Hitler or Göring or any of the rest of them. All that was Erika's kind of problem. What mattered now was why Erika hadn't answered the telephone when they'd called from TV Center, where Beate was dropping off her tape of the rally at the Brandenburg Gate.

Out of the night headlights drifted toward them, then whipped past, and the darkness descended all around them once again. Occasionally red taillights flared ahead, faded away or were passed. It was like floating through an endless night in space. There were Beethoven and Bach on the radio, and past the slightly open windows the night was crisp and cold.

Why hadn't Erika answered the phone? Was she still at the house?

If not, where would she have gone in the middle of the night? Or had she been found? Had someone else pulled a Paulus, found an angle and traced it all the way to the mountains, to the house, to Erika Koller? And at the back of his mind, Cooper wondered if Werner Paulus was quite the white knight on a charger he appeared to be. When it came to that, what did he know about Werner Paulus except hearsay? It was Berlin, what did he know about the workings of Berlin? Nothing.

Cooper was still bothered by the fact that Beate hadn't told him about Erika's hiding place—and therefore her safety—much sooner. When he brought it up again she snapped at him, told him he was going to have to get used to it, and anyway he knew now so why didn't he just drop it.

"But if anything has happened to her," he said, "you're going to bear some of the responsibility. If you'd told me—"

"I'm the one who found her a place to be safe," she said. "I'm the one who helped her, hid her. I'm the one who's been protecting her from the rest of the world. I'm not likely to accept any guilt you throw my way. If you hadn't come to Berlin . . . well, who knows, nobody was getting killed before you got here. Draw your own conclusions."

"Stupid, irritating Kraut!"

"*Dumkopf!* Insensitive, violent Yank—for God's sake, you actually killed somebody!"

"And therefore *you* are alive. Maybe I did make a mistake. Rock and roll, rock and roll."

"Idiot!" But she had started to laugh.

Later, they heard yet another radio report concerning the death of Joachim Stiffel, leader of the neo-Nazi movement, at the Brandenburg Gate rally. Many people had been trampled and injured during the rally but there had been only the one death. And that had been by gunshot. The police were saying nothing more. Clearly, Berlin was rife with speculation. Was it an accident, a gun going off in a crowd? Not likely. It was a perfect execution wound. Who was responsible? Was it a power struggle among the leader and his followers? Was it a member of the anti-Stiffel public who'd had enough, who'd been overcome by the memories of the Holocaust and the implications of his movement? Was it one of the immigrants exacting revenge for the killing of the infant the previous week, the bombing of the hostel, the deaths of others?

Beate had been lucky. She'd been close enough to the discovery of Stiffel's body to get in, get some tape, get some interviews with others who'd seen the dead Nazi at their feet. One middle-aged man had said something to the effect that only the good die young, that Stiffel and his followers were the only thing standing between Germany and the hordes of "Third World rabble, the diseased and the criminals. Watch, AIDS will be everywhere and it will start with the foreigners, not the Germans!" A much younger man had laughed at the thought of a dead Stiffel, had said: "He was a creep, you know? He got just what he deserved . . . everything he did was built on hate." A woman in a fur coat, looking out of place at the rally, was crying. When Beate moved in to ask why, she got the most unexpected answer of the evening. "I'm crying because Putzi, my dachshund, was killed by a hit-and-run driver this afternoon—I saw him drive away, I just know he was a Nazi!" "But what about Stiffel? He's been shot—" "Who cares? Putzi was my best friend in the world, the only person I could trust." Beate was beaming. It was perfect. The human comedy. "So why are you here?" But the woman just waved her away, then turned: "Because every patriot in Germany should be here. We must pray for the Fatherland."

Chancellor Glock had spoken to the crowd demanding a return to peace . . . or there would be war! Well, the possibility of martial law in Berlin, anyway, and then, the good burghers of Berlin would discover how peace and lawfulness could be imposed . . . The streets would be made safe again for everyone, good Germans would see that their government cared for them . . . The crowd raved its approval. It was past time for arguing and his fist pummeled the podium, the blows ringing out across the crowd like the beating of a huge drum. Glock was not given to flights of oratory, and there had been desultory booing and shouting and applause. But the threat was clear. He might not be exciting but he tended to be a man who believed in his threats. When he said Germany needed a return to discipline everyone knew he had the power to make it stick.

Wolf Koller had spoken too and the crowd sensed that here was their charismatic leader. They knew Glock was his surrogate. They knew Koller was the man from whom Glock derived so much of his strength: a vote for one was a vote for the other. Standing on the stage high above the crowd, making a rare appearance in such a public setting, Wolf Koller looked like a younger version of Herbert von Karajan and he conducted the immense gathering as the maestro might have handled the Berlin Philharmonic. There was a grace in his movements and words, a sense that what he said somehow represented the German soul, that he was reaching into the wellspring and bringing out the elixir of their very being. He exhorted his fellow Germans to live up to their heritage of discipline and self-control and steel, to change Germany through legal means rather than by taking to the streets, to work for a better Germany . . . a Germany truly for the *Volk,* for the real Germans . . . a Germany that was a beacon of sanity which could cast its light into every dark corner of Europe so that other nations would learn from its example —instead of sending their sons and daughters to be cared for by an economically strained Fatherland. The hope of Germany should first be for Germans . . . And that great Germany was just within reach . . . A Germany, he declared portentously, that might be just around the corner . . .

And yet, if Werner Paulus was correct, Wolf Koller was responsible for the chaos, the violence, that he now demanded must end. If Paulus was correct.

As the long drive through the night passed the halfway point, Beate tensed herself to bring up the subject of Lee to Cooper. It was bothering her, the idea of his being so involved with his sister. It wasn't healthy, she thought, it wasn't right or natural . . . She wanted to know what was really going on between them, and the cover of darkness provided the best time to ask.

"You must realize, Beate, that her being my sister is just a coincidence. She was a stranger to me. I have almost no memory of her as a child. She went to England with my parents when she was tiny . . . they were caught there during the opening rounds of the war."

"Well, what are you going to do about her?"

"I'm afraid she's going to die. Then I won't have to do anything about her. Then I'll have to do something about me."

"Do what about you? You don't mean you'd kill yourself or something stupid like that?"

"I suppose I'm too cowardly for that. But I don't know if, or how, I'll be able to handle losing her twice in one lifetime. If I lose her again, I'll . . . well, there's no point in thinking about all that now, is there?"

"So, do you still want her to come back to Boston with you?"

He thought in silence for a moment, then said: "Maybe she'd refuse again. And then where would I be?"

"She'd have to be crazy to do that."

"I once had a great friend who thought she was nuts. He called her 'crazypants.' Maybe he was right. I just don't want her to die now, not after all this."

"No, no, no! Look at all you've gone through for her. Twice. It *is* a fairy tale. You've come back a second time, she's no longer young and you're not quite the brave boy you once were, and you still want her. You won't give up. It's a female fantasy, John. Undying love . . . She's found a man who is eternally in love with her."

Later another radio report, this time the BBC World Service, caught their attention. A parliamentary crisis was looming in Moscow. The anti-Yeltsin forces were coalescing around the old KGB man, Rossovich, who had found new life and a popular appeal as an MP. He was calling for Yeltsin's resignation and had delivered his most extreme speech yet, blistering Yeltsin for failing the new Russia on every economic and political front. Now Rossovich was urging the expulsion of "non-Russians, people who have never shared our culture or our values," which meant he was once again playing on the ancient anti-Semitism other dictators had encouraged and used. He was calling for a return to military greatness, hegemony over all that had until so recently been the USSR, as well as a return to expansionism—particularly the partitioning of Eastern Europe into spheres of influence, beginning with the cutting up of Poland and Czechoslovakia by Russia and Germany. Peace would be imposed on the charnel house of what had once been Yugoslavia. And, as a final stroke, he exhorted his followers to demand the return of Alaska to its rightful owner, Mother Russia.

The cultured tones of the BBC announcer stopped for a momentary pregnant pause, presumably of disbelief, and then said, "Mr. Yeltsin has responded to Mr. Rossovich's remarks by saying that Mr. Rossovich is entitled to his point of view, however provocative cooler heads throughout the world might find it. He went on to remind his questioners that in Russia free speech is a newly valued freedom and Mr. Rossovich must certainly be given the right to air his views. Curiously," the BBC man continued, "Mr. Yeltsin, who controls access to state-controlled television, allowed the showing of a two-hour biography of Mr. Rossovich last night, a program adulatory and totally sympathetic to the former KGB director. Mr. Yeltsin's motives in this matter have occasioned a good deal of confusion in journalistic and governmental circles. There has been no official reaction from Washington as yet but Admiral O. Z. Chapman, the national security advisor, did remark to a CBS reporter that it sounded "like Yeltsin has got himself a new Hitler-wannabe on his hands."

The sky was lightening to a glowering gray. The road was virtually empty and their eyes locked. "New Hitler?" he said.

"It always comes out of economics, doesn't it? Hard times in

Russia, losing the Cold War . . . and a fascist comes out of the wood-work—"

"Not exactly out of the woodwork," he said. "I mean, Rossovich is far from a mystery man. He's been hanging around the corridors of power a long time—"

"You'd think they'd turn to someone new with fresh, progressive ideas, not somebody who starts out with anti-Semitism and going to war! Politicians make me furious! So stupid! They understand nothing—"

"You're right. The stupidest thing on God's earth is the politician who still thinks going to war is the cure for anything. Of course, this guy's just talking—isn't he? I think the Alaska thing is just to get everyone's attention."

"What bothers me," she said, "is that photograph we saw in Bruni's office. The one with Rossovich in his wheelchair and Wolf Koller leaning down talking to him—I wish they didn't know each other . . . *How well do they know each other?*" It was a question they couldn't answer.

Cooper nodded. "We've got Wolf and Kilroy. We've got Wolf and the Chancellor. We've got Wolf and Gisevius. We've got Wolf and Stiffel. What do they all have in common? What brings them together? Who *killed* Stiffel? We're assuming Wolf saw to the murder of Karl-Heinz . . . It makes my brain hurt."

Beate looked at her watch. "We'll be there in less than an hour. Maybe we'll start getting some answers."

The huge Daimler-Benz limousine moved away like a Stealth bomber, heavy and black and almost invisible, insulating the two passengers from the rabble beyond. The Brandenburg Gate grew small through the one-way glass in the rear of the passenger compartment. The ventilation system made a very timid sound, or was that just the whispering of the tires? It was soft and dark and leathery within, an environment chosen to induce calm, but in the present instance the environment had failed miserably. The tension poured from Wolf Koller like a kind of poison.

Koller sat in the middle of the deep leather seat, Dr. Gisevius watching him from the facing jump seat. Behind them in a second limousine were Chancellor Glock, Konstantin Orlovski, and Clint Kilroy. Orlovski looked at his gold Rolex in the hope of finding a friendly face. Clint Kilroy sat next to Orlovski wondering what he'd ever done to deserve this much concentrated bullshit. The silence was oppressive, as if no one was willing to let the others hear his thoughts.

Kilroy looked around at the faces cast in unhealthy shadows by the dim side lamps. The Chancellor seemed sunk in a sodden depression: he was perspiring profusely; his face was gray and deeply lined and he looked, all in all, like a man about to suffer a major turd-floater of a coronary. Orlovski looked like a sybaritic ex-Red who was longing for the good old days in Dzerzhinsky Square, a few hours of nail-pulling followed by a vodka oblivion. It was enough to make Kilroy wish he'd drilled Koller in the heart that night and saved everybody all the aggravation. Shit, life was too short for all this. He wondered what was going through Koller's mind in the lead car. Kilroy thought things were beginning to get to Wolf. He reckoned he saw the first cracks in the facade of Wolf's perfect grasp of power and it made him nervous. Wolf wasn't used to improvising. Kilroy sat back, having no desire to make conversation with any of his limo mates.

Up ahead Wolf Koller was on the phone. "Herr Stiffel died instantly, I take it?" He listened attentively. "The killer escaped unnoticed. Well done. I presume Stiffel had a mother somewhere? Get some money to her, anonymously, for a modest funeral. I doubt if his fellow neo-Nazis are generous in such matters. And God knows, he served our purposes." He listened again, said once more: "Well done." He clicked the phone off, stared out the window into the blur of lights behind the tinted glass. The rain was spitting all over the limo. He was waiting for another call.

When it came he answered quickly: "Yes?"

The man on the other end said: "Herr Schmidt's researches into your daughter's whereabouts have borne fruit. He used your idea about checking on Beate Hubermann's family place." Wolf Koller had once heard Erika talking about a wonderful mountain place in Bavaria where the Hubermanns took holidays. Near Berchtesgaden. He'd told Schmidt, and the security director had tracked it down. He'd discovered that a woman who didn't look much like Erika was in residence—she could, however, be Erika in disguise. The house or lodge was referred to by the neighbors as Schloss Adler in a joking reference to the proximity to Hitler's Eagle's Nest.

The voice on the phone said: "Shall we continue?"

"Yes. Use the jet. It's all a question of time now. You have your orders. No variations, no inspirations. Follow your orders to the letter." It would have been so much simpler if she hadn't sent him the postcards, the threats. But it was too late to worry about that now. She knew about

SPARTAKUS. That was all that mattered. "Tell me, how is Security Director Schmidt feeling?"

"Not at all well, sir."

"I fear for his survival," Wolf Koller said.

"I think he's beyond help, sir."

"A tragedy. And his wife?"

"She is no better than he, sir."

"Shocking. A whole family wiped out and no one but themselves to blame." There was no hint of sympathy in Koller's voice. Once his men had broken Karl-Heinz and Koller had learned about the bugging of the secret flat, he knew they all had to die. But first he had to make sure Bernd Schmidt had tracked Erika to earth. Then Koller had let fate run its course and the Family Schmidt was no more.

The two limousines slid onward through the blowing mist. In the second Kilroy was smoking a cheroot, trying to put himself in Ned Cheddar's shoes, trying to think it through because, while the fat man was safe in Georgetown, he might find his ass in a wringer at any damn moment. Something had to be done about Cooper. And there was Lise Koller. When Cooper came nosing around he'd been told that she'd been taken to a private hospital. Not which one, of course. But what were they going to do with her? How was it going to end? Cooper . . . he just didn't seem to get the idea that he was supposed to go home. He'd refused to take Koller's advice. Maybe John Cooper had Wolf Koller's number somewhere in some cosmic game of chance. Clint Kilroy couldn't think of anything scarier than that.

Chancellor Glock was watching Kilroy from beneath heavy lids. He spent a good deal of time thinking about Wolf Koller, how his mind worked and what he really wanted from SPARTAKUS. Though large and forceful in appearance, the Chancellor was politically timid: he made no bones about it to himself, he didn't know what exactly it was that he wanted. Which was why he needed Wolf Koller: to point the way to greatness, to German destiny. But now, with SPARTAKUS, Chancellor Glock was losing his nerve. Using back channels to send chemicals to Saddam Hussein, joining with the Israelis in arranging more arms for Iran were just good business—but SPARTAKUS was too big. It took a man like Wolf Koller even to imagine something like SPARTAKUS. But the risks were so huge . . . What would the Americans do? What would the whole world do? And, on a more mundane level, what was Kilroy's role here? There was something in the relationship between Kilroy and Koller that lingered just beyond the edge of Chancellor Glock's comprehension. The Chancellor had tried to figure out Kilroy's role and given up without success. No one else seemed to be able to speak quite so bluntly, or with such an edge, to Koller. Kilroy alone seemed unafraid of him. So, what was his part in SPARTAKUS? And was Wolf's master plan going to work? For the first time, Chancellor Glock was not merely envious of the respect with which Wolf Koller was treated—he was afraid he might be associated with a disaster. If SPARTAKUS came to grief . . .

In the first car Dr. Gisevius leaned forward, forcing himself into Wolf Koller's consciousness. "I don't know who John Cooper thinks he is. He just bullies his way into the situation . . . What are we going to do with him? We can't ignore him, he's in the equation. And he keeps forcing himself on us—"

"You're right," Koller mused with his fingers pressed to his lips. "He wouldn't stop twenty years ago and he won't stop now. He hasn't learned a bloody thing, I'm afraid. I wish he weren't mixed up with this insufferable Beate Hubermann. She's a troublemaker, my people at German TV tell me she's a far leftist. She sees herself as a crusader for everything from the Greens to women's rights. And now she's got hold of Cooper, and who knows what kind of filth she's filling him with . . . she's full of hate, she hates anyone who steps up and takes action, that automatically makes them fascists in her mind . . . she helped corrupt my daughter, she and that offensive swine Karl-Heinz Schmidt . . . now all the Schmidts have paid for their treachery." Koller was brooding, staring out into the night, fingers tapping on his lips, his voice failing to reflect the emotion in his words. He was running through options in his mind. "I can't let these people destroy the work of a lifetime. I can't let them wreck my family. For all I know they're behind this attempt on my life!" The emotion blazed up, as if a stone had been pitched into glowing embers. With one arm in a sling and a soft cast, he rapped the hand on his good side against the window, a large signet ring clattering against the glass. His disgust had boiled over. "I am trying to help create the true New World Order. The Americans understand nothing. That nincompoop George Bush—and Clinton is no better. Everything begins and ends in Europe. It is Europe's destiny to set the agenda and carry it out and stand at its center . . . and I understand that. I look to the future and I see Germany's role . . . Even the Chancellor understands it. And entirely negligible people—like Cooper and his German girlfriend and, God help me, my daughter—cannot be allowed to wreck it. They must be stopped. We are right on the edge of the greatness . . . what failed fifty years ago and what was killed in the bud twenty years ago will not fail again. And now, like a test, Fate has placed this fool Cooper—"

Gisevius interrupted: "*Fool* is not the right word, Wolf. Try *Nemesis*. That's closer. Fate put him here twenty years ago, too."

"He's in our path. He must be removed . . ."

Gisevius said: "Calm yourself, Wolf. You have a fever. There's a touch of infection in your wound and the antibiotics haven't knocked it out yet. You've got to keep yourself from getting all worked up. We need you—*Germany* needs you—at full strength now."

"Cooper, my wife, my daughter . . ." Koller was whispering, almost as if it were an incantation of some kind. "The Chancellor is weakening, he's jealous, he's a coward . . . I don't trust him, Fritz. What if there are several leaks within our organization—"

"Impossible. Don't dwell on the impossible. There's no point in being paranoid. Remember, Cooper didn't come here to get you . . . he came here for his sister—"

"Yes, and last time he came for his sister, too—"

"No, last time he came to avenge the murder of his brother! *This* time he's come for his sister—you can end the Cooper problem and the problem of Lise in one stroke. You can do it tonight . . . Bring Lise to Wannsee. Tonight. No one would know she was there . . . why can't she simply die there? Tonight . . . Think of the public sympathy, think of the release for her, for us all, an end to suffering—"

"No, no, that won't do. I want her to die with dignity. I want her to die with a view of the mountains, the cold clean snow and the sunshine, like the welcome of God. I want her to slip away with the Elgar cello piece playing, the mountains slowly fading from her view. That is the way it must be."

Gisevius sighed, leaned back against the leather. "They'll die together, then. Rafaela and Lise. Your two women." He sighed again, murmuring almost to himself. "The women of Wolf Koller . . ."

"It's as it should be, Fritz. Try to understand, my old friend."

"I do, I understand."

"And there is the third woman," Koller said. He held out his hand to Gisevius. In the palm were two postcards. One with Kirk Douglas ready to do battle, the other with the faces of Douglas, Jean Simmons, Laurence Olivier, Peter Ustinov, Charles Laughton, and Tony Curtis, the stars of *Spartacus*.

"Read them," Koller ordered. "Aloud."

" 'The world will know the truth in days. Now I must know another truth. I am on my way, like an arrow.' "

Koller spoke from the shadows. "She knows. Erika knows everything. She's going to use it against me."

Gisevius was at a loss for words.

She had finished the videotaping. It had taken almost two hours to get it right, even reading from the script she'd written, and her hands were damp and trembling. She took the script and threw it into the fireplace and lit it. Then she sat down in the deep armchair and began planning what to do next. She had sent the postcards to her father. He was warned, though she had no idea if he'd realize they had come from her. She found his insensitivity indescribably profound at times. But he was warned. He'd be sick with worry now. He was dealing with being shot. She wanted to add to his problems, overwhelm him. And in some ways he was defenseless. Against the sniper. Against his daughter. As long as he couldn't find her. And now she was almost through with hiding . . .

And then she heard the sound of a car coming up the narrow rutted path from the road that clung to the mountainside. The headlights felt their way through the evening's ground fog. Her heart nearly stopped, then broke into a sprint. Had they found her, was it all over?

There was no way to fight them off . . . She thought of the Luger in the drawer, the cartridges, but she was shaking, there wasn't time . . . There was nothing to do but brazen it out, play the innocent, the troubled girl who had no idea she'd caused such a commotion. She hurled herself out of the chair, grabbed the videocam and the tripod and the cassette and thrust them all into the closet. She was waiting near the door when she saw a single figure get out of the Range Rover . . .

Then, hearing his voice, watching him come into view, she opened the door, stood smiling and happy on the porch.

"Professor," she called. "You've come!"

She brought a tray of espresso and chocolate cakes in from the kitchen. She put them down on the table by the couch. "There, Professor, just like the Café Einstein."

The bearded man looked up, eyes deepset and one of them twinkling with life behind his glasses. "You're too kind. I expected to find you sickly and pale and stretched out on your bed . . . it must be the resiliency of youth. I was very worried when I heard about your mishap—"

"It wasn't a mishap," she said. "Let's be honest. I tried to kill myself and you know why—"

"Now, now, don't punish yourself—"

"I'm not punishing myself. I won't do it again. Maybe I had to try it to get it out of my system." She paused, shifted gears, mentioned the call she'd made to him a few days previously. "I'm very glad you were home when I called. Beate would say I was mad to break security and I'm sure she's right but . . . I had to. It's so isolated here and I knew you'd worry and I wanted to see you. You're very good to come—I hope nobody followed you."

"I don't think anyone did."

"How long can you stay?"

"My students can do without me for a few days." He caught her eye. "Things are quite mad back in Berlin. Someone shot your father, I suppose you know—"

"Yes, I heard all about that on the radio. He's all right, I take it."

"Oh, yes. He's hard to kill, I expect. Or he leads a charmed life."

"Sooner or later the charm will wear off. Someone is bound to kill him."

"Not necessarily. He's well protected." He smiled warmly, reassuringly. "But I thought you could probably use some cheering up, out here in the mountains. I was very relieved to hear from you. Your friend Beate is pretty much a miracle worker. If she hadn't found you, *kaput,* you'd be dead. What a waste! And being dead is no fun."

She laughed. "You know that, do you?" She heard some of the sounds of the night. It was still, then something. One of the trees was creaking in the wind. It felt as if snow was coming.

"Of course. I died once. A long time ago."

"You certainly made a remarkable recovery."

"Funny, isn't it?" He took a bite of one of the cakes and washed it down with a sip of the thick black coffee. He changed the subject as if he were afraid he might begin talking and end by telling her everything. It was always a temptation with Erika: she could keep a secret, and this one would interest her greatly; it touched upon her own life. But he could never quite let go. The habit of twenty years was too strong. "So, what have you been doing to pass the time up here?"

"Thinking. Reading. I went to Bayreuth one day. Here in the lodge I've been snooping around. I found a few things . . . you might call it the heritage of the house." She told him about the militarist past, the portrait, the old snapshot, the SS.

He nodded. "I understand. Anyone who looks into the past runs that risk. But the people who lived then, they're nothing to do with you. What those people may have done or believed—none of that's your burden. Try to believe me, Erika. I know this to be true . . . What are you going to do now?"

Suddenly she was near tears, edging up on a kind of psychic exhaustion. "I don't want to go back. But I have to. I'm going to end all of this business with my father and me." She forced a grin, wiped at her eyes. "Unfinished business. I must see Mother, of course. I think about her all the time."

"They're looking for you. Your father has his own people looking for you. They'll find you, sooner or later. Even disguised this way, they'll find you."

"He's afraid of me. He's afraid of what Karl-Heinz told me . . . oh, yes, I know he's dead too. That was my father's work, you needn't try to hide that from me. Karl-Heinz told me if he died violently it would either be the Americans or my father . . . Mostly he feared my father. He was behind Stiffel, you know—Karl-Heinz told me that too. Well, I've got plans for Father."

The Professor stared at her for a moment. "With any luck, it will take a while for them to find you."

She smiled wanly. "It doesn't matter. I'm ready to go back. There's no point in waiting. I'm so worried about Mother. If I could just get word to her—"

"Don't even think of it. He'd find out."

"I'm sure you're right. She's been so sick . . ."

He nodded sadly. There was nothing he could say. He couldn't tell her about Delaney, or the old terrorists from the past turning up, or Orlovski and the green suitcase, or the comings and goings at the Wannsee house, or the man who'd made the mistake of finding him watching the house from his car . . .

They watched the news before going to bed. The big story was the Brandenburg Gate rally. The reporter's face filled the screen, the flames licking the night sky. Bodies burning. They were reviewing the coming of the neo-Nazis to Berlin.

"You see, it's not dead," she said.

Upstairs in the hallway she kissed his cheek. "No one has ever been kinder to me than you have. And you've asked nothing from me."

"Sleep tight, sweetheart."

The wind off the water blew the rain across the picture window, bent the shadowy trees. It was dark on Lake Wannsee. Gisevius was staring disconsolately out the window, seeing his own reflection and the others in the room behind him. He had decided not to tell Wolf about the burglar he'd interrupted in his office. No point in provoking more paranoia: Wolf needed as few distractions as possible, and he already had too many.

Kilroy was wishing he were somewhere else. Anywhere else. Even Belize City, and he'd never thought he'd see the day when he was longing for Belize City. The Chancellor was afraid to look at Koller: let sleeping dogs lie. Orlovski was longing for a liter of vodka. It was Germany, he concluded. There was something different about Germans.

"Now," Koller said, with that metallic chill in his voice. "Listen to me, my friends. You are all aware that someone shot me in the privacy of my own home. By luck I survived. Who could have done such a thing? That's what I ask myself . . . and I don't know, but I have theories. It is possible that I am being betrayed by one close to me—tonight I have taken certain steps to eradicate that possibility. But I—we, my friends— have enemies. There are people who would stop us from completing our great mission . . . And now someone has come to the edge of my property and murdered one of my security guards and left his body bleeding by the side of the road. This . . . is . . . not . . . Chicago. Do you understand? This is not the Mafia. This is simply not acceptable. What's going to happen next? Will it be one of us? Me? Or possibly you?"

Wolf Koller turned to stare at Kilroy and saw the bottomless eyes and felt a shiver run along his spine. He had never known anyone like Kilroy before. Koller believed deep in his heart that Clint Kilroy would as soon kill you as talk to you. It was a quality he admired. "I want to hear your thoughts, Clint." The question was, could he trust Kilroy? To whom did Kilroy truly belong? To Ned Cheddar? Or to Wolf Koller? Which of his masters was he more likely to betray?

"I think somebody's fuckin' with you, Wolf. But I don't know who it might be . . ."

Koller turned to the Chancellor. "And you, my friend—you are famous for your survival instincts . . . do you know who might be trying to stop SPARTAKUS?"

Glock snorted. "Every country in Europe, for a start. The United States. The Israelis. The intelligence services of these nations—" He smiled bloodlessly. "I would look outside rather than within your own circle . . . But you do not need me to advise you on your own security. If you know of weaknesses, so be it."

The Chancellor stood up, straining the buttons of his double-breasted suit. He went to the drinks table and poured himself a brandy, engulfed the snifter in his massive hand. He lifted the snifter in a toast.

"To confusion," he said bitterly.

The Professor came awake and smelled the cold and the snow. But it was something he'd heard that had awakened him. He lay quietly beneath the wool blankets. The bedroom window beneath the eaves was open. He heard something again. The crunching of a footstep in the freshly fallen snow. Well, it wasn't the man come to shovel the walk. He got out of bed, standing in the darkened room. He'd kept his socks on because it was a cold night. Now he padded across the room and looked down. Snow was sifting past the trees, swishing in the boughs, blown by the wind. He heard the creak again. *Bloody hell . . . Can't a man get a decent night's sleep?* He thought he saw a shadow moving below the window. It didn't make any difference, shadow or not. They couldn't hurt you as long as they were outside.

He put on the robe he'd found in the closet. It was a heavy, sky-blue woman's robe of some nubby material, warm. Then he picked up the gun from the nightstand. It was the same gun he'd used to kill the man at the house in Wannsee. That was always the danger in killing somebody. You kill one, pretty soon there are others and you have to kill them, too. He regretted it, which meant he'd been in the business too long. It had been years—decades—since he'd killed anybody. Hadn't it? Had he forgotten anyone?

He moved through the darkness, down the hallway to Erika's room, whispering to her from the doorway.

"I'm awake," she said.

"Good. There's somebody outside. I'm afraid they're up to no good. Don't worry. Nothing to be afraid of." He laughed softly. His knees were knocking. He hoped it was the cold. He told her to stay in her room until he came and got her. "Get dressed," he added. "This won't take long."

He went back into the hallway and padded down toward the stairway. They couldn't do any harm until they came upstairs. So all he had to do was keep them from coming upstairs. He wondered if it would work out the way logic told him it should. After all, they thought they were dealing with a lone girl. He hoped they hadn't noticed his Range Rover parked back in the trees, where he'd moved it. He wondered: were they coming to kill her or just bring her home to Daddy?

They were inside now. They were pretty good. They hadn't made much noise. He heard them now whispering to one another. The Professor yawned. Nerves. He was wide awake.

They were puttering around downstairs, bumping into things. He listened while they fumbled around in the kitchen, in the parlor, while they swore at one another. A lone girl. They weren't taking this very seriously. They had no intelligence about the building. No preplanning. No planning, period.

They were tiptoeing up the stairs in front of him when he shot hell out of them. Then they were yelling and falling down the stairs and a shot went wild into the ceiling and the screaming was really pretty awful. The Professor reloaded, stood off to the side, and turned on the lights with the switch near the top of the stairs. He peeked around the corner.

Carnage.

From the way it looked, the opening volley of shots had caught the first one in the chest and groin. The second man had gotten turned around when the body came hurtling back at him and two more shots had caught him in the back. The first one was dead and the second was sucking wind from a lung that was beyond repair. He died while the Professor was looking down at him. The Professor wondered if there was backup anywhere. He hadn't done this sort of thing in a long time. His technique had been primitive and inartistic. He was rusty.

Erika was standing at the top of the stairs looking down at him. He must have looked like a bad dream in the woman's fleecy robe. All he needed was a mobcap and his hair in curlers. "I don't think you want to come down here."

She came down. Her face was drawn with shock. She stared down at the first man who lay on his back, eyes open, his chest bloody. She spoke without feeling, as if her soul were in the grip of winter.

"He works for my father. I've seen him at the house doing security

work. Father sent him here with a gun . . . Father sent him to kill me."
The Professor reached out to comfort her, to provide a shoulder if she
wanted to cry. It wasn't necessary. "I'm right about all of it. I knew I was
right. Karl-Heinz was right. He'll kill me because of his bloody damn
SPARTAKUS! He's like a monstrous child, smashing and breaking and
destroying anything in his way. He thinks he's God, he thinks he has the
power of life and death over people—"

"Come on," the Professor said. "Throw some things in a bag. It's
time to get out of here. I don't know if these guys came alone—I've got to
get you somewhere safe."

She nodded and went upstairs. He collected the two guns, thought
about moving the bodies, then wondered just where he thought he was
moving them.

When she came downstairs he already had his clothes on and was
making instant coffee in the kitchen. She went to the closet, plucked the
videocassette from the darkness, and dropped it into her shoulder bag.
When he came into the hall with a cup of scalding coffee for her she
sipped and warmed her hands around it. Her eyes were red but she'd
done her crying in private. "He's going to kill my mother, too. She's so
sick, she'll be easy to kill."

There was nothing he could say to that.

Outside it was cold and the snow stung their faces and the wind
was whacking at the tall trees and the house. He couldn't see their car but
found his own back under the boughs drooping from a towering fir tree.
It was a good thing he'd switched the run-down old VW for his Rover
before leaving Berlin. They'd have had a hell of a time in the Beetle. He
got her settled under a blanket, threw their bags into the back, and felt
the reassuring roar as the Rover came alive. He left the lights out and
rolled quietly all the way down to the road. It was clear of traffic. The tire
tracks had been filled in with fresh snow, if the intruders had made any.
Where had they left their vehicle?

He had driven for about twenty minutes when he found out. A
panel truck had appeared in his rearview mirrors, refusing to pass on the
winding road, hugging his tail. He knew what was coming and there
wasn't a helluva lot he could do about it but try to out-drive the other
guy. The men he'd killed hadn't come alone. These guys were the
backup.

It turned out all wrong.

He felt the panel truck ram the Rover hard from behind and then he was skidding on the mixture of ice and snow and then he knew he had no control of the vehicle and there were no guardrails on the road and they were going over the side . . .

They were both buckled in. He tried to lean over in front of her, hoping to cushion any blows, trying to keep her free of broken glass . . .

It seemed as if the car had been bouncing downward for about a day and a half when something smashed the windshield and the cold air and glass and dirt and rocks blew through like a hurricane and the car swiveled sideways and began to roll and a door ripped away and he hoped to sweet God the gas didn't explode . . .

And then he could no longer hear or see or feel.

36

WIND-UP TOY

Cooper snapped on the lights at the foot of the stairs and saw the mess. He rubbed the toe of his shoe in the stains on the throw rug and the wood flooring. It was still just damp enough, like a new scab, to smear on the smooth wood. From upstairs came the sounds of Beate looking around in the bedroom. She came to the head of the stairway and shook her head.

"She's gone." She watched him for a moment, hearing the wind blowing across the light snow cover outside. The morning light was gray but bright, glaring off the snow beyond the windows. "What are you doing?"

"There's blood all over the floor. There's a bullet hole in the ceiling"—he pointed up and then down at the plaster dust—"and another bullet hole in the wall down here. There's some blood sprayed on the wall, too."

"Are you trying to tell me they came here and killed her?" She grabbed hold of the balcony railing. They were both tired.

"I don't know. But just look at the blood down here, which is more blood than there should be. And you say she's gone—what about her clothes?"

"Gone. She left a few things behind."

The heat hadn't been turned on and it was cold. In the kitchen there were some unwashed dishes. Coffee cups, a Chemex coffeemaker, a plate with a stale cake and some crumbs on it, spoons, forks. Two coffee cups, one with very faint lipstick smudges, one without. She saw what he was thinking. "The other bedroom has been used, too."

"There were two people here?" he asked. "A man or a woman?"

"I can't tell. John, do you think . . . did somebody die here?"

He shrugged. "No body. Maybe not."

"They've got her, haven't they?"

"Look, we just don't know—"

"Somebody was shot here, Cooper. I doubt if Erika shot anyone . . . so somebody else was doing the shooting, Cooper . . . That son of a bitch Koller—he's got her! Or he's killed her." She slammed her hand down on the counter and knocked one of the cups onto the floor. It shattered, loud as a gunshot in the quiet house. "I feel so helpless . . . What should we do?" She turned to look up at him. He'd never seen her actually look to him for help.

"There's no point in staying here," he said. "There's nobody here but us chickens—"

"What is that supposed to mean?"

"It means there's no point in staying here. Whatever is happening is happening back in Berlin . . . All we can do is try to find her. There's nothing left to do but go back to looking for Koller and all the . . ." He felt himself about to blow and he couldn't stop it in time. "—all the fucking rest of 'em!"

They were walking across the virginal snow, virginal but for their own footprints and tire tracks. Any other prints had been filled in with fresh, dry snow, and he wasn't much of a tracker, anyway. Why was it always the snow? Everything always happened in the snow . . .

They got back into the car and headed back toward Berlin.

It was dark and the wind off Lake Wannsee was biting and cold, got its teeth into you and kept on chewing toward the bone. Cooper stood alone and cold in the shelter of high shrubbery, the wind blowing rain down the back of his neck. The snow had stopped when they left the mountains. He was watching the low-slung modern white house. The rain made a peculiar sound striking the water of the lake, bouncing off the covered docks, spattering on the stones of the patio, pinging off metal patio furniture. Boats thumped against the pilings beneath the coverings.

There was big-band dance music coming from somebody's house not terribly far away. Overhead and behind him the trees thrashed in the wind, the fallen leaves soaked up rain underfoot.

Wolf Koller's house was dark. But Cooper thought he'd give it one more look around before leaving. He stepped out of the pitch darkness of the shadows and crossed the patio, peered into the windows. Behind him, all around him, the summer furniture crouched ominously, half of it already tucked up in its winter plastic shrouds. He was tired, eyes burning. He'd grabbed catnaps on the way back from the mountains while Beate had done the driving. She hadn't been able to sleep while he drove and then he'd dropped her at TV Center. She would keep going on caffeine and an amphetamine or two. He yawned, feeling like an intruder on Gatsby's estate out on Long Island, turning back to look out across the water, seeing the light on somebody's dock and wondering which Egg it was—he could never remember which was Gatsby's Egg, East or West. He let his weary mind ramble across Redford as the doomed Gatsby in a much better picture than it got credit for being, then thought about Alan Ladd, who'd played the part before him. He wished he were back in Boston, where he could slip into his own theater and watch something old, something good . . . Where Claudia Cardinale would always be young and he could make believe it didn't matter . . .

There were no signs of life in the house, but he didn't want to set off any security alarms. He sighed, taking yet another last look into the darkness beyond the windows. He was frustrated and lonely and wet and worried about Erika and, now, with the empty house, about Lee.

And suddenly he felt something he knew damn well was the muzzle of a gun in his back.

And a voice was saying something very calmly in German that he couldn't understand, and he was afraid if he did the wrong thing it would get him killed, all because he couldn't speak German . . .

A hand pushed him and he marched around the side of the house and underneath the deck extending out from the second floor of the back of the house. Once they were out of the rain, the hand clamped down on his shoulder to stop him. Then the pressure of the hand turned him around.

It was Werner Paulus.

Cooper had no idea where he was but he and Paulus were sitting in a café drinking coffee. The place smelled great. Overpoweringly of coffee. Paulus was waiting for Cooper to finish his explanation.

"So, since the mountain place was empty—we had nowhere else to go. I took her back to work in Berlin and then I drove out here. I didn't have a plan. I just wanted to find out where Wolf Koller was . . . maybe I just wanted to see him, to see if I thought he could actually have arranged to have his daughter disappear—it still doesn't seem quite possible to me."

"I understand."

"But as you saw, the house is locked up. What about the house in Grunewald?"

Paulus shook his head. "Empty there, as well. They are all gone, it seems. Kilroy, the help, Wolf, Gisevius . . . the Chancellor . . ."

"And my sister," Cooper added. "Everybody's gone up in smoke."

"You know that Stiffel is dead?"

"Yes."

"Do you know anything about Bernd Schmidt?"

"Karl-Heinz's father? What do you mean?"

"Now Bernd Schmidt seems to have disappeared, as well, along with his wife. A sharp-eyed neighbor saw them being taken away by some men in a car . . . the biggest car in the world, it would seem from the neighbor's description. A Cadillac, very old, perfect condition."

"Does that mean Koller put two and two together about the Schmidts, father and son, and decreed the father must also pay the price?"

"That's my presumption. For all I know Schmidt was behind the shooting of Wolf and Wolf found out about it. And maybe he wasn't. And who killed Stiffel? I don't know, but I can guess."

Cooper got around another espresso and consented to have another large bite of something very chocolate. It was too warm in the coffeehouse. A day or two in residence, he reckoned, and the chill would be baked from his bones. "Well, a man like Koller can't disappear for long, surely. He's too important—and for that matter, the Chancellor can't just vanish into thin air. I mean, he has to turn up every day. Or the whole country notices." He sipped coffee, warmed his hands on the cup. "You don't act like a man who's retired, Chief. You can't convince me that you're doing all this out of habit."

"No, I don't suppose I can. So I won't try. I am employed. I have a boss. But I'm retired from the police."

"Well, wait a minute—who are you working for?"

Paulus chuckled, waving a finger back and forth in front of Cooper. "Most confidential."

"Then you must know what's really going on. You must—or you'd just be stumbling around in a daze—"

"I have an idea or two. But the people I work for, not even *they* know what's going on. And *they* set it in motion. It's a bit of a joke, really."

"Who started it?"

"You wouldn't believe me if I told you."

"Why would you say that? I'd believe anything—you're the eighth dwarf and you work for Snow White. Sounds reasonable to me."

"I've been working for my present masters for many years."

"How's that possible? You were a cop for ages."

"Yes, for a very long time. That was what you Americans call my 'day job.' I was working for someone else all through the years. And I'm still working for them."

Cooper thought a moment. "Are you a good guy or a bad guy?"

"Don't you find that such distinctions are just a little silly these days?"

"Don't ask me. Let's talk about Wolf—where the hell is he? And where is my sister? Why would he go into hiding now?"

"Fear? Maybe he's afraid whoever tried to kill him will try again. My guess is that he's not thinking as clearly as he believes he is. He's like his father, he's getting excited and stressed just when he should stay calm . . . Look at it from his point of view. Murders all around him, some he's responsible for, others he's not . . . And then he had the Schmidts murdered . . ."

"His own private Night of the Long Knives."

"Yes."

"But who is he afraid of? Who's applying all this pressure?"

"He only needs to know that the pressure is there—somebody is closing in on him, and his plan, whatever it is, is in jeopardy. So he's got to move quickly." Paulus considered the last of his coffee, the end of his cigarette. "Wife, daughter, leaks, time passing—there are a lot of pressures on Wolf. Where is it coming from most intensely? I don't know. But with all due respect, Mr. Cooper, I don't always trust the Americans.

They are not as simple and open a people as they would sometimes have us believe. They bumble around, they give the impression that the right hand doesn't know what the left hand is doing—but that's often by design, I've discovered—"

"I don't know what the hell you're talking about. If you're looking for someone to share your lack of trust in the Americans, look no farther. But how much knowledge of the American government and its way of doing things do you actually have?"

"Ah, more than you might expect . . . I've made quite a study of it over the years." He was smiling rather sadly, Cooper thought, and no doubt with perfectly good reason.

He waited in Beate's office. It was hot in the cubicle and he was falling asleep when she came around the corner and swept in, threw herself into the chair behind the desk. She picked up a coffee cup, peered into it, quickly put it down. He stared at her from eyes that felt like Kuwaiti oil well fires.

"Wolf and all the rest of them, they've disappeared. Both houses are empty as . . . as—"

"I understand." She sighed and rubbed her eyes. "We're a fine pair." She tried to work up a laugh but it came out another sigh. "He's going to win."

"Whatever that means." Cooper stood up and stared out into the main room, which was almost empty. Some of the video display terminals glowed in the dim, institutional light of evening. "That's what really, truly, deeply pisses me off. We don't even know what Wolf's winning means, except that it's not good for Erika and Lee. I keep wondering if he would actually kill his daughter—"

"The Chancellor is back in Bonn, and two Russian diplomats have been spotted going in back doors to secret meetings. Agriculture guys. That's the word that's out. Agriculture guys . . . Russia is supposed to starve again this winter, and that's been one of Wolf Koller's favorite public relations opportunities . . . so there's all this talk about some new trade deal in the wind, lots of aid to the Russians, something to polish up Germany's image in the rest of the world. Saving the starving Russkies, instead of supporting neo-Nazis at home. Anything to take people's attention off the neo-Nazis . . . or to keep them from asking about why the hell we're not trying to stop the Serbs from committing genocide—"

"Everything they say about European civilization is wrong," Cooper said groggily. "Europe doesn't have a long memory. Europe hasn't learned anything from history. Europe has always had one simple rule of conduct . . . Look out for Number One. Europe is not about idealism, selflessness . . . Europe is about staying alive . . . which is something they do so badly. One of life's little ironies."

"And America is selfless, I suppose," she said. She was smiling at him.

"Not exactly. But more so than anybody else, I guess."

"I guess the Yanks will never learn, then. I'm so tired. Let's get out of here. Let's go home."

She linked her arm through his as they left. Home was where she lived. It was his home in Berlin. This sort of thing sneaked up on you.

Since it was hard for him to walk, and since it had been a long flight, and since he was tired, and since it was raining and slippery, he waited in the taxi on the tree-lined street in Charlottenburg. He didn't know it but he wasn't far from the world-famous bust of Nefertiti. Not far from the Charlottenburg Palace itself, which lay through the rain and fog dead ahead. But he didn't know that either.

He looked up at the lighted window, glowing yellow in the night. A man was staring down into the street, holding a curtain back. Then he let the curtain fall into place.

The man in the taxi was smoking a cigar, blowing the thick clouds out the window, when the man from the window came trundling out beneath an umbrella, his skin gray and pockmarked, carrying a bulky package, long as a fly rod but much thicker. He was an American.

"You know how to use this thing?"

The man in the backseat nodded. "Who said it was any of your business, soldier?"

"You can do a helluva lot of damage with one of—"

"If I can't, you're in a lot of trouble."

"Be fucking careful is all I have to say."

"Good for you. You said it. Thanks for the help."

The taxi pulled away from the curb.

The man in the backseat unwrapped the package, carefully laying back the sheets of brown paper. The contents seemed to get bigger the more he unwrapped. It was an optical illusion, of course, depending on the implications of the object itself.

The gun had a handle like a very big pistol. Attached by a hinge at the top of the handle was the folding stock, which was at present pulled forward toward the business end of the barrel. He pulled it back, fitted it against his shoulder to get the feel of it, then tilted it forward again, returning it to its original configuration—that of a gigantic revolver with a second hand grip halfway along the bottom of the barrel to hold the damn thing steady.

In front of the trigger guard was a very large, round magazine, which held twelve shotgun shells. Beneath the barrel, on the front of the round magazine, was a large butterfly key, which, when the spring within was wound tight, kept the magazine in a state of constant tension. When the trigger was pulled and the first shotgun shell fired, the spring was released and the next shell was almost instantaneously moved into the chamber for firing. The result was rather like having a machine gun that fired twelve shotgun blasts in three or four seconds. It made a hell of a noise. It was called a Streetsweeper. They were all custom-made.

The man thought the gun was the scariest wind-up toy ever invented. It was almost impossible to fire accurately from the shoulder. The recoils were just too powerful to control. The funny thing about this weapon was that it was entirely legal, at least in the good old US of A. It was neither an automatic nor a semiautomatic weapon since the user had to pull the trigger each time it fired. Just went to show you. He laid it across his knees and stared out into the rainy night.

He had no idea where the hell he was.

They were waiting in the dark, upstairs beneath the skylights.

Cooper and Beate were both exhausted, didn't even stop in the kitchen for a final shot of coffee or anything else. Erika and Lee would have to wait for tomorrow. They were just too tired to go over it anymore, to try to think what they were going to do the next day. Cooper knew that he wanted to think about something Paulus said . . . what was it? . . . oh, yes, he'd said that he'd had another employer through the years, someone he was still working for, and Cooper wondered . . .

it sounded promising, somehow . . . But tomorrow, he'd have to think about it tomorrow . . .

When they reached the top of the stairs, began throwing down their wet coats, the lights came on and there were three men in overcoats who shouldn't have been there. Two of them were holding nine-millimeter Berettas like the good old Denlingers in the Minnesota snowstorm . . . that was how Cooper's mind was working, slowly, methodically, trying to figure out what was going on, and then it hit him what was happening . . . They were motioning to them to raise their hands, speaking German, which made it all the more frustrating for Cooper, who couldn't understand a fucking word, and Beate was pale, looking like death, and she was trying to talk to them, asking some questions, and it was all so pathetic and confusing and frustrating and they were all sort of concentrating on Beate, explaining to her what they wanted done, and something—something physical, something he could hear at the back of his head—something snapped in Cooper's brain or cerebral cortex or wherever things finally snap and he went straight out of control, went fully and completely off the edge of sanity, did a half-gainer into the dark side of his psyche, flung out one huge arm and smashed a backhand through one of the faces, very surprising, and the man went backwards over one of the low couches and banged into the coffee table and squeezed the trigger and blew a hole in one of the immense twelve-by-twelve beams, and Cooper threw himself as hard as he could into the arms of another one and rushed him backwards, feet driving the way they had in high school a hundred years ago when he'd been a football player and he kept pushing and knocked the guy backwards into a bookcase and over the arm of a chair and some of the stringy-looking plants that had been gasping their last on the shelves went flying through the air and Cooper smashed his head into the man's face and felt something give and then someone was on his back and he staggered upward, slamming backwards into the wall, hoping to break every bone in the motherfucker's body and then someone was swinging at his face and Cooper grabbed a halogen lamp and used it like a club across somebody's face and someone drove a fist into his guts and he felt the breath leaving his body in a helluva hurry and he saw little white and silver and red explosions before his eyes and he heard Beate screaming and somebody yelling in German and then somebody fired a gun once, then again, and Cooper was sure as hell he'd been fucking shot and he swung the halogen lamp again and again and he seemed to be spinning meaninglessly in the center of the room and he thought he saw one of them holding a gun to Beate's temple and then he felt himself going, he felt like he was going to throw up, his legs were getting mushy, he wished he hadn't made such a mess of her apartment, he wished he weren't dying but figured it was kind of an exciting way to go but then he thought of Lee, what would happen to Lee, and he was going over, felt himself toppling from a very high place . . .

It was raining and raw when they eased the enormous Cadillac across the street from the wrought-iron pissoir standing by the park. They backed the car up to the tall doors of the apartment building and half-carried, half-dragged the big man out into the rain and pushed and pulled and swore and crammed him through the door and onto the deep leather seats in back. The woman had shut up after being given a forearm across the face. She sounded like she was having trouble breathing but that wouldn't make much difference very soon. One of the men climbed into the backseat with them and placed a rough cloth sack over her head and tightened it with a drawstring. He yanked the big man's head up and got a similar bag over his head and drew the drawstring tight as he could, feeling it dig into the man's throat. He'd put up such a fight! Jesus, what had the guy been thinking of? Maybe they should have killed him right on the spot . . . what difference did it make? But there was one lesson you learned early on in this outfit. Follow the directions. Look at what happened to the poor Schmidts . . . The man had liked Schmidt, had hated to do it, but in the end, once people stumble around and whine a bit, it's easier, you're glad to get rid of them, glad to kill them and run them through the Motherland . . . Motherland . . . that was their nickname for the compactor at the disposal warehouse . . . you sent them back to the Motherland . . .

37

NED IN THE NIGHT

Ned Cheddar lay in bed, eyes wide, sleep nowhere in sight, restlessly thinking, thinking—was he playing this right, did he still have the touch of genius that Emory Leighton Hunn had seen in him years ago? E. L. Hunn, the Master of the Masters. He'd learned it all from E. L. Hunn and now he was wandering in a dark wasteland, unsure of his own motives anymore, unsure of how best to reach his goals, the new master trapped and struggling in his own terrible web . . .

The idea had been clever, in the beginning, if not terribly original: to use Wolf Koller—whom he had used to their mutual advantage over the years—to advance the German policy, to spread a certain discord in the newly united Germany through the services of Joachim Stiffel. A Germany beset by a neo-Nazi movement was a Germany under a microscope, a Germany hampered and restrained by the glare of the spotlight. A Germany rendered less powerful than its national character, its land mass, and its economic power would imply. It was the German containment policy. *Keep the Hun Helpless* was what they called it at the think tank where policies were concocted by academics and retired generals and God only knew who else.

Somehow—and Ned Cheddar couldn't isolate the moment unless he thought of it in terms of John Cooper, and it wasn't Cooper's fault—somehow the whole thing had run off the tracks, had too much of a head of steam, Wolf Koller had turned it into something else . . . Wolf

Koller's ego, his sense of the German destiny and his role in achieving it, that's where the blame lay, and now Ned Cheddar couldn't sleep for fear of waking up to something called SPARTAKUS that would change the whole goddamn world . . .

Delaney had watched Stiffel being assassinated right in front of him—that had to be Koller's idea; he'd used Stiffel and now he was used up and knew too much about Koller's involvement in the neo-Nazi movement to go on living. And Koller had had Karl-Heinz and the Schmidts killed . . .

It was now a war. A war Ned Cheddar had not declared and did not understand. All because of SPARTAKUS, which was more important to Koller than his relationship with Cheddar and thus with America.

Emory Leighton Hunn had always called these private wars the secret wars, the wars nobody ever heard about, the wars that lay behind the wars in the newspapers. And no doubt this was now a war.

What was it that Hunn was always quoting, that bit of Shakespeare about what happens to men once war overtakes them? Cheddar could almost quote it but not quite, and there was nothing to do but get up, put on his reading glasses, slide into his Brooks Brothers slippers and waddle over to the bookcase, find the ancient *Complete Shakespeare* with its yellowing pages and tattered dustjacket and paper thin as the Bible. He got it back to the bed and leaned back against the pillows, glasses on the end of his nose. It was *Henry IV,* wasn't it? No, no, it was *Henry V,* the St. Crispin's Day thing . . . something about Englishmen lying abed today regretting they weren't at Agincourt or someplace . . . ah, there it was . . .

> In peace there's nothing so becomes a man
> As modest stillness and humility:
> But when the blast of war blows in our ears,
> Then imitate the action of the tiger;
> Stiffen the sinews, summon up the blood,
> Disguise fair nature with hard-favored rage;
> Then lend the eye a terrible aspect.

It was a war, all right. And there was only one question at the end of the day. Who best would imitate the action of the tiger?

No, sleep was impossible. He was nearing the heart of the problem, he had to pin it down. It was time for an all-nighter, just like the old days, get out the long yellow legal pads. He was using his own fountain pen, a Montblanc Lorenzo de Medici, rather than the tacky government-issue ballpoints that cluttered his desk drawers. He had to make it come clear in his mind so he could arrange the endgame as felicitously as possible. Where did he stand with all these madmen?

The fountain pen in his fat fingers was doing adagios and arabesques across the yellow paper.

Clint Kilroy was an admirable assassin. Cheddar had worked with him for a long time and knew all about what he'd been up to before he became Kilroy. It was because he knew so fully Kilroy's past that Kilroy had been obliged to come to work for him. Only death could break the bonds by which Kilroy was fettered to Ned Cheddar. Kilroy was very good at killing people, though you had to admit he wasn't getting any younger. When the time came to finish off Wolf Koller once and for all—as now seemed quite inevitable—Kilroy was the man for the job . . . Ned Cheddar sort of hated the idea of killing Koller but it had always been the fallback position, though Wolf Koller could scarcely have imagined it. Of course, there was always the chance that Koller would kill Kilroy, or have him killed, first, but Ned Cheddar had to believe that Koller had enough else on his plate to keep him from zeroing in on a few of the oddities of his relationship with the American spymaster. After all, it was Ned Cheddar who had made Wolf Koller's political power possible, by offering secretly the full aid and comfort of the US of A. It was Ned Cheddar who had thought up the idea of using the neo-Nazis and the scummy little turd Joachim Stiffel, using them to further the foreign policy aims of the United States of America—at least as Ned Cheddar saw them. It was clean, antiseptic: everyone above Cheddar had absolute deniability, so there was no paper trail, no Ollie North festival of paper-shredding in the future because Ned Cheddar knew Ollie North and Ned Cheddar was no Ollie North. In the first place, Ned Cheddar knew what the hell he was doing because he'd been doing it for a long time. Subverting governments, for example, was something you had to learn over a period of years. Ollie North knew what he wanted to do, not how to do it, and in the end his ass was in the wringer. A lot of asses were in the wringer. Ned Cheddar's substantial posterior—well, they hadn't yet made the wringer that could handle it. And people like Burke Delaney and Clint Kilroy weren't on anybody's paybooks, nor was Wolf Koller. Nobody on earth could tie Ned Cheddar to Koller . . .

Ned Cheddar didn't know for a fact who had killed Stiffel but he figured it must have been Koller, putting a permanent stopper in the mouth of a man who knew too much. Stiffel could finger Wolf Koller but he didn't have a thing on Burke Delaney: but it had been Delaney who'd been Stiffel's case officer on the neo-Nazi operations, just as Kilroy had been Ned Cheddar's representative in the Koller camp. It was fine with Cheddar, Koller putting paid to Stiffel, whose usefulness—to anyone— had come to an end. It just saved Burke Delaney from having to do it.

Ah, old Burke. A link to the past, to the days of building the tunnel under the Wall, to the Old Guard, a man who'd won his letter when the game was played on real grass. Burke Delaney was a true field agent. There weren't many left alive and only a handful who were still able to play the game. If Burke had been able to do much of anything else, he'd probably have put himself out to pasture long ago, that was the truth of it. He was the equivalent among the good guys of these old farts coming out of the woodwork. Burke was even older than Sebastien the Red. Unlike Sebastien, Burke had never been officially consigned to the boneyard, but otherwise it was much the same. Cheddar wasn't quite sure what he was going to do with Burke in the short term. They would improvise.

If Burke Delaney presented a comparatively simple and straight-forward situation, the Professor was something else. While Burke was alive and kicking, the Professor had been officially dead for twenty years. Was he going to stay that way? Or would he have to die again? Twenty years . . . The man the Professor had been back then was investigating Nazi underground movements in South America when he'd been blown. Someone had tumbled to what he was doing and they weren't happy about it. The Nazis were going to kill him, you had to expect that. Ned Cheddar in those days was not yet quite the twisty-minded genius he was to become in stories around the spook campfires later on. And the Professor was so valuable, so skilled, that Cheddar embarked on one of his more elaborate bits of legerdemain. A double was found, a few slight adjustments to the man's physical self were made, poor bastard, and he was murdered by the Nazis, who naturally thought they'd done the right man. And the newly "dead" Professor was turned into one of the Cheese's double agents. The Russians thought he was truly defecting: he made them believe it. That gave you an idea of the man's extraordinary nerves, his ability to give a performance, the grace under pressure. The Russians eventually made him a "Yank Reader," as they were known at Moscow Center—an equivalent of American Kremlinologists. He'd even been used by them to baby-sit the famous third man himself, Kim Philby, during his middle period in Moscow. But all the time he was working for Ned Cheddar, who thought the Professor, or Kiril as he was known in the East, was the coolest man under pressure he'd ever known. At the moment, however, Ned Cheddar wondered why he couldn't find the Professor when he might need him most . . . Where the hell was he?

The final names on Ned Cheddar's list belonged to Wolf Koller and John Cooper. By the time he got to them he'd had the house steward, a Marine bodyguard, bring him a pizza. Pepperoni, sausage, green pepper, not enough tomato sauce. And a light beer.

Wolf Koller.

Wolf Koller, the self-proclaimed savior of the Fatherland, whom Ned Cheddar had chosen to serve the purposes of the United States of America. It was all so simple, really. With the reunification of Germany, it was very important to keep people in the rest of the world—that is, Europe and America, which was still really the rest of the world in Ned Cheddar's private mind—nervous, if not actually scared shitless, about the big new Germany. Cheddar had decided in the privacy of his Georgetown kitchen one night, waiting for a chicken to finish roasting in its coating of garlic and herbs, that the easiest button to push was the Nazi button. Or in this case, the fringe neo-Nazis. Bring the Nazis back for an encore. In reality, not too serious perhaps, but serious enough to keep people looking over their shoulders. Serious enough to generate an immense amount of publicity. The point was to keep the Germans obsessed about themselves: keep their hands off the rest of Europe. Ned Cheddar didn't tell much of anyone about his plan. Since so much of his budget was hidden, since the man he picked to back the neo-Nazis—Wolf Koller—was so much in tune with the Nazis, there really wasn't much need to tell anyone else. He didn't tell the President and he certainly didn't tell Wolf Koller. Like every maniac, Wolf Koller had a blind spot: he bought Ned Cheddar's argument that there was too much liberalism in Germany, too much leftist sentiment, too much of a leaning toward chaos, too damn many refugees—what was needed was a firm hand, a bit of the old medicine, and by bankrolling the new Nazis, however revolting and unwashed he might find them personally, Wolf Koller could move the *Volk* and the government to the right, toward the authoritarianism he valued so highly. As Cheddar pointed out when Wolf was wrinkling his nose at the likes of Stiffel, he didn't have to invite them over for dinner. The neo-Nazis would never gain any real power, but Koller's people, those he supported and put forward, would eventually fill the government. It was all a question of creating an atmosphere. That's what the neo-Nazis had been meant to do—to create the nervousness that would lead the nation to the right, into Wolf Koller's sphere.

And then came SPARTAKUS.

SPARTAKUS was news to Ned Cheddar and he hated news that was really news. He only liked the news he knew was coming. SPARTAKUS meant Wolf Koller was thinking for himself, slipping out from under Ned Cheddar's control.

Wolf Koller was the creator of SPARTAKUS and Ned Cheddar had analyzed the raw data at his disposal and had just about figured out what was going on.

But where did the joker—John Cooper—fit in?

He had put down his legal pad and finished the pizza and beer and turned off the light over his bed and he'd begun to drift a bit when he ran directly into John Cooper.

What was he going to do about John Cooper?

And, God help us all, he had to keep John Cooper and the Professor apart. Far apart. He could only imagine what a hothead like Cooper might do if . . .

He sat up.

He disentangled himself from the bedclothes and reached for what he hoped was a final piece of cold pizza but was disappointed. The plate was empty.

Well, he'd just have to wake the steward.

He couldn't be expected to think these things through on an empty stomach.

38

LOOSE NUKES

The Professor still had a hellish headache and was lucky that it wasn't worse. Never, he supposed, had a Range Rover tumbled quite so far, or for such a long time, without inflicting at least broken bones. There had been a time in Albania when he'd taken a turn too fast in the rain and the radio man had been killed and a time in Peru . . . But no, somehow none of that had happened this time. He'd thrown up as a result of the jostling, and Erika's seat belt had yanked the breath out of her and she'd fainted, missing much of the fun. The world seen from within a tumbling and rolling Range Rover was not to be missed, really.

He was recalling the experience as their bus arrived at the Zoo Station in the heart of Berlin. He looked at Erika, napping in the seat beside him. She seemed very peaceful but he was still surprised each time he looked at her. The blond hair, the change in its length, the clothes, the makeup. Beate had turned her into a different person. The Professor was surprised at how well it had worked. He tapped her shoulder, whispered in her ear, and she fluttered her eyes, looked lost for a moment, then focused in on his face. "Where are we?"

"Zoo Station. Or what the bombers left of it." He pointed out the barricades blocking several entrances.

"So soon?" She yawned, running her fingers through her still unfamiliar hair. "How are you feeling?"

"I'm all right. You've had a good sleep. How are you?"

"Stiff. Mainly stiff. My neck is a little sore. I'll live."

"Damn right you'll live, my dear."

They pushed through the swarms of drug dealers, whores, and other Berlin-bound passengers and got a taxi outside. It was night and it was raining and he wondered in passing if the rain would ever stop. It wasn't a hard rain. Just persistent. And cold right through to the bone.

He gave an address just off the Ku'damm, one of the small, independently leased hotels. It was owned by a man named Klaus, an old West German agent he'd crossed swords with a time or two in the past. Now they tended to joke about it. After all, they'd both survived. Many hadn't. They'd shot it out once in a deserted U-Bahn station where a prisoner exchange went bad and a couple of men had died, but neither of them, as luck would have it. Once the Soviet Union disintegrated and the Wall came down and Germany was one again, the Professor had looked him up and they'd put down a great deal of schnapps and shared some old secrets and had a good, if somewhat rueful, laugh about the whole thing. For them, that world didn't exist anymore. It was like a way station in their pasts, a country they'd once visited, the Cold War. The world had moved on and it seemed like a million years ago. And here he was, all those years after his carefully staged "death" and the years in Moscow Center, tied by ribbons as fragile as spiderwebs to that bastard Ned Cheddar . . . He thought of him as a bastard in the way that men do, with a kind of grudging affection.

There he'd been, in the guts of Moscow Center, working as one of Ned Cheddar's agents, baby-sitting Kim Philby, and actually enjoying himself a good bit of the time. He hadn't really minded the privations involved in living in Russia during those years. For a time he'd had many of the benefits accorded Philby himself, good vodka, very nice accommodations, all the latest recordings, a good stereo. And he'd made some good friends in Moscow, including Konstantin Orlovski, for that matter, who was now enjoying some of the consumer goods of the West.

They took the rickety elevator up to the cozy lobby with its big overstuffed chairs and hissing radiator and very green palms with a slight coating of dust. A young man in a bright green sportcoat was figuring up room bills behind the desk. He looked up at the nondescript bearded Professor and the girl with the short blond hair and the black leggings and long black sweater.

"Fetch Klaus, will you, lad?"

"He has retired for the evening."

"Not for me he hasn't. Tell him the Professor is waiting in the lobby. Tell him it's Kiril. Tell him it's Beethoven's Fifth." He was tired and waved the boy away. "Just get him, sonny. Just hop to it." His mind was a little sloppy. Beethoven's Fifth was the old designation for life-and-death.

Erika had folded herself into one of the deep chairs. A television was playing somewhere. She was half asleep, absentmindedly chewing a thumbnail, like a small child.

Klaus came out wearing a smoking jacket and an ascot knotted behind a starched white shirt. Striped trousers, carpet slippers. He was nearly bald with some gray hair slicked back over a narrow, bony forehead and a thin, rather funereal face. It lit up at the sight of the Professor. "Look what the cat's brought us! What are you up to, Kiril?" His eyes roved over the pretty girl.

"My niece. Don't be a dirty old man, Klaus. I mean, don't let it show. You're looking very natty this evening."

"I'm entertaining, dear boy." He leered slightly.

"I thought you were long past that. Good for you. I need a room."

"You'll have to sleep with your niece . . ." He grinned. His face had a gray pallor.

"Klaus . . . we're very tired. What have you got?"

"A very comfortable room." He pointed across the lobby. "You've used it on occasion in the past."

"Excellent. I'm afraid I don't have enough cash at the moment—left in a hurry."

"Your credit is always good here, Kiril."

Klaus held out his hand and the boy in the green jacket gave him the key and he led the way across to the huge door. Erika roused herself and the Professor ushered her ahead of him. The door swung open and Klaus attended to the necessaries, bowed his way out.

The bed was huge. Erika smiled at him. "I'll never know you're there."

"I snore."

"I'm so tired it won't make any difference."

Erika showered and came out of the bathroom wrapped in a flannel robe she'd packed when they had made their escape from the mountain lodge. She crawled into the bed under the heavy feather duvet and was asleep by the time he shut the bathroom door and got his own shower going.

He soaked up the hot water, held on to the railing in the glass stall. He had cracked a couple of ribs, he knew that because he'd done it before: not broken, just cracked. They hurt but they'd get better. And he'd suffered a concussion in the bouncing, crashing car, but he saw no point in mentioning it to Erika, who would just have worried. They'd found the local doctor in the nearest hamlet and he'd wrapped Erika's sprained ankle so tightly that she hardly limped. She'd forgotten there was anything wrong with the ankle. And they'd both been downing enough ibuprofen to keep them more or less pain-free. The Rover had been rather smashed up and they'd left it for a garage to pick up later. He hadn't really wanted to be bothered with details at a time like that. He hadn't mentioned the people who had driven them off the road. They'd still be stranded doing paperwork and answering questions if he had.

Erika had pulled herself together, had gotten off the my-father-wants-to-kill-me number because there was no point in going on about it and the Professor wouldn't stand for it. *Focus, focus, focus is everything. Tears come later.* That was his message, the message of experience.

After the shower, and the toweling off, which was not without a certain coefficient of pain in the rib cage, he'd tottered out into the room where Erika was snoring in a ladylike way and two of the table lamps were still turned on. He sat down in a big armchair in front of the television set and flipped on CNN.

He was just trying to unwind. He didn't care what was on the television. Even that irritating style and fashion show with that woman who made him grind his teeth . . . It didn't matter. But it was a piece about the breakup of the Soviet Union; the reporter was going on about the agreement Yeltsin had made with Bush. The Russians were supposed to sell almost eight billion dollars' worth of weapons-grade nuclear material taken out of warheads to the United States. The United States would then work some kind of magic on the stuff and resell it for peaceful purposes . . . that part alone set off all sorts of alarms inside the Professor's brain, concussed or not. God only knew what the Americans would actually do with the stuff. It would probably wind up with the fucking Contras or some Noriega type who was momentarily in favor . . .

The Professor remembered the deal Bush and Yeltsin had made. The world had breathed a helluva lot easier as a result. Another great step away from a nuclear war.

But they hadn't acted on the deal yet.

He was no longer paying attention to the television. He was thinking about the country where he'd worked for so long. He was thinking about the old KGB man, Egon Rossovich, who'd have been up to his eyeballs in any such negotiation. He was thinking about the way Rossovich had hated Gorbachev for going soft, in his view, and how much he must hate Yeltsin's plans for a market economy, capitalism, the works. He was thinking about Ukraine and how jealous of their autonomy and power they were, how much they wanted to act out their own destiny, independent of "those Muscovite assholes, peasants, doctrinaire pissants," as he'd heard them refer to the Red Menace of the past. He was thinking about the sad state of the Russian military, where captains and majors—who could find no housing in Moscow and the other cities—were out in the sticks standing guard duty because there were no longer enough enlisted men to fill out the ranks. In the previous spring's annual draft only one in five of those drafted had actually bothered to show up for induction. The military was in trouble. They had lost their reason for existence and sooner or later they were going to want it back . . . And Rossovich had been running his mouth into military ears for a long time now . . .

And Konstantin Orlovski, Rossovich's handmaiden, was running around ducking into secret meetings with Wolf Koller, the Chancellor, and people like Gisevius and Sebastien and Clint Kilroy . . . Koller was making an appeal to German nationalism and the Chancellor was worried about the need for martial law . . . and the Professor remembered how everybody had wondered about the "loose nukes" floating around in what had been the old Soviet Union after Yeltsin and Bush had agreed on the deal . . . and how was the deal going to be enforced?

Loose nukes.

And he remembered how Wolf Koller's companies had been involved with selling stuff to Khomeini, Quaddafi, and more recently Saddam Hussein and how the Americans had had to wink at all of it because they themselves had created Saddam . . . The Americans were always "creating" some maniac who would eventually turn on them and bite their nuts. It never failed.

And Stiffel was dead now and the neo-Nazis were in disarray and the German nation needed some strong leadership and a new kind of identity if chaos was to be avoided . . . Something had to get them past the obsession with immigrants and the arrival of the East Germans in the job market and the torrents of violence and the squabbles in the EEC . . .

He'd lost touch with what was on the television and snapped back to it when they switched to a live broadcast from outside the Moscow White House, where the Parliament was ensconced, where a crisis seemed to be coming to a head. It had been cooking for weeks but someone had turned up the heat. Dawn was just blurring the horizon, crowds were singing songs and locking arms and carrying banners and shaking their fists at TV cameras. Tanks had been drawn up to defend and preserve the government of Boris Yeltsin. The scene was reminiscent of those tense days when the coup had been attempted against Gorbachev. The Professor imagined a future full of such scenes, years and years of them, before democracy took hold or was stamped out. After all, the integrity of power was all that mattered over there. The integrity of consensus, the bedrock of democracy, had no tradition whatsoever. To most Russians it meant nothing and the struggles for power seemed to have almost no bearing on their lives, which would be hard as hell in any case, as they had always been.

The CNN correspondent came on, face reddened by the icy wind. He had a cold and kept sniffling as he spoke with the crowds of protesters strung out behind him.

"Morning comes to Moscow and these ten thousand protesters have been out here in the cold all night, facing the tanks in their ominous silence. Boris Yeltsin is still inside the White House, which you see over there—he clings to power, leader of this troubled, fragmented new nation. Yeltsin refuses to leave the White House, Parliament has dispersed to wait it out, to visit constituents, and some to join the ten thousand here who are calling for Yeltsin's resignation and the installation of a new government . . . and the betting on the future keeps turning up the name of former KGB man, wheelchair-bound Egon Rossovich, long a political traditionalist behind the scenes. Rossovich does not approve of Yeltsin's reliance on American support, on democracy, on capitalism American-style. There are rumors in the street that Rossovich is waiting for the crucial moment, when Yeltsin is at his weakest, to unveil a striking new plan for Russia's future, an economic plan that will catapult him into national leadership. But let me emphasize, no one knows what is coming next . . . and no one is absolutely sure who is giving orders to the army which stands here, represented by the tanks, and doesn't move a muscle. If the crowd charges the White House and tries to rout Yeltsin out of office, will the tanks open fire on their countrymen to preserve the government? Or will they charge the White House as well, in the name of a new Russia led by Egon Rossovich? Is the future of Russia to be democratic, or a new old-fashioned dictatorship in the control of a strongman? Only time will tell . . .

"One thing is certain: Muscovites are facing another bleak winter.

Civil unrest, not enough to eat, little in the way of consumer goods—and it's worse in the countryside. Inevitably, starvation will be widespread this winter—everyone is predicting it. And where do the Americans fit in? Is more aid on the way? Will the Americans or the UN intervene if the army over here breaks in two and goes to civil war? What of the great European powers who certainly have an interest in the future of Russia? What of Germany—can Germany afford to let Russia fall apart? Or become more militaristic? Where would a new Cold War take the Continent? These are but a few of the questions being asked at dawn in Moscow and around the world. Meanwhile Yeltsin clings to power and the maneuvering behind the scenes goes on. And Egon Rossovich has not been seen in several days, not since he last spoke to the nation and advocated a variety of new proposals, including the reclaiming of Alaska from the United States, forming new and closer ties to the Arab militarists, and using nuclear tactical weapons against any pockets of opposition to the plans he has for Russia. But where is his economic rescue plan? What does it entail? And where is Rossovich himself? Those are the questions of the moment and I am Kirk Robbins in Moscow for CNN, waiting for the new day, waiting to learn if today is the day for Russia to reinvent itself yet again . . ."

And then the Professor understood it all.

He sat there with a bemused grin, wondering at the audacity of it.

Of course, somebody had to stop it.

Tomorrow. He was too exhausted to think about it anymore tonight. He'd call Paulus tomorrow . . . and Delaney . . . Ned Cheddar had to be involved . . . and then he was asleep with his pain and his concussion and the girl he'd rescued snoring softly in the bed.

Ned Cheddar got up and dressed and, with his armed Marine bodyguard, went for a predawn walk in his Georgetown neighborhood. Young bureaucrats were up and about and plotting ways to keep their jobs or wrest a job from somebody else; the Secretary of Transportation was out with his Alsatian bitch—a fine figger of a dog, Cheddar thought—having a run. The car and driver were waiting in the driveway of the Chairman of the Joint Chiefs of Staff. The driver was buried in *The Washington Post*. It was a very secure neighborhood. One of the President's advisors from back home was already backing out of his driveway and heading in to work. Washington was an early-rising town. It was misting and very quiet but the sense of pulsing life was everywhere. Several front windows were showing Christmas tree lights already.

Cheddar was thinking. He was analyzing what in later years he would reveal had come to him "in a dream." It would make a good story and parts of it were true. The thoughts of Wolf Koller and the constant reports he was getting from the Kremlinologists, the Yeltsin watchers, the boys on the scene in Moscow, the watchers at the think tanks—they'd all worked their way into his dreams and had arranged and rearranged themselves, forming one picture after another, all through the three hours he'd slept. Each dream picture had had something wrong with it, each but the last one. Even while lost in the dream, Cheddar always knew it was a dream: within the dream, he would say to himself, *I know this is only a dream but I think it makes sense, I'll remember it and analyze it when I wake up.* This kind of dreaming he found enormously useful, even though most of the results of his dreams fell quickly apart when he tested them in the light of day. Today was different. This dream picture held up. He couldn't shake it.

He knew what Wolf Koller was up to.

He understood SPARTAKUS.

Wolf Koller was dictating a new German foreign policy.

The crazy son of a bitch was putting together another Russo-German pact.

The German economy. The Russian nuclear arsenal . . . and to hell with what Bush and Yeltsin had wanted to do . . . to hell with Clinton and his team . . .

Germany and Russia. A new Axis. Economic power and nuclear weaponry.

With the rest of Europe in a squeeze play, caught in the middle.

No wonder everybody was having a fit.

Wolf Koller . . .

It would take a Wolf Koller even to think of such a thing. It was beyond politicians. They'd tell you it couldn't be done. They'd tell you the shot wasn't on the table.

Wolf Koller would just tell them to think again.

Wolf Koller would see the deal. You get, we get.

No wonder people were getting killed. This deal was bigger than people. The Professor thought of Wolf Koller putting it together . . . Wolf Koller worrying about Karl-Heinz and Lee and Erika and then

John-fucking-Cooper coming out of nowhere. No wonder he was a little testy.

You had to hand it to him.

Wolf Koller was taking the play away from everybody else, leaving all the Ned Cheddars playing with themselves in the sandbox.

Wolf Koller was going to change everything. Change the world.

Of course, somebody had to stop him.

When the Professor finally woke up Erika Koller was gone. He couldn't imagine a worse turn of events. Would she have enough sense to stay hidden? Or did she have some agenda that might get her killed?

It was a lousy start to the day.

39

DÉJÀ VU ALL OVER AGAIN

Cooper decided that all in all this was just about what he deserved for being a lovesick dimwit, for having considerably less brains than a small child, for not being able to leave well enough alone, for poking his nose into other people's business, for generally being such a dumb bastard. And he was also going to be responsible for the death of Beate Hubermann. She'd never done anything so awful to Wolf Koller or the neo-Nazis. Nothing worth dying for. But in Wolf Koller's mind she must represent all the terrors of the media, the fear of exposure . . . And she'd been spending too much time with John Cooper.

What all the rigmarole, the ride in the old Caddy had to do with it, he had no idea. But he knew they were going to kill him. And Beate. He felt as if his head had been split open, and there was blood in his eyes and his hands were tied behind him and his sense of balance was shot and from the smell of things he'd thrown up somewhere nearby. Maybe they were going to kill him because he'd thrown up in the Caddy. It really didn't matter why, did it?

The three men murmured to one another, paying little attention to their cargo. One of them sat in the back, next to their prisoners, holding a gun in his lap. So this was what it all came down to: he'd lived his life and had made a mess of it over his sister, and now he was going to die and his sister was probably already dead and there was nothing he could do about it.

It was probably best that he'd had the shit kicked out of him first. There wasn't much fight left in the old boy and, if it came to that, not much will to go on with any of it if Lee was dead or dying. It just went to show you that the bad guys finally were going to win. They hadn't won twenty years ago. He and Olaf Peterson had had a pretty good game back then and had pulled it out in the bottom of the ninth. But you couldn't win them all. He wasn't going to win this one. He wondered what Peterson would say, or think, or do, when he heard what had happened to his old comrade on his second invasion of Germany. Would he remember John Cooper with a grin and wish him well wherever he was . . .

He was drawn back to the present by Beate's moan and the jostling of their bodies as the Caddy crossed into a driveway and headed into a fenced lot, which led to a warehouse long as a football field. He felt or heard a kind of throbbing all around him, something from another world, as if the earth and the air were vibrating, a Martian invasion, Michael Rennie about to walk down from the spaceship . . . God, maybe he was losing his mind, maybe that was the way the psyche protected you at the very end, maybe you believed you were someplace else, in a movie . . . He wanted to be in a *Thin Man* picture, everybody having drinks and lots of colorful characters making smart chatter and that dog Asta and Myrna Loy telling William Powell that it said he'd been shot in the tabloids . . . Jesus, somebody once told him Myrna Loy and William Powell hadn't even liked each other . . . what a world, what a world . . .

The car rolled to a stop and Koller's men opened the back doors. The one with the gun had a bloody nose and a cut lip from his encounter with John Cooper and the halogen lamp, and when Cooper staggered out of the backseat the guy tripped him and knocked him down and said something in German and kicked him in the ribs. What difference did it make? It just made him think less about dying . . .

They were pushing Beate along, toward a small doorway in the side of the warehouse. Cooper discovered how hard it was to get himself upright with his hands tied behind his back. He turned to the man with the gun and said: "Untie my hands and I'll rip your head off and spit in the hole." He'd heard that at the movies. The guy didn't say anything, just shoved him forward toward the doorway. The vibrations were everywhere. He felt as if maybe a big fucking monster lived in the warehouse and his breathing made the world shake and he was hungry. Dinner was on the way.

It was dimly lit in the warehouse and there were trucks for what appeared to be collecting trash and compacting it and huge dumpsters full of rubble and it smelled of oil and hydraulics and cement and dirt and something that had been scorched. At the end of the space was something, the monster, with huge doors and hydraulic devices. Cooper sighed. He didn't want to die. His heart felt as if it might explode: he couldn't will it calm. He prayed he'd be dead by the time he got fed to the monster.

They were pushed and shoved toward a table and into some wooden chairs. One of the Germans said something to Beate and she said something and he said something and she nodded and turned to Cooper.

"We're waiting for someone. There's someone who wants to talk to us."

"Before they kill us?"

"I suppose so. I don't think it's going to be very nice."

"Being murdered probably never is," he said. He was playing the scene tight-lipped. Bogart or Bill Holden. Coop in *For Whom the Bell Tolls* only he wasn't going to be able to take a lot of the Fascisti with him before he went.

"There are questions they're going to ask us—when the man gets here—"

"It's Koller. He wants to know how much we know about SPARTAKUS."

"But we don't know anything—"

"Somehow I don't think that's going to save us," Cooper said, trying to smile. "I'm sorry, Beate. You don't deserve this."

She smiled at him. There was blood around her nose and mouth. "Nobody deserves this. It's just bad luck."

"No, it's the Cooper Touch. Sometimes I get the Nazis, sometimes the Nazis get me."

He didn't see it coming but the blow hit him across the back of the skull and knocked him off the chair. He tried to right himself and then the pain exploded in his head and he slipped and fell down hard on the cement floor and the guy came over and stepped on his face, pushing one side against the cement and slowly increasing his weight.

Another one finally yanked the first one off and Cooper felt a burning sensation where the boot had been. The second guy helped him up and put him back on the chair and said something in German but he couldn't hear it anyway. He felt as if his eardrum had broken and was leaking. The rumbling and vibrating were in his head now, they were wearing him out. He sank back in the chair, wondered how long they would wait for their interrogator.

An hour passed, an hour of the vibrating and the low-pitched rumble and the pain in various parts of his body and trying to think of what he could say to Beate and knowing there was nothing that would make any difference. Her eyes were closed, as if she were meditating herself onto a different plane of existence, distancing herself from the mess Cooper and his sister had gotten her into, and Cooper was only half awake when he heard something through the din. Had the small doorway opened somewhere back in the darkness . . . or a different doorway? Or was it his imagination? Was he awake or was he dreaming? Nobody else seemed to notice.

Then he heard another noise. A tapping or shuffling, something that wasn't supposed to be there. Or, at least, hadn't been there before.

He looked around into the deep shadows, straining to see if Koller had arrived. But there was nothing. Just the low-pitched rumbling and the vibrations and . . . there, the funny noise, something tapping on the cement, or something sliding, like a man dragging a heavy sack of something . . .

The three men had now heard it. They peered into the darkness and one of them swore and called out something, probably Who goes there? or its equivalent but there was no answer. Just the occasional tapping or sliding.

Koller's guys were really pissed by now. Pissed but helpless. The space was so vast, the shadows so deep, the noise so insistent, the ability to pinpoint the tapping and the scraping so paltry. Each of them had now produced a gun, one a machine pistol from the recesses of his long coat. They were standing, staring into the darkness as if they were the last of the Dalton gang.

It was *High Noon.*

They were scared but maybe they were just spooked.

Then came an act of God. Kind of.

The man came out of the shadows, or maybe he hadn't come out, maybe he was just there, and the darkness had been blown away for a moment, revealing him.

He wore a long sheepskin coat that hung open.

He was leaning on a crutch under his left arm.

The crutch. That was the tapping.

He took another step out of the shadows, revealing slightly more of himself. You couldn't see his face.

You could see the thing he had in his right hand, resting on his hip. Cooper had never seen anything like it. It was some kind of shotgun. With a big round magazine like an old-fashioned tommygun.

One of the bad guys yelled out something and fired a shot at him. The man shuddered momentarily when the slug hit him, then he was coming toward them and—

The next thing Cooper heard was like the earth erupting. It came fast, an awesome, rocking noise that filled the warehouse and cannonaded off the walls and blew its way through the rumbling and vibrations, and bodies and blood and chunks of clothing and flesh filled the air and splattered on Cooper's face and across Beate in the chair, shattering explosions, disaster and death and worse spilling out of the barrel of this gun from hell and the air was full of disintegrating Germans. The first one, the one who'd fired the shot, caught a blast across the chest and most of his arm came off and he did a funny little dance step backwards and went down and the second one was trying to duck to one side and got it just above the shoulders and his face wasn't there anymore which left a whipping aerial of spinal cord behind a geyser of blood pumping out of his throat. The third one stood his ground, getting off a round or two before the blast cut him across the middle and turned him into two half-men and Beate was screaming and looking away as the air filled with crap and the man with the mother of all weapons came slowly forward through the fire and brimstone and the noise of the gunfire, which seemed to echo on and on and on. He came out of the shadows like some movie's avenging angel and of course that's what he was, the avenging angel, the guardian angel—it was a part he knew well, he'd been there before. His progress was slow with the crutch and the sort of shuffling sound was his one foot sliding along the cement floor.

He loomed over Cooper.

"Honest to God," he said, "you find yourself in deeper shit than anyone else in the history of man." He paused and grinned. There was blood seeping through holes in the sheepskin coat. He bent down on one knee, grimacing with pain, began untying Beate's wrists. "What the hell would you do without me?" He coughed. "I'm not always going to be there, y'know."

"You always have been," Cooper said softly.

Cooper turned to Beate, who was staring at this man, her face speckled with bits of other people's blood. She looked as if she was in shock, staring in that funny way.

"Beate Hubermann," Cooper said, "Olaf Peterson."

The man leaned forward, extending his right hand past the enormous gun cradled in the crook of his arm. "I'm the man who looks after our friend Cooper here."

Cooper watched him gently brush her hair out of the blood on her face. She looked up at Olaf Peterson as if she were seeing the face of God. Her face was streaked with tears.

Tonight was not the night of his death.

Olaf Peterson had seen to that.

Again.

"John, he's been shot." Peterson was slowly leaning toward her, into her arms.

"That snot-nosed little prick over there." He pointed with the huge gun. Then it slipped from his grasp and clattered mightily to the concrete.

Olaf Peterson's sheepskin coat swung open, revealed a large splotch of blood like a dark red rose.

He collapsed in Beate's arms, as if she were a welcoming angel at the gates of Glory.

40

ERIKA AT LARGE

Feeling the weight of the Luger she'd found at the Hubermanns' lodge, feeling it heavy and terrifying in her coat pocket, Erika stood at the corner of the Ku'damm across from Kranzler's, by the international newspaper kiosk, her head pushed into a telephone enclosure. The traffic pulsed and rushed all around her. She was waiting while the special call routed through two other switching boards, snaking its way into her father's sanctum sanctorum at Koller Industries International. When she'd gotten no answer at the Grunewald house, nor at the Wannsee house, she'd been sure he was at his hideaway, for which only half a dozen people had the number. In case of emergencies. She had it, her mother had it, Dr. Gisevius had it. There couldn't have been many others. Now it rang once, twice, the machine answered anonymously, then she spoke and heard the quick pickup, her father's voice.

"Erika! My dear—where are you? Are you all right? We've been worried sick . . . what's this all about?" He sounded concerned but calm, his paternal mask securely in place. Not at all as if he'd tracked her down and sent his people to murder her.

"You know the Loretta beer garden?"

"There are several—"

"You know which one. The place where you had your people dump the body of Karl-Heinz Schmidt."

"I have no idea what you're talking about. Why not come here, darling? Or I can meet you at home—are you quite all right?"

"You heard me. Noplace else."

"You sound very upset."

"Just because you sent your thugs to kill me? Why should I be upset by that? It's in character. I'm warning you to come alone—if you don't, you'll wish you had, I promise you."

"Wait a moment. It will take me some time to get there. I'll need a couple of hours."

"That's unfortunate. You have only an hour. And if you're not there in an hour, on foot, and alone, you'll be reading all about SPARTAKUS in tomorrow's newspapers. Walk across from the Ku'damm. I'll be watching. When you get to the Ferris wheel, wait for me. Do you understand? Wait for me."

"Now, Rikki, I know you're upset, you're angry and confused, but let me assure you—"

She hung up the phone. *Rikki.* God, how she resented his use of the nickname he'd given her as a baby . . . She'd worshiped him as she grew up, until she was eight or nine and she began to realize how he treated her mother. The disdain, the impatience, the fear, all wrapped together—she hadn't known what to call his attitude, but she felt it, it hung like a pall over the household, over the rest of her growing up. *Rikki, darling, would you do this, Rikki, sweetheart, your riding master is waiting for you . . .* He had bought her a horse, an Arabian, but by then it was too late: she hated him and loved her mother. But it was more than love. She knew her mother needed protection from him and she took it upon herself to provide it . . . *Kids,* she thought, *poor little kids . . .*

She had to get out of the cold, slashing wind. She picked up a newspaper and took it with her to a café and read while drinking coffee with hot milk and eating a sticky bun. She had left the hotel, left the Professor snoring, at a little after noon, and had walked and walked, making sure of what she should do, checking it over and over again for flaws, until she realized her plan was flawless—if she was willing to perform one simple act at any moment. And that was to kill her father. As long as she had that card to play, she was safe. Sitting in the café, she thought she could do it if she had to. She looked at her watch. It was time to go.

It was dark now. She saw him get out of a taxi and stand for a moment, pulling his hat brim down, glancing around in case he might spot her. Failing in that, he strode off purposefully, his coat draped over his shoulders like a cape to accommodate the arm and its cast. She let him walk ahead while she watched from the other side of the street. There was no car following him, no one on foot. He didn't check his watch, he didn't stop and look around, he just went on his way. Unescorted. Sure of himself.

The Ferris wheel loomed out of the rain against the night sky. He crossed the busy street and stared for a moment at the brightly painted logo of the parrot, then leaned casually against the fence beneath the Ferris wheel. The blank eyes of the deserted ticket booth seemed to be watching her as she crossed the street. At that moment she realized he could have his people already in place at the beer garden, out of sight, ready to rush her, but if she held to her willingness to kill him, none of the rest of it really mattered.

The cold wind cut like a knife. It raked her short blond hair as she came toward him. She was wearing tinted glasses, black leggings, a belted leather jacket, lace-up boots. He looked right at her, through her, turned away, having no idea who she was. She took a few steps past him, then stood looking up the street, into the gleaming headlamps of the oncoming traffic.

"Hello, Father."

His profile turned to face her. His mouth was open with surprise. "I didn't recognize you. What have you done to yourself?"

"It's my disguise."

"Disguise? What are you talking about? Here, let me get a good look at you." He began to move toward her and she stepped back, hand up to ward him off, shaking her head.

"I've been trying to stay alive. Two of your goons died the night before last. They almost had me. But I had a protector. I don't need one tonight, do I, Father?" She smiled.

"I don't know what you're talking about—you must be mad."

"Is that it? Are the rest of us all mad? Mother, me, anyone else who doesn't agree with you? Do you think that will hold up, Father? You'd better give it some more thought—"

"What do you want with me? If you're not going to make any sense, come to the point."

"I want to see Mother. Where is she?"

"Your mother is much too ill to speak to you, or see you for that matter. How could you even face her, putting her through this nightmare the way you have? Blood on the floor, knives, no body . . . You knew perfectly well what condition she was in when you pulled your little stunt—"

"You're wasting your breath. Take me to her. I am going to see her or you're going to die before she does. It's only fair to tell you, I have a gun. It's loaded. I won't hesitate to shoot you if you try anything—just take me to her. After I see her, I'll decide if I'll kill you for what you did to Karl-Heinz . . ."

"A gun . . . my daughter holds me at gunpoint." He spit the words with pure contempt. "My daughter threatens to kill me . . . Your mother is at Dr. Lipp's hospital. You know where it is."

"Oh, you're coming with me."

She stepped to the curb and waved down a taxi, gave the driver the address of the private hospital that looked out into the Grunewald forest. She knew that among the other cars passing in the street her father could have several watchers keeping an eye on him, sliding back and forth, never letting him out of their sight. There was nothing she could do about that.

In the cab he said softly: "What has happened to you, Rikki? What brought you to this point?"

"You happened to me, Father. You brought me to this point. One more thing you will never be forgiven."

"You can't go on this way—"

"No, Father, you're the one who can't go on this way. Haven't you figured that out yet?"

"Don't be fatuous, Rikki."

The rest of the ride was passed in silence. She never relaxed her grip on the Luger in her pocket.

The hallway smelled of antiseptic, the sounds were muted. Dr. Lipp's hospital retained all the character of the private mansion it once had been. You could almost smell the previous occupants, the faint whiff of cigars and cologne and elaborate meals from the direction of the kitchen far belowstairs. Almost, but not quite. The hospital smells prevailed. There were still huge paintings in heavy gilded frames on the walls, ancient carpets muffling footsteps.

There was a small red light above the door to her room. Wolf Koller swung it open and Erika followed him inside. There were several vases of flowers on small tables. The light was very dim. A small table lamp near the window, a faint light from the bathroom. Bach played very softly on a small stereo in a bookcase. It was a luxurious private bedroom, quite unlike a hospital room. It was a home away from home for those inconvenient members of the upper, upper class.

The woman on the bed lay quietly under a smooth blanket, only her face visible. The shadows played cruel tricks on the face, which in utter repose looked as if life were already extinguished. Erika waved her father around the bed, to stand between the bed and the wall, cutting off his exit. She surprised herself with her coolness.

When she turned her attention fully to her mother she felt herself momentarily giving way. Lise was pale to the point of grayness. Her eyes were sunk deep in the sockets. Her lips were drawn back slightly, as if they were being stretched across her bone structure. "Mother," she whispered. "It's Erika. Can you hear me?" She thought she saw the eyelids flutter. She took her mother's hand and squeezed it softly. There was a slight answering pressure. So weak. "Mother, I'm all right . . . don't worry about me . . ." Lise's head turned slowly, her lips moved, but there was no sound; her hands shifted under the blankets. Then nothing.

"What have you done to her?" Erika kept her voice calm, her eyes burning into her father's. "What is this? She wasn't like this the last time I saw her—nothing like this. What's going on?"

"She's sedated, of course. She raves unless she's sedated. She wouldn't know you. Or me. She doesn't know herself most of the time—"

"You're killing her, you bastard!" Her fingers tightened on the gun in her pocket.

"Erika, don't be ridiculous. She's very, very ill. She may have only days left . . ."

She leaned down and kissed her mother's cheek. There were tears running down her face when she looked back at Koller. "Then that makes two of you with only days left. If anything happens to her, or me, you can forget all about SPARTAKUS. *All* of your plans—forget them, if anything happens to either of us—"

"I know nothing about this SPARTAKUS, you're making no sense—"

"Karl-Heinz told me everything before you had him killed. Do you hear me, do you understand?"

"I don't know what he told you—I'm sure it was warped and irresponsible . . . but what you must realize is that you can't stand in the way of history. You can't let your personal hatred interfere with the fate of the Fatherland! You must see that, Rikki, or you'll be trampled by history—"

"Oh, spare me the fate of the Fatherland! I don't care about the fate of the Fatherland, don't you understand? Our family is all that matters to me, to hell with the Fatherland! *Your* family, your generation and the generations before, all the way back to the spiked helmets, you've made a hellish mess of the Fatherland—it's a mess now and you're determined to make it worse . . . all that's left for me is the family!"

Wolf Koller was standing at the end of the bed, his face rigid, his eyes glittering like coals. "The family? You care nothing for the family. You've made a mockery of it, my daughter, you've forgotten how close we were, how I held you on my shoulders at the parade so you could see . . . you've forgotten how I taught you to swim and kept my hands under you so you'd never sink, so you would have nothing to fear, you've forgotten meeting St. Nicholas and holding my hand because you were frightened—none of the reasons you loved me has survived, not one. And that was the family, Rikki. You and I were the only hope of our family— the rest of it, your mother—she's mad and she's made it a joke, it has always been a joke as far as she's concerned, from the day they told me I must marry her—"

"*They? Who* told you?" She felt tears on her face, hated herself for listening to him.

"Associates of mine, people who were worried about her instability—"

"You mean the Nazis, why don't you just say it? The men who surrounded her first husband . . . oh, she told me all that, she told me that you were one of them—"

"More insanity! And you believed her! You don't know that she spent the first year of our marriage in a mental institution! And she's your authority! My God!"

"I know all about Dr. Warmolts and his clinic and the shock treatments, all about what happened in Bayreuth. And I know this, too—she didn't have a baby while she was there. I know all that's a lie . . ."

She could see his white teeth as he grimaced, moving closer to her, along the foot of the bed. "It's not a lie that I love you, Rikki . . . it's not my fault that it worked out the way it did—it's not the way I wanted it, you must believe that—"

"So," she continued, out of breath, "one final issue, Father . . . *who am I? Who is my mother?*"

"For God's sake, you must listen to me—there are answers to your questions. Your mother—" He shook his head, unable to speak.

"Is she dead? Did you kill her, too?"

He shuddered at the impact of her words, then reached out for her, pushing off the corner post at the foot of the bed. His wound made him stiff and clumsy. As he reached out for her hand, she stepped aside and pushed him away, half terrified, half wishing she could let him enfold her and soothe her and kiss her tears away as he had when she'd run to him with a skinned knee or a broken doll. But now he gasped with pain and surprise and staggered back against the small table, upsetting a vase of flowers. He was turning, trying to protect his arm and the bullet wound. His face was contorted with pain and his voice was pinched, hoarse. "Erika, please—don't do this. Try to find it in your heart to—" He was struggling to keep from falling. On the bed, Lise stirred, moaned softly at the sound of their voices and the vase smashing. "I am your father, Rikki—I will always be your father, you can never change that."

She was sobbing now at the sight of him, the look on his face, the pain in his eyes. *I am your father. I will always be your father* . . . He was right, he lived in her. There was nothing she could do about that.

She took the videotape from her pocket, wiping her eyes with a gloved hand, mastering her emotions. "I've spent today having ten copies of this tape made. On my say-so, or when my friends can't locate me, they will be delivered to the major German newspapers, *The New York Times, The Times* of London, *The Washington Post,* the intelligence agencies of America, England, and Israel. It's your fate, Father, not *ours.* Take a look at the tape . . . I'll be in touch in a day or two. Be prepared to tell me who I am, Father. Surely you must know—aren't you all-knowing? All-powerful? Isn't the future of the Fatherland entirely up to you?" She stared into his ashen face. "Now, I'm going . . . No, stay where you are, Father. I can find my way out. Enjoy the tape . . . and take very, very good care of Mother."

Wolf Koller sat slumped in the chair by the window, watching the street below for the appearance of his daughter, waiting for the pain in his arm and shoulder to recede. Erika . . . he loved her because of the woman who had borne her. But she was a monster. Women! The undoing of so many great men . . . The women close to Richelieu had been his greatest burden! Now it was Wolf Koller's turn—how could his personal life have gotten a stranglehold on everything else that mattered?

He took the cellular telephone from the pocket of his coat and called Sebastien, who had followed them from the beer garden and now waited outside. "She'll be out any moment. Follow her. I must know where she goes. She's on foot—she'll probably have them summon a taxi for her. When she settles somewhere, call me immediately."

Finally he got up, feeling stiff and slightly feverish. Was it the wound or was it psychosomatic? Erika was enough to give anyone a fever! He made his way to the bathroom and bathed his face with cold water.

For just a moment he'd thought he had reached her, appealing to her childhood, to the way she'd worshiped him and he'd adored her. Maybe he *had* reached her.

His daughter . . .

He had doubts about what she might do with the videotapes. Or even that she really had the ten copies. She had wanted to try it out on him first. What had she taken away from the meeting? How much did she hate him?

She knew that he'd had Karl-Heinz killed—but she wasn't afraid of him. She'd taken steps to protect herself, but still, his blood flowed in her veins. How far would she go to destroy him?

Two of his people dead in the mountains . . .

He stared for a moment at the videotape; then, clutching it in his hand, he used the cellular phone to call one of his drivers to come and pick him up.

He was very tired and he'd been shot and his wife was dying and his daughter was trying to destroy everything he'd worked years for and he'd spoken with Rossovich only hours before and the Russian was coming to Berlin to sign the new alliance . . .

And the women were tearing him down.

He sighed, and left the room without paying the slightest attention to Lise on the bed.

He was trying to decide if he could risk killing his daughter now. Was she bluffing about the tapes? Or was she playing for keeps?

41

THE ENDGAME BEGINS

Cooper woke up in a strange room, hearing a faint scraping of sleet blowing against the window. It was a small bedroom; the window was open a few inches to allow fresh air in, and when he tried to move he felt as if people had been beating him up, which, he began to remember, they had. Then it all came seeping back into his brain, and he slowly swung his feet out of the bed and sat up. It was Werner Paulus's guest bedroom. Paulus had been waiting outside the warehouse when Olaf Peterson had come in and started killing people . . .

They had left without wasting time. Three bodies needed explanation and Paulus, who knew about such things in great detail, deemed it advisable to disappear as quickly as possible. It didn't matter if Koller might be on the way. Anybody might be on the way. The idea was to get the hell out.

They had taken Olaf Peterson to the emergency room of a hospital where the Chief was well known. The doctor receiving the patient left it to Paulus to make the report of a gunshot wound to the authorities. They all waited two hours—during which Cooper's various abrasions and bruises had been disinfected and dressed—and learned that the slug had missed Peterson's spine but had managed to damage liver, spleen, kidney, and lung. The lung was collapsed and the slug was still in the chest cavity. Peterson's condition was grave and he would be in surgery for several hours. There was considerable internal bleeding. An exploding cartridge, what used to be called a dumdum bullet, could do untold damage once it was inside a human being. Exhausted, they had all finally returned to Paulus's flat, where the Chief felt no one would come looking for them. Beate agreed, although she insisted on returning home the next day. She and Cooper had both been given sedatives at the hospital and sleep came easily.

But now it was time to get dressed.

He was going to have to stand up.

Paulus and Beate were sitting at the table in the kitchen drinking coffee strong enough to go ten rounds. Coffee with an attitude, which was just the way Cooper liked it. Paulus poured him a cup and Beate blinked sleepily at him. "You're alive," she said as if she were surprised.

"Yes. Funny, isn't it—I feel dead. Only worse." He wasn't kidding. He thought the pain in his kidneys was the worst but that was just splitting hairs. "Peterson," he said. "What have you heard?"

Paulus looked back from the counter where he was grinding more coffee beans. "He's out of surgery. They got the remains of the slug. He's in bad shape. But I'd say he's also very tough—it's fifty-fifty, the doctor tells me. They will know more in twenty-four hours."

Cooper nodded. Beate, seeing his expression, squeezed his hand.

"Last night," she said. "It still seems like a dream, I can still hear the tapping of that crutch—those guys were really, ah, you know, like ghosts. They were—"

"Spooked," Cooper said. He smiled at her. "They were spooked all right." When the whining of the coffee grinder stopped he said: "I've got to get this straight. How did you and Peterson hook up? How did he find us at all? The last time I saw him he was laid up in Minnesota in a snowstorm—"

"Yes," Paulus said, "I don't wonder you're curious. It is an odd story . . ."

When Paulus had gotten a feeling—*Fingerspitzengefühl* at its best —for the situation, he had thought back over the whole business of twenty years ago, which had become a bit of a legend in German intelligence circles. And the name that was missing from the present situation was Olaf Peterson's. Olaf Peterson was the man who'd kept Cooper more or less alive. And Werner Paulus was very worried that Cooper wasn't going to get out of this one the same way. So, he had put in a call to Olaf Peterson in Cooper's Falls, Minnesota.

Peterson hadn't been able to ignore the flattery. And he'd been grousing to himself ever since seeing Cooper the night after the big snowstorm. It was all happening again, another chance at some real action, and it would never come his way again. You didn't have to be a genius to figure that out. The years were getting in the way. One of these days somebody was going to get the bad news about the X rays and there was going to be six months left and there wouldn't be any more great adventures and then how the hell would he feel if he'd missed the last big show? John Cooper had provided Olaf Peterson with the single most interesting experience of his life: better than the Minneapolis murder investigations, better than women, better than any goddamn thing, and that was the truth. Even now he could remember every damn minute of it. But twenty years was a long time to draw sustenance from the crack and flash of the big game . . . and then the chance had come again. But Peterson had told himself he was too old, his broken leg was too big a hindrance. He'd seen Cooper set off alone . . . and it damn near killed him. And it was sure as hell going to get Cooper killed.

And then, when his regrets were eating him alive, a third chance. Werner Paulus calling from Berlin . . . Your friend John Cooper is well and truly in the shit, though Paulus would never have used that particular word, and he's going to need your help . . .

You don't ignore the lifeline twice, not when you're drowning in the knowledge that you've blown it, that you've missed the last go-round . . . that you've let an old friend down at the end . . .

Paulus had arranged to have the guy waiting for him in Berlin with the Streetsweeper shotgun. It was a condition of Peterson's coming.

Paulus had been waiting in his blue Mercedes across the street from Beate Hubermann's apartment building when Peterson's cab had pulled up right on schedule. Together the two men had waited, seen Koller's foot soldiers bringing them out of the building. Paulus knew they were taking their victims to the warehouse where the disposal equipment destroyed evidence. There was so little Paulus didn't know about how men like Koller got things done. But an automobile accident had slowed them down—not their own vehicle but a truck and two cars on a slick street clogging traffic, making the rescue just a bit too close for Paulus's comfort.

Paulus had waited outside to take care of any late arrivals. But no one had come and Peterson had made sure no one made an escape from inside the building. The only thing that had gone wrong was the shooting of Peterson. But, then, God would always have His little jokes.

"Now Wolf Koller knows he is up against people who will fight back. He's losing assets." Paulus measured his words. "Everywhere he looks, things he couldn't have foreseen are coming unstuck. He's come up against people as ruthless as he is—when they're pushed . . . I hope it puts the fear of God into him." He sipped coffee. "I don't know where Erika is, but I think I know where Koller will take your sister, if he hasn't already. It's his secret place—"

"Well? Where?"

"We'll get to that in a moment. But first Erika—we must prepare ourselves for the idea that she may be dead."

"I pray that's not true. But what I have to know, Chief, is where is my sister?"

When she left Dr. Lipp's hospital Erika hardly knew what was happening. She knew her adrenaline had gone off like a bomb, catapulting her through the scene with her father, and now she was bouncing off her emotions like something in a video game. She got back to the Ku'damm on a bus she caught several blocks from the hospital, remembered nothing of the ride: the images of her father and mother were burned into her conscious, Lise seeming like death, her father in pain, reminding her of the snapshots of childhood when she'd loved him. She trembled for a long time, hugging herself tight on the bus. It had been so long in coming, the final, desperate confrontation she'd lived through in her mind so many times . . . and she had seen him at her mercy and there was no satisfaction in it, no pleasure for her. But neither were there the fear and hatred she'd felt so long: she'd somehow settled the score, she had done all she could do to him . . . And on the bus she felt herself slowly coming down from the high, trying as hard as she could not to think about all the Freudian implications of her relationship with him . . .

All that was left was to put the final pressure on him, once he'd seen the videotape. Then he would have to move her mother to some other hospital where she could get the proper care, beyond his control. Because it was all in the video . . . SPARTAKUS, the murder of Karl-Heinz, Lise's condition, and Erika's fears for her safety . . .

She went to a café and sat in a corner, shivering with the rain and cold, still trembling inside her clothing with the effects of what she'd just done. She drank the steaming black coffee fast, burning her tongue to force herself back to reality. She was suddenly hungry and ordered a rich chocolate cake and more coffee, this time café au lait with lots of sugar. She supposed she'd better get used to being an orphan of some kind, because she was destroying her father and there was surely a good chance her mother was going to die. All that was obvious. And for the first time she began to wonder what she could do on her own, what she might make of her life . . .

Of course she could still work at the gallery . . . she could go back to school, maybe in England or even the United States . . . But what in the world was she thinking of? Her father wanted to kill her, he'd sent men to kill her—she was a fool to assume all that was over. If Wolf Koller was still sane, if he believed her threat about the tapes, then it might be over, but that was a big if . . . She had to stop thinking like a child . . . She remembered what F. Scott Fitzgerald had written so many years ago, something her mother had pointed out to her. *Nobody feels sorry for a girl on a yacht.* Lise had told her that she'd be living her whole life as a girl on a yacht, figuratively speaking, because she had done so herself. And there was no point in expecting anyone to worry about your welfare, your happiness, because in the minds of everyone else, a girl on a yacht had no problems. Get used to it, Lise had said. She might tell the world about her megalomaniac father, the Nazi, who wanted to kill his own daughter, who wanted to embody the future of the Fatherland, but there wasn't going to be any sympathy for Erika Koller.

Well, she could live with that. She had lived with Wolf Koller all her life. She could handle anything that came her way . . . She hoped.

And she knew she had one friend.

She arrived at Beate's flat in Kreuzberg, leaned on the bell, and breathed a sigh of relief when she heard the answering buzz. She took the five flights of stairs two at a time and arrived panting like a sprinter, eager, smiling, and then shocked at the sight of Beate's face.

Beate's eyes widened; then tears sprang to her cheeks and she threw her arms around Erika. They were both quietly crying for everything that had happened, all the pain. "You're not dead, you're not dead," Beate whispered into her ear.

Erika pulled back, took hold of her shoulders: "But you—what has happened to you? Your face!"

Beate tried to smile but it hurt. There was a cut in her lip and a scrape over one eye and the eye was going black from another blow. "It's the result of an encounter with the bad guys." She winced at the smile. "But I'm fine . . . There's a lot to tell you. And a lot to hear, I'm sure."

Erika stared at the wreckage of the upstairs rooms, the broken lamp, the shelves swept clean, books and papers scattered around, a table overturned, all the mess made by the fight John Cooper had put up. "Who did this?"

"Your uncle, actually. One of the good guys trying to keep us from getting killed. I've just come back but forget the mess, let's have a glass of wine."

"My *uncle* did this?"

Their exchange of stories went in fits and starts, each trying to piece together the whole picture and realizing that it was a big job. Beate concluded with the story of Olaf Peterson's arrival out of the night to save their lives, and Erika told of how she'd confronted her father and how she'd left things with him.

"You're saying you know what SPARTAKUS actually is? And you've videotaped it. Did you really make ten copies to be sent to—"

"No. I didn't really know how. I thought you—"

"Yes, yes, I can dub it. You've still got one?"

"Yes, I did that one at an electronics store. The salesman was young and liked the way I looked—he showed me how to do it with two VCRs." She sipped at her second glass of wine. "Now you must listen very carefully, Beate. Let me tell you the story. I'm speaking to Beate the journalist. I'll tell you everything Karl-Heinz told me . . . It's why they killed him. Why my father is so afraid of me—I can't bear to think of what he might do once he sees the tape . . .

"It was the last thing Karl-Heinz told me, that last night, and I told him it was crazy, not even my father would try to do such a thing. I thought he must be making some of it up but now I know he was telling the truth . . . It's why he was killed.

"Listen to me. It's all about the Russians. My father has made a secret deal . . . and he's convinced Chancellor Glock that it's the beginning of a new age of German world leadership . . ."

When she'd finished she said: "The Americans can never let this happen. They can't let it happen, can they, Beate? That's what Karl-Heinz said. It's up to the Americans in the end . . ."

Her eyes were so huge and, suddenly, filled with uncertainty.

Wolf Koller sat alone in the near darkness of the deserted mansion in Grunewald. His footsteps had echoed in the foyer and it was cold in the large, empty rooms. He had told his driver to wait in the car. And now he was slumped in a deep chair, his coat still over his shoulders, with the remote control for the VCR and television set in his hand. A snifter of cognac sat beside him on the end table. His head ached: he was subject to migraines when he went past his stress threshold. He looked at his watch. No time to waste. He had to get moving soon. Gisevius and the ambulance carrying Lise were well on their way. The others would be gathering soon. He couldn't keep everyone waiting . . .

He turned the television set on and pressed the play button. He took a sip of cognac while he waited for the picture to come into focus.

He saw his daughter's face. He loathed the absurd "disguise." She was so beautiful, he hated to see her beauty marred. He didn't recognize the background in the shot. Her face nearly filled the screen.

"My name is Erika Koller. My father is Wolf Koller. He is about to set into motion a plan which will lead to the domination of Europe by the Germans and the Russians. He has directed the murders of several people in order to protect the secrecy of his plan—when it is announced, it will be too late to stop it . . . Let me tell you about the plan he has chosen to call SPARTAKUS . . . SPARTAKUS because it represents the revolt of the slaves, the revolt of the Russians and the Germans who have become in his view slaves to the American empire . . ."

Wolf Koller was unable to take his eyes off the screen. *She had it all.* If she leaked it to the press or to the Americans . . . well, that couldn't happen until the signatures were in place and Yeltsin was out . . . The announcement by the two parties must come first, then it would make no difference, her story would be drowned out by all the other noise surrounding the announcement, her other charges deemed hysterical.

History would never forgive him if he failed to stop her.

He took his cellular phone again and called Clint Kilroy.

Ned Cheddar was indulging in blood sausage and pork hocks, sitting in the kitchen of the Georgetown house, with the table full of telephones and yellow pads and decoded onionskins. He'd just about gone mad for a period of hours during which none of his operatives in Berlin and its environs had called in as scheduled. He'd been reminiscing with one of the team of guards while he waited but now he was beginning to run short of patience.

Ned Cheddar hadn't been to Europe in twenty years; for that

matter he hadn't left the States since a trip to Chile and the "Dead Zone" in Argentina, where he'd arranged for some enemies to join the ranks of the disappeared. He had finished up in Manila, which had been dicey since he hadn't really been sure whose side he was on. Aquino was fine and all but there were certain ties to Marcos, questions of what passed for honor in the shadow world. Now in Berlin there was no need for ambivalence. He was finding out that he was being betrayed by people he was betraying, and that made him almost irrationally perturbed. It was clearly too late to reform Herr Koller.

Finally the telephone rang while he was ruminating for a moment, regretting that he hadn't decided to go to Berlin himself. The balloon was going up, as they'd said in the long-ago days of his youth, and he was on the sidelines. In Berlin he might have gorged himself on the blood sausage and sauerbraten at Hecker's Dele not far from the Kempinski, he'd have had his fill of Berlin beer . . .

But now Clint Kilroy was talking, and Cheddar could hear the puffing on the black cheroot. The old boy was sounding every day of his age. Cheddar realized it was about time to cut him loose, let him go back to Texas and play with his grandkids before he had that last heart attack or the big blowout in his guts. Still, there was this one last mess to clean up.

"I finally found out what's going on with all these old guys coming out of the woodwork. Got it from Sebastien." It was odd listening to Kilroy talk about men junior to him as the old guys but Cheddar knew what he meant. "They're all *dead* terrorists—who didn't die after all. Koller rounded them up, or maybe Bernd Schmidt—that's his security genius, suddenly among the missing with Frau Schmidt, incidentally— rounded them up for him, gave 'em all new identities, new papers, new histories . . . they were all working for Koller's old girlfriend in the bad old days when they were blowing up airports and school buses and such. You remember her, Rafaela Dorfmann, more recently seen as the psychotic terrorist and child-killer. Apparently she really did get blown up in her little factory, but some of the others couldn't be identified. Koller knew the whereabouts of Rafaela's people, though, and he jiggered the papers to make it look like some of them died in the blast—" Cheddar could hear a clicking noise. Kilroy was picking his teeth with a fingernail.

Kilroy went on: "As I say, Schmidt and his wife are among the missing and from what Sebastien told me, they're not coming back. And they're not on holiday in Tahiti, either. Schmidt's kid, our young friend Karl-Heinz, is to blame for the passing of Mom and Dad—Sebastien hinted that Koller's people wrote off the whole damn family. We shouldn't expect to find any remains."

"So I've been given to understand," Cheddar murmured.

"I've been following your instructions, picking Koller's brain. He thinks you're very remote from all of this, funding his movement through me—he sees me as the man in charge of things for you, the paymaster. After all, he knows who I am—which, incidentally, is beginning to make me just a little nervous if you and he have some sort of falling-out, as would seem likely . . . Let's not have him raking up the past, singing the old songs. You see my point."

"With me as your protector, Clint, you're as safe as can be. You know that. The haven I offer is immutable and forever and in perpetuity throughout the universe."

"Right. So the only person I really have to worry about is you."

"When I go," Cheddar wheezed, "you go."

"I hate deals like that."

"You've lived with this one a long time."

Kilroy said: "Can I go now?"

"You certainly may not. Have you spoken with the Professor?"

"I haven't seen hide nor hair of him since he decided to follow Orlovski. He called me, told me about seeing him with Sebastien . . . since then he's gone to ground."

"Behind his beard the Professor is a very bright man," Cheddar mused. "And busy, I might add. He called in . . . He has found Erika, brought her back to Berlin . . . and lost her again." He lapsed into silence.

"Well, how nice for him! Was there any plan to tell me?" Kilroy drawled. "What *is* going on here?"

"It doesn't matter to you," Cheddar said. "We're getting down to the short strokes, Clint. What else have you got for me?"

"There was one helluva shootout at Koller's big disposal ware-house the other night. Three dead. All of them Koller security men. Sebastien told me it looked like somebody put a grenade inside 'em."

"Yes. What else?"

"Cooper's disappeared. His own personal Barbara Walters looks like a truck hit her, and some little blondie is taking care of her at her place, showed up this morning."

"Beate Hubermann looking like a truck hit her," Cheddar mused. "Somebody beat her up, presumably." He snorted. "It doesn't matter, for the moment. But one is curious about who else is out there killing bad people at Koller's warehouse. And what about this little blondie?"

"Not little. Tall, short blond hair, very hip, all leather, tight pants or leggings or something—"

"Well? Who is this girl?"

"I don't know . . . but something happened at that flat, Burke and I had a look yesterday, before Hubermann came home from wherever she'd been. The place was a shambles. No Cooper, no Beate Hubermann, furniture knocked over, lamps broken, looked like John Wayne had just defended the fucking Alamo in the living room—"

"Wait a moment," Cheddar said slowly, finishing the last beer. "What girlfriend of Beate's? Somebody we don't know? Didn't we have one of our snoops do a workup on the young lady? I don't want to hear that we've started missing people—"

"Don't yell at me, yell at the snoops. But this blondie is not on the list—or in the photo file."

"Then I submit to you that this *blondie* is Erika Koller. They've given her a makeover and they're hiding her out in the open."

"You know, Cheese, you just might be right."

"I want you to stay with Koller. Don't let him doubt your loyalty. Keep his paranoia under control. I've got work to do from this end and time grows short, my friend. I'm going to try to stop SPARTAKUS and keep Koller in the family fold. If I pull it off, it'll be a monument to my career . . . a monument to some damn thing, anyway. But I need you to stand ready. I repeat, don't give Koller a reason to doubt you. We must keep you close to him in case you're called upon to . . . exercise your special skills."

"I don't know how many more I've got in me, Cheese."

"This one, I'm sure, old friend. At least this one." Cheddar sighed. He heard Kilroy hang up; Kilroy was coughing as if a lung were coming loose. He had too many things wrong with him. Damn it, the man deserved what time he had left back on the spread in Texas.

Wolf Koller was staring at the static on the television screen when he noticed that Clint Kilroy had joined him in the darkened room. He had been unable to move after watching the tape of Erika's report on SPARTAKUS. He felt as if a great gloved hand were pushing him down,

down beneath the surface of a roiling sea . . . He was surrounded by enemies. They were drowning him. They were trying to destroy the work of his life.

"Clint," he said softly. "Are you with me?"

"I'm right here, Wolf. I got your call and came right away."

"It seems to me that it's taken forever."

"No, I came right away. What's going on here? Where's Gisevius?"

"Everyone has gone to the mountains. There's a storm coming up there—we have to get there before it hits. Are you with me, Clint? Can I trust you? You once told me that, while you worked for Cheddar, you were personally loyal to me—that Cheddar didn't realize where your heart lay . . . is that still true, Clint?"

"Sure as hell is, Wolf. You know who I really am, so how can you doubt where my loyalties lie? You can trust me with anything."

"I'm glad to hear that, my friend. We have reached the turning point—this way success, that way the blackness of the abyss."

"Oh, hell, Wolf—there's always tomorrow."

"No, you are mistaken there. There is always tomorrow only if we prevail. SPARTAKUS will deliver us to the morrow . . . there is no other way. Forces, huge forces have been set in motion. The continent of Europe will never be the same again . . . if SPARTAKUS succeeds." He sighed heavily and clicked off the television set. The hum of the static stopped, and silence collapsed around them.

Kilroy shifted his weight on his tailbone. It made him nervous when Wolf started sounding like Hitler in the bunker with the Russians barking up his ass. Doom and gloom. It drove him nuts. Though he supposed Wolf had a point. Still, how could a man like Wolf Koller afford to trust anyone?

"So, what are my instructions?"

"I want you to kill my daughter." He paused, whether out of emotion or a sense of theatricality Kilroy didn't know. "She is hiding at the flat of Beate Hubermann. You must kill them both or SPARTAKUS is at risk. Everything is at risk. She has several videotapes. Or she *says* she has. Find them if they are there, bring them. Then, come to the mountains. Clint—it doesn't have to be elegant. It has to be quick."

"All right."

"There was a time when I almost believed that you were the one who shot me that night—that Cheddar had discovered SPARTAKUS and he'd told you to kill me. I nearly lost my faith in my mission . . . but now I know I can see it through, I can overcome my enemies. I have found new strength . . . my last illusions have been stripped away. And I see the truth . . . you are true, Clint. You are my special weapon."

"I understand," Clint Kilroy said softly.

"Don't fail me, Clint. It's like the war. Orders are orders." He stood up, extended his right hand. "I'll see you in the mountains."

Kilroy clicked his heels, an old reflex. What he saw on Wolf Koller's face might possibly have been a grim smile. It was too dark to be sure.

The rain had turned icy and the street shone like glass. A car coming toward him applied a little acceleration and immediately fishtailed, spinning until it bumped a parked car and stopped. He could feel his arthritis in every goddamn joint and he was nervous about having to walk on the slippery surface. He was just that age. You fall on your ass, break a hip, it's the home and then the mortuary real damn quick. That's what you got from messing around with crazy people. Sometimes he thought he didn't know anyone who wasn't crazy, anymore.

He was standing by the wrought-iron pissoir, leaning on it, out of sight. The windows in Beate Hubermann's flat at the top of the building across the street were yellow with light. The light glowed through the skylight on top, as well. From time to time he saw shapes moving, shadows on the walls. The gun he carried was bulky with the silencer, and he kept his gloved hand around the grip in his pocket. He had to figure out how to gain admission to the flat—that was the hard part. The rest would be nothing.

He was concentrating on the yellow rectangles far above when he heard the voice behind him.

"Don't even think about it, soldier."

Clint Kilroy felt the muzzle of the old forty-five Army-issue pressing against the back of his head. He winced slightly at the thought of what the slug would do to his brittle old skull. He knew the voice.

"Well, Burke, what are you doing here?"

"Keeping you from doing anything stupid."

"Burke, may I remind you that we're on the same side?"

"I don't know who the hell you really are, Clint, but I know they used to call you the Iceman. That's what you do for a living—kill people. But you're not gonna kill these two women. They're off the field of combat. Don't turn around just yet."

"Oh, bullshit," Kilroy said. "Kill me if you want to but I'm turning around. Christ almighty, Burke." Facing Delaney, he said: "The Cheese told me not two hours ago that I was supposed to stick with Koller. Be sure as hell I didn't give him a reason to doubt my loyalty. I'm just following orders." Clint Kilroy realized that a dog was sniffing his shoes, then realized that the dog was connected to Delaney by means of a leather leash. "I don't believe it," he sighed.

"As good a man as I've ever teamed with," Delaney said. "Name's Schuyler."

"What a handle for a dawg," Kilroy lamented, then reached down and scratched one of the bull terrier's ears. "Anyways, pard, the Cheese wasn't whistlin' Dixie. I'm not aimin' to rile Koller—"

"If you don't cancel the down-home bullshit, I'm gonna shoot you just for that."

"Wolf Koller just ordered me to kill his daughter and the Hubermann woman. They don't mean diddly to the Cheese—and if the fate of the world depends on my following Wolf Koller's orders, then I'd better kill 'em." The dog was rubbing against Kilroy's leg.

"Kill his daughter? Erika?" The breath emptied from Delaney's lungs. "What a piece of work this guy must be. And you're gonna do it?"

"I don't have a hell of a lot of choice."

"That's right. You don't. 'Cause the Cheese's special orders to me, not thirty minutes ago, were to make sure nobody harmed the daughter. Guess he didn't figure Koller would send you to do it for him . . . anyway, those were my orders. And I've got the drop on you, Clint . . . whoever the hell you are."

"I'm not an unreasonable man. There's a telephone at the corner. Let's call Cheese."

"From a phone on the corner?"

"Why not? Safest phones in the world."

It took a couple of minutes but then Cheddar's phone was ringing in Georgetown.

Ned Cheddar answered. "This had better be good, gentlemen. My lunch is getting cold. Now talk to me."

And they did.

42

LEOPOLD STECHER

Kilroy had never made the drive to Wolf Koller's mountain hideaway before, and it was taking forever. Once they left the highway and began the slow climb, gradual at first, then more of an ordeal, there was snow sifting across the road and patches of ice. The first big storm of the winter, everybody said, and, God knew, that figured. This whole thing had been nuts from the very beginning so why should the weather cooperate? None of them had known what the hell they were getting into when the Cheese had sent him on that fool's errand to Boston to chat up Cooper, and now it was too late to think it over and go at it in a better way. Cheese acted as if he could handle it but that was all it was, an act. The fat man wasn't a field man, didn't think like a field man, hated getting off his fat fanny to do anything more strenuous than making an omelette and that was, from Kilroy's point of view, a bad sign. If Cheese had known what the hell it was like out here, running around, watching every word you said for fear of letting loose the hounds of Hades, he might have figured out a better way of handling all this. Then again, maybe not.

Kilroy didn't particularly like this idea of going to the mountains. He didn't much like the attitude Wolf Koller was hauling around with him, and being stuck with him in the middle of a snowstorm didn't have much to recommend it. Somewhere along the line the Wolfman had begun slipping the rails, and Kilroy wasn't sure where it had started. Had it been Cooper's arrival? That seemed to accelerate the downward slide for all of his plans. In the end, it all seemed pretty simple to him: Wolf Koller was Ross Perot with a gun. There was no point in chewing at it beyond that. Kilroy knew that if he hadn't sneezed when he pulled the trigger on Koller, everything would be different now: the Cheese's instincts had been right in the first place. Well, shit. Kilroy had a very strong belief that the world was getting worse and worse because it never learned its lesson. It never learned any lessons. Nations really were like rats in a maze. It was enough to make you want to just kill everybody and get it over with. But that too would be a big job.

He looked over at his passenger. Konstantin Orlovski had been napping through the afternoon but was now awake and watching the countryside, the thick stands of firs and the snow and the ice. Orlovski had never been a guest at Koller's lair. Every so often he checked his gold Rolex and told Kilroy that they were making pretty good time considering the treacherous road. The emerald green suitcase was in the backseat. It contained the rough drafts of the documents which would be approved by Rossovich, Koller, and Chancellor Glock.

Koller had brought him up to speed on Rossovich's involvement in the plan, though he had learned its specifics only through Cheddar's speculations. "This weather isn't great for Rossovich's flight," he said, making conversation. "Things like this always happen at just the wrong time. I've seen a herd of cattle caught in a storm like this up the Panhandle and I've seen planes crash flying in food for the poor buggers—"

"Rossovich will get here," Orlovski said. "Don't worry about Rossovich. Watch the road. Make sure we get there."

"Sure, sure, you bet."

Kilroy had noticed Orlovski watching him from the corner of his eye in the last couple of days. Kilroy figured that Orlovski knew who he was, or who he had once been. After all, Soviet intelligence was pretty good at keeping track of old enemies, and Kilroy certainly qualified as that. Somewhere in the back of Orlovski's mind, some half-forgotten file had fallen open, and a tattered picture or an old identity card had come sliding out and the penny dropped and Orlovski was now trying to figure it out. Maybe it was something for Kilroy to worry about, maybe not. After all, Orlovski saw that Koller relied on Kilroy. But Orlovski knew Clint Kilroy was not the American he pretended to be, and so he would wonder: Did Wolf Koller know? And if he did, why would either Koller or Kilroy be carrying on with the pretense? Did it matter? Orlovski must be wondering these things. Was Kilroy playing Koller for a fool? Was Kilroy *really* working for the Americans?

Kilroy tried to rummage around in the Russian's head and concluded that it was a boggy swamp in there. He was never going to figure out what the Russian really thought until it was too late. Russians were the craziest bastards on earth.

They passed a small clinic clinging to the side of the mountain, looking out over a stunning landscape, and kept turning, kept going higher. They'd been in the car for a long time.

Slowly Kilroy pulled over onto the narrow shoulder. He had his orders from the Cheese and there was no time like the present. He sighed and turned to Orlovski and said: "You know, Konnie, it's a terrible thing to be an old man. I've been sitting in this car forever, and my right leg has seized up. Cramp. Gotta shake it off."

"Would you prefer I drive, Mr. Kilroy?"

"Let's get out and walk for a minute, see if I can get limbered up. Jesus, it hurts like a Brahma bull fell on it." He opened the door and slid out, favoring the bad leg, making sure his gun was ready to go. Cheese had his heart set on that fucking suitcase. Cheese reasoned that if you horse around with a bright green suitcase in the middle of the play it had better show up at the end. Kilroy supposed he might be right, and he'd never minded killing Russians anyway. It was good to stay in practice.

It was starting to get dark and they were in the lee of the mountain, which made it darker and colder and windier. He heard Orlovski getting out on the other side. Kilroy stamped his feet, shook his head. Their destination—Koller's mountain lodge—was only about five hundred yards directly up the hill, but of course you couldn't go directly up the hill. You had to follow the winding road and fart around until you finally got there, but Orlovski had no idea they were so close.

"Come on, keep me company." Kilroy set off along the high bank, which dropped down eight or nine feet and then formed a culvert before it began to rise abruptly into the snow and trees, black in the fading light. He'd walked about fifteen yards when he realized Orlovski hadn't come with him.

He turned around and looked back and there was Orlovski, the sly bastard. Kilroy sighed.

The Russian was standing partially shielded by the passenger door, leaning on the top of the door, steadying his arm. He had some kind of a gun in his hand and Kilroy reflected once again that he was way too old for this shit.

"Come on, Konnie, what the fuck are you doing? I'm the only thing out here to shoot at and you sure as hell don't want to shoot me . . . so what the fuck are you doing?"

"Leopold Stecher," Orlovski called to him.

Kilroy put a hand to his ear. "Come again?"

"You are Leopold Stecher."

"Never heard of the man."

"Leopold Stecher was an SS assassin. You were a young man then. But you are still an assassin."

"Konnie, you're talking a load of crap. Now cut the shit and come take a walk with me and have a piss or stay the fuck in the car but stop horsing around." Now he actually was beginning to get a cramp in his leg. What next? *What the hell next?*

"Everybody was looking for you after the war. Leo Stecher. A top war criminal. You never minded murdering people in public. Jews, Poles, Russians, anybody, men and women and children, we have a file on you in Moscow Center as long as Stalin's memory. I guess the Americans found you . . . and put you to work. You must have been very valuable. We always wondered who they found who knew so much."

Kilroy laughed, slapping his gloved hands together in front of him. *Shoulda killed this shithead while I was driving the car. Didn't want to mess up the upholstery. And now look at the crapper I'm in.*

"I was an American intelligence officer, Konnie. Worked for Wild Ass Bill Donovan, it's all in the record, you crazy bastard. You been lookin' in the wrong file, son. Now it's cold and my leg's gettin' worse, so put the gun the fuck down! I've really had enough of this shit." He was very slowly edging toward the bank, trying to get a peek over the edge to see what was waiting down there. He wore black, leather-soled shoes, very slippery.

"You're Leopold Stecher," Orlovski shouted into the wind, "from Detmold. You were a ruthless murdering Nazi fucker—"

"I'm from West Texas! I'm telling you you got me mixed up with Stecher or Martin Bormann or somebody but I always been nothin' but Clint Kilroy—"

"You enjoyed it, killing people—"

"Still do, but less so now, and that don't make me this guy you're talkin' about . . ." His Texas down-home accent was getting more pronounced.

"After the war you went to work for the OSS and you turned in all your old pals and took up the same line of work for the OSS and then the CIA and God knows who else . . . I know who you are, you bastard!"

The first bullet whined away in the wind, close enough to make Kilroy flinch. And then he was gone, just gone, like a magician's trick in the fading light. Hocus-pocus. Another bullet whistled away and buried itself in the snow on the hill behind where he had stood.

Kilroy felt as if he were falling out of an airplane and thought how preferable that would be to what he was actually doing. He was too old, way too old, he could break a hip doing this. He really didn't care if he lived or died. It was instead the challenge of wriggling out of the trap he'd thoughtlessly let himself step into.

He just let himself drop down the slippery slope into the culvert, damn near killed himself, only eight feet or so but it felt like the West Face of Mont Blanc, he was so old and so brittle. But he had the keys to the car and Orlovski was bound to come looking for him.

He flattened himself against the back of the shelf of snow and dirt and rock, out of sight, underneath the overhang of frozen, snowy thatch, and took out the gun he'd been planning all along to use to kill the Russian. He was panting as if he'd run five miles. He hoped the wind would drown out his heavy breathing. Orlovski couldn't see him from above. He could hear him prowling along the edge, staring down into the snowy underbrush, trying to keep from getting killed. He was intent on looking, discovering where Kilroy might be hiding. Kilroy wondered if he should just calmly step out from his shelter and rely on surprise to give him the time to aim and fire . . . or should he wait for Orlovski to come down the embankment, and shoot him while he was getting his bearings? What to do, what to do? He hated suspense. As a young man, his instincts would have taken over and he'd have known what to do. Ah, fuck it . . . He stepped out from under the overhang.

But Orlovski wasn't peering down at him.

The Russian had tripped in the snow and was falling, all confused and wrapped in his coat and grunting and crashing and he landed at Kilroy's feet. Both men were so startled that they practically levitated, each shouting with surprise. Orlovski was feeling around in the snow for his gun and Kilroy backed up, caught his heel in a root or some damn thing, and sat down abruptly.

When the snow had blown free of them they sat facing each other in the near darkness like two obstreperous children. Orlovski couldn't take his eyes off Kilroy's face while his hand patted the snow looking for the gun he'd dropped. Kilroy could see it from where he sat.

Kilroy had to laugh. He couldn't help it. Like two kids trapped in a playpen, not knowing what to do.

Kilroy nodded toward the butt of the gun in the snow. "It's over there. By your foot."

Orlovski reached for the gun, still patting the snow, his eyes locked on Kilroy's.

Kilroy shot him twice in the face.

43

ESCAPE

She lay in the bed wondering how long she'd been there, wondering where she was, but perfectly well aware of who she was. Scared to death. Because none of this made any sense. She was sure she'd never been here before. Through half-closed eyes the place reminded her of a church but it clearly wasn't. There was a cathedral ceiling and lots of glass and darkness beyond the glass, and inside it was all polished wood and had an antiseptic smell and there was indirect lighting blooming in the corners but mostly it was dim and relaxing. Maybe if she'd known where she was she'd have gone back to sleep. But she'd been sleeping so much she was tired of sleeping and she wanted to find out what was going on.

They hadn't given her an injection in a long time and she hadn't seen Dr. Gisevius in a . . . day? Two days? Time meant so little when you were groggy and hopelessly weak and . . . and . . . How had she gotten to this place? She couldn't remember any of that. Dr. Gisevius was always giving her injections, whispering that it would ease the pain, but she didn't know what he was talking about, there wasn't any pain, she was just tired and confused and her memory was shot to pieces . . . but now, it was peculiar, she felt that her mind was very clear, she was able to think about who she was, who her husband was, her doctor, her daughter, about whom she was very worried. And she knew why she was worried. And John Cooper, her brother . . . where was he? It wasn't like John just to abandon her and she didn't think she'd seen him in quite a while, not since their argument in the garden at Charlottenburg, which she also remembered perfectly well . . . and she remembered where she'd been sitting when Wolf had been shot through the window from somewhere out in back. Had they ever caught anyone for doing that?

When she'd first awakened in this new place a doctor had come and talked with her, a doctor she didn't know. He seemed pleasant enough, almost fatherly, but he didn't seem to have much authority, not much presence, not at all like Fritz Gisevius, who always reassured her that everything was going to be all right, that she shouldn't worry, that if things got bad he could give her another injection and she'd simply go to sleep. The new doctor wasn't like that at all, he seemed shy and not quite sure what to do about her . . . she hadn't seen Dr. Gisevius in days, it seemed, but she was feeling much better, just a little weak from lying in bed, but her head was clearer, her mind sharper . . .

In the quiet room, with the plants and the soft lighting and the big window with the blackness beyond, she heard some kind of mechanical sound, a hospital sound, like a respirator, some mechanical huffing and puffing, very low and quiet and something dripping, steadily, slowly . . . She leaned up on her elbows, blinked, pushed against the tightly tucked-in sheets, twisted to look around and saw the other bed . . . she hadn't noticed it before but there it was, a bed with hospital sides up and a figure that wasn't moving, and she whispered in the stillness, *hello, hello, can you hear me, are you awake* . . . But there was no answer. She raised herself farther until she was in a sitting position. She was wearing one of her own nightgowns and a robe lay over the back of a chair drawn near her bed. She sipped some cold water from a glass and carafe on the bedside table. There, that was better . . . She was surprised at how good she felt . . . almost like a normal person. She remembered how sick she'd been since seeing John at Charlottenburg, how she couldn't remember who she was and how she'd been unable to eat and could only sleep and have terrible dreams and Dr. Gisevius, looking so worried, would lean over her with his syringe and slide it into her and tell her that soon it would all clear up but it hadn't, it had only gotten worse and worse . . . and now she felt so much better. She wondered where he was, she wanted to tell him that she was all right . . .

She tried working her legs out from under the sheet and finally got them free and dropped over the side. Her feet didn't quite reach the floor but she could swing her legs and get the blood flowing again and get the needles and pins worked out and she kept listening to the pumping machine and saw that it was hooked to the person lying in the other bed. Slowly she lowered her feet to the floor. The floor was warm and polished and she felt quiet little wings of warm air scurrying from vents and it was not at all like any hospital she'd ever seen before. No busy walking about and talking and rolling carts clanging along in hallways. She felt as if she had been transported to the far side of the moon, to a new kind of hospital, or maybe a special kind of mental institution—well, she certainly wasn't crazy, she had no doubts about that. She wondered where Erika was, if she'd come back. She missed Erika so much . . . she remembered the day they'd brought the little baby to her . . . she remembered how Wolf had told her she was unable to have children of her own, how she'd been unable to speak about it without breaking into sobs and Wolf had hated her crying . . . she remembered Wolf handing her the baby, with big eyes and thick black hair and the tightest little fists and how the little creature had nestled against her, how warm, how dependent on her, the first living thing who had ever truly needed her . . . Erika. She and Wolf had named her that night, and it was Wolf's gift to her, the baby she thought she would never have. She had abided by Wolf's decree that Erika must never know she was adopted, that the whole world must believe she was their natural daughter . . . Koller blood, that was the thing . . . She wondered if Erika was home yet, if she'd been found yet . . . alive.

She roused herself from her momentary reverie, stood up and crossed the space between her bed and the other bed, toward that quiet figure and the machine and the dripping. *Hello, hello, am I disturbing you, do you know where we are . . .*

Peering at the figure, she suddenly drew back.

There wasn't a whole person under the sheet. She didn't believe she screamed but there was a moment of sudden terror in her brain, in her throat—

Only half the head seemed to be in place, bandaged, some gray hair, a misshapen set of features, the other side just gauze and cotton wadding . . . there didn't seem to be a shoulder or an arm or much of a body on one side . . . what she could make out of the face was a woman's but it was a face without life, a face, and a woman, who would have been so much better off dead . . . being kept alive this way was like a punishment, something prescribed by Satan . . . she shivered and flinched, her own hand momentarily touching the cold claw that had once been this woman's hand . . .

"Don't touch her."

She turned to face the voice. "No, I was only trying to speak with her. And then I saw that she—"

"She doesn't speak, Lise." It was Dr. Gisevius. "And you shouldn't be out of bed. You're not well enough. . . . Do you know who I am? Do you know your name?"

"Of course, Fritz. Don't be foolish."

"Who am I?"

"Dr. Fritz Gisevius. And I'm Lise Koller. But I'd like to know *where* I am. I'd like to know what's going on and where Wolf is . . . how long have I been out?"

"You're very weak, Lise. Your memory could go at any moment—"

"But I feel fine, Fritz. Better than I have in months."

"You need to go back to bed. Rest. I'm very glad to hear that you're feeling better—" He was wearing a dark suit, double-breasted, and a dark cashmere overcoat was draped over one arm, and he carried his small doctor's kit in the other hand. She'd seen the kit so many times.

"I'm not going back to bed, Fritz. I feel all right."

"Are you hungry?"

"I want to know where I am. And who is this other woman? Tell me, Fritz. Right now."

"All in due time. But first, back into bed." He was coming toward her slowly, a strange expression on his broad, flat face, his squat bulk threatening in the dim light. "You could faint at any moment. You could fall and hurt yourself—we don't want that, do we?"

"I do have a headache," she said softly.

"You see, my dear. You're not quite as well as you think you are. We're going to make you feel fine again, there's nothing to worry about, but it's going to take some time. Now you need some rest, my dear. I'll give you a sedative and you'll get some sleep and we'll talk about it in the morning. I'll tell you all about the other woman and this lovely little hospital—Wolf thought you'd be more comfortable here. Your recovery will be quicker in this quiet place." He came near her, reached out to take her hand; she felt his thick fingers close on hers, draw her back to the bed. He pulled the sheets back. "You've had a long, tiring day. You should be asleep. Tomorrow we'll have a long talk—"

"No! I'm not sleepy, I'm not tired, I've been in bed for days and days, getting weaker and weaker, and now I'm feeling much better . . . and I haven't had one of your injections in, how long has it been, Fritz?

What are the side effects of those injections? Have you thought about that?" He was refusing to let go of her hand. "Let me go, damn it!"

"Now, now, Lise, I can't do that. I can't take responsibility for your condition if—"

"I'm not asking you to take responsibility! I'm asking you to pay attention to what I'm saying. I feel all right, Doctor! Doesn't that matter to you?"

He held her hand tight. "It's an illusion, my dear Lise. I could never forgive myself if you did yourself an injury . . . now, I must insist that you take a sedative, then you can sleep." He had the needle in his right hand. The kit lay open on the white sheet.

"You're hurting me, Fritz! What's going on here? What do you think you're doing?"

"I'm just helping you, dear Lise—"

The needle was poised over her arm. She saw the trail of punctures on her bare flesh. *They are trying to kill me . . .* Suddenly she grabbed the silver water carafe and swung it as hard as she could at Gisevius's face, struck him head on, heard the frames of his glasses crack apart. The frames were driven into the flesh beneath his eyes and he cried out. The needle jabbed downward into her arm. She hit him again with the carafe and his grip loosened on her hand. He fell backwards against the bed, clutching his face, his glasses hanging, broken, down one cheek. The third swing of the carafe emptied the water across his head and chest and he screamed as the broken glass frames were smashed deeper into his face. His hand fell away and she pulled back, was free of him.

The pain in her arm was escalating. The needle had been driven deep into her arm and still hung there, fluid leaking into her arm, running down and dripping from her wrist and fingers.

She took hold of it, tried to straighten the angle, finally just yanked it out and felt a cold rush of feeling flooding her arm from within. It frightened her, she didn't know what was in the needle, what was now in her bloodstream . . . She felt suddenly cold all through her body, as if she were freezing from within . . . she had to get out . . . Gisevius was on his knees trying to find the lenses of his glasses. Blood was smeared across his face. He looked like a bear, an injured animal, fuming and angrily turning in circles on the floor.

She darted past him. He sensed the movement, flung out an arm, ripped at the hem of her nightgown, his fingers sliding down her calf, and she fell, crawled away from his grasping fingers, got to her feet, her head spinning, not feeling all right anymore, having to get away, maybe she was insane, but having to get away from Gisevius . . . She was sick to her stomach and her legs felt weak but she couldn't stay here now . . . He'd kill her, he wanted her dead, he'd been killing her with the injections, her mind was spinning and she knew she was mad, it was Fritz Gisevius, he couldn't want to kill her, it was her friend Fritz . . . He was on his feet, staggering toward her, and she ran, down a corridor, past an office with the blue glow of a closed-circuit television screen registering on her mind, a picture of the room she'd just left, the bed where the half-body lay, then she was pushing past, the cold inside her eating at her, through a door and into the night . . .

It was cold, as cold outside as she was inside, and the wind was blowing down off the mountain, it was snowing and the snow bit like razor blades at her face, cutting through the thin fabric of her nightgown, she was sliding in the snow, barefoot, she was climbing toward the road in the darkness, reached it, began to run, but it was hopeless, she was going to die . . . one glance behind her, and she couldn't even see the building she'd fled, the night had swallowed her whole.

44

GÖTTERDÄMMERUNG

Ned Cheddar was not happy with Chancellor Glock.

That would have been bad enough but there was more, there was worse, damn it.

He was now going to have to depend on Chancellor Glock. Cheddar felt the uncomfortable sensation that came from having your nuts caught in the nut grinder. He was running out of time, he was a long way from the action, and he really hated having so much at stake and so little absolute control. He felt like a man wearing a blindfold, feeling around with gloves on, trying to identify everything by touch. It was driving him crazy and it was making him hungry.

Glock . . . He'd worked with Glock off and on through the years, beginning back when Glock had been a West German intelligence officer. In those days, when the villain was always the Commies, they'd worked together on exchanging spies with their opposite numbers in Moscow, funneling the warm bodies through East Berlin. Glock used to take delivery on the Glienicke Bridge and call Cheddar to let him know that all had gone well. They'd worked together on furthering American diplomatic and NATO aims when Glock had been a liaison officer at NATO HQ. And they'd prepared for the reunification of East and West when Glock had moved on to become a politician, on the verge of the top spot in Bonn.

But Cheddar had never entirely trusted Glock's instincts. Deep in

Glock's heart, like an eternal flame in the Black Forest, there burned the fire of German nationalism. He couldn't help it: it was just part of the man. Hell, you couldn't really blame him. But if you were Ned Cheddar you didn't have to like it. When Wolf Koller had emerged from the shadows as the primary engine driving Glock's political career . . . well . . . Cheddar had tried not to worry. He believed he could keep both men on the leashes he held in his Georgetown fortress. But Koller had slipped the leash, had sneaked away and created SPARTAKUS and had set it in motion with the acquiescence of Chancellor Glock, and now Glock was in it up to his neck.

Now, it was crunch time.

The cavalry, led by the immense figure of Ned Cheddar, had just crested the rise and seen the treachery on the plain below and . . . well, so much for metaphors. Cheddar was going to make Glock choose between the shining path of American truth and honor and decency and whatever Wolf Koller was selling. Ned Cheddar wished he felt a little better about the whole business.

He picked up the telephone and called Bonn. He was informed by one of the Chancellor's aides that the Chancellor had left for a long weekend at the mountain lodge of Wolf Koller.

"Do you think you could patch me through? Is he traveling by car?"

"Yes, he is. There's a problem with patching you through, however. A big snowstorm is building up in the mountains—it's making it very difficult to establish radio and telephone contact. Give me a message, please, and I'll keep trying."

"No, I think not. Give the patch a try. Keep trying. I'll hold on here. Tell him Ned Cheddar's very anxious to speak with him."

Several interminable minutes went by, Cheddar's heart skipping an occasional beat, his fat fingers drumming on the desktop. He took deep breaths, tried to force himself to stay calm. The aide finally came back on the line. "The connection was breaking up but I got through long enough to tell him it was you, sir. They are now changing their route, heading for the nearest town. The lines there may be better than the cellular connection. He said to tell you he'd call you direct."

"Well done," Cheddar sighed. "Thank you very much."

When he hung up the telephone he checked his watch, figuring in the five-hour difference between Georgetown and the Harz Mountains. Once he'd made a note, he remembered the cheesecake and orange-cranberry sorbet in the refrigerator. He rang the kitchen.

When the call came through only thirty minutes later, which seemed an eternity to Cheddar, the connection was good. Cheddar sank back, his desk chair wheezing. "Chancellor, good to hear your voice. It's Ned here. Thank you for making the detour." You had to attend to the formalities now that he was Chancellor, no longer somebody you could yell at.

"I could hardly do otherwise, could I? Your message was urgent . . . and I was on my way to Wolf Koller's lodge. What is it you have to tell me?" He sounded edgy. Guilty, actually, was what he sounded. Cheddar smiled to himself. Dear old Glock was afraid he'd been caught with his hand in the cookie jar.

"Yes, it's your trip I want to discuss. May I say that there is nothing good that can come of your visit to Wolf Koller? I doubt if there is a single imaginable result which would serve you well. Do you understand what I am saying, Chancellor? I'm thinking only of your own good, the good of your career . . ."

"I have no idea what you mean." The Chancellor's voice came hesitantly.

"Let me try to make it clearer, Chancellor. Your further relationship with Wolf Koller at this time is detrimental to affairs between our two great countries. I'm sure that in the long run you know where the interests of your country will remain. Wolf Koller is a passing comet. The United States is the sun from which you personally draw your power, your influence, your stature among nations. I know full well that you would never put that crucial friendship in danger . . . I am merely reminding you, as your greatest friend, that you have quite enough on your plate. Germany needs stability and the support, moral and otherwise, of its friends. German greatness does not lie with the machinations of Wolf Koller."

"May I be frank, Ned? Being the junior partner in a relationship with the United States might not be all that Germany and Germans hope for. To be a senior partner within Europe . . ." He left the sentence, and the thought, unfinished. His voice changed subtly. "And what will Wolf say? He is a very impetuous man . . . but a strong ally. I owe him a great deal and I don't wish to discover what kind of enemy he is."

"I can't believe you are comparing Wolf Koller to the United States as a useful ally. Surely not. And believe me, Chancellor, you would much prefer Wolf Koller as an enemy than . . . me. Think about it. My own belief is that the storm raging around you is going to keep you from reaching Koller's lodge. I'm sure many travelers will be stymied by the storm."

The Chancellor grunted. He was a realist, in the end.

"You should also understand that we know all about Wolf's foreign guest . . . and we know every jot and tittle about SPARTAKUS. However, follow my advice, and there will be no reason for the two of us ever to speak of it again."

There was a lengthy pause filled with the Chancellor's heavy breathing. "I have no choice, do I?"

"Not if you know who your friends are, Chancellor."

"Yes. My friends . . ."

"Now, there's something else I need you to do. At once, I might add. From the telephone you're using at this moment."

"Yes, I'm sure there is. Well, we might as well get on with it . . . But there is one thing I must say, Ned."

"Yes, Chancellor?"

"If Germany had not lost two great wars, you would not be speaking to me this way."

"I agree absolutely, Chancellor. But then, Germany did lose them. We all must play the cards we're dealt."

"What do you want from me, Ned?" The dream of a stolen triumph was dead, and you could hear it in his voice.

The Professor had been irritated but not entirely surprised to awake and find that Erika had flown the coop. She was a resourceful girl, and she sure as hell had her own agenda. His friend, the hotel's owner, offered to have the boy in the green jacket at the desk flayed and quartered for failing to keep track of her. The Professor shook his head. He thought he probably knew where she'd gone. Even if he was mistaken, he thought she was bright enough to stay out of harm's way.

He called Ned Cheddar again. This was no time to go off on your own without checking in with the master. You couldn't be too careful.

"I haven't found the girl," he said, expecting a blast from Georgetown.

"Don't worry about the girl now. Where's Cooper? He seems to have gone off my screen."

"I don't know. I never know where he is."

"I don't like it. We should know—well, look, we have business to discuss. We've avoided this long enough. Now we're out of time, my friend."

"You mean Cooper."

"I mean the Brothers Cooper. Plural. John and the late Cyril . . ."

"Do you think he knows—"

"Come on, Professor. He hasn't met you, he hasn't laid eyes on you . . . no, it's not John Cooper I'm worried about. It's Cyril—"

"Why? I'm not going to make any—"

"*Cyril!* Listen to me, damn it. You and I go back a long time. I've made decisions for you, I've kept you alive—"

"And I've delivered for you, each and every time. Don't forget that, Cheese. All those years at Moscow Center. You gave me the name . . . *Kiril* . . . I've been your good and faithful soldier—"

"And I have seen to it that you have money in Switzerland, more than you'll ever need. But there's something I haven't given you. I haven't given you your *real* life back—"

"Listen, you can rely on me. *This* is my real life now."

"But you have been a good soldier . . . and now you can have it back if you want it. You can be Cyril Cooper again . . . I only want you to promise me one thing. Are you with me?"

"All right. What is it?"

"If this endgame with Koller brings you and John together . . . *if* it does, don't be a fool. Don't do anything noble or foolish or risky just because he's your brother. Is that absolutely clear?"

"All right. It's clear."

"There'll be time for a reunion—if that's what you decide you want—when this SPARTAKUS mess is over and done with. But you have to get through it alive. We want everybody to get out of it alive. Right?"

"Right. The reunion comes later."

"Exactly. Now, what's the weather like in Berlin?"

"Cold and wet."

"All right, my friend. I have plans for you . . ."

Clint Kilroy was standing by the fireplace, which was roughly the size you'd need for a day of ox-roasting. He listened to the wind howling in the chimney and in the chinks, which were part and parcel of the huge rustic lodge. Wolf Koller's father had built the lodge and had invited

Reichsmarschall Göring and his entourage there on several occasions to hunt on the mountainside. Göring had liked the place, Kilroy in his previous incarnation had heard him say so on more than one occasion. It was pretty swanky for roughing it, which was probably why Göring liked it. Big wall hangings, Siegfried and Rhine maidens and a cast of characters endlessly doing their thing on vast expanses of woven material shot through with gold threads, a largeish animal head here and there, some ornate statues of men wrestling with bears and possibly winning—it was all a bit on the heavy side, but there were still people who liked that sort of thing, he supposed. The wind racketing away, the snow rattling in the chimney, the crackling of the huge logs all contrived to keep him from hearing the possible approach of his putative master. Kilroy was not looking forward to explaining the absence of the Russian and his emerald green suitcase.

Chancellor Glock was on his way from Bonn to meet Egon Rossovich right here, in this room, and with him to sign the statement of intent of the new European Alignment. They were also to initial the alterations on the documents in Orlovski's emerald green suitcase. Then, upon his return to Moscow, Rossovich would unveil the economic plan and the Parliament, along with the army, would turn against Yeltsin and it wouldn't be just a new Europe, it would be a new world. The storm raging outside with all the potential for screwing up flights and communication was bad enough. But Kilroy hated having to tell Koller some lame story explaining Orlovski's absence.

The sounds of the storm did indeed prevent Kilroy from hearing Koller arrive behind him, and when he heard the voice he gave a start that made him wince. The problem with Orlovski had left his whole body aching.

"Clint," Koller said, dispensing with bullshit. "Where is our guest?"

"Orlovski."

"Yes, where is Orlovski?"

"He didn't show up at the meeting place—now look, Wolf . . . I couldn't wait, I knew you wanted me here—-"

"He didn't show up?" Koller was already tensing up, his fist clenched, a vein pulsing in his handsome forehead. His free hand moved protectively over the cast on his arm.

"I'm sure he's on his way—"

"Why would you say that?"

"Because I can't think of any other explanation."

"I see." He paced rigidly away and crossed to a drinks table and awkwardly poured himself a brandy, extracting the cork with one hand. He didn't ask if Kilroy would like to join him. He looked up at the window, where snow was rattling on the glass and the wind was hammering for entry. Outside it was white as night fell. Koller looked at his watch. "Rossovich should be entering German airspace about now. You checked on the helicopter bringing him from Berlin?"

"Everything's ready to go."

"They're waiting in Moscow for his call."

"It's going to be fine, Wolf."

"And . . . your other mission. The two young women . . ." He couldn't look at Kilroy, his eyes locked on the flames licking the blackened back wall of the fireplace.

"It's all taken care of." He had left Burke Delaney on the street watching over Erika and Beate. A grumpy old guardian angel with his dog. It had been a relief when the Cheese had nixed killing them. But Kilroy hoped he wasn't around when Koller found out the truth. Cheese had better have a plan.

"Yes," Koller said softly. "I congratulate you on carrying out a . . . difficult . . . task. Tell me, was there any difficulty?"

"No. There wasn't any pain for anyone. Don't torture yourself about it."

Wolf Koller stood at the window watching the storm blowing across the sloping lawn and the trees and brush beyond. The snow was well over a foot deep and drifting in the wind. The lights from the house penetrated just so far, and beyond lay what seemed to be the infinity of space.

"Glock will have his own copies of the agreement with all the corrections," he said to himself, "and we have our copies. If Orlovski doesn't get here because of the snow"—he shrugged—"it won't make any difference." The wind kept gusting, hammering the house. The huge beams groaned, and hanging iron lamps swayed overhead, long shadows moving across the room. Wolf was pressing his temples as if he had a terrible headache. He opened his eyes, staring at his own reflection in the window. "There are so many unexplained incidents of late . . . don't you agree? I was shot." He lifted the arm, pain cutting across his face. He had Kilroy in his sights. He turned and picked up his snifter of brandy. "No explanation. My guard was shot and killed at my home in Wannsee. No explanation. Someone killed the people I sent to find my daughter. No explanation. My daughter has disappeared with some unknown persons in a Range Rover that drove off a cliff but didn't kill its occupants . . . again, no explanation. Someone broke into one of my warehouses and in cold blood murdered three of my security people . . . no explanation." He sipped the brandy, rolling it on his tongue.

Watching him, Kilroy wondered if he might be on the verge of seeing an example of spontaneous human combustion. He'd seen men, powerful men of great character, come completely undone from far less pressure than Wolf Koller was experiencing. Everything had gone wrong for Koller, on all sides, and all of it beyond his power to repair. Yet he persevered, almost as if in a kind of trance. He could have pulled out of the Russian deal at any time, but retreat wasn't in him. He would break before he would bend. When he broke—*if* he broke—everything might get very ugly. But, at least for the moment, Wolf was winning the battle for self-control.

"A most regrettable week, wouldn't you say, Clint? Wouldn't our Mr. Cheddar agree? Have you told Mr. Cheddar, by any chance, of our run of bad fortune?"

"You know I'm leaving that to you. I'm merely an errand boy for Mr. Cheddar, helping to coordinate the use of the late Herr Stiffel and his followers. I'll brief him if you instruct me to—otherwise, it's up to you." Kilroy was beginning to feel a little chill of fear, not something he was used to. Koller was too damn calm for a man whose seams were close to bursting. "All of your work with Mr. Cheddar—you must admit—has been very successful. It's created exactly the atmosphere you wanted—a perfect setup for the new Greater Germany to assume its rightful place in the European Community—"

"But as you know, I have taken a further step into the future of the Greater Germany." Koller darted a glance at the fireplace again, where the wind had rushed down and showered sparks across the tiled grate. It was getting to him. It was all getting to him. His forehead was covered with a fine patina of perspiration.

"I'm just a foot soldier, Wolf. It is your 'further step' that I have left to you to discuss with Mr. Cheddar. Or not. It's your call, Wolf."

"Is that true, my friend?"

"How could it be anything else? I didn't know a damn thing about Rossovich and Russia until you told me—after you'd seen that tape your daughter made? You know you can trust me—"

"I wonder about you sometimes, your devotion to this cause . . . Where exactly does your devotion lie? Is it to the late Mr. Hunn and his student Cheddar, for rescuing you at the end of the war and saving you from the hangman's noose? Or is it to me? Is it to Germany and everything your heritage stands for? I wonder about these things. I have put a great deal of trust in you . . . what if you are betraying me?" His face softened; he crossed to Kilroy and put a hand on his shoulder, which in Kilroy's view was much better than the knife in his back he'd half expected.

"You know me so well—" Kilroy began.

"My *father* knew you so well. That's why I have such implicit trust in you. You are one of us. You served in the time of our greatest need. You took the personal oath to the Führer . . . You are the living link between me and my father and the Führer himself."

"I appreciate your confidence in me." Kilroy felt like an idiot playing the lucky man whom Wolf Koller, almost twenty years his junior, had chosen to smile upon.

"But, Leo, I sometimes wonder . . . is your actual identity precisely the reason why Ned Cheddar chose you to deal with me?"

"I don't understand. Of course that's why he chose me—why the hell else? We share so much, our whole heritage . . ."

"But he could be sure that I'd believe in you. He could be sure that I would believe everything you did, everything you told me . . . while you were betraying me. I wonder, could that be the way his mind works?"

Kilroy decided to roll the dice. "Look, I hate to interrupt you in the middle of a threat, Wolf, but my pedigree is of a rather higher order than yours. You were just a snot-nosed little kid, *you* didn't know Hitler —*I* did. Did he shoot pool with you? Hitler shot pool with me. I played with his fucking dog and I knew Eva . . . Are you a part of history? Or am I? Do I have the confidence of America's spymaster? Do I hold the fate of your plans in my hands? You talk about your veneration for your father, for the Führer . . . then I suggest that you think twice before threatening me. I am your lifeline, Wolf, and if you pull this off with the Russians, I'm the guy who might be able to blunt the reaction of the Americans. I'll let you in on something, pard—you're gonna need somebody to absorb the recoil on this one because Cheddar is gonna think you stuck the old SS dagger right up his ass . . ."

While he was talking, Kilroy reached the conclusion that this was the biggest chance he'd taken since the day, nearly fifty years before, when he'd made the decision to give up his former colleagues to the war crimes people and save his own neck and go to work for the Americans. He'd never really regretted it, considering the alternatives—a rope around his neck or, if he was lucky, a steamer passage as a deckhand to godawful Paraguay, where he would live out his life in hiding—but at the moment he knew his life was balanced on the knife edge of Wolf Koller's well-justified suspicions. Kilroy didn't know if you could trust the Americans. Were they moralists, in the final crunch, or were they realists? He had bet long ago that they would be realists. He'd been right, more often than not. Now he was betting that Wolf Koller's reverence for the past still held him in its grip. Otherwise, Clint Kilroy knew that his skinny old ass was grass.

Koller stared at him for a long moment, then slowly nodded. "Of course. You're right. I must trust someone. You are like one of the Disciples—you have dined at table with Hitler. I choose to trust you."

"A wise decision," Kilroy said, feeling his bowels relax. Jesus, he really was too old for this craziness.

"Good, good. Well, we must make the best of this situation." Koller had turned brusque. Kilroy thought he looked—in the eyes, in the slightly higher-pitched timbre of his voice—as if he was well along the road to going completely nuts. The mask of calm determination was growing little cracks, providing glimpses of the fellow within. Wolf Koller was telling himself he could still pull something out of his hat, but the fact was his world was collapsing around his ears and he knew it, he just refused by effort of will to believe it. Back in the final days when the Red Army had entered the tunnels leading to the Führerbunker, Clint Kilroy had been there, assisting Bormann, and the main thing on his mind was trying not to be in the room when some crazy Nazi bastard like Himmler or Goebbels decided you should join the group bumping themselves off. Young Kilroy, Leo Stecher then, figured he could survive, go to ground if he could just get the fuck out of the bunker and run away into the rubble. Nearly half a century down the road the trick was still to stay alive, until Koller accepted reality or went completely nuts and you could kill him with a clear conscience, so to speak. A day or two, that ought to do it, one way or the other. Men's dreams died at different speeds.

"Chancellor Glock is coming from Bonn. He's on his way now. He's coming by helicopter. The weather worries me, Clint." He was staring out into the storm again, his voice sounding far away, back in the trance. "I wonder if Erika sent the tapes . . . you didn't find the tapes she said she made?" Kilroy shook his head. As if trying to convince himself, Koller said: "I don't think she made them . . . did she tell the Hubermann woman? You found no other tapes?"

"None." Kilroy was praying that this conversation would soon end, that God would deliver him from Wolf Koller's candid fears and reflections.

God's messenger, Sebastien the Red, appeared in the arch leading to the two-story hallway.

"Herr Koller," he said, "there's a telephone call for you."

Koller glanced at Kilroy and nearly smiled. "Orlovski?" he murmured.

"Sure," Kilroy said, "that's probably him now."

Kilroy heard Wolf raising his voice, shouting into the phone, from where he stood by the fire, warming himself. The encounter with Wolf Koller had lowered his body temperature drastically. Coupled with the results of falling around in the snow with Orlovski, it was too damn much. And now Koller was yelling on the telephone. It didn't sound like anger: more like a man trying to be heard on a bad line. Kilroy couldn't tell who was calling, knew only that it wasn't Orlovski. He saw and heard all the signs of its being a very long night.

Sebastien was smoking a cigarette and staring out one of the bay windows into the storm. The snow was piling up, wiping out the shrubbery and walkways that crisscrossed the immense lawn. The penumbra of light that eventually gave way to the pitch-black forest surrounding the property seemed deeper each time Kilroy looked. On one side of the property, stone emplacements sat atop the cliffs, like sentry boxes commanding the valley beyond. Their eyes met—Kilroy's and Sebastien's—in the window's reflection, and Kilroy said: "Bad news, I guess," nodding toward the sound of Koller's voice. "Who was it?"

Sebastien shrugged. He had never quite trusted Kilroy and Kilroy supposed it was a jealousy based on how close Kilroy was, by necessity, to Koller. Of course Sebastien had no idea who Kilroy had been a lifetime ago, not that it would have impressed him. Sebastien was a killer, not a thinker, the perfect makeup for a terrorist, which he had been as a young man. Now his opportunity to pursue his favorite activity was severely limited. Kilroy assumed it was Sebastien who had murdered Joachim Stiffel in the crowd at the Brandenburg Gate but he didn't really know. In any case, he was only a killer. As such, Kilroy held him in wary contempt. You could never turn your back on him but he was never going to out-think you. Sebastien wasn't about to tell Kilroy anything, the identity of the caller or anything else. So be it.

When Koller returned he was shaking his head, arguing with the facts. "It was Glock's assistant. Everything's going wrong—the chopper pilot wouldn't try to get up here so Glock is coming by car. It was a terrible connection. But the man thinks they're an hour away, maybe two. It's in the hands of God." He sighed. "What does this mean about Rossovich getting here? He's going to run into the same weather . . . he may have to stay in Berlin until the weather clears. I don't like it."

"Don't worry about what you can't control." Kilroy poured more brandy and handed the snifter to Wolf. "Everything's going to be all right."

"So you say." Koller tried to smile.

They could hear the phone ringing.

Koller's face brightened. "It must be Orlovski this time—it's the weather. He'll be late."

Kilroy nodded. "Gotta be."

Sebastien appeared again and summoned Wolf. Kilroy felt the tension being ratcheted up.

When Koller finally returned, his bronzed, elegant face was grayish white and the bags beneath his eyes seemed to have been recently packed for a long, long voyage. His voice cracked hoarsely when he spoke.

"That was Gisevius. I don't know what . . ." He hesitated, looked from Sebastien to Kilroy with a finger to his lips. "Lise has escaped from the clinic." His voice sounded as if there were a river of blood in his throat. "She's out there in the storm in her nightgown . . . She'll die out there . . . she's so weak." His voice trailed off and he swallowed hard. He wanted to kill her but, Kilroy thought, somewhere deep in his animal heart there must be some vestige of love for her; he didn't want the cold and the snow to claim her.

Kilroy said: "How did it happen?"

"Does it make a difference? Something about her sedation wearing off, she was hallucinating, or so he says, she—she *overpowered* him, his word, and ran away into the night . . . apparently she hit him with a water pitcher, broke his glasses and he cannot see. He says he's badly cut up . . . he wants me to come down to the clinic in case she wanders back." He looked at his two listeners. "You two must get out there and look for her—she can't have gone far. She's alone, barefoot, barely clothed, weak from her illness, she probably headed for the house so you can cut down straight overland—"

Sebastien said: "But—"

"Don't argue with me!" Koller unexpectedly shrieked, his voice splintering again. "Go! Just go, both of you! We've got to find her."

Kilroy left the room and found his overcoat. He winked at Sebastien. Sebastien frowned at the intimacy, put his second gun in the pocket of his sheepskin coat, and slipped into a pair of green wellies. Kilroy saw the wisdom in that and looked around in the boot box until he found a smaller pair that would fit over his shoes. He went back into the room, where Koller stood staring into space. He looked like a man who has seen the future and can't find himself anywhere in it.

When he heard them leaving the lodge, Wolf Koller roused himself from the distracted state that had descended on him utterly, like the hood on a parrot's cage, when he'd heard that Orlovski had not kept the appointment with Kilroy. There had been nothing but bad news ever since that moment . . . The fact was, there had been nothing but darkness all around him since he'd talked with Erika in Lise's hospital room. And now—Gisevius had been sobbing, whether with fear or frustration Koller didn't know, begging him to come to the clinic. Begging, his voice shaking, his chins cascading and trembling—Koller could see it in his mind. Koller was moving almost as if he were in a dream, a very bad dream that wouldn't end. Could it all be saved? He didn't know but if he kept going, if nothing more happened to wreck his plans, if the weather let up, maybe, just maybe, Glock would get through and Rossovich would somehow arrive in his chopper and together they would all shepherd the plan through and the two great powers would be joined again, this time for good . . .

The only car ready to go was the little Mercedes sports model. He got in and the motor started immediately. But the car had been sitting outside so he got back out and brushed the snow off the windows while the engine idled. He'd be at the clinic in a few minutes . . . maybe he'd see Lise in the storm . . . he backed up, and turned the car out toward the curving road that wrapped around the mountainside. As the long private driveway sloped downward he realized that it was icy beneath the snow. He automatically corrected for the ice and spun softly out of the skid and straightened out, felt the bump as he reached the main road. The headlights pushed without much effect into the thickly falling, blowing snow. He turned left onto the outside half of the road, which was smooth and untraveled, a white blanket, like something from a child's picture book.

He crawled along, carefully, desperately, for the first mile, two miles, then grew impatient. The car was holding and he stepped on the gas, felt the car leap forward. His eyes continually searched for Lise in the stretch ahead, and he saw her again and again, only to have her shimmer away as a flurry of snow or a shadow of blowing snow caught in the light or a roadside tree behind a curtain of snow. His mind was wandering, he was remembering her when they'd first been lovers, when she'd been so lost and afraid, her husband dead, her brother gone back to America. She'd known that Gunter Brendel had been a weak man and she'd seen that Wolf Koller was anything but weak and she'd clung to him, begged him not to leave her, betray her, forget her . . . and he'd always wondered why she hadn't made the break and gone with John Cooper, gone back to America, where she'd been born . . . He hadn't pried, but he'd always thought she should have gone with her brother, but then he didn't suppose he knew the whole story . . .

The whole story. The whole story of SPARTAKUS was on the tape Erika had left with him. Christ. He hadn't slept since meeting with her. Every time he closed his eyes he saw her face on the tape, heard her revealing the whole story—everything. And not only SPARTAKUS but all the rest of it, the killing of Karl-Heinz, the men sent to find her, even the story of the fake pregnancy, which resulted in her arrival on the scene, everything but the identity of her real mother—that she didn't know . . . A transcript of what she said on the tape might sound mad, but watching her—the clarity of her delivery, the calmness—no, it was his worst nightmare, people would *believe* . . .

The car began to slide when he thought about Lise and the past and how it had all come undone, how she'd come to hate him, how he had begun to fear her. She had grown increasingly irrational and angry, and that was when the idea of her illness had come up between him and Gisevius . . . There was nothing wrong with her other than her own delicate, high-strung psyche: it was the way she was, and there was no changing it. But Gisevius could medicate her so that it would appear that she was growing mentally ill; Wolf Koller didn't quite understand the pharmacological aspects of it but he saw the results—the memory losses, the hallucinations, the paranoia, the terrible frustrations, and she never mistrusted Fritz Gisevius and his legendary bedside manner. Fritz had been very good all along. He had carefully kept the audiotapes of his discussions with Wolf about his wife and her illness. Just in case there was ever any question about the treatment and his diagnosis. And when she died, well, people would have noticed her peculiar behavior, it wouldn't come as a surprise. Wolf was thinking about all that when the car, having gathered a fair head of steam, slipped out of control and he couldn't bring it back into line and the slide was gathering speed and his bad arm was caught in the spinning steering wheel and he began to scream, felt as if his arm were being ripped out of the socket, as if the bullet hole were being torn open, and he knew he was disappearing into the swirling snow and then there was a tremendously loud cracking sound and the windshield was gone in a shower of glittering razor blades and the snow was blowing in his face and the breath was knocked out of his body as if he were a rag doll and he had visions of his arm being pulled off and flung out into the snow . . .

Sebastien, being a younger man than the doddering old American, set off into the snow at a speedier clip, but before he knew it he was just about lost in the blizzard. Then he tripped over a hidden tree root and went ass over teakettle and cut his hand on a broken branch and couldn't find the glove that had been torn off and it was so damn dark and he was out of breath and when he put his hand in his pocket to keep it from freezing and falling off he discovered that when he'd fallen, the second gun had dropped out of the pocket and was back there in the dark and the snow somewhere and there was no way in the world he was going to find it. Well, he still had one gun and one gun was all he needed.

It seemed to take a long time to reach the road but he knew that as long as he was going downhill he was bound to reach it sooner or later. Koller's brainless wife was probably wandering around in the road, half dead from the cold, and maybe it would be better not to find her until she was all the way dead. Less trouble for everyone. She drove the boss crazy and she could be a real handful. He'd driven for her a couple of times and he'd wanted to kill her himself by the time they got home. Now where the hell was she?

And where the hell was Kilroy?

If the old bastard found Lise, he could stop looking for her and go get warm someplace. He called Kilroy's name several times and could barely hear it himself over the wind. He got out his flashlight from the other pocket—naturally it was the *gun* he'd lose—and tried to get a better idea of where he was. But the snow just reflected the light in his eyes and he was suddenly almost blinded. He snapped off the light and began trundling downhill.

He couldn't really blame himself for plummeting headlong off what seemed like a cliff but turned out to be a drop of only eight or ten feet which he took running and stumbling and finally falling hard into the snow and bouncing off some hidden object. The breath had been knocked out of him and he lay on his back gasping, sucking wind and snow, cursing Wolf Koller and Lise Koller and Fritz Gisevius and all the hounds of hell that had brought him to this point. He wanted to shoot them all. He wondered if he'd broken anything. He howled Kilroy's name to no avail. *He wouldn't come if he could, the Yank bastard.* He was a bitter man, lying there on his back, trying to breathe, his face cut and chapped by the application of ground and snow. *Kilroy, you son of a bitch . . .*

Then he began calling Lise Koller's name. He called it several times and realized he'd gotten his breath back. He leaned up on one elbow and then extended his hand to get a purchase upon which to raise himself and he touched something soft, or only half frozen anyway, that gave beneath his touch, and he thought he'd found Lise Koller. He struggled to right himself and the thing moved again under his hand, slippery and squishy, and he drew back in disgust and made a little moaning sound. He felt for the flashlight with fingers that had lost most of their feeling, finally found it, struggled to get it out of his pocket, and flicked it on. It wasn't Lise Koller. His hand was pushed into the half-frozen muck that had once been about two-thirds of Konstantin Orlovski's face. The onetime most wanted terrorist in Europe, Sebastien the Red, thought he was about to faint.

Paulus was driving because he knew the way and Cooper was sitting in the passenger seat in front. Olaf Peterson's incredible gun lay across the backseat. They'd stopped at the hospital before leaving Berlin, then called once from the road. Olaf Peterson was going to make it. He wouldn't be paralyzed. Cooper was looking forward to seeing him, hearing what kind of crazy shit he'd say . . .

The road conditions were treacherous, worse the higher you went.

Paulus passed through the little town he'd gone through on every previous trip, the service station and the bakery, and everything was closed up
tight, no lights at the station, nobody walking around behind the driven
snow. It was blowing hard. The town was closed. He didn't know if the
road might be closed later on and there was no point in mentioning it.
Don't go looking for trouble was what his wife had used to say to him
long ago, whenever he was returning to the barracks from a leave in the
early days of the war, before he left for North Africa. Don't go looking
for trouble. Enough will find you on its own. Sometimes he'd feel a
certain pang of longing for her that he didn't think he could survive. And
then it would fade, life would go on. He wondered if he'd be with her
soon enough. He wondered in the cold and snowy night if, when he died,
they would be reunited in a different, peaceful place. She had died young
and he'd be dying old and would that be a problem? What happened
when you died old, did you go to heaven old or were you restored to your
prime? Or was it all just a lie to make you go to church? There was just
no figuring it out ahead of time.

    "How much farther to the clinic?" Cooper was worried about his
sister.

    "Not long."

    "And you're sure she's there?"

    "I'm not sure, no, son. But I'd say the chances are very good. It's
logical. He has another patient he keeps there."

    "You're kidding . . ."

    "No, he set up the whole thing for the care of this one person. A
woman he was in love with a long time ago, before he met your sister. She
was more or less killed in an accident—"

    "What happened?"

    "It doesn't matter. It wouldn't mean anything to you. At any rate,
she survived. But she never regained consciousness, she never took another breath on her own. Only about half of her body is there and she's
wrapped up like a mummy and it's all quite pointless. But he wouldn't let
her die. He's kept her there, attended to day and night, for about twenty
years. It's madness, of course. But, then, it's part of what Wolf Koller is."

    "And you think he's added my sister to the patient list."

    "Yes, I do."

    "What does he plan to do with her?"

    There was no answer and Cooper sank back in the corner of the
darkened cocoon, feeling the wheels sliding, struggling for traction. Big
storm. Just like Minnesota. Peterson would have loved this. Just like the

old days. But Peterson lay in a Berlin hospital unconscious. Cooper wondered where his mind might be roaming as he fought his way back to the surface, back to life.

The first thing Wolf Koller realized when he came to in what had once been a collector's item of a Mercedes was that he had just vomited. There was no getting away from that. He was covered in it. The second thing he realized was that he had suffered some kind of a cut on his scalp or forehead and was bleeding copiously and feeling lightheaded. He could taste the blood running down his face, getting in his eyes, soaking into his scarf, and adding its scent to the recently regurgitated brandy and food. And finally among his discoveries was that his arm hadn't actually been ripped off and flung out into the storm. It was still attached, though he seemed to have lost any power to move it. It hung limply in its cast. He carefully lifted it, feeling pain that reminded him of a kidney stone he'd once had, only worse, and slipped it back into the sling. He cried out with pain and his tears mixed with the blood and if he didn't get out of the wreckage of the car he was going to vomit again . . .

He pushed the door open—against gravity since the vehicle had tilted and ripped the bark off a tree and taken out part of a guardrail— and got himself hoisted halfway out of the car. He was hanging over the bottom of the doorsill when the wind caught the door and slammed it back down on him, cutting the back of his head, a deep gash beneath the handsome mane of wavy gray hair. He didn't lose consciousness but retched from the pain, dry-heaving into the snow, then pulled himself with his good arm and pushed with his legs from inside the car until he was more out of the car than in and dropped head first into the deep snow. Slipping and sliding, crawling, he got to his feet, knowing in the recesses of his mind that the whole thing was out of control, that he was hurtling headlong into the abyss and he didn't quite know why, couldn't quite discern through the disaster, through the smoke and fire of his life, who had betrayed him, who had brought him down . . . Cheddar? Schmidt and his son? Somehow, was it Cooper, twenty years later, doing it all again? If Cooper hadn't come to Berlin, would it all have gone right?

He fell again, plunged his face into the snow again, wiping away the blood and vomit with it, talking to himself, hating the pain and the

frustration and the failure, hating everything, hating everyone . . .
Maybe it had been Kilroy. Kilroy had been Leopold Stecher and had
betrayed all his colleagues from the old days to Dulles and all his new
men to the Americans . . . maybe it was in Kilroy's nature . . . how
could you ever trust a man who had become a different man in the
middle of his life and never looked back, who gave up his old friends to
the enemy . . .

When he got up he stood staring wordlessly at the car, feeling the
blood pounding in his head, feeling the insane weariness and the pain in
his arm and all the other pain. He took the machine pistol from the
pocket of his trenchcoat and shot the car. It didn't make any sense. He
just wanted to shoot something. A bullet to the engine block.

Then, limping and unsure of his footing, he set off in the snow
toward the clinic . . .

Sheltered in the stand of trees across the road, Clint Kilroy stood
watching, chewing reflectively on a frozen bit of twig. He watched the
whole scene Wolf Koller had played and slowly shook his head.

He didn't suppose Wolf Koller had ever heard of Murphy's Law
but the fact was he was living it.

Dr. Gisevius stood in the middle of the large main room of the clinic,
waiting for Wolf Koller.

His glasses, broken in half, hung loosely from one ear. One lens
was gone, the flesh around each eye puffy from the damage Lise Koller
had inflicted upon him. He was standing there hating what he had become, hating where he was, and he didn't know what to do about it. He
was a powerful, important, respected man and now he was ensnared in
the cancer that was Wolf Koller's ambition: but their lives had been
entwined forever, their mutual loyalty never questioned. There was nothing to do but see it through.

Where could Wolf be?

Gisevius was soaked through with perspiration. He paced around
the room, his legs feeling weak and heavy. He had bathed his eyes,
swabbed disinfectant into the cuts, bandaged them. It hadn't stopped the
bleeding. Now all he could do was wait. He went and stood by Rafaela
Dorfmann's bed, watching the pathetic thing stretched out before him.
Where had her mind been these twenty years, hovering between now and

beyond? Was there anything going on inside the remains of the once beautiful head?

He leaned down, trying to catch the sound of her breathing, but it was too weak, the respirator drowned it out. He felt for her pulse. It was almost nonexistent. A month ago, when he'd last seen her, the pulse had been strong. Was she finally slipping the bonds that held her tight to the earth?

He was going to have to explain what had happened with Lise, how it hadn't been his fault, how he'd been blameless, and he'd remind Wolf that he'd suggested arranging for her demise before leaving Berlin. Wolf would have to listen to reason.

How had she concluded that the injections were the cause of her "illness"? Or was it just the instinctual, brainless will to live? Somehow she had known, had sensed she shouldn't let him inject her anymore . . . yes, they should have killed her back in Berlin, a stronger injection, no one would ever have known. God in heaven, the man wanted her dead, what difference did it make where? Dead was dead. But Wolf Koller loved playing God, deciding the moment of life and death . . .

He was staring down at the floor, half-looking for his missing lens, his vision distorted, his head pounding, blood pressure inflating at an alarming rate . . . his eyes were swelling shut, he could see out of only one eye now, who'd have thought she would have so much strength after what they'd done to her, the dosage they'd used, carefully increased over time, and then he heard Wolf Koller calling his name, felt the cold air seeping down the hallway . . .

"Good God, Wolf, what happened to you? Are you all right?"

Wolf stood in the doorway, leaning on the frame, then came forward. "I wrecked the car . . . out of control on the ice." He was caked with snow and ice, which was melting where he stood. He grabbed a towel from a rack and wiped his face. "I've hurt my arm and shoulder. The bullet wound."

"Let me have a look, Wolf."

"Not now. I need a painkiller. Give me a shot."

Gisevius went to his bag, prepared a hypo. Wolf bared his good arm and Gisevius injected him. Wolf talked his way through the pain. "Has she come back? Have you seen her? Were you serious, she's wearing only her nightgown? How could it happen, Fritz? How could you let her get away?"

"I wasn't expecting it. She's been so weak . . . but too much time passed between her medications . . . she was strong." He shook his head in confusion at her transformation. The cuts around his eyes had begun to bleed again. "Wolf, there's something else. It's Rafaela . . ."

Wolf's eyes snapped open. He was slipping the leather jacket back over his shoulders. "Rafaela? What do you mean?" Anxiety overflowed, overcame the pain and the worry about Rossovich and Lise and Glock. *"What do you mean?"*

"She's slipping away. Her pulse is almost gone. The respirator isn't doing the job anymore." He put his meaty hand on Wolf's shoulder. "There's no more life in her, Wolf. There's nothing more to do. Twenty years . . . You can only do so much."

"Are you telling me she's gone?"

"Going, Wolf."

Wolf pushed past him, went to Rafaela's bed. He sat on the bed beside her, took her hand. "My darling," he whispered into her ear. "My darling . . . goodbye." He leaned down and kissed the cold corner of her mouth. He stood up and slowly moved to the head of the bed, pulled the plug connecting to the respirator from the wall. The silence was profound, as if a riotous party had just ended.

Wolf sat down on the bed, took her hand in his, his fingertips on the pulse. When he stood up, after the passage of less than a minute, there were tears on his face. He ignored them. "Fritz . . . you should not have let Lise escape."

"I know," Gisevius said. "It was an impossible situation. I couldn't see. My face was bleeding—"

"I want you to go find her. I've got Sebastien and Kilroy looking for her. I want you to go help them." His voice was calm, uninflected. "Please, Fritz. Go."

"But Wolf, the storm . . . I can't find her in the storm, I can't see, my glasses . . . I'm afraid I'll lose my way in the snow . . . Wolf . . ."

"You can help find her, Fritz. You let her go, you can't object to helping find her. I'll wait here in case she comes back. You'll be all right. But hurry, she's out there in her nightgown . . . Fritz, do you understand, if she dies in the storm it will be your doing."

Gisevius backed away, felt for the doorway. He was going into the storm, he couldn't help himself. He felt he'd been hypnotized.

Alone, Koller spoke to the dead woman.

"I must confess to you, my dearest love. Tonight I have not only ended your life . . . I have killed our daughter." He might have said more but he was sobbing as he gathered the remains of Rafaela Dorf-mann in his arms.

Sebastien had grown used to the ruin of Konstantin Orlovski's face. Des-perately trying to escape from the culvert, Sebastien discovered that something bad had happened to his leg when he pitched off the edge and into the darkness where the stiff had been waiting for him. He had broken something. Leg. Or, with luck, ankle. Now, he figured, he was honorably out of this ghastly night, but he couldn't help thinking about how somebody had wasted the Russian and the only candidate he could come up with was that goddamn Kilroy. Which meant . . . which meant that . . . well, it meant that Kilroy wasn't being honest with Koller and therefore he might be the guy who'd sold Wolf Koller out.

An American, you knew it was going to be an American, it had to be an American, once you started dealing with those bastards . . . But where was Kilroy? Was Kilroy going to come sneaking up on him there in the culvert, helpless, broken-legged, in pain, and finish him off? Well, he'd be pretty fucking sorry if he tried . . . Sebastien still had one gun and all the humanity of a plastique bomb . . . killing an antique Ameri-can would be child's play . . . He heard a noise behind him, jerked around and fired wildly into the darkness but then the quietness en-veloped him and he realized just how cold he was, began to think what might happen if nobody came to find him. He tried to draw himself up, tried to get up on one knee, but the knee came down on Orlovski's chest which was frozen and very hard and it slipped off and Sebastien fell with his full weight, knee on a stone, and lay in the snow and then he began to call out to anyone, to Lise Koller, to Wolf Koller, to Kilroy, to anyone who might hear him and save his life because he didn't want to die, he wanted someone to have mercy on him . . .

Beate Hubermann had made hot, sweet chocolate and produced the last of her cache of Oreo cookies. She and Erika were listening to Fred Astaire on a CD collection. Erika was curled in a deep chair, balancing the cup on her knee. Beate had been telling her about the time she'd spent with John Cooper, what sort of man he was. Finally Beate raised the matter of his relationship with Lise Koller.

"Do you remember the conversation we had, about John Cooper and your mother? The things your mother told you—what happened between them twenty years ago."

Erika nodded. "Did he talk about all that?"

"Yes. He says that they've only spent a few days of their adult lives together, that they can't even remember one another as children—He says they love each other, that their being brother and sister just doesn't matter."

Erika cocked her head. "They're like strangers, you mean?"

"That's it. He says he's loved her for twenty years—from the time they met."

"Do you believe him?"

"Oh, I don't think there's any doubt of that. But it is incest . . ."

"Beate, look what my mother's life has been. And it's not as if they're going to be having children."

"No, I suppose not."

"And . . . my mother once told me that she wished she'd gone with him twenty years ago but she hadn't known how to do it, how to leave everything she knew . . . . She said she'd realized it not long after she'd sent him away . . ." She set her cup down sharply. "But what difference does it make anyway, Beate, if my mother is dying?"

"None, if she's dying. But you haven't met Cooper. I'm not sure of the word that best describes him. Maybe it's just *determined*. He has a way of willing things to happen—or that's the way it seemed to me."

"Then they're two very strong-willed people. If they both will my mother to live, maybe she will. Somehow."

"If she lives, he's going to want to take her away. Back to Boston. Or Cooper's Falls . . ."

Erika was silent for a moment before replying. "Then she'll go."

She heard someone calling her name.

She felt more dead than alive, frozen, wet and terrified and hopeless, hiding in a turnout dug out of the mountainside near the road, a cubbyhole where road signs, flares, barricades, deicing materials, shovels, and picks were stored to help deal with bad storms.

She was out of the wind and snow but it was too cold, it didn't make any difference, she felt as if she couldn't last much longer . . . she knew she was freezing to death but she couldn't answer the call, it was Wolf or one of Wolf's men, they would take her back to Dr. Gisevius, they would hold her down and he would come at her with the needle . . . unconsciously she rubbed the hole in her arm where the last needle had gone in and she couldn't remember if the cold she was feeling was from the injection or from the coldness all around her and it didn't make any difference . . . she was going to die and John Cooper would never know, would never hear again from her lips how much she loved him and cared about him and needed him, he would never know . . .

Wolf Koller didn't know how long he'd sat on the bed where Rafaela Dorfmann had lain for so many years, how long he'd held the seemingly weightless remains of her body. There was almost nothing there but he cradled her corpse in his arms nonetheless and felt his body tearing itself apart with sobs wrenched from whatever it was that passed for his soul.

Rafaela was dead at last.

Lise was lost in the storm.

He'd had Erika killed.

Fritz was stumbling around blindly in the snow.

Wolf Koller felt as if the lifeline securing him to planet Earth, to humanity, to all that was the story of his life—he felt as if the lifeline was fraying and he was in danger of floating away into the darkness where he would twist and turn forever and the pain would never go away.

But Rossovich was coming. He had to get the landing lights on for the chopper. And Chancellor Glock might arrive at any moment.

His will began to return. He had rested. He was ready to fight onward. He had to get back to the lodge.

He couldn't mourn Rafaela forever.

Paulus said to Cooper: "The clinic's just up ahead. About half a mile, I think—around this long curve in the road. It's hard to tell in this snow." His arms and back and legs were stiff and sore from battling the storm and the heater was losing its punch. It was getting cold in the car. He hoped he was right, that Lise Koller was at the clinic. But he wasn't sure what they should do when they got there. She'd surely be under guard. But Cooper was in no mood for being put off . . . and he had the enormous shotgun. It was a deadly situation but Paulus couldn't see an alternative: he was afraid Wolf Koller might kill his wife. It worried him, though, that he and Cooper had no backup.

Had he let sentiment, his concern for John Cooper and his sister, get the better of him? Well, there were times when you had to take a chance on the right thing. So . . . It was sentiment. He was old and soft and he'd fallen for Cooper and his quest.

Cooper stared out into the storm, wondering what the hell he was going to do when they got to the clinic, if Lee was there at all . . . what condition would she be in? What if she was already dead?

The figure came out of the snow almost as if it were a part of it, a creature created by the storm, moving like a ghost, slowly, amorphous, into the path of the car, and Cooper shouted reflexively at Paulus to stop. Paulus slammed on the brakes and the Mercedes spun to one side and skidded past the ghost, somehow managed to avoid hitting it, and Cooper had flung the door open, was scrambling and falling and getting up as he left the car and went running off into the snow like a madman. Could it be Lee? Could she have wandered out of the clinic in some half-drugged state? Was she crazy after all?

Paulus was turning the car around to shine the lights after Cooper. He leaned over the steering wheel, straining to see what was going on up ahead.

"Is it Lee?" he breathed, alone in the car. Something caught in his throat as he watched the huge man in the headlights struggling with the shape in the snow.

The car moved crablike back into the deep ruts and surged toward the two figures. Paulus swung the door open, straining to see through the snow that blinded you even at a distance of five feet.

Cooper was half-dragging, half-pushing the snow-covered figure into the backseat, climbing in afterward.

It wasn't Lee.

It was Fritz Gisevius.

In the warmth of the car, brushing and chipping at the ice and snow covering Gisevius, who slumped next to him, Cooper said: "We've got to get him to some warmth." Gisevius was almost unable to move and was almost dead weight. "You're gonna be all right, Doctor. What the hell were you doing out there?" There was no answer. Cooper leaned into the front seat: "He can't stop shaking. Christ, he could die from hypothermia. Underneath the snow he looks like somebody hit him in the face with a bat."

Paulus nodded. "We'll have to take him to the clinic. That's it, up ahead there."

The shape of the clinic, the A-frame, loomed up in the unearthly glow of the headlights hitting the snow and he pulled across the road, let it roll into the courtyard driveway.

Cooper got out of the car and guided the somewhat more responsive figure toward the clinic doorway. The door was partly opened. Paulus, carrying Peterson's Streetsweeper, pushed it all the way open and went in first, then motioned to Cooper to follow.

Once they were inside Gisevius opened his eyes and looked up at Cooper. "Is Wolf still here?" He was exhausted and nearly frozen but he was alive.

"The place seems to be empty," Cooper said.

"Down there," Gisevius whispered hoarsely. "In the main room. I left him there." He was suddenly racked by uncontrollable trembling. The wind whistled at the windows.

The large room, with the huge window fitting into the contours of the A-frame at the far end, was empty but for the two hospital beds. Someone lay on one of the beds.

"Lee?" Cooper was suddenly afraid. The body was so small.

"No," Paulus said. "That's the other woman I told you about—"

"She's dead," Gisevius said. He was thawing out. He was staring into the corners of the room. "Wolf!" he called loudly. "Wolf—where are you?" There was no answer.

"Where's my sister? Was she here?"

"She was here, yes . . . Wolf wanted her in these ah, these . . . these lovely surroundings . . ." Gisevius was struggling to get hold of himself, to resume his normal manner.

"Where is she *now*?" Cooper asked very deliberately. "So help me God, you're going to give me straight answers this time or I'm throwing you back outside and the storm can have you." Slowly, he took the doctor by the soaked, half-frozen lapels. "I don't care if you die—do you understand me? I just don't care! *Where is she?*"

Gisevius didn't even try to pull away. He floated his blurry gaze toward Paulus, found no help there, and sank his head down onto his chest. "She ran out into the night—I tried to stop her. I couldn't—"

"What the hell are you talking about? I saw her the other day, she was made of paper, ancient, dry, gray paper! And now you've got her running out into this storm and you're unable to stop her—don't lie to me!"

"The injections—she'd been too long without her injections, they'd worn off—"

"You're telling me that without medication she can run off . . . but with your medication she's three-fourths dead? What were you trying to do to her? Kill her?"

Gisevius began to gasp for breath, struggling inside his clothing, shaking, gagging. "Asthma," he said, his face darkening. Cooper released his grip and Gisevius staggered backwards, steadied himself on the bed where Lee had lain. He fumbled in the pocket of his suit, came out with an inhaler and fired it into his mouth, fell back on the bed, gasping.

Cooper leaned over him. "Where is she?"

Gisevius was shaking his head, pointing down the hall. "Out there . . . in the snow. Wolf was here . . . waiting for her . . . to come back. But now he's gone . . . Kilroy and Sebastien . . . are out . . . looking for her." He sucked the inhaler again.

Paulus stood beside Cooper. "Leave him with me. She may find her way back here. You'd better get moving—she may have headed toward the lodge. It's just up the road. Or if the others find her they may take her there. She'll die in this weather, John—she must be found."

Cooper looked down at Gisevius. "Is she sick? Or is it your injections?"

Gisevius turned his head away, closed his mouth tight.

"All right," Cooper said. He picked up the inhaler. "I'm taking this with me. I hope you won't need it." He pushed the inhaler into his pocket, turned to leave.

Gisevius immediately began coughing, sucking air with raspy, raw noises. He was reaching out with shaking hands, trying to reach the life-giving device. Cooper stared down, shook his head.

"Fine," Gisevius gagged. "She's fine . . . it's the medication . . . that makes her sick."

Cooper held tight to the inhaler. "You miserable bastard," he said softly. "You rotten—ah, the hell with it." He dropped the inhaler on the bed. He turned to Paulus. "I'm too fucking good to people," he said and went in search of his sister, Lee.

It was the twilight of the gods . . .

Wolf Koller was thinking in mythological terms by the time he saw the glow of the lodge through the thick wall of fir trees and the raging, blowing snow. In all the years he'd owned the place, he'd never seen this kind of storm, it was *Götterdämmerung* . . . was it the end of the Reich he'd hoped to create? Had it all ended before it began . . . doomed . . . would he sleep a thousand years and a thousand more and never waken . . .

He kept plodding toward the lodge with its heavily rustic outline, which owed so much to the chalets of Switzerland, the sloping roof, the perfect setting, a place so he could be near his beloved Rafaela . . . he'd loved her so much, her incredible beauty, her animal appeal, she was a kind of animal, merciless, a killer . . . he had taken her baby girl, *their* baby, and made it his own . . . and he had kept her alive . . . she was always alive in Erika's dark beauty, but now Erika was lost to him, too . . . Rossovich . . . could he possibly get here in this storm? . . . he could rise above his private horrors once Rossovich and Glock were there, it could still come right . . .

Behind him, when he'd left the road and climbed down into the culvert between the hill and the road, he had thought he heard a noise of some kind, a kind of croaking sound—he'd thought it might be Lise, helpless, dying in the cold. He'd listened again, had heard only the roar and whine of the wind shifting off the mountainside as it piled the snow everywhere, and he'd climbed upward toward the lodge, through the trees and the knee-deep snow, calling her name but seeing not a living soul. And so it was that he passed within some twenty-five feet of the famous terrorist, Sebastien the Red, who was in the process of dying alone in the frozen culvert, dying of the cold, of the fear that was making him panic, of the hypothermia produced by the fear, who was dying because every so often somebody got just what he deserved.

Olaf Peterson's modified shotgun, the Streetsweeper, lay across the passenger seat as Cooper pushed on up the road that wound toward the lodge. He thought Lee might have kept close to the road, might have realized she needed something to follow. The wind buffeted the car and as he slowly, steadily negotiated a turn, a great mound of snow was barely revealed as a wrecked car, a Mercedes sports model, smashed through some kind of railing up against a tree. It was disappearing, becoming part of a drift. He kept going, feeling the wheels sliding and then catching, again and again, while he peered out the windows, desperately trying to see something, anything that could be Lee. The truth was, Lee could have been ten feet beyond the car and he'd never have seen her. He was sweating, edging toward panic, but he had to keep going. And finally he reached the lodge's driveway, its outline still visible because beneath the snow it was bordered with shrubs, which stood like little round men guarding the house.

He took the gun from the front seat and left the car, plunging into the snow. The front door of the lodge was open an inch or two and the snow was filling in the deep footprints of someone who'd departed not too long ago. Snow had drifted into the front hall. He went in, stood still, listening. He closed the door. The wind seemed to be everywhere, licking the walls like flame. He heard the cracking of the logs in the fireplace and went into the two-story great hall with its wrought-iron chandeliers and the matching sconces on the timbered and paneled walls. The fireplace was huge, smoke blackened up the front, and the scent of burning wood filled the place. Gusts of wind blew smoke into the room. Several partially filled glasses stood on end tables along with a bottle of brandy, one of Calvados, and several other bottles of liquor. A long stairway crossed one wall and led to a balcony circling the room, with bedrooms opening onto the balcony and darkened halls leading away.

He listened again. Nothing. He sensed that the house was empty. He climbed the stairway, carefully holding the heavy shotgun in readiness, and from the balcony looked down past the heads of several lions and tigers and wild boar mounted on the walls. It was still empty. He pushed open each of the six bedroom doors, found nothing, and checked out the shadowy hallways. Nothing.

Lee was still among the missing. And Koller was out there somewhere looking for her. And there wasn't a damn thing John Cooper could do about any of it. He could hear a branch scraping against the house. The crackling fire.

Then . . . the opening door. The sound of footsteps. Not the same door he'd come in. Somewhere else.

He was trapped on the balcony, the sound of his own breathing pounding in his ears. He flattened himself in the shadows against the wall and waited, hearing sounds he couldn't identify, and then—throwing off a sheepskin coat—Wolf Koller came into view below him. Koller poured himself a brandy, swallowed it, poured another and went to stand before the fire. He put the brandy on the mantelpiece, ran his hands back through his thick mane of gray hair. He was staring into the fire, his back to Cooper.

Without turning around, Koller spoke.

"Mr. Paulus, is it? Wherever you are, come out and have a drink. There's no point in hiding. I saw your car outside—every man in Berlin with a security division knows that license number . . . It looks like a long night, Chief—I don't want to drink alone."

Cooper moved to the balcony railing. "It's not Paulus . . . it's John Cooper. I've come for my sister—"

Koller remained facing the fire. "You do make yourself as inconvenient as possible, don't you, Mr. Cooper? I thought you were going back to America—didn't we decide all that?"

"Don't be disingenuous. Your goons tried to kill me the other night. We killed them instead—and I decided to stay awhile. I'm not leaving without Lee—"

"No point in going over old news, Mr. Cooper. Come down, have a drink . . . One of my men will find Lise soon. We might as well be comfortable while we wait." He was warming his hands at the fire. "We'll have to discuss this situation—since you're here, you may as well see history made tonight. A new Europe created before your eyes—"

"I don't give a damn about Europe, old or new—why is that so hard for you people to understand? All I care about is my sister and her daughter. As far as I'm concerned, you're totally absolutely nuts, and I don't want to take a summer vacation with you on Lake Wannsee and laugh about old times. All I really want to do with you is kill you. You see, I've talked to Gisevius. He got the point, he understood that I was going to kill *him* unless he told me the truth—that the two of you have been slowly murdering my sister. I realize that murder is not exactly a new enterprise for you, but unless you can produce my sister, alive and well, tonight, I'm going to shoot you dead. That's all you really need to know about tonight." Cooper was holding the Streetsweeper as if he were about to fire. "Why don't you turn around and face your accuser—see how you're going to die unless I get Lee back—"

Koller turned deliberately and from his belt he pulled a pistol. The familiar shape of the Luger traced itself across Cooper's mind, and, using one hand, not like the American cop shows on TV, presenting his slender profile as a target, Koller fired, all in the flicker of a second. The slug blew a chunk of wood out of the balcony railing six inches from Cooper's hand and buried itself in the wall behind him.

He was slow to react, shocked by the event itself, the instant violence, and in what seemed a painful eternity he finally threw himself low, landing behind the huge wooden banister and its anchor at the top of the stairs. Another slug thumped into the wood. He pushed the barrels of the shotgun through the slats of the railing and pulled the trigger once, quickly, and the back of the long leather sofa a few feet to Koller's left exploded in a cloud of stuffing.

The great hall was seventy feet long with French doors along the back wall. Koller was moving quickly, a shadow darting among chairs and potted trees and casual tables and carved pillars. Cooper saw him, here, there, in and out of the shadows, and began to descend the stairway, crouched on his knees, using the heavy slats for cover. Suddenly Koller was gone and the room was silent. Cooper waited, feeling faint and lightheaded. This was war. Jesus. He hadn't been at war in a long time . . . and back then he hadn't been alone . . . now all he had of Olaf Peterson was the gun . . .

A movement, like a bat flitting across a room in the twilight, a searing sensation along the side of his face, and Cooper was jerking backwards, registering the crack of the shot. Falling and landing on the floor at the bottom of the stairway, knowing he had to do something fast, he tilted the gun in the direction of Koller's last appearance, behind a grand piano in front of the windows. He pulled the trigger again—twice—and he heard the racket as the first blast blew out the side of the piano in a jagged cacophony, ripped off a leg and sent it crashing to the floor, the second clanging off a wrought-iron floor lamp and taking out one of the French doors. Cold air spilled into the room, snow blowing in. He put his hand up to his face and it came away sticky with blood. There was a sliver of banister stuck like an icepick in the side of his face; he felt its wicked splintered edge and squeezed it between two fingers and pulled it out, feeling his cheek tear and warm blood flow.

Cooper was out of breath, panting, trying to imagine where Koller had gone after the last fusillade when he heard the noise, the beating of great wings over the sounds of the storm, the wings of a helicopter like something in a surreal dream, a helicopter flying through the snow and wind as if it were on a suicide mission . . . and then he half-saw and half-heard another movement along the wall of French doors and a figure smashed outward through the wreckage his shotgun blast had caused and reflexively he stood and fired again, smashing a lamp, shredding a potted palm tree, and blowing out another door of glass . . .

Koller was gone. Cooper could see the figure, a dark blur, and then, like magic, there was light, a ghostly glow of lights coming on beneath the snow, turning the scene outside an icy, eerie blue . . .

He was out of his head and he knew it. So perhaps he wasn't all the way out. He was still clinging to some kind of reality . . . Some shard of glass or wrought iron, given flight by one of the blasts from Cooper's enormous gun, had lodged in or near his eye and he was having trouble seeing. Blood, or some mysterious sticky fluid, was leaking from the eye, but he couldn't spare it a thought now, not now with the pounding of the chopper's rotors. He hit the switch on the outside wall and the lights came on from under two feet of snow. The blast from the last shot was echoing inside his head and particles of glass still seemed to fill the air. He ran out into the snow . . .

He heard the pounding, the beating over the wail of the wind and the howling of the pain spreading through his own body . . . He had jammed his shoulder against the frame of the French door as he leaped through and his wounded eye was driving a stake of pain into his brain . . . how could a helicopter get through this weather? It was impossible. Flown by a madman . . . but it had to be Rossovich from Berlin, somehow they'd gotten him through, and now there was a maniac with a shotgun shooting up the house . . . if only he could somehow get their attention, signal the pilot, wave him away . . . maybe tomorrow the storm would be over and the evening's disasters would be cleaned up and Cooper would be dead and Lise would be back in the clinic and Chancellor Glock would have arrived and all this would recede into the darkness of a bad dream . . . Was it hope he felt sputtering in his frenzied brain?

Where was the helicopter? Were those its lights blinking through the blowing snow . . . The noise was overwhelming, the snow was swirling . . . he knew he presented a target for Cooper, standing in the huge square of blue light, but he had to keep them from landing. He stood, waving his good arm as if he were cursing the storm and the night, and from behind him came the voice of Cooper, shouting at him, screaming his name . . .

Then the sound of the helicopter props abruptly cut out and he

would have sworn he heard a huge fluttering, whispering sound overhead . . . like a gigantic bird falling with a broken wing, wounded,
doomed . . . he stopped, cocked his head, forgot the pain radiating
from his chest and arm, and listened for the chopper . . . and then did
he hear the sound of something, a mighty beast, thrashing through the
treetops, hurling trees from their rooting places, ripping and tearing at
the trees and the mountain itself?

A downdraft caught the chopper just when the Professor thought he'd
found the helipad about a hundred yards from Wolf Koller's mountain
lodge. A big bluish square of light had suddenly appeared below, as if
they were expecting him. Well, they were expecting *someone*—Cheese
had said Rossovich himself was expected at the lodge. Cheese had put a
stop to that: by order of Chancellor Glock, via a suggestion from the fat
man in Georgetown, the customs people had denied Rossovich entry at
Berlin and were holding him for the next flight back to Moscow. Christ,
it was amazing what the fat man could do when he put his mind to
it . . .

There wasn't much you could do about a downdraft, though.
Maybe it was a windshear, that was the latest terminology, but then he
was far from the latest model of chopper pilot. He'd flown them a few
times when he was working for Moscow Center and they needed to pull
some poor bastard out of a spot—there had been one nasty job in Den-
mark when he'd been the only guy in the vicinity to do it, God help 'em
all—and he'd kept current, kept his license, but being current and li-
censed weren't a really big help in a storm like this one. When he'd left
Berlin in the chartered chopper the weather had been cold and wet, and
the storm hadn't yet reached brute force in the mountains. Cheese had
thought having him there, at the mountain hideaway, was good backup if
Koller got a hair up his ass about Kilroy and decided to kill him. The
Cheese didn't know precisely what was going on at the lodge but he
knew what wasn't: Rossovich wasn't going to make it and Chancellor
Glock was already heading back to the safe, gray confines of Bonn. Anything was possible at the lodge, Cheddar had told him over the radio
halfway between Berlin and the mountains, and the Professor was on his
own, could make his own decisions in the field, but Cheese wanted him
to stay out of it—because of the Cooper problem—if he possibly could.

Exactly how he could stay out of it, with Wolf Koller thinking

Rossovich was going to be alighting from the chopper, the Professor didn't know.

Then the snow began and the winds were flopping the aircraft around like a Ping-Pong ball and he couldn't see landmarks through the snow and it was a miracle he found the place and the downdraft yanked at him and now the goddamn chopper was spinning and the blades had cut into a power line that was sparking as it fell away into the forest and the stabilizer was gone, he was going down, forward and sideways and every which way all at once, and he was thinking about how the hell he was going to get out and maybe he wouldn't have to worry about the Cooper problem after all.

Time was going slowly now, he thought he'd glimpsed some poor bastard down below waving his arm, it was like a dream, time was like a dream of half-death, half-life, he was moving through a vast silence now, a void of darkness with the chopper's spotlight spinning out of control, the only sound the faraway smashing of the rotors and cockpit through the trees and he felt as if he just might be having a kidney removed without aid of anesthetic but it was all happening to someone else, some poor shit who was dying . . . Then it all came to a stop and he broke out of the cocoon of silence and he could hear himself yelling wordlessly and he could smell fuel running free. Off through the snow, like a twisting snake, the live electric wire the helicopter had severed was skittering and spitting . . .

He was on his side, trying to stay calm as he unbuckled the seat belt and pushed at the Plexiglas in the door, smashing at it with his shoulder, feeling it finally give way and wedge up against a tree trunk. He wasn't going to be able to move the tree or the helicopter . . . or was he? The damn thing was hanging in the arms of the trees and the ground was maybe fifteen feet below and the cabin of the chopper was swaying slightly, moved by wind and gravity. He waited until there was some give in the door and pushed hard, shoved the handle of an emergency shovel between the frame and the door, and it held. He squeezed his shoulders out, reached for a protruding limb, and hoisted the rest of his body out of the cockpit until he was hanging free on the limb. Looking down, he tried to see what he could in the swinging light, tried to judge the lay of the land, which appeared to be sloping downhill, and let go, dropping himself like a sack of wet laundry. He felt his legs absorb the shock of the landing and rolled himself tight and went with gravity, hoping his head didn't smash a rock, but he was still wearing his helmet so it would have to be one helluva rock and then he was worrying about his legs and his back and then he was brought up short against another tree, covered with snow and trying to sit up, and with a hellish whoosh the chopper went up in a blinding red and orange and yellow flash, a giant flower of flame and black, putrid smoke, a heavy roar, and a few pieces of metal and plastic blew past him and caught in the trees and dropped around him and he could smell the spray of oil and fuel while he tried to make himself small against the base of the tree. Then it was over. Some of the trees still burning and the snow hissing and turning to steam in the inky darkness. It was not quite the arrival he'd planned and he expected he'd have all sorts of visitors pretty soon and he was prepared, both with a machine pistol and some papers identifying him as an agent from Cheese in case Koller decided to get shirty. Since Cheese had not been informed of the SPARTAKUS plan, at least not by its creator, the Professor was going to have to play dumb, saying . . . saying something Cheese had told him to say and which the crash had scared out of him . . . Cheese had told him it would all be all right . . . But the Professor was a man in his mid-fifties, though fit, and so far the trip had been anything but all right and when he tried to stand up he felt his leg splinter and give way and he knew the bone had just cut through the skin at the front of his leg and he began to scream, then sank his teeth into the sleeve of his flight suit, and when he opened his one good eye he saw, through the tears, a man coming toward him, sinking knee-deep in the snow . . .

Wolf Koller watched the beast thrashing through the treetops, spewing branches and long splintered pieces of tree trunk, he smelled the oil and fuel as the lines burst and he ran toward the noise, saw the severed electrical wire dancing in the air, striking trees, curling back on itself as if it were alive. He staggered on, falling, struggling through the deep snow on the trail of the rampaging helicopter . . . no one could survive such a crash . . . what if Rossovich was dead . . . then he would start again to put the plan together, clean up this mess and go back to work, it could be done, he knew he could do it . . . and he began to hope that Rossovich *was* dead, that there would be no explanations to make, no dragging the Russian through the mire of his own private problems . . . Rossovich would be dead, Lise would be dead, he'd kill Cooper . . . Kilroy had finished Erika and Beate Hubermann, there was still hope, out of all the dying, his Phoenix, his new Europe, might still rise again . . . the Chancellor might not get through the storm, Gisevius was all right . . . He was dripping with sweat from the exertion and then a ball of fire ballooned up out of the black hillside beyond the blowing snow, the exhalation of the fire-breathing dragon, the distinctive smell of burning oil and gasoline . . . and then some trees were flaming up like enormous candles. He shook his head, as if he could clear it of the fires of his hallucinations . . . and in the blowing snow and the shadows thrown by the flames he pushed onward, finally saw a man standing in the snow, and then the man was toppling over and the sound of a scream reached him, and Koller stopped, watching, the live wire hung ahead of him, like a deadly snake dangling from a tree limb . . . he carefully walked around it, sinking deep into the snow with each step . . . "Rossovich," he called, "is it you? Rossovich? It's me, Wolf Koller . . . are you hurt?" He took another agonized step toward the fallen man. "Egon? It's Wolf . . ."

Ten feet from the body lying in the snow, Koller stopped. It had spoken.

"Not Rossovich, I'm afraid . . . Rossovich isn't coming . . . the Chancellor isn't coming . . . you're all through, Wolf—"

"Who are you?"

"I'm the pale rider of your dreams . . ." The man coughed wetly. Koller heard the strength fading. "And my name is Death . . ." The man coughed again, laughed raggedly. "You're all done . . ." He was holding something in his hand, trying to lift it.

"Whoever you are," Koller panted, lightheaded from the struggle through the snow, "you are alone . . . there's nothing you can do to me . . ."

Calling on his last reserves of strength, the Professor pulled himself up into a sitting position, leaning against the tree. He was faint. He couldn't hold out much longer. Behind Koller, back in the light of the burning wreckage, another man had entered his field of vision. Sweat was running into the Professor's eyes but he could see the man was coming fast, kicking up snow, carrying a shotgun. The Professor said a small prayer. The machine pistol in his hand was too heavy, he couldn't keep the muzzle pointed at Koller.

"Johnnie . . . I'm over here, I could use some help . . . John Cooper . . . Is that you, Johnnie? Haul ass, man . . ."

Koller spun, saw Cooper coming, saw him fall forward in the snow, saw him struggling to get back up. Had he seen the wire hanging from the tree?

As the gun fell from the Professor's hand his finger tightened on the trigger and several slugs went wildly into the trees, one banging and whining off the remains of the chopper.

Koller shot him twice in the chest with the Luger and when he turned back to fire at Cooper he was met with another enormous blast, then another, and Koller felt his leg blown out from underneath him, was suddenly sprawled in the snow feeling nothing, no pain, just an unendurable cold and he knew he was in shock and he knew there wasn't much left of his leg. He had dropped the Luger in the snow and when he stretched out his arm his fingers just brushed the grip. The pain was beginning now and he closed his eyes and when he felt a boot pushing at his ribs he opened them and Cooper was standing above him, looking down, holding the gun. Koller said: "Its name is Death." He realized he was whispering.

"What are you talking about?"

"That thing you carry—its name is Death . . ."

Cooper leaned down over the other man, the man propped against the tree. He was breathing with terrible difficulty and had torn the front of his jacket open. He had a beard and he reached out and touched Cooper's arm.

"Are you John Cooper?" He coughed and blood welled up in his mouth, just like in the movies. Cooper had seen it play out like this before. "I can't see so well . . ."

"Yes, I'm John Cooper."

"Shake," the man said, lifting his hand, pulling off his glove. "Shake hands . . . shit, I'm dying here . . . shake hands with . . ."

Cooper took the man's hand. There was only the slightest pressure left in the guy.

Cooper put his mouth near the dying man's ear.

"Make believe it doesn't matter . . ."

When he slowly let the stranger's body go limp against the tree, Cooper stood up, stared down at Wolf Koller.

Koller stared back at him. "I'm bleeding to death, Mr. Cooper. Siegfried will sleep for another thousand years." He smiled faintly. "Put me to sleep, Mr. Cooper."

"With pleasure," Cooper said.

He held the gun a couple of feet from Wolf Koller's face. "That's good," Koller said.

John Cooper hesitated for a fraction of a second, long enough to hear Olaf Peterson whispering out of the past, and then he pulled the trigger.

Cooper made his way back to the lodge, numbed by the cold and confused. Who was the man who had died in his arms? Was he supposed to know him?

That was the way it had been once before in Germany. No matter how hard you tried, you never knew what the hell was going on. You just hoped you'd get out alive.

He saw the lights of the lodge ahead, the smashed French doors . . . There was someone moving in the room.

Someone was waiting for him.

He crossed the expanse of snow, caked with snow himself. He moved slowly. He was finished by the time he reached the great hall and walked through a hole where once there had been a door.

She was stretched out on the couch that Cooper hadn't blown to pieces. Covered with blankets. Her face raw with color from the cold. He saw an eyelid flicker. She was asleep. She was alive.

"Well, Cooper, boy." The sardonic voice, the drawl. He turned and saw the wraithlike figure of Clint Kilroy standing in the shadows at the end of the vast fireplace. "Have a rough night?"

Cooper looked at him, remembered something, a joke Cyril had once taught him. "No thanks," he said. "Just had one."

Kilroy smiled and stepped out of the shadows.

"I found your sister out there." He waved toward the storm. "An orphan of the storm, you might say. Wandering around like a little lost calf . . ." He looked at her. "I'm not what I once was, but I picked her up and damned if she wasn't light as a feather. Or I had the strength I only remember. Anyway, she's okay."

Cooper knelt beside her, looked down on her face.

She woke when the snow and ice in his hair dripped onto her face. She came awake smiling.

"Oh, John . . . Johnnie . . . what have you been doing? You're all wet and . . . Mr. Kilroy says Erika is back . . . she's fine, I can see her back in Berlin . . . John, you came for me . . . Is it all right, John? Is it okay now?"

He leaned down and softly brushed his lips against hers. He felt the curve of her smile against his mouth.

"Never better, Lee. Never better."

"Oh, Johnnie . . . don't let go of me . . ."

"Never again, Lee." He kissed her hair. "Never."

The last of the Coopers.

It was all that mattered.

ABOUT THE AUTHOR

THOMAS GIFFORD is the author of *The Assassini, Praetorian, The Wind Chill Factor,* and other novels. He lives in New York and Dubuque.